THE FURYCK SAGA

WINTER'S FURY

THE BURNING SEA

NIGHT OF THE SHADOW MOON

HALLOW WOOD

THE RAVEN'S WARNING

VALE OF THE GODS

KINGS OF FATE
A Prequel Novella

THE LORDS OF ALEKKA

EYE OF THE WOLF

MARK OF THE HUNTER

Sign up to my newsletter, so you don't miss out on new release information!

http://www.aerayne.com/sign-up

VALE OF THE GODS

THE FURYCK SAGA: BOOK 6

A.E. RAYNE

AMAZON ISBN: 9781710742916

For more information about A.E. Rayne
and her upcoming books visit:

www.aerayne.com

www.facebook.com/aerayne

This book is dedicated to you, dear reader.
Thank you so much for coming on this
epic journey with me.

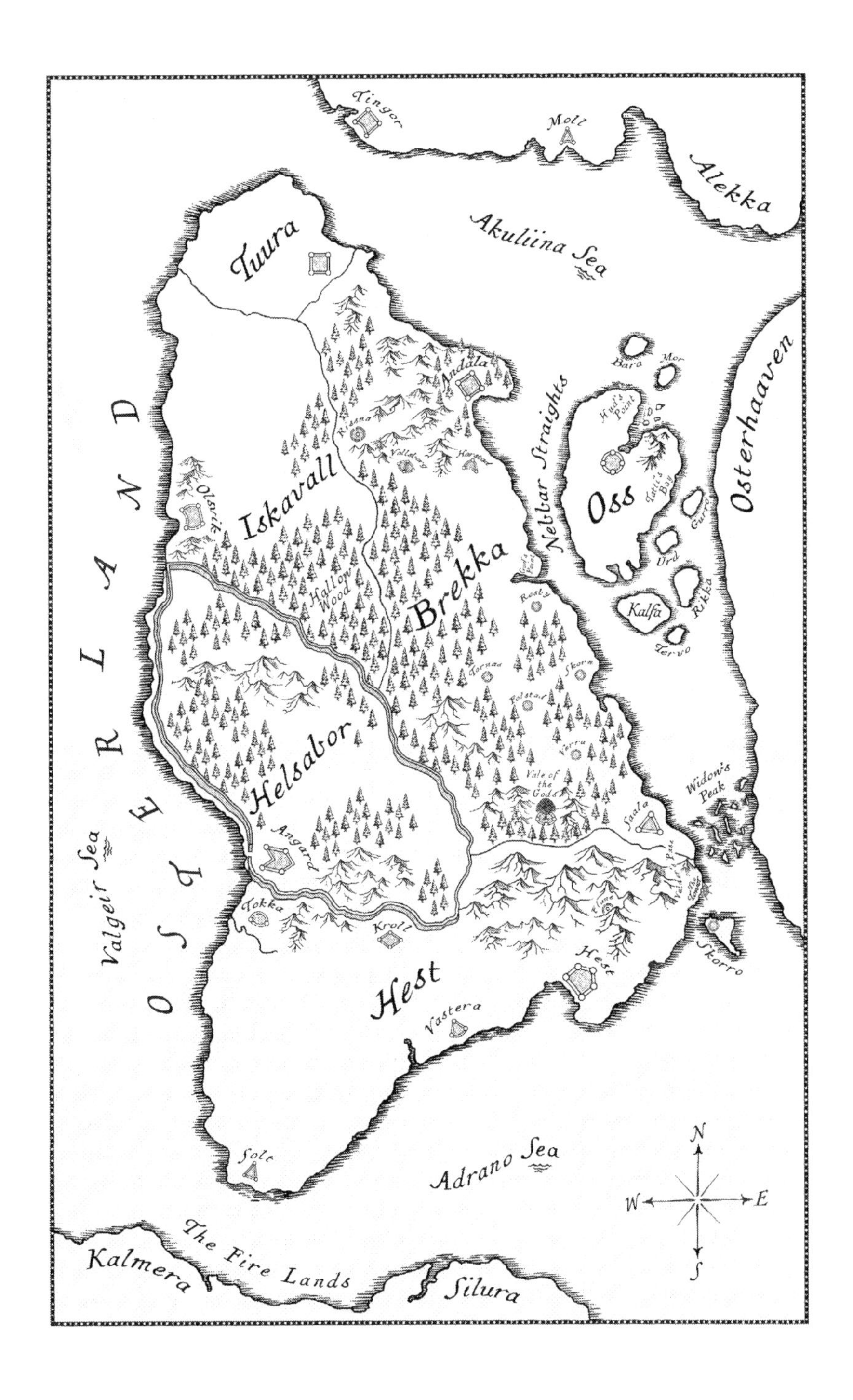
Tingor
Moll
Alekka
Akuliina Sea
Tuura
Andala
Osterhaaven
Bara
Mor
Nebbar Straights
Oss
Iskavall
Olsvik
Hallow Wood
Brekka
Urd
Kalfa
Rikka
Tervo
Rosby
Tornaa
Vale of the Gods
Widow's Peak
Saala
Helsabor
Angard
Tokka
Kroll
Hest
Hest
Skorro
Vastera
Valgeir Sea
O S T E R L A N D
Solt
Adrano Sea
N
W
E
S
Kalmera
The Fire Lands
Silura

CHARACTERS

In Andala

Jael Furyck, Queen of Oss
Aleksander Lehr
Thorgils Svanter
Gant Olborn
Edela Saeveld
Eydis Skalleson
Brynna 'Biddy' Halvor
Axl Furyck, King of Brekka
Gisila Furyck
Bram Svanter
Fyn Gallas
Entorp Bray
Ayla Adea
Bruno Adea
Rork Arnesson
Ulf Rutgar
Bayla Dragos
Karsten Dragos
Nicolene Dragos
Berard Dragos
Hanna Boelens
Marcus Volsen
Astrid Ranveg
Derwa Fylan
Alaric Fraed
Torstan Berg
Branwyn Byrn
Aedan Byrn
Kayla Byrn
Beorn Rignor
Sybill Ethburg
Ontine Ethburg

CHARACTERS

In the Kingdom of Hest

Draguta Teros
Jaeger Dragos, King of Hest
Eadmund Skalleson, King of Oss
Meena Gallas
Amma Furyck
Evaine Gallas
Brill Oggun
Ballack
Tanja Tulo
Berrick Ives

In the Kingdom of Helsabor

Briggit Halvardar, Queen of Helsabor
Morana Gallas
Dragmall Birger
Else Edelborg
Sabine Sellen
Lillith Sellen

In the Kingdom of Iskavall

Raymon Vandaal, King of Iskavall
Getta Vandaal, Queen of Iskavall

In Vallsborg

Beryth Ulrik, Lady of Vallsborg

In Verra

Rexon Boas, Lord of Saala

PREVIOUSLY

Jael, Thorgils, and Aleksander had escaped from Harstad with the healer, Astrid, amidst a dragur attack, and after the loss of Jael's baby. They made it back to Andala, only to suffer another assault from the dragur, who were finally defeated; turned to ash by the combined effort of sea-fire, and Edela and Eydis, who found a symbol in the Book of Aurea to end them.

With the dragur gone, Jael quickly turned her attention to meeting Raymon Vandaal to discuss a combined assault on Draguta. Despite a concerted effort by his wife, Getta, to dissuade him, Raymon offered his help to Jael. Getta was furious and turned to the comfort of her old lover, Garren Maas. Garren, having discovered that Raymon was Ranuf Furyck's son, tried to overthrow his king on their way back to Ollsvik. Jael had a dream and was led by the raven, Fyr, to stop Garren before he could kill Raymon, though she was not in time to prevent Raymon's mother from being murdered.

In Hest, Jaeger was panicking.

He thought they had killed Draguta, but she had disappeared, and the threat of her return hung over the castle like a storm cloud. With Morana unable to speak or even move on her own, he had no one to protect him, and though he was hopeful that Meena could read the Book of Darkness, he knew that she was unlikely to offer any resistance to someone of Draguta's ability.

Draguta, meanwhile, had hidden in a small village where she

summoned Eadmund to her, knowing that his presence would encourage Evaine to help her remove the Book of Darkness from Jaeger's clutches. Once Evaine had escaped Hest with what she believed to be the book, Draguta was able to bind Jaeger to her with the items Evaine had retrieved from the castle.

Now freely able to return to Hest, Draguta began putting her plans in place. She found Rollo, the most skilled warrior in Flane, who she tasked with training Eadmund. Hard. Harder than he'd ever been trained before, knowing that one day soon she would use him to fight off her arch-enemy, Jael Furyck. Evaine wasn't happy, for despite being reunited with Eadmund for the first time since her escape from Oss, she could tell that he was now bound to Draguta as well. And that split loyalty did not favour her, as she discovered when Eadmund killed her father and then threatened to kill her.

In Andala, Edela was being kept busy, first finding a way to undo Briggit Halvardar's sickness curse, and then working to break Evaine's spell on Eadmund. But, having cut the rope binding Eadmund to Evaine, Edela found another rope she couldn't touch at all.

Growing impatient with Morana's slow recovery, Jaeger took Else's advice to bring in Dragmall, Hest's volka. Dragmall suggested that Morana had been cursed, and though he was reluctant to help her, he realised that to keep Else and Meena safe from Draguta, he needed to try.

Draguta's attention wandered to Helsabor and Briggit Halvardar, though she still had one eye on Jael Furyck and the Book of Aurea. In the end, she sent Rollo and a crew of men to Andala. They arrived at the fort pretending to be traders, waiting for the cover of Draguta's next attack, so they could abduct Eadmund's son, Sigmund, and Amma Furyck; Amma who was pregnant and worried that Jaeger was the father.

As Draguta's giant barsk dogs ravaged Andala, Runa was killed, and Gisila was seriously wounded, and the Andalans were left devastated, with Jael and her shellshocked men trying to pick up the pieces before they turned their attention to Hest.

Hest and Draguta and the Book of Darkness and Eadmund.

Where everything would end.

Soon.

PROLOGUE

'You won't come back.'

Jael didn't know the voice.

She frowned. In the darkness, it was hard to get her bearings.

But he was there. Somewhere.

His voice, a warning.

She shivered, turning away from the threat that she could feel; the unfamiliar sense of fear.

Her breathing was panicked now, her body starting to shake, her bottom lip quivering.

She didn't want him to see.

If he saw...

Her chest rose and fell in time to her thundering heart.

'You won't come back from this. Not now.'

Jael glared up at him. He was taller than her.

Stronger.

'You don't know me,' she insisted, cross with the weak tremble in her voice.

Where was Aleksander?

Panic.

She didn't look around, her heart thudding louder. Faster.

'You think your father will save you, little girl?' he sneered. 'Little bitch. He can't save you. No one can save you now, Jael.'

Jael hated Ronal Killi. But that wasn't Ronal's voice.

Ronal was standing over her, his friends behind him – his

bigger, older friends – and she was lying on her back, a broken sword in one hand, blood running into her mouth from where he'd punched her, cutting her lip.

They were in the forest.

He had followed her.

Jael was mad that she hadn't heard him.

She'd beaten him in front of his father, humiliated him in the training ring again and again, and he'd waited to take his revenge. He'd waited for weeks, eyeing her slyly. Watching her. Whispering to his friends about her.

Leering at her.

And now?

The forest was so quiet. Jael couldn't even hear Tig, though he was nearby, somewhere, she knew. She hoped Ronal wouldn't hurt him.

And then Ronal lunged, wrapping his rough hands around her throat. Jael jerked her head from side to side, slippery pine needles in her hair, the crunch of leaves in her ears. Ronal was squeezing her throat, laughing, leaning over her.

Or was he?

Shadows masked his pudgy face.

'I have you now, little bitch. You're mine, and *I* will end you.' He laughed.

Someone laughed.

'You thought you could stop me? You? Ha! You don't know me. Don't know what you're up against. And you won't. Not until it's too late, little *bitch*.'

'Jael!'

She could see Ronal's eyes now as he swung his head in the direction of the trees, his friends urging him to hurry.

'I'll get you, Jael,' Ronal hissed, spitting in her face before spinning away. 'I'll get you.'

And then boots running, and suddenly Aleksander was there.

'Jael?' Gripping her hand, he pulled her up, into his arms. 'What did they do to you? Are you alright?'

Jael shook her head, confused. 'What are you doing here?' She was panting, struggling to catch her breath.

Not in the forest anymore.

Aleksander saw the sheen of sweat on her brow, her dark hair wet on her face, her eyes unable to focus on his. He gripped her hand, feeling it tremble. 'You were screaming. Having a nightmare.'

It was dark in the chamber, but Jael could see the silhouette of her brother in the doorway; Gant too. 'I'm fine.' She shook her head, wanting to be alone. 'I'm fine. Go back to bed.' And tugging her hand away, she waved it at them. 'Just a bad dream.'

Nodding their sleepy heads, Gant and Axl disappeared into the corridor.

Aleksander didn't move.

The lamp beside the bed flickered, highlighting the deep frown between her eyebrows.

'What happened?'

'I don't know. It was about Ronal. That time he attacked me in the forest.'

Aleksander frowned just as deeply, confused. 'Why him?'

Jael rubbed her eyes, trying to think. 'Something he said that day. I keep hearing it. The same words.'

'What?'

'You won't come back. He said that over and over. He wanted to kill me. I heard him telling his friends that he was going to.' She shivered.

Aleksander squeezed Jael's hand, trying to get her to focus on him. 'You killed Ronal.'

'Ronal was a boy,' she snarled, eyes sweeping the furs where a disturbed Vella was trying to make herself comfortable. 'A nothing boy.' She stopped, staring into Aleksander's eyes again. 'A boy. And I had a sword. And I killed him with it. And nobody's life was in danger. Nobody's but mine.'

Aleksander's shoulders relaxed, and he smiled, understanding now. 'And you did it alone. But you're not going to be going to

Hest alone, are you? You're a queen now. A queen with armies from Brekka and Iskavall and the Slave Islands. Alekkans too. You're not alone, Jael.'

'No, I'm not,' Jael mumbled, wriggling away from him, feeling a cold draft slip under the door. She pulled the fur away from Vella, over her arms. 'But it's not enough. Armies and men aren't enough, are they? Not for who we're going to face. *What* we're going to face.' She lowered her voice. 'I'm going to lead those men to slaughter. Take them away from families who'll never see them again. *I'm* going to do that.'

'What choice do you have? Staying here would see them slaughtered *with* their families. You have to go. *We* have to go. We all do.'

Jael could feel her wedding band, cold against her finger, listening to the echo of that voice in her head.

Aleksander was right, she knew.

But perhaps, so was he?

'You won't come back,' he threatened again. 'I won't let you.'

PART ONE

Walls

CHAPTER ONE

Eadmund threw back the fur and sighed.

He couldn't sleep. His dreams were torturing him, leaving him tired and confused. He saw Evaine, naked, writhing on the bed before him; Morac dying on the floor, his mouth wrenched open, wine in his beard. He heard the hungry wail of his son, the agony of Rollo as Jael killed him, and Draguta's voice loudest of all. It was an urgent echo in his mind and body, never letting him go.

Defeat Helsabor with Jaeger.

Bring back Briggit Halvardar and her Followers.

And then what?

Eadmund rolled onto his side, hearing the angry creak of his narrow cot. Something was nagging at him. Like a word hanging near the tip of his tongue; a thought almost formed. He couldn't grasp it, couldn't see it, but it was there. Or in Helsabor.

But what?

The tent flap was dragged open as his determined steward bustled inside. Berrick. Draguta had insisted that he accompany Eadmund to Helsabor. A king, she had barked, poking a stern finger at him, could not act like a common man. A king must be treated like a king, especially in front of the men that king wished to follow him into battle.

So now Eadmund had Berrick, a slightly-built, snivelly sort of man who shuffled about in a constant state of prickly irritation. A man who insisted upon waking his king while it was still dark.

'You're awake.' It wasn't a question.

'It appears that I am.' Eadmund coughed, taking the silver goblet Berrick offered him as he struggled into a sitting position, a sharp pain searing through his right eye. For some reason, it reminded him of Jael, and he almost smiled.

Then, imagining Draguta's disapproving face, he frowned.

'King Jaeger is outside, talking with Gunter and Berger. Going over plans.'

Berrick liked to gossip. He reminded Eadmund of Morac: a slippery-tongued old grumbler, always manoeuvering himself into the position that would most benefit him.

'Well, then,' Eadmund sighed, clearing his throat again and handing back the empty goblet. 'I'd better join them.' His shoulders tightened into fist-sized knots as he swung his legs over the side of the bed, watching Berrick lay out his armour.

Dropping his head to his hands, Eadmund closed his eyes, not wanting to think about Draguta or Jael, or Jaeger most of all. He tried to think of his son instead, knowing that Sigmund would be with Draguta soon and if he didn't do what she wanted...

Standing with a groan, Eadmund reached for his trousers, unable to raise a smile.

***

'Aarrghh!' Jael dropped onto her backside with a plop, gritting her teeth, not enjoying the cocky look in Karsten's blue eye. 'Fuck!' She threw herself at his legs, gripping and twisting, toppling him to the ground. 'You fuck!'

Thorgils burst out laughing at the surprised look on Karsten's face just before it slammed into the dirt; Jael over the top of him now, hauling him onto his back, her forearm jammed into his throat.

Berard joined in. 'Karsten's not going to take that well!'

Thorgils slapped him on the back. 'You're right about that.' And just as he said it, Karsten twisted his legs around Jael's, trying to flip her over. 'Though I've a feeling Jael's not going to let him do much about it.'

Berard's eyes widened as Karsten and Jael grappled, arms flailing like battling worms; blinking as Jael chopped Karsten in the throat with the side of her hand; watching as his brother collapsed back onto the ground again.

Thorgils roared with laughter as Karsten rolled, struggling onto his knees, gagging, trying to breathe. Jael threw herself onto his back, arms around his throat, securing him, kneeing him in the hip, forcing him down onto the ground.

Karsten couldn't breathe as he lay there, dirt in his eye, in his mouth, his neck in Jael's vice-like grip, feeling her arms tighten. He couldn't move her. He tried, and despite being certain that he was stronger than the Queen of Oss, he couldn't break her hold. Eventually, reaching out a hand, he tapped the ground.

Jael released her arms, standing up, watching as Karsten rolled over.

He blinked into the sunshine, trying to see the angry creature who towered over him without a hint of humour in her eyes. Two eyes. Green and bright and mean. Two eyes, not like him who lay in the dirt with the one eye she had left him after taking the other.

Jael's face softened as she held out a hand, pulling him to his feet.

'That wasn't quite the beating I had in mind,' Karsten rasped, bending over, hands on thighs. He shook his head, sweat flying from his red face. 'Not at all.'

Jael smiled, picking up her sword. 'Well, don't give up. I'm sure you'll catch me on a bad day.' And walking towards the railings, trying to suck in a breath, she could almost see the look on Karsten's face as he muttered irritably behind her.

'Not bad,' Thorgils admitted with a raised eyebrow. 'You might be able to defeat Jaeger with that.'

'Jaeger?' Karsten spat, grabbing the water bag Berard was holding. 'Jaeger's mine.' He glared at Jael, wiping a hand over his dripping blonde beard, daring her to disagree. 'And only mine.'

Jael shrugged. 'I've a feeling there'll be plenty to go around when we get to Hest, so help yourself.' She shook her head, ignoring the water bag Karsten was offering her. 'I'm going to check on Ivaar, then, Thorgils, we need to go and find Beorn. I want to test out those catapults. Make sure they're going to get up a hill, otherwise what's the point in taking them to a place like Hest?'

'Jael!'

Jael spun around feeling her aching body tense at the sight of a puffing Biddy pushing her way through to the railings. 'What?' She hurried out of the training ring, her throat tightening. 'What's happened?'

'It's Gisila,' Biddy panted. 'You need to come!'

***

Meena tied up her boot with shaking hands.

They had been shaking since the night when Dragmall had rescued Morana. Since they had escaped from the city with Else.

Jaeger had left too. Gone to attack Helsabor with Eadmund Skalleson.

Having discovered that Morana had fled, and knowing how Draguta would feel about that, Jaeger had been reluctant to leave Meena behind. In the end, though, he had simply kissed her and suggested she keep out of Draguta's way. Hide in the chamber until he returned.

Which she had.

She had only left it to sneak down into the kitchen for a few leftover scraps, and though she had no appetite, and there was likely no point in feeding herself now, she did, trying not to let her mind wander to Berard, knowing that he was not safe, as much as she was not safe. Draguta could, and would simply reach into any chamber, in any fort, and hurt anyone she liked, however she liked. They were all figures on Draguta's map table now, waiting to be lifted up and moved around.

Or thrown away when they were no longer needed.

Meena swallowed, knowing how much Draguta had enjoyed torturing Morana by leaving her a prisoner inside her own body. Perhaps she wasn't going to try and kill her at all? Perhaps she had something even worse planned?

The sudden banging on the door had Meena scrambling off the bed in a shaking mess of red hair and chattering teeth. She squeezed her hands together, unable to speak.

The banging continued, and, eventually, Meena shuffled and shook towards the door, unlocking it slowly, dragging it open.

To Brill.

Meena blinked, trying to read something in the servant's dull eyes.

'My mistress wishes to see you in the hall,' Brill said, struggling to even lift her head to look at Meena. 'Now.'

***

Jael hurried into the chamber past Entorp, who was unpacking his satchel onto a small table, releasing all manner of strange odours as he uncorked his jars of salve. 'Mother?' Axl was on one side of the bed, dark rings under his eyes as he glanced up at his sister.

Edela and Eydis were there too.

'Mother?' Jael dropped to her knees, gripping Gisila's hand as her mother opened her eyes.

'Aarrghh!' Gisila cried, writhing in agony.

'Ssshhh, now,' Edela soothed, moving behind Jael to reach Gisila's head. 'Entorp is coming with that salve. It will help, I promise. And Derwa is off in the kitchen getting something for the pain. Don't worry. Try to stay calm.'

Jael looked up at her grandmother as Gisila closed her eyes, clenching her jaw. 'Has someone gone for Gant?'

Edela nodded, smoothing her hand over Gisila's furrowed brow, humming low in her throat. 'Ssshhh, now.'

Gisila loosened her grip on Jael's hand, her body relaxing in the bed. She opened her eyes, blinking at the brightness of the candlelit room. 'Amma? What happened? Runa...' Her voice was faint, just a breath, and her body was quickly taut, twisting in pain again.

Axl swallowed, his eyes on his sister. 'Amma's gone. Eadmund's son and his wet nurse too. Runa's dead.' His voice was flat, for although Axl was relieved that his mother had come back to them, his heart was aching for Amma. He was struggling to stay still, to remain in Andala while they prepared for their departure. While they trained and readied their weapons and made their plans.

He wanted to leave. Now.

Gisila gasped as Entorp placed his hands on her stomach.

'I've tried to warm them up, but I'm afraid they're always a bit cold,' Entorp said bashfully. 'Perhaps you should do it, Edela?'

Edela shook her head. 'I think it's best if I stay up here. Gisila won't mind, will you?' she smiled. 'After all, she's had a lifetime of my cold hands.'

'Amma should be in Hest soon.' Jael said, watching her mother squirm as Entorp applied the salve around her stomach wound, surprised that the smell of it didn't affect her anymore. She blinked, not wanting her mind to wander back to the time when it had. 'Edela's convinced that they won't hurt her.'

Their grandmother's confidence in that had gnawed away at Axl for days. 'Why? Why won't they hurt her? Jaeger killed his first wife, so why are you so confident, Grandmother?' He distractedly patted his mother's hand as the pleasant aromas of yarrow and goldenrod permeated the room. 'Why?'

Edela sighed, sensing Eydis twitch on her stool near the end of the bed. There really was no choice but to tell him now. 'Amma is pregnant. I suspect Draguta took her for that very reason.'

Axl's mouth remained open, his weary mind struggling to

comprehend her meaning.

Despite being just as tired, Jael was quicker. 'Because it's Jaeger's baby?' she guessed, her eyes on her brother.

'I suspect it might be,' Edela mumbled, watching Axl's jaw working away.

No one knew what to say about that, so they remained silent, confusing Gant who had just walked in. 'What is it?' he panicked, looking from Axl who was frowning, to Edela who appeared troubled, to Gisila whose eyes were still closed. 'Gisila?'

Gisila opened her eyes, turning towards his voice, groaning again as the pain bit. 'Gant.'

He hurried to the bed, barely noticing that Jael was there as she hopped out of the way. 'Gisila.' Kneeling on the floor, he took her hand, surprising no one. Over the past few days, they'd all seen just how much Gant cared for Gisila, but what they hadn't seen was how Gisila felt about Gant. But now, with tears running down her cheeks as he bent over her, kissing her forehead, now, there was no longer any question.

Everyone stared at them, except for Eydis, who sat perfectly still, listening.

'Where have you been?' Gisila whispered. 'I thought you'd be here.' Closing her eyes, she smiled through the pain. 'I told you not to go anywhere, remember?'

Gant smiled back, tears in his eyes. 'I remember. And I won't. Not again, I promise.'

Jael frowned, but Gant was too busy watching Gisila to see.

Axl was too busy glowering at his grandmother to notice.

But Edela's eyes were on Jael, knowing precisely what that meant.

***

'If we approach through there, we'll get too many killed before

Draguta has a chance to do anything.' Eadmund was growing impatient with Jaeger's inability to think; to care enough about his men to want to protect them. He thought in bursts of anger and impulse with little regard for carrying a thought through to its conclusion.

Thinking like that would get them all killed.

'I'm not here to listen to your opinions!' Jaeger barked, his voice hoarse. He'd been feeling increasingly unwell since they'd left Hest. Three days on horseback in teeming rain, terrorised by a sharp westerly wind had left him chilled to the bone, and he felt irritable that Eadmund was talking to him so far away from the fire. His body was hot and cold, shivering and sweating interchangeably.

But he wasn't about to let Eadmund Skalleson know it.

'Draguta sent both of us to claim Helsabor. I don't think she imagined all the plans would be yours,' Jaeger growled.

Eadmund shrugged. 'It's no loss to me whether you die in Angard, but Draguta... she wants you on the dragon throne. Her heir. Have some plans, as many as you want, but if they're not good enough, you'll be a king without any men. Maybe not a king at all. Briggit Halvardar and her Followers might kill you before you've even drawn a sword.'

Jaeger jammed his teeth together, annoyed. Annoyed because Eadmund was right. Dreamers were trouble, and Briggit would be watching them.

Waiting for them.

'Draguta wants us to succeed. She won't sit on the sidelines. She'll be there, helping us. She wants Briggit and Helsabor,' Jaeger grumbled throatily, eyes narrowed against a rare burst of sunshine, though he could see that the moody sky would not allow it to linger for long. He took the cup of wine his servant offered him, suddenly wistful for Meena. 'You think Briggit can hurt us when Draguta has the Book of Darkness? Ha! It's a wonder she puts so much faith in you when you have none in her.'

Eadmund stepped forward, studying Jaeger's angular face. He could see the gleam of sweat shining on skin that looked unusually pallid; the amber eyes that were oddly red, blinking, tired-looking; the strained sound of Jaeger's voice. 'I know that not everyone can be stopped by that book. Look at what Jael did. What she continues to do. What her grandmother and my sister can do with their own book. How they can stop Draguta.' Eadmund shivered suddenly, certain that Draguta was listening. 'If you want to return to Hest, to your castle and your throne, you'd better be prepared to use your own head. I'm sure you're used to your father or your brothers saving you from yourself, but now there's only you, and I wouldn't be confident that anyone will come and save your sorry arse this time. I certainly won't.'

Jaeger's anger exploded like a jar of sea-fire, but he bit down on it, feeling the wine swirling around his aching throat, knowing that his men were watching and that Draguta would be at her seeing circle, interested to see how nicely they were playing together. He smiled, though his eyes were sharp. 'Seems to me that if anyone needs to worry about what Jael Furyck can do, it's you. You being the one Draguta wants to kill her. So shut your fucking mouth about me.' And striding towards his horse, Jaeger decided that they'd done enough talking.

It was time to get their men to Angard.

***

Jael sat on her mother's bed, thinking about Eadmund. She could almost feel his tension building like a wave in a storm-whipped sea, and she felt troubled by what that might mean. Thinking about Eadmund led to thoughts of Sigmund, and then Runa. Fyn. Bram too.

'Jael?'

She blinked, coming back into the room. Edela was talking to her, Biddy and Eydis hovering nearby as she sat on the bed. Everyone else had left, and Jael knew that she should go too. Gisila had closed her eyes, and there was so much to do in the fort. 'What did you say?'

'I was asking about your dream. Axl said you were screaming last night.'

Jael's eyes darted to the right where Ido and Vella were licking up remnants of the broth Biddy had spilled on the floor. Ido was limping and whimpering, but not prepared to miss out on any of his sister's fun. Jael relaxed her face before turning back to her grandmother. 'No idea. Just a flood of images, voices, words. Like being in a blizzard.' She saw Eydis frown. Edela too.

Dreamers, she knew, could read minds, so why was she lying to them?

Neither of them said anything, though, and Biddy was too busy fussing around Gisila to notice.

'Have you seen Fyn today?' Jael asked, changing the subject.

Eydis' neck lengthened, her spine straightening, suddenly more alert. 'No. No one has seen much of him since Runa's pyre.'

'Not even Bram?' Biddy wondered. 'I should have gone to see how he is. Taken him a stew. Poor man. Will you two stop licking the floor. Shoo now! Get outside!'

Ido and Vella scampered and limped past Jael as she turned to Biddy. 'Bram's keeping busy. Thorgils has an eye on him, but I'll need to go and find Fyn. He's avoiding me too.' She stood, grimacing as she put her weight down on her right ankle, surprised to discover that she must have twisted it fighting Karsten.

'Jael, wait.' Edela struggled to her feet, stiff after days of sitting by Gisila's bed. 'I'll walk with you.' And she creaked around the bed towards her granddaughter who ushered her through the door with a look back to Gisila, who appeared to be sleeping comfortably now.

The hall was humming with activity, preparations for the army's departure intensifying with each passing day. Since the night of the barsk attack, the need to make themselves safe had been at the forefront of Jael's mind, but they were never going to be truly safe until she took the army to Hest to defeat Draguta.

'I had a dream about Eadmund last night,' Edela said, her

voice low as she slipped her arm through Jael's.

Jael wanted to stop, but she didn't. Everyone's eyes were on her, and she could sense how many people had questions they needed answered, including Axl who was trying to extract himself from a conversation with Bayla Dragos. 'What about?' Her heart beat faster.

'He is preparing to attack Helsabor.'

'What?' Now Jael did stop. She pulled her grandmother close, out of the way of Branwyn who was trying to shoo a chicken outside. 'What do you mean? Eadmund? On his own?'

Edela stared into Jael's tired eyes. 'With Jaeger Dragos. With the Hestian army.'

Jael stood back, frowning. 'Helsabor?'

'Eadmund does Draguta's bidding. He will only be there because of her.'

'So Draguta wants Briggit Halvardar?'

'She must. And all those Followers too. They will have heard about what happened in Hest. What Draguta did to the Followers there. They will not be friends or allies. She will seek to defeat them, I imagine. To remove another threat. And the Helsaborans under Briggit are a powerful threat indeed.'

Jael felt strange. Draguta attacking Helsabor was a gift she had not anticipated, though the idea that they might face one enemy instead of two was encouraging. 'But why now? Why would she send them there instead of here?'

'Why?' Edela shrugged, her eyes on the doors as Fyn made his way inside, head low, hoping to avoid everyone as he quickly found some food. 'Perhaps Ayla may have some thoughts? She saw inside Briggit's head many times while she was ill with that sickness. Why don't you speak to Fyn and I'll go and find Ayla.'

Jael nodded, a sad smile on her face as she watched Fyn scrambling to fill a plate with flatbreads and cheese, his floppy auburn hair hiding his face. 'Alright, but come and find me. I'd like to know why Draguta wants Briggit so badly.'

Edela's thoughts had quickly turned to Ayla and whether she was speaking to Bruno, and she only mumbled in response as she hurried to the doors, almost tripping over the puppies who were busy tangling themselves around her legs, trying to lick her broth-covered boots.

Jael turned away, taking a deep breath as she headed towards Fyn.

***

Amma couldn't stop hearing the sound of the sword as it punctured Runa's chest. It was a noise so sickening, so terrifying, that she had frozen with terror, convinced that she would be next, so it had almost been a relief when she'd realised that the men wanted to take her too.

To Hest.

That's all they'd said when they pulled her out of the fort, filthy hands over her mouth, dragging her towards their ship.

To Hest, where Jaeger Dragos would be waiting.

Amma glanced at Sigmund, who lay asleep in Tanja's arms. The sea was calm at long last, and if she hadn't been so terrified, she might have felt hungry. But one look at Tanja's tear-stained face reminded her that she had every reason to feel terrified, and none at all to feel safe.

The crew had thrown a few furs at them, a couple of water bags, some food, and then ignored them. Most of them didn't appear threatening, and Amma didn't feel fearful of what they would do to them. She knew that they would be under orders not to hurt her.

She hoped they would be.

Sigmund too.

And they needed Tanja. They had obviously realised who she was when they snatched her out of her sweetheart's arms, running a sword through his chest as he tried to protect her, just as they had Runa's.

And Gisila.

Amma's face was numb from the biting wind, but she could feel the tears as they slid down her cold cheeks, dripping onto the nightdress covering her knees.

Was Gisila even alive?

Was Axl?

Amma remembered the blood; Gisila lying in the corridor so still, the axe she had tried to fend the men off with tossed away. Turning to Tanja, she held out her hands. 'I'll take him,' she said quietly. 'You need some sleep.'

Tanja barely blinked, but she tucked Sigmund's swaddling cloth more tightly around him, and the fur around that, before handing him to Amma. She leaned against the high back of the stern, closing her eyes, blinking them open as the ship hit a wave with a smack.

Amma peered down at the sleeping baby, trying to see if he looked like Eadmund, but she couldn't. Her mind wandered to who her own child would look like.

Wondering whose child it was.

CHAPTER TWO

Fyn didn't want to feel sad. He didn't want to grieve. He didn't want to feel anything. But his mother was dead, and the loss of her was inescapable. It covered him like a snow cloud; the pain a constant ache in his chest. He couldn't stop seeing her: the look in her eyes, her face strained with shock, her body soaked in blood. It was all he could think about.

Jael was talking to him.

He wished he hadn't come back to the hall. He didn't feel like talking to anyone, but Fyn knew that he couldn't let Jael down. In those brief moments he managed to escape the heavy weight of grief, he knew that he didn't want to let her down.

Seeing that Fyn was struggling to talk, Jael had taken him to the stables, and they'd saddled Tig and Alf, who had been her cousin Aron's horse, and they'd disappeared into the forest together. The smell of pyres had followed them. Pyres and sea-fire and dragur and burning barsk. It shrouded Andala like a funeral cloth, irritating their throats, stinging their eyes.

Death. Death hung over them.

Death that had been. Death that would come.

Fyn didn't want to speak.

So Jael did. 'When I was in Harstad with Thorgils and Aleksander,' she began. Gripping the reins tighter, she could feel her lips wobble. It was only real if she talked about it, so she hadn't talked about it to anyone. Not since her mother. And barely then.

'I nearly died.'

Fyn nodded. He knew that.

Then hearing the odd tremble in Jael's voice, he turned to her, certain there were tears in her eyes, suddenly curious. 'What happened?'

'I had a baby.'

The look on Fyn's face was one of horror and surprise.

'She died. She was... small. Too small.' Jael blinked. 'Edela saw that she'd come in the winter. It was not her time. She was already dead when she was born.'

Fyn wanted to reach out and touch Jael, but she was too far away.

'Aleksander made her a pyre, and I said goodbye to her. And I never even saw her eyes. I never heard her voice or saw her smile. Nothing. And the pain...' Jael bit her lip. 'It is deep, and I want to hide from it.' She grinned suddenly, shaking her head. 'I am hiding from it.'

'I'm sorry, Jael.' Fyn's eyes were more alert than they had been in days. 'So sorry.'

'What I'm trying to say, Fyn, is that I can feel your pain. I know what it felt like to lose my baby. What it feels like worrying about Gisila. And I'm sorry for you. Grief is hard to bear. The loss of someone you love... it's so final...' She didn't want to go on.

Fyn retreated into himself again, letting his hair fall over his face. 'My mother was so worried about me. Always wanting me to be safe, but I didn't stop to think about her,' he sniffed, tears coming like a flood. 'I didn't stop to think about whether she was safe!'

'No, none of us did. We thought the threat was outside the fort, not in it.' Jael edged Tig towards Alf. 'But now we know. And when we leave, we'll do what we can to keep everyone safe.' She felt a dull ache in her stomach, that voice echoing in her ears again. 'We'll do everything we can. Everything.'

Fyn looked into Jael's eyes, seeing her pain for a brief moment before it vanished, replaced by that familiar look of determination. He nodded. 'I don't want to lose Bram too.' It was barely a whisper; he was almost too shy to admit it.

Jael smiled. 'No, me neither, but don't worry, there's plenty of time to sort the fort out before we leave. Now, come on, it looks like it's about to piss down.' And clicking her tongue, she tapped her boots against Tig's flanks, urging him ahead of Alf, her ears open, listening for whatever threat might be coming next.

***

Brill almost had to drag Meena down the stairs, into the hall. She had made such a stuttering fuss about having to see Draguta that Brill was worried she was simply going to run out of the castle, which would not please her mistress at all.

And, Brill knew, it wouldn't help Meena.

Draguta had a way of finding everyone.

Almost everyone.

'You came!' Draguta smiled, her red lips glistening as she sat up straighter on the tall dragon throne, smoothing her white dress over her knees. 'I was growing so worried, thinking you would simply fade away up in that chamber.' She narrowed her ice-blue eyes as Meena approached, her voice dropping to a throaty growl. 'Or run away.'

Meena gulped, unsure whether she should attempt to look at Draguta, or just keep her eyes on her boots. She was unsure what to do with her hands either which were jerking uncontrollably in front of her new dress. Eventually, she grabbed one and held them both over her stomach, trying to keep her mind clear, her head bent, hair tumbling over her face like red brambles.

Draguta stood, leaving the throne behind. 'Meena, Meena, my little Meena,' she cooed. 'How did you end up like this, I wonder? You are not the ugliest girl I have ever seen, yet you look as though you were raised in a cave by a family of trolls!' She circled Meena whose eyes jumped wildly, not knowing when Draguta would lunge at her, but certain that, eventually, she would.

Her experience with Varna and Morana had taught her that.

'Morana...' Draguta purred, digging beneath Meena's hair, lifting her chin.

Meena shivered.

'Morana is gone! And neither of us are sad about that, are we? In fact, I imagine we are both thrilled by her sudden disappearance.' She stopped, peering down at Meena's bulging eyes. 'Wouldn't you say?'

Meena didn't know what to say. She didn't know what she thought.

But she did know what she thought of Morana.

'Yes.'

Draguta laughed, straightening up. 'Thanks to you. Thanks to you, Morana is gone!'

Meena's eyes were quickly back on her boots, trying to keep her mind clear of everything but the gaping holes in them.

'You did so well. So well indeed!'

Meena looked up, too confused to be scared now, her mouth hanging open.

'Oh! You didn't realise that the voice in your head was me? Me telling you about the ship in the cove? About Dragmall and his special tea? About where to go and what to do and what to think and say? All me! Ha! Well, I suppose there was a reason I chose Fool's Cove to send you to!' And laughing some more, Draguta turned back to the throne, her mood jubilant.

Morana had run away as she'd hoped, thanks to a malleable Meena. Jaeger and Eadmund were on their way to destroying Helsabor and retrieving Briggit Halvardar and her vermin Followers. Jael Furyck was broken and weak and...

She frowned, sitting down.

None of it meant anything while her sister was still in the wind.

Alive and hiding.

Draguta drummed her fingers on the skull armrests, irritated, trying to convince herself that soon her sister would have no choice but to reveal herself.

No choice at all.

***

Ayla almost wished that Bruno hadn't recovered from the sickness so quickly. If he were still bed-bound, she would have been able to avoid him. To not have to see him as she tended to the wounded and did what she could to help Edela prepare for the army's departure. But once he was on his feet, Bruno had been determined to follow her around, hoping to be of use, wanting her to speak to him again.

Ayla was finding it hard to even look at her husband.

It was childish, she knew, but Bruno had hidden so much of who he was from her that it felt as though their marriage had been a lie. She could sympathise with the loss of his sister, but she couldn't understand why Bruno hadn't told her about the prophecy.

About how he had stolen it.

Sold it.

Ayla frowned as he approached with a basket.

'Biddy thought you might need something bigger,' Bruno smiled weakly, hobbling towards her. He had been on his feet all day, and though his body was urging him to find a bench, he wasn't about to listen. He'd had enough of sitting down while everyone else worked.

Ayla took the basket, placing it on the dirt beside her. 'Thank you.' She turned back to the garden where she was harvesting salvia and mugwort. They were filling Edela's cottage with supplies for teas and spells, dream walking herbs too; anticipating what they would need to do to help protect the fort from Draguta; well aware of how vulnerable they were going to be once Jael left.

'Shall I help?' Bruno wondered, bending down beside her.

Ayla didn't look up. 'You won't know what to do with these plants. It takes a skilled hand.'

Bruno smiled, trying not to let his wife's sharpness dissuade him. 'I can see that, but you could show me.'

Ayla sat back on her heels with a sigh, brushing hair out of her eyes with the back of a dirty hand. 'There's too much to do to have this conversation, Bruno. Too much. I don't want to talk now.

I want to focus. I need my thoughts clear. I want my head free of anything but what I need to find. What will help us stay safe. We are all in such terrible danger. The sun is shining, and everyone is walking around, carrying out their tasks, but Draguta could attack us at any time, so I can't be worrying about you. I can't be fighting with you.'

Bruno dropped his head, admitting defeat. 'Makes sense,' he mumbled, struggling back to his feet. 'I'll go and find Bram and Ulf, then. I'm sure they could use another pair of hands.'

Ayla felt terrible, watching as he turned and limped away, seeing how much of a struggle it was for him just to walk. But she didn't move. She didn't go after him. She couldn't. There was too much to do.

'Well, I don't suppose I need to ask how things are going?' came a familiar voice.

Ayla spun around, embarrassed. 'I'm... it's hard.'

'I imagine it is. And I'm sorry for my part in it.' Edela wobbled down to the dirt beside Ayla. 'But I think that, eventually, the truth brings us closer together.'

'Or perhaps it pushes us further apart?' Ayla sighed, shaking the dirt from her hands, wiping them on her apron. 'Has something happened? Is it Gisila?'

Edela smiled. 'Gisila has opened her eyes! She is in a lot of pain, but I think, with Entorp's help, she is going to be alright.'

'Oh, Edela, I'm so happy about that.'

'Yes, so am I. But that is not why I came. I've been having strange dreams, and I need your help with them.'

Ayla was quickly frowning again.

'Draguta has sent Eadmund to attack Angard. Eadmund and Jaeger Dragos.'

'Oh.'

'And I need to know why. Jael is about to leave for Hest. I need to know everything I can so we can help her. So she knows what might be coming.'

'Of course. I will see what I can find out. I seemed to slip into Briggit's world easily while I was ill. I will try again tonight.'

Edela smiled. 'Good! Now, how about you leave me here. I'll gather in the rest of the salvia, and you can go and find that husband of yours. He's a good man, Ayla. I can feel that. And you were without him for so long. Life is short, as poor Runa showed us. We don't know what's hiding around the corner, so my advice is to make the most of the time you have. We all should.'

Ayla ducked her head, nodding it. 'I'll try. Thank you, Edela, I will try.' And rising to her feet, she took a deep breath, feeling the heaviness in her shoulders threaten to push her back down, knowing that she had to find a way to forgive her husband before it was too late.

***

Eadmund didn't feel comfortable.

He was surrounded by Hestians. Men he didn't know. Men he was sure he wouldn't like if he did know them.

Men who weren't loyal to him.

He missed his Islanders: Thorgils and Torstan; Beorn and Arlo; Fyn and Bram.

Jael.

They had left Kroll early, after a quick breakfast of smoked pork and salt fish, which had left him both hungry and nauseous. Now, Jaeger was leading them towards Tokka, a small settlement near the coast, positioned in the shadow of Helsabor's wall, from where they would begin their assault on Briggit Halvardar's kingdom. Draguta had changed her mind about wanting to separate her kings, deciding that it made more sense for Eadmund to keep an eye on Jaeger. Though, how it was all going to work, Eadmund still wasn't sure. They didn't have ships, and the terrain was too mountainous to take any form of siege engine with them, so they would be relying on Draguta to protect them from whatever trouble the Followers would make once their attack began.

Turning back around, Eadmund inclined his head for his second-in-command, an older man named Berger, to come alongside. He reminded Eadmund of Gant: a grey-haired, experienced warrior, economical with his words but sharply attuned to everything happening around him. A man, he was sure, prepared to counter any attack within moments.

They were navigating a narrow path that snaked around the edge of jagged red-rock mountains. For the first time in hours, there was enough room to ride two abreast and Eadmund was eager to get Berger onside.

'My lord?' Berger's lips were hidden beneath his coppery-grey beard, as though he was sucking them in, not wanting to speak to Eadmund at all. He shielded his eyes from the sun with one hand, masking those too.

'How long would you say till we're at Tokka?'

'We're over halfway there, lord. If we keep to this pace, two more nights and we should arrive outside the wall.'

'And will it be like this all the way?' Eadmund wondered, staring into the distance, noticing that the path was narrowing again. And rising.

'No, my lord, it will get much steeper. Narrower too. Best you keep to the cliffside. Hold your reins tight, keep your horse calm, and pray there's no more rain. It's already slippery underfoot.'

Eadmund couldn't help but glance up, searching for clouds, but for the first time on their journey, there were none to find in a sky that was blue and clear, stretching across them all like a bright cloak.

Bobbing his head, Berger shrunk back into his saddle, hoping that would be the end of it.

It wasn't.

'Stay alert,' Eadmund warned, nudging his horse ahead. 'Eyes everywhere. Dreamers are watching. Dreamers who know how to make dragons come to life, and turn ravens into weapons. Wolves and serpents too. Eyes everywhere.'

Frowning, Berger let Eadmund slip ahead, gathering his own horse's reins tighter, feeling his shoulders rise as he lifted his head, checking the sky.

***

No one was alright.

Everyone was walking around with tired and grainy eyes, wrapped in bandages. Broken limbs. Broken hearts. Stumbling around a broken fort.

No one was alright.

'Jael's not right.' Gant turned to Aleksander, listening to the growl of his empty stomach. He knew he wasn't eating enough, but between worrying about Gisila and the fort, and supervising preparations for their departure, he'd been struggling to care about food at all.

Aleksander's eyes remained on Jael who was deep in conversation with Thorgils, both of them leaning over the railings of the training ring. They were putting the Islanders through their paces, trying to focus everyone, though most were still struggling to cope with what had just happened: the dragon, the dragur, the barsk. 'No, she's not. She's having nightmares.'

Gant frowned. 'Understandable with what she's been through lately.' He glanced around, but they were alone. 'With the baby. With Gisila.'

'She's dreaming about Ronal Killi.'

'Ronal? That little shit. Why?'

'I don't know.' Aleksander's frown was as deep as Gant's. 'He terrorised her for years. She didn't tell you or Ranuf. I don't think she even told me everything, but I think it was bad.'

Gant was surprised by that; surprised to think that Jael had ever been bothered by anyone. From the time she'd had a sword in her hand, she'd been unstoppable, not intimidated by men or boys. 'But she killed him. He got what he deserved. After he killed Asta, she ended him.'

'She did,' Aleksander agreed, though he'd always thought there was more to the story than Jael had ever let on. He sighed, realising that he was trying to distract himself from what lay ahead of them by continually looking backwards.

His eyes wandered to Jael, and he knew why. For all that had happened to push them apart, he was still struggling to let her go, to see a future without her in it. It was the last thing he needed to think about he realised with a shake of his head.

Jael watched Gant and Aleksander, knowing that they were talking about her. Worrying about her.

She didn't blame them. She felt worried too.

Since the night of the barsk attack – when Gisila was stabbed, and Runa was killed, and Sigmund and Amma were taken – it had felt as though she was crossing a frozen lake. And as much as she knew that she had to, not one part of her wanted to keep going forward.

Thorgils was talking so quickly that she'd barely been listening until something jumped out. 'What? What do you mean, stay here?'

Thorgils' face reddened. 'I just think that... even with the wall finished, we're going to need some warriors, good warriors, to defend everyone. After what happened to Runa, I...'

Jael could sense his fear for Isaura. 'Agreed. And we'll have them.'

'Bram can't lead them. He's not strong enough yet. Runa's death has hit him hard.'

'No, he can't. But nor can you.'

Thorgils squirmed.

Jael frowned. 'I need you, Thorgils Svanter. You have to come.'

'I...'

'You do realise that being your queen, I can make you.'

Thorgils lifted an eyebrow. 'Is that so? And you'd try that, would you?'

Jael smiled. 'No. No, I wouldn't. Only those who want to should come. I just thought you'd be one of those who'd want to.'

Their attention was diverted to the ring as Fyn jabbed his sword at Torstan's chest, knocking him to the ground.

Jael's eyes sprung open in surprise. 'Keep that up!' she called, enjoying the scowl on Torstan's face as he scrambled to his feet, dusting off his tunic, crouching, ready for more. 'And what about Fyn?' she wondered, turning back to Thorgils. 'He's going to need you.'

Thorgils grew even more uncomfortable.

'Not to mention Eadmund.'

'Alright, alright!' he grumbled, holding up a hand. 'I surrender. I'll come. I'll come!'

'Of course you'll come,' Jael grinned. 'I never doubted it. Now, you keep an eye on that lot, and I'll go see how the wall's coming along. Looks like we're only a few days away from having it finished!' And she turned away before Thorgils could see the worry in her eyes.

The worry that they weren't ready for what they were about to face.

Wall or not.

***

Once she had welcomed Meena back into the fold, Draguta had been reluctant to let her go, for despite being such a pathetic creature, she was very useful. In more ways than Meena had even been aware of herself.

Draguta smiled from her rickety stool, watching as Meena stirred the cauldron. 'That's the way. We have a busy time ahead of us, you and I. The sooner those potions are ready, the sooner you'll be able to rest, so keep going, even though your arm is breaking. Keep going, little mouse, we're nearly there!'

Meena's eyes bulged, reminded of Morana, wondering why Draguta had let her escape. Draguta's eyes were suddenly sharper, and Meena blinked, her attention quickly back on the cauldron.

They were in Morana's chamber, Draguta not wanting the potions to infuse her bedchamber with their foul odours. They had been there for hours, and Meena was growing faint with hunger. It had been days since she had eaten properly, and likely days before that, she realised. And the suffocating heat in the chamber with the fire going...

Meena tried to catch her breath as she leaned against the wooden spoon, stirring the dark bubbling liquid.

Draguta smiled, standing. 'I shall leave you now, and you shall attempt to stay upright. I would hate to come back and find you swimming in that cauldron, girl. You wouldn't want to know what that potion is capable of!' She laughed, pointing a long finger at Meena's grimacing face. 'Do not stop now, not for a moment. I shall see. Remember that!' And striding to the door, she sighed contentedly, sensing how perfectly everything was coming together.

Meena lifted her eyes for a moment before hurrying them back to the cauldron, peering into the swirling liquid, shivering all over.

CHAPTER THREE

The sea air was bitterly cold, the wind a sharp blade across her face, but Morana didn't care. She could almost feel how close they were to land. Oh, how she longed for land, though she was hardly enamoured with their destination.

Angard, Helsabor's capital city.

Once they'd discovered where they were heading, Dragmall had started describing the city in great detail to Else, reminiscing about the places he remembered, the friends he'd left behind many years ago. Morana could tell that he was eager to go back to the place of his birth, though she was too busy thinking about how to evade Draguta to care to find out why. There were Followers in Angard, she knew. Followers who would help protect them. Morana had carved symbols around the ship, glowering at the helmsman who pressed his bearded lips together, turning away from her evil eyes. Every time she thought of a new symbol, she added it to the deck, to the mast, to wherever she found a clear piece of wood. Symbols she hoped Draguta couldn't see through.

Dragmall had helped.

Else had not.

She had been far too busy sniffling and fretting about Meena, who was likely dead. How could she not be after helping her escape like that? Morana smiled, letting the wind chill her body until her crooked yellow teeth were banging together; until she had to close her eyes and wrap her arms around her thin cloak to stop herself jerking about.

Morac was dead.

She had dreamed it, seen what Eadmund had done to him, certain that Eirik would have celebrated that small helping of revenge. And sad though she may have felt for a moment, her brother had never been of any real use to her. Evaine was just as hopeless, pointless now that she had lost Eadmund.

And none of it mattered anymore.

Morana was far away from Hest, from her family, from all that she had been.

She was heading for Briggit Halvardar and The Following, and an opportunity to start again.

***

'You're not worried?' Sabine asked. She was worried. Had been since the dreamers had seen the men marching into the mountains. All of them coming from Hest.

Coming for them.

'Worried about what?' Briggit snorted, watching flames dance in sconces around the walls of the long marbled hall, their flickering lights shimmering like golden waves. Briggit and her favourite companions, Sabine and Lillith, were eating alone. After spending the day with her soldiers, listening as they outlined their plans for the defense of the city, she had been looking forward to a different topic of conversation, though that had not eventuated. 'You think I should be worried about what Draguta will do? What her spellbound puppet kings will do?' Briggit finished her wine, licking her full lips. 'Draguta's an old woman. Long dead and not alive enough to know that she is no match for me. No match for any of us. Besides, it saves us the time of going to defeat her in Hest. Now we can just wait and finish her here. She is doing us a great favour by dragging all those men over the mountains in this terrible heat, just to be defeated! A great favour, indeed!'

'But she killed the Followers in Hest. All of them!' Sabine's dark-blue eyes blinked double time as she grasped Briggit's heavily ringed hand. 'She wants to kill you, and the Book of Darkness will make her near unstoppable.'

Briggit shook her off.

Sabine's fussing irritated her. She was an exceptionally pretty woman. Such luminescent skin, and lustrous brown hair that curled effortlessly over pert breasts. Briggit narrowed her eyes, sharp eyebrows rising slightly before she stopped herself.

Pretty but irritating.

Slouching back in her chair, she turned to Lillith who was not pretty at all, but far less annoying. 'Have you organised the meeting?'

Lillith nodded calmly, ignoring Sabine. The sisters had been fighting for Briggit's attention and her love since childhood, though Lillith had always been aware that Briggit had no interest in love. Not the love of humans at least. 'Yes, they will be here soon.'

'Excellent. Then I shall bathe, and you will gather what we need. Both of you. We have a great challenge ahead of us, and we must be prepared to face it. Do not fear, Sabine!' she laughed, leaning forward to stroke her fretful face. 'We will be ready. United. Draguta will not defeat us. She will not surprise us. We will be waiting for her.'

Sabine turned her blinking eyes towards her sister, who, for the first time, almost looked anxious.

'Don't be long,' Lillith warned. 'The Followers will be waiting.'

Briggit smiled, sliding out of her chair, her green dress slithering behind her. 'I'm glad to hear it. But don't worry, Lillith darling, they will wait for me. Of course they will. I am their queen, their leader. What choice do they have?'

***

Jael headed to the cove to look for Beorn who had escaped the fort before she could find him. She had been up before the roosters, conscious of how quickly they all needed to move now. They were hoping to leave the fort within seven days, eager to get to Draguta before she could cause any more harm. Eager to get Amma and Sigmund and Eadmund back too. Jael had sent a note to Raymon, asking him to prepare his men as quickly as possible, stressing the need to meet in Vallsborg earlier than expected.

And now she had to have everyone ready to depart.

She couldn't stop. Couldn't rest. Couldn't take a moment to think, though she knew she needed to.

And turning around, Gant could see that Jael looked ready to fall down.

'How about some ale?' he grinned, handing her a cup.

Jael was puzzled as she took it, grateful for something to drink. 'You walked all the way from the fort with that cup? Just for me?'

'Well, when I left the hall, I thought I'd find you somewhere closer!'

Jael took a quick drink and offered him the cup, but Gant shook his head, standing awkwardly in front of her, his eyes unable to focus anywhere near her face. Sighing, Jael finished the ale, leaving the cup in the sand. 'You're not coming.'

Gant blinked in surprise, drawing his eyes back towards her.

Jael shook her head. 'How many of these conversations am I going to have? First Thorgils, now you. Who's next? Aleksander?'

'How did you know?'

'I saw you with Gisila. I heard you. And, I suppose, well, I was going to ask you to stay.'

'You were?' Gant followed her towards a tussocked bank where she plonked herself down, eager to give her ankle a rest.

Jael turned to him, watching as he made a seat in the grass beside her. 'I don't want to. I want you with me. I need you with me. But who else can look after the fort now? We can't just leave a small garrison and an injured Bram and hope for the best. What's the point of going to defeat Draguta if she destroys everyone we love while we're gone?'

'Which she may try to.'

'She may.' Jael wasn't sure that she knew what Draguta really wanted, and she wasn't sure she wanted to find out. 'I hope not, but while the Book of Aurea remains here, she'll be a threat. She's been trying to take that book from the beginning. I don't imagine she'll stop when we leave.'

'No, you not being here will make it easier for her to try something. You and that raven of yours.'

It was unsettling, how little control they had over what was about to happen.

They could both feel it.

It was as though every thread of their lives was now dangling out of reach, leaving them grasping helplessly in the dark.

'You'll have three dreamers and a powerful book,' Jael reminded Gant. 'That's more help than I could ever give you.'

'You're sure?' Gant wondered. 'Sure you don't need a dreamer yourself?'

Jael blinked, surprised that it wasn't something she'd considered. 'Well, I don't think Edela is up for the journey, and I wouldn't take Eydis. She needs to be with Edela.'

'But what about Ayla? You're going to need some help, Jael. I imagine it'll be hard, fighting and dreaming at the same time.'

Jael laughed, glancing up at the sky as the clouds rushed overhead, darkening now. Turning back to Gant, she tried to remember a time when she hadn't felt suspicious of clouds. 'Mmmm, I can't see myself dream walking while trying to cut off Draguta's head.'

Gant could hear the tension in her voice. Reaching out, he placed a hand on her arm. 'I want to come with you.'

'I know.'

'You'll be fine without me.'

Jael didn't reply.

Gant squeezed her arm, trying to get her attention. 'There's nobody I'd trust more than you to do this, Jael. Nobody. Not even your father.'

Jael peered at him in surprise.

Gant's eyes were serious. 'This is your destiny. It's always been your destiny. That sword was made for you,' he said, his eyes on Toothpick's moonstone pommel. 'The gods believed in you. And Ranuf and I spent all those years teaching you what to do. You're going to be fine, I promise.'

Jael didn't know what to say. She saw Beorn in the distance as he walked down onto the sand with Snorri and Villas, all three helmsmen flailing their hands as they argued. Nodding quickly, she stood. 'I need to speak to Beorn before he disappears on me again. You should get back to Gisila, see how she is.' And smiling awkwardly, Jael headed across the sand.

Gant watched her go, imagining Ranuf sitting beside him, knowing that he was abandoning his children when they needed him most.

And not for the first time.

Dropping his head, Gant saw the cup in the sand, and he picked it up, his eyes meeting Jael's for a moment before she turned away.

***

Edela had left Biddy and Ayla on their knees in her garden. Entorp too. His salves were running low after the barsk attack, and when he wasn't tending to Gisila, or helping Biddy, he was back in his cottage, making more. Edela smiled, pleased to have so much help, though none of their preparations would be of any use if she didn't become more familiar with the Book of Aurea. It was hard to concentrate, though, with Gisila so weak and in so much pain. So Edela had brought the book to Gisila, and she sat with Eydis, beside her daughter's bed, the two of them studying the book together. Or, at least, she was studying the book, and Eydis was fretting beside her.

'You are welcome to leave,' Edela murmured distractedly, running her finger over a strange symbol, trying to force it into her memory; hoping to store as many symbols as possible in her mind; knowing that she wouldn't have time to fumble in the dark, searching for answers when they were under attack. 'I'm happy to sit here by myself. Perhaps you should get something to eat? It certainly smells like something nice is on offer out there. Or go and check on Fyn?'

Eydis frowned. 'No.' She was rubbing Vella's fluffy head as she sat beside her, wishing she had something to eat. 'Fyn doesn't need to talk to me. He needs to train. They all do. And I need to find what I can about the book in my own way.'

Edela looked up in surprise, hearing the resolve in Eydis' voice; she sounded just like Jael. 'Yes, you do, but surely you can only do that in your dreams? When you're asleep?'

'No, the book comes to me when I'm wide awake, and only then can I see what I need to do. How I can help.'

'Well, Dara Teros is out there somewhere too, isn't she? She must be. If only she would help us now. This book is useful, more than useful, of course, but it is not mine. I don't know it as she does. I don't know where all the answers are hiding. Those that I'm going to need, at least.'

Eydis heard the worry in Edela's voice. Worry for her daughter, and her granddaughter. Worry that she wouldn't be able to help them when it was time. 'But together we'll find a way, won't we? And Ayla. Dara Teros too. She saw what Draguta would do. She wrote it all in the book. It will help us, Edela. I know it will.'

Edela smiled, though she felt under attack from nagging doubts. She kept thinking about the knife that had killed Draguta, about how Bruno Adea had sold that scroll to Briggit Halvardar's mother.

Voices swirled around her head, mocking her, goading her, warning her that she was too old and useless to help anyone.

***

Jael gripped her wooden sword, distracted, not concentrating.

'Sure you're ready for this?' Ivaar called, scuffing his boots in the dust. A few hot days had dried out the mud in the training ring, making the surface more amenable than usual.

Jael looked up, staring into his piercing blue eyes, sensing how much Ivaar was ready for this fight. She wasn't. She didn't have any appetite for it at all. But by the looks on the sweaty red faces of the men who had stopped training to watch, plenty of others were too.

Her stomach rumbled, and Jael realised that she should have headed back to the hall for breakfast before agreeing to take on Ivaar. 'Ready to feed you some dirt!' she called half-heartedly to a loud cheer, led by Thorgils who had pushed himself up to the front with Torstan. And scuffing her own boots into the dirt, Jael took a deep breath and lunged, cracking the edge of her blade against Ivaar's, wondering if she should let him win.

Get it over with. Find some food.

Ivaar lunged, slapping his sword against Jael's waist, lifting an eyebrow as he skidded past her, regaining his balance, turning to face her again.

Jael sucked in her cheeks, realising that it was hardly going to inspire anyone if she let Ivaar Skalleson have his way with her. She loosened her shoulders, shaking her head, almost feeling better for a moment, knowing that she would need to get sharper and quicker and stronger if she was going to defeat Draguta.

And Eadmund.

If that was what Draguta was planning.

Rushing at Ivaar, Jael swapped her sword into her left hand, confusing him. Confusing him further when she dropped the sword entirely. Ivaar's attention switched sides, and Jael threw herself at him, arms around his waist, knocking him to the ground, his face turning to her in surprise.

His sword gone.

And for a moment, he looked just like Eadmund.

Hands empty now, Ivaar quickly reached for Jael's arms, but she was already rolling off him. And scooping up her sword, she was over him in a heartbeat, jabbing the tip of the wooden blade against his pulsing throat. 'That was too easy, Ivaar Skalleson. Why not get up and we can do it again?'

Ivaar growled, listening to the roars of laughter and the disappointed jeers that it was all over so quickly. He nodded. 'Again.'

***

Sigmund's terrified wail echoed around the cavernous stone hall.

Amma wanted to join him, but she was too busy trying to calm him down. Tanja appeared to have frozen, and Sigmund was sobbing loudly against her chest, his head wobbling around as he tried to squirm out of her arms. 'Here,' she said. 'Let me take him.'

Tanja released the baby who cried even louder as he was removed from her familiar arms by a nervous Amma, who jiggled him awkwardly, trying to put him over her shoulder.

She had no idea what she was doing.

They were standing in the middle of the hall, the enormous dragon throne in front of them, tables to the right. They were empty, but Amma could almost see her father and Osbert sitting there, both of them red-faced and drunk, toasting to the future success of their alliance with Haaron Dragos.

An alliance which had forced her into marriage with a monster.

One she thought she had escaped.

Amma wanted to run, but they were not alone. Slaves lined the walls. Shaven-headed, silent slaves who were watching them. And men. The helmsmen and some of his crew who had delivered them to Hest, and now waited to hear what prizes they would be offered. 'Ssshhh,' she murmured in Sigmund's ear as he fought against her, refusing to stay still. He felt hot.

She felt hot.

And then a voice she didn't recognise.

'Amma Furyck, or, I should say, Amma Dragos,' Draguta purred, striding into the hall, Brill and Meena trailing dutifully behind her. 'How delightful to finally have you returned to us. To your rightful home. To your husband's bed.'

Amma swallowed, not wanting to think about her brief time in her husband's bed. She tried to focus on soothing Sigmund, and on the tall, elegant woman who stopped, looking down at her with intense, almond-shaped blue eyes.

'And this must be Sigmund Skalleson.' Draguta turned to Brill, irritated by the horrific noise coming from the red-faced baby. 'You will retrieve his mother, unless she's killed herself. Find her and bring her here. She has work to do.' And ignoring the trembling Tanja and the wailing Sigmund, Draguta turned on her heels and headed for the throne, her white dress swishing softly behind her. 'Come closer, Amma,' she ordered, taking a seat. 'And give the baby to the girl. She may go and feed him, or whatever task must be done to stop that squawking.'

Amma's boots would not move, but Tanja's did. Having been offered a chance to leave, she was keen to take it, so grabbing Sigmund out of Amma's arms, Tanja left to find a corner where she could hide and try to stop his tears.

Left alone, Amma felt exposed, and as Draguta made herself comfortable on the throne, snapping her long fingers for a slave to bring her guest something to drink, she realised that she had no choice but to go to her.

'Do you know me?' Draguta wondered, narrowing her eyes, watching as Amma crept closer, realising that the girl was wearing nothing but a nightdress. 'Have you all been talking about me in Andala, I wonder? Planning what to do with me?' She smiled, sensing Meena shaking by the entrance. 'Girl!' she barked, her face hardening. 'Come and join us and we can all share our stories about Jaeger!'

Meena edged forward, eyes down, avoiding looking at Amma Furyck.

Amma was too busy trying to remember everything she had heard about Draguta to notice. 'I...' She wasn't even sure if Draguta wanted her to speak. 'I... I have heard about you.'

'Well, I would hope so! I didn't imagine that Jaeger would have a cloth-headed fool for a wife.' She smirked at Meena. 'No, a Dragos king needs a clever wife. A woman acutely aware of her place. One who knows what is required of her. A Dragos wife and a Dragos mother.' Draguta's eyes drifted down to Amma's belly.

Amma's eyes widened, and she instinctively wrapped her arms around herself. It was so warm in Hest that she didn't feel cold, though she did feel exposed and embarrassed to be standing there in her nightdress. Although neither of those feelings were as demanding as the terror she felt of not knowing what Draguta planned to do to her. Or where Jaeger was and what he would do to her too.

'Jaeger?' Draguta mused, reading her thoughts. 'Jaeger is not here.' She could see the instant relief in Amma's brown eyes. They were blinking and twitching like a rabbit about to have its neck wrung. Her nostrils were flaring too. Such a timid creature, she thought with a smile. 'Jaeger will return soon, and his absence gives us a wonderful opportunity to prepare you for your new role. By the time he arrives, my dear, you will know exactly what is required of you. You will know everything you need to do to please your husband. And Meena, here, will help you.'

Meena cringed, finally forcing herself to look at Amma, who appeared even more terrified than she was. And realising that, Meena tried to smile encouragingly at her, but Amma promptly burst into tears, sobbing just as loudly as Sigmund.

***

Evaine had not been out of bed in days.

She was bereft. Unable to think or act. Unable to see a path forward.

It was all so pointless without her father. Without Morana.

Without Eadmund.

She lay in the darkness, the unbearable, muggy darkness of her bedchamber, trying to remember when Eadmund had last looked at her with desire. When his hands had been on her body, holding her, touching her with need.

He had loved her. He had loved her.

But now?

She rubbed her eyes, wondering what time of day it was. Her servant, Elfwyn, was cooking. Perhaps that meant breakfast? Or supper? Evaine didn't know.

Stretching her legs, she ran a hand up her thigh, imagining that Eadmund was there, lying beside her...

The knock on the door was not loud, but Evaine frowned, annoyed to have been brought back into the present. 'Tell them to go away!' she barked moodily. 'Whoever it is! I want them to go away!' And she dragged a fur over her head, not caring to even guess who had come to her door.

Evaine turned over at the sound of a cough, staring at Brill whose long, thin body stooped awkwardly in the doorway. 'What do you want?'

Brill wrinkled her nose at the rank smell of the chamber. 'My mistress wishes you to come. To the castle.'

Evaine rolled back over. 'Well, I don't care what she wants. I'm not going anywhere. Why should I? She took Eadmund from me! Turned him against me! Why should I do anything Draguta says?'

Brill sighed, sensing that she was going to have a lot of trouble with Evaine. 'Because your son is here,' she tried. 'She wants you to come for your son.'

Evaine blinked. In all her grief for Eadmund and her father, she had forgotten all about Sigmund.

Her son with Eadmund.

And smiling, she rolled over, pulling back the fur. 'Tell Draguta I'll be there shortly.'

CHAPTER FOUR

Else shuffled down the busy pier behind Dragmall whose eyes were fixed on the palatial castle commanding Angard's square. Memories bubbled up of a happy childhood spent following his father across the cobblestones as he traipsed from the citadel to visit Wulf Halvardar, who had demanded his presence with great regularity. Dragmall had always felt a charge visiting the castle. It was bright and luxurious, filled from floor to ceiling with gold and marble and noise. So much noise. The citadel had been a place of darkness and solitude and study. A dull and depressing place to be as a child, though Dragmall had had little choice but to stay there with his father, being motherless from the age of three.

Hearing a barking cough, he spun around as Morana crept up to his right, her eyes on the armoured guards striding towards them, two of whom aimed for their small party, the rest walking towards their helmsman and his crew.

Dragmall stiffened, feeling Else grip his arm as they waited for the guards to stop.

'And you are?' the younger of the two asked imperiously, hand on his sword.

'Here to see the queen,' Morana snarled. She was cold and tired and impatient to get into the castle. Draguta would no doubt be watching, and she wanted to get to safety quickly.

The young guard looked her over, barely suppressing his disgust. 'And why would the queen want to entertain a party of beggars?' he wondered. 'You've come to the wrong place if you're looking for handouts!'

Morana shook her black-and-white hair, chanting under her breath, and within a heartbeat, both guards were stepping away, out of their path, leaving them free to head for the castle.

Dragmall and Else didn't move, though, not certain what Morana had done and not sure they wanted to go into the castle with her.

'What choice do you have?' Morana grumbled, spinning around. 'No choice! None at all. Now hurry up before Draguta is breathing down our necks. We need to get inside that castle!'

The thought of Draguta was more terrifying than anything Else could imagine, so she stumbled forward, hurrying after Morana. And with a heavy sigh, Dragmall picked up his feet and followed her.

***

Jael watched Ayla out of the corner of her eye. She was looking over the shields with Entorp. As well as tending to those who had been wounded in the barsk attack, he was also supervising the application of symbols onto every piece of equipment and armour they were taking.

Marcus was helping him.

Despite all that had befallen the fort, Marcus looked lighter. The heavy weight of worrying about Hanna had been lifted. She was still bedbound but getting stronger by the day. Astrid was caring for her, and he had a lot of confidence in her broths, which, despite their foul smell and unpleasant taste, had strengthened Hanna considerably. She was desperate to get out of bed, and Marcus could see no reason why she wouldn't be walking within days.

Turning her attention away from Ayla, Jael tried to pick up the conversation.

'These are the most protective symbols Edela and I can think of,' Entorp sighed wearily. 'But whether they will do anything against Draguta and her creatures...'

'I'm not sure that's why we need them,' Jael said, running her finger over the freshly engraved symbol in the shining boss of her new shield. 'I don't think we can stay safe from whatever Draguta is planning, but we want to protect ourselves from the Followers, wherever they are. Not many have tattoos for protection, so hopefully, these symbols can help us.'

Marcus nodded. 'And it's not just Draguta we need to worry about. There's Briggit too. She will have a role to play. Her and The Following.'

'Well, according to Edela, Draguta's sent Jaeger and Eadmund to attack Helsabor.'

That surprised both men.

'It makes sense,' Marcus said, chewing it over. 'They are a threat to her. Perhaps an even greater threat than you. The Followers need the Book of Darkness to bring Raemus back. And they require Draguta for that.'

'Why?' Entorp wondered. 'If they can take the book, use it themselves, why do they need her?'

'There is a page that describes the ritual to bring him back. It was torn from the book. I imagine Draguta knows where it is.'

Jael frowned. 'Perhaps they will welcome Draguta's attack, then? It's an opportunity to defeat her and take the book.'

'I would say so,' Marcus mused. 'But whatever the case, it will keep both Draguta and Briggit busy. Hopefully, too busy to worry about us for a while.'

'That would be good,' Jael smiled, watching Ayla walk away from Isaura. 'Keep going with the symbols. We have to do what we can. And don't forget the helmets. Swords too. Keep going!'

Entorp nodded, turning back into the smoking armourer's hut, slightly daunted by the task that lay ahead of them all.

Marcus stayed outside, his eyes on Jael, trying to think of anything else that would keep her safe while she tried to kill Draguta.

If only they knew where the shield was.

***

Morana watched Briggit Halvardar as she perched on the edge of her golden throne, dressed as though she was entertaining guests at a grand feast. Her gown was an eye-catching deep-red, embroidered with golden flowers that blossomed over an ample bosom. Her ebony hair shone, hanging simply past her wide face, resting on a pair of olive-skinned collarbones.

Morana scowled, not liking the look of Briggit Halvardar or the equally over-dressed women who stood on either side of their queen, peering at her as though she were a pig, turning on a spit.

Vanity, in Morana's experience, was an indulgence of the foolish.

The weak.

And there had always been far too much vanity on display in Angard.

Varna had taken her and Morac to Angard when they were small children. She had visited the city again as a woman, meeting Neera Halvardar and her daughter, Briggit. Liking neither of them. They were self-absorbed creatures, overly obsessed with their status as members of the ruling family. They professed to follow Raemus, to seek his return, as the Hestian and Tuuran Followers did, but Morana had always suspected that the only people Neera and Briggit were loyal to were themselves.

'Our mothers are dead.'

Morana blinked, irritated by the preening queen who stared at her, dark lashes fluttering over golden eyes.

'They are. And we do not mourn either of them.'

Briggit laughed, motioning for Morana to come closer.

Else and Dragmall had been ushered into the castle, left in the entranceway, happy to hide in the shadows, far away from flaming candles and mind-reading dreamers. So far Else had been unable to close her mouth. She had always imagined that Hest was the greatest kingdom in all of Osterland, with its majestic stone castle and its busy harbour, once filled with an impressive array of ships for war and trade. The Dragos' had always been keen to show just how rich and powerful they believed themselves to be, but this?

Angard's castle, though similar in size to Hest's, differed entirely in its interior. There were no dull grey flagstones lining the floor, no rough, plain walls that needed to be enhanced with colourful velvet tapestries. Briggit Halvardar's castle was made of marble, gleaming and light, and Else couldn't stop staring as she peered around, whispering in Dragmall's ear, hoping the queen would be content to speak to Morana and not request their presence at all.

Briggit's cat-like eyes held Morana's dark gaze. 'No, we do not mourn our mothers. They were useful for a time, but ultimately, weak. In the way. Obstacles to be removed so we could reach our one true goal.'

Briggit spoke like a true Follower, and Morana shook with pleasure to hear it. Vain, beautiful, but perfectly succinct. 'Agreed. And now we can, with my help.'

Briggit laughed, her freckled nose in the air. 'Your help? And why do you think I require your help, Morana Gallas?' She turned to Sabine who stood to her right, encouraging a smile from her pretty face. 'I appear to be sitting upon a golden throne, in command of a wealthy, powerful kingdom, while you are grovelling before me in need of a bath.'

Morana straightened her spine, shaking hair out of her eyes. 'I know Draguta. I know Eadmund Skalleson. I know Jaeger Dragos. And all three are coming for you.' She flapped a filthy hand in Briggit's direction. 'Dismiss me if you wish, but we want the same thing. I have spent my life fighting to be here, at this moment, as have you. Why not help each other get what we both want? I can be of use to you. I can help you stop them all. I can help you claim the Book of Darkness.'

Briggit frowned, leaning forward. Morana looked like a beggar witch, but she knew of her reputation.

She curled a finger in her direction.

Morana edged towards the throne. 'I have touched it. Used its spells. I have attacked with it. Maimed and killed with it. I know that book better than anyone here. Anyone in your kingdom.' Her eyes were on Lillith, who was a girl, just as Briggit was a girl. Neither of them understood Draguta and the book as she did.

Briggit's eyes were aflame as she leaped out of her throne, striding towards Morana. 'Yes, you have, haven't you? So why did you leave it behind? Why are you here, in my kingdom without it? Has Draguta sent you? For me?'

Morana laughed, ready to fall down with exhaustion. 'Draguta? I doubt she could be that clever. No, she imprisoned me, hoping to torture me for the rest of my life. I escaped.' She jerked in anger at the memory of being imprisoned in her own body, staring at that door, day after day. Unable to speak, eat, lift a limb on her own. 'Draguta made a mistake not killing me because now I can help you kill her. And then we can do what she was meant to. We can return Raemus to his rightful place. Together. We can bring him back.'

Briggit's eyes lit up as she studied the snarling creature before her, black-and-white hair sweeping the ground, her body twitching with rage. Briggit could feel it. She could see what Draguta had done. How Morana had been trapped in a chair, force-fed like a child. 'You seek revenge?'

Morana was dismissive. Impatient. That was not the point! 'I seek Raemus. Now. Everything else is just wasting time. And if we don't kill Draguta, we'll have no chance.'

Sabine and Lillith glanced at Briggit, neither of them liking the look of Morana Gallas, but the queen turned back to her guest with a beaming smile. 'I couldn't agree more!' She tried not to inhale as she motioned for a servant to come forward. 'I shall have Tilda find you somewhere to stay. A comfortable house, I should think, Tilda. And the baths. You shall ensure my... guest is given some soap. We will speak this evening, Morana. Discuss our plans. For your sake, I hope you'll have something tangible to offer, otherwise, I shall have to send you straight back to Draguta, and, after your little escape, I doubt she'll make the same mistake twice.' And striding back to her throne, Briggit left her servant to remove the ragged woman from the hall, wrinkling her nose as Morana's earthy scent lingered.

***

Meena was struggling to control her thoughts. They kept escaping, flipping away from her like a slippery fish. She couldn't grasp hold of them at all.

Once she had been jealous of Amma Furyck. Now she was supposed to befriend her. Help her.

She couldn't speak as she opened the door to Jaeger's chamber, holding out her hand, motioning for Amma to go inside.

Amma didn't want to go inside.

She remembered this place; what it had felt like when Jaeger had dragged her up here on their wedding night.

It didn't feel real.

She kept thinking about Axl, trying not to cry again.

Seeing that Amma wasn't moving, Meena walked ahead of her, into the chamber. 'You have to come,' she mumbled, growing even more uncomfortable.

Amma didn't know what to make of the strange woman. She only caught sight of her face occasionally as Meena shook her hair, bent over and twitching as she moved.

Amma didn't trust her. In Hest, she was sure, she couldn't trust anyone.

Meena realised that she would have to stay elsewhere. She was grateful for that, remembering the chamber Berard had given her; wondering what Jaeger would think when he returned. Turning to Amma, she could see the fear in the girl's eyes as she stood there not wanting to look around. Not wanting to see the memories of her time in Jaeger's bed.

Meena felt much the same. 'You must stay here now,' she tried. 'This is where you belong.'

Amma blinked, biting her lip.

Meena looked away, noticing her cloak on a chair, and she hurried to pick it up. 'I will leave you, and... send someone. I will send someone. You must have a servant. A maid. Someone to... help.'

'Wait.' Amma didn't want her to go. 'Do you live here?'

Meena twisted her cloak around her fingers. 'I... I... no. I... yes.'

'Oh. So you and Jaeger...'

Meena stared at the floor.

'I don't want to be here!' Amma panicked, hoping she could find an ally. 'I was taken. Those men took me. I don't want to be here!' Her eyes filled with more tears, and she dropped her head, shuddering.

Meena dragged a hand away from her cloak, wanting to take Amma's, to comfort her, sympathise with her. Then she saw a flash of Draguta's displeasure, and she flattened her hand back against her cloak. 'You belong here,' she muttered. 'This is your home now.' And hurrying past Amma to the door, she didn't look back. 'I will send someone. They will help you.'

Amma turned as Meena raced outside, shutting the door behind her, her shoulders drooping, tears streaming down her face.

***

Jael's eyes were everywhere as she walked Ayla through the fort. There was nowhere to go. Nowhere to sit. Nowhere to be alone. All the benches and tables had been removed from the square as the catapults were brought in for everyone to carve symbols onto. Jael wanted to believe that those symbols could work, but the voice in her head laughed at her.

She saw Axl, working with Aedan and he nodded, dark rings under his eyes. He wasn't sleeping, she could tell. Worrying about Amma, she knew. But what could they do about Amma except hope?

And wait.

Jael shook her head, listening as Ayla told her more about her dreams.

'Briggit believes that she'll defeat Draguta. She welcomes her attack. She is confident and prepared. Happy.'

'Well, she'd be the only one. Though, if she can defeat Draguta or Draguta can defeat her, that would make our job easier.' Jael tried to smile, but her lips wouldn't budge. Ivaar had not given up easily that morning, and she'd ended up with a kick in the mouth that had swollen her lips.

Ayla didn't look convinced. 'Together or apart, each one of them is still a grave threat. And neither of them will release the book, whoever becomes its mistress.'

'No, it won't be easy, which is why I need you, Ayla.'

Ayla stopped, surprised. 'Me?'

'I want you to come with me. To Hest.' Jael watched Ayla's eyes widen with fear. 'I need you to help us. There's no guarantee that Edela can do anything from here. Hopefully, she'll be able to protect the fort, but as for helping us... perhaps it's too much to ask of her? And I need to focus on my men. On leading us into battle. I can't be a dreamer when we get to Hest.'

Ayla felt her body tense. She saw fire. Darkness. She felt terror.

And her throat tightened.

Then she saw Bruno hobbling towards her, and she nodded. 'Of course. I'll come. Of course.'

Jael was pleased. 'Good. You'll need to do more than dreaming, though. I will need a healer. Someone to help Astrid.'

Ayla's eyes widened some more. 'You're taking Astrid?'

'I am. She doesn't know it yet, but yes, I am. Astrid's had some experience now with Draguta's creatures so she'll be the perfect person to help us.'

***

Astrid didn't look convinced. 'Hest?'

'You'll be with me. I won't let anything happen to you,' Jael insisted.

Astrid sighed.

'You'll be fine. I saved you from those dragur, didn't I? And besides, we're going to need someone with your skills. Someone to care for the injured.'

'Well, I can hardly say no to that,' Astrid admitted, glancing at the door as though readying an escape.

'I wish I could go,' Hanna said from the bed. Her cheeks had filled out, and she almost looked like the woman Jael remembered from Tuura. 'But no doubt I'll be stuck in this bed until you return!'

Jael smiled. 'I can't say anything about that, not being a healer, but you look fine to me.'

Astrid frowned, having grown very protective of Hanna since she'd moved into Marcus' cottage to care for her. 'Not quite, but close. Another day or two. That's what we agreed, wasn't it?'

Hanna scowled at her. 'We did.'

The knock on the door had her sitting upright, looking with interest to see who it was. Being bedbound, the only excitement in her day was receiving visitors, and now, after a day with no one, she had two at once.

Jael froze as Aleksander came in.

Aleksander froze, surprised to see Jael there. He quickly stepped back towards the door, bumping against it.

Astrid didn't notice; she was too busy thinking of all the things she would need to prepare before their departure. Too busy worrying about who would look after Hanna. Certainly not Marcus, who could barely look after himself.

'I...' Aleksander's voice was faint. He coughed. 'I should go. You have visitors.'

Jael laughed, though her eyes were sharp, and she felt almost as uncomfortable as he looked. 'No, I'll go. I'm going. You stay.'

Aleksander couldn't look at her. He couldn't look at Hanna either. He tried to focus on Astrid, who turned back to the cauldron, ignoring them all.

Hanna watched them both with interest.

'Come and find me when you're done,' Jael said, reaching around Aleksander for the door handle, wanting to go and find something cold to put on her swelling lips. 'We need to organise a wagon for Ayla and Astrid. I want them to have somewhere to work while we're on the road. Better if they're not on horses. And we need to keep everything dry for them too.'

Aleksander frowned, not understanding any of that, but he nodded as Jael left, almost wishing he could go with her.

Hanna smiled, all of her attention on Aleksander now. She was pleased to see him, despite the fact that he looked ready to bolt after Jael. 'Come and sit down. Astrid's just made a broth. Perhaps you'd like some?'

Aleksander shook his head, waking himself up. He remembered Astrid's broth. 'No, no,' he muttered quickly, carrying a stool towards the bed. 'I'm not hungry.'

Hanna laughed. 'I don't blame you.'

Aleksander sat down on the small stool, trying to meet Hanna's eyes. She smiled at him, and he found himself relaxing, forgetting Jael. Well, not forgetting Jael, but the warmth in Hanna's eyes helped remind him of why he'd come. 'You look better.'

'I feel better. Impatient to get out of this cottage. I want some fresh air!'

'You won't get any out there, I'm afraid. It smells better in here.'

'I find that hard to believe,' Hanna laughed.

'Well, you might think that broth smells bad, but you'll change your mind when you walk around the fort. It's not good.'

Hanna noticed all the cuts on Aleksander's face; the bandage wrapped around his wrist, his upper arms. 'You've had a busy time out there while I've been stuck in this bed.'

'We have. About to get even busier,' he grinned, remembering all the things he should be doing. 'A lot busier.'

'And what can I do?' Hanna wondered. 'To help? Soon I'll be out of bed. Maybe tomorrow.' She ignored Astrid's frown. 'I want to do something.'

'Well, you could help Astrid,' Aleksander suggested. 'We have to put together bags of herbs and salves. Tinctures too. Bandages. Splints. Whatever we can think of to take with us. I've a feeling we're going to need a lot.'

Hanna's smile was gone now, and she glanced at Astrid, who looked just as worried. 'I will. I can do that, can't I?'

'Yes, yes, you can,' Astrid said. 'It's the sort of thing you can sit at a table and do. You can be useful, I'm sure.' She was distracted, thinking of how far she had come since her time in Harstad.

Thinking of how far she was about to go.

***

Evaine strode into the hall with her head high. She had taken her time to get ready, and though her hair was dirty, Elfwyn had spent a long time brushing it, which had given it a sheen that was almost presentable. She had barely eaten since Eadmund had left, and her golden gown swamped her petite figure, but her eyes were sharp, and her shoulders were straight, and she carried herself with the determination not to be cowed by anyone.

Especially not Draguta.

Draguta inhaled sharply, motioning for Evaine to join her at the map table. She had been fascinated to realise that she could make it come to life. Having painted her symbols around the long perimeter of the table, she could now watch where everyone was. She could see how far away Jaeger and Eadmund were from Angard. How disinclined they were to ride together. Though soon they would have no time for grumbling and bickering. Soon they would need her support, and she would be ready.

'You require a bath,' she said, turning to Evaine. 'You will use mine. I cannot bear to be around such filth.'

Evaine looked as though she'd been slapped.

'And you will not disgrace Eadmund by being so slovenly again. Lying abed all day as though you were a wastrel with no prospects! You have prospects, Evaine. Plenty of them. How are you so blind?'

Evaine frowned, stepping forward. 'Prospects?'

'Your son is here. I have brought you your son.' Draguta placed a finger on the figure of a faded blue man. 'I have brought him for you and Eadmund.'

Evaine scowled. 'Eadmund killed my father. He wants to kill me!'

'But he didn't and he won't. You are the mother of his son. And seeing you with the baby will only confirm that.' Draguta peered at Evaine whose eyes were brighter now, though the stink of her was still strong. 'Watching as you tend to your tiny son? Seeing how much the baby needs you? He will soften towards you over time, I'm sure.'

Evaine wasn't. She had seen the hateful look in Eadmund's eyes when he'd threatened her. She wasn't sure she cared if he loved her anymore.

She shivered uncontrollably, her body protesting the lie.

'And his wife? What of her?' Evaine jutted out her chin, feeling her teeth scrape against each other. Just thinking about Jael Furyck made her want to spit.

'Eadmund will kill her,' Draguta said, already seeing how that would go. 'He will kill her because he is bound to me. He will kill her because I want her dead. But not yet. Not until everyone is in place. Not until I have everything I need. And then, my dear, Eadmund will be all yours, so go and wash that smell away and then, hurry to your son. You want to be ready for when Eadmund returns, don't you?'

***

Thorgils had dragged Fyn around the fort with him, not wanting him to slink away and hide from them again. He knew that Fyn wasn't the type to shirk his duties, but he also knew how deeply unsettling the loss of a parent was; even the loss of a parent as mean and angry as Odda had been.

It felt strange to be an orphan, Thorgils realised, but Fyn still had Bram. Though Bram appeared as distant and lost as his new-found son.

'There you are!' Thorgils boomed, surprising his uncle who had taken a break from supervising the wall repairs to head for the piers to check on Ulf. 'Thought you'd gone back to your cottage for a nap!'

Bram didn't look in any mood for Thorgils' jokes or his company. He ignored him and glanced at Fyn instead. 'Wondered where you'd gotten to,' he said. 'Thought you were going to come and help with the wall. We could use someone a little lighter up on the scaffolding. Taller too. We've too many short fat men up there. Not sure it'll hold.'

Thorgils laughed, pleased to almost see a twinkle in Bram's eyes. 'Well, they wouldn't want me up there, then.'

Fyn smiled, watching as Jael approached with Eydis. 'I can do that,' he mumbled.

'Do what?' Jael's attention skipped past Fyn to Karsten and Ivaar who she could see arguing in the distance.

'Bram thinks Fyn should be up on the scaffolding, helping to finish the wall, him being as light as a bean.'

Jael nodded. 'Good idea. And that way, we'll know just where to find you.'

Eydis wanted to say something to Fyn. To see if he was alright.

She didn't imagine he was alright.

'I had a dream about Morac last night,' Jael announced suddenly, noting the sharpening of everyone's eyes as they turned their gazes on her, constantly surprised by how similar they all were.

'Lucky you,' Bram grumbled, trying not to let his attention wander.

'He was dead.'

'What?' Fyn looked horrified.

'Dead?' Thorgils' eyes popped open. 'How?'

'I don't know,' Jael admitted. 'Evaine was there, sobbing over him, but no one else. He was lying on the floor, quite dead.' She had been confident that Fyn wouldn't feel sad about that, and the look in his eyes confirmed it.

'Well, I hope whoever did it made him suffer,' Fyn growled. 'He deserved to suffer for what he did to Eirik. For how he treated my mother.'

They were all quiet for a moment, remembering Runa.

'Well, whoever did it, or however he died, what matters most is that Morac Gallas is no more,' Bram declared. 'And that's the most important thing of all.'

'Agreed,' Thorgils added. 'That just leaves us with Morana and Evaine. Two more Gallas' dead and I'll be happy. Then the Svanters and the Skallesons will finally be free.'

Jael watched Bram and Fyn nodding, and she found herself frowning, knowing that it would take more than killing Morana and Evaine to make them free.

It would take so much more than that.

CHAPTER FIVE

The rain was driving Jaeger mad.

He was not used to it. Living in Hest, he was not used to rain at all, but the further west he travelled, the more it felt as though the dripping granite sky was clinging to him. Him and his equally sodden, miserable men who rode and marched behind him in the sloppy mud. Silently. The only sounds Jaeger could hear were the squeak and squelch of wet boots, the groan of wheels, the snorting and blowing of impatient horses growing bored with the slow progress of their trek towards Tokka.

Jaeger had left Eadmund to ride further back. Much further back. There was no need for them to keep up the pretence that they were leading this invasion together, not when Draguta wasn't there to snap at them. These were Hestians. His army. Nothing to do with Eadmund, who could fall off a cliff for all he cared.

Jaeger grunted, sick of thinking about Eadmund. He nudged his horse, leaning forward as they started climbing, conscious of how slippery the path was becoming.

Another reason to hate the rain.

His mind wandered from Hest to Helsabor, bored but anxious. He had seen The Following work their magic. He had seen what skilled dreamers could do, and he knew that they were being watched – by Draguta, of course – but he was certain that Briggit Halvardar was following them as well. He didn't feel happy about that, worrying that every rain cloud drifting towards them would reveal some new threat. He had been sleeping in disturbed bursts of panic, not even wanting to close his eyes; listening, trying to hear over the constant pelting of the rain, hoping to get a warning of what was coming for them.

Surely something was?

One more day, one more night and they would be in position.

If Briggit didn't try something first.

***

Else and Dragmall were pleased to have escaped Briggit's attention.

Though they could not escape Morana's.

Briggit's servant had found Morana a cottage in a noisy street near the castle, and Morana had insisted that Dragmall and Else share it with her. It was much more than a cottage, though, it was a fine stone house with three rooms, a bedchamber for Dragmall, one for Morana, and a number of beds in the main room, any of which were perfectly acceptable for Else.

It was the ideal arrangement, Morana thought, sipping the mint and licorice tea that Else had hastily prepared; an odd combination, but surprisingly refreshing after such an arduous journey from Hest. An arrangement that would give Dragmall and Else security, and Morana assistants who were bound to her, not by magic but by their desire to remain safe, under her protection.

She glanced at Dragmall, who had barely spoken since they'd arrived in the house. He sat opposite her, at the long wooden table in the main room. There were two fires, and Else was busy fussing over one, flipping hotcakes, collecting them onto a tray.

'I'm not hungry,' Morana grumped. 'Stop fussing. I'm not hungry!'

'Well, I am,' Dragmall sighed. 'At long last, I believe I may have rediscovered my appetite.'

Morana was surprised. 'I had thought you would simply fade away now that your part in proceedings is over.'

'Over?' Dragmall's stomach rumbled, and he looked longingly at Else's tray, wishing she would hurry up. 'You want to dispense with my services, then? Now that we've rescued you?'

Morana pursed her hairy lips, eyeing the old man.

He was a volka.

She didn't like volkas.

Those she had known were sanctimonious and condescending. They spoke to her as though her knowledge was less than theirs. They saw themselves as wise men. Only men. They had never put any stock in what dreamers said.

But Dragmall was different, she knew. She could feel it.

'You wish to be of service to me?' Morana scoffed. 'I doubt that!'

Else finally delivered the tray of hotcakes to the table. 'They're a little... crumbled, I'm afraid,' she apologised, red-faced and flustered, unfamiliar with the kitchen.

Dragmall thought they looked perfectly fine, and he quickly helped himself to one, spooning a dollop of honey onto it before rolling it up. 'I do not appear to have much choice in the matter,' he admitted, shovelling the hotcake into his mouth. 'Without you, I'm not sure what The Following would do to us. You and Briggit have made an arrangement, and while we remain with you, I suspect she will not harm us, so I don't believe that Else and I have any choice.'

'No, I suppose you don't. But as to whether I have any use for you...' Morana glared at Else, who quickly dropped her eyes. 'Though I cannot deny that I am only here because of you. Here, with an opportunity to defeat Draguta.'

'And you think that's possible?' Dragmall wondered. 'That you could kill her? She survived once.'

'She did. Twice if you count that she was dead before we brought her back to life.' Morana scowled, thinking about Yorik and the Followers, and how callously Draguta had murdered them. How much pleasure she had taken from their deaths. She would pay for that. And more. 'But now we are here. And now we have help.'

'You mean Briggit?'

'And her Followers. They will defeat Draguta. They have plans. Sound plans.'

Dragmall raised his snowy eyebrows. 'Draguta has the Book of Darkness, Morana. You know what that book can do. She has her seeing circles. She is watching. She will be prepared for whatever plans Briggit has made.'

'She may watch,' Morana sneered, glancing around the walls of the room where she and Dragmall had drawn symbols, hoping to keep Draguta from peering inside. 'But then what? The Followers are united and powerful. And so is Briggit. More powerful and knowledgeable than Draguta realises.'

'What do you mean?' Else had returned to her skillet, though her attention quickly drifted away from her hotcakes.

Morana smiled. 'I mean that Briggit has the prophecy.'

Else looked confused but Dragmall didn't. His father had told him all about the Tuuran prophecy. He frowned. 'The prophecy was destroyed not long after it was written from what I've heard, so how can Briggit have it?'

Morana was confused. 'How do you know that?'

'I am a volka, Morana. Like The Following, volkas have centuries of knowledge to call on. We are the collectors of history. Curators of myths and legends.' He looked around at Else whose eyes were back on the skillet. 'Whatever Briggit has is not the prophecy. It is likely an account, taken from someone who read it or dreamed about it. Memories. And who knows how accurate those memories are. No one ever found the actual prophecy, but one dreamer was convinced that the girl who wrote it had burned it. Thrown it into the flames.'

Morana's mouth hung open as she listened. 'And you know this how?'

'My father. He was the master volka here for decades. The most knowledgeable man in the kingdom.'

Morana scowled.

Dragmall frowned. 'The prophecy was a document so powerful that perhaps its author rightly feared that it would end up in the wrong hands. So, whatever Briggit has may be relevant and useful. Or it may just be the misrememberings of one dreamer. And who knows where their loyalties lay?'

***

The city of Angard gleamed beneath a brief sun shower as Briggit glided out of the castle, down the steps, heading for the harbour. The cobblestones were slick, and Sabine was fussing beside her, mumbling about slowing down.

Briggit smiled, listening to her panic, smiling wider as she glanced at Lillith who appeared oblivious. How different those sisters were, she mused, her attention suddenly on the exceptionally tall man who was striding towards her, squaring his shoulders as he approached.

'My lady!' Ebbert Foyle called. 'The sun has come out just for you! We were all drowning not five minutes ago.'

'Well, I imagine the gods realise how powerful I'm about to become!' Briggit's eyes drifted towards the harbour, the piers so full of warships that there was barely enough room for the merchants to moor. Though that thought did not displease her. She had little patience for the complaints of those greedy men, and no need for their gold. 'And how are your preparations coming along, rain or not?'

Ebbert's smile broadened, his armoured chest puffing out. 'They are complete. We are ready.'

Briggit was surprised by his confidence. Or not. Ebbert had proven himself very loyal after the death of her grandfather. And her father. And her mother. And her uncles. All her soldiers had. But then again, once she had bound them, they'd had little choice.

'I'm pleased to hear it. And what will you do tonight?' Briggit wondered, her eyes roaming Ebbert's lean body, admiring how snugly his shining mail shirt hugged his chest. He barely looked a day over thirty, though he was approaching fifty. 'Where will you wait for the attack?'

'I shall be here, my lady, with my men. On the square. We will protect the castle. If they get over the wall, or into the harbour, we will be ready.'

'Hmmm, if they get over the wall...' Briggit smiled at the thought of it. That wall had mattered so much to her grandfather. And his grandfather. Centuries of wall building, for what? To keep their gold all to themselves? Hoarding it like dragons? 'Well, perhaps you should join me for supper before you camp out here with your men? I'm sure Sabine and Lillith would enjoy the company.' And waving her hand at her two frowning companions, who did not like to share, Briggit strode past Ebbert, wanting to inspect the men who straightened up as their queen approached, pushing their shoulders back. 'Well, come along,' she laughed. 'Come along, my little pets. Let us see how well Ebbert has prepared his warriors.' Briggit felt a lift as she walked, knowing that everything was about to begin.

Draguta Teros thought that she would crush Angard and take her kingdom, but the Followers of Helsabor were Raemus' finest and they had never been defeated.

***

Draguta felt different. Each day she awoke feeling changed from the day before. Power was surging through her, and she was fighting to contain it. To calm her twitching muscles and her sparking anger.

Control.

The ultimate power lay in self-control.

To not act reflexively, but to think strategically. To plan and wait and percolate, so that every little piece, every part of her plan would come together as designed at precisely the right moment.

To jerk and thrust impulsively in one direction would only leave her dissatisfied.

Disappointed.

Draguta leaned over the map table, picking up the black figure of a man. She stared at it, wondering how she could put her faith and trust in one as impulsive and reckless as Jaeger. Though, she smiled, thinking about her son, Jaeger was a true Dragos. A pulsing mass of muscle and energy, seething and demanding and hungry for power.

For victory.

He wanted to conquer, and for her, he would.

Helsabor would be theirs. Jaeger would place the head of his army in charge, and then, perhaps, Draguta mused, returning the black figure to the table, picking up the blue one, perhaps she would make Eadmund the King of Helsabor? Surely, he would prefer the wealthy golden kingdom to the salty little rock of Oss?

Spinning around suddenly, she saw Meena creeping down the stairs, trying not to be seen as she headed for the doors. 'Girl!' she snapped. 'You are going somewhere that I have not asked you to go! Somewhere far away from my potions!'

Meena, sighed, turning into the hall.

'And where is Amma? What have you done with the girl? You are supposed to be watching her. Looking after her and my potions!' Draguta growled, leaving the map table behind.

'Brill took her to the markets,' Meena mumbled. 'And I need more roseroot.'

'Oh. Well, that sounds surprisingly reasonable,' Draguta admitted. 'Though by the look of you, you're hiding something.' She peered at Meena, whose thoughts revealed nothing, and quickly bored with trying to pull on that stubborn thread, she turned towards the throne. 'Well, hurry up, then. You must be ready by tonight. I have plans. We have plans. Ensure that you are ready, girl.'

Meena could feel her heart fluttering inside her chest, reminded of what it felt like to hold a bird; feeling its panic, its urgent need to fly far away.

***

Karsten kept staring at Berard. He was trying to push himself between Ulf and Bayla who were embroiled in a discussion about finding a new cottage.

Bayla still wouldn't let that go.

He shook his head, turning back to Jael. 'I don't want Berard to come.'

'What?' Karsten had tagged along as Jael headed to inspect the wagon they had chosen for Ayla and Astrid to travel in. It would need a roof. Sides. Symbols. It needed protection from the weather and from Draguta too. Jael was going to leave Beorn in charge of that, which hadn't pleased him as he appeared to be in charge of so many things now. 'Berard thinks he's coming. He wants to come. He's been in the training ring every day trying to get stronger.'

Karsten laughed. 'Berard could train till Vesta and be no better than he is now. He needs to stay here and not get himself killed.' His eye was back on his brother, watching as Nicolene joined his mother, agreeing with Bayla's side of the argument no doubt. He'd heard nothing but complaints from both of them about the state of their cottage. 'He needs to stay here.'

'And you want me to tell him?'

Karsten nodded. 'It's better coming from you. He won't listen to me. I'm just his brother. But you? You're very persuasive, and Berard listens to you.'

'Not sure it's much of an argument, saying you don't think he's good enough to come. I doubt he'll listen to that.'

'Berard's never been good enough with a sword. Never. But he's the only brother I'll have soon. And if something happens to me...' His eye met Nicolene's and, surprisingly, she smiled. 'If something happens to me, who will look after them?'

Jael followed his gaze. The Dragos family was so far removed from the one she had met in Hest. Half the size. No fine garments. No impressive castle. No swagger to any of them any more. Not even Bayla.

'He should stay here. This fort needs someone like Berard. Someone with a quick mind. There are enough of us who can use a sword. We don't need him.'

'Well, I can't argue with that, but I've a feeling Berard will. He's got a good reason for wanting to go to Hest.'

'He has,' Karsten agreed. 'But just like my father, he wouldn't stand a chance against Jaeger. I need to end him. Berard needs to stay here in case...'

Jael could hear the lack of confidence in Karsten's voice. 'Jaeger will die,' she promised him. 'If you can't kill him, if something happens, I won't let him live.'

Karsten stared into Jael's eyes, surprised to find that he didn't want to dig them out with his fingernails anymore. 'Good. Don't. Whatever you do, whatever happens to me, don't let Jaeger live.'

***

After two goblets of mead, Briggit was beginning to wonder why she was letting Morana Gallas live. Though, she reminded herself, staring at the morose dreamer, she was a Follower. A Follower of reputation and standing, and Draguta's sworn enemy. Still, she felt wary as she leaned forward, helping herself to a cherry from the bowl which sat on a low table between them.

After an uncomfortable supper in which Morana had barely spoken, Briggit had brought her into one of her private chambers, wanting to discuss her plans.

Wanting to know what Morana knew of Draguta's.

'That ridiculous woman is an empty vessel,' Morana began. 'A complete disappointment!' Dark eyes intensified, the memory of Yorik's death returning in a rush of angry fire. 'I raised her. We all did. And yet it was all a lie! She didn't want Raemus. She just wanted to be a queen. To rise again and rule. A crushing disappointment.'

Briggit could read Morana's thoughts. They were loud and furious, dark and twisted, and she started to relax. 'And now you wish to end her, once and for all?'

Morana nodded. 'She was a mistake. My mistake. If I hadn't raised her, I would still have that book. Yorik and his Followers would still live. All of them.'

'All is not lost, Morana,' Briggit assured her. 'I have nearly three hundred Followers here with me. Almost one hundred of them dreamers.'

Morana's black eyes popped open. 'That many?'

'Oh yes, the Followers may have hidden in Hest, and in Tuura, but in Helsabor they have roamed freely for years. Our base of power has been growing for some time.'

'And now?' Morana couldn't read Briggit's thoughts at all, but Briggit was happy to share them.

'Draguta made herself valuable by tearing out the ritual to bring Raemus back. She knows where that page is, so we take Draguta and her book. And when Raemus returns, we will watch as he kills her.'

Morana ignored Briggit's smug smile. 'But first, we must stop her from killing us. She is sending Eadmund Skalleson and Jaeger Dragos here. Thousands of men with weapons. And she has that book.'

'Yes, she does, but do not worry, Morana, I have been planning this for some time. We are prepared to defend ourselves, and we will.' Leaving her goblet on the table, Briggit stood, motioning for Morana to follow her through the balcony door. 'Come with me, and I'll tell you exactly what I have planned.'

***

Brill was a strange creature, Amma decided. Strange but kind. And that was a comfort. In this terrifying place, with the horror of being reunited with Jaeger to come, Amma was grateful for some kindness.

Brill had taken her to the markets, to the tailor, who had measured her, noting the bump where her stomach was starting to protrude. Amma wasn't sure how she felt about that anymore. It appeared obvious now that the child was Jaeger's. Why else was she here?

Yet, it was hers too.

She shook her head, conflicted as she followed behind Brill who was pushing down the crowded street, forging a path for them both. It was hot, steaming, and Amma could feel her dress clinging to her. She wiped her face, wanting something to drink.

And then Meena was there.

Amma smiled, convinced that Meena was just as nice as Brill. Both of them appeared trapped beneath Draguta's thumb, though. And that position, she could see, had rendered them almost mute, shaking with nerves.

Much like her.

'Draguta wants you to come,' Meena said, ignoring the people jostling her, and the determined flies buzzing around her face. 'She is in the hall. Waiting.'

Amma nodded, butterflies flitting around her stomach as she fell in beside Meena, both of them quickly leaving Brill behind.

'What will she do to me?' Amma asked quietly. 'What will she do to everyone?'

Meena swallowed. She couldn't talk to Amma.

She couldn't tell her anything.

'She wants you to be Jaeger's wife. To have his baby.' Meena didn't feel comfortable talking to Amma about Jaeger. She kept seeing visions of him lying on top of her, stroking her face. She blinked. 'Draguta wants you to be the mother of the Dragos heirs.'

Amma sighed, tripping over a broken cobblestone. She fell to her knees with a crash, her basket falling with her, spilling out the fabrics and brooches she had half-heartedly bought.

Meena dropped to the ground. 'We must hurry now. Draguta does not like to be kept waiting.' Her eyes were on the cobblestones, grabbing two plums that had rolled away.

'Help me,' Amma whispered, gripping Meena's arm, trying to get her attention. 'Please help me. I need to go home. To Andala. You can come. You'll be safe there.'

Meena blinked, wanting to yank her arm away.

Andala.

She thought of Berard. If she said anything, anything at all...

'I can't help you. You are safe here. Draguta wants your child to be born. You are safe here,' she insisted, scrambling back to her feet, holding out a hand. Her eyes met Amma's, and though neither of them spoke, their shared feeling of terror was undeniable.

Amma could sense it as she stood, bending down for her basket. And nodding her head, she tried to remember Axl and Jael.

Axl and Jael were coming for Draguta.

And if she could just hold on, if she could just survive, then they would come for her too.

CHAPTER SIX

'That looks sore,' Axl mumbled between mouthfuls.

His sister was finding it difficult to eat with swollen lips. Ivaar, who sat at the opposite table, was struggling not to enjoy it.

Jael could tell, and she wasn't about to give him the satisfaction of thinking that she was in pain. Dropping the crab claw back onto her plate, she reached for her ale. 'Not really. Still works.' And eyeing Ivaar, she raised her cup, deciding that they would need a rematch. She didn't like the idea that anyone could lay a hand on her.

Or a boot.

'You seem better today,' Jael said, turning her attention to her brother.

'Better?' Axl grabbed his own cup with a heavy sigh. 'I don't think so. Maybe.' He shook his head, confused. 'I'm happy about Gisila. She's healing quickly.'

'She is.'

'But it's been so long without Amma. She'll be in Hest now, won't she? If they made it there.' His frown intensified, making him look like their father.

Jael smiled to see it, but she didn't want her brother to play that game. She knew how it felt, wondering where Eadmund was, what he was doing, who he was doing it with. 'Focus on what you can do, Axl. The wall is looking solid now, and everyone's working hard to prepare the army. Focus on what you can do, not on what you can't. And you can't do anything about Amma. Not yet.'

Axl scowled, irritated. He looked around for Gant, but he wasn't there. Nor was Aleksander. Throwing back the last of his ale, he eyed his sister. 'We need to talk about what will happen if...' His eyes darted around and he waited while his steward filled his cup before disappearing back into the kitchen.

Jael lifted an eyebrow. 'If?'

'If I don't return.'

'Been thinking about that, have you?'

'Of course, haven't you?' Axl lowered his voice, sensing his sister's discomfort.

'About coming back? No,' Jael lied, 'I'm focused on getting there. What happens when we get to Hest is up to the gods.'

'Or not, depending on who you listen to these days.'

Jael stared at her brother, wishing she could see something that told her he would come back. Dreams came to her intermittently. They did not seem to bend to her will as much as she bent to theirs.

She saw nothing about what was coming.

But she did hear that voice.

'True. But we'll do what we can, whatever we can, to bring everyone back, including Amma and Eadmund.'

'And if we don't return? What will happen to Brekka? Who will be king here? What Furyck will rule?'

That was a good question.

'The gods wouldn't let the Furycks die out. They wouldn't. Furia wouldn't.' Jael hoped it was an argument that Axl could believe in. 'If something happens to you, I'll come back. I'll rule here. I won't let Brekka fall.'

Axl looked relieved to hear it.

'Until your child is old enough.'

'Doesn't sound as though it's my child.'

'Not your blood, perhaps, but it will be your child in your heart.' Jael thought of Sigmund, reminding herself that they would need to bring him back too. Runa had died trying to save that baby, and Jael would do whatever she could to bring him home.

Him and his father both.

***

Eadmund wanted Berrick to leave his tent.

It was early, but he was weary. Five days of slowly trekking through perilous mountains had been arduous, and, at times, terrifying. The weather had turned foul again, and he felt a heaviness in his body he hoped sleep would cure.

It had to.

They had finally arrived at Tokka, a crumbling rock of a village clinging to the edge of a cliff near the coast. It reminded Eadmund of Flane, which brought back taunting images of a naked Evaine. Eadmund quickly closed his eyes on that memory, smelling the sea, wishing for a patch of earth that wasn't barren or mud-slick, and company other than his irritating steward, who had been fussing around him ever since their arrival that afternoon.

Tomorrow, they would attack the wall around Angard. They could see it from their camp - if you could call it a camp. It was more of a shelf of rock where the Hestians had gathered to eat and stay warm, huddling around fires, trying to dry their wet clothes and warm their shivering limbs. Despite the heat of the days, the nights on their journey had often been as cold as Oss.

Eadmund, like Jaeger, was sleeping in a tent. He didn't feel comfortable about that, but Berrick had insisted, and though his steward was hardly someone to listen to, Eadmund knew that Draguta would be happier if he slept like the leader she wanted him to be. 'You can go,' he grumbled sleepily, rolling over. As well as raining, the wind was picking up again, screaming around the walls of the tent, snapping them noisily. Eadmund yawned, wondering if the gods were trying to disrupt Draguta's plans.

Wondering if he wanted them to.

'Yes, my lord,' Berrick muttered. He was not looking forward to another night out in the rain, but Eadmund had made no move to let him sleep inside the tent, so he had little choice but to leave. 'I will come in the morning, before dawn.'

Eadmund didn't reply. He was already seeing the familiar face of Morac, who had haunted his dreams since he'd left Hest. He didn't blame him, certain that he would do the same to the man who'd murdered him.

But Eadmund didn't care. He thought about his mother.

About what Morac and Morana had done to her.

He didn't care.

Trying to turn his mind away from Morac's corpse, and Berrick's muttering, he saw his mother again. He heard her gentle voice as she smiled, motioning for him to follow her. And sighing deeply, feeling his body sink into the cot bed, Eadmund slipped into a dream.

***

Briggit felt calm.

She could hear the storm battering the thin glass of her bedchamber windows.

The wind was becoming violent, and she wondered if they would shatter.

Perhaps that was what the gods intended?

Ebbert had been a good distraction, but he was sleeping beside her now, his bare feet hanging over the end of the bed, and her mind had wandered to Draguta. She was both a curse and a gift. The woman who had placed herself between Raemus and his Followers, thereby making herself indispensable.

The woman who had the power to give her everything she wanted.

And she would.

Briggit's dreams were vivid slashes of colour.

Blood red, golden light.

She saw Draguta, and Draguta was on her knees. She ran her hand over Ebbert's back. He stirred but did not wake, his scarred muscles tensing.

Draguta was on her knees.
And then what?
Briggit smiled.
She had seen that too.

***

It was as though Draguta's mind was a beehive and all the bees were talking to her, buzzing with a desperate fervour. She could read their thoughts, their fears and desires. Mostly their fears.

There were so many of them.

Sighing with happiness, she headed into the catacombs, not noticing how stale the air was, or how it clogged her throat. It was dark, though she had all the light she needed from the torches carried by Brill and a burly slave she had commandeered to help her. With no Jaeger, no Eadmund, and no Rollo, there was no one to do her heavy lifting anymore, so she had replaced them all with a new man named Ballack. A man twice as wide as Jaeger, and uglier than an inbred troll. A strong-jawed, hulking beast of a man with arms big enough to move a stone coffin. 'That way!' And pointing to the archway, Draguta hurried ahead of the shaven-headed slave and her shuffling servant. 'Come along, come along, we can't take all night! We have work to do. More things to prepare. All this dawdling, waiting, hesitating! I am growing bored! The pieces of my puzzle are taking far too long to fall into place. I say we give them a little... push in the right direction!'

***

Eskild could feel the battle of dark and light inside her son, and she wanted to help. To intervene. She had exposed what had remained hidden for all those years, revealed it all, and Eadmund had killed Morac, and left Evaine.

But it wasn't enough.

Soon Draguta would make him kill Jael, and with it, every part of himself.

And if that were to happen...

Eskild needed to help him. In here, she hoped, in Eadmund's dreams, Draguta couldn't find him. Couldn't get to him. Couldn't twist him into self-destructive knots. Couldn't make him kill for her.

Eadmund didn't recognise where his mother was taking him. It was a small fortified village. Not Oss. Not an island.

Brekka?

'Come with me,' Eskild said. And she walked through the door of a thatch-roofed cottage, into a brightly-lit room.

Eadmund followed his mother, his eyes quickly on a tired-looking Thorgils, wrapped in bandages, sitting on a stool beside a bed. Aleksander was there, frowning, a woman he didn't know standing beside him.

And Jael.

Jael was in the bed.

Eadmund blinked, hurrying forward.

She was in pain, he could see. Crying out. He couldn't move any further, though. He couldn't help her.

'That's it,' the woman urged. 'As hard as you can. Push as hard as you can!'

Jael screamed out as Eskild gripped Eadmund's arm, feeling the tension coursing through it as he stood beside her. And with a powerful roar, Jael threw her head forward, gritting her teeth, squeezing Aleksander's hand. Sweat shone on her brow, her braids stuck to her forehead, her face cut and bruised.

Exhausted, she dropped back onto the pillow, dark hair splayed across the pale linen, Aleksander checking to see if she was alright. Her eyes remained closed. Eadmund wanted to get closer, but his boots wouldn't move.

He wanted to be there, holding her hand.

Jael opened her eyes as the woman wrapped the baby in a blanket.

The baby.

Eadmund listened, but there was no sound. No sound but the exhausted panting of his wife, who lay in the bed, tears streaming down her face.

No sound as the woman carried the baby away.

No sound as Thorgils watched her, tears falling down his own cheeks.

Just as they were falling down Eadmund's.

'We will make her pay for this,' he heard Aleksander say. 'We will make Draguta pay for what she's done.'

Eadmund turned to his mother, who held his gaze, her eyes reflecting the pain in his. And when he turned back, they were no longer in the cottage, and Jael was sitting against a tree, a tiny bundle in her arms.

He edged closer, wanting to hear what she was saying. Wanting to be with them.

'I was lying when I said I didn't want you,' Jael almost whispered. 'I was lying. I wanted you very much. More than you will ever know.'

Eadmund watched as Jael wiped her tears from the baby's face.

'I'd thought of a name for you, you see. It was Lyra... Lyra Skalleson.' And bending forward, Jael sobbed, gripping the baby to her chest.

Their baby.

Their daughter.

Dropping his head, Eadmund wiped the tears from his eyes, watching as they dripped on the grass.

Their daughter.

***

Jael shut the door and leaned her back against it, sliding down to the floor. She felt just as impatient as Axl and Karsten, though she'd never let them know it. She wanted to ride to Hest, slice her sword across Draguta's throat, tear her open. Make her pay for what she had done to all of them.

Dropping her head to her knees, Jael sighed, wondering if she had the energy to drag herself into bed.

She doubted Draguta was quaking at the thought of being attacked by a gaggle of exhausted, injured, broken warriors, led by the most broken one of all.

Lifting her head, Jael grimaced, feeling around her lips.

Hardly a fiercesome leader, she grinned, struggling back to her feet, knowing that she needed sleep if she wanted any chance of thinking clearly in the morning.

Or dreams. Perhaps she needed more of those?

Sitting down on the bed, Jael wasn't sure which was preferable, then she remembered what Edela had said about Eadmund attacking Helsabor. Helsabor which was ruled by a dreamer queen and her army of dangerous Followers. Eadmund was trading one enemy for another. Jael frowned, tugging off her dusty boots, wanting to grasp those threads, to have some control.

Any control at all.

Pulling off her socks, she placed her bare feet on the floorboards, feeling the rough surface against her heels, wishing she could push them straight into the earth. She had an overwhelming urge to ground herself. To remember who she was.

'A warrior,' her father barked. 'You're a warrior, Jael.'

And smiling, welcoming his voice, Jael lay back on the bed, closing her eyes, trying to remember his face as he stood before her in the training ring, glaring down at her. Trying to encourage her, motivate her, prepare her.

So many times she had wanted to give up, but he'd never let her.

Countless times he'd pushed her into a situation she thought she wasn't ready for. And she'd never let him down.

'You're a warrior, Jael,' Ranuf growled. 'And now it's time to fight.'

***

There were boxes everywhere, lids discarded now as Draguta dug into each one. She had faint memories of the contents of some. Strong memories of others.

What she was looking for was tiny.

It was the key to their attack on Helsabor. And despite her earlier confidence, Draguta was starting to wonder if someone had come into the tomb and helped themselves to it. But who?

Had those revolting Followers known about this place?

Nothing appeared to have been disturbed, though. But where was it?

'You!' she shouted at Ballack who was edging towards the stairs, wanting to find some air. 'Get back here and do some digging for me. And you!' she grumbled at Brill who looked just as uncomfortable as she tried to suppress a cough. 'A box is missing. It must have been put inside something else. It's not large.' She was muttering, almost under her breath. Taegus had given it to her. A prize, he had promised. The perfect weapon. He wanted her to have it.

She had to find it.

'Keep looking!' Draguta screamed. 'I must have it! Hurry!'

***

Morana could hear Dragmall snoring through the wall. She was certain that Briggit would be able to hear him from the castle. And though it was hard to think of Briggit without sneering, Morana had to admit that she was a surprisingly shrewd woman. Those cat-like eyes were conniving, yet careful, and Morana couldn't see beyond them.

She wanted to.

She wanted to know why Briggit was so confident that she could defeat Draguta. Morana had seen what Draguta did to Yorik and his Followers, though her attack on them had been a surprise. This time they would know.

They would be waiting.

The crash of thunder that shook the house was louder than Dragmall, and Morana was grateful for some respite from his hideous noise. Thinking of Dragmall reminded her of the prophecy, and she wondered if the old volka was right. Could it be that what Briggit had in her possession was no more than a story? Something masquerading as the true prophecy?

And if that were so, then Morana needed a plan.

A way to survive whatever Draguta intended to throw at them.

***

Draguta sighed, sinking to her knees with a smile, gripping the box. It was impossibly tiny, smaller than she had remembered. She had never used it before, though she could still see the gleam in Taegus' eyes when he had presented it to her.

The Ring of Taron.

It did not shine like the baubles worn by the ladies of Hest. It did not gleam or glimmer or catch the eye. Its plain silver setting held a large, oval, black onyx stone. Impenetrable. Dark. Deadly.

Draguta blinked, lost for a moment.

That was the last time she had seen Taegus; just before his mother, that bitch Daala, had killed him. Anger flared as she rounded on Brill. 'Now, go!' she snapped impatiently, wanting to be alone. 'And take that beast with you. Leave the torch, though. I will be up soon. And then we will go and wake Meena.'

Brill hurried away, not wanting Ballack to leave without her.

Draguta didn't hear them. She didn't hear anything but the

pounding of her heart as she held her breath and popped open the lid again, inhaling the odour of neglect, and death.

Lifting her eyes, she smiled.

And victory.

***

Jaeger hoped Draguta would be ready.

At her seeing circle. Watching.

She needed to be. They couldn't get into Angard on their own.

Turning away from the wall, he headed back to his billowing tent, knowing that although his body was already vibrating with anticipation for the impending battle, he had to get some sleep. His sword arm needed rest, as did his mind. Sitting atop a horse day after day had both bored and exhausted him, wearing him down with tedium. He was ready for battle. A release from all the tension.

In his mind, at least.

Reaching his tent, Jaeger turned around to look up at the wall, stretching back his neck. He wasn't sure that he could even see its ramparts. The storm clouds were low, dark, rolling, the wall disappearing into them.

'My lord? This way.'

Jaeger frowned, certain he recognised the voice, rubbing his aching eyes as he walked towards it, surprised by how heavy the rain suddenly was. He didn't hear the voice again. Nor did he hear any footsteps, but suddenly, he was entering a wood. He shook his head, convinced that he hadn't seen a tree in Tokka since they'd arrived. He swallowed as a figure appeared before him. 'Egil?' Jaeger was confused, turning around, starting to panic as bare trees thickened into a lush deep-green forest, enclosing him in a grove. He could hear the sound of rushing water now, the distant hooting of owls.

And turning back around, he came face to face with his father.

'My son,' Haaron growled, his condescending smile bright in the moonlight.

There was no rain. No storm clouds anymore.

'How I have missed you.'

Jaeger felt warm all over. His tunic was too tight. Too heavy. He reached up, yanking at the collar, pulling it away from his neck. He couldn't breathe. 'Fuck you,' he spat, turning again. But when he stopped, his father was still there. 'Get out of my way, old man. I ended you! You're irrelevant to me now. Get out of my way!'

'Irrelevant? Am I?' Haaron smirked. 'I imagine you wish that were so, Jaeger. I am dead. Your brother is dead. Berard has one arm. And Karsten is coming to kill you.'

'He can get in line.' Jaeger turned again.

Haaron was still there.

'Get out of my way!' Jaeger seethed, pushing past his father – through his father – but when he reached the trees, there was no way out. Nowhere to go.

Haaron laughed. 'You think you can escape, Jaeger? For what you've done? For what you're about to do? You think you can escape those you've hurt? Killed? Your brother is coming,' he warned, following Jaeger as he spun around, trying to find an escape. 'He is coming to end your miserable life.'

Jaeger jerked awake, panting, looking around the tent.

'My lord?' His servant was bending over him, a lamp in his hand.

Jaeger could hear the rain thumping onto the tent roof, dripping through it.

'My lord, it is time to begin.'

PART TWO

Weapons

CHAPTER SEVEN

Jael blinked in the darkness, wondering for a moment where she was. Turning her head to the right, she was half expecting to see Fyr perched there, watching her from the chair in the corner of her chamber.

But she was alone.

Not even the puppies were with her tonight.

Closing her eyes, she tried to fall back to sleep. From experience, she knew that if she didn't do it quickly, her mind would wake up and then there was no chance. No chance of sleep again.

Then she saw a flash of Eadmund, and panicking, Jael opened her eyes, sensing that he was in danger. Lying perfectly still, she tried to focus on his face, hoping to see what was happening. Wanting to find him.

'It's too late,' she heard him say. 'I have to go.'

And then he was gone, and Jael blinked into the dark void of her chamber.

Alone.

***

'But, my lord!' Berrick charged out of the tent after Eadmund, cringing into the crashing storm. 'You've forgotten your cloak!'

He had been trying to help prepare Eadmund for the battle, but Eadmund had been impatient, focused on leaving the tent as quickly as possible. He was still sleepy, not concentrating on getting dressed.

'I don't need it!' he called, hurrying into the darkness, the rain cold on his face, eager to get to his men and far away from nagging Berrick.

Berrick watched him go with a grumble before turning back to the tent, happy to hide from the storm.

***

'A storm! A storm! Of course there's a storm!' Draguta laughed, full of good humour despite the hour.

They were in the hall, standing around the map table: Draguta, Brill, Meena, Ballack and a handful of yawning slaves ready to assist their mistress, wondering what she was talking about.

All of them waiting to hear what Draguta needed from them.

But Draguta was barely there. Her glazed eyes were focused on Tokka as an odd-looking Jaeger shrugged on his mail shirt; watching Eadmund at the other end of that tiny settlement, running through the rain, heading for his men.

It was dark, but the lightning, when it came, was helpful.

Draguta was grateful.

Grateful to those desperate gods who were so powerless now.

Grateful for their help.

'Girl!' she snapped at Meena, suddenly back in Hest. 'You have my first potion ready?'

Meena looked puzzled.

'You do have them in order, as I requested?' Draguta grumbled. 'How else were we going to tell them apart? The first one is the mead, yes?'

Meena was tired, having only just fallen asleep when Brill

hammered on her chamber door, dragging her out of bed, but she nodded, understanding now.

'Well, bring it to me. I need it now! And the fire, Brill, get that higher. Ballack can help you. I assume you have more wood than that? We will need it!'

Her assistants rushed around as Draguta's eyes were drawn back to the map table where the blood-red symbols glowed around its wooden edge, guiding her, showing her everything she needed to see. 'Hurry up!' she demanded. 'They will not wait for any of you! Get those herbs smoking, Meena Gallas! It is time to begin!'

***

Mud. Jagged shards of lightning revealed nothing but mud.

Jaeger was shivering, shaking as he ran, his mind a twisted pile of bracken, tangled with jarring thoughts, half trapped in his dream, worried that Draguta wasn't watching. That she wouldn't be able to help them.

There were men all along the wall. Looking up, he could see silhouettes moving - little black shadows, tiny as ants - and they were moving quickly, alert to the danger below. 'Go! Go! Go!' he ordered, motioning to the right with one hand, to the left with the other. 'Hurry!' And Jaeger's men crept towards the wall, half following Gunter, who would head down the hill, drawing fire. The other half trailed after Jaeger. Eadmund and Berger were further east where they would wait for his signal. 'Stay out of their line of sight!' he called hoarsely, though the rain hammered down on them, drowning his words. Jaeger shook even more, imagining for a moment how pleasant it would feel to be sitting by his fire with Meena. Blinking rain out of his eyes and his wandering thoughts far away, he tried to concentrate.

Shouts along the ramparts.

Flaming arrows lit up the angry sky, flying fast enough to beat back the threat of rain.

Jaeger ran, pinning himself against the stone wall, his chest heaving as he waited, listening, hands flat against the dripping stone.

They had planned this out. He had talked it through with Eadmund until they both wanted to kill each other.

Draguta had insisted that they just needed to be ready.

They just had to wait for her.

***

Briggit nodded at Morana Gallas, who hid beneath her dark hood as she joined the queen and her Followers in the rain-lashed square, directly in front of the castle. Briggit had not wanted to hide away. She did not want to miss what Draguta would do.

Monsters and creatures from the Book of Darkness?

Those that had belonged to Raemus himself?

Briggit didn't want to miss this.

She had cast a circle in the square before night had fallen, scraping it into the cobblestones, sacrificing three slaves and one horse; mixing their blood with herbs and spices, her own blood too. She had poured the mixture into the indentations in the stone and cast a spell. A spell to keep them safe within the circle while they battled their enemies. A dreamer circle of protection that would not be broken, could not be broken, of that Briggit was certain.

She watched Morana take her place on the opposite side of the circle. She was a knowledgeable dreamer, Briggit knew, and her hatred of Draguta was like a weapon. She would help keep the circle secure.

Draguta might think that she could come into her kingdom, and take whatever she wanted, but she had never fought The Following of Helsabor. Their magic had been taught to them by Raemus himself.

Handed down for generations. Never forgotten.

As Draguta would soon find out.

***

Jael was more tired than she'd realised, and she had fallen back to sleep quickly, her mind focused on Eadmund, but when she found herself in a dream, she saw Draguta stalking around a map table.

They were in Hest's hall.

The fire burning in the long stone hearth crackled noisily. Jael glanced around, but there was no Amma. No Sigmund. There was that bug-eyed girl she remembered from her time in Hest, an enormous shaven-headed slave, a morose-looking servant, and Draguta herself.

Jael shook, staring down at her bare feet, cold on the flagstones.

She walked closer, wanting to hear what Draguta was saying, listening to the sound of a storm. Thunder booming. Rain and wind too. Men screaming, running. The sound of horses.

Jael could feel the rain dripping on her, splashing her feet.

She was so cold.

Placing the silver goblet near the edge of the map table, Draguta slipped a knife from her belt; a beautiful ivory-handled knife, symbols etched along its haft.

Just like Toothpick.

Jael shivered as she leaned forward, watching Draguta slide the blade across her palm, dropping it to the table as she squeezed her blood over the map, forming what looked like a circle.

Draguta was chanting as she smoothed the bloody line with a long finger. 'The second bowl now, Meena Gallas.' Her voice was distant, quiet, but Meena had been waiting for her, and she carried the bowl forward quickly.

Jael swallowed, watching as Draguta drank from it before picking up two wooden figures from the table and dunking them into the bowl. Pulling them out again, she placed them back on the table, dark liquid oozing over the map.

'And now my boxes, Ballack. The big one first.'

Jael turned, watching as the slave came forward carrying a large wooden box. He placed it on the table beside Draguta, attempting to open the lid.

She shooed him away, her eyes glazed. 'That is not for you.' And watching as Ballack retreated to the blazing fire, Draguta opened the box, pulling out...

Jael frowned, feeling herself stumble, worried that she was losing the dream as everything started to blur.

What was that?

***

Morana watched Briggit, pleased that she had been included in the circle for the defense of Angard. Nobody knew Draguta as she did. Nobody knew what the Book of Darkness could do.

Nobody living at least.

'She is coming!' Briggit called, her voice reverberating around the Followers. The dreamers, all women, were dressed in simple black robes, forming the outer circle, of which Morana and Briggit were a part. The inner circles contained the rest of the Followers, mostly men. 'Can you feel it? That bitch thinks she can kill us! Destroy the last stronghold of The Following! But our people are Raemus' finest! Our ancestors were taught by him! This was his home once! We are his people! We will succeed for him!'

Morana scowled, unimpressed with the wild-eyed dramatics of the queen.

She could feel the warmth of the ritual mead in her chest. She could taste the familiar iron tang of blood in the air. 'Draguta will know that we are here!' she called across the circle, rain splashing her face. 'She is watching!'

'I hope so,' Briggit smiled, her bloody teeth bright in the storm.

***

Eadmund leaned against the wall, panting, wet through, his body jolted by each boom of thunder. It was coming in louder and louder bursts now, dropping lower.

His teeth were chattering. He should have grabbed his cloak.

Berger was there, his usually hooded eyes bursting open. 'My lord!' he screamed, pointing at the wall as hot coals were tipped down from the ramparts; sparks flying as the coals flew through the rain.

'Look out!' Eadmund cried, running away from the wall, wet boots slipping on gravel. Fire arrows shot down from above, landing in front of them, sizzling as they dug into the sloppy ground. 'Back to the wall!' It was no surprise, of course, but they were caught between being burned alive or being burned alive. The challenge of the terrain had been so great that no siege engines had been able to travel, and the wall was too sheer, too tall to climb, as no doubt the Halvardars had intended. 'Archers!' he bellowed. 'Fire at will!' His archers were hidden behind boulders staked around their rocky campsite. 'Fire! Now!'

***

How long was she going to take? How long was she going to take?

Jaeger was shivering uncontrollably, sheltering against the wall, watching the burning arrows spluttering around them. The rain fell even harder, finally dousing the flames, but the hot coals were more stubborn, their burning heat fighting the rain's determined deluge.

He wondered where Draguta was.

What she was waiting for?

He felt strange, his body tingling, everything suddenly turning hazy.

***

Draguta sighed contentedly, her eyes on the items she had removed from the wooden box.

Jael shuddered, suddenly reminded of the ravens, the dragon, the barsk. She edged closer, trying to see what Draguta was holding, and as Draguta turned, the flames from the hearth flickered, making them shimmer, sparkling like blue and green waves. Scales, Jael realised with a frown. They reminded her of fish scales. And she froze, thinking about the sea serpent she had killed.

'When all old kings are murdered, when ravens rule the sky...' Draguta's voice was that of a girl. She did not sound like herself at all. 'Ravens?' she laughed, her own voice returning with a roar. 'Why use a bird when you can use a beast?'

***

Eadmund's guts were griping, but not from fear. It was as though he had eaten something rotten. He could taste it in his mouth; his mouth which was suddenly full of bile. He blinked, trying to focus, but he couldn't clear his mind.

'Aarrghh!'

His men were screaming, on fire, as some of the flaming arrows struck their targets, hot coals continuing to tumble over the wall, burning liquid too. He could smell fish.

He needed to focus.

There was no sign of Draguta, but they couldn't remain holding the same position much longer. He had to do something. He couldn't let the Hestians be slaughtered.

And then Eadmund felt a sudden rush overhead; a gust of wind so strong that he was knocked to the ground, pressed flat against the sodden earth.

His men were all down too. Flattened. Unable to stand as the long shadows passed overhead, the force of the wind pinning them where they lay.

***

'Hold the circle!' Briggit cried, though she did not open her mouth. She had no need to speak when she could communicate with her mind, far away from Draguta's open ears. 'We hold here!' And gripping Sabine's and Lillith's wet hands, she began to chant.

Ebbert had his men lined up in front of them.

He was the first to die as a powerful sea-green dragon swooped down over the wall, blowing a hot stream of fire all over him and the men who stood beside him, consuming them in a rush of murderous flames.

'Shields up!' screamed Ebbert's second-in-command from three rows behind. 'Shields! Protect the queen! We must protect the –'

Briggit smiled, pressing her boots against the wet cobblestones.

Dragons.

She could stop a few dragons.

***

Jaeger hadn't known what Draguta was going to do, and picking himself off the muddy ground, his men with him, he wasn't even sure what he had seen. Lightning exploded from the rumbling storm clouds, shooting down into the enormous shapes flying over the wall.

Dragons, Jaeger realised. Bigger than ships.

Readjusting his armour and his sword, he lifted his eyes up to the top of the wall as the burning Helsaborans started falling over it.

Screaming. On fire.

Dying.

***

Draguta's two dragons, the largest one an eye-catching, shimmering blue-green, the other one smaller with jet-black scales and burning red eyes, plunged down from the storm clouds, flying low over the square, turning the scattering army to ash. Their flames could not penetrate the circle of dreamers, though, as the Followers remained united, peering at the terrifying beasts who roared and threatened them as they incinerated the soldiers trying to protect them.

Briggit could feel her heart racing, heat swelling around her, watching in awe as the magnificent beasts dipped and dived, their wings spanning the width of the castle, their mouths opening and closing like bellows.

'Run!'

Voices rose in panic around them, soldiers scuttling like beetles, fleeing the flames, trying to escape the exposed square, looking for shelter.

The black dragon screeched, holding its wings wide as it swooped down towards a line of charging soldiers. Soldiers who were running in the direction of the castle, though they did not even make it to the steps before they were consumed by the killing flames.

Morana could feel the Followers' hands gripping hers, surprised that there was no tension in them.

There was tension in Morana's hands.

A lot of tension.

She had not anticipated that Draguta could conjure up more dragons. Those fire-breathing bloodthirsty giants of the sky had terrorised thousands before Daala had ended them.

After she had ended Raemus.

As Morana watched the dragons turning, preparing to target the square again, she panicked, feeling the rain trickling down her back, her eyes on the blood in the indentations of the circle that would soon be washed away.

***

'What do we do?' Berger cried, eyes on Eadmund. 'We can't climb the wall!'

They could barely hear each other over the roaring of the dragons, and the terrified cries of the Helsaborans; those on the ramparts; those on the other side of the wall. The dragons may have been burning and killing their enemies, but how were they going to get into Angard to finish the job?

'We wait!' Eadmund insisted, his voice ringing in his ears. 'Stay alert! We need to be ready!'

'Ready for what?'

Eadmund shrugged. He didn't know.

***

Briggit could feel the circle moving. Tremors of fear like waves were starting to shift it. 'The circle will hold!' she insisted, trying to keep them all together. 'I can stop the dragons! We are safe, do not fear!'

But the dragons were quickly turning and diving over the wall again, side by side now, each fiery mouth bellowing more flames as they flew low towards the castle, aiming for the circle.

Briggit's body was pulsing with energy as she closed her eyes, trying another chant, knowing that Draguta's monsters could be defeated.

Everything could be defeated with magic.

***

Jael could hear Eadmund.

His voice. The storm. The screams.

She could hear it all.

But she stood in the hall behind Draguta who had put down the dragon scales and picked up another box, this one so tiny she had to strain her neck to see what was inside.

'Oh, Briggit,' Draguta smiled. 'You think the dragons are my real weapon?'

And popping open the lid, she pulled out a ring.

CHAPTER EIGHT

Dragmall held Else close, feeling her heart thump against his chest.

'Who will stop it?' Else whimpered. 'Can they stop it?'

They were hiding in a corner of the house, listening to the terrifying bellow of the dragons swooping over rooftops, shaking the walls. They could hear the panicked cries of the men and women who were fleeing the square; those in their homes as their roofs collapsed, fires sparking in thatch.

The smoke was quickly overpowering, seeping under the door, through the gaps in the windows, filling the house with thick, eye-watering clouds.

Dragmall pulled Else closer. 'Draguta wants Briggit,' he croaked, hoping to convince them both, trying not to cough. 'She will not want her dead, will she? What fun will she have then? Don't worry now. Don't worry.'

***

The fire-breathing dragons soared over the square, avoiding the harbour, Draguta's sharp voice in their ears keeping them well away from those precious vessels. They attacked the last dregs of the army instead; those whose formations had broken, whose courage had abandoned them. They sought out running soldiers still holding useless swords and shields, incinerating them.

And they kept going.

Her army in panicked flames, collapsing around the circle, Briggit kept chanting, an unnaturally calm presence amidst the thundering chaos. Eyes bursting open, she yanked her hands away from Lillith and Sabine, pushing her way through the Followers, into the middle of the circle. Drawing her knife, she cut across her palm, digging into the wound, needing blood.

The circle of dreamers quickly closed around her, the roars of the dragons louder than the sound of thunder as it clapped above their heads, threatening them all.

On her knees, black hood falling over her wet face, Briggit drew a symbol, murmuring a chant.

She knew this. She had seen this in her dreams.

This symbol would work.

And throwing back her hood, she watched the flames shooting overhead as the dragons screeched, in pain, their wings suddenly dropping. And then they were spiralling quickly, falling with a speed that had Briggit's heart stopping, her head craning back, trying to judge where they would land.

On her circle? Her harbour? Her castle?

She held her breath. Waiting.

The dead dragons fell through the smoky clouds like anchors being dropped into the sea. Those Angardians still in the square scattered, screaming, the storm crashing over their heads.

And then the dragons.

The black dragon hit the square with a crash that had the Followers in a heap, knocked over by the sheer force of its impact. The dragon's neck snapped, its head shattering the cobblestones as it skidded to a stop before the piers, the tip of its long tail slamming down just outside their circle.

The sea-green dragon smashed into the narrow rows of houses bordering the harbour, one wing dipping into the water, the rest of the dragon's shimmering body turning the houses to rubble, sparking the thatch into flames.

Briggit swallowed, trying to focus.

Sabine was over her quickly, wanting to help her back to her feet.

'Get away!' Briggit snarled, standing up, her hand dripping with blood. 'Get back into the circle, you fool! You think she's done?' She spun around, glaring at them all with demanding eyes. 'Do you think Draguta is done?'

***

'She's quite right,' Draguta mused, holding the ring on her finger. It was far too big for her delicate hand. Big and powerful, and ready to kill. 'I am not... done. But your queen is.'

***

Eadmund couldn't hear the rush of the dragons anymore. He couldn't hear the men on the ramparts. He could hear the screams of the dying, though.

The burning. The frightened and the running.

And he could hear Draguta.

'Are you ready?' she asked. 'Are you ready for me?'

***

Morana felt herself trembling as she waited, holding her breath, smoke in her eyes. For all that it had taken to escape Draguta's prison in Hest, how was it possible that she was to be killed here?

Or, more likely, taken right back to that ridiculous woman. Back to that chamber. Back to the place where she couldn't move an arm or a leg.

Helpless.

She would welcome death before she allowed that to happen again.

Morana thought of Raemus, gripping the Followers' hands, ignoring her fears. Ignoring the panicked voice in her head warning her that she was in danger. She needed to move, it urged, before it was too late!

Sabine could feel the tension in the air. A heavy fug of smoke blew towards them, and she coughed, needing water. She couldn't breathe. 'We need to run,' she tried, hoping to get Briggit to see sense. 'Draguta will kill us all!'

Briggit ignored her, pushing her boots firmly against the cobblestones. 'We do not break the circle! Draguta is no match for The Following! No match for our symbols! No match for me!'

And then she felt it beneath her boots. A vibration.

As though the earth was shaking.

***

Jaeger sheathed his sword, confused, almost losing his balance as the ground undulated beneath his boots. 'Take cover!' he yelled. 'Get away from the wall!'

***

Jael held her breath, watching as Draguta placed her ringed finger on the map, pushing it down, straight through the bloody line she had drawn.

Rising up on shaking tiptoes, Jael leaned over the table, peering at the line.

The line around Helsabor.

The wall.

***

'Get back!

Eadmund could hear Draguta's warning. 'Get back!' he bellowed, running with his men, away from the wall. 'Hurry! Run!' And throwing his shield onto his back, he pushed Berger forward, racing after him, trying to keep to his feet as the terrain shook and shuddered all around them. The sky was lightening, the storm was retreating, but it was still almost impossible to see where they were going.

And then the wall exploded behind them, shards of rubble flying everywhere.

***

'No!' Briggit shrieked, watching in horror as an enormous hole was ripped through the wall, rubble flowing down onto the square like a waterfall, cascading over those who had been hiding from the dragons. 'No!' She swung around, looking for a soldier. Anyone. Anyone who had men.

Men with weapons. Arrows.

She needed archers.

Where were her archers?

'Into the breach!' she ordered, finally seeing a man who wasn't on fire. 'Get your men to the wall! Now!'

The man was shaking, not moving, and then Briggit saw why: his left arm was missing, just a bloody stump remaining, dripping blood and gore onto the broken cobblestones. She didn't care. He could use the arm he had. 'Find archers! Get men! Get to the wall! You must defend it!' And spinning back around, she tried to quell her panic.

Dreamers. Dreamers. Dreamers.

Dreamers could defeat warriors.

'We stand and fight for Raemus!' she bellowed. 'For Raemus!'

***

'Let's go!' Jaeger roared, the dull streaks of dawn light revealing a gaping hole in the wall. He coughed, dust in his throat, irritating his eyes as the tumbling rubble started to settle. 'Follow me!' He stumbled, tripping over a collapsed part of the broken wall, grimacing, thinking about his ankle – the ankle Jael Furyck had done so much damage to – and he smiled.

First Helsabor and Briggit.

Then Jael Furyck.

And moving more quickly now, Jaeger lifted his sword in the air as the Hestians surged after him. 'For Hest! For Hest! We will claim Angard for Hest!'

***

Briggit heard the Hestians rushing into the city like a roll of thunder.

It had been her grandfather's greatest fear that Angard was too close to the wall. But it was where his ancestors had chosen to build the castle; where the harbour was most amenable, protected from invaders, surrounded by a circle of ship-wrecking stones.

Still, Wulf Halvardar had fretted enough to ensure that that part of the wall was higher than the rest, wanting to ensure that no enemy could climb such a sheer mountain and claim his prized gold.

Not imagining that anyone would ever go straight through it.

'We can fight men!' Briggit yelled, pulling her circle closer, urging her hooded Followers to stand with her. 'Let them come! We don't need swords! We can fight men!' She thought of how many men she had dispatched to her borders, knowing that Draguta had sent the rest of her army to the east. That appeared to have just been a ruse, though warriors with swords and shields weren't the defense Helsabor needed now.

'We will defeat them!' Briggit insisted, her voice rising over the screams and the terror and the rumble of Hestian warriors in the distance.

Morana wasn't so sure.

She was continuing to panic as the clouds of smoke pumped towards them, rain soaking her robe. She felt hot, as though Draguta was standing before her, breathing warm air on her face. She could almost see those red lips curling into a satisfied smile, knowing that it didn't matter what Briggit did, or what she said. Draguta had them trapped.

She had been defeated too many times now.

She would not walk away from this.

She would claim a decisive victory.

She would crush the city and The Following.

***

Dawn was hurrying towards Angard now, dust from the smashed wall clouding the sky like dirty fog. Eadmund was struggling to see. He blinked to clear his eyes, moving towards the wall, stumbling on the uneven surface, littered with rubble. Shards of stone and rocks and broken pieces of mortar jabbed into his boots. The hole in the wall was wide enough for his men to pass through in numbers, and he could see the opening as they approached.

Though not through it.

What was waiting for them on the other side was shrouded in clouds of dust.

'Archers!' he bellowed, his voice hoarse. 'Line up behind us! Wait for my call!' And nodding at Berger who was coughing beside him, his eyes blinking out of a dust-mask, Eadmund gripped his sword and started to climb into the city.

***

Jaeger.

Morana could sense him before she could see him, and suddenly there he was, a hulking shape emerging from the smoke, striding across the square towards their circle, his dusty warriors fanning out behind him.

Draguta's king now.

She didn't know what to do.

The smoke and dust were mingling together, and she couldn't breathe. Nor could anyone else. The Followers were coughing, bent over, struggling to see.

It was suddenly impossible to stop coughing.

The smoke.

There was something strange about the smoke.

Morana yanked her hands away from the old dreamers on either side of her, covering her mouth and nose, trying not to breathe. Her eyes were watering as she spun around, not caring about Briggit or her defense of Helsabor anymore, but suddenly very conscious that Draguta had already won.

And she was not going back to Hest.

The clouds descended, choking them, and Morana dropped to her knees, oblivious to the cobblestones scraping the skin off her shins as she crawled away with speed, forcing her way out of the circle, the bloody line smeared and broken as she hurried across it, disappearing into a cloud of smoke.

She was not going back to Hest and Draguta Teros.

***

Jael stepped back, wanting to cough, feeling the dust in her throat, knowing that Eadmund was in the midst of it all. She could hear him shouting, ordering his men to stay alert as they approached.

She watched Draguta whose eyes were round and big and fixed on the map, on what she could see, and Jael could only hear.

Jael turned away, wanting to take a deep breath of fresh air, wanting to see Eadmund, but suddenly she was back in Andala.

She blinked. At Furia's Tree.

Her shoulders slumped, her head falling forward, the weight of what she had witnessed threatening to drown her. She sank to the ground, onto her knees.

No one could know.

No one could know.

***

Once Eadmund and his men had made it through the hole in the wall, he could see that there was no one to fight. Those who hadn't tipped off the ramparts when the dragons had flown over, had been killed by those same dragons as they terrorised the square with their flaming breath. Those who hadn't been killed by the flames had been crushed by the shattering of the wall.

And those still standing couldn't breathe well enough to fight.

They held up swords and hands, trying to see through thick waves of smoky dust.

Some fell to the ground, unable to stay awake. Others stumbled around, trying to find an escape.

The corpse of the black dragon was like a range of mountains stretched across the smoky square. Eadmund couldn't see beyond it but he could hear the crackle of fire, and see the glow of flames in the distance as he clambered over the rubble. The guard towers backing onto the wall had been crushed. He saw bodies flattened, in pieces, lying at strange angles, limbs buried in layers of dust.

Charred corpses everywhere.

Eadmund scanned the chaotic scene before him, and despite the swirling smoke, his head suddenly cleared, and he remembered that Draguta wanted to claim Helsabor for Hest. He held up his own sword. 'Surrender!' he called to the men pulling themselves up out of the rubble. 'Surrender now!' He bent over, coughing, realising that there was barely an enemy in sight. Not any standing. And not any who looked ready for a fight.

Shoving his sword back into its scabbard, Eadmund reached out and grabbed hold of a hand, pulling a bleeding soldier out of the debris. 'Help them!' he ordered, turning back to his men. 'Get them out of here!'

***

Briggit stood tall, watching Jaeger Dragos and his men advance on her circle, determined to fight till her last breath.

Draguta would not take her.

She would not take Sabine or Lillith either.

She would not take any of her Followers.

And nor would Jaeger Dragos.

Holding out her hands, she smiled as he approached, motioning for his men on either side of him to surround the Followers. 'You cannot enter this circle!' she shouted. 'Try it! Try it and see what happens!' And gripping Sabine's hand, Briggit started chanting, her eyes on Jaeger, daring him to come closer.

Jaeger could hear the shrieking woman, but he was struggling to see which one of the hooded creatures she was. The haze of smoke was thicker than anything he'd experienced on Skorro, but as he stepped closer, gripping his sword, the smoke parted to reveal the ranting Queen of Helsabor.

Briggit Halvardar glared at him, dripping wet, covered in dust, black robe clinging to her, hood half-covering her shining wet hair.

Jaeger jerked to a halt, smiling.

He could hear Draguta's voice urging him on, and sheathing his sword, he lunged into the circle, wrapping a filthy hand around Briggit's throat.

Briggit's eyes popped open in horror and confusion.

Jaeger's men quickly rushed the circle, seizing hold of the panicking Followers surrounding her.

'No! No!' Briggit shook her head, gagging, trying to wrench herself away from Jaeger as he dragged her to him, her boots scraping across the cobblestones.

Across the line of the circle.

The impassable circle.

How?

Holding Briggit an inch from his smug face, Jaeger kissed her roughly. 'First, we'll have some wine, and then, I'll have you!'

***

Draguta's sigh was satisfied.

It had been quite a defeat. Complete, she thought to herself.

Crushing. Though Briggit had killed her remaining dragons with that symbol of hers and the irritation of that needled her. She would have to think of something else for her looming battle with Jael Furyck and her Brekkans.

Spinning around with a smile, she eyed a confused Meena, determined not to let any small niggles tarnish her victory. She would focus on all that she had achieved. Helsabor belonged to her, and so did the South.

And now it was up to Eadmund and Jaeger to finish the job and deliver her prisoners, her gold, and her ships with haste. Draguta's eyes gleamed as she sought out Brill, who was slouching by the hearth. 'Wine, I think, don't you?'

***

Briggit hated the smell of Jaeger Dragos; the stinking, strutting arrogance of him. She tried to twist away from his hold, consumed by an unfamiliar flicker of panic, wondering where Sabine and Lillith were. The dust was swirling now, cutting her off from her Followers. She could hear them shouting out in protest and pain, though she couldn't see them. But she was not prepared to lose a single one of them.

Not to a brute like Jaeger Dragos.

Jaeger dragged the queen across the square towards the castle steps, surprised to see how much Angard reminded him of Hest; what he could see of it in the dust cloud, at least. The sun was coming up, and the smoky glow from the fires burning around the square was making everything even harder to see.

But he could see Briggit.

'Get your hands off me!' she spat. 'You will not touch me!'

'Seems that I will,' Jaeger laughed as he stopped on the steps, pulling her to him. 'Would you like to try and stop me? Perhaps a curse? A spell?' And he threw her backwards, watching as she fell onto the steps, her black robe sliding up over her knees.

Briggit was quickly scrambling to her feet, ignoring the pain, arms out, twisting, chanting. She jammed her hands forward, yelling her spell at him.

Cursing him.

Jaeger laughed. 'I do have an itch.' He fumbled, grabbing his crotch. 'Right here. Something... something doesn't feel right. Perhaps you could help?' And he seized Briggit's hand, pushing it between his legs.

'Grrrr!' Briggit screamed, spitting at him. Something was shielding him from her curse. She spun around, trying to see what was happening, trying to find someone to help her. She couldn't see anything at all, but she could hear the cries of the dying.

The coughing.

And kicking Jaeger in the shin, Briggit slipped her small hand out of his and ran up the steps, almost on her hands and knees, wondering why the circle had not held.

Wondering what Draguta would do next.

CHAPTER NINE

There was no feeling quite like it.

Success. The delicious taste of success.

'Wouldn't you agree?' Draguta asked, finishing her wine and turning to Meena.

Meena stumbled in surprise, banging her hip against the map table, certain that Draguta hadn't posed a question. 'I... yes.' What point was there in saying anything else? She hadn't drunk the mead, so she hadn't seen what had happened.

There was relief in that, but confusion also.

What had Draguta done?

Meena had guessed what the shimmering scales were for, remembering the dragon that had attacked Andala, but the ring?

What had she done with that ring?

'Think of all those ships!' Draguta exclaimed, holding her hands to the fire. 'All those majestic ships! Soon they will fill our harbour, and we will have a fleet mighty enough to conquer any kingdom! And Briggit's gold will help us buy even more!' She spun around, reaching for the replenished goblet Brill was delivering on a silver tray. 'Think of it! Silura, Kalmera! Why should we limit our ambition to dreary Osterland? Imagine what treasures await us in the Fire Lands and beyond?'

Meena felt sick, her head spinning with the smoke, her fears about what Draguta would do next as loud as thunder in her ears. She wanted to leave. To run out of the castle, out of the kingdom.

Far away from Hest and Draguta.

She had to leave!

***

'We have to leave!' Morana burst in through the door, barely looking at Dragmall and Else who were still huddled in the corner of the main room, choking on smoke, listening to the panic out in the square, wondering if it was safe to go outside.

It wasn't.

'We have to go! Now!' Morana grabbed Dragmall's satchel and headed for the door.

'Morana!' Dragmall was quickly on his feet, pulling a shaking Else with him. 'Where will we go? Where can we go?'

'You tell me!' Morana growled, spinning around, fear in her eyes. 'Who would you rather be killed by? Draguta or Briggit? Either way, we're dead, so you'd better find somewhere for us to hide. Now!'

Dragmall shook his head, realising that the hole he'd dug with Morana Gallas was getting deeper by the day. 'I know of a place,' he said, reaching for Else's shaking hand. 'But we must hurry.'

***

Jaeger had left Eadmund and their men to round up the Followers, and quell any resistance out in the square, of which there appeared to be none. The clouds of dust were dispersing, aided by a determined wind, though the smell of scorched flesh and smoke was still clogging the air, making it difficult to breathe. Fires continued to burn throughout the city, and the sound of flaming thatch crackled and popped in the distance.

Jaeger had taken Briggit into the castle, wanting to find something for his dry throat. He could barely speak, and his back was dripping with sweat, though he felt happier than he had in days, knowing that he had captured the prize Draguta wanted more than any other.

The most beautiful prize he had ever seen, if he didn't count Evaine Gallas.

Which he didn't.

Jaeger drank the wine Briggit's slave had poured into a golden goblet, wiping a dusty hand across his dusty mouth. 'A bit... sour,' he declared. 'Much like you.' He had thrown Briggit onto her golden throne, shackling her in the iron fetters Draguta had designed to enslave her prisoners. Fetters engraved with symbols that would keep Briggit's magic at bay.

He hoped.

Briggit watched him strutting around in front of her like a peacock. She didn't know what he was going to do. It bothered her. Draguta had done something to him. Shielded him. She couldn't hear his thoughts, couldn't tell what was coming next. Looking down at the iron shackles he had clamped around her wrists, Briggit noticed the tiny symbols carved into them. Her shoulders tightened, dark eyebrows knitting together in displeasure.

Jaeger Dragos didn't frighten her, though. Not a boorish, empty-headed oaf like him. 'Well, why not go back to your own slum kingdom, then, where the wine is sweet, and the girls are all wet between their legs for you!'

Jaeger laughed. Beautiful. Quick. Smart.

A queen.

There was nothing not to like about Briggit Halvardar.

'True, but I do like to travel. See the world. Sample the delicacies on offer.'

'Well, go on, then,' Briggit dared, pushing herself up out of her throne. The Followers were being dragged into the hall now, masked in dust, shocked, confused, some bleeding. She saw Sabine and Lillith cowering together, watching her. The Hestian soldiers were shoving and pushing them all down to the floor, threatening them with swords and fists. Briggit scowled, avoiding their eyes which inevitably turned to her, wanting to believe that she had a plan.

Briggit wasn't sure that she did.

She was still in shock that her circle had broken. The symbol she had used was the most powerful symbol of all. Raemus' symbol. One very few knew about, if any. She had not seen the breaking of the circle in her dreams, nor the destruction of the wall, but no one needed to know that. Especially not Jaeger Dragos. 'Do what you must. It will not trouble us.'

'Ha! Not trouble you to lose your heads? You can grow another, can you? With your spells? Your symbols? A new head?' Jaeger walked towards Briggit, bending over. She was small, but there was strength in her. He could feel it almost vibrating in her lithe body. The way she glared at him, the intensity in her eyes.

He could feel her power, and it excited him.

'You will not take our heads. Your mistress wouldn't be happy if you did, would she?' Briggit challenged, her mind whirring. 'That is not why you're here. You're here for me. For all of us. For my ships and my gold. Take just our heads back to Draguta, and how will she reward you?'

Jaeger tried to still his pulsing body, his face impassive. As charged as he felt by the conquest of Angard, he was suddenly overwhelmed with the need to sit down. Or fall down. His head was thumping, though he wasn't going to show any weakness before Briggit. He was a king, and she didn't need to know how ill he felt, or how desperate he was to please Draguta. 'You're right,' he agreed, lowering his head until he could smell her sweet breath. 'And soon you'll be with her, and she will have her fun with you, but, until then, I'll have mine.' And grabbing her shoulders, Jaeger brought Briggit close, kissing her lips, pushing his tongue into her mouth.

Briggit squirmed, biting his tongue, pushing him away, kicking him between the legs. Jaeger stumbled, fury flashing in his eyes. He swung back a hand, ready to slap her.

But Eadmund grabbed it. 'I don't think so.'

Jaeger spun, trying to yank his hand away, but Eadmund held on, his eyes never leaving Jaeger's face.

'Draguta wants the queen. She wants her Followers. And we will take them to her in good order. Not beaten and abused and raped by you.' Eadmund stepped closer to Jaeger, eyeing him, daring him to disagree. To fight him. The thrum of battle was still surging in his body, and there hadn't been any action to sate it. He almost wanted Jaeger to try and thump him.

Briggit slunk back to her throne and sat down, watching with interest.

Eadmund Skalleson. Poor Eadmund Skalleson, she thought to herself.

If only he knew...

'Fine!' Jaeger spat. 'You deal with her, then! I'll see how the men are doing preparing the ships. I want to get out of this shithole fast! Back to a real kingdom. My kingdom.' And tugging his hand out of Eadmund's, he strode away.

'Thank you.'

Eadmund turned to Briggit, watching as she sat, watching him. She reminded him of Draguta: sharp eyes trying to read his thoughts, wanting to dig inside his heart, his memories.

There was nowhere to hide from a dreamer, he knew.

He nodded. 'I'll watch you now. Jaeger won't hurt you.'

'And you?'

'I've no interest in you or your people. I'm here to do a job. Once you're in Hest with Draguta, I'll be done. Then I'll go home.'

Briggit laughed, taking the goblet a slave offered her, struggling with the fetters. 'Done?' she mocked, sipping the wine. 'Eadmund, you are so much cleverer than that. Done? When Draguta owns you? When she has plans for you?' She sat forward, her dark robe sliding across her legs. 'You really think you'll ever go home? That she will let you?'

The floor was made of marble. Cool. Slippery. Light.

Eadmund thought of Oss.

Dark, cold, weather-beaten Oss, and he felt his body sink, knowing that Briggit was right.

***

Jael's dream had left her in a daze. She could barely swallow as she walked through the hall, avoiding everyone's eyes. She didn't want to see her grandmother. Aleksander. Anyone.

It was early, but she had to go somewhere. To be alone.

To think.

But what was there to think about?

She shook her head as she walked, not knowing where she was going until she reached the bottom of the path. And looking up she saw Ayla sitting on Edela's moon-watching bench.

Jael opened the gate, walking towards her.

Neither of them spoke at first. It was a cool morning, the sky exploding above them in red and pink stripes. The view was breathtaking from this high up on Edela's little hill, though neither of them appeared to notice.

Ayla glanced at Jael, unsure of how to begin. 'I had a dream last night.'

Jael kept staring straight ahead, her eyes on the roofs of Andala's cottages, watching trails of smoke weaving through the thatch. 'About?'

'Briggit.'

'I had a dream about Draguta.'

'Oh.'

They knew then that they had seen the same thing; a palpable terror rendering them both silent for some time.

'You can't tell anyone,' Jael said, at last. 'Not yet. No one can know.'

Ayla frowned. 'Not even Edela?'

'I...' Jael sighed. 'It's hard to keep things from Edela.'

'What Draguta did...' Ayla shook her head, long brown curls bouncing across her shuddering back. 'What she did... I...'

Jael was just as speechless. 'Why hasn't she done that here? Why hasn't she crushed us like that? Taken everything she wanted? Killed us all?'

Ayla didn't know. She gripped her hands, watching her silver wedding band gleam in the morning light, suddenly worried for Bruno, wondering how much time they had left. 'Perhaps now she will? Perhaps she didn't know how to before?'

'She had a ring,' Jael said. 'Draguta was at the map table. She had another one of those circles, drawn around Helsabor on the map.' Jael closed her eyes, trying to remember everything she had seen. 'She painted around the wall with her blood, then she took the ring out of a box and put it on. She ran her finger through the line she'd made.'

'And she made a hole in the wall.'

'Yes.'

'She can destroy a wall with her finger. She can conjure up dragons to burn us all.' Ayla could barely think; panic consumed every part of her. 'How can we leave the fort now?'

'How can we stay?'

Neither of them knew.

'What else can she do with that ring?' Ayla wondered.

'Anything,' Jael breathed. 'Anything she wants.'

'We can't tell anyone,' Ayla agreed, shaking her head. 'Except Edela.'

Jael lifted her eyes, watching the stripes of colour bleed across the sky.

Wondering where Draguta would strike next.

***

Much of Angard was new, but the new had been built around the old and as Morana, Else, and Dragmall ran through the back streets of the city, everything suddenly became narrower. Darker. Older. The meandering streets wound around the overhanging buildings like cobblestoned mazes and Else swallowed as she stumbled along behind Dragmall, worried that he didn't know where he was going.

But he did.

'In here!' Dragmall whispered hoarsely to Morana, heading down an alley that was barely big enough for him to push his shoulders through. 'Hurry!' And running, panting, he found the doorway.

Iron strong. Locked.

Fumbling in his leather satchel, he brought out an old, rusted key and shoved it into the lock, holding his breath as he jiggled and turned it.

Morana held her own breath, listening to the shouts in the distance. Someone was running, being chased.

She hoped it wasn't them.

Dragmall pushed open the door, cringing at the noisy creak of the ancient hinges. 'Through here! Hurry!' And pulling Morana, and then Else inside, he locked the door after them, suddenly aware of how dark it was.

'Where are we?' Else croaked, hoping there would be water somewhere. Her mouth was so dry that she was struggling to swallow. Everywhere stunk of smoke. Dust was in her eyes, her mouth.

'Come on!' There was no time for explanations. 'Just a little further, I promise. Just a little further.' And Dragmall disappeared into the darkness.

Morana turned back to the door, listening, but she couldn't hear the shouting now. No boots. Nothing. She squinted, looking more closely at the door, noticing the symbols carved around its frame.

And smiling, she turned back around, hurrying after the quickly disappearing Else.

***

Draguta had been walking around the map table, peering into

her seeing circle, and she felt confident that at least Eadmund appeared to have everything under control. 'We must celebrate!' She no longer experienced hunger, no longer required food at all, but others did. 'Bring Amma. And let's have Evaine here too!' She smiled at Meena, enjoying her obvious discomfort. 'We can celebrate our victory together!'

Neither Brill nor Meena moved, so Draguta glared from one to the other, and soon they were scuttling out of the hall, half-asleep, but determined not to incur her wrath.

Draguta watched them go, her eyes drifting to the boxes on the table.

All of her attention suddenly on the smallest one.

'What a gift you are,' she murmured, picking it up. And popping open the lid, she ran a finger over the black stone, feeling it vibrate with power. 'A very precious gift, indeed.'

***

Eadmund felt confused as he walked down the castle steps. Confused and ready for something to drink. Though it was dispersing, the dust cloud had dropped lower over the city, caressing the tops of buildings, and the ridged back of the black dragon; sinking low enough to cover the head of the enormous marble statue of a man in the middle of the square.

Eadmund wondered who it was, though he didn't really care.

Jaeger strode towards him, having run his eye over Briggit's impressive fleet of warships, happy that they would be travelling back to Hest in comfort, once they had loaded their prisoners on board, and scoured the castle looking for Wulf Halvardar's gold. 'It's not your place to tell me what to do!' he snarled, poking a finger at Eadmund's face. 'Not in front of my men. Not in front of my prisoner!'

Eadmund blinked the spittle from his eyes. Jaeger always

stood too close, and he had to fight the desire to step back, not wanting to give him any ground. 'Your prisoner?' he grinned, remembering Skorro and how crippled Jaeger had been by the smoke; by his injured ankles. He blinked, trying to concentrate, but his thoughts were drifting, floating like the cloud of dust. 'She's Draguta's prisoner, and your only job is to get her to Hest in one piece so Draguta can decide what to do with her.'

Berger came up to them, dragging a snarling Follower by the sleeve of his black robe. 'Caught this one escaping. Hiding down an alley.'

Eadmund frowned, glancing at Jaeger. 'How did he get away? I thought you'd surrounded them? Trapped them in that circle?'

Jaeger shrugged.

Berger shook his head. 'No idea. But he was running for it. Planning to hide, I suppose.'

'Well, take your men, look everywhere. Down every street. In every building. Draguta wants all of the Followers. Every last one of them.' He turned back to Jaeger whose attention was on the harbour. 'We have to secure the wall.'

Jaeger looked surprised. 'There's a fucking hole in it!'

'Which needs to be defended. Angard belongs to Hest now. But only for now. If we don't round up every last Follower, if we don't secure the castle and the wall, they could easily turn things against us. You saw what Draguta was capable of, but we've no idea what trouble the Followers could stir up if they escape.'

It was Jaeger's turn to frown. The thought of displeasing Draguta disturbed him, and for the first time since he'd stepped inside the city, he felt his anger cool. 'We need to be on the ships tomorrow. We can tidy things up today. It won't be too hard. We've crushed them. Ripped the heart out of this place.'

'No, it won't be hard, though I'm sure Draguta will be watching nonetheless,' Eadmund warned as Jaeger's attention turned back to the castle. 'I'm sure we can convince Briggit to help us find anyone who's gone missing. It won't take long.'

***

'What is this place?' Morana grumbled as they descended the narrow stone stairs. She placed her hand on the wall, surprised by how wet it felt. 'Where are we?'

Dragmall had already left the stairs behind, and he was heading down the dark tunnel when Morana caught up with him. 'Centuries ago the volkas were under attack from a dangerous queen who wanted to rid Helsabor of our kind. A woman who feared the truth, so she tried to burn it. Bury it. Pretend it had never existed. The volkas dug tunnels, hid beneath the city. Hid their books. Their artifacts. Themselves.'

It reminded Morana of the catacombs in Hest, only damper and darker, and not as pleasant smelling. She couldn't smell death anywhere, just the reek of sewage. The smell of a place that had never seen the sun.

Else couldn't stop shivering. The darkness was gripping her like a pair of evil hands, and catching up to Dragmall, she slipped her arm through his, squeezing tightly. 'Will we be safe here? Does anyone know of this place?'

They were at a crossroads of sort, tunnels leading left and right.

'We go this way,' Dragmall said. 'And as to whether anyone will find us, I don't know. Perhaps Briggit and her Followers have been here? From what I've heard, the volkas are no more.' He felt sad, as though he was creeping into a tomb, which, in truth, it was. Some volkas had been buried here over the years. Some recently.

Volkas and their hidden treasure; together for eternity.

'But we don't know what Briggit is capable of anymore, so we shall have to wait here and see,' Dragmall sighed, hoping to sit down soon. He needed a moment to gather his thoughts. 'We shall have to wait and see what Draguta will do to her.'

***

'Is no one going to compliment the meal?' Draguta wondered with surprise. 'No one?' She turned to Amma who sat to her right, picking at a lamb sausage. Blood was oozing from it, and she was trying not to vomit. 'Are you unwell? Or is the food not up to the standard you are used to?'

Amma opened her mouth, her eyes meeting Evaine's.

Evaine who sat on Draguta's left, in between her and Meena.

'I am not unwell, but I... my appetite has changed,' Amma tried to explain. 'Because of the... baby, I think. I cannot tolerate certain foods. Some things make me feel... ill.'

Draguta's eyes were wide with interest. 'Well, I do seem to remember some such feeling myself from many years ago.' She peered down at Amma's plate, noting the bloody juice. 'Perhaps you'd like something sweeter? I believe the cooks are baking cakes this morning. Isn't that right, Meena? You saw that, didn't you?'

Meena didn't want to be brought into the conversation. She didn't want to be forced to eat with Draguta at all, convinced that she was only placing her near Evaine and Amma to tease and torture her. 'I think so,' she mumbled, gobbling down a boiled egg. Having been momentarily assured of her safety, her appetite had returned, and she was eating as much as she could of the bounteous spread, not sure when she would be invited to eat again.

'Well, there you are, cake it is!' Draguta smiled, placing a hand on Amma's belly. The girl was wearing a new lilac dress, though it didn't appear to have been adequately sized as it was already straining across her breasts, Draguta noted with displeasure. 'Cake, and then, I think, a return to the tailor's.'

Amma flinched, afraid to move at all, though she very much wanted to. Draguta's hand felt like ice. She nodded, her bottom lip wobbling. 'Cake would be nice.'

Draguta laughed. 'What a nervous little thing you are. Not like Evaine over there, eating as though all the food in Hest was about to spoil!'

Evaine scowled, not wanting to be made fun of. Lifting her head, she eyed Draguta. 'I've had no appetite since my father's death. It was very upsetting what Eadmund –' She stopped herself, not wanting to go on.

Amma's eyes were suddenly alert.

'What Eadmund did?' Draguta mused. 'What did you expect him to do? Let Morac live when he had taken his own father's life? You would have had no respect for a man that weak. No respect for a king who let another man rule him. No, Eadmund is the perfect sort of king. Unlike Jaeger,' she added, turning back to Amma who was not as pleasing to look at but far more pleasing to talk to than Evaine. 'But we will work on Jaeger together, won't we? Stop those little impulses he has. Calm down all that fire. There is no need for it now, is there? Not when he has us.'

Amma didn't want to talk about Jaeger. She didn't want to think about the baby being Jaeger's or being Jaeger's wife. Forcing herself to smile, she reached for her cup, sipping the warm milk, trying not to vomit.

***

Jael and Ayla agreed to meet again at Edela's in the afternoon once Jael had explained their dreams to her grandmother. Though, Jael wondered, perhaps Edela had already seen it herself? She hoped not. That sort of nightmare was nothing her grandmother needed to witness first hand.

Trudging back to the square, Jael's mind wandered to breakfast, though she had little appetite after watching Draguta decimate Angard. She wasn't looking where she was going, and she walked straight into Karsten. He stumbled backwards, not having been looking where he was going himself, spilling the basket of apples he was taking back to the cottage for the children.

'Sorry!' Jael exclaimed, shaking her head. 'I must have been walking with my eyes closed.'

Karsten shrugged it off. 'Guess it's the curse of being a dreamer.' He dropped to the ground, picking up the rolling apples, Jael bending down to help him.

She frowned suddenly, staring at him. 'Who is Meena?'

Karsten looked surprised. 'Meena? Why?'

'I had a dream about Hest. She was in it. Red hair. Big eyes. Shaking all over.'

Karsten laughed as he stood. 'Sounds about right. She's a... mystery that one. Morana Gallas' niece. Varna's daughter.'

'Oh.'

'And Jaeger's plaything, much to Berard's annoyance.'

'Berard?'

'Mmmm, she had the Book of Darkness. Her and Berard... they took it together. They were going to leave with Hanna when Morana caught them. Meena dropped the book. Jaeger took off Berard's arm.'

'Oh.'

'She stayed behind.' Karsten frowned. 'I don't know why. To help? Berard wanted her to come. It's part of why he wants to go to Hest. To save Meena.' He saw the puzzlement in Jael's eyes. 'He loves her.'

And suddenly it felt as though the clouds had parted and for the first time all morning, Jael could breathe.

CHAPTER TEN

The crypt had nothing in it that would light a torch, and though Dragmall had a tinderbox in his satchel, he was reluctant to do anything to attract attention. So they sat in the dark and the cold and the silence.

All day long.

Morana would have usually grumbled about the confinement. She would have stood up and stalked around the small crypt. She would have griped and moaned and mocked Dragmall and his volkas for the poverty of their hidden city beneath Angard; the bleak, miserable darkness of it all. But she sat still and quiet on the dirt floor, feeling the damp seep through her cloak, laying her head back against an unforgiving stone wall, though at least in here, away from the tunnels there was less of a stink.

She couldn't stop thinking about Briggit's circle. The magic in that circle was like nothing she had ever felt. All those Followers had been united, led by Briggit, who was a powerful dreamer, that much was obvious. It could have held Draguta out, and certainly Eadmund and Jaeger and the Hestian army, so why had she panicked, thinking it would break? Why had she broken it?

Why had she run?

Now she would be hunted by everyone. No Follower would welcome her. They would all shun her. And Draguta would not rest until she had caught and killed her.

Or imprisoned her again.

Morana dropped her head to her knees, feeling all the air leave her chest. The only allies she had were old and terrified. Pitiful creatures. And though Dragmall had been able to secret them away in here, she wondered how long they could last. There was no food. No water. No light.

A rat scurried across the dirt floor, chasing another. And another.

Else squealed, scrambling to her feet, Dragmall hurrying to comfort her.

But Morana didn't even lift her head.

***

Edela felt well-rested, though she could tell that Jael wasn't, but her uptight granddaughter didn't say a word until Biddy and Eydis had left with the puppies.

Biddy had not planned on taking Eydis with her to meet Entorp. They were going to be making salves, and she didn't imagine that Eydis would be very enamoured with that, but she could tell that Jael wanted to speak to Edela alone, so she had dragged Eydis along.

And now Edela and Jael were alone in the cottage, and Jael didn't know how to begin.

Part of her hoped that her grandmother would just read her mind.

She didn't.

'Shall we go for a walk?' Edela suggested, moving to the edge of her chair. 'Get some air? Maybe that would help?'

'No.' Jael leaned forward, gripping a cup of fennel tea that was still too hot to drink. She placed it on the floorboards and sighed. 'I had a dream.' She shook her head. 'It didn't feel like it was a dream. I was there, experiencing it. Ayla had the dream, too, in a different way.'

Edela shivered, wondering what was coming; sensing that whatever it was would not be good. 'What about?'

So Jael told her about the dragons and Eadmund; the wall and the ring; Briggit Halvardar and her circle; Meena Gallas.

Edela's forehead furrowed into deeper and deeper rows, cold hands clenched in her lap. 'I see,' she said when Jael was done. 'I see.'

She didn't see.

She couldn't breathe.

'We are in such danger,' Jael said, feeling Toothpick leaning against her leg. 'The gods had this sword made for me, but what can I possibly do with it now? A sword against Draguta?' She shook her head. 'A sword that has no power anymore, against a ring like that?'

It had seemed impossible before, Edela thought. Almost impossible, but they had still been determined to destroy Draguta and the book; to rescue Amma and Sigmund; to free Eadmund.

And now?

'We have to find a way to stop Draguta before we leave to meet her,' Jael insisted, sensing that her grandmother had frozen. 'And I think I know something we could try.'

***

Draguta had freed Meena to spend time with Amma, insisting that she show her the coves where she could swim if she chose not to bathe in the castle. Draguta had smiled as Meena reddened before her, reminded of how she had manipulated her, sending her here, there, and everywhere like an eager puppy.

A puppy with no mind of its own.

Amma appeared relieved to have someone to talk to as they walked, but Meena couldn't think of what to say to her. She knew that Draguta had gone to her chamber, perhaps taking to her bed, but she could just as easily be watching, listening to every word they said.

Which wasn't something that occurred to Amma. 'When will Jaeger return? Will he return?'

Meena could hear the desperation in her voice, and she felt sorry for the girl, wondering what Jaeger would do to his wife when he did return, though she didn't have to wonder for long. 'He will return soon. They are in Angard. Helsabor. Draguta wants their ships and their queen. They will not delay. Jaeger and Eadmund will be back soon.'

Amma was looking forward to seeing Eadmund, to see if she could talk to him about Jael. About herself. About whether he could help her escape.

Meena blinked, surprised that she could hear Amma's thoughts so clearly. Sighing, she worried if, in fact, it was just Draguta again, playing games with her. 'Eadmund is Draguta's,' she said anyway. 'He will not go against her. He will not help you. He is Draguta's.' She wanted to warn Amma away. It would do her no good to get herself in trouble with Jaeger or Draguta. No good at all.

The gravel road leading towards the coves suddenly steepened, and Amma stopped, turning to Meena. 'Who are you? Jaeger's woman? Draguta's servant? I don't know who you are, or why you're here. Why you stay? You don't appear to want to be here any more than I do.'

Meena wanted to tap her head as she dropped it forward, hiding her face beneath her hair. 'I'm nobody,' she mumbled. 'Just nobody.' And looking up at Amma's worried face, she tried to smile. 'But you are not. You are a queen now. And that will keep you safe. Being a good queen, doing what Draguta wants. And Jaeger.' Turning away, she plodded onwards, feeling a slight breeze ruffle her hair.

Amma hurried to catch up with her. 'Will you help me, then? We could help each other.' She tried to get Meena's attention, but Meena refused to even look her way. She was working hard to clear her mind of anything to do with Amma, or Eadmund Skalleson, or Berard.

Especially Berard.

***

Jael hadn't known where to take Berard, so, in the end, they had walked to the cove, to Sea Bear, sitting in the battered wooden house. There had been no one on the beach, which didn't surprise Jael. They were all busy in the fort, focused on preparing weapons and supplies. On getting their horses ready. And themselves.

But as for ships?

They couldn't risk taking the ships.

Though Jael knew that now they couldn't risk anything at all.

Not without help.

'No, no, no!' Berard was on his feet, backing away, whacking his head on the pole hanging down from the hinged flap in the roof of the house.

Jael remembered when they had made the houses for the attack on Berard and his brothers. And now, here they sat, allies. Hopefully, more than allies. Hopefully, two people who had the power to save a lot of lives.

'Meena...' Berard began, staring down at Jael with frantic eyes. 'She is not...' He stopped himself, remembering Meena slitting Egil's throat, taking the Book of Darkness, charging down the stairs with it.

She had stayed behind when she could have left.

She was stronger than he'd ever realised. Stronger than him. 'What would she have to do?' he sighed, sensing that he had little choice but to go along with Jael.

The wind was strong, and Jael could hear it whistling through the holes in the walls. 'The people we love are in danger. A danger so grave that unless some of us do brave things, all of us will die.'

Berard nodded. 'I know. It's just that Meena is quite timid. Nervous. I'm not sure she will respond well to you. And Draguta...' He didn't know Draguta, but if she was worse than Morana, he could only imagine what she would do to Meena if she caught her.

'Draguta has hurt a lot of people, and if Meena doesn't help us, she will hurt a lot more,' Jael insisted.

Berard frowned, and digging into his pouch, he pulled out a leather strap with a few strands of red hair attached to it; not quite a lock, more of a matted knot. 'I took the hair from her chamber,' he admitted, cheeks reddening. 'If it will help?'

Jael smiled. 'I hope so. It should certainly help me get to Meena in her dreams. Hopefully, what happened in Angard will make her want to act. I can't imagine that she wants to stay in Hest with Draguta and Jaeger.'

Berard saw flashes of Meena, giddy with happiness, moving into Jaeger's chamber.

He hoped that Jael was right.

***

Briggit studied Eadmund Skalleson with interest.

Her visions of him over the years had been of a bumbling drunk, empty-headed and ale-addled, stumbling from one woman's bed to the next. An embarrassing stone anchor around his father's neck. And yet, here he was, sitting next to her at the high table, sober and serious, and totally in command of everyone, including Jaeger Dragos, it seemed. Briggit smiled, grateful that she'd not had to endure that revolting man writhing all over her, shoving himself inside her as though he was doing her a great favour. 'More wine?' she asked pleasantly, determined to act like the queen she no longer was. Wanting to believe that she still had the power to order everyone about.

Jaeger laughed. 'Was that a request?' He could see very well how confused Briggit appeared. He wondered what plans Draguta had for her. What she would do to her once she was in Hest. It would be such a shame for a woman like that to go to waste, tossed on Draguta's scrap heap with the rest of the Followers.

The sound of Jaeger's voice made Briggit want to vomit. She was pleased that Eadmund had positioned himself in between them. 'I have no desire for wine, I was merely enquiring whether you wanted any more.' The Followers had been removed from the hall now, dragged onto the ships, and Briggit's attention returned to Sabine and Lillith, wondering if she would ever see them again. She didn't want to sit around eating and drinking as though they were holding a celebratory feast. Not when so much was uncertain. When so much was yet to be played out.

She wanted to head for her bed. She needed to find a dream, though looking down at her fetters, she realised that it was likely impossible now.

Eadmund stood with a weary groan. 'I'll check on the men. See how they're coming along down at the harbour. We need to be ready to depart in the morning.'

'So soon?' Briggit was surprised, sitting up straighter, her eyes sharp. 'You think you can conquer my kingdom in a day and then leave?'

'I think we've conquered your city, and now the rest of our army is conquering your kingdom.' Eadmund frowned, not liking the sound of that. The Hestians were not his. Not his army. He didn't want to become one of them. He had to hold onto who he was.

He couldn't let that go.

'Well, I wish them luck!' Briggit glowered. 'The Helsaborans will not be defeated so easily.'

'I'm sure Draguta will intervene if she sees any problems,' Jaeger mumbled between mouthfuls of bacon-wrapped chicken. He was already planning on taking Briggit's cooks back to Hest as well. The food easily surpassed anything he'd eaten before; prepared under great duress too. He reached for his wine which was excellent, wanting to remember to send some men down to the cellars to clear it out, determined to find room on board for as many barrels as would fit. 'She means for Helsabor to be in Dragos hands now. And as you've just seen, she has every tool at her disposal to make that happen.'

Eadmund walked away from the table, wondering at the wisdom of leaving Jaeger behind with Briggit. 'Why don't you head up to the ramparts?' he suggested, turning back around. 'See what else we need to do before nightfall. You'll have a good view from up there.'

Jaeger frowned. 'And why would I want to do that?'

'Because it would please Draguta, of course, unless you plan to rule with only your cock. You'll find yourself very busy in bed, but you'll have a kingdom in ruins.'

Briggit smirked, leaning forward to stare at Jaeger who ducked his head, muttering under his breath, not wanting to do anything Eadmund said, but very aware of how right he was. Draguta wanted a king who was a strong leader. A man in control. In charge. She would not be pleased to see him sitting around, eating and drinking as though all the work was done. So, pushing himself away from the table, he stood, smiling at Briggit and ignoring Eadmund. 'I'll check on the ships. I want to make sure they're filled with gold. It would be a shame to have to leave any behind!' And throwing back the last of his wine, he headed out of the hall, determined to act like the king Draguta wanted him to be.

***

Gant watched Axl with mixed feelings. He was his king, and sometimes he felt like his son. Either way, he wanted to protect him and keep him safe, as he had kept Ranuf safe for all those years.

Axl was standing outside the armourer's hut, trying on his new helmet.

His new mail.

He looked older, Gant thought, watching him from a distance. Bigger. His arms had grown, becoming stronger, thicker from all his training, which was why he needed new armour. But he was still a boy in terms of experience, and Gant was letting him leave for the biggest battle any of them would ever face.

Without him.

'Your turn next?' Aleksander grinned, slapping him on the back. 'New helmet? New arm guards? I think we'll all need new arm guards after the barsk chewed through them!' He felt a familiar mix of excitement and nerves brewing, sensing that they were getting closer to leaving. At least he tried to tell himself that was what it was.

Gant frowned. 'I'm not coming.'

'What?'

'I thought Jael would have told you. I'm not coming.'

Aleksander didn't know what to say. He suddenly felt ten-years-old again.

'You don't need me. None of you do. Not anymore. As Karsten would say, I'm just an old man. A grey-beard.'

'Maybe. But I'd take old and experienced over young and useless any day.'

Gant laughed. 'Axl has you. And you have Jael.'

'And Jael?'

Now they both looked uncomfortable.

'Jael doesn't need anyone just yet,' Gant decided. 'Not yet. But according to Marcus, the prophecy says that she does need Eadmund. As far as I'm aware it doesn't say anything about needing me!'

'No, don't suppose it does. Me either.'

'So,' Gant said, his voice low, 'that's something to remember, isn't it? You have to help Jael get Eadmund. You have to help her free him.'

It wasn't the most appealing task Aleksander had ever been assigned, but he nodded. 'Of course. I will. But without you?'

'You think I won't be busy here? Trying to keep everyone safe?' Gant laughed, though he could hear the strain in it. 'You'll have more than enough help. Karsten's useful. Ivaar too. And who could forget Thorgils? You're all experienced. More experienced than Axl.'

'But not as experienced as you.'

'No, and lucky for everyone here, I'm the best person to try and keep them all safe.' Gant doubted that was true, though it was something to say to try and convince them both.

Aleksander watched Axl head towards them. Despite his impressive new armour, he looked miserable. Tired. Ready to scream. Aleksander didn't blame him. If Jaeger Dragos was keeping Jael prisoner, he would've felt the same. If Jaeger Dragos was keeping Jael prisoner, he wouldn't be in Andala at all. 'Have you told him? Axl?'

Gant shook his head. 'No. Looks like I'm about to, though.'

'Rather you than me. Then again, maybe our king will refuse to let you stay, him being in charge as he is,' Aleksander grinned, looking up, certain he'd heard a rumble of thunder, though the gathering clouds appeared harmless enough. 'Good luck!' And heading away, he wondered if he had time for a quick visit to Hanna.

***

'We have to do it tonight,' Jael decided, her eyes on the sun which was already heading for its bed. 'We can't wait.'

'I agree,' Edela said, though she didn't feel confident about how it would go. 'But I think I should be the one to do the dream walk.'

'Why?'

'You are weak,' Edela reminded her. 'You and Ayla. Both of you have been ill recently. More recently than me.'

Jael frowned, avoiding Ayla's sympathetic eyes. 'No. You'll be dream walking when we leave. I've no doubt about that. You should conserve your energy.'

Edela wanted to argue, but it made sense. 'I imagine you're right.' They were walking in her reinvigorated garden, Ayla bending down every few steps to add a cutting to her basket, preparing for an afternoon of tincture making.

'Are you sure you'll be alright, Edela?' Ayla wondered suddenly. 'Without me?' She straightened up, wiping a dirty hand on her red apron.

Edela tried to smile confidently, though she felt uncertain about how she would handle the load. Their dreams about the ring had terrified her. She couldn't stop imagining the moment when Draguta had pushed her finger through the wall, breaking it open.

All that ancient stone.

She had seen that wall in her dreams many times over the years. It was tall enough to touch the clouds, she was sure.

How was it even possible?

Edela hurried all her fears away from their enquiring eyes. 'Oh, I'll be fine. Eydis will no doubt be far busier than me. You've no need to worry about us. As long as we have our supplies and our symbols, we'll be fine.'

Jael turned towards the gate. 'I'll come back tonight, then. Think I'd better go and find Aleksander, check on Gisila, and maybe have something to eat. If I don't, Biddy will hunt me down!'

Ayla smiled, watching her go, her tension building.

Soon Jael would leave, and she would go with her.

And if Meena Gallas didn't help them, they were all surely going to die.

***

Amma had been struggling to breathe in her new dress, so Meena had taken her back to get it adjusted. Panicking that the tailor was taking too long, she had left her there, worried that Draguta would be stalking the castle looking for her. She had no instructions or lists, and though she knew that there would be time before Jaeger and Eadmund returned with their prisoners, she didn't know what Draguta was planning in the meantime.

Hopefully nothing.

Meena's mind wandered to Else as she walked. To Dragmall too.

She wondered what Morana had done with them.

To them.

She was so lost in her thoughts, letting them run freely for the first time in days that she didn't see Evaine coming around the corner of the castle, heading for the markets.

'What is wrong with you?' Evaine snapped as Meena stood on her foot, banging into her. Stepping back, she eyed her venomously. 'Why don't you look up when you walk, you stupid girl!'

It often surprised Meena to realise that she and Evaine were cousins. Evaine treated her as something stuck to the bottom of her shoe. She frowned, noticing the girl carrying Evaine's baby, watching with interest. The baby stared at her, sucking on his pudgy fist. Meena felt lost for a moment, not bothered by Evaine's spitting fury. She thought of how lovely it would be to hold a baby, a happy baby. Not Jaeger's baby. And reminded of Amma, and then Draguta, she blinked, turning to Evaine. 'I may be stupid,' she said, 'but I've never put a spell on anyone to make them love me.' And moving quickly past a rigid-with-horror Evaine, she almost skipped up the castle steps two at a time.

Tanja ducked her head, hiding a smile. She didn't really feel happy at all. She thought of Andala and felt wistful for the young man she had dreamed of marrying. And of Runa who had tried to save Sigmund. She thought of Draguta and shook, but the baby wriggling in her arms gave her some hope. According to everything she'd overhead, Eadmund would be returning soon.

And when he was here, there would be a chance to escape, of that she was certain.

***

Eadmund stared up at Briggit's ostentatious castle. Not one part of him wanted to live in such a place. He turned away, scanning the carnage of the scorched square. The smell was intensifying thanks to the presence of the dragon's corpses; a smell he remembered from his time in Andala. It had been raining again, and now everything was damp; blood running across the cobblestones in dark-red rivers; charred remains turning soggy; broken pieces of wall and people everywhere.

The Hestian army was hard at work, removing the bodies, securing the Helsaborans, putting those who were able to work, tending to the wounded, clearing up the rubble, making a path so that people could get in and out through the hole in the wall.

Draguta wanted Helsabor as the next step in her quest to claim all of Osterland. She wanted Briggit Halvardar and her Followers, but what was she going to do with them once they were in Hest?

Eadmund stretched out his neck, realising that he hadn't seen Jaeger in hours, wondering if he had snuck past him and gone back into the castle to find Briggit. He hoped not. Turning around, he realised that he would have to check. Draguta would be furious if Jaeger laid his hands on Briggit.

Frowning, he looked to the left, past the decomposing black dragon, to where the square stretched towards a series of streets. Tall, narrow houses, once pale stone were dirty with wet dust now. He shivered, blinking his eyes open wider, peering through the rain. It was getting heavier, but he was sure he'd just seen a glimpse of his mother.

CHAPTER ELEVEN

Draguta ran a hand over the soft, white bed furs, enjoying the luxurious feel of polar bear. Dead polar bear. Sacrificed for a greater good. Sacrificed for her pleasure.

A greater good, indeed.

She lay down on the bed, her eyes on the late-afternoon sun streaming in through the balcony doors in lengthening rays, a deep golden light filling the chamber. And she sighed, suddenly weary. It was as though her body required regeneration. Rest. A renewal of energy. And yet there was so much more to do. So many more lives to bind and end. So many more enemies to destroy in Osterland and beyond. There could be no rest until then. Not until they were all vanquished and she ruled alone, obeyed and feared by all.

Twisting the soft fur in her fingers, Draguta closed her eyes, hoping to find her sister waiting for her in a dream.

***

'Are you going to do it tonight?' Berard wondered. 'The dream walk?' He had hunted Jael down, realising that there were things he should say. Things he hoped would convince Meena to help them.

'We'll try,' Jael said. She was distracted, watching as the tanner fitted new leather armour over Tig. She wanted to make sure it fit. That he was not exposed. That he would still be able to run freely. Her mind was not on Berard or the dream walk at all.

Berard could tell. He grabbed Jael's arm, trying to get her attention. 'Meena is very... she may not listen to you. She will be scared of you, I imagine. Intimidated.'

'Of me?' Jael looked surprised.

'Well, you are quite intimidating on first meeting.'

'But then?'

'But then... no... you're still intimidating after that,' Berard decided.

Jael laughed, giving him almost all of her attention. 'What are you saying? That I should try to be nicer than I usually would? Softer?' She wrinkled her nose, doubting she was capable of that.

'Well, yes, if you could, I'm sure that it would help.' Berard was flustered. Thinking about Meena had produced a rush of emotions, all of them demanding his attention. But mostly, he felt worried. 'I think Meena needs encouragement. A reason to help.'

'And?'

'I want you to tell her that I'm coming to rescue her. That I'll be there soon. She needs to help us and stay safe until I come. I'll rescue her from Jaeger. From Draguta and Morana. I will come!' Berard was red-faced, getting himself worked up, imagining how much his brother must have hurt Meena since she'd been stuck in Hest with him.

Remembering her conversation with Karsten, Jael placed an arm around Berard's shoulder, drawing him away from Tig and the tanner, towards the stable doors. 'You're not coming with us, Berard,' she said gently. Hoping she sounded gentle. 'I need you here. To help Gant and Bram with the fort.'

'What?' Berard's face reddened further. He shook his head crossly. 'No! No, I want to come, Jael. I need to come. To help Karsten. To save Meena!'

Jael sighed, realising that honesty was probably the better strategy. Certainly the fastest. 'Karsten doesn't want you to come.'

'What? Why?' Berard stood taller, imagining just what his brother had told Jael. 'He doesn't think I'm good enough. He never has! None of them ever did! But he can't stop me. I have to go!'

'But I can stop you, and I agree with Karsten.' Jael stared into Berard's frantic eyes. 'He doesn't know if he'll come back. He doesn't want to leave your family alone. He needs you to stay, to be with them. To protect them.'

Berard frowned, quieter now. 'He doesn't think he'll come back?'

'Well, there's no guarantee, is there? But Jaeger will die, one way or the other, and who will be left to sit upon the dragon throne? Who will be left to care for all those children if something happens to Karsten? You can do more good here, Berard. More good than you could with a sword.'

Berard dropped his head, sighing.

'We will kill your brother, I promise. We will kill Jaeger.'

He nodded, looking up. 'Alright, alright. But you must tell Meena that we will save her. That I am... waiting for her. I... want to see her again.'

Jael smiled. 'I will.'

'It might help,' Berard insisted, turning at the sound of the tanner's yelp as Tig bit him.

Jael closed her eyes in embarrassment. 'I have to go. Don't be too hard on Karsten. He's trying to do the right thing. And it is the right thing!' she insisted, hurrying to Tig who looked ready to bite the grimacing tanner again.

Berard watched Jael go, listening as she grumbled at her badly behaved horse, his mind flitting from Meena to Karsten and finally to Jaeger.

Jaeger, who had to be stopped one way or another.

In the end, he realised, it didn't matter who did it.

As long as they killed his brother.

***

Eadmund had walked down to the piers, relieved to see that Jaeger had not snuck back into the castle. He was actually doing some work, overseeing the ferrying of the gold from the castle to the ships. They would be taking nineteen of Briggit's fleet back to Hest.

Their ships now.

That would leave enough men behind with Gunter to maintain order in Angard. More troops would be scouring the rest of Helsabor, putting down any resistance they met, conquering one settlement at a time.

Claiming each one of them for Hest.

Jaeger smiled at the thought of it, then frowned, glaring at Eadmund. 'Why not?' They stood on the end of a pier next to a forty-man warship, the sky darkening above them, rain falling steadily.

He was growing tired of being wet.

'We need to tie up every loose end before we leave. It makes sense for you to get the Followers back to Draguta quickly. I'll stay another day, make sure there are no problems,' Eadmund said, not needing or wanting Jaeger's approval for why he was choosing to remain behind. 'I want to make sure we've got every Follower. I'm not convinced we do.'

Jaeger realised that he didn't care either way, and besides, at least he would arrive back in Hest first, with all of Draguta's prizes.

'I'll be bringing Briggit with me.'

'No.' Jaeger stepped forward, jutting his bearded chin at Eadmund, daring him to step away.

He didn't, enduring the smell of Jaeger's sour breath.

'Draguta asked me to bring her back. You heard her!'

'I did, but I also heard her say that she didn't want Briggit touched,' Eadmund reminded him. 'And I think you've already broken that promise. Let Draguta reprimand me, but I'm not leaving Briggit alone with you. Not for four days on a ship.' And not waiting for an argument, Eadmund strode down the pier, back to the square, his eyes drifting to where he thought he'd seen his mother, realising that he needed to find somewhere to get a good sleep before he started hallucinating.

Jaeger watched him go, deciding that the time had come to do something about Eadmund Skalleson. Draguta was becoming far too fond of him, far too reliant on his leadership. But in Hest, there could be only one king.

So it was time to think about removing the other.

***

Ayla stood outside the cottage door, thinking about Hest. About Draguta. About Helsabor and Briggit.

About her dream.

She couldn't stop shivering. It felt as though they were being pushed towards the most terrifying conclusion. As though life as they knew it was coming to a horrifying end.

The door swung open, and Bruno stood there staring at her. He smiled, his weary body almost sighing with happiness. 'Do you plan to come in or should I come out?'

Ayla's hands were muddy, her fingernails black. She had been digging in Edela's garden for most of the afternoon. Distracted. Not realising how filthy she was until now. 'No, I'm coming in,' she smiled, staring up at Bruno, pleased to discover that her feelings of resentment towards him had retreated, or perhaps vanished altogether. She was overwhelmed with the need to hold him close, to spend some time with him.

Before she had to let him go.

***

Thorgils hadn't said a word since he'd sat down at the table, which nobody appeared to have noticed because with four children eating, it was impossible to even hear yourself think.

But Isaura noticed. She reached under the table and squeezed his hand. 'Are you sure you don't want another turnip?'

Thorgils loved turnips, she knew, but he had barely made his way through one.

He shook his head, blinking, realising that he'd drifted off, but he was suddenly aware of Leya's red face and the tears on Selene's cheeks. 'Is everyone alright?' he asked, smiling at the girls; at Mads who glared crossly at him.

There were a few nods, a few more tears.

Isaura tried to lift the mood. 'Selda made an apple cake,' she smiled, jiggling Mads on her knee. 'Would you like some?'

Mads frowned, wondering what he would have to do for that treat. But Isaura was too busy worrying about Thorgils to try and coax anything out of him.

'How about you?' She nudged Thorgils' arm. 'Cake?'

'Cake would be nice, then I have to leave.'

'Oh?'

'A meeting in the hall.'

'Another one?'

'I doubt there'll be many more, don't worry,' Thorgils grinned, reaching for the piece of cake Selda handed him. 'We have to go over what still needs to be done, which by the looks of things out there is a lot.'

'At least the wall is finished. That's something.'

Thorgils nodded, his mouth full of warm apple cake. 'It is... finished... finally.'

'And you think it's high enough? That it will keep everything out?' Isaura looked anxiously at her children, realising that it was not a conversation to have around them.

But Thorgils felt confident in his answer. 'It's high enough. Those barsk wouldn't have been able to jump it. Don't worry, we've a good wall there. A strong, tall wall. You'll be perfectly safe in here once we leave, won't you?' And he smiled at the girls whose attention was suddenly on the cake Selda was serving. 'Perfectly safe indeed.' Thorgils turned to Isaura, seeing the worry in her eyes, the fear that they would never see each other again.

He reached under the table and squeezed her knee, trying to make her smile.

She did, and they held each other's gaze for a moment before Mads screeched, annoyed that Annet was getting a bigger slice of cake than him.

***

Briggit forced herself to be patient, watching as her slaves and servants busied themselves serving the two kings. They no longer looked to her, no longer appeared to consider her their mistress. She glowered at them, her eyes sharp, wanting to remember which ones had been so disrespectful.

As if she could be defeated so easily.

'You will remain here in the morning,' Eadmund said, reaching for his goblet. He was thirsty, disappointed that there was only wine on offer, but feeling no inclination to demand any ale. He just wanted to head for bed, to get away from Jaeger and Briggit. 'With me.'

'Why?' Briggit's attention was solely on Eadmund now. 'Why is that? Aren't you taking me to Draguta?'

'You want to go to Draguta?' Jaeger laughed. 'You obviously don't know anything about her!'

Briggit ignored him. 'Why am I staying here?'

'Just for another day,' Eadmund promised. 'I need to ensure everything is under control before we leave. Jaeger will take the Followers with him, but you'll stay with me. We'll depart when I'm ready.'

Briggit frowned, though she felt a sense of relief at being kept away from Jaeger and his worm-like tongue. 'I'm pleased to hear it. My people need me.'

'Your people?' Eadmund was confused. 'Your people will

remain here. Those who still live.'

Briggit shook her sleek black hair. 'I mean my Followers. They need me to protect them. To keep them safe. To guide them.'

'Well, I don't imagine you can do any of those things anymore,' Eadmund said. 'Draguta doesn't appear to like Followers. I don't think she's inviting you for a visit.'

Jaeger grinned, gnawing on a leg of mutton. 'You could say that. She killed every last one of Hest's Followers. One clap of her hands and they were piles of burning ash.'

'You were there?' Briggit asked, eyes alert, heart throbbing in her chest.

Jaeger nodded, pleased to have claimed her attention. 'I was.'

'And she spared your life? She killed all those noble Followers, and spared your miserable life?' Briggit snarled. 'Well, that tells me everything I need to know about Draguta.'

Eadmund didn't say anything, but he doubted Briggit's confidence would last long, not once she was in Hest. Not once Draguta took what she wanted from her.

Whatever that was.

***

Else was surprised to discover how hungry she was.

Her stomach rumbled endlessly, provoking Morana's wrath. Morana who wanted to sit in the darkness and the silence and contemplate how they could keep themselves safe from Draguta and all their other enemies. 'Will you shut up!' she barked, her voice echoing around the empty chamber like a clap of thunder.

Else shook and Dragmall sighed. 'It won't help any of us if we start fighting amongst ourselves,' he murmured, though he felt as irritated as Morana. Else's stomach was a loud distraction, and he too was trying to find an answer to their predicament. He felt ancient, too old to be quick-witted and clever. Too weak to fight anyone. Coughing, he edged away from the wall, pushing himself up, onto his feet.

'Where are you going?' Else panicked, blinking in the darkness.

'I can't feel my legs,' Dragmall groaned. 'I need to stretch them. Perhaps find something to make a fire. It's very cold down here. We may need to light one soon just to keep warm.'

Morana was torn. She was freezing too, but the idea that they might attract attention concerned her, though they were very far away, hidden down here in the catacombs. 'Why not take Else with you?' she grumbled. 'Give me some peace!'

Else remained where she was, though, not wanting to trek through the darkness, tripping over more rats. She felt tired, exhausted with worry, dreaming of her little bed in the servants' quarters in Hest's castle. How warm it had been tucked behind the kitchen where the heat from the fires had kept her toasty all night long.

'The best thing you can do is try to get some sleep,' Dragmall yawned. 'Whether it's night or day, we all need to think clearly. Sleep will help with that. I won't be long. I'll just see what I can find.' And, hands out, he stepped towards where he imagined the entrance of the crypt to be.

Dragmall remembered this place. It had been his father's secret place. And his father had given him a key to it; told him to keep it with him always; warned him that what was hidden in the catacombs was a secret so great that nobody could ever find out.

Though Konall had told his son.

Before he died, Konall had told his son what that secret was.

***

Everyone looked bored by the thought of another meeting, Jael could see. She didn't doubt that they'd rather spend their last few nights with their loved ones, but she needed information. To hear it. To share it. They needed to be prepared to leave, but they also needed the fort to be secure. Those remaining behind would face as much of a challenge as those who were leaving.

Jael shut all thoughts of Draguta and her ring out of her mind. She hoped that she could do the same with her face, not wanting anyone to see the bright shards of fear she could feel jabbing her. Her every waking thought was accompanied by a taunting laugh.

That voice, so confident now.

'The wagon will be finished tomorrow,' Beorn said. 'Tonight even. We're working on it in the stables.'

Jael was pleased. 'Entorp, Marcus, will you carve symbols on it tomorrow? Aedan, why don't you help them? And take Ayla and Astrid with you. They need to fill it with their supplies, see what else is needed, what can fit inside.'

All three men nodded.

Jael turned, looking for Aleksander. 'And how about those sea-fire jars? Are they secure in the wagons?' She had been worried, not liking how loose they were in their boxes.

'We've stuffed straw around them, so they're tucked in like babies now.'

'Good. And what about our supplies here?' she asked Bram. 'You'll need to keep making sea-fire.'

'I've had men in the forest for days, gathering everything we need. Up at the caves too. We'll have enough to make more. A lot more,' Bram said confidently.

Edela had been visiting Gisila, and she made her way through to the throne which Jael stood in front of, talking to those who had come to report to her. Axl sat behind her, trying to listen, but his mind kept drifting to Amma. Edela smiled at him as she passed, reaching for her granddaughter's arm. 'I want to move into the hall,' Edela said. 'We need to be here, in the hub of things. Able to respond quickly. I shall need help with symbols. I want to move the tables, carve a circle into the floor. Herbs around the doors, the walls. We must protect ourselves any way we can. And we must start here.' She scanned the rows of anxious men and women, resting on one woman in particular. Someone she didn't know, didn't recognise. Tuuran perhaps.

Edela sensed that she needed to speak with her, though she was too distracted to give much attention to that now. 'Once everyone has departed, we will have our own plans to organise. And once Gant is done here, he and I will discuss what they are going to be.' And turning to him, Edela winked. She felt sick, her stomach twinging at the thought of how empty her words were. At how helpless they all were.

At Draguta's mercy.

Jael's dream had ripped away any illusion that they had a hope of defending themselves, and she was struggling to keep moving forward.

But what choice did they have?

'That sounds like a good idea,' Jael said, sensing the fear gripping her grandmother just as much as it was gripping her. 'I think we're finished here. Unless anyone else has anything to add?' She looked around, but the hall was filled with exhausted, dead-eyed men and women who looked more inclined to head for their beds than carry on talking. So, nodding, Jael stepped away, wanting to have a word with Aleksander before he snuck off again, no doubt to see Hanna. She was too distracted to think about how that felt anymore.

Edela waited while Gant talked to Ulf and Bram, her eyes back on that woman who had remained behind as everyone dispersed, returning to their ale cups and benches, or leaving for their homes.

The woman stepped forward, her curly grey hair tucked into a scarf that complemented her plain grey dress. She was Gisila's age, Edela thought; perhaps younger. Short and wide, a ruddy complexion. Enormous, furtive blue eyes that didn't stop moving.

'Do I know you?' Edela wondered. 'Have we met before?'

The woman smiled nervously, shaking her head, her eyes jumping all over Edela's face. 'My name is Sybill. Sybill Ethburg. From Tuura. I remember you, but I don't expect you know me, though I was friends with your daughter Branwyn when we were children.'

'You were?' Edela smiled. 'Well, how far we have all come

from those days. Not where any of us imagined we'd end up.'

'No, most certainly not.' Sybill squirmed nervously, unable to keep her hands still.

'Is there something you wanted?' Edela wondered. 'Something you need to tell me?'

Sybill took a deep breath, calming her shuddering body. 'It's something I thought might be able to help you.'

Edela looked on with interest.

'My daughter, she is a dreamer.'

'Oh?'

'I never wanted anyone to know. I knew about The Following, you see. My neighbour... she was one. She would watch us. She suspected Ontine was a dreamer, but I insisted she wasn't. I didn't want to send her to the temple. I didn't want them to take her. To trap her.'

Edela stood perfectly still. 'I see.'

'She is my last child. My eldest daughters, they died as young girls. Ontine was a late arrival, a surprise. I am... very protective of her.'

'She has never trained as a dreamer, then?' Edela asked. 'She has no training?'

'No, but she has dreams,' Sybill insisted. 'She saw how powerful The Following would become, but by then, it was too late. They would not let us leave the fort.'

'Well, I should like to meet her,' Edela decided with a smile. 'If you think your daughter would like to help us? We could use all the help we can get. Especially dreamers. I had not thought there was another one in the fort.'

'No.' Sybill looked embarrassed. 'You will not think much of me, hiding her away, but she is my only family now. My most precious gift. I... I did not want to put her in danger. But now, I realise, we must do everything we can. Each one of us, no matter how afraid we might feel.'

'We must, yes,' Edela agreed. 'You were right to come forward. I know it is frightening, but only by working together will we have a chance to be free from the darkness that wants to consume us all.'

Sybill nodded, looking more confident now. 'Shall I send her to you? Tomorrow?'

'Please. Yes. I would like to meet her. Come to my cottage after breakfast, and we will have a talk, all three of us. Tell her not to be nervous. I don't bite!' Edela grinned, her attention on Jael who was watching her, inclining her head to the doors. Edela swallowed, wanting to get rid of Sybill quickly now. 'I shall see you in the morning, then.'

Sybill smiled, bobbing her head as she slipped away.

Edela didn't notice. She was already on her way to Jael, glancing around, happy to see that no one was watching them.

It was time to prepare for the dream walk to Meena Gallas.

CHAPTER TWELVE

The odd feeling that his mother was watching him stayed with Eadmund as he left Briggit's hall and took her to a bedchamber for the night. The room he had chosen was on the second floor. Small. A single bed. Barely furnished.

Cold.

Briggit didn't look enamoured to be sleeping in it.

Eadmund didn't care.

He would sleep on the floor, between the bed and the door. There was no window in the chamber, which is why he'd chosen it. The only way in or out was through the door, and he would sleep in front of it.

He didn't trust anyone else to look after her.

He didn't trust anyone to stand up to Jaeger.

Eadmund plonked Briggit on the bed, securing her feet with another pair of fetters, throwing a fur over her. She wriggled irritably but did not complain as she edged up the bed, trying to get comfortable.

'Your mother was from here,' she murmured as Eadmund grabbed a blanket and a pillow for himself, lying down on the floor. 'Wasn't she?'

Eadmund froze, hearing the invitation in Briggit's voice, knowing that she likely had more to say.

Not knowing if he wanted to hear it.

'Why not go to sleep, or perhaps I should take you down

to Jaeger? That might shut you up.' He wanted Briggit to leave him alone. He'd had more than enough revelations about his past recently.

She needed to leave him alone.

Briggit sniggered. 'You won't do that, Eadmund. You're not like Jaeger. You're not the sort of man to stand by while a woman is raped by that brute. If only you'd been there to save poor Evaine...'

Eadmund swallowed, his lips clamped together. 'What are you saying?' His words were stilted, not wanting to leave his mouth.

'You didn't know?' Briggit mused with faux surprise. 'Mmmm, while Evaine was waiting for you to escape your wife's clutches, Jaeger pounced. Raped her. Beat her. He has turned into a reckless brute, hasn't he? All down to that Book of Darkness, no doubt. It's a wonder Draguta wants him on the dragon throne. A vicious thug like that?'

Eadmund felt hot all over.

He had no love for Evaine. None. What she had done to Edela. To him. Manipulating him. Putting a spell on him.

He had no love for Evaine, but for Jaeger to do that...

Clenching his jaw, Eadmund suddenly remembered the faint bruises he'd seen on Evaine's face when he'd arrived in Hest. A fall from a horse, she'd insisted. He squeezed his hands into white-knuckled fists, fighting the urge to hunt Jaeger down and smack him in the mouth. And then what, he asked himself, knowing that Draguta would not take that well.

Then what would he do?

Eadmund could hear Briggit laughing, and he rolled over, wishing for his soft bed on Oss and his prickly wife with the cold feet.

Trying not to think about Evaine.

***

Evaine had happily moved back into the castle, relieved to escape the dark, stuffy house she had shared with Eadmund and the terrible memories of her father's death. And though her hungry son was lying in the corner with the constantly crying Tanja, Evaine felt a sense of comfort in no longer being alone.

She had Eadmund's son, and that gave her a chance. A chance to own him again. To be his again. To have him bend to her will again.

And he would.

She yawned, rolling away from the mewling baby and his sniffling wet nurse, wondering how she could bring Eadmund back to her; thinking about the ways she could crawl back into that place in his heart she was sure he still kept for her. Eadmund had loved her before the spell. He had wanted her long before then. They were meant to be together, she knew. If only Draguta would hurry up and kill Jael Furyck. Get it over with. Free Eadmund.

Then they could be together.

Closing her eyes, Evaine smiled, hoping she could find her way to Morana in a dream.

***

Edela had asked Biddy and Eydis to leave, again, and it worried Biddy as she headed away from the cottage. Eydis was just as troubled as she walked down the path, holding Biddy's hand.

'Don't worry,' Biddy assured her. 'We'll hear all about it tomorrow. I think they've got a lot on their minds. We all have. Best we leave them to it.' The puppies had charged off into the chilly, dark night, and Biddy was conscious of not losing them. She wanted to keep them close, especially Ido who wasn't able to walk very far without whimpering, begging to be picked up. 'Come on,' she smiled, glancing back at Edela who was waving from the doorway. 'We'll be back in the morning. Perhaps we can bring Edela something for breakfast?'

Eydis heard the worry in Biddy's voice as she hurried to keep up with her, the feeling that something was not quite right, and the frustration that they weren't allowed to know what it was.

Edela watched Biddy and Eydis leave, quickly shutting the door as they melted into the darkness. 'How long should we wait, do you think?' she asked, hurrying back to the fire. She was shaking, likely with nerves, she knew, but still, the heat from the flames would be welcome.

Jael kneeled on the floor, glancing at the bowl of blood beside her. 'I think a bit longer, just to be sure.' She was impatient to start, but she had the sense that they needed to give Meena time to get herself to sleep. It was probably still too early to catch her dreaming.

Edela nodded. 'And what did Berard think? Will Meena help us? She is a Gallas, after all, and I've yet to hear about a member of that family who isn't on the wrong side of this fight.'

Jael had the same fears. 'I'm not sure,' she admitted. 'But I'll know more once I reach her. Hopefully, it will be obvious which side she wants to be on.'

Hopefully...

***

'I have to go,' Meena insisted. She had been sitting with Amma, keeping her company. They had eaten in Jaeger's chamber together. There had been no sign of Draguta all day, and neither of them had wanted to eat in the hall with Evaine.

Meena had been surprised to find how much she enjoyed Amma's company. She missed Else terribly, and Amma had helped to fill that void. She was quiet and gentle, and though obviously scared, she was being very brave.

'Yes, I suspect it is late,' Amma mumbled, glancing at the

bed. It was a very comfortable bed, with a soft mattress, but she couldn't sleep in it. The memories of Jaeger held her tightly, rigidly, not letting her relax enough for sleep to come. She was afraid that she would wake to find him looming over her, tearing off her nightdress.

Shivering, she wrapped her arms around her stomach.

'I'll go and find you some wood,' Meena said, standing up. 'You are cold.'

Amma shook her head. 'I don't think I am. It's warm in here. I'm just... worried. Jaeger will be here soon, won't he?'

Meena nodded, not looking forward to that either.

'And what will he do, do you think? To me?'

Meena opened her mouth, then shrugged, glancing quickly at the door, wanting to escape. She immediately felt bad and turned back to Amma with a sigh. 'You need to please him, do what he wants. That's the only way. You are his wife. That is his child,' she said, pointing to Amma's belly. 'He will try not to hurt you, I know, but Jaeger... he cannot control himself. The book... the book controls him.'

Amma blinked rapidly, not really understanding but nodding nonetheless.

Meena tried to smile reassuringly, edging towards the door. 'Draguta wants your child. She will protect you. You must believe that. She sees everything. She will protect you.' Those words rung in Meena's ears as she gripped the door handle.

Draguta sees everything.

She might want Amma. Need Amma. Protect Amma.

But as for how much longer Draguta would need her...

Meena pulled open the door. 'I will come again in the morning if Draguta doesn't need me. Don't worry, you're safe here.'

Amma sighed, watching her disappear through the door, suddenly feeling very alone.

***

Gant didn't want to disturb Gisila, but she'd insisted that he sleep with her. She didn't want to sleep alone anymore, so he lay on his side, listening to her as she told him what had happened that night.

'One man had Amma... Sigmund. I saw Runa...' Gisila closed her eyes, remembering the moment that man had ripped the axe from her hands, throwing it away. 'I felt so helpless. Still. All these years after Tuura. Why hadn't I let Ranuf show me anything? Any way to defend myself at all?'

Gant touched her hand. 'I'm not sure it would have helped. They didn't care about you. And there were two of them. You would've struggled to fight them off even if you knew how to.'

Gisila closed her eyes, knowing he was right. 'Poor Amma,' she sighed, opening them. 'She must feel so scared. You don't think they've killed her, do you?'

'No. Edela seems confident that they won't. She is Jaeger's wife, and he seemed quite enamoured with her when we were there. And carrying his baby might just be a stroke of luck for Amma.'

Gisila gasped, a stinging pain jabbing her stomach as she tried to adjust her legs.

'Do you need anything?' Gant wondered, propping himself up on an elbow.

'Only to feel safe. To be free from all these threats. To turn back time to three years ago, even a year ago, when we were safe.' She stared into his worried grey eyes. 'When I thought we were safe.'

Gant lay down again, holding her hand. 'I can't agree with you there. Three years ago, we had Lothar. And then you were his wife. And now...'

'Now?'

'Now we'll fight whatever comes our way together. You and me.'

Gisila's body sunk deeper into the mattress. She was in pain and terrified of what was coming, but deep down in her heart, happier than she could remember feeling in years. Leaning forward, she kissed Gant, the bristles of his beard rough against her lips. 'You and me,' she smiled. 'Together.'

***

Meena wasn't sure if she had ever been happy, but if there had been one moment in her life when she might have felt true joy, this was it.

She was seven-years-old.

Her red hair was tame, long, falling down past her waist in tight braids tied with blue ribbons. Her face was clean, her eyes bright as she ran alongside her father. He was unhappy, she could tell, his heart broken by the death of his second wife, but Meena hadn't liked her, and she felt elated to have her father all to herself again.

But then there was Varna.

Her grandmother walked on Meena's other side, a terrifying, odd figure. A smelly old crone who stooped and shuffled and spoke in strained rasps. There was no smile in her eyes, no warmth in her gnarled hands that kept pointing and poking at her. But her father was there, a comforting presence keeping Varna away, so Meena ignored her grandmother as she ran, chasing the birds which flew up high, squawking. They would be happy here in the city, her father had promised. They would stay in the castle with Varna until they found a cottage.

It would be a new start, just the two of them.

Meena ran and ran, shuddering to a halt as the sky rumbled above her, dark clouds clustering, lightning zigzagging above her head. Spinning around, she saw that her father had gone, but Varna was still there, peering at her with wild eyes, strands of thinning grey hair whipping around a sunken face.

'You foolish doormat!' she growled. 'What sort of dreamer are you? Blind, deaf, and dumb. Awake or asleep! What use are you to anyone? A dough-headed fool! An embarrassment to our family! All that's left. Almost...' Varna turned away. 'What use are you to anyone?' she muttered, her voice lost beneath a boom of thunder.

Meena stood watching her grandmother shuffle into the darkness, happy that she was gone, relieved that she was dead, reminded of her pinching fingers and her biting tongue. She shivered, closing her eyes, wanting to see the sun.

To feel warm.

Safe.

'What about me?' came the voice.

Meena spun around, coming face to face with Jael Furyck.

'What use can you be to me?'

***

Eskild couldn't get through to Eadmund. She needed to, though.

Urgently.

But something was shielding him from her. Something Draguta had done.

One of the many things that Draguta had done.

She watched her son dreaming of Oss, tortured by memories of Jael and Evaine, and she couldn't force her way through into any of them. He was alone, drifting, in danger of being consumed by Draguta.

Lost to them forever.

But there was a chance. A chance that she could change his course.

If only she could break into his dreams.

***

Meena stumbled, glancing around. She wanted to leave. 'M-m-me?' Dropping her eyes, she tried to think, not knowing what Jael Furyck wanted with her, or what she was doing in her dream.

Jael reached out, grabbing her arm, trying to calm her down. 'I have come for your help, Meena.'

It was suddenly so dark that Meena didn't know where they were. She blinked, listening to waves pounding the shore. At the cove. They were at Fool's Cove. And she remembered how Draguta had led her there; tricked her into not even knowing her own thoughts.

Was this Draguta now? Playing games with her?

Jael watched Meena twitch and wobble, her big eyes flitting about in panic. 'Meena, I have come from Berard. He sent me.' She hoped Berard's advice would help. 'He is so worried about you. So sorry that you stayed behind.'

Meena froze. 'Berard?' She turned quickly, her eyes on the cliffs. 'Draguta will be watching!' she almost shrieked. 'You have to go! I don't care about Berard! Go! Go back to Andala!' She ripped her arm out of Jael's grasp. But as she ran, stumbling through the heavy sand, Jael easily caught her, grabbing her again.

'You have to take the ring.'

Meena stuttered to a stop, her shoulders sinking, her head low.

'Draguta will kill us all with that ring. I am coming. I will come. For you. And Amma. And Sigmund. And Eadmund. But I cannot stop her if she has that ring. You must take it. Destroy it.'

Meena's mind was blank, her thoughts running away, as terrified as she was.

Jael turned her around, staring down at her trembling figure, trying to see her eyes which were now lost beneath all that hair. 'I know it is terrifying, more than terrifying, but we all have to do something brave. Each one of us has to take a step forward. And if we do, if we all try to defeat Draguta, if we fight together, we have a chance.'

Meena didn't speak.

Jael wasn't sure that she was even breathing. 'You might die,' she said quietly. 'I might die, but I would happily die knowing that my death saved everyone else. Wouldn't you? Or would you rather stay here as Jaeger's prisoner? As Draguta's? What sort of life would that be? A slave to them all!'

'I... how? How could I?' Meena kept having to remind herself that Draguta was watching. 'I can't. I wouldn't. Draguta saved me! She keeps me safe. I won't betray her!' She wondered if Draguta was trying to test her loyalty.

If this was Draguta.

Jael could read her thoughts, but what good they were, she didn't know. 'I've spent a lot of time with Berard since he arrived in Andala,' Jael tried. 'I've spoken to him about you. Karsten told me about how you stayed behind when you had a chance to leave. That was brave. You could have left, couldn't you? But you didn't. You wanted to help, Meena. You stayed for a reason, and here it is. Now. You must take the ring. Destroy it before it's too late.'

Meena didn't say anything. She pushed her boots deeper into the cold sand, wanting to push herself straight under it and disappear from them all.

'Berard is waiting for you,' Jael said, her ears buzzing; familiar enough with dream walking now to know that she was losing her grip on the trance. 'We will come. Soon. Take the ring, Meena. Please! Take the ring!'

And then she was gone, and Meena was blinking at the dark shapes of merchant ships out at sea, Jael's voice ringing in her ears.

CHAPTER THIRTEEN

They arrived earlier than Edela had anticipated, both of them as twitchy as mice. Edela had not seen Biddy or Eydis yet, and she hadn't felt inclined to make herself anything more than a cup of dandelion tea for breakfast.

'Have we woken you?' Sybill worried as she sheltered on the doorstep, trying to keep out of the rain, her eyes on the yawning old woman who stood before her in a yellow dress, enormous silver brooches holding up her apron straps.

Edela shook her head. She felt as though she'd just woken up, though she had been awake for some time. The smoke from Jael's dream walking had played havoc with her sleep, and she felt as though she'd been working hard all night with nothing to show for it. 'Please, come in,' she smiled, looking from Sybill to her daughter who was tall and thin; an attractive looking girl with intense dark-blue eyes framed by thick eyebrows; long golden-brown hair trailing down her back in a single braid, a few strands escaping to frame an angular face. She seemed slightly more confident than her timid mother as she ducked her head, entering the cottage.

Edela followed them inside, hoping that Biddy would return soon. She didn't have the energy to fuss about looking after guests. 'Please, take a seat,' she mumbled. 'Can I make you some tea?'

The two women shook their heads as they each took a stool, waiting for Edela to get comfortable in her chair.

'I must confess that I've forgotten your name,' Edela admitted, her eyes on the girl who was almost as tall as Jael. 'Your mother mentioned it last night, but with all the hubbub in the hall, I quite forgot it. Though that might just be old age!'

Sybill smiled at her daughter, encouraging her to speak.

'My name is Ontine.'

'Oh, what a pretty name,' Edela said. 'And how old are you, Ontine?'

'I'm nineteen. Twenty come winter.'

'And not married? Lucky you!' Edela grinned, feeling better now that the flames were once again warming her frozen toes. She took a sip of her tea, noticing that Ontine looked ready to cry.

Sybill hurried to explain. 'Ontine had a sweetheart. They were promised to one another. He was killed in the fire. He ran back into the fort to save his horse. We escaped Tuura, but poor Victor never made it out.'

'Oh.' Edela felt terrible. 'I am sorry.' She looked up as the door opened and Biddy and Eydis came hurrying in from the rain, followed by a dripping Fyn, who took one look at Ontine Ethburg and turned bright red.

Biddy looked surprised, her eyes on Edela's visitors. 'I didn't know you were expecting company this morning.' She felt odd, wondering why Edela was suddenly keeping so many things from her.

'I should go,' Fyn mumbled into his wet tunic. He had seen Ontine around the fort, many times, though he doubted she'd ever noticed him. It was a shock to see her sitting there, staring at him. He swallowed, wanting to leave.

'Oh no, you won't!' Biddy grabbed his arm before he could slip through the door. 'I promised you a hot breakfast, and now that we're all wet, you need it more than ever. You sit over there with Eydis. On my bed. Dry those puppies before they shake all over us. I'll get to work.'

'This is Sybill and Ontine,' Edela said, sensing that Biddy was huffing around the kitchen with hurt feelings. 'Ontine is a dreamer. They have come to see if they can help us.'

Biddy's eyes were wide, though not as wide as Eydis'.

Eydis couldn't see either of the visitors, but she could sense Fyn's interest in one of them, and it immediately unsettled her.

'Well, we need all the help we can get,' Biddy decided, unpacking her basket onto the table. 'Especially dreamer help. Fyn, come over here. We need to get that fire going if I'm going to make some flatbreads. Eydis can dry the puppies.'

Fyn almost tripped over his wet boots as he stood, making his way towards Biddy, catching Ontine's eye and blushing further.

'I've got some soft cheese and honey in here. Raspberries too, if you'd like some, Edela? And tea,' she decided. 'Something to warm us all up. That rain is freezing!'

Edela was nodding, eyes on her guests. Sybill and Ontine were looking at each other awkwardly, too shy to say much. Fyn was trying not to look at anyone as he added logs to the fire.

And Eydis, who couldn't see a thing, suddenly had the overwhelming feeling that everything was about to fall apart.

***

Hanna's eyes brightened as the door opened, before falling, seeing that it was only her father who had rushed inside to escape the sudden downpour. 'You should come and sit by the fire. Dry yourself off.'

Marcus shook the rain from his hair, rubbing it out of his eyes. 'I will. It's not warm out there this morning.'

'No?' Hanna tried to sound interested.

'You were expecting someone else?' her father wondered, pulling a stool towards the fire where his daughter sat, failing miserably to mask her disappointment. 'Someone tall and dark-haired perhaps? Good with a sword?'

Hanna scowled. 'I'm happy for any company. Any visitors would be welcome.'

Marcus smiled, glancing around. 'Where has Astrid gone?'

'She left with Ayla to prepare their wagon.'

'Oh.'

'I imagine she'll be gone for most of the day.'

'I could go and find him if you like? Aleksander?' Marcus felt odd saying it, but he hated seeing Hanna look so miserable. And he didn't blame her for wanting company that wasn't his. She was a woman. Not a girl. He couldn't expect her to be happy locked in a cottage day after day with no one to talk to.

Hanna squirmed uncomfortably, preparing a protest before dropping her shoulders. 'No. He... I think it's best if you don't. He loves Jael Furyck.'

Now Marcus squirmed. 'I couldn't say. He did, yes. But she is married, isn't she? Quite determined to get her husband back from what I've seen. Aleksander just needs time to let her go.'

Hanna listened to the rain pattering on the roof, reminded of Tuura and her horrible cottage. She turned to her father. 'My mother never let you go.'

Marcus almost bit his tongue. 'What do you... what do you mean?'

'When she was dying, she told me that she had never stopped loving you.' The memory upset her and Hanna felt tears coming. 'It took some time to claim her, the illness. She spoke at first, told me all about you. That I should find you when she was... gone.'

Marcus couldn't speak. His greatest regret had been leaving Hanna's mother. The emptiness inside him had remained, not filled by his service to the temple or his privileged position as the elderman.

Hanna rushed to fill the silence, feeling guilty for hurting him. 'She didn't blame you. She wasn't angry. She accepted that you loved the temple. It was just... hard for her. She missed you.'

Marcus nodded, memories surging forward, surprisingly raw. 'I... missed her.'

'So, it's not always easy to let go, then.' Hanna held her father's hand, leaning against him. 'Even when you know you have no choice.'

'No,' Marcus conceded sadly. 'No, it isn't.'

***

Jaeger hadn't slept much, and it showed.

He had gone with Gunter and some of his men to a brothel, which despite the attack on the city, was still doing business. Though after the destruction of Briggit's army, it was Hestian business now. The night had been entertaining, distracting, but ultimately, unfulfilling. His mind had wandered to Meena and then Briggit. Sometimes, he'd thought of his pregnant wife, who he knew would be waiting for him in his bed, but mostly he'd thought about Draguta, and how much he wanted to please her. And though Jaeger wanted to get rid of Eadmund, and claim all of her attention for himself, he realised that killing Eadmund would have the opposite effect. Draguta would not thank him at all. Eadmund was her favourite new toy, and he knew that she had plans for him. Plans he couldn't disrupt if he wanted to stay on her good side.

The sun was out, and Jaeger was relieved to be almost dry as he ran his eye over Berger and his men who were busy securing the contents of Briggit's wine cellar onto the warships he'd be taking to Hest. He nodded in approval, feeling his head pound, remembering how much mead he'd drunk in the brothel. It was powerful stuff, stronger than anything he'd tried before.

He was taking casks of that too.

Turning to glance up at the wall and the enormous hole Draguta had made in it, he smiled, pleased to think that he wasn't Briggit Halvardar or Jael Furyck. Or Raymon Vandaal, come to think of it. They would all suffer at Draguta's hands. Each one of them powerless against her might.

She had torn through an impenetrable stone wall. With what?

He didn't know, and he wasn't sure he wanted to.

Jaeger frowned, his attention on Eadmund, who was storming towards him, fists clenched as he charged down the pier.

Jaeger turned to Berger. 'Make sure they secure those Followers properly. I don't want them able to use their hands. Or their minds.' And turning back around, he walked towards Eadmund, a sneering smile on his face, anticipating the sanctimonious drivel the King of Oss was about to deliver.

But Eadmund didn't say a word as he walked straight up to Jaeger and pushed him off the pier.

***

'I have never had a better sleep!' Draguta declared from her place at the centre of the high table, her eyes on Amma who sat to her right. The girl was carrying Jaeger's heir, and she wanted to ensure that she was taking proper care of herself. 'And you?'

Amma coughed, watching as Meena crept into the hall, eyes jumping back and forth, not knowing whether her presence was required. 'I... yes, I did, thank you.' She had cried herself to sleep and dreamed terrible things about the attack on Andala – the many attacks on Andala – but she didn't want Draguta to know that. She wanted to be strong.

She thought about Jael. She wanted to be strong.

'And Meena, my odd little mouse, how did you sleep?' Draguta wondered, motioning for Meena to join them, much to the displeasure of Evaine who sat at the table yawning, wishing she could go back to bed, determined to find another chamber for Tanja and Sigmund. She simply couldn't endure another disturbed night's sleep.

Meena stammered forward as all eyes turned to her, feeling her armpits moisten, her face warming as though she was standing in the midday sun. 'I had bad dreams,' she muttered, her weary eyes roaming the table, looking at everyone's plates. She was not hungry, but she needed something to look at that wasn't Draguta. 'A lot of them.'

'Oh?' Draguta's face revealed nothing. 'Well, I'm hardly surprised, for what I accomplished yesterday was the stuff of nightmares.' She smiled at Brill who had entered the hall with

Ballack, both of them looking ready to be put to work. 'Though we are not done yet, are we, Meena Gallas? No, if you think your nightmares were terrifying last night, wait until you see what I have planned next!'

All eyes moved to Draguta now, but she turned her attention to her plate, picking up a spoon and pushing it through a pile of blood-red cherries. She would not eat, and nor did she need to. Her sleep had refocused her purpose and restored her power, and despite an odd absence of dreams, she felt ready to get back to work.

'Evaine,' she smiled. 'Why don't you join Meena today? See what you can do to help her. There is no point to you if you're not useful to me in some way, and moping about the castle, pining for Eadmund does not aid me in the slightest.' She ignored the horror in Evaine's eyes and Meena's squirming discomfort. 'You will never have a chance to reclaim Eadmund if you are not here, will you? And you will not be here much longer if I can find nothing for you to do. Your son appears far more attached to his wet nurse than his mother, so I don't think he would miss you. And, as it stands, nor will Eadmund, so hurry along now and prove your worth. There is a list waiting upstairs for you both. I'm sure Meena will show you everything you need to do.'

Evaine hadn't closed her mouth, nor moved her spoon which she held in mid-air, gaping at Draguta. Eventually, she found herself almost nodding, realising that she was willing to do whatever it took to bring Eadmund back to her.

Even if that meant digging in the dirt with her feral cousin.

***

Eadmund left before he threw himself into the harbour after Jaeger and drowned him. He could feel the weight of Draguta's displeasure, heavy on his shoulders as he strode back through the castle, up to the chamber where Briggit was being guarded. He didn't want to see her at all, but he had to keep a close eye on her. He had the feeling that she was plotting an escape. How could she not? After what Draguta had done to Angard? How could she not fear what was waiting for her in Hest?

He swallowed, trying not to think about Andala and Jael, and what Draguta would do to them. He couldn't do anything about that, he told himself. He couldn't.

Eadmund's eyes were ahead of him, following his boots down the darkening corridor, not aware of where he was going until he heard a voice. He turned towards the nearest door. It was closed. Locked. He turned again, looking around, but no one was there. And sighing, he started walking again before pausing, frowning, turning back to the closed door.

Kicking it open.

The chamber was empty. It looked much like the one he had slept in. There was no fire in the hearth; the bed was undisturbed. Nobody had been in there at all. He had heard the Hestians pilfering their way through the castle, looking for Followers and treasure, but this chamber had not been touched.

No one was there.

Eadmund was just about to head back into the corridor, when his attention wandered to the long window opposite the door. It was open, a sheer curtain fluttering over it. And striding across the chamber, Eadmund pulled it away from the glass, inhaling the familiar scent of winterhazel.

He shivered, blinking, certain the dreamers were playing games with him.

His mother had always smelled of winterhazel.

Stepping close to the window, he looked down on a darkened street that disappeared around a corner.

But no one was there.

Letting the curtain fall back across the window, Eadmund headed for the door, hearing the sudden bellow of Jaeger Dragos who was somewhere in the castle, yelling his name.

Smiling to himself, he turned one last time, watching the curtain as it ruffled in the breeze.

***

Berard had been quick to find Jael that morning. She was shovelling porridge into her mouth, eager to get on. It was too hot, though, and she had to keep adding buttermilk to the bowl which only made it harder to eat quickly. 'I don't know,' she mumbled, wiping her mouth. 'I honestly don't know, Berard. She seemed very frightened.'

'Do you blame her?' Berard's voice was low, frantic eyes darting around the busy hall. Thoughts of Meena had kept him awake all night. What Jael was asking her to do would likely get her killed.

'We shouldn't talk about this,' Jael warned. 'Or even think it. Keep your mind clear.'

Berard nodded. 'I'll try.'

Jael turned to glare at him. 'I mean it, Berard. Clear.' She had no idea what Draguta could see or hear, and despite every part of the hall and the fort itself being covered in symbols now, including her own body, she had the feeling that Draguta already knew all of their plans. And that would put Meena in even greater danger if she decided to help them.

Pushing away her bowl of porridge, Jael frowned. The dream walk had left her unsettled. Meena Gallas was a nervous creature, and her evasive eyes had not given her any confidence about where her true loyalties might lie.

She had remained in Hest. With Jaeger.

Perhaps there was another reason for that? Perhaps she was bound to him?

Or Draguta?

Berard had grabbed a flatbread and was helping himself to a plate of smoked salmon.

'Focus on keeping your family safe. Helping Gant and Bram. Ulf too. There's a lot to do.' Jael had the sense that someone was trying to get her attention, and turning around, she saw Entorp by the doors, inclining his head towards them. 'I'll find you later. We can speak then.' And leaving before Berard could say any more, she headed for Entorp, only to be stopped by Ivaar. She frowned. 'Yes?'

'Sleep well, did we?'

The dream walking had exhausted Jael's body, and her mind felt hazy, cloaked in some sort of fog. Neither of which helped her mood, which was fractious. 'No. What do you want?'

'I want to talk about Eadmund,' Ivaar said. 'About what you'll do to him. About what that will mean for Oss.'

Jael was quickly exasperated. 'You want to talk about that damned throne again?'

Ivaar looked insulted, but he blinked it away. 'If something happens to Eadmund. If you have to... kill him...'

Now he had Jael's attention.

Ivaar stepped back. He'd thought about what to say many times, but those eyes of hers undid his certainty. 'I will support you. On the throne.'

'What?' She hadn't been expecting that.

'If you have to kill Eadmund, I'll support you. As queen. You... have my support, Jael. For what you've done. For what you'll do.' Ivaar stopped, thinking about his father. He thought about him constantly now. 'You were Eirik's choice, the only reason he changed his mind about Eadmund. He wanted you to rule his kingdom. He believed in you.'

Jael relaxed her face, dropping her shoulders. Ivaar had changed, she knew, but it was sometimes a surprise to see just how much. 'Well, he wanted both Eadmund and I. And I haven't lived up to his expectations on that front.' She saw Entorp twitching in the distance, and she wanted to get to him.

'Not yet. But I've seen you fight. I've seen Eadmund fight. You can stop him, Jael. If it comes to a fight, you can stop him.' Ivaar leaned in close, looking down into her eyes. 'You can hurt him and stop him. Not kill him. We could... try. Practice. I could show you some ideas I have.'

Jael raised an eyebrow. 'Thought about this a lot, have you?'

Ivaar grinned. 'No, whenever I thought about stopping

Eadmund, it didn't involve sparing his life. But I don't imagine you want to kill him, do you?'

'No, I don't.'

'Then we can practice. If it comes to a fight, you'll be ready.'

Jael appreciated the offer, and she almost smiled at her brother-in-law, nodding at Entorp who had grown impatient and was now approaching. 'I'll meet you in the training ring. Midday. I have a lot to check on, but we should do that. Midday.'

Ivaar nodded. Pleased. He didn't know why he wanted to help Jael not kill his brother. Why he would care to help either of them live and keep the throne that he'd always believed should be his. Then, turning as a little pair of arms wrapped around his leg, he looked down at his blonde-haired son and smiled, thinking of the way his father used to look at him.

He knew why.

***

Eadmund's forearm was across Jaeger's throat as he pushed him back against the wall, against the ancient tapestry that Jaeger was soaking with his wet hair. He was dripping all over the floor, flicking drops of water with every angry shake of his head.

'Grrrr!' Jaeger pushed back against Eadmund, but his boots were wet, slipping on the marble floor and he slid, trying to keep to his feet, still pinned to the wall in the hall, his men gaping, watching, wondering what would happen next.

'You raped Evaine!' Eadmund spat, wanting to remove his arm and slam his fist into Jaeger's nose. 'Raped her!'

'And?' Jaeger sneered. 'You don't love her. What do you care?'

'About you raping someone? The mother of my son?' Eadmund leaned in, jamming his arm harder against Jaeger's pulsing throat. 'You think you're powerful? A true man? A noble king? A Dragos? A man who does that?' He stepped away, disgusted, watching

Jaeger coughing, holding his throat, glaring at him. 'You're not a man!'

'What are you staring at?' Jaeger rasped, pointing at the handful of men standing around, bearded mouths hanging open. 'Get everything onto the ships! And the gold. We need more chests! As many as can fit!' Draguta had insisted they drain at least half of the Halvardars' coffers, though Jaeger didn't think the ships could take that much weight.

He'd never seen such riches.

Turning back to Eadmund, his anger spiked again, but the cold hand of Draguta was on his shoulder, and her sharp voice was in his ear. He jutted out his chin. 'Lucky for me, I don't need to give a fuck about what you think. We're going back to my kingdom on my new ships with my new gold to my castle!'

Eadmund laughed, staring into Jaeger's frantic eyes. 'That power you think you have? That power you think you feel? That's just fear,' he sneered. 'Fear that you have nothing without Draguta. Without that book. That you're nothing without either of them.' And realising that he was just as powerless, Eadmund turned away, pointing more men towards the entranceway. 'Make sure all the Followers are on board. Your king would like to leave!' He turned back to Jaeger. 'Touch Evaine again, and I'll come for you.'

Jaeger snorted. 'Why would I want to? My own wife is waiting for me in Hest. Lovely little Amma. Waiting in my bed. Evaine is all yours. I've had my fun with her. Now she's just used goods.' And turning, trying not to grimace as he swallowed, he spun away, wet boots squelching as he followed his men out of the hall.

Eadmund watched him go, clenching his jaw.

Amma.

He saw Axl hurrying her across Hest's square the night they'd all escaped, leaving Lothar's headless body behind.

Amma in her nightdress. Terrified Amma.

Dropping his head, he sighed.

CHAPTER FOURTEEN

Edela had taken Ontine for a walk, leaving Eydis behind with Fyn and Biddy.

Eydis had been upset since Runa's death - since Amma and Sigmund had been taken - and she had not been very forthcoming with Ontine. In fact, she had almost been rude. Edela smiled, remembering how much Fyn had blushed around the girl. How hard he had struggled to even get out a few words. Eydis, though not being able to see any of it, had obviously heard something in Fyn's voice and made up her mind about Ontine straight away.

Which would help neither of them.

Edela needed to know more about Ontine, though. She had to find out if she could use the young dreamer. If she could trust her.

The sun having banished the rain, they were free to walk around to the cove, which was a private, if not muddy route to take. It was a chance for Edela to pry more information out of Ontine, far away from her overprotective mother. 'How do you like Andala, then?' Edela wondered. 'It is not like Tuura, is it?'

Ontine frowned. Thoughts of Tuura made her feel sad; thoughts of Victor, who she'd planned to marry since she was a girl. 'It isn't,' she said quietly. 'It is grander and warmer. Brighter. Bigger. But I prefer Tuura. It was my home.'

'Though now it is rubble and ash, thanks to The Following.'

Ontine shivered. 'They destroyed everything. Took everything from us. Now there is no Tuura for the first time. How is that possible?'

Edela tried to see behind Ontine's words, but her thoughts were murky, which was no surprise. She was tired, struggling to take control of the myriad of fears and ideas flapping around her weary mind. 'Tuura will rise again. I don't believe that there can be an Osterland without a Tuura. Once this is all done, I'm sure you and your people can return home and start again.'

Ontine looked daunted by the thought of it. Scared too. 'If we're not all killed soon.'

'Well, true, but I would prefer to think of something more cheerful, wouldn't you?' Edela grinned, her eyes twinkling. 'I always prefer a story with a happy ending.'

Ontine didn't smile. She was a serious girl.

She didn't say anything either.

'Do you want to be a dreamer?' Edela wondered. 'When it is all over? Do you see that in your future?'

'I do.' Ontine nodded enthusiastically now. 'I want to help people. To offer guidance and solve their problems. I do.'

Edela was pleased to hear it. 'And now? When we are in such grave danger? When we face a real threat? Our lives at risk? Do you want to help now?' She stopped, turning to look up at Ontine who towered over her, with narrow shoulders that rounded slightly, giving her a hollow chest. Sharp eyes though, Edela noticed as Ontine mulled it over.

'Yes, I am scared, but... if I can help you, I will.' She frowned. 'If you want my help? I have no training. I'm not experienced in anything. I have dreams, but they come and go as they wish with little help from me.'

Edela smiled, slipping her arm through Ontine's as they came to the slippery rise, certain that Biddy would be fussing at this point. 'Well, lucky for you, I happen to know an old dreamer who might be able to help you with that.'

***

Evaine was no help at all. In fact, her presence was a hindrance Meena didn't need, and she was starting to wonder if she could just disappear into the bushes and leave her cousin behind. She sat back on her haunches, brushing hair out of her eyes with dirty fingers, and sneezed.

'How much longer are we going to be?' Evaine grumbled for the fifth time from the comfort of the stone bench she had perched on since they had arrived in the winding gardens. 'Won't Draguta be waiting? I'm sure my son needs me. I am a mother, you know. I can't sit around in a garden all day, watching you dig around like a grubby mole.'

Meena eyed her, sensing an opportunity. 'You should return to the castle, then. See your son. Draguta will understand.'

Evaine saw the eagerness in Meena's eyes, the desire to get her in trouble with Draguta, and she frowned. 'Or perhaps, you should point me towards something I can... gather. Something that doesn't require me to kneel.' She saw a flash of Jaeger and what he had done to her, and she swallowed.

Meena looked surprised, but she pulled Draguta's list from her purse and ran her eyes over it. 'There is the heart of a chicken. You could go and do that?'

Evaine grimaced.

'Or, cardamom. We need to go to the markets for that. Black salt too.'

Evaine was off the bench in a flash, snatching the vellum out of Meena's filthy hands. 'I can do that!' And without another word, she was striding back down the path towards the stone archway, eager to get away from her cousin and the taunting memories of Jaeger Dragos dragging her into the bushes.

Meena watched her go with a smile, hoping she could remember the rest of the list, but not caring in the slightest if she couldn't.

It was such a relief to finally be alone.

***

Fyn and Eydis found Jael on her way to the tailor's with Entorp.

Jael didn't know why she was on her way to the tailor's, but Entorp wouldn't tell her. She glanced at Eydis. 'What happened to you?' she wondered, peering at Eydis' sour face.

Fyn, who hadn't noticed that anything was amiss, suddenly turned to her. 'Are you alright, Eydis?'

Eydis could sense everyone staring at her, and she felt uncomfortable and embarrassed, realising that she'd been acting like a child. 'Yes. I am...worried. That's all. Everything feels so uncertain.'

'It does,' Jael agreed, turning to Fyn. 'Why don't you take Eydis to the hall? I know Biddy was going to start preparing it for Edela. You could help move things around? Maybe help with carving the symbols too?'

Fyn nodded, eager to have something to do. He was struggling to turn his mind away from his grief. Everyone was too busy focusing on their own tasks to notice most of the time, but Jael could see that he needed direction. And she needed someone to keep an eye on Eydis, who didn't look happy at all. She didn't blame her. With so much terror swirling around the fort, and with the fear of what would happen with Eadmund, it was a worrying time for them all.

Eydis let herself be pulled away by Fyn and Jael's attention was quickly back on Entorp who was attempting to push her inside Arnna's cottage. 'I'll come and see you later!' she called over her shoulder, stopping short as she turned around to the tiny, almost hairless Arnna who was holding the most magnificent leather arm guards in her hands.

And when Jael glanced at the table, she could see dark leather trousers and a new blue tunic. Her faithful old helmet had been polished, free of its usual dents, her mail shirt repaired and gleaming. A new pair of boots sat there too – longer than she would usually wear – black leather, shining silver buckles.

She blinked.

Entorp smiled. 'We wanted to make you a new outfit,' he said shyly.

'You did?' Jael had no idea that Entorp and Arnna had ever spoken to each other, let alone conspired to produce a beautiful new set of armour for her.

'Well, it was my idea,' Arnna cackled, bent over and shoving the arm guards at Jael, who took them with unblinking eyes. 'But I needed some help. Someone to show me how to keep you safe. Entorp came in quite handy for that.'

Jael could see as she ran her eyes over the black leather, noticing the symbols carved into it. Some were almost familiar now, she realised. 'You have been busy.'

'Well, not just us,' Arnna admitted. 'Bertil played his part too, dying all that leather just the right shade of black. I do hope it will fit,' she grinned toothlessly. 'But for that, we'll need to get rid of you.' And peering up at Entorp, she pointed a tiny finger at the door. 'Wait out there, and I'll call you in when she's ready.'

Jael turned to Entorp as he headed for the door, her eyes still full of surprise. 'Thank you,' she smiled. 'I... thank you.'

Entorp ducked his head, pleased that he could do something to help. He knew that those symbols were likely useless against Draguta, but hopefully, they would help protect her against any other dreamers who sought to hurt her.

If Draguta didn't kill them all first.

***

Dragmall had barely spoken since they'd woken up.

He imagined it was morning as he had woken at the same time, give or take an hour, since he was a young man. His stomach was certainly acting as though it was morning, joining Else's in a rumbling chorus of hunger pains.

Morana was tired, her body aching. She had tried to dream, but she had seen nothing except pointless memories of her childhood on Oss with Eirik and Morac. It had left her feeling morose, as though she was looking backwards, instead of to where she needed to go next; instead of finding a way out of this stinking dark pit. The catacombs reminded her of the Dolma, and she shivered, sensing how close that bleak hole was to claiming her.

Else mumbled away to Dragmall who didn't answer.

He appeared to be conserving his energy.

For what, Morana wondered? What could he see? 'You're a dreamer,' she stated blankly. 'Aren't you?'

Else blinked, turning to Dragmall, trying to see his eyes, but they were hidden. Under this blanket of oppressive darkness, everything was hidden.

It was a question Dragmall had rebuffed for years. But now? 'I am.'

Morana looked pleased to have drawn the truth from him.

Else was gobsmacked. 'You are? But you've always insisted that you weren't. All these years, you said that you weren't!'

Dragmall sighed. 'Being a male dreamer is no easy path to walk, Else. Not one who aspired to being a volka. The volka. They did not recognise a dreamer's gifts at all. When my father married my mother, he tried to stop her dreaming.'

Morana frowned. 'Why did your mother put up with that?'

'She didn't,' Dragmall admitted. 'She just hid her gifts. Taught me instead.'

'So, you have dreams?' Else asked. 'You're a real dreamer?'

Dragmall laughed. 'I don't know what a real dreamer is, but I have dreams, I see things, yes.'

'And do you see a way out of here?' Morana rasped desperately. 'I can't see anything. Only this. Only darkness.'

'I see Eadmund Skalleson and his men. They are looking for those who escaped.'

'Oh!' Else was quickly panicking beside Dragmall, gripping his arm, moving closer. 'And will they find us?'

'Here?' Dragmall shrugged. 'They will be hard-pressed to. This place is warded from those who seek its location. Or, at least, it was...'

Morana leaned forward. 'What do you mean?'

'Everything has gone,' Dragmall said. 'The Followers killed the volkas. I saw that in my dreams last night. When Briggit rose to power, she had them all killed. But first, she tortured them. She found a way into their secrets. Most died nobly, but one man sought to have his life spared. He told her about this place. About what was hidden here.'

'Which was what?' Morana felt strangely removed from her senses. Her thoughts were trapped, just as they were trapped, and she couldn't find a way back to herself; back to all that she needed to help her get out of Angard alive.

'Treasure. Valuable treasure,' was all Dragmall would say. 'Treasure Briggit has taken.'

'And if she's been here, taking the treasure,' Else breathed, 'then she knows how to get in here.'

'Yes.' Dragmall wrapped his arm around Else, pulling her close. 'Yes, I'm afraid she does.'

***

The Followers were on board, still dressed in their damp and dusty black robes, shackled in the iron fetters, spread out amongst the fleet.

Waiting for Jaeger.

Eadmund frowned, knowing how possible it was that Jaeger was going to do something catastrophic on his way back to Hest, but he felt the need to remain behind for another day. He wanted to ensure that they were leaving the city under control. That no Followers were hiding, planning to launch another attack, hoping to reclaim the Helsaboran throne for Briggit.

Briggit was not inclined to help him as he dragged her around each ship, looking over the shackled Followers who stared up at their queen with a mix of fear and anger as they sat slumped against the gunwales, guarded by Hestians with swords; hulking, dull-eyed warriors who didn't need swords to hurt them. A Follower shackled in iron would simply sink if he or she were tipped over the side, unable to do anything to save themselves. 'There are hundreds,' she grumbled, her eyes on Sabine and Lillith who were wedged into the throng of huddled Followers, watching her. 'I cannot tell you if everyone is here! How could I?'

Jaeger snorted. 'You expect us to believe that? Perhaps you'd like to join them? Sail back to Hest with me? I have room.' His blood-shot eyes were suddenly alive with interest, lingering on her breasts.

Briggit ignored him, waiting for Eadmund to intervene.

He didn't. 'Perhaps Jaeger's right? If you're not prepared to help, why should I keep you away from him?'

'I doubt Draguta would be impressed to hear that.'

'I doubt Draguta would be impressed to hear that you hid your Followers from her.'

Briggit suddenly realised that she hadn't seen Morana Gallas.

She inclined her head, wanting Eadmund to lead her away from Jaeger, which he did, gripping her arm. 'There is one place you could check,' Briggit murmured. 'If anyone was hiding, perhaps they hid there? It's a secret place, beneath the city. I could... show you.'

Eadmund didn't trust her, and his nod was a reluctant one. 'Alright, show me.' And turning back to Jaeger, he waved a hand. 'I'll see you in Hest!'

Jaeger glowered at him before turning around, heading for his helmsman, happy to think that he would be without Eadmund for at least four days. He would arrive back in Hest, the glory of their victory and Draguta's attention all his to claim.

***

Draguta turned away from the map table towards Amma, Meena,

Brill and Evaine, curious as to why only Jaeger was at sea but pleased that he was bringing shiploads of Followers to her. 'We must organise a grand feast to honour our conquering kings and their doomed prisoners! And we must look the part, all of us!' She glanced at Meena and Brill, unable to hide her distaste. 'Well, not all of us, but Evaine and Amma, you must look your best. And Brill, you will do something about this hall. Never has a king been forced to reside in such a durgy pit of mediocrity! Except for Eadmund Skalleson, of course,' Draguta smiled, striding towards the entrance. 'Though having seen Briggit Halvardar's palace of gold and marble, we must make an effort, mustn't we? Perhaps that wretched tailor can whip up some new curtains? There must be something we can do to improve this heap of rocks!' She was far ahead of them already and realising it, Draguta spun around, her eyes snapping from one face to the next.

'Meena, you will take Amma back to the tailor's. See what can be done about another dress. Something more festive this time. More elegant. That creation is...' She ran her eyes over Amma's figure, which was still being squeezed by the pretty lilac dress. 'Plain. Have him return you to the castle when he's done. He can bring samples for the new curtains. Evaine, you will come with me. We must think of how we are going to welcome Eadmund home. He has done well... so far. And we must reward him for his loyalty. Show him the path forward. How vital he is to what will happen next.'

Evaine's mood lifted, her eyes more alert as she followed after Draguta, who, with a few urgent strides, had already turned down the corridor.

Meena and Amma looked at each other with resignation as they headed for the castle doors and Brill just waited in the hall, not knowing who to follow.

'Hurry!' they heard Draguta bark as she headed for the kitchen. 'Hurry up, my little snails!'

Meena shuffled alongside Amma who was walking quickly, wanting to get far away from Draguta and Evaine. She knew Amma was talking to her, but she was thinking about her dream.

She hadn't seen Draguta's ring again, and she wasn't sure she wanted to either. Ballack had taken the dusty boxes away from the hall after the attack on Helsabor, but she doubted that Draguta would have had them returned to the catacombs. She would have kept a treasure like that with her. Up in her chamber. Meena did not doubt that it was up in her chamber.

But how could she get in there without being seen?

And if she got away from the castle, where would she go?

Sighing, Meena reached out to tap her head, quickly stopping herself, her hand in mid-air.

'Meena?' Amma turned to her, not having had a single reply to any of her questions. 'Are you alright?'

Meena nodded quickly. 'Yes, but we must hurry. Draguta wants us to hurry!' And grabbing Amma's hand, she led her towards the markets, determined to leave all thoughts of the ring and Jael Furyck behind.

***

Aleksander had left Jael behind in the hall, arguing with Beorn, which was nothing new, he smiled to himself as he knocked on Hanna's door.

'Come in!'

He was pleased to hear how strong her voice sounded, and when he walked inside, even more surprised to see her sitting at the table all alone. 'Where's Astrid?' he asked, suddenly nervous. They hadn't been truly alone since Tuura.

Hanna didn't appear bothered by that. 'Helping Ayla. Preparing their wagon.'

'And your servant?' Aleksander couldn't remember the woman's name, though she had a memorable face, always scowling at him, trying to shoo him out the door.

'Marta? She hasn't been here since Astrid came to stay.'

'Oh.'

Aleksander was standing awkwardly near the table, and Hanna sensed how ready he was to run for the door. 'You could sit down,' she suggested. 'If you wanted to?'

He nodded, taking a seat opposite her, adjusting his sword, struggling to sit still.

Hanna poured small ale into an empty cup and passed it to him. 'You're leaving in a few days, then?'

Aleksander took the cup. 'Trying to.' He smiled, thinking about Jael, then blinked, realising that he was sitting with Hanna. 'There's still a lot to do.'

Hanna looked worried, her smile disappearing for the first time since he'd arrived. 'It will be dangerous, fighting Draguta and that book. So very dangerous.'

'It will. But there's no choice. It will be dangerous here too, I'm afraid. We all need to fight this in our own way. Every one of us.' Aleksander's eyes were on his ale as he spoke, and he was surprised when Hanna grabbed his hand.

'I nearly died,' she almost whispered. 'I thought I would. I... had all these feelings. Saw things. My whole life rushing before my eyes. Memories coming and going.' Her head was down, looking at his hand, and then she sat up, staring at him. 'I saw you.'

Aleksander was holding his breath. He didn't know what to say.

'I saw you in Tuura. I remember that. I wanted to see you again. I remember that too.'

'What happened in Tuura... it was...' Aleksander stopped and took a deep breath. 'I'm sorry. I was... lost. Still am.'

'You are?'

'Some days. Other days the path is clear, but most days I don't know where I am or where I want to be.'

'Or who you want to be with?' Hanna prompted shyly.

Aleksander stared at her, suddenly aware of voices outside the door. Familiar voices.

Marcus' voice.

He pulled his hand away. 'I should be going. I'll come again, before we leave.' Hanna looked disappointed, and Aleksander felt guilty, cross with himself for always sticking one toe in the water before pulling it out. He was confusing her as much as he was confused himself. He stood quickly, moving towards her. 'I want to come back,' he said, kissing her forehead. 'To see you.'

And then Marcus was there, and Aleksander's cheeks were flushed and so were Hanna's and Marcus was looking from one to the other with a pair of stern eyebrows, wondering what he had just walked in on.

***

Ayla was pleased with the wagon. Under Beorn's supervision, a wooden roof and sides had been added, a door and a window too, with steps that could be taken out to help them dismount. There was enough space for small short beds. A fire. Stools to sit on. Shelves even, where they would store their jars and sprigs of herbs. Bandages and salves too.

Bruno was standing beside her, and he was far from pleased, Jael could tell. 'I've assigned four men to guard the wagon at all times. They will walk alongside it. Plus the driver. They'll all keep Ayla and Astrid safe.' Jael found it hard to talk so absolutely, especially with the constant presence of that voice teasing her, twisting her words so that she was struggling to believe anything she said. Bruno frowned so intensely that Jael worried that he could hear them. 'Their job is to stay with the wagon, whatever happens. To get Ayla and Astrid to safety. To protect them while they try to help us,' she added, her words fading into a deafening silence.

'Bruno.' Ayla slipped her arm through his, trying to coax a smile out of him, though all her thoughts were on Briggit and Draguta and her fear that a simple wooden wagon would be useless against either of them. 'This is the best we can hope for. I have to go to Hest. Jael needs my help. I can't stay here and hide under the bed with you. Not this time. I need to do something.'

Bruno nodded. 'I know. And I agree, you can't hide from this. Neither of us can. But I want to come.'

Both Jael and Ayla were surprised by that.

'You do?' Ayla stood back, staring at him.

'Of course I do,' Bruno insisted. 'Stock that wagon with arrows. With swords and axes. And me. I'll be in there too. I will protect you. I may not be able to walk far, but I can use a bow, and, if it comes to it, I can protect you with a sword too. I can hold off anyone long enough for you to do your work.'

Ayla smiled, and so did Jael. She wasn't about to say no. She needed to keep Ayla safe. Ayla, who would hopefully be able to see what was coming before she did. 'It sounds good to me,' Jael grinned. 'As long as you're not a snorer. You're going to be rather close in there!' She turned as Ivaar came up to her with Aleksander, who had decided to watch the fight.

'Ready?' Ivaar asked, trying to avoid looking at the Adeas.

Jael nodded, eager to get Ivaar away from Bruno who didn't need the distraction of trying to kill him. She peered at Aleksander. 'Coming to offer your advice, are you?'

'On ways not to kill Eadmund?' Aleksander laughed. 'Not likely.' And he fell in beside Jael and Ivaar as they left the wagon and the frowning Adeas behind. 'But if you're looking for how to kill him... I could help you with that.'

'I'm sure you could, but for now, let's try and focus on saving him. I think Eydis has had enough to deal with lately. You don't want to take away her favourite brother.' Jael winked at Ivaar, who wasn't comfortable enough yet to feel like winking back at her.

Or smiling.

Dropping his shoulders, he followed after them.

Bruno watched them go.

'No.' Ayla grabbed his hand, trying to get his attention. 'We have no time for that. Ivaar will face his own reckoning for what he's done. As will we.' She stared into Bruno's eyes. 'The gods have a plan. It may not seem like it at the moment, but they do. You must trust in them. Let Ivaar go.'

Bruno sighed, his anger simmering, off the boil. Ayla was talking to him again. Talking of a future where they'd be together. A future they would build once Draguta was defeated.

He had to find a way of turning his attention to what was important. And, for all that Ivaar had done to both of them, he wasn't important. Not now.

Revenge, he admitted with a frown, would have to wait.

CHAPTER FIFTEEN

Briggit had the shackles off her ankles, but her hands were still bound, so Eadmund helped her to walk, tugging her across the square, around the mountainous corpse of the black dragon. He was relieved not to be staying in Angard for much longer, reminded of how much the dragon had started to stink in Andala.

'Draguta is not the mistress you need,' Briggit murmured, her voice dripping with intent. She was trying to tempt him with something, but he didn't care to know what.

He wasn't about to listen.

'I can free you from her spell. Once I have the book...'

Eadmund ignored her as they walked across the square, enjoying the warmth of the sunshine which was bright for the first time since his arrival in Angard, its harsh glare revealing the true destruction Draguta had wrought upon the city.

'You love your wife. I could reunite you. Free you to be with her again.'

The pain in Eadmund's heart was sharp as he thought of Jael, remembering his dream of her holding their daughter. But he quickly shut those thoughts away. They would not help him get out of Helsabor and away from Briggit Halvardar. 'As you say, I'm bound to Draguta,' Eadmund muttered. 'So hold your tongue and save your breath because you're bound to her too, in your own way.' He looked down at Briggit's fetters. 'Don't talk about freeing me, when you're as much of a prisoner as I am.' And Eadmund clamped his teeth together, trying not to scream. 'I need to get you back to the castle, so show me where to go.'

'Show you?' Briggit was surprised, her eyes popping open. 'Oh no, I must take you. It is complicated. You will not find your way there on your own.' She wanted to lead him, to trap him. If she could just find where Morana Gallas was hiding, Morana could help free her.

Eadmund stopped, staring up at the castle, at a window on the second floor, watching a pale-grey curtain flapping against the glass. He turned, glancing down the narrow street, smelling winterhazel again. Shaking his head, he turned back to Briggit. 'I think I will,' he murmured, pushing her towards the castle. 'Once I've secured you back inside.'

Briggit panicked, pushing her boots against the cobblestones as Eadmund pulled her away. 'I must come with you! You won't know where to go!'

She needed to go with him. She had to go with him.

Eadmund stopped, gripping her shoulders, looking down at her. 'Thank you,' he said coldly. 'But no.'

***

'This could be the strangest thing I've ever done!' Jael called to Ivaar, who stood back against the railings, his eyes narrowed against the afternoon sun. The rain had gone, and though it had not lingered, the training warriors had quickly turned the moist surface into a choppy mess.

'I think I'd say the same!' Ivaar called back.

There was a lot of noise in the ring. A lot of grunting, growling, clashing warriors who were feeling the pressure to be ready for their departure.

Ivaar wasn't sure why he wanted to save his brother. If he wanted to save him. As if he could undo everything Morana had done to his family? He shook his head. He couldn't. But he could do something about what was coming. And maybe this was it. 'Let's go!' he yelled, running forward.

Jael ran to meet him, trying to imagine that he was Eadmund. But Ivaar was gaunt and wiry. Eadmund was wide, broad shoulders, thick arms - muscle now, she had seen in her dreams. Perhaps she should have tried fighting Aleksander?

'Focus!'

She heard Aleksander from the railings where he'd been joined by Gant.

'I'm going to try and kill you,' Ivaar grinned, enjoying this part, at least.

'Well, we'll see about that,' Jael said, ducking his first blow, whacking his arm with her wooden blade.

'I'm going to keep coming!' Ivaar called, edging closer, scything his sword in front of Jael's face. 'You need to stop me!'

'You think I can't stop you?' Jael growled, trying to think of how she could stop him.

'You can't kill me! Can't be killed by me! How are you going to stop me? You can't go for my belly! I'll bleed to death!' Ivaar frowned as Jael ducked and swayed, avoiding the tip of his blade; stepping back, making him do all the work.

He was right, Jael realised. How to stop Eadmund without killing him?

She'd never really considered that sort of end to any fight.

Breaking away from Ivaar, she strode back to the railings. To Gant.

He inclined his head towards her. 'Nothing fancy. You won't have time for fancy.'

She knew that.

'Here.' And Aleksander pulled Jael close, handing her something, pulling her even closer as she concealed it, tucking it down her trousers.

Gant smiled. 'Nothing fancy!' he warned as Jael strode back into the ring.

'Not sure you'll have time for a conversation in the middle of battle!' Ivaar called. 'With Draguta urging Eadmund to kill you!'

'You talk too much!' And gripping her sword in her right hand, Jael stepped forward, her eyes never leaving his. Ivaar was no dreamer, and nor was Eadmund, though he would likely have Draguta's help. If it truly was her intention to play the game of having them try to kill each other, then Draguta would be watching.

And Draguta would be in Eadmund's head.

She would warn him.

Jael swung her sword, cracking it against Ivaar's, pushing forward, hammering him again and again, ducking his blows, aiming hers at his throat, trying to unbalance him. Ivaar jumped back, and Jael lunged, anticipating it. Stretching her leg, she smacked her boot into his balls, knocking him to the ground. Ivaar cried out in pain, his head thumping back onto the muddy ground, barely holding onto his sword which had threatened to fly out of his hand.

Jael ran to him, kicking the sword away, throwing her own after it, elbowing him in the nose – a fair return for his kick in the mouth – and dropping to her knees, she pulled out the length of rope Aleksander had handed her, tying it around Ivaar's ankles as he tried to sit up.

He did, reaching for her and Jael hit him again, the side of her hand straight across his throat. He jerked back, unable to breathe and she grabbed him, rolling him over, dragging his hands behind his back now, taking out the second length of rope, hurrying to tie a knot.

And dropping the moaning Ivaar back to the ground, Jael stood up, nodding at Aleksander and Gant. 'That could work.'

Ivaar, face in the mud, his hands and feet bound, was struggling to breathe, listening to the laughter booming around the ring.

Jael flipped him over. 'Very helpful, Ivaar,' she grinned. 'Though it looks like I broke your nose. Sorry about that.' She tried to stop smiling as she bent down, untying his hands, letting the rope fall away.

Ivaar spluttered, grabbing his throat, wanting to wipe that smug smile off her face, but he saw an image of his father nodding his approval, and he sighed. 'Well, it's one option at least,' he croaked. 'There are others. Maybe you can try with Aleksander? I might... need a seat.'

Jael smiled, pulling him up. 'I can do that. Thank you.'

And she meant it.

***

Eadmund could still hear Briggit's furious ranting as she was dragged back into the castle. He had left her with Berger and two other men. He wanted her watched closely, hoping that Draguta's magical fetters would keep her from doing anything to control his men while he was gone.

He shook his head, wanting to get Briggit out of it.

His attention was quickly focused by laughter.

Laughter?

He was walking down a dark, narrow alley; dirty, sky-high stone houses crowding him as he walked; loose cobblestones threatening to trip him. Cold. It was surprisingly cold. Eadmund shivered, listening again, wondering at the wisdom of letting Briggit return to the castle. Though, perhaps she had been planning to ambush him? Lead him towards those Followers who were hiding, not bound. Who would kill him and free their mistress.

He drew his sword, his hand clammy on its leather grip.

Eyes everywhere.

Up and down. Doors. Windows. Around corners.

No one was there.

Not a Helsaboran. Not a Follower.

No one he could see, at least.

Eadmund crept forward, into the shadows. It was getting darker, the streets growing narrower. Too narrow for a cart. Houses towering over him.

He heard the laughter again, and he recognised it.

And then the smell. Spinning around, he tried to see who was there.

Someone was. Leading him...
Leading him where?

***

'They will not stay in Angard for long,' Dragmall insisted wearily. The damp and cold of the catacombs was making things even more unpleasant. They were all exhausted by the gloom. The heaviness of the darkness was suffocating. 'Draguta wants Briggit and the Followers. We all know that. She wants them in Hest.'

'You think they'll just leave?' Morana scoffed. 'This place? After all they did to claim it? After what Draguta did?' She sighed, bored with the conversation. Hungry too. Her own stomach had finally joined in the rumbling chorus. 'And if they do?'

'We'll be free to come out, won't we?' Else suggested, her voice just a croak. She was aching for something to drink, her dry throat becoming painful now. 'Won't we? If they have taken the Followers and left, we can come out. Decide what to do.'

Dragmall didn't move. Every hair on the back of his neck was standing on end. He could feel it. It was a strange sensation that travelled down his arm, fluttering in his protesting stomach.

Morana could sense it. 'What? You don't agree?'

'I... I don't feel safe here. Do you?'

Morana shook her head. 'No. Not here. Not while they are still up there. If they are –'

They held their breaths, listening to the creak of a door handle.

***

At first, Eadmund thought the door was locked, but eventually, he felt some play in the handle as it turned. He pushed it open, groaning hinges inconveniently loud in the silence. He cringed, looking around, swapping his sword back into his right hand.

It was dark, but tiny beams of light from the alley illuminated the symbols around the door. Around the walls.

Eadmund shivered, turning one way and then the other, looking from the doorway to the darkness.

Eskild watched him, sensing her son's trepidation.

He didn't know what he was about to walk into, but she did.

She tried to urge him on. He just needed to keep going.

Into the catacombs.

***

They hid.

It was not hard. Everything was cloaked, veiled in a darkness so thick that no one could see a hand in front of their faces. There was no source of light. No obvious sense of where air was coming from at all.

It was not hard to hide.

Dragmall felt Else shaking beside him. He had been holding a hand over her mouth, whispering in her ear to be quiet. Now, he released it, keeping her close, hoping he could trust her not to cry out.

Morana was beside Else, her hands on the great stone tomb they crouched behind, listening. Her hearing had deteriorated over the years, she knew, but once she had been able to hear a pine needle drop in a forest. Now, she held her breath, waiting, hoping to get a warning.

Of who it was.

She couldn't tell.

It panicked her.

She couldn't tell who was coming.

***

Eadmund could feel the trickle of sweat snaking its way down between his shoulder blades, another dripping down his temple. He kept one hand out in front of him, the other tightening around his sword grip.

He tried to calm his breathing, to silence the noise of his boots scuffing the dirt.

It was so dark. He kept turning, afraid that he would miss something.

Walk into something.

He couldn't smell anything now except sewage.

Distracted for a moment by the overpowering reek, Eadmund tripped over a rock. Stumbling, he tried to keep his balance, but he pitched forward, throwing out his hands to break his fall, his sword lost in the darkness.

Scrambling quickly onto his knees, stirring up clouds of dust, he tried to find it, crawling left and right, back to where he'd started, but his sword was gone.

***

Eydis couldn't stop thinking about Eadmund. He was in danger. The sudden feeling of a hand around her throat told her that. She couldn't see what was threatening him, but she could sense it. It felt as though Draguta herself stood before her, squeezing the air from her lungs.

She was dizzy, struggling to breathe.

Fyn was ignoring her, talking to that girl. That dreamer.

Eydis didn't trust her.

She shook her head, not wanting to get distracted. Something was wrong. Eadmund was in danger now. She could feel the heightened sense of terror, her body almost convulsing with it.

They were near the training ring, Eydis remembered, though all the loud voices around her had blurred. Suddenly she was freezing. Shaking.

And then she was falling, hitting her head on the dirt, collapsed into an unconscious heap.

***

'Could this be what you're looking for?' came the hoarse voice in the darkness. 'This sword? Your sword?'

Morana had quickly given it to Dragmall, who stood beside her now, his breath coming in panicked bursts. She could feel his fears, loud for a moment before they retreated, and she turned all of her attention to Eadmund.

'Your mother,' she growled. 'That dead bitch led you here, didn't she? For me?'

Eadmund wasn't sure who had led him here. But here he was, at last, face to face with Morana Gallas. He couldn't see much more than a shape, but he knew it was her.

He knew that voice.

His knee was bleeding, stinging with pain. He must have landed on something sharp. Blood ran down his leg, into his boot.

It was too dark to see who else was there, but there appeared to be at least two of them. Someone was holding his sword. He saw the glint of its blade occasionally. It wasn't Morana, but she was near it. Eadmund doubted she needed his sword to hurt him, though he would need it back to hurt her.

Morana frowned, wanting to see inside Eadmund's head. But whether it was the symbols carved around the catacombs or something Draguta had done to him, she couldn't see anything. 'You shouldn't have come, Eadmund. This was never your destiny. To die here? With no one watching? Ha! That wasn't what your gods imagined for the mighty Esk's son, was it?' She laughed, coughing suddenly as the dust Eadmund had stirred up caught in her parched throat. 'And what of your wife?' she wondered, her voice teasing him, her confidence surging back. 'Who will kill her now? Jaeger? I suppose that's the only choice Draguta will have left. To send the Bear to kill the Bitch! Ha!'

Eadmund couldn't throw himself forward. He thought about it, but being unable to see, he could just as easily throw himself onto his sword, and then what use would he be?

Morana could sense Eadmund's hesitation as his boots moved around in the dirt, deciding what to do; planning how he would overcome her; underestimating what dreamers could do.

Dragmall gripped the sword, his hand shaking.

'The only bitch I know is you, Morana,' Eadmund seethed, his voice as heavy as stone. 'You who killed my mother. Who killed my father and my wife. Who turned my brother against me! Who forced me into Evaine's bed, and took me away from Jael! From my home!' Eadmund's body was jerking now, losing control. 'The only bitch I know is you!'

He wanted to kill her. To rush into the darkness and grab her by the throat, but he hesitated, panting, coughing.

Waiting.

And then Morana spoke.

'Kill him.'

And Eadmund lunged in the direction of her voice. Low. Wrapping his arms around her legs, knocking her to the ground.

She hissed and growled, wriggling away from him, chanting.

And suddenly Eadmund was screaming. The pain in his ears was as though a thousand birds were screeching inside his head. Rolling away from her, he clamped his hands over his ears, crying out. 'Aarrghh!'

Morana laughed, spluttering, blinking. She'd hit her head on something, and her own ears were clanging as she scrambled back to her feet. 'Well, what are you waiting for?' she demanded, looking up at Dragmall's towering shadow. 'Kill him!'

And then she blinked, her senses alert to a sudden shift in

things.

Turning away, she scuttled into the darkness, running, stumbling, arms out in front of her.

Dragmall reached down and found Eadmund's hand, pulling him to his feet, trying to give him the sword, but Eadmund ignored him, drawing a knife from his belt instead, his ears suddenly clear. He listened to Morana's boots as they raced away. And then a light.

In the distance, he saw a light.

A bright, warm, golden light.

And in the middle of that light was his mother.

Flicking his wrist, Eadmund threw the knife at the running Morana.

'Aarrghh!' she screamed, seeing Eskild before her as she tumbled through the air. 'You bitch –'

And then she was down, the knife through her skull.

Eadmund held his breath, blinking, trying to see but the light faded quickly, and everything went dark.

***

'Eydis!' Ivaar was kneeling by his sister, Fyn on her other side, Jael hovering over them both. 'Eydis?'

Eydis groaned, opening her eyes, confused.

'What happened?' Jael felt a sense of dread, heavy and dark. 'Is it Eadmund?'

Eydis felt odd having Ivaar so close, and she quickly recoiled from him. 'Eadmund... yes, he was in danger. I could feel it, as though it was all around him.' She shook her head, trying to remember what had happened. 'I couldn't see him. He was hidden, in the darkness.'

Jael frowned, bending down, crouching on her heels. She hadn't expected that. Not while he was bound to Draguta, who would surely be keeping him safe. 'What happened to him?' She swallowed, wanting to see Eydis relax, to know that Eadmund was alright.

Eventually, she did. 'I didn't see. Usually, I can see in my dreams, but it was too dark... I don't know.'

Fyn looked worried, handing Eydis a water bag. 'Here,' he smiled. 'Something to drink. Water.' And he placed her hands around the mouth of the skin.

Eydis could hear his concern, remembering that Ontine was somewhere nearby, watching her being fussed over like a child. She took a quick drink and handed back the bag, wanting to get up. 'I don't know what happened,' she insisted. 'But Eadmund is not safe. I sense that. Not even with Draguta. While he is there, with all of them, he is not safe at all.'

***

Eadmund felt around in the dirt, on his knees, eventually finding Morana's body. She was warm, but she wasn't breathing. Else and Dragmall came with him, not wanting to lose him in the darkness.

Dragmall held out the sword as Eadmund rose to his feet. 'It's best if you finish things,' he suggested haltingly. 'To be sure.'

Eadmund took the sword and stuck out a boot, feeling where Morana's neck was, knowing that, despite the darkness, it was safer to finish her now. And swinging his sword with both hands, he brought the blade down across Morana's neck, chopping off her head.

He bent over, sobbing, remembering all that he had lost. All the voices in his head. The crying and the dying. The pain and the loss.

All that Morana had taken from him.

All that he could never get back.

Eadmund dropped to his knees, onto the dirt, his sword still in his hand, not wanting to lose it again.

Morana Gallas was dead.
But so was part of him.
And nothing he could do would ever bring it back.

CHAPTER SIXTEEN

Jael was distracted, not listening as Bram mumbled away beside her, showing her around the new defenses he had organised at the main gates. The stakes the barsk had sailed over had been doubled, and a new row, closer to the walls stood higher out of the ditch now, their lethal tips threatening anyone who dared come close. It would certainly keep out an army of men, he insisted.

Perhaps the dragur, Jael thought. The barsk.

But not Draguta with that ring.

'Jael? Do you think it will be enough?'

Jael turned to Bram, blinking away the memory of that map table, and the screams and the rain and the crashing shock as the wall ruptured. 'The barricades? I think so,' she lied. 'Anything trying to throw itself over the walls will have a painful time, I'm sure.'

Bram thought he detected a lack of confidence in Jael's voice. She had a lot on her mind, he could see. 'I wish I was coming with you,' he said, walking her back through the gates.

'You do?'

Bram nodded. 'It would be some way to go, wouldn't it? Likely to impress Vidar, a battle like that.' He sighed. 'Everyone around me is dropping dead. Eirik, Odda, Morac... Runa. My friends. My family.' He stopped, turning as someone called his name. 'Wouldn't be such a bad way to go.'

Two men were motioning Bram over to a gate tower, but Jael

grabbed his arm. 'I'm sure Fyn wouldn't agree,' she said sharply. 'And you may think you've lost everyone, Bram Svanter, but you've only just found him, and he deserves a father. After all he went through with Morac? After losing his mother? Fyn deserves a father, so I hope you'll be waiting here when I bring him back to you!' And feeling herself getting more irritable by the moment, Jael dropped Bram's arm and strode away.

Bram blinked, watching her go.

'What did you say to Bram?' Thorgils asked, looking at his gob-smacked uncle as he hefted another barrel of ale onto a cart. 'He still hasn't shut his mouth!' He laughed, seeing the fire in Jael's eyes. 'Need some more sleep, do we?'

Jael glared at him. 'What I need is for you to talk less and lift more. Get moving, or you'll be working into the night!' And leaving behind a second open-mouthed Svanter, Jael headed in the direction of Aleksander, realising that he was possibly the only person who stood a chance of calming her down.

***

They left Morana's body inside the catacombs, Dragmall locking the door, stuffing the key inside his leather satchel.

'Why didn't you lock yourselves in?' Eadmund wondered, turning to Dragmall as they stood in the dark alley. 'If you had the key, why didn't you lock the door?'

Else had been wondering the same thing, though she was sure that Dragmall had locked the door.

'I knew your mother, Eadmund,' Dragmall said sadly. 'Our families were friends for many years. I knew her as a girl, before she left to marry your father.'

Eadmund blinked.

'I am a dreamer. A volka and a dreamer. I saw some things, heard some more. I unlocked it when I knew you were coming.'

Else blinked.

'But you were with Morana.' Eadmund was confused. 'You helped her escape Hest.'

'At the time, I believed it was the better choice to make. Either we were going to be killed by Morana or Draguta was going to do it. In the end, one of them would triumph. One evil would defeat the other. I simply made what I hoped was the right choice.' He pulled Else close. 'We both did.' Dragmall tried to see anything in Eadmund's eyes that would give him a clue as to what he would do with them.

A clue as to what he should do about Eadmund.

'And now? You wish to stay here?' They weren't Followers, Eadmund told himself. Draguta required him to bring back all the Followers.

They weren't Followers.

Dragmall looked hesitant. 'For now, yes, I think so.'

'Then stay,' Eadmund said, motioning for them to walk with him. 'Stay here.' Smoke drifted towards them, and he thought of the destruction of the city; the totality of Briggit's defeat. 'Though, I'm not sure how safe you'll be, or what will come next. It will be an uncertain time.'

Dragmall shrugged. 'Well, I suspect much of that will be up to you.'

'What do you mean?'

Dragmall felt exposed. Though the alley was dark with shadows and those houses still standing appeared deserted, he suspected that the Angardians were merely hiding, waiting until they could be assured of their safety.

He had symbol stones in his leather satchel, but Draguta would likely see through them. What did it matter, he supposed? Now? When everything had been blown apart. 'You are meant for something,' Dragmall said softly. 'The dreamers knew it. The volkas knew it too. They did not agree on much, but that is where they came together.'

Eadmund froze. 'Meant for what?'

'There is a shield, made hundreds of years ago, right here in

Angard. Commissioned by the gods, both old and new. For you.'

'A shield? For what? Why?' Eadmund felt confused, disturbed, memories stirring; wondering if Draguta was watching.

Dragmall wondered the same thing. 'To defeat our greatest enemy. Both you and Jael. Together. She has her sword. And for you, the Shield of Esk.'

'Esk?'

'Oh yes, you are Esk's son. That God of War is your forbear on your mother's side. You are his as much as Jael is Furia's daughter. When the gods learned of what would come, they realised that only humans could save us all. Raemus' Book of Darkness was filled with spells they had no power to stop, so they chose you, you and Jael. It was in their plans, you see, for you to come together.'

Eadmund swallowed, not wanting to think about Jael. About what Draguta wanted him to do to her. Draguta who he had no choice but to please.'I need to get back to the castle,' he muttered, wanting to ignore everything Dragmall had said; it sounded similar to something Jael had told him. 'I have to check on Briggit. We have to leave. You stay, but I have to leave.'

'Eadmund!' Dragmall hurried Else along the narrow street after the quickly disappearing king. 'Wait!' Eadmund was a fast walker, and he panted as he tried to catch him. 'The shield!'

Eventually, Eadmund stopped, convinced that Dragmall would keep following him if he didn't, and he didn't want to get the old man in trouble with Draguta. 'I can't help you. This shield? I don't know where it is, and even if I did, what could I do with it? Draguta would destroy it. She has no wish to be defeated, and I've no wish to defeat her!' he insisted, conscious of the stabbing pain in his heart that betrayed his lie. 'I won't use it against her. I can't.' Eadmund wanted to leave. Quickly. 'Don't do anything foolish, Dragmall. I'm letting you both go. You helped me. I'm letting you go, so go. Now! Please.'

Dragmall nodded. 'Of course. I understand. I do. We will find our own way now, thank you.' He could see a familiar street disappearing around the corner up ahead, and he took Else's hand. 'I wish you luck, Eadmund, whichever path you choose to take.

Your mother was a good woman. I was very sad to hear about what happened to her.' And hurrying Else away, he left Eadmund standing alone in the shadows, Morana's blood splattered over his boots, thoughts of Draguta swirling around his head.

And the shield.

He blinked, shutting it all away as he strode down the street, wanting to get back to Briggit.

***

Amma was full of questions that Meena didn't want to answer.

'But what will she do with the queen?' Amma wondered as they walked behind the tailor and his long train of servants who were taking armloads of fabric samples to the castle. 'Briggit Halvardar? Will Draguta kill her? Keep her prisoner?'

Meena shrugged, knowing that it wasn't her place to comment either way.

'Or Eadmund? What does she want with Eadmund? What use is he when she has Jaeger?'

Meena was feeling wistful for the time when Amma had been too timid to speak at all. Though, she supposed, at least it filled her mind with something other than thoughts of the ring.

She gulped as thoughts of the ring suddenly filled her mind.

Jael Furyck too.

'We have to wait,' Meena mumbled, scratching her head. 'Until they arrive. Then we will know.'

Amma had dreamed of Axl, and though she wasn't a dreamer, she had seen him preparing to leave Andala. It felt as though he was always preparing to leave for somewhere. But now she knew that he was coming to Hest.

To defeat Draguta. Jaeger. The Book of Darkness.

And she felt a lift because of it. If she could just hold on...

If she could just survive...

She glanced at Meena. 'The Dragos' are in Andala, you know. Those who still live. Berard and Karsten. Queen Bayla. Karsten's wife.' She frowned, never having found any reason to like Nicolene. 'They hope to return. To defeat Jaeger. To take back the throne.'

Meena shivered, thinking about Berard, remembering what Jael Furyck had said about him waiting for her. But if she didn't retrieve that ring, there was no chance. No chance that she would ever see him again.

***

Karsten was checking through his armour, bending his new leather arm guards. They were stiff, and from experience he knew that they would need some wearing in before they felt part of him. He hoped he wouldn't have to use them until they reached Hest, though that was unlikely.

Berard was frowning at him.

'You know I'm right,' Karsten insisted. 'You do. Otherwise, you'd be sorting your armour next to me.' Kai and Eron were crawling all over him, and his brother was scowling at him from a bed, and Nicolene was standing by the door watching him. Bayla had taken Haegen's children for a walk, trying to stop herself from fretting, though if they were there, Karsten was sure they'd all be watching him too. He was starting to agree with Bayla.

They needed more room.

'You're right,' Berard admitted, dropping to the floor, leaning his back against the bed. His stump was throbbing, reminding him of just how right Karsten was. It was his mind that felt ready for a fight, but his body kept trying to warn him that he was not ready. Not to face Jaeger, who would have only grown stronger since they were in Hest.

Karsten smiled triumphantly. 'Good! And don't think you won't get some action here.' He glanced at Nicolene, who looked worried by the thought of that. 'You need to lock up this place every night as though you're going to war. Wood. Weapons. Get your tinderbox out. Barricade the door. Keep the fire going.'

Now Nicolene was frowning. 'Boys, come away from your father,' she scolded, grabbing Kai's hand. 'Let's go and see the sun before we all die from the gloom in here!' And with a pointed look at her husband, she ushered her sons outside.

Karsten laughed. 'Not sure which is the most daunting, going to face Draguta, or being locked up in here with Bayla and Nicolene and five children!'

Berard was wondering the same thing. 'Ulf's going to stay.'

'Is he?' Karsten was surprised by that. Surprised but pleased.

'Well, with you gone, there'll be a bed free, and Bayla insisted. I think she'd feel safer with two more arms.' He grinned, trying to lighten the mood.

'Poor Ulf,' Karsten laughed. 'Bayla has him wrapped around her finger now. He'll never be free!'

'Well, I'm glad,' Berard said. 'We need all the help we can get with the bad luck we've had lately.'

'Mmmm,' Karsten agreed. 'But here's where our luck is about to change. Don't you feel it? The winds are blowing, Brother, and I feel a change coming.'

***

'We're all going to die!'

Aleksander laughed. They had walked away from the fort until they were alone, and Jael had finally felt free to explode in a mess of fears and worries, her shoulders sinking with every step. 'Maybe, but we'll die trying, don't worry.'

'Don't worry?' Jael couldn't tell him what might be coming, but she needed to give him some kind of warning. 'It's worse than you think, you know, what Draguta is doing. What she's capable of.'

Aleksander's good mood slid away. 'What have you seen?'

'Enough to know that we're all going to die!'

'Jael.' And stopping her, Aleksander gripped her arms, trying to get her attention. Her eyes were darting all over the road, not stopping anywhere near his face. 'Say what you need to. I can handle it. Say anything you like. You've always been able to.' He smiled, feeling her start to relax.

She shook off his hands, rubbing her eyes. 'I need more sleep. Fewer dreams, more sleep.'

'The gods didn't choose you because they thought you'd give up before we even began,' Aleksander tried. 'They chose you because they knew you'd fight. They saw who you'd become, and they made you full of fire, Jael Furyck. Ready for war.' He felt a deep sadness as memories washed over him. 'I believe in you,' he said. 'So turn off all the voices in your head. Shut them all out. Don't listen to any of them. Put one foot in front of the other. That's it. Leave everything else alone.'

Jael frowned.

'You can't look back. What has happened is done. What is coming will come. And you'll have all of us, right there beside you. All of us. Fighting with you. We'll never stop. We'll never let you down. You're not alone, Jael. You've never been alone.'

Jael pushed herself forward, against his chest, encouraging him to wrap his arms around her. 'You've gotten very good at this over the years,' she murmured into his tunic. 'Though I'm not sure Hanna will be so enamoured with you fixing me once you're married.'

Jael felt Aleksander freeze, and she laughed, staying right where she was, enjoying for one moment the feeling of being safe.

Soon, she knew, it would all change.

***

By nightfall, Eadmund felt confident that all of the Followers had been found. Well, not confident, he supposed. It was impossible to know what those dreamers could do to hide themselves, but he was, at least, convinced that he had done everything he could to find them. The ships he was taking back to Draguta were stuffed from prow to stern with Wulf Halvardar's precious chests of gold, and now those ships were being guarded by a swathe of almost-sober men, and Eadmund had one more night to endure in Briggit's castle before they set sail for Hest.

He was growing more and more uncomfortable in the company of dreamers. Dreamers and volkas who all appeared to know more about him than he ever had.

Briggit had been brought into the hall for supper, and though the smell of roast salmon had her lips moist with hunger, she found herself more interested in Eadmund Skalleson, who seemed both sad and angry, and very, very distant. 'It must be hard for you,' she cooed, 'knowing that soon you will have to kill your wife.'

Eadmund crunched into a carrot, not caring to hear what Briggit thought about anything. 'It must be hard for you,' he countered, 'knowing that soon Draguta will kill all of your Followers. And then you.'

Briggit sat alone at the high table.

Eadmund sat further away with some of his men. The Hestians. He didn't like the food or the company, but it was better than sitting near Briggit.

Briggit glared at him. 'You underestimate the power of a dreamer. The power of The Following. So does Draguta. As she'll soon find out.'

Eadmund eyed the queen over his goblet, watching her nibble on a slice of smoked cheese. 'Draguta is more powerful than any dreamer you know of, wouldn't you say? After watching what she did out there?' He turned his head towards the entranceway, looking for an escape. 'I expect she's more powerful than the gods now.'

Eadmund's words ruffled Briggit's confidence. She couldn't deny that she had been surprised by the explosive power of

Draguta's attack. It was still a mystery how she had pushed through the wall and shattered that impenetrable stone.

With what?

Briggit didn't know.

But she settled back into her chair with a serene smile masking her fears. It didn't matter. Draguta was only a dreamer. A dreamer with a book of symbols that didn't belong to her.

She could be defeated.

CHAPTER SEVENTEEN

Draguta had spent most of the day in her chamber, enjoying the solitude and the silence. Industrious sounds from the harbour had drifted up through her balcony window, making her sigh with satisfaction. Those men appeared to be working hard constructing the piers. And they would need to. In only a few days, the harbour would be filled with more ships than Haaron Dragos had ever imagined.

With even more to come.

Draguta ran a blood-tipped finger around the edge of the seeing circle, watching the symbols glow, searching for clues.

Dara was out there somewhere. Hiding.

Her little sister.

Once her favourite sister. Not like Dalca and Diona. The three of them had been similar ages, but Dara was ten years younger. The baby. And how they had all doted on her. Doted on her and dismissed her, not noticing what a talented dreamer she was. Not seeing what she would grow up to become.

Draguta frowned, annoyed that she had been blinded by her sister's loyalty for all those years as she nurtured her, mothered her, gave her a home, taught her everything she knew. Blinded until the knife was in her neck and she was dead, entombed in that stone coffin for centuries.

The ultimate betrayal.

Reaching out, she pulled the tiny box towards her, flicking

open the lid.

The Ring of Taron was a dark treasure. A tool so powerful that she could strike anywhere with it.

Anyone.

Any time.

Running her finger over the black stone, she smiled, turning to the Book of Darkness which sat in front of her, waiting.

Waiting for Briggit, for Jael Furyck, for Dara.

Wherever that bitch was...

***

It was impossible to hide forever.

But if she came out? Revealed herself? What then?

Dara considered it hourly. She was not sleeping, though sleep was not a requirement for someone like her. It was a habit she had broken long ago. She would live for centuries and beyond if Draguta didn't destroy everyone first.

It was raining.

She watched it falling in front of the cave, dripping from its stone mouth, washing mud inside. Dara was not cold, but there was a fire spluttering at her feet.

A cave inside a grove inside a forest.

Protected by the gods.

They were keeping her safe. Hidden from Draguta.

But for how long?

And for what purpose?

If she came out, revealed herself, what then...

Would Draguta stop? Turn her attention to the revenge she so desperately sought? Leave everyone else alone?

Yet once it was done...

Dara poked the flames with a long charred stick, her thoughts teasing her. Jael and Eadmund were so far apart. Eadmund did not have his shield. Jael's sword appeared useless now. Eadmund was not even on the right side of the fight that was coming.

What if they could not defeat Draguta now? After all this time, after all that she had done, what if they could not defeat her now...

But if she came out, and revealed herself?

Dara lay down on the dirt, her head resting on her arm, thinking of her mother, and her sisters before they were claimed by the book. Draguta had once been a girl of such delicate beauty. Admired and desired by many, broken by the deaths of their parents, corrupted by the Book of Darkness which had slowly turned her into...

A dark, unstoppable force.

Her sister, who needed to die. And quickly. But everything was shifting and changing so unexpectedly that Dara wasn't sure whether it was possible to kill her anymore. And if that were the case, she didn't know what she was going to do.

Closing her eyes, she let the dripping rain trick her into thinking that she needed to sleep; lulling her towards a place of peace and stillness where she hoped to find a dream.

***

Draguta turned around, blinking. 'Come in!' She had drifted away, in a trance, lost in a thick wood of trees, searching for clues.

It was suddenly so dark. Where was Brill?

Meena shuffled into the chamber, eyes on the flagstones.

'How long ago did I send for you?' Draguta grumbled moodily. 'I sometimes wonder why I keep you alive!'

Meena wondered the same thing. 'I was with Amma,' she tried. 'She is... lonely.'

Draguta's face broke into a smile. 'Well, not for much longer. Jaeger will be here soon, and then Briggit too, so we must hurry along with our preparations.' She flapped a hand towards her bed. 'I wrote a list. You will wake Evaine before the sun tomorrow, and the two of you will collect those items. Quickly. In order. There is even a chant to repeat for each plant as you harvest it, though that is not something to bother Evaine with. And the knife,' she said, turning, pointing to the knife which lay next to the piece of vellum. The knife Meena had thrown at Draguta's head, killing her for a time.

Meena gulped.

'Yes, that knife,' Draguta purred. 'It is a powerful knife still, so you will cut the plants with it. Remove the bats' wings with it too. Best you slit their throats first. We may as well use some of their blood.'

Meena's eyes were round with horror.

Draguta was pleased to see it. 'I am you,' she warned as Meena crept towards the bed, stuffing the list into her purse; carefully slipping the knife into her empty scabbard. 'I am in your head. I take every step you take. I hear what you say. I feel your breath. Betray me, Meena Gallas, and I will cut out your tongue with that knife.' Her ice-blue eyes narrowed into threatening slits as they studied the shaking woman. 'I have no need for your voice. It is only your hands and legs that offer me any assistance.'

Meena could feel tears of terror stinging her eyes, and she bit down hard on her teeth, wanting to show no fear. It was impossible, though. She had seen the ring box on the table, briefly, as she'd come into the chamber, and she was working hard to keep all thoughts of it far away.

Far away from Draguta.

Her only mistress now.

***

Eadmund wanted to find his mother in a dream, but his mind was so troubled that he couldn't even fall asleep. Briggit was lying on her bed on the other side of the chamber, and he felt disturbed by her presence, unable to relax. Her scheming eyes always studied him so intensely, masking more secrets than he wanted to imagine. He feared what she might do if he closed his eyes.

Thinking about secrets led Eadmund to Dragmall and he was reminded of how much the old man had revealed.

Esk's son. A shield. Jael.

His mother.

Eadmund's shoulders loosened as he thought of Eskild. She had led him all the way to Morana. To the truth. To the truth about Morac too. And he'd taken revenge. In the end, they'd both had their revenge.

But how empty it felt with no one left to share it with.

His mind was drawn back to thoughts of the shield, and he had a strange sense of deja vu. As though he had always known about it. As though he had seen it in his dreams. The memory of the shield was there, just out of reach and Eadmund sighed, closing his eyes, trying to slip into a dream.

Hoping to find his mother waiting for him.

***

The puppies knew that something was wrong. They always did.

And lately, a lot had been wrong.

Ido yelped as Jael rolled over, trying to move his sister and not crush him. 'Sorry,' she murmured into the darkness, wishing she'd left a lamp burning. 'Lie down, there you go.'

It was good to have their company. She felt so alone in their bedchamber, knowing that danger was lurking outside the fort, inside the fort, and most of all at that moment... inside her dreams.

She was not looking forward to falling asleep.

Not tonight.

So she tried to remember Eadmund and Oss. After Tarak's death they had been inseparable, almost hiding out in their house.

In their bed. Even Biddy had barely seen them. Occasionally, she would have to knock on the bedchamber door to make them come out and eat.

Jael's face broke into a smile in the darkness, and she felt her body relax, her mind staying in that place, remembering their comfortable bed and Eadmund's warm feet and his deep voice murmuring in her ear, soothing her to sleep.

***

Meena stared at her grandmother's bed, which had been Morana's for a time. She shivered, reminded of her aunt's screeching cackles; the sneer with which she had always considered her; the sting of her coarse fingers pinching her skin.

Dull moonbeams shone down from the window high above, revealing the true misery of the chamber, and she sighed.

The first few nights after Amma had come to stay, Meena had slept in the bright and warm chamber Berard had found for her, but tonight she'd returned to the place she had lived in since the death of her father.

She thought about him often. He had never been cruel. But he had been sad.

Too sad.

Meena blinked, looking down at the piece of vellum she had pulled out of her purse. It was going to be a long morning, she could see, especially having to endure Evaine's company. Folding it back into her purse, Meena took off her belt and laid it over a stool, watching the glint of the knife secured in her scabbard.

Thinking about the ring.

Not thinking about the ring!

She was afraid to fall asleep. Afraid that Jael Furyck would come into her dreams again, and try to convince her to help them. Meena squeezed her hands together, twisting her bare fingers which had never worn a ring.

Fingers that would likely never wear one now.

Looking around the chamber, she decided to light a fire. It was not cold, but a fire would make her feel better. Even without Morana or Varna, it was a depressing place to be, so getting up from the stool, Meena sought out the tinder box which Morana had kept under her bed. Bending down, she grabbed the little box with her fingers, touching a book as she did so. Frowning, she rocked back on her heels before leaning forward again and wriggling under the bed, pulling out the old, musty books, one at a time.

One, in particular, caught her eye, and she dusted off its cover, noticing the symbols scratched into the dark-red leather. The first page revealed its contents: Dreamer Ailments and How to Cure Them.

Perhaps something in the book could help get rid of her nightmares?

***

Else hadn't spoken since Dragmall had gotten the fire going in the empty house they had decided to camp in for the night.

It had taken time to find wood, to sweep out the old hearth, to find something to light it with. But the flames, once they burst into life, took away some of the stark terror of the past few days. It was comforting to see light again after the pure darkness of the catacombs, and they both started to relax.

'It's hard not to think about what happened to Morana,' Else said, at last, her body sinking back against the very uncomfortable chair. Frowning, she bent down, trying to push one of the legs back in, worried that it was about to collapse.

Dragmall yawned. 'It is, though it was the right thing. Morana hurt a lot of people, Meena included.'

'Do you think Meena is dead?' Else wondered. 'She must be,

mustn't she? For helping us? Draguta would have killed her.'

Dragmall had seen nothing of Meena. His mind had been focused on trying to get them away from the danger in Hest. And then the danger in Angard. And he had, but now their path was becoming more precarious by the day. 'I imagine so. Draguta seems to prize loyalty highly, but we mustn't think about Meena. Not yet. There is still so much for us to do, Else.'

Else turned to him in surprise. 'Do? Us?'

'Oh, yes,' Dragmall smiled. 'Though we are going to need more than a few flames to help us. We are going to need some sleep tonight, and something to eat when the sun comes up tomorrow. And I know just where we can go for that!'

***

The noise was a furious swarm of screams and clashing weapons.

Jael wanted to put her hands over her ears, but she needed to know what was happening. She couldn't see where the noise was coming from, or who was fighting. It wasn't dark, but clouds were swirling threateningly above her head, sinking lower as she spun and spun, searching for clues.

She was standing in a valley, gravel beneath her boots, high mountains sweeping in on either side of her, shelves carved into their rocky faces like platforms.

Memories were stirring now, and as Jael turned away from the entrance to the valley, looking in the opposite direction, she saw a magnificent old tree bursting out of a grassy ridge, surrounded by...

Followers.

Followers in dark robes and big hoods, forming an enormous circle around the tree. And at the head of that circle, a woman dressed all in white.

'Jael!'

She turned, hearing a familiar voice. 'Eadmund?' But the din of the invisible battle quickly drowned him out.

And then silence.

Nothing but silence as she stood there waiting.

Listening.

And then she heard it.

'No! Please! No!'

Shivers ran up and down her spine as she listened.

It was her voice. And she sounded in pain.

***

Eskild's face was glowing, her pink cheeks round with a smile she couldn't stop. She looked up at Eirik, beaming. 'He's perfect.'

Eirik's eyes were on his newborn son. 'He is. Looks just like you.'

Eskild laughed. 'Well, we'll know soon enough, but for now, I think he looks like a baby troll.'

'I think he looks like the next King of Oss.'

'But what about Ivaar?'

Eirik frowned. Ivaar would not speak to him. He had become sullen and withdrawn since his mother's death. Understandably. He was having a hard time with Eskild. A harder time to come with his new brother, Eirik thought to himself. He would have to talk to him.

'Ivaar is your heir. He should be your heir.'

'He should, you're right, I just... love you.' Eirik bent down, kissing Eskild's hair. 'If I could choose, I'd choose our son to rule here when I'm gone. Yours and mine. It feels right. As though he's meant to be the king.'

'Ivaar just needs some time,' Eskild murmured, watching her baby squirm, his mouth open, readying a cry. 'Give him some time, my love. It has not been easy for him. And besides, I've a feeling

Eadmund will have other things to do one day. He might be far too busy to sit on a throne, listening to arguments about chickens and fences!'

'Other things?'

Eadmund watched, wistful for them both.

He saw the look in his mother's eyes as she turned to him. 'You are meant for more than this, Eadmund. Draguta will never rule your heart. And if you want to save everyone you love, you will have to fight harder than you've fought for anything in your life.'

Eadmund froze.

'You need to find the shield. Listen to me now. It is here, in Angard, waiting for you. I have seen it. And when you find it, you will remember it. I used to draw it for you. We would draw it together, remember? The magic shield? You will know it. Look for it, Eadmund, please. Before you leave. Look for the shield.'

CHAPTER EIGHTEEN

Meena sat back on the chair, enjoying the cheering light from the flames she had just brought to life, surprised by how well-rested she felt. She hadn't had a single nightmare. Not one. Not one terrifying thought or image had entered her mind all night long.

Varna's book must have helped, she realised, thinking about the tea she had hastily prepared before bed, grateful for the shelf of tiny jars and pots that Varna had kept her dried herbs in.

A tea to stop her dreams.

She doubted that Varna had ever used the recipe herself, though it was a book that had not been written in her grandmother's hand. Some dreamer obviously felt the need to turn off their dreams, if only to get some rest. Then, reminded about what had happened with Dragmall, Meena wondered if it had even been her idea to make the tea in the first place. She gulped, trying to convince herself that she knew the difference between her own thoughts and Draguta's.

But she didn't.

Her mind jumped quickly from Draguta to the ring, and she shook her head, picking up the book again. It was not yet light enough to see much, but the flames illuminated some of the words as she read, trying to force her attention onto something else.

How to Conceal Your Thoughts from Dreamers.

Meena held her breath, her fingertip lifting off the page, fighting the urge to turn around and check the door. It was unsettling to be in the chamber. She still expected to find her grandmother hunched over on her bed, shouting at her to add another log to the fire.

Pressing her finger back on the vellum, Meena's eyes quickly darted down the list of ingredients required for the potion before turning the page, casually browsing the next ailment.

Ingrown Toenails.

***

Eadmund had the sense that dawn was coming. The chamber was dark, but his body had developed a familiar rhythm recently, and he was wide awake, anticipating the sun's rise.

He wasn't sure how he felt about it.

Briggit sounded asleep. He hoped she was. He wanted to be alone with his thoughts. The remnants of his dream were still lingering, and Eadmund felt sad, wanting to see his parents' faces again, to hear his mother's voice as she told him to find the shield. But Draguta's voice was there too, warning him away.

What need did he have for a shield? A shield from her?

He was her shield now.

Her shield against Jael, and all those who wanted to hurt her.

Eadmund rubbed his temples, desperate to be freed from his warring thoughts; the constant battle of them as they fought each other, trying to claim him. But, Eadmund realised, rolling onto his side, watching Briggit stir.

There was no fight.

Draguta had already won.

***

Evaine was so furious at being woken before dawn that she wanted to scream, but she was far too tired to even open her mouth as she traipsed towards the winding gardens after Meena.

Meena had no desire to spend any time with Evaine, and she didn't speak either. And so, as the sun rose and the morning dew slowly evaporated in the cool light of day, Meena dug in the earth, occasionally mumbling a small chant as she sliced through a stalk and carefully laid the cutting in her basket.

Evaine glared at her, though she was too bored to even complain as she watched her cousin, not offering her help at all. Eventually, she stood, stretching her back, eager for some breakfast. 'I shall go to the markets. What do you need from there?'

Meena was halfway through a chant, and she didn't appreciate the interruption. 'Nothing,' she muttered. 'Not today.'

Evaine frowned. 'Nothing?'

Meena didn't reply, but she waited to ensure that Evaine wasn't going to say any more, and finally satisfied, she started her chant again.

'But how long will this take?' Evaine grumbled, enjoying the perturbed look on her cousin's ugly face. 'How long?'

Now Meena was mad. 'You need to be quiet!' she hissed. 'Draguta will not be pleased to see what you're doing. She will see, you know. She is always watching. And listening. She will hear you talking when I'm supposed to be chanting and then how will you get Eadmund back? Without Draguta helping you, how will you trap him again?' Meena shook and trembled, fighting the urge to push Evaine over. She squeezed her hand around the haft of the knife and turned back to the row of flowers. 'You will be quiet,' she almost growled, her eyes on the bright-blue head of the cornflower she had been attempting to cut. And grasping its stem, she closed her eyes, wishing Evaine away.

***

Gant smiled, pleased to see Jael coming towards him, though when she stopped by his table, he could tell that something was wrong. Her eyes were darting around the hall, barely focusing on him at all. 'Bad dreams?' he wondered as she took a seat opposite him.

'Odd dreams.'

Gant's eyebrows were up. 'About?'

'I saw a battle. Heard a battle,' Jael frowned, shaking her head as he offered her a plate of smoked eel. 'I think it was our battle. The battle.'

'But you couldn't see it?'

'No, but I saw where it was.'

Gant waited for her to go on, his knife in mid-air.

'The Vale of the Gods.'

That was a surprise.

'There were Followers surrounding the Tree of Agrayal. A hundred or more.'

'Followers?' Gant's knife remained in mid-air, the wedge of cheese before him uncut. 'And who else?'

'I saw Draguta. She was with them in a circle, but I couldn't see anyone else. It was loud, though. I could hear a battle.'

'At the Vale of the Gods?'

Jael nodded.

Gant shook his head. 'That is some place. Perhaps the perfect place. But it won't be easy to get to. Not with the catapults.'

'No, but we'll need them.'

'You will. Especially if Draguta has all those Followers on her side.'

'Mmmm.'

They sat in silence, both of them trying to recall their visit to the vale years ago, when they had gone with Ranuf and Aleksander. They had stood on a mountaintop, looking down into the vast arena, imagining the battles that had taken place over the centuries between the Oster and Tuuran gods.

The Vale of the Gods was a place of blood and magic and death.

And sacrifice.

Jael remembered the sound of her own voice, the painful cry that had the hairs on her arms standing on end as it had risen above the invisible fray.

Wondering what had happened.

***

Briggit had eyes that made Eadmund squirm.

It was as though she was studying him naked. He tried to avoid looking anywhere near her face, not wanting her to see his discomfort, knowing that it was all part of her game. She couldn't hurt him with spells, couldn't do anything with her hands, so she was using her eyes, teasing him, unsettling him.

'What are we waiting for?' Briggit wondered irritably. Eadmund had dragged her down to the hall, leaving her sitting alone at the high table while he instructed his men on the final preparations before their departure. She had barely slept, unused to sleeping by herself, worrying about Sabine and Lillith who were sailing to Hest with Jaeger Dragos for company.

The thought of that had put her in a foul mood.

'We're waiting for me. I want to ensure that we've thought of everything. I imagine you have. I imagine you're not sitting there as happy to be a prisoner as you're pretending to be. No doubt you've got plans, ideas about what you'll do. Ways to escape. Ways to hurt Draguta and retake your kingdom. To claim victory over hers,' Eadmund said sharply, walking towards the table. 'And it's my job to anticipate every problem you're going to cause.'

Briggit burst out laughing, her eyes aflame with irritation. She was hungry and growing impatient for her breakfast. 'How pathetic you are, Eadmund. Did you ever think it would come to this? Finally made a king. Finally worthy of being the king your father always wanted, yet now you're a slave, just as all your forbears were. Draguta Teros' slave!'

'Says the queen in fetters.'

'Yes, but only my hands are imprisoned. Only my hands are Draguta's. You are lost to her! Bound to her forever. Every single part of you. You will never be free!'

'And you?' Eadmund wasn't sure if he was more incensed or troubled. He leaned over, hands splayed on the table, glaring at Briggit. 'How will you be free?'

'Ha! You think I should make it easy for you? But surely if you figure it out on your own, you'll earn Draguta's praise? Won't that be worth it, Eadmund? Or maybe you're trying to please your wife too? Perhaps you'll try and find the shield? Go against Draguta? Make your wife happy?'

Eadmund almost stumbled backwards, confused.

'Oh, you think I'm reading your mind?' Briggit smiled. 'Maybe these fetters don't work at all? Perhaps Draguta is already failing to imprison me and my power?'

Eadmund wasn't sure what Briggit was doing to him, but he didn't want to waste his time trying to find out. He wanted to leave. He needed to get back to Hest to see his son. He tried to focus on Sigmund. Not Evaine. Not Draguta.

Not Jael.

'But you won't find the shield here,' Briggit mused, not about to let him escape from the hook she had so carefully baited. 'You won't find the shield, if that's why you're waiting. That shield is hidden somewhere it will never be found!'

***

Dragmall had to pull Else towards the castle.

She didn't want to go near it.

'The Followers have all gone,' Dragmall said encouragingly. 'All of them. We know that.'

'Do we?' Else was surprised. 'Do we know that?'

Dragmall smiled. 'I do, yes. Only Briggit remains, and she is shackled, waiting to sail back to Hest with Eadmund. I saw it in my dreams. Her sight is blocked by Draguta's symbols, so she is no enemy to us now.'

'And you're really a dreamer?' Else followed him more willingly, wanting to know all those things he had hidden from her. 'You can see that?'

'Yes, I can,' Dragmall sighed. 'Which is both a curse and a gift, seeing and sensing evil. There was so much of it in Helsabor, and now it is all moving to Hest. To Draguta.'

Else stopped, waiting while he turned back to her. 'Why don't we leave?' she wondered. 'I know this was your home, but I'm not sure I could ever feel safe here. Eadmund may have let us go, but once Draguta discovers it, she might try to find us.'

'Well, I'm sure she's already discovered it, Else, knowing the power of that woman. And yes, I believe we should leave. Absolutely. But first, I need to find the shield.'

'You said that it was taken. Not in the catacombs anymore. How can we find it?'

'Well,' Dragmall mused, taking Else's hand and slipping it through his arm while she was distracted, making it easier to quicken their pace towards the alley which led around the back of the castle. 'I believe that Briggit took it, and if that's the case, it shouldn't be hard to find, especially if I can take something of hers to help me. Now, come along. We need to find our way to the kitchen before your empty stomach has everyone coming for us!'

***

Amma had come to the hall looking for Meena. She hadn't seen her all morning, and she was starting to feel anxious. If something had happened to Meena, she would have no one to talk to. No one who wasn't terrifying and threatening.

No one until Jaeger came back...

Evaine looked her over with a sneer as she walked towards her with Tanja who was carrying a gurgling Sigmund. After finally running out of patience standing around while Meena talked to the plants, she had returned to her chamber to change her clothes and have Tanja fix her hair. Now, once again, she felt presentable, like the lady she was and the queen she would soon be. 'Have you lost someone?' she asked, eyeing Amma. She was such a timid, dull girl, though she was carrying Jaeger's child, and Evaine knew very well how powerful that made her. Amma's son would be the next King of Hest, just as Sigmund was Eadmund's heir.

Eadmund, who would soon be here too.

'He will!' Draguta exclaimed, gliding into the hall behind them. 'Eadmund and Jaeger and all those slavish Followers who probably haven't bathed in years, if ever!' She rubbed her hands together, striding towards the throne, her white teeth gleaming. 'I cannot wait!'

Taking her place on the edge of the throne, she eyed Amma. 'Your hair will not do. It is so plain. For a girl like you? The Queen of Hest? The woman who must look the loveliest of any in the kingdom?'

Amma stopped moving, her brown eyes full of surprise.

Draguta laughed. 'You were not aware that you're the Queen of Hest now? Or is it that you'd prefer to be the Queen of Brekka?' She smiled, watching Amma's discomfort flush her round cheeks. 'There is no point in thinking of that anymore. Your future is here, with Jaeger. With your son. With me.' Draguta eyed Sigmund who promptly burst into tears. 'Unlike that child there, who has no future in Hest at all. Though, I'm sure he will make a good ally when he takes the throne from his father one day.'

Evaine wasn't sure what that meant, but the bounteous spread of food on offer had immediately claimed her attention, and she was barely listening as she motioned for Tanja to take a seat.

Amma wondered if she had to stay.

'You must eat!' Draguta insisted, pointing her to the table. 'That child requires nourishment, so eat, and then I shall have Brill try some styles with all that hair. We will find something befitting the queen, won't we, Brill?' She looked around, but there was no Brill anywhere, and Draguta frowned, certain that she'd been following her.

She was always following her.

And where was Meena? Surely she should have finished that list by now?

Draguta glared at Ballack who was a steady, if mute presence now, guarding whichever room she happened to be in; waiting to lift something, to move someone. 'You will go and find Brill. Send her to my chamber. I shall meet her there shortly.' Her attention turned to Evaine who was busy filling a plate with hotcakes, one eye on the pot of honey, oblivious to the distress of her son who Tanja was struggling to soothe. 'And why are you here, Evaine Gallas?'

Evaine froze before slowly turning around. 'Meena sent me away. She didn't want my help.'

'Is that so?'

Evaine nodded vigorously. 'In fact, she was quite rude. Ordering me about as though I was her servant. Me? My son's father is the King of Oss. Why should I dig in the dirt under her orders!'

Draguta eyed her with a look that had Evaine shrinking backwards. 'Well, why indeed? Perhaps because you wish to retain your place at my table? In my castle? In this world? If I were you, Evaine, I would hurry back to the gardens and help your poor cousin before I forget why I decided to let you stay.' She flapped her hand at Evaine. 'Run along now, there's a good girl. And do tell Meena to hurry up, or we may have to revisit our conversation about whether or not she requires a tongue!'

***

The ship Eadmund would be sailing back to Hest in was bigger than any in his fleet, though the craftsmanship far fell short of anything Beorn would have been satisfied with. He smiled, remembering his crotchety master shipbuilder and how hard Jael liked to work him.

His attention was diverted to Briggit, busy snapping at Berrick who insisted on fussing over her as though she was his mistress instead of his master's prisoner. Eadmund shook his head. No doubt Berrick was still weighing his silver, trying to decide which side would win. But between Draguta and Briggit, Eadmund didn't think there was much of a decision to make. He wasn't really sure that that was where the actual question lay.

Eadmund turned away, happy that Briggit was restrained, tucked into the stern opposite the stocky helmsman who eyed her with trepidation, one hand on the tiller, watching how carefully she studied him.

Briggit had a way of making everyone think she had a plan.

Eadmund hoped she didn't. He just wanted to get to Hest and deliver her into Draguta's hands.

Walking towards the prow, he inhaled the salty tang of the sea as it beckoned, listening to the gentle rock of the waves slapping the hull. It reminded him of Oss and his father, and turning around, eyes on the mist-touched castle in the distance, Eadmund felt the relief of leaving the city, and the satisfaction that the headless body of Morana Gallas would rot in the darkness, far away from the Slave Islands and those whose lives she had destroyed.

Forgotten by all.

Remembered by none.

***

Meena felt sick as she crept down the corridor to Draguta's chamber. Evaine had found her in the winding gardens and reluctantly helped her collect the last items on the list, warning her that Draguta was in a terrible mood, ranting about how long she was taking. That had sent Meena into a panic, which Evaine added to by deciding that she needed to return to check on Sigmund, leaving Meena to carry the weighty baskets to Draguta's chamber on her own.

Reaching the door, Meena stopped to catch her breath, worried that Draguta would have seen into her dreams and watched her reading Varna's books.

Sighing, she knocked anyway, knowing that Draguta would be inside listening to her dithering outside.

There was no reply.

Glancing up and down the corridor, Meena couldn't see anyone coming. She couldn't hear anyone inside either. Torn between needing to go in and wanting to run away, she turned the handle and pushed open the door. 'My lady?' she croaked, her voice failing her. Clearing her throat, she tried again, edging further into the luxurious chamber which smelled strongly of jasmine, with a hint of blood. 'My lady?'

But there was no sign of Draguta at all, though she would not be far away.

She would have to stay.

Meena's eyes roamed the chamber, almost reluctantly, resting on the table where Draguta must have been sitting. The chair was moved back, a piece of vellum and an inkpot near a seeing circle.

And a tiny box.

Meena's eyes raced away from the box, back towards the door.

Draguta was always one step ahead of them all. Always anticipating what everyone was planning. So if that box was sitting on the table, out in the open, Draguta knew that someone might try to take it.

Perhaps that was why she was here all alone?

Shivering, Meena placed the baskets on the floor, listening for footsteps approaching, but the only noise she could hear was a loud argument drifting towards her from down on the square. She picked up one boot and edged towards the table. And then another step, and soon she was standing beside it, hands by her sides as though that was where she had been waiting all along.

The voice in Meena's head was a high-pitched warning, alerting her to danger, but Meena turned towards the table, one hand reaching quickly for the box, shaking fingers fumbling with the lid.

The ring was in there.

She snapped the lid closed, shaking herself back into a standing position, eyes bulging, turning towards the door.

Which opened.

And in came Draguta and Amma, with Brill trailing silently behind them.

Meena couldn't swallow. She tried and tried, but she couldn't swallow. And feeling the tightness in her throat, she panicked, suddenly hot and dizzy, still unable to swallow.

And then everything went dark.

CHAPTER NINETEEN

Dragmall had spent years in the castle with his father, Konall. Wulf Halvardar had respected Konall, and though the king had been a man with a small view of the world and an over-sized view of his part in it, he'd had a thirst for knowledge that a volka was perfectly positioned to quench. And, as a boy, Dragmall had tagged along. As a boy, and then, as a young man. He knew the castle well. And he knew how to slip up through the kitchens and into the bedchambers. Wulf Halvardar's daughter, Neera, had been a beauty and there had been a time when he had...

Else pinched his arm so sharply that Dragmall yelped. 'What?' And looking around, he glimpsed a man turning the corner into the corridor they were hurrying down. Dragmall yanked Else in through the nearest open door, holding his breath, his hand over her mouth, feeling her tremble against him.

They waited behind the door, wondering if the man had seen them. It was not the most carefully thought through plan, Dragmall realised with a frown. He had charmed a tasty breakfast out of the kitchen staff, some of whom recognised him from the visits he would make over the years, especially as his father's health started deteriorating. Though, perhaps all that food had dulled his thinking because he had failed to consider how he would get the shield out of the castle.

It was hardly something he could hide in his satchel.

Footsteps grew louder and then passed by. Eventually,

Dragmall released his hand from Else's mouth, feeling the gallop of his heart ease.

'Who was that?' Else was worried that she was about to sneeze. The dust from the rubble and the smoke from the fires, many of which were still burning in the city, had her eyes watering and her nose twitching.

'Hestians. No Angardians will be roaming the castle freely, I suspect,' Dragmall whispered, keeping his voice low as he poked his head around the door. 'Not for a long time. Come on, we need to move quickly now. It's just down the corridor a way. The chamber up there, on the right.'

Else tiptoed after Dragmall, terrified that they were about to be caught and shipped straight back to Draguta.

***

Meena opened her eyes, staring at Brill's worried face.

'She lives!' Draguta declared, turning to Amma. 'Now we can get back to thinking about your hair. Brill is excellent with hairstyles, though I prefer a simpler look for myself. But you? You must draw the eye, my dear. Especially Jaeger's. We want to impress him, don't we? Make him proud to have you by his side. We need you to look like a true queen. His queen. It will help him to... focus. To... calm down.'

Amma's face was frozen, terrified for herself but also worried for Meena. 'I... yes, but Meena? We must give her some water. She couldn't breathe. It's very warm. Perhaps we need to open the balcony door wider? Let in some air?'

Draguta lifted an unimpressed eyebrow. 'I suspect we must, or how else will I get the rest of my ingredients? Evaine has proven herself useless already, so, yes, find her something to drink, Brill.' And pointing distractedly at her lanky servant, she turned back to Amma. 'Come out onto the balcony, and we can enjoy the sunshine.'

Meena was pleased to hear them leave. She took the goblet Brill handed her, smelling the wine.

'There is no water,' Brill mumbled apologetically.

Meena sipped the wine, though it was not something she had ever enjoyed. She screwed up her face as the pungent liquid scalded her throat, then handed the goblet back to Brill and sat up, coughing, wondering what had happened. Her eyes drifted towards the tiny box on the table, and, gulping, she looked away, forcing all thoughts of the ring out of her head.

She couldn't take the ring.

She couldn't.

***

Briggit's grand chamber had a bed wider than any Else had seen in Hest. Big enough to fit seven people, she was sure, and so high that there was a little golden step beside it.

'Wouldn't surprise me if she did,' Dragmall muttered.

Else turned around in surprise. 'Did what?'

'Have seven people in her bed,' Dragmall said, lying down to look underneath it. 'From what I've heard, Briggit has an appetite for that sort of thing.' He wriggled out from under the bed, covered in cobwebs. 'And more besides.'

'Oh.' Else's eyes snapped back to the door. 'We should hurry.'

'What we should do is find that shield,' Dragmall sighed, glancing around the chamber which shimmered like a sea under the sun. There was an abundance of gold on display, from the bedhead to the goblets and ornaments on the tables, and the tapestries stretched across the marble walls. There were even gold-threaded curtains. Dragmall spun around, trying to ignore the garish furnishings which were not where his attention needed to be.

'But where is it?' Else wondered. 'Surely it's not big enough to be hidden in there?' She ran her eyes over the small wardrobe he was trying to force open.

Dragmall had his knife in the wardrobe's lock, and he was jiggling it around, eventually flicking it open. But pulling open the doors revealed that the shield wasn't there. He spun around in frustration, his eyes suddenly on the wall. The bright beams of morning sunshine had illuminated something, and as he walked closer, he could almost see the scrape of a circular outline above a marble shelf.

Chewing on a hairy lip, Dragmall eyed Else. 'Well, looks as though we still have work to do.' And he glanced around the chamber, wanting to find something of Briggit's to take.

Something that might help get him into Briggit's head.

***

Jael felt hot, which was unusual for her. She wasn't sure that it was a warm day, though standing close to the fire wasn't helping, so she moved around the map table, away from the flames, scanning the hall for a jug of water.

'It would make sense,' Karsten was saying from her left. 'Though what it will mean for us, I don't know.'

Jael dragged her attention away from her hunt for water, back to the table. 'It won't help us to fight there, that's for sure.'

The Islanders stared at the map with puzzled expressions, not having a clue what Jael and Karsten were talking about. Aleksander stepped in. 'The Vale of the Gods is a place few ever go. The Tuuran and Oster gods built it together as their very own battle arena. A place where they could wage war against each other and themselves. Mountains all around here,' he said, dragging a finger around the area of land near the south of Brekka. 'A hard climb in through the northern part of the vale. And here,' he murmured, pointing further down, 'is the Tree of Agrayal. Set up on a low ridge. A place of sacrifice. And beyond it more mountains.'

'It's hard to get in or out,' Karsten added. He had visited the vale with his father and Haegen when he was young. They had never fought there. No one would dare incur the wrath of the gods by doing so.

No one but Draguta Teros it seemed.

'So our catapults, our sea-fire... it's all useless?' Beorn wondered from Jael's right, glancing at Thorgils who was pulling on his beard with a frown.

'Well,' Jael began, 'not necessarily. The clifftops would be useful.'

'Not likely we can drag the catapults up there,' Aleksander said.

'For archers, I mean,' Jael explained. 'Archers on the clifftops, catapults outside the entrance. That would give us the range.'

Frowns dug deeper. More beard pulling.

Jael left the table for that cup of water, giving her a moment to think, and when she returned, Gant was talking.

'If Draguta's going to be waiting for you in the vale, there's little choice. You want her, you have to go and get her. Most times, one side picks the field of battle, and if Jael's dream is right, this will be it, so all you can do is prepare. And think. We've been there.' He looked at Aleksander and Jael. 'We know it. We can come up with some ideas.'

Aleksander nodded. 'We can. Besides, we'll have an army twice the size of anything Draguta can bring. Sea-fire and dreamers, and Jael and her sword. We'll have plenty of weapons.'

No one looked convinced. And though Jael's face conveyed confidence, she couldn't help her mind from wandering to Eadmund and his shield and how much she was going to need both of them.

***

Having left the castle behind, Dragmall and Else made their way back to the catacombs, much to Else's displeasure.

This time, they took a burning lamp.

'Do you really think she put it back?' Else wondered, following behind Dragmall, who was walking quickly now that he could see where he was going.

'I hope so,' he muttered, not turning around. 'It wasn't where my father kept it, so I assumed that it was not here. But where else would she have hidden it?' He had taken Else down to the almost empty cellars, and to the vault where Wulf Halvardar had hidden his chests of gold. Hestian soldiers were guarding that carefully, and Dragmall had had to do some quick talking to get them out of that situation in a hurry.

And now, here they were, trailing through the dark, dank depths of the catacombs again; the smell only intensifying thanks to Morana's decapitated corpse. They had come across it, and Morana's head, which lay nearby, being gnawed on by rats, both of them relieved to think that she was dead, though Else couldn't help feeling sorry for her, lying there all alone as she was without a proper burial or pyre.

'Focus, Else,' Dragmall grumbled, sensing that she was falling behind. 'We must hurry.'

'Must we?'

'Yes. If we are to find the shield and get back to Hest in time, we must.'

Now Else did stumble. 'What? Get back to Hest? What do you mean?'

Dragmall realised that she wouldn't come if he didn't turn back for her, so he turned back for her. 'Eadmund needs the shield. And Eadmund has gone back to Hest. And once we find it, so must we.'

Else's shoulders sank. 'Oh.'

Dragmall smiled. 'Come on, Else. I'll keep you safe, don't worry. Just try to keep up with me. I don't want to lose you in here!' And grabbing her hand, he pulled her along, into the darkness.

***

Jaeger couldn't stop thinking about Hest as the ship reared up in the storm. Over and over again it dipped down, diving towards the dark-green, white-tipped waves; rising up again just at the last minute, reaching for the thunderous sky, before crashing down onto the water, jerking his spine.

Warm, dry, sunlit Hest...

The high-pitched whistle of the wind had seared itself into Jaeger's eardrums, so that it was the only sound he believed he would ever hear again. The weather was the worst he had ever experienced at sea, and most of the crew had spent the journey emptying their stomachs over the gunwales, not drinking any of the wine they'd been looking forward to sampling.

Jaeger's only consolation was the thought that Eadmund would be suffering too. Even a day behind them, he was still guaranteed to be blowing around in the shit-storm of waves and rain and that howling, haunting wind most of all.

Jaeger put his numb hands over his frozen ears, leaning his dripping face on his wet knees, trying to picture his warm bed, layered in thick furs, Meena lying next to him.

***

They searched the catacombs for hours. Until the flaming torch threatened to blow out. Until Else's stomach started complaining again. Until both of them wondered whether it was day or night.

But there was no shield in the catacombs.

There were, however, an awful lot of rats.

Else kept shrieking as they ran over her boots. She could hear them shuffling about, running from them. Running towards

Morana's corpse.

They were everywhere.

Dragmall didn't notice.

They sat down on a stone bench, both of them grateful to rest their feet.

'It's not here.' Else was tired and cold.

'It's not,' Dragmall agreed. 'But it is somewhere.'

'And being a dreamer, you can't find it?'

Dragmall frowned. 'Well, I did before. I saw that it had gone from here. That it was in Briggit's chamber. I saw a vision of her looking at it from her bed.'

'And now?'

'Now, I can't see it in my mind at all. It's as though it's hidden.'

'Which it obviously is.'

Dragmall shook his head. 'Not like that. It's as though it's invisible. Hidden from dreamers.' He sat up straighter. 'Hidden from dreamers...'

'What? What is it?' Else wondered as Dragmall stood, stepping away from the bench. 'Where are you going?' she called, watching him disappear into the darkness. 'Dragmall?'

***

Draguta sat at the high table, fresh from a long soak in the hot baths. She felt slumberous, well-rested, and very much looking forward to her evening. Once Meena returned and got to work, she would try and find her sister. The spell she was planning was something new that she had discovered in the Book of Darkness, which had surprised her. She thought she knew that book better than anyone. Better than Raemus himself. Certainly better than Morana Gallas, whose stench still tainted the pages she had defiled.

Turning to Evaine, she noticed her scowl. 'You will not tempt Eadmund back to your bed with that face, Evaine. He will not be moved by a sour look and a snarl.' She lifted her goblet, taking a long drink. 'No, Eadmund is a man of heart. He feels things deeply. If you want him to develop actual feelings for you, if you want him to love you without magic, you will have to stop being so self-absorbed. You are not helping yourself at all.'

Evaine sat back, blinking.

'Though, with a mother like Morana Gallas, it is no wonder you cannot control that part of yourself. That mean, snivelly, witchy part of you? That is pure Morana.' And placing her goblet on the table, Draguta turned to Amma. 'Unlike lovely Amma here, whose heart is full of goodness. Her face glows with it, can't you see? That is the sort of face a man wants to look at.'

Evaine didn't want to look, but, feeling compelled by Draguta's words, she leaned forward and stared at Amma who cringed with embarrassment.

Draguta laughed, watching as Meena crept into the hall. 'You took your time!' she growled, her good humour gone in a flash.

Meena nodded, agreeing.

'Well, then, do not dither about here. Get up to my chamber. Evaine can go with you. She can help you prepare everything. I need every pair of hands, for I do not wish to be trying this potion with breakfast!' And glaring at Evaine until she pushed herself away from the table and slowly traipsed across the hall after Meena, Draguta turned back to Amma, picking up her hand. 'Though not the hands of the Queen of Hest. These hands will not be used for any menial tasks, will they? How delicate they are. How perfectly suited to pleasing your husband.'

Amma didn't know if it was the smell of the wine, the look in Draguta's intense eyes or the terrifying images stirred up by her words, but she scrambled up from the table, hands over her mouth, running outside to vomit.

***

The smell of the catacombs was turning Else's stomach, and the fear she had that Dragmall would not return was making her panic. She called for him occasionally, but there was no answer, and so she sat, cloaked in the darkness. Alone but for the rats who appeared to be alert and active and no doubt still gnawing away on Morana.

Eventually, Else stood, squinting into the darkness. 'Dragmall?' Putting her hands out, she crept forward, one tentative step at a time. 'Dragmall?'

And then a light. A flickering glow in the distance.

Else gasped, holding her breath, blinking rapidly.

Hoping it was Dragmall.

She squinted some more. The light was faint, not coming forward in any great hurry. She began to edge towards it, wishing she had more than an eating knife to defend herself with, but she drew her knife anyway, holding it out just in case.

'Were you planning on eating me?' Dragmall grinned as he approached.

Carrying an enormous shield.

PART THREE

Travellers

CHAPTER TWENTY

They were going to be late, which Raymon supposed was only fair since Jael and Axl had kept him waiting the last time they'd met. He sighed, memories stirring of Rissna. Of Jael saving his life. Of the moment he'd discovered that his father was, in fact, Ranuf Furyck.

It had not been that long ago.

Since returning to Ollsvik, Raymon had lived in a fog, a thick cloud of grief and paranoia, lost and alone. He needed to move forward, to strengthen his hold on the throne. To quash any further rebellions. To organise and lead his army to meet the Brekkans. To fight for their freedom and their lives.

But he wanted to crawl into his bed and hide.

It was his birthday, his eighteenth birthday, and his wife had not remembered. No one had. He didn't expect them to. But his mother would have. She would have planned a feast and had a thoughtful gift made. She always had.

Raymon missed her desperately. His grief was a searing pain inside him, and then a great empty hole and then, most of all, utter helplessness, knowing that there was nothing he could do to bring her back.

He would never speak to her or see her again.

The finality of it all was too hard to bear.

'Your mother would want you to be strong.' Getta spoke without feeling. She watched Raymon gather the reins into his hand. He had kissed her goodbye, though it felt as though he wasn't even there. He had barely spoken to her since their return to Ollsvik. She didn't know why. Perhaps it was because of Jael? Had her cousin said something to Raymon about her involvement with Garren? Had Jael known about that? Dreamed about it?

Raymon hoisted himself onto his heavily armoured horse. He felt relieved to be leaving. The fort echoed with reminders of his mother, his childhood, the man he'd believed to be his father. His desire to escape it all was strong, hammering inside his chest, urging him to leave. 'Take care of yourself,' he mumbled. 'And Lothar.' It might be the last time he saw his wife, he realised, though he couldn't bring himself to give her more than that.

Getta panicked, suddenly feeling vulnerable. 'Don't do anything silly. You are not experienced, Raymon. Let others lead. You must return to the kingdom. Your people need their king. Lothar needs his father.'

There was no affection in her eyes for him, Raymon could see. She was worried for herself, for her position as queen. It was as though he could see Getta clearly for the first time. As though he was viewing her through his mother's eyes and what he saw was everything Ravenna had warned him about.

Raymon nodded, thinking about his son. 'I will.' He wanted to come back for Lothar. He knew that. And, settling into the thick sheepskin covering his saddle, he turned to the new head of his army, a steady, older man named Soren, who blew a few shorts bursts on his curled horn. 'Goodbye, Getta.'

Getta tried to smile at her husband, but her frown wouldn't budge. The drizzle was intensifying, and she was eager to get inside. 'Goodbye.'

***

Marcus had brought Hanna to the hall to find some company that wasn't his. He could see by the beaming smile on her face that she was enjoying herself, though he kept his eye on her as she chatted to Berard.

Berard was miserable, his head drooping as he considered his cup of ale with a heavy sigh.

'You want to save Meena, don't you?' Hanna asked, trying to get through to him. 'Prove yourself somehow?'

'I...' Berard didn't know how to say it, but he looked down at his pinned sleeve with a sigh. 'I only have one arm. Last time Meena saw me, I had two.'

Hanna's eyes drifted to Aleksander who had just punched Jael in the arm, the two of them laughing with each other, joined now by Thorgils and Isaura. 'I'm not Meena,' she said, forcing herself to stop staring, 'but if I were, I'd be thinking about how brave you were to try and save me by fighting Jaeger. You have one arm because you tried to save her, Berard. Because your violent, murderous, two-armed brother tried to kill you. If I were Meena, I'd be grateful. I'd want to see you again.'

Berard looked embarrassed before scrambling to his feet. 'My mother...' he mumbled apologetically, watching a sharp-eyed Bayla beckoning him in the distance. 'I'd better go before she starts screeching. No doubt she's looking for someone to find us a new cottage again.' He rolled his eyes and headed towards his glowering mother, trying not to think about Meena.

Karsten quickly took his place, offering Hanna a plate with a slice of cake on it. 'Something to make up for you having to endure my brother,' he grinned at her.

Hanna looked bemused. 'I wasn't enduring Berard. Why are you so mean to him?'

'And why are you so kind?' It was a genuine question, Karsten realised. Few people had ever paid much attention to Berard, and Hanna's interest in his brother had always struck him as odd.

'You honestly don't know why?' She could hear Bayla in the distance, grumbling at Berard, pointing to her grandchildren, obviously needing some help. 'Because he is nice. Have you never noticed? Never noticed how nice your own brother is?'

'Well, when you've got three brothers, it's easy for one to slip through the cracks,' Karsten grinned. 'Jaeger was always complaining, Haegen was always showing off, and my father was always yelling at all of us. Berard just hid in a corner hoping no one would blame him for anything.'

'I'm almost jealous,' Hanna admitted. 'I never had a brother or sister, or a father growing up. And then when my mother died, I was completely alone.'

The smile left Karsten's face. 'You were?'

'Until I found my father. I used to dream about how it would feel to be part of a family.' Hanna had seen Aleksander leave the hall, and all of her attention was on Karsten now. 'You should hold onto the ones you have left, Karsten. You're lucky in more ways than you realise.'

Karsten was going to mutter something about her obviously not having spent enough time in his mother's company yet, but he stopped himself. He felt the loss of Haegen, his father, Irenna too. His family was being chipped away at, and it made him feel oddly vulnerable. He couldn't imagine what it would feel like to be completely alone. 'Well, if you're looking to be part of a big family, you could come to Hest, look after all the Dragos children,' he suggested with a grin. 'They like you well enough.'

Hanna laughed, her eyes on her father, who kept watching her, waiting to see if she needed to go back to the cottage. But she didn't. She had been enjoying the company and the conversation. She didn't want to feel like an invalid again. 'Well, if we get out of this mess I'm sure I'll have to make a decision about what to do next, though I can't imagine my father would want to go to Hest. I've a feeling he'll want to return to Tuura, to see what can be resurrected there. It's where he always wanted to be.'

Karsten tried not to look disappointed. 'Well, the offer's there. I'm sure Berard would like to have you around.' He could see Nicolene approaching, and pushing himself off the bench, he winked at Hanna before turning and heading towards his wife.

***

Dragmall had been up early, hurrying around the city. There were abandoned houses everywhere; some left empty by those who had died in Draguta's assault on Angard, others deserted by the men and women trying to flee the invading Hestians. He was able to find a new set of clothes for both of them, and despite being ill-fitting and reeking of smoke, they helped to change their appearance. Dragmall had filled a basket with food and wine, his satchel with more food, and then he'd found an abandoned wagon. Two horses. An old sword. And a stack of furs which he laid over everything.

The shield itself had symbols carved into it, and, using his knife as a chisel and tapping on it with his whetstone, he had added more; the same symbols as the tomb he had found the shield hidden inside; the place where the volkas had kept their most valuable treasure, protected with symbols that even dreamers couldn't see past. Though he had not been surprised to find they were gone, knowing that those volkas had been betrayed by one of their own.

'But how long will it take to get to Hest?' Else wondered, wishing she was asking a different question. She was whispering while they waited to get through the narrow path the Hestians had cleared through the rubble, not wanting to be overheard by the soldiers who were checking everyone as they exited the city, looking for Followers.

'I don't know,' Dragmall whispered back. 'Days. Possibly five?' He sat up straighter as a soldier approached, feeling his heart quicken.

'Where are you going?' the flat-nosed man asked gruffly.

He looked as though he'd been in a few fights, Dragmall thought, staring at the man's squashed nose, trying to calm his mind. 'To Kroll. My wife and I do not feel safe in the city. We wish to get to our daughter. To be reunited.'

Another Hestian had wandered down to check on their wagon, lifting the furs, rifling through the basket of food.

They looked old, the flat-nosed soldier thought, though that in itself was no free pass. There were a lot of old Followers, he knew. He'd helped secure them onto the ships himself. 'And how do I know you're not Followers looking to escape?'

Else almost bit her tongue. She gripped Dragmall's arm, trying not to look suspicious, hoping they wouldn't find the shield Dragmall had secured under the wagon, and kill them both.

'Followers?' Dragmall was dressed like a trader, he hoped. Or a farmer. A servant, even. He was wearing a faded beige tunic, a pair of tight, darker brown trousers; too short for him by far. He had on a wide-brimmed hat, though he tried not to slouch beneath it, not wanting to appear evasive. 'They have all gone, haven't they? No, we are most certainly not. Do we look like Followers?' Dragmall smiled, turning to a clearly terrified Else.

Else shook her head. 'We did not like the Followers. We're glad they're gone. We are just eager to see our daughter.'

The soldier who was ferreting through the wagon looked up suddenly. 'What's this? Come here, Sten!'

***

'I didn't know there was cake,' Jael smiled, helping herself to some of the small ale in Hanna's jug. 'Looks good.'

'It is,' Hanna said, feeling awkward. Jael Furyck made her nervous.

Jael could tell. 'I came for Berard. Thought I saw him with you earlier.'

'Yes, but he left to speak to his mother.'

'Oh.' Jael was eager to leave and find him, but the sudden urge to say something to Hanna was strong. 'I hope you'll all be safe here when we're gone. We've done as much as we can now to protect the fort. It's never been more secure.'

'I hope the same for you. That you all return, though that's not likely, is it?'

Jael didn't take a seat. She had just spotted Berard being grumbled at by Bayla, and she wanted to grab him before he tried to escape. 'No, it's not, but I'll work hard to bring Aleksander back to you.' She said it quickly, and it felt strange. So strange that she didn't go on.

Hanna's eyes popped open, her mouth following.

And then Jael was gone, with a flash of an awkward smile as she hurried to catch up with Berard.

***

Dragmall swallowed, squeezing Else's hand. 'Oh, that?' He tried to keep his voice light as he turned around, but he could feel his right leg shaking against Else's. He could hear the tremor in his voice. 'That's just a stick. For walking. I... struggle without it.'

The soldiers glanced at each other, then back to Dragmall and Else.

'Looks like more than a stick to me,' the flat-nosed soldier mused, his eyes on the tiny symbols running up and down the ancient staff he'd pulled out of the wagon.

'I can leave it behind if you'd prefer,' Dragmall suggested with a smile. 'It's not something I have a great attachment to. I can find another for sure.'

The soldier shook his head, laying the staff back in the wagon. 'Keep it. And get moving. Looks like rain soon.'

Dragmall nodded, trying not to clap the reins hard. He didn't want to appear in a panic or a hurry, though he was certainly eager to escape the city quickly. 'Thank you. Good day to you both.'

Else bobbed her head, holding her breath as Dragmall nudged their wagon forward, listening to the groan of the wheels as it eased away from the broken wall.

Leaving Angard behind.

***

Marcus left Hanna in the hall under Biddy's watchful eye, accompanying Edela back to her cottage, eager to speak to her alone. And though Edela was curious about what he wanted, Marcus didn't say a word until he was sitting at her table unfurling a stack of scrolls in front of her.

'I took as much as I could when we escaped the temple fire. It has taken some time to go through them all, though, what with Hanna being ill and the attacks on the fort. I did not give them my full attention for some time, but I've been studying them closely over the past few days, hoping to discover something useful.'

'And?' Edela's eyes were on the first scroll. It looked ancient, its vellum a dark yellow, the sprawling texts cramped together in a style no longer used; almost impossible to read, especially for someone with her eyesight.

'This interested me.' Marcus pulled a stool around to sit beside Edela, leaning over the scroll, pointing to the bottom section where the text condensed even further. 'It tells of a battle with The Following.'

Edela felt herself stiffen, blinking now.

Marcus ran his finger under a long line of text. 'Six deranged Followers were hunted down by the noble Tuuran army under the command of Geras Arlund. The cornered Followers cast a dreamer circle of protection. A circle the army could not penetrate.' Marcus looked back at Edela.

She was confused. 'I don't understand.'

'The Followers did not allow themselves to be taken. They held that circle. It was not breached.' Marcus turned back to the scroll, finding another passage. 'Despite their concerted efforts, the circle remained intact. Geras' soldiers employed arrows, fire, swords, and spears. They brought in skilled dreamers who knew dark magic, but the circle would not fall. The evil Followers killed every Tuuran but one, the very man who escaped to tell this tale to me.' Marcus could sense that Edela wasn't even breathing as he turned to her. 'They were Followers from Helsabor. It is believed to be where Raemus hid. The Followers there were his most loyal servants.'

'And you think they used his magic to make the circle?' Edela's eyes were searching Marcus' face, trying to anticipate where he would go next.

Marcus nodded, shifting the scroll to one side, revealing another beneath it.

Edela's attention was quickly drawn to a symbol near the top of the scroll. She reached out, touching it, following its intricate dark lines with her finger. 'This symbol held the circle, didn't it?'

'It did.'

Edela's finger was still on the symbol. 'It is like nothing I've ever seen. It feels dark. Like Raemus.'

'Perhaps Draguta knows of it? Perhaps it is in the Book of Darkness? She may be able to find a way through it.'

'Or,' Edela mused, 'she may not...'

***

That night they gathered in the hall for the last time.

Thorgils felt sick, not wanting it to be the last time. He saw many familiar faces - eyes bright, beards wet, hands slapping backs - all of them feeling the same flutter of anticipation, the same fear that they wouldn't come back.

That these goodbyes would be their last.

Swallowing, he turned to Isaura with a forced grin, but she ducked down to tend to Annet who was tugging on her sleeve, and he came face to face with Ivaar.

His smile faded.

'A word,' Ivaar muttered, two cups in his hands. 'I'd like a word.'

Red eyebrows high with interest, Thorgils followed Ivaar to a table where they sat down, Ivaar passing him a cup of ale. Thorgils studied him with a frown, but Ivaar didn't say a word. Eventually, Thorgils grew impatient. 'And?'

'We could kill each other, I know,' Ivaar said, looking up, his eyes black and blue from the punch that had broken his nose. 'Or perhaps once that was true. I've no appetite for it anymore. Not for that.'

Thorgils snorted, doubting it.

Ivaar shrugged. 'I can't change what you think. I'm not sure you know everything Morana Gallas did. Maybe you do...' His voice drifted away as he lost focus, feeling uncomfortable.

'I know some things.'

'I... want you to look after my children,' Ivaar said, eyes on his cup. 'Raise them well. As Skallesons. As Islanders. I want you to give them a home if something... happens.' His eyes were up, searching Thorgils' face.

Thorgils gave nothing away, but he nodded. 'I will.'

'There's nothing for them to be proud of,' Ivaar added. 'Nothing that I've done. But you could tell them about me. One day. Especially Mads. He's so young. I don't expect he'll remember me.'

Thorgils gripped his cup, his shoulders tense. 'Sounds as though you've already decided how things will go.'

Ivaar's laugh was hollow. 'For me? I think so. My luck left me long ago. When I was a boy. When my father went to Helsabor and met Eskild. Haven't had any since.'

He sounded bitter, and Thorgils tried not to feel sorry for him, though with Ivaar being so pathetic, it was hard not to. 'Well, I know a thing or two about luck, having lost Isaura to you for all those years.'

Their eyes met, and neither man knew what to say.

'But,' Thorgils went on, 'then I got her back, so luck can change. If you hold on long enough, luck can change.' His eyes moved past Ivaar to where Fyn and Bram were talking to Jael. 'You never know what's waiting around the next dark corner. I'll look after your children, Ivaar. I'll protect them with my life till the day I die, I swear that to you, but why not try holding onto some hope? We're all going to need some of that soon, aren't we?'

Jael watched Thorgils and Ivaar deep in conversation, and she smiled. Goodbyes had a way of bringing together the most unlikely couples. She turned back to Bram and Fyn who, she could see, were starting to warm to one another. Runa would have been happy to think that her death had brought them together; happy to know that she had left Fyn with a man capable of caring for and loving her son.

Eydis snuck up behind her, wrapping an arm around her waist. 'Hello,' she smiled.

'Thought you'd gone back to the cottage with the puppies,' Jael smiled back. 'I haven't seen them in some time.'

'Biddy shut them in your chamber. She wanted to make sure they slept with you tonight.'

Jael was pleased. 'They won't be happy, no doubt. I'd better take them a treat. You will take care of them, won't you? Promise me.'

'I will, Jael,' Eydis reassured her. 'You never have to ask.' She could sense that Fyn was there, and she felt awkward, wanting to say something to him before the morning. Before it became a big rush and panic as everyone hurried to do all those things they'd forgotten about.

But she didn't know what to say.

'I hope you'll stay safe, Eydis,' Fyn said, beating her to it. 'Bram's promised to keep a close eye on the hall. He's going to sleep here every night, aren't you?'

His father nodded. 'I am. Got my bed all set up too. Not just me either. I've organised an army to stay inside and protect you.' He hoped he sounded reassuring, though his chest was still giving him grief, and he was struggling to feel confident in his ability to do much. Runa's death haunted him, and he was finding it hard to forgive himself for that too.

Eydis did feel better knowing that Bram and his men would be staying in the hall. 'I hope you'll be safe too,' she mumbled to Fyn whose attention had just drifted towards Ontine who'd arrived with her mother.

He didn't answer her.

'I'm sorry to interrupt,' Ontine said shyly. 'I was just wondering if you knew where Edela was? She asked me to come.'

Jael watched Eydis stiffen, and seeing the way Fyn's attention had suddenly been consumed by Ontine, she wasn't surprised. 'I think she's visiting Gisila. She'll be out soon, no doubt.'

'Thank you.' And smiling shyly, Ontine followed her mother back into the crowd, Fyn's head swinging around after her.

Bram met Jael's eyes, and he grinned.

Jael squeezed Eydis' hand. 'Come on, why don't we go and find Biddy? I could really do with some hot milk.'

'Milk?' Bram was horrified. 'What do you want milk for? A night like this and you want hot milk?'

Aleksander joined them. 'Hot milk?' He winked at Jael. 'Sounds perfect to me.'

***

Meena couldn't wait to go to sleep.

Instead of dreading it, she had spent the past few nights looking forward to hopping into bed, ensuring she had everything she needed to prepare the tea that would stop her dreams.

The recipe she had found in Varna's old book had been working so well that she was starting to feel like a different person. Her thoughts were no longer attacking her. Her body was no longer trapping her. She almost felt free.

Meena crawled under the furs, letting her mind drift towards the blissful darkness that awaited her, knowing that nothing would be hiding in the shadows, waiting to torment her. She closed her eyes, her mind immediately wandering to Andala and Berard, hoping that he would stay safe from whatever was coming. And then her thoughts skipped to Jael Furyck, and her eyes burst open, staring into the darkness, all thoughts of sleep suddenly gone.

Meena took a deep breath, shivering uncontrollably, not feeling cold at all.

If she were to try and take that ring...

CHAPTER TWENTY ONE

Jael woke with a start, sitting upright.

Her chamber was dark, though a lamp burned on the table beside her bed, flickering the last of its flames across the wall.

She felt as though she'd had a dream, but she couldn't remember any of it. Trying to catch her breath, she turned around to her pillow, punching it into shape, her eyes resting on the raven who perched on a chair watching her.

Fyr.

Jael blinked, her heart racing now as she hurried out of bed, bare feet on cold floorboards. Gripping the door handle, she turned it, opening the door, padding into the corridor. Light spluttered from sconces along the walls, but no one was stirring. She could hear her brother snoring. Her eyes dropped to the dark stain of Runa's blood which was still obvious no matter how many times the servants scrubbed the floorboards. The stain from her mother's wounds had lingered too.

Jael frowned. She had no sense of impending danger, but she headed into the hall anyway, wanting to be sure. Pulling back the curtain, she could see that some were already beginning preparations for their early departure. Fyn and Bram were mumbling sleepily to each other, stretching long arms above their heads.

Jael turned back into the corridor, deciding that she must have imagined the raven, but when she opened her chamber door, she was still there.

She sat down on the bed, confused, watching Fyr's white eye, then the black one as they blinked at her. Listening. Trying to understand why the raven was there. What she was warning her about?

Was she still asleep?

And then, flapping her sleek feathers, Fyr fluttered over to the bed, stepping along the fur towards Jael.

Jael held her breath, sitting perfectly still as the raven stuck out one dark claw, placing it down on Jael's knee, hopping onto her leg, staring up at her with a twitching head. Jael looked down at those mismatched eyes, conscious of the sharpness of Fyr's beak, reminded of the attack in Tuura. And then all the tension in her body eased as she watched the raven, who had her head cocked to one side now, studying her.

It was as though she was communicating.

And Jael smiled, understanding perfectly.

***

Amma was almost yanked out of bed by a determined Brill who knew that Draguta was waiting in her chamber, up early and ready to help prepare her for the arrival of her husband.

It was dark, and Amma felt like crying, but eventually, seeing how worried Brill was and not wanting to get her in trouble, she sighed and sat up.

'My mistress wants you in her chamber quickly. We will need time to get you ready for your husband.'

'We?'

Brill nodded, still half asleep herself. Draguta had not been sleeping, therefore she had not been sleeping either, and the lack of sleep and the constant demands all through the night were starting to wear her down. 'She wishes for you to look like a queen.'

 280

Amma was getting irritated with the idea of being a queen, certain that Jael had never spent even a moment thinking about her appearance. And, knowing Jael, she never would. 'Does that mean Jaeger is coming today?'

'My mistress says so. She saw it in her circle. He will be here this morning.'

Amma shuffled towards the edge of the bed in her nightdress, one hand on her small bump, trying to quell a sudden rush of nausea; unable to tell whether it was from the baby or the prospect of seeing her husband.

Reaching out, she took the hand Brill was offering, unable to raise a smile.

***

'I have to go.'

'You just got here!' Gisila complained as her daughter edged towards the door.

Gant stopped Jael with a look, and she turned around, huffing back to the bed. 'I have to go, Mother. There's a lot to do, and if I'm not out there, no one will be doing it!'

'And if I never see you again? Is this the last thing you want to say to me? Just an angry grumble about something that doesn't matter?' Gisila was propped up on pillows, feeling stronger, but still in a lot of pain. She grimaced. 'Let them organise themselves. Let Aleksander do it, or Axl. I want to say goodbye to you.'

If Gant hadn't felt so tense about everyone leaving, about not leaving himself, he would have laughed.

Jael scowled, hating goodbyes. 'Gant will look after you,' she tried.

'I know that,' Gisila snapped. 'We're not here to talk about Gant, are we? We're saying goodbye to each other.' She tried to get her daughter's attention, placing her hand on Jael's, trying to bring her closer. 'We may never see each other again.'

'Well, I appreciate your confidence, Mother.'

Now Gant did laugh. 'Never thought anyone would be worse at goodbyes than Ranuf, but you really are, Jael. I'll go outside, see how everyone's doing, so take your time. No one's going anywhere without you.'

It wasn't even dawn.

Jael had ensured that everything was packed the night before so they could depart as the sun was rising. She was eager to make the most of the day, hoping to reach a safe campsite before nightfall.

Safe.

It seemed like a terrible joke now.

Gant shut the door behind him, and Jael felt her shoulders tighten further, knowing that soon she would have to say goodbye to him as well.

She sat down on the bed, careful not to disturb her mother, who looked pale, she thought, her eyes flickering across her face. Worried too. 'I don't know what to say,' Jael admitted. 'What can I say?'

Gisila touched her daughter's arm. 'You're not confident, are you?'

Jael hardened her stare. 'Confident? Going to face Draguta and her monsters?' She laughed, and it sounded like the taunting voice in her head. 'I'm confident enough in what we can do, but what they can do...' Jael wanted to leave it there. She was making everything worse. This might really be the last time. 'We'll do everything we can, Mother, and I'll look after Axl, I promise.'

'And Aleksander?'

'I think it's more likely he'll be looking after me, but of course I will.'

'What will happen if none of you return?'

'None of us?' Jael frowned, staring into her mother's eyes, watching pain and fear meld into a look of pure terror. 'Then you'll find a way, won't you? You were the Queen of Brekka once. And if that happens, you will be again. You will find a way.'

Jael's voice was iron-edged, and Gisila felt the burn of tears threatening her eyes, which would surely make her daughter bolt for the door. 'I will,' she promised. 'I will.' She dropped her head, sensing that she was about to lose control. 'Please, Jael, be careful. Please.' And she burst into tears.

Jael leaned forward, her arms awkwardly around her mother, feeling her sob against her shoulder. 'I promise. I'll do everything I can to come back. To bring us all back.' Tears were threatening her own eyes and Jael realised that she had to pull herself together. Sitting back, she inhaled sharply.

'You should go,' Gisila said, wiping away her tears. 'Isn't that what you're about to say?'

Jael grinned. 'Yes, I should. But I'll be back, don't worry.'

'Ahhh, if only that were possible, but, being a mother, it's not. Do what you must, Jael. What you were born to do.'

Jael nodded, heading for the door. She paused, gripping the handle, turning around.

'Your father was always so proud of you,' Gisila smiled, more tears coming quickly. 'I know he never said it, but he was. He would be so proud of you now.'

Jael turned back to the door, unable to say any more.

***

Meena had risen early, feeling well-rested and determined to do something about the ring. And though it was highly likely that Draguta had already seen inside her thoughts and possibly her dreams, she was going to try the spell to shut Draguta out of her mind. She had already been to the markets for some black pepper and saffron, and now she was almost running towards the winding gardens, hoping to get there and back to her chamber before Draguta was down in the hall, bellowing her name.

Stumbling to a stop just outside the stables, she spun around, sensing that Jaeger was there, watching her. Dawn was coming, and there was enough light to see that no one was there at all. But he would come today, of that she was certain.

Jaeger and ships full of Followers.

And what would Draguta do to them?

Meena hurried past the stables, not wanting to think about the Followers. She couldn't do anything about them, but if she got the ingredients she needed, maybe there was a chance she could keep Draguta out of her head long enough to do something about the ring.

***

The sun was on its way, the square filled with a cacophony of pre-dawn noise that drowned out the caterwaul of the roosters. The lines of saddled, armoured horses stretched from the harbour gates to the main gates, and beyond. The horses appeared confused to be leaving before the sun had done much more than peek above the horizon, though by the time everyone had stopped rushing about, saying goodbye, hurrying to find last minute items, and discovering unexpected problems, it would surely be light.

'Least there's no rain,' Thorgils yawned, his eyes on Isaura who was going through his saddlebags in a nervous panic. 'Here,' he said, pulling her back. 'I've told you it won't fit. Give it to me, I'll stuff it down my trousers.'

Isaura's eyes were frantic as she turned around; red-rimmed and swollen. She didn't want him to worry about her, but she had spent most of the night crying, worrying about him. 'That won't make it smell very nice. Or you!' she grumbled, but Thorgils took the long package from her and stuffed it inside the narrow gap down the front of his trousers, patting it with a smile. Isaura shook her head as he brought her in close. 'It's fine,' he tried to convince her. 'No doubt it'll start raining the moment we head off, so I'll be able to keep it nice and dry in there. No stopping to undo my saddlebags either!'

They were talking about salt fish and saddlebags.

Thorgils felt Isaura grip him hard, burying herself deeper into his arms, wanting to be close to him, to remember every part of him. 'Come back,' she breathed. 'Please. Come back to me.'

Thorgils bent his head until it was sitting on top of Isaura's. He smiled, enjoying having her all to himself. The children were still asleep, staying with the servants, out of everyone's way. Sniffing her freshly-washed hair, he smiled sadly. 'I will. And when I do, I think we need to do something very important, something long overdue, don't you?'

Isaura stilled, pushing herself back. 'You do?'

He nodded. 'I want to make you my wife. More than anything. If you'll have me?'

Isaura laughed at the look on Thorgils' face. All his confidence had suddenly vanished as he blinked rapidly, studying her, trying to gauge her reaction. 'Of course! It's all I've ever wanted too.' And pushing herself into his arms again, she heard him sniffing away his own tears. 'So you have to come back. Do what you must, but come back to me, please, Thorgils.'

Thorgils could hear her mumbling as he held on tightly. He could feel the warmth of her, the love in those arms, the thudding of her heart as her chest pushed against his, and he looked up, tears streaming down his hairy cheeks, meeting Jael's eyes.

Jael blinked, turning away.

Everywhere she looked there were tears and hugs and all the things she found so uncomfortable; the sky was brightening enough to see it all now.

'Trying to skip out on your goodbyes?' Aleksander grinned from behind her.

Jael spun around. 'Trying to.'

Her eyes didn't linger near his face, though she knew that he probably felt as strange as she did. Well, perhaps not as strange, Jael realised, remembering Draguta's ring. 'Ride with me,' she said, her hand on his arm guard. 'This morning. Just the two of us. There's something I have to tell you.'

***

Draguta gaped at the sight of a dishevelled Jaeger as he stumbled down the pier towards them. He looked like some beggar who'd crawled out of a sewer: all rumpled and filthy, pasty-skinned and bleary-eyed.

Even his hair had lost its golden sheen.

She was not impressed, having spent hours preparing Amma to greet her victorious husband. And turning to the girl, she could see that Amma did indeed look beautiful. Elegant. Like a lady. A queen.

Jaeger didn't even look worthy of emptying her chamber pot.

'Well,' Draguta grumbled, taking Amma's hand. 'We will return to the castle. And you, Jaeger Dragos, will clean yourself up into something resembling the king of this magnificent kingdom. I do not wish your poor wife to have to inhale your fetid odour, or lay her eyes on your decaying body a moment longer!' She spun around, spinning Amma with her, striding back down the tiny stretch of newly built pier towards the square.

Jaeger looked bemused, watching as his men stumbled over the gunwales, all trying to fit on the new wooden boards of the pier. There wasn't enough length yet for more than two ships to moor at any one time, so they were going to have to take turns unloading their cargo and prisoners.

'And you will bring those dogs into the square!' Draguta bellowed over her shoulder. 'Guard them until I return!'

She didn't even slow down.

Jaeger watched them leave, too nauseous to feel disappointed. His body was rocking, every part of him damp and aching. He didn't feel right at all. Whatever sickness was lingering would not retreat.

Lifting a hand to his clammy head, he felt the heat of his brow.

Yet, he was shivering, in need of a fire. Unable to stop thinking about Meena.

Wondering if she was still alive.

***

Assured that Draguta had left the castle to greet Jaeger, Meena had hurried up to her chamber, eager to begin.

She still had the piece of silk Jaeger had torn off one of Draguta's discarded dresses in his desperation to have her dream for him. And she would need it. The spell called for Meena to use an item from the dreamer she wished to keep away.

And Meena very much wanted to keep Draguta far away.

One eye on the door, she ripped the strip of white silk into smaller pieces and added it to the bowl at her feet which contained a pungent mix of her own blood, black pepper, garlic, and a long list of herbs and spices. Glancing at the open book on the floor beside her, Meena squinted, realising that she had forgotten to get bay leaves, but she knew that Varna had a jar of them on her shelf. So, scrambling to her feet, she hurried across the chamber, knowing that Draguta would only be preoccupied for so long.

She had to hurry.

***

Aleksander felt flustered as he glanced around the square.

Unusually muddled.

There was so much to think about, but he hadn't been sleeping well for some time, and he was struggling to think quickly. Perhaps it was the thought of saying goodbye, he realised.

The idea of not returning.

Spinning around, deciding to go and find Gant, he threw up his hands, grabbing Hanna's arms before she fell backwards. 'Sorry!'

Hanna smiled, shaking her head. 'I was just about to say hello. I didn't think you'd heard me coming.'

'No, no.' Aleksander glanced around awkwardly. 'It's a bit noisy this morning.'

'It is,' Hanna laughed, though her eyes were filled with worry. 'No one wants to leave anything behind.'

'Or anyone. Though with Jael bellowing from one end of the fort to the other, I'm sure no one's sleeping.'

Hanna could see her father eyeing her in the distance. He was talking with Edela, though he appeared ready to head her way. 'I... I hope you'll defeat Draguta, and... return soon.'

Aleksander nodded, taking a deep breath. 'So do I. It would be nice to end this. To feel safe again.'

'Hopefully, we will be. Soon.' Hanna wanted to reach out and take his hand.

Aleksander didn't know how he felt, but he knew that he very much wanted to get back to Andala and find out. He smiled at Hanna, unable to take his eyes off her, lost for a moment in the possibilities of what might be.

Then Marcus' voice carried towards them, and he blinked, realising that he had better keep moving. Walking past Hanna, his arm by his side, he reached out his hand and touched hers. 'Look after yourself.' And leaving her behind, he disappeared to find Gant.

Hanna watched him go, unable to stop staring until her father walked into her line of sight with Edela, Ayla, and Astrid.

Edela was trying to get rid of Marcus, who was mumbling about too many things she didn't want to think about now. She was about to suggest that he go and find something else to do when Jael arrived, which was easily the biggest distraction of all.

'Do you have everything?' Jael looked from Ayla to Astrid who stood next to her grandmother, all three of them almost shivering with nerves. 'Anything else we can get you?' She barely acknowledged Edela, knowing that that goodbye was coming soon.

Astrid shook her head. 'The wagon is so full. I'm not sure we could fit anything else in if we tried.'

'Except us, hopefully,' Ayla smiled. She felt butterflies flapping around her stomach, knowing how much danger they were going to expose themselves to; grateful that Bruno had decided to come along.

'Well, we need to get going,' Jael said, trying to remember what else she had to do. 'So, if you've finished your goodbyes, you should hop inside.'

Ayla nodded, glancing around. 'I'll just go and find Bruno. He snuck into the kitchen, I think, looking for more food.'

Astrid stepped away with Marcus and Hanna, leaving Jael and Edela alone.

'What about you?' Jael asked quickly. 'Do you need anything else?'

Edela laughed. 'It's a bit late for that now, isn't it?' She grabbed Jael's hands, squeezing them tightly. 'We don't have to say goodbye if you'd prefer.'

'Really?' Jael almost sounded happy.

'Not now, at least. I can come and visit you in your dreams if you like.' Edela winked at her granddaughter, pulling her into her arms. 'You are the funniest creature I know. The bravest. The strongest. The most beautiful.'

'What?' Jael snorted over Edela's shoulder. 'Did you have wine for breakfast?'

'I did not,' Edela insisted, pushing her granddaughter away, admiring her new leather outfit. Arnna knew Jael so well, and it fit her perfectly. 'But you should know what I think. What I feel. There are always things we don't say, but we should say them at times like this.'

Jael's mouth hung slightly open. 'I...'

Edela laughed. 'I'm not looking for compliments! I just wanted to tell you all those things in case...' Feeling tears coming, she pushed a stone into Jael's hand. 'Keep this on you. In your pouch. I've given Ayla one, but you need one too.'

Jael looked down at the stone, turning it over, seeing the dark symbol painted on both sides. 'What's it for?'

Edela leaned in close. 'It's a door. To me. To you. There are so many symbols on you, your armour, your weapons. Symbols all around this fort too. But this, I hope, will give us a door through all of them. In case we need each other.' Her voice trailed off, her attention on Biddy who was sniffing as she arrived with Eydis and the puppies.

Jael nodded, quickly slipping the stone into her pouch.

'You weren't going to leave without saying goodbye to us, I hope?' Biddy grumbled, her lips making odd shapes, tears already in her eyes. She had said goodbye to Axl and Thorgils. Fyn and Aleksander too. She wasn't sure she could take much more.

'I was hoping to,' Jael admitted. 'There've been too many goodbyes lately. I'm sure we'll be alright without one more.' Though she grabbed hold of Biddy and held her close for a moment, trying to ignore her sniffling which rapidly turned into a flood of tears.

Sensing that Biddy had stepped out of the way, Eydis pushed herself forward, wrapping her arms around Jael's waist.

Jael squeezed Eydis hard. 'I love you,' she whispered, bending down. 'With all of my heart. And I'll do everything I can to bring Eadmund back to you, I promise.' A tear ran down her cheek, and Eydis reached up, wiping it away. Jael blinked, wondering how she had seen it.

'I know you will, Jael,' Eydis cried. 'I know you will. But please stay safe. Please protect yourself. I want you to come back too.'

'We'll be here helping her, won't we, Eydis?' Edela soothed, her hands on Eydis' shoulders. 'Don't you worry now.'

'The puppies...' Jael could feel their paws on her legs, and she dropped down to the ground, letting them lick her, her hands on their fluffy heads, watching their tails flapping wildly from side to side.

'I'll keep them safe,' Biddy mumbled, searching for the cloth she had tucked up her sleeve. 'And Edela, and Eydis too. Don't you worry.'

Aleksander arrived with Fyn, still wondering what Jael wanted to talk to him about.

'And you,' Edela smiled, slipping an arm around Aleksander's waist before he could skip away. 'You will come back in just the one piece, thank you.'

Aleksander bent down, holding her gently. 'I like the sound of that. And then I might go away somewhere. Somewhere quiet. Where the sun shines all day and the birds are just birds. Where there's no chance of creatures coming to eat me in my sleep!'

Fyn felt awkward.

He could see Bram out of the corner of his eye talking to Thorgils, and he wanted to see him before they left, but not until he had spoken to Eydis. She was like his little sister. He cared deeply for her, but he didn't know what to say.

Eydis didn't know what to say either.

'Fyn,' Jael said, sensing his hesitation. 'We need to go.'

Fyn nodded, watching as Jael and Aleksander headed for the horses. 'I hope you'll be alright while we're gone, Eydis. Biddy and Edela will be here...' His words faded into a mumble, and he shook his head. 'I'll miss you.'

Eydis was mad at herself for ever being mad at him. She was just a little girl. She meant nothing to him, she knew. Not like that. But he was her friend, and whatever happened, she wanted him to know it. 'I'll miss you too, Fyn,' she said, leaning forward, slipping her arms around his waist. 'Make sure you look after Jael. And yourself.'

'I will, I promise.' He could feel her shudder against him as he tightened his embrace.

Bram frowned, wondering if Fyn was avoiding him.

'Keep a close watch on Eydis,' Jael said firmly, trying to get his attention. 'She's lost a lot recently, like you.'

Bram nodded as Fyn approached. 'Don't worry, I'll have a good eye on all of them.' His attention jumped from Jael to Fyn, who was looking shyer than usual as he stopped in front of his father. 'And how about you, then? Hope you doubled your sheepskin on your saddle? Nothing worse than not feeling your arse for days on end!'

Fyn couldn't help it. Thoughts of his mother filled his heart, and his eyes brimmed with tears. And then, so did Bram's. 'I hope you'll still be here when I get back,' he said haltingly.

Bram pulled Fyn into his arms, holding him tight. 'I'll be here, don't you worry about that,' he promised, clapping his son on the back. 'I've learned my lesson, harsh though it may have been. I'll have both eyes open this time. You just make sure you find your way back to me, you hear? Me and Eydis. We'll both be here waiting for you.'

There were too many tears, Jael decided. And no one looked happy, whether they were staying or going, so nodding at Gant who was approaching with Ulf, she took a deep breath, indicating for Thorgils to blow his horn. Gant had given it to him, and though Jael doubted the wisdom that had seen him pass it to Thorgils, it was something to distract him with for now.

'Up on your horses!' Jael hollered, taking a deep breath and straightening her shoulders. 'Let's make a start!' And inclining her head for Gant to walk with her, she took one last look at Edela, Biddy, and Eydis. The puppies weren't going to be left behind yet, though, and they quickly bounded after them.

Gant didn't speak as they headed for Tig who was making a fuss, impatient to get going. Being saddled meant a departure as far as he was concerned, yet Jael had shown no sign of coming anywhere near him since she'd strapped it on his back.

'I wish you were coming,' she said, her eyes on Tig who seemed to be in a bad mood. 'One less goodbye.'

'Ha!' Gant laughed, though he felt disturbed by the thought of everyone leaving without him. It was the right decision to remain behind and protect the fort, he knew, but it wasn't easy to watch everyone else leave.

It wasn't easy to say goodbye.

'I hope the dreamers can help you,' Jael said. 'You've got three of them now. They should see whatever's coming. Perhaps talk to Edela, though? She has some new information I think you're going to need.'

Gant tried to think of what to say. They'd always ridden off together. Her and Aleksander. Him and Ranuf. 'I expect to see you back soon. All of you.'

Doubt flashed across Jael's eyes, and Gant grabbed her arm, wanting to focus her. 'This is it. All those years of training. All those battles. Everything we taught you. Everything the gods have given you. This is it. Here. Now. And you're ready. You have the skill and the talent, and most of all, you have the desire, because Draguta took your husband, and,' he lowered his voice, glancing around, 'your baby. Don't let the weeds grow and twist around your confidence, Jael. Don't let the clouds come in. You can get Eadmund back. You can save us all. You can. I believe it. I believe in you.'

Jael smiled through her tears. 'I saved the best for last, it seems, Gant Olborn.' She turned as Aleksander joined them. 'I'll be seeing you,' she said, watching his eyes, grabbing Tig's reins.

Gant nodded. 'I'll be seeing you, Jael Furyck.'

CHAPTER TWENTY TWO

After a long soak in the hot baths, Jaeger was allowed to greet his wife. And despite feeling more inclined to head for his bed to get some sleep, he could not deny that seeing Amma had been worth the wait. Draguta had certainly worked hard on his reluctant bride.

She looked ravishing.

But despite the beautiful ivory dress which accentuated her ample curves and the exquisite jewels which dropped from her ears and looped across her breasts, it was hard to ignore the fact that Amma was still the timid little girl who had run away from him on their wedding night, choosing Axl Furyck over him; leaving him in a heap on the burning square while her family destroyed his fleet and set fire to his piers.

He stared at her, wondering again what had happened to Meena.

Draguta glared at Jaeger as he sat on the dragon throne, looking just as ill but far cleaner. 'You have done well,' she said shortly. 'Bringing those Followers to me. All in one piece too. All except for one. The one I wanted most of all.'

Jaeger emptied his goblet of wine, and, with no intention of standing, waved his hand for a refill. 'Blame Eadmund. He wanted Briggit all to himself.'

Amma, who stood there feeling like a doll being admired by a child, was surprised to hear that, though she tried not to signal any interest in their conversation. Now that the discussion had turned away from her appearance and Draguta's disappointment in Jaeger, she wanted to leave them to it. But Draguta's firm grip on her arm did not lessen, and so she stood beside her while they spoke, worrying that another wave of nausea was just around the corner.

'Eadmund?' Draguta looked as though she had inhaled a waft of fresh manure. 'You are blaming Eadmund for that? Not yourself and your inability to control any part of your body? Not one part! No, Eadmund was right to intervene as he did. I required Briggit Halvardar delivered to me in one piece. Not chewed on and spat out by you!'

Evaine walked into the hall, ready for breakfast, stumbling to a stop at the sight of Jaeger sprawled on the throne.

'Ahhh, another of your victims!' Draguta announced dramatically. 'The castle is full of them! But realise that your wife has been returned to you now. I have returned her to you, and you will treat her with the respect due to the Queen of Hest. Especially the Queen of Hest who is carrying your unborn son.'

Jaeger pushed himself upright, though the effort made him sigh heavily.

Amma didn't look pregnant, he thought, studying her belly with a frown. But Draguta was certain there was a child in there. His. His son. And what was he going to do about that? 'Where's my wine?' he growled impatiently, slumping back into the throne again, wishing they would all go away. As desperate as he had been to please Draguta, now all he could think about was falling asleep.

Evaine, happy that no one was paying any attention to her, backed straight out of the hall, heading for the kitchen, nerves jangling. If Jaeger was here, that meant Eadmund would be arriving soon. And despite the fact that he'd killed her father and threatened her own life, she knew very well that Draguta's plans for Eadmund meant that soon he would be looking for a new wife.

And she was determined to be ready.

***

Eadmund was trying to stay away from Briggit.

Despite the driving rain, the waves curling over the ship, drenching them all and the painful howl of the wind, he could still hear her sharp voice, always calling out to him, demanding something to drink, wanting a fur, a dry cloak, insisting that she be moved to another part of the ship where the waves couldn't reach her. It was a constant stream of complaints and Eadmund realised that he had asked for it by not letting Jaeger take her as Draguta had wanted.

He didn't know why he had intervened.

Eadmund sighed. He did. Of course he did.

Jaeger's intentions were perfectly clear, and Eadmund didn't want anyone's rape on his conscience, though now he had Evaine's. He frowned, leaning out over the shields that lined the gunwales, enjoying the numbing effect of the wind on his face. He wished it would numb his feelings too.

'Eadmund!'

Rolling his eyes, he turned around, glaring through the salt spray. The buffeting wind was angry and strong, and though it made for a nauseating ride, Eadmund hoped it would get them to Hest quickly. He had to get away from the nagging Queen of Helsabor and her scheming eyes.

The ship was rocking, riding the surging waves with a groan and a bang. A few of the crew were at the gunwales emptying the contents of their breakfast over the shields. Eadmund almost felt ready to join them.

'I need to sit down!' Briggit screeched, swaying against the creaking mast where Eadmund had secured her after the helmsman had complained. He didn't like the way she kept staring at him, as though she was cursing him with her strange golden eyes.

They all felt much the same, Eadmund knew.

'If you don't bring me down I will blow away!' Briggit cried.

Eadmund almost hoped she would, but it would hardly please

Draguta.

'Alright.' And untying the ropes around her ankles, and then her arms, Eadmund pulled her away. Briggit's wrists were still bound in the symbol covered fetters, which he hoped were doing something to contain whatever trouble she was brewing. 'Come over here!' And dragging her towards the prow, he decided to secure her far away from anyone, slipping the rope through an oar hole. They would certainly not be needing to slot the oars in in this weather.

'No!' Briggit didn't want to be near the prow, which was dipping and diving into the freezing water. 'Not here!' she yelled into the wind, sea spray slapping her face.

Eadmund pretended not to hear her as he pushed her down onto a sea chest, working the rope into a knot, pulling it tight. 'Sit there, and you'll be fine!' Or, he thought to himself, Ran might choose to swallow you whole. Either way, she'd be quiet, far away from the rest of them.

Briggit glared at him, then spat in his face.

Eadmund backed away, watching the wave as it tipped over the prow, drenching the seething queen. Turning around with a smile, he headed back to the stern, imagining how nice it would feel to be on board Ice Breaker, sheltering in her little wooden house.

***

It felt strange without everyone in the fort, and so quiet that Gant was finding it hard to concentrate. His mind was on Jael, Aleksander, and Axl, wondering if they had been attacked yet. He kept going back into the hall to see if Edela or Eydis needed anything, but Edela was busy organising her circle, and she kept shooing him away, sending him off to check on someone else.

Which he did.

He found Bram who was giving Berard some pointers for working with a spear, which, Gant realised, might suit him better than using a sword. They nodded as he passed, not encouraging his company either, so he headed towards the ramparts, wanting to check the surrounding countryside, to see if there was any threat lurking in the distance.

'Gant Olborn, isn't it?'

Gant froze, turning slowly with an awkward smile. 'My lady,' he said, nodding at Bayla Dragos.

She smiled. He was a handsome man. A man with manners. A well-kept man, she could tell, not like Ulf who looked as though he'd never owned a new pair of trousers in his life. 'You are in charge here now?'

'I am, yes.' Gant felt his insides clench, wishing he wasn't in charge of anything.

'Well, perhaps you can help me?' Bayla smiled warmly, showing off a set of straight teeth. 'I am seeking new accommodation for my very large family. I have five poor children to care for, you see. Five children and a one-armed, helpless son. Pathetic creatures, all of them. And somehow, I am expected to house them all in a tiny windowless shack. A shed. It even has a dirt floor! I'm sure you wouldn't ask Gisila Furyck to sleep in such a hovel, would you?' She had heard the rumours about Gant and Gisila, and she could see the discomfort on Gant's face, which quickly confirmed that those rumours were indeed true.

'No, I wouldn't, of course not.' Gant had seen the castle Bayla Dragos had lived in, so he wasn't surprised that she wanted new lodgings. And now that the army had left, he was in a position to do something about it. 'Leave it with me, and I'll find you somewhere new today.' He hoped that would be that. He wanted to get up on those ramparts and check the valley.

Bayla was elated. 'Today? Well, that is fast work, I must say.' She eyed Ulf who was approaching with trepidation. 'You see?' she called. 'You just need to ask the right man! To get anything done, you just need to ask the right man!' And hitching up her dress, she flashed Gant a glowing smile and strode past Ulf, her long nose in the air. 'I shall go and prepare the children and Nicolene for our move!'

Ulf looked at Gant who blinked, happy to have resolved that issue so quickly, though now he needed to go and find Bayla somewhere to move her family into. Glancing up at the ramparts, he sighed, turning to Ulf. 'Come on, then, if we can find the Dragos' a new home, we'll both have some peace and quiet!'

***

Jaeger was pleased to finally shut the door to his chamber, surprised by how relieved he felt that Amma wasn't in it with him. He just wanted to fall asleep. Not even wine was more important to him than that, though he had drunk more than enough downstairs, much to Draguta's annoyance.

Falling onto the bed, he dragged a fur over his shoulder, curling onto his side, trying to remember if he had ever felt so weak. So ill. He just needed to fall asleep, he told himself. Just a little sleep would help, and then he would return to his old self. Then he would feel as though he could stand without needing to lean on something.

Closing his eyes, Jaeger imagined that he was still at sea, being thrown around on board that enormous Helsaboran warship.

His ship now.

His aching body started to relax, and he felt himself drift away, thinking of all those black-robed Followers kneeling in the square in the scorching sun, guarded by his men, waiting to die.

Draguta hadn't been able to stop talking about her plans for them.

She'd insisted he be awake for that.

***

Draguta had been so irritated by Jaeger's unkempt appearance and his poor attitude that she had hurried Amma out of the castle, deciding to take their minds off what a disappointment the king's return had been. She was determined to cheer them both up with a visit to the markets, hoping to find fabrics and ornaments to start decorating the baby's chamber with. For he would have his own chamber, Draguta insisted. A place where he would sleep with his wet nurse. Where Amma could visit. Jaeger too.

Amma was almost panting as she tried to keep up with her, wishing that Meena had come along. Or even Brill. She didn't want Draguta all to herself. And she didn't want to think that she would have a baby and then hand it off to someone else to care for. She wasn't sure how she felt about giving birth to Jaeger's son, but she knew she would love her child. That she would want to be with him.

'But you're a queen!' Draguta announced, turning to Amma, her ice-blue eyes sharp and insistent. 'A queen must focus on ruling, not rearing. That is a thankless job best handed out to someone born of the lower classes. Not like you, Amma. And besides, you will still be his mother! You must not give in to such morose thoughts.'

Amma swallowed, reminding herself that thinking was likely to get her in trouble. 'I'm sorry,' she tried, attempting to clear her mind. 'It's all so new. I'm sorry.'

It pleased Draguta to hear it. 'I understand. Of course I do. And Jaeger has not helped, has he?' She frowned, her thoughts drifting back to Jaeger's arrival, a realisation dawning. 'Come along, now,' she muttered, her stride lengthening as they slipped beneath the striped awnings covering the entrance to the markets. 'I want to get to the tailor's first. I must see how he is coming along with those curtains. I want everything ready by tomorrow, though the speed that man and his minions work, I'd be surprised if he even emerges from his house before next year!'

Amma stumbled after Draguta, banging into a scowling merchant, trying not to let herself panic. Trying to remember that Axl was coming.

Axl was coming for her.

***

It would take two days to get to Vallsborg to meet the Iskavallans, and then another five or six to arrive at the vale. At this slow pace, maybe more.

Axl wanted to scream.

'You're quiet,' Thorgils grinned, bringing his horse alongside. He'd been riding further back with Rork and Karsten, making plans for the Iskavallans, with Torstan too who was full of nerves but not much conversation. He had even stopped to speak to Ivaar, and he'd been hoping to speak to Jael, but he could see that she was deep in conversation with Aleksander at the front, neither of them inviting company.

Axl looked up at Thorgils, squinting into the sun streaming past his bushy red head. 'It was hard to say goodbye.'

Thorgils nodded. 'It was, but it feels good to be moving.'

'Mmmm, good and bad.' Axl glanced up at the sky. 'Do you think she's watching us? Draguta?'

'I expect so.' Thorgils wriggled, jamming a hand down his trousers, already hungry.

Axl stared at him. 'What's that?' he asked as Thorgils revealed the long package.

'Salt fish. Want some?'

Axl shook his head, his eyes on his sister and Aleksander, wondering what they were talking about. By the look on Aleksander's face when he glanced around, it wasn't an enjoyable conversation.

Aleksander was struggling to get his head around what Jael

had told him about Draguta's ring and Helsabor's wall. He peered into her eyes, then up at the sky, behind him, into the trees, then back to Jael again. 'Can she hear us? See everything we're doing?'

'If she wanted to, I imagine she could,' Jael murmured, listening to Axl and Thorgils chatting behind them. 'But I don't believe she's at that map table day and night. I remember seeing visions of her with Eadmund in a cottage. I think she can draw those symbol circles anywhere. I think they help her to see.'

'Us?'

Jael nodded.

'So why the game?' Aleksander wondered. 'It must just be a game for her, mustn't it? We're out of the fort. She could kill us now.' He shook his head, still in shock. 'She could have killed us with that ring while we were in Andala.'

Jael didn't want to say anything about her dream walk to Meena. She needed Meena to live. To get that ring and live. But until then?

Shrugging, she turned around, her eyes on a bird in the distance. 'Draguta seems to like a performance. So yes, I think it's all a game. And all we can do is wait until she decides to play again. Wait and be ready.' She watched as the bird flew straight towards her. 'Though, here's hoping we get some warning. With dreamers in Andala and Ayla here with us, we should get some warning.'

The bird was a raven. And that raven was Fyr.

She landed on Jael's left shoulder, sharp claws wrapping around her new black leather vest.

Fyr turned her white eye on Aleksander, who blinked back at the bird in surprise.

'And then, of course, there's Fyr,' Jael laughed. 'I've a feeling she's going to come in very handy!'

***

Meena shook with terror as Draguta loomed over her in an obviously foul mood. 'Swanning around the castle were we? Imagining I wouldn't notice? Wouldn't see?' She leaned forward, towering over Meena who stood on the castle steps, shrinking, trying to shut all other thoughts out of her head.

Trying not to think about the potion she had just drunk.

The one that would hopefully stop Draguta reading her mind.

'I... I didn't know what to do,' Meena mumbled, worried that she had blood on her lips; that she smelled like garlic. 'There was no one in the castle. I... you weren't here, and I couldn't find Amma.'

Draguta's frown didn't ease as she thought of Jaeger, though she stepped back, realising that his miserable return was hardly anything to do with her trembling assistant. 'Well, here we are!' And suddenly she was smiling, turning to Amma who was silent behind her, not wanting to go back into the castle yet. 'Why don't you keep Amma company, while I go and have a little chat with Jaeger.' She noticed the distaste on both their faces. 'Jaeger, who is your king. Your king, who rules here, whether either of you likes it or not. Your king, who rules you.' She straightened her shoulders, determined not to let Jaeger ruin everything she had been working so hard for. 'He had an arduous journey, though once he has recovered, he will be ready to help me end Jael Furyck and his deformed brothers.' She enjoyed the flash of horror in Meena's eyes. 'Axl Furyck too.' She heard Amma gasp.

It made her smile.

And striding up the steps towards the castle doors, Draguta suddenly felt much better.

***

'You've got a bird on your shoulder.'

Jael grinned. Aleksander had slipped back to talk to Axl, and Thorgils had taken his chance. The sun was hiding behind a bank of swirling grey clouds, and she could almost see him without squinting.

He looked nervous.

'You don't like birds?'

'Magical birds?' Thorgils shrugged. 'I've nothing against them. But are you sure this bird is on our side?' He leaned forward, staring at Fyr who had remained perched on Jael's left shoulder for most of the morning. Occasionally, she would fly off, but she returned quickly, back to her perch.

Fyr peered at Thorgils in turn.

'I'm sure,' Jael said. 'She wants to help.'

Thorgils' frown deepened. 'Know that, do you?'

Jael wasn't sure what she knew. 'I think so.'

'Well, as long as she's not going to call her friends and peck us to death in the night, I suppose I'm happy about that.'

'Ha!'

'You seem better. More relaxed,' Thorgils smiled, sticking his hand down his trousers.

'What are you doing?'

'Getting my salt fish.'

'From there?'

'Want some?' Thorgils flapped the packet at Jael, which he had to admit, did look a little sweaty.

'No... no, I don't.'

Fyr seemed to be sniffing the air, though, and Thorgils kept the packet close to his belly as he pulled out a soggy strip of fish.

'Surprised you've any left. We've been gone for hours now.'

'Ha! Well, this is just a snack. I've got more in my saddlebags.'

'I don't doubt it.' Jael felt like stretching her legs, but they weren't going to stop for some time. Vallsborg was two days away, and she wanted to get there with everyone still intact. Including Thorgils. 'Save some room for supper, though. I might let you share my stew.'

Thorgils looked intrigued. 'Got plans, have you?'

'Aleksander's brought along some trout. Said he'll make me a stew tonight, so yes, I do.'

Thorgils raised an eyebrow. 'I might just leave you to it, then, Jael. I'll be back here, having a word with Aleksander.' And breaking off a big chunk of his salt fish, he let Jael slip ahead.

Which she did.

And for the first time all day, she was alone, her eyes on the line of trees in the distance, on the clouds which had dispensed with the sun, on Tig who seemed alert. She spun around, smiling at Aleksander who was frowning at Thorgils, trying not to imagine that Draguta was watching, waiting, preparing to kill them all.

CHAPTER TWENTY THREE

Leaving Amma and Meena behind, Draguta headed into the castle, up to her chamber, and then to Jaeger's, where she knocked on his door.

It took some time before Jaeger opened it, and he looked half asleep, paler than ever, and now that she was standing close to him, Draguta could see how bloodshot his eyes were.

He was not well.

And she knew why.

'Sit at the table,' Draguta ordered, marching past him, glancing around the empty chamber, her eyes sharp with disapproval. It had all the charm of a latrine. 'You must find a new servant, Jaeger. Amma has spent a lot of time with Meena while you were gone, but she is no servant, that one.'

'Meena?' Jaeger's red eyes widened. 'Amma was with Meena? You didn't kill her?'

Draguta laughed, taking a seat at the table, placing the Book of Darkness on it, watching Jaeger's attention stutter, drawn immediately to the book. 'I didn't kill her, no. That was generous of me, wasn't it?'

Jaeger's eyes didn't leave the book as he sat down opposite Draguta. 'It was. But why?'

'Because she did not go against me. She released Morana because I wanted her released. I was in Meena's big empty head, telling her to help Morana escape. It was all my plan. I needed someone in Angard to help me break Briggit's circle. I saw how she planned to defend the city. I knew that circle would be impenetrable if it had remained intact, so I sent Morana. She was the perfect assistant once I had bound her to me. Though she was so desperate to escape that I doubt she suspected a thing.' Draguta pushed the book towards Jaeger's eager fingertips, wanting to leave all thoughts of Morana Gallas behind. The woman had been useful, and now she was dead. There was no need to dwell on her any longer. 'Touch it.'

Jaeger looked surprised by the offer, but he hurried to take it up.

'You have been away from the book for too long,' Draguta murmured. 'Look at you. At how ill you are. It is as though your body has been deprived of its source of nourishment. Without the book, you have withered and sickened. And now, being in its presence again, you have a chance to renew. To replenish yourself.'

Jaeger already felt more alert as he pressed his hands against the soft dark leather. 'But why? I haven't been near the book since you returned. It has been in your chamber.' He didn't feel resentment about that anymore. The book was Draguta's, he knew.

'The Book of Darkness is more powerful than you realise, Jaeger. You have been near enough it to be changed by it. You have seen what happens when you are without it. Do you deny that you have missed it? That you need it?'

Jaeger could feel a pulsing energy surging through his body, a sensation that felt even better than wine. He could almost feel his head lifting as his body strengthened.

He nodded.

'Well, then, I think it is time we come to an arrangement, you and I,' Draguta purred, pulling the book away from him.

Jaeger looked bereft, his arms stretched across the table, fingers extended. 'Arrangement?'

Draguta could hear the panicked throb of Jaeger's heart, his hunger to touch the book again.

She smiled.

'Our arrangement will be quite simple, to the mutual benefit of us both. You will act like a king, and I will allow you to touch the book. Often. I will let you keep your strength. Increase it even, if I see the need.'

Jaeger's eyes narrowed. 'Act like a king? Meaning?'

Draguta inhaled sharply, smelling the wine on him. It was no wonder his eyes were bloodshot. 'You will rule here, Jaeger, as a man in control of himself. In control of his body. Not one who wishes to rape and fist fight anyone he pleases. That is not a king. That is the behaviour of one who has not been raised in a castle. It is not the behaviour of a Dragos! You will sit upon that dragon throne and rule here with a strength admired by all, as my son, Valder, did all those years ago.' She felt wistful for a king who did not need to be told what his role was; for a man who did not need to be scolded as though he was a boy.

She thought of the family she no longer had and felt even more wistful.

'And if I do that, you will let me near the book?'

'I will. You will begin to feel better just being in the castle, but I imagine you have felt weakened for some time. Since that moment you gave all your blood to Yorik Elstad for me. Since I came and took the book from you,' she mused, watching him. 'I imagine you would like to feel more powerful than this, for how will you possibly have the strength to defeat your brother when he comes to kill you?'

Jaeger licked his salty lips. 'I don't imagine you're talking about Berard.'

'I don't imagine I am,' Draguta smiled.

***

Karsten had almost fooled himself into thinking that they were simply riding to Vallsborg. A place he'd never heard of. A settlement near Hallow Wood. Just riding. Taking their men, expecting to be there in two days, hoping the weather would stay fine.

He had to keep jerking himself out of that sense of certainty. The feeling that everything was normal. Predictable. That they were safe. Just like he was trying to convince himself that his family would be safe back in Andala.

He looked up, eye on the clouds which appeared to be darkening in the distance. Shaking his head, Karsten laughed, still finding it hard to believe that they had to worry about clouds.

'Enjoying yourself?' Thorgils wondered. He wasn't. They were riding slowly, having to stop every now and then when a catapult or a wagon got stuck. The terrain was generally flat now that they'd left the hills surrounding Andala behind, but their path was strewn with rocks, big and small, holes too, and the catapults were struggling. And every time they stopped, Thorgils was sure that his heart had stopped too as he glanced around, wondering if Draguta would strike.

'No, I'm not.' Karsten looked serious now, turning in his saddle. 'I just want to get out of here. There's no cover. Nowhere to hide if we're attacked.'

'True. But nowhere for anyone to hide who might want to attack us,' Thorgils pointed out. He felt like some ale. The sun had long since disappeared, but it was still a very warm day, especially for an Osslander who was not used to such heat.

That didn't comfort Karsten. 'Not sure we have the sort of enemy who feels the need to hide. Besides, how do you hide a dragon? Or some giant black dogs? No, I think Draguta will just pounce. Out of nowhere. Attack us head-on.'

Thorgils swallowed. 'She's never attacked us during the day, has she, so we're probably safe for now. Safe till tonight anyway.' He looked at Karsten who shrugged. 'Well, nothing we can do but keep going. Too late to go back now!'

Karsten nodded, trying to turn his attention to something that wasn't magical. Like Jaeger. His murderous brother. The King of Hest.

A man who would soon be dead.

Now that was something to try and focus on. Something he had the power to make happen with his own two axes.

Jael turned around, watching Karsten and Thorgils, both of them with furrowed brows, serious and quiet. Everyone was quiet. It made the day seem as though it had gone on forever, yet it was only early afternoon, and they were still hours away from their campsite.

'Do you think we'll get there by nightfall?' Axl asked.

'I don't know. We're taking longer than I'd anticipated. The catapults aren't the best travelling companions.'

Aleksander grinned. 'You say that now, but when they're flinging sea-fire at the Hestians, you'll be thinking more fondly of them, I'm sure.'

'I'm sure I will. And hopefully, we can get to the caves by nightfall. It would be good to get some cover.' Fyr had flown off, and Jael kept watching the sky, wondering if she would return.

'Have you had any visions?' Axl wondered. 'Do you see anything coming?'

Jael shook her head. 'No. Nothing. Not yet. Hopefully, I will, though. And Ayla's here, don't forget. She's much better at this than me, so don't worry. We can't change anything now. It's all up to Draguta. There's nowhere for us to go but forward. The next move is hers.'

***

Draguta sat with Jaeger for a while longer, and when she had his agreement that he would commit to becoming the ruler she envisioned, she handed him the book, though not for long. But his desperation to touch it, and his realisation that he needed it had proven useful. Now he would be less likely to get himself in trouble, she was sure. He was bound, unable to go against her, eager to please her, and now he knew what would happen to him if he failed to live up to her expectations.

They had an agreement.

She smiled as she walked back into her chamber with the book, hearing the low moaning chorus from down on the square. After a coolish start, the clouds had dispersed, and the heat was beating down on the harbour like a hammer striking an anvil.

Draguta couldn't have been happier. The Followers were out there, suffering, begging for mercy, wanting an escape from the heat. Desperate for shade. A breeze. Water. Well, she had instructed the soldiers to give them water. Of course she had.

Just not that much.

Still, Briggit would arrive soon, and they needed to live... at least until then.

Placing the book on the bed, Draguta turned her attention to her new seeing circle. She ran a finger around one of the symbols, watching the long train of warriors trekking across Brekka, heading for...

... their deaths?

She smiled, seeking out Jael Furyck.

And there she was, riding at the front. Draguta could almost feel the fear pulsing inside her as she held her head high, bravely leading her army to war as the noble warrior she imagined herself to be.

But it wouldn't be a war, Draguta sighed contentedly.

It would be a massacre.

***

'Meena!' Jaeger was striding towards her as she hurried back into the castle with a basket of bats. He threw his arms around her, genuinely pleased to see her. 'You look different,' he murmured into her hair. 'So different.'

Meena's arms stayed wrapped around the basket as he inhaled her, trying to press his body against hers. 'So do you,' she mumbled awkwardly.

Jaeger stood back, looking her over. 'I've been ill, but I'm recovering now.' And he was. He felt different already. Just being near the book was helping him, he was sure. 'What happened to you?' He ran a hand over her hair, smoothing it down. 'You look taller.'

Meena laughed. She couldn't help it.

'You do,' Jaeger insisted, an arm around her back as he ushered her into the hall. 'Taller and happier.'

Meena couldn't deny that the last part was true. 'Draguta didn't kill me, so I suppose that's a reason to be happy.'

Jaeger smiled. 'Come to my chamber tonight,' he whispered, not wanting anyone to overhear. Not wanting Draguta to know. They had an agreement, and though it didn't explicitly state that he should avoid taking Meena to his bed, Jaeger was sure it was implied.

Meena frowned. 'What about Amma?' She glanced towards the entranceway, feeling guilty. Amma had chosen to remain in the markets, wanting to stay far away from the castle and her husband.

Jaeger walked Meena towards the map table, almost expecting his father to be waiting for him, readying an insult, his brothers on hand to share in the joke.

Except for Berard. He'd never laughed along.

Shaking away his nostalgia, Jaeger turned back to Meena and what he needed her to do. Bending down, he lowered his voice. 'I want you to find a chamber for Amma. Somewhere far away from mine.'

Meena was confused. 'Why?'

Jaeger's eyes were darting around her head, wanting to see which slave was trying to listen. Wanting to know if Draguta had any spies. But closing his eyes, he realised that she didn't need any. 'I want Amma kept away from me until the baby comes. It's best if she's nowhere I can reach her.'

'Oh.' That was a surprise.

'I thought about it a lot on the journey from Angard... what happened to Elissa. What happened to my son.' He had thought about it. There had been no one to talk to and nothing to do but hunker down on that rain-drenched ship, trying not to vomit, wondering if he would die. The storm at its worst had threatened to sink them. Many times. And his thoughts had wandered to his father and his brothers. To his mother, who had loved him most of all. But mainly, Jaeger had thought of the son he didn't have. The son who would have carried on his name. Who would have ruled Hest one day, if he hadn't killed him. If he hadn't lost control and punched Elissa, ending both their lives.

'Amma needs to have this baby,' Jaeger whispered, his eyes haunted as he stared at Meena. 'Keep her away from me. Please.'

***

Edela had a problem, and she was struggling to solve it.

In the end, she went to Biddy for help.

'It's Eydis. She won't even talk to Ontine. When Ontine is near her, she moves away.'

'I've noticed,' Biddy said, hands full of bandages she wanted to put down. She felt flustered, worrying that they wouldn't be organised before night fell. 'But what can you do?'

'Well,' Edela sighed, 'I was hoping you could tell me. What can I do?'

They stared at the two girls who sat on opposite sides of the circle Edela had cast in the middle of the hall, both of them not knowing what to do with themselves.

Biddy frowned. 'Let me put these bandages on the table, then I'll grab Eydis. You take Ontine. She'll be fine. It's just Eydis who has the problem. I'll have a word with her. Set her right. She's not going to be any help if she won't get out of this mood.'

'Good. Good idea. You'll be better at that than me. I really do need to spend some time with Ontine. If an attack comes tonight, I need her to understand how she can help without getting in the way.'

Biddy nodded, heading to the nearest table while Edela motioned for Ontine to join her for a walk, leaving Eydis all alone. Having deposited her bandages, Biddy sat down beside her.

'Hello,' Eydis smiled, recognising the smell of rosemary, a little fish too. 'Have you seen the puppies? I haven't heard them all day. I hope they didn't run after Jael.'

Biddy laughed. 'If they'd done that, they'd have been sent back here with their tails between their legs! Nobody wants those big babies for company.' She thought of how Ido and Vella had tried to defend her against that giant warrior, and she felt bad. 'They were in the kitchen just now. Freya's crumbing fish which always means a mess, so I doubt they'll be leaving till she's done.'

'That's good.'

Biddy took a deep breath. 'Edela is worried about you and Ontine,' she began gently. 'About how you will work together when the time comes. You don't seem to like the girl. Is that because of Fyn?'

Eydis immediately lifted her shoulders, dropping her head. 'No.'

Biddy smiled. 'No? He did seem quite taken with her, didn't he?'

'Did he?' Eydis lifted her head.

'He did. She is pretty, and boys usually tangle themselves in knots to impress pretty girls. They can't help it. But pretty doesn't matter in the end. Once they're done making fools of themselves, they move on to something real. To someone real. Someone they care about. Someone who has more than long eyelashes and a heaving bosom.'

Eydis laughed. 'Has she got a heaving bosom?'

Biddy was pleased to see Eydis come to life. 'Not that I've noticed, but then I haven't looked too closely!' She held Eydis' hand, giving it a squeeze. 'Fyn cares about you, and you know it too. But you're young.' She saw Eydis frowning. 'It doesn't mean you don't feel things. Doesn't mean your feelings aren't real. But it does mean that there's time. Time for Fyn to grow into a man. For you to grow into a woman, and one day, if it's meant to be, it will.'

Eydis squirmed, but she didn't deny anything that Biddy was saying.

'And none of it will even matter if you don't put it all to one side and focus on being useful. On helping Edela. That's why you're here, Eydis. She needs you. You've saved us all, many times, and she'll need you to do it again. We all will. And you can't help any of us if you're too busy thinking about Ontine and Fyn.'

Eydis felt even more embarrassed. 'I'm sorry,' she mumbled. 'Sorry for being silly.'

Biddy wrapped an arm around her shoulder. 'Nothing to be sorry for. It's perfectly normal to feel jealous. We all do sometimes. Even me many years ago. But now's not the time for it. Now you need to get to work. So when Edela and Ontine come back, you have to make it right. Show Edela that you want to help.'

Eydis nodded, feeling bad that she'd ever caused Edela to worry, but at the same time, she couldn't shake the feeling she had about Ontine.

There was just something about the girl she didn't like.

And it had nothing to do with Fyn.

CHAPTER TWENTY FOUR

Everyone was in shock that they'd made it to their first campsite without being attacked by fire-breathing dragons or pecked to death by possessed birds.

Nothing had happened, apart from the weather turning foul which hadn't made things easier, especially not for the catapults or the wagons, whose wheels had to contend with sucking mud as well as rocks.

'At least you're dry,' Jael grinned at Ayla and Astrid, who did indeed look dry after spending the day inside their covered wagon.

'We are,' Astrid smiled, her arms loaded with the branches she was taking to the nearest fire. 'Or we were. Now we'll be as wet as everyone else.'

Jael, who was soaked to the bone, shivered in response. 'Well, the faster we get those fires going, the quicker we can all dry out.

Astrid hurried away with her branches, while Ayla turned around to look for Bruno, leaving Jael to wait for Aleksander who was running through the rain towards her.

'Happy?' he wondered, coming to a stop, shaking his hair all over her.

'With what? Being wet and cold?'

'With still being alive. One day down and we're all still here to tell the tale!'

Jael didn't look impressed. 'You've just cursed us. I imagine Draguta's watching you. You and your big mouth.'

Aleksander shut his big mouth for a moment. 'Well, I was thinking about that. Might help us to have her launch an attack now. The more of her creatures we kill before we get to the vale, the less there'll be waiting for us.'

'Ha! A nice thought, but I don't imagine she'll throw everything she has at us before we get there.' Jael glanced around, lowering her voice, conscious of the rain getting heavier and her desire to get out of it growing stronger. She pulled Aleksander into the cave they would be sleeping in. 'If Draguta wanted us dead now, we'd be dead. We're still alive because we have a part to play. We have no control over anything, so we just need to keep going.'

Aleksander nodded. 'Well, let's keep going over to that fire before you break some teeth. And I've got to get cooking. I promised you a stew tonight.'

'You did.' Jael rubbed her wet hands together, looking out into the rain, wondering where Fyr had disappeared to. 'And I can't wait!'

***

Ontine was pleased to get out of the hall, away from Eydis Skalleson. It was unsettling to be around the girl, and despite Eydis being blind, Ontine sensed that she was always watching her.

It made her uncomfortable.

'You needn't worry about Eydis,' Edela assured her, enjoying the last of the sunshine, though she felt her shoulder blades aching at the thought of how much they still had to prepare. 'Eydis has had a difficult time of late. Her father was killed, her brother taken. She has had to leave her home. And she is motherless. It has been a hard time for her.'

'Oh.' Ontine looked surprised. 'I sympathise with her loss. It has been a painful time for us all.'

'It has. We are all struggling with loss of some kind, aren't we?'

Edela said, thinking of Branwyn. 'But only by working together will we be able to prevent any more. We must come together now.' She smiled at Alaric and Derwa who were deep in conversation with Sybill at one of the tables in the square. 'You are older than Eydis, by what, five years? So you must lead the way, Ontine. Show her that you wish to be friends. She is a lovely girl, but rather reticent around strangers, so you can help her. Be a friend.'

Ontine nodded, sensing that Edela was already keen to get back to the hall. The old dreamer kept turning around, twitching. 'I will, of course. I just want to help. Not be a distraction.'

Edela stared up at her, trying to focus. 'Yes, I know you do. And you will. I have a few more stones to paint symbols onto. Perhaps you could sit with me, and I'll explain what may happen and how we will need to respond.' She shook her head, realising that she had no idea what was going to happen next. 'Well, how we will prepare ourselves, at least!'

'I would like that. It would help to know what to do... before it happens.'

Edela nodded, hoping she could find out what Draguta was planning before she attacked.

Before it was too late.

***

Thorgils ended up eating most of Jael's stew that night. It was as though he could tell that she had little appetite when he plonked himself down next to her, and he was quick to pounce on her bowl when she stopped eating.

'Are you ever not hungry?' Jael wondered.

'Never.'

Karsten grinned, finishing off his own bowl, wiping his beard on the back of his sleeve. 'That's the best meal I've eaten in a while,' he declared, surprised he was saying that to Aleksander. 'You'll make someone a good wife one day.'

Jael glanced at Aleksander, who was suddenly very interested in the fire.

'I'm sure Hanna would agree!' Thorgils laughed.

Jael was surprised by that, but not as surprised as Karsten.

'Hanna?' He stared at Aleksander, who, having poked and prodded the perfectly healthy fire, slowly turned around. 'You and Hanna? Wouldn't have picked that.'

Aleksander tried to put an end to it. 'I knew Hanna in Tuura. Nothing more. We're... friends.'

Thorgils lifted his eyebrows, nudging Karsten. 'Special friends, from what I hear.'

Jael frowned. 'Who do you hear anything from?'

But Thorgils didn't say.

And as no one else was speaking, Jael decided to leave them all to it. 'I'm going to check on Ayla and Astrid. See if their company's any better!' And standing up, she stepped around the fire and out into the rain.

Thorgils watched her go. 'So where were we?' he wondered, looking from a moody Karsten to a squirming Aleksander. 'Oh, that's right... Hanna.'

***

Marcus brought Hanna to the hall for supper, leaving her on a bench beside Berard while he disappeared to see what he could do to help.

'You look better!' Edela declared from the floor where she was crawling around on aching knees, placing her symbol stones. Her back was niggling her, and she looked wistfully at those sitting on benches.

Hanna smiled. 'I feel better, thanks to Astrid's broths, though I'm looking forward to eating something else while she's gone!'

Edela nodded distractedly, pointing Ontine to a bunch of herbs. 'Bring those into the circle. Yes, right there. I want everything to hand. Biddy! Where is that tinderbox of yours?'

'I thought we could do something with the children tomorrow,' Hanna suggested, turning to Berard. 'Organise some fun.'

'Fun?'

Hanna laughed. 'Didn't you have fun when you were a child? Or was it all practising for war?'

'Well...' It had been so long since he'd thought about his childhood that Berard wasn't sure. 'I think there was fun.' He frowned. 'Karsten and Haegen had fun tricking me. Hiding from me. Sometimes they hid me.'

'Hid you?'

'From our father. When he asked them to find me. They'd lock me in a wardrobe or a chest instead. Run away with the key so I couldn't get out. Then my father would grow wild and send servants to look for me.'

'How mean! And what happened when they found you?'

'Oh, my father would be even more furious at me for being such a gullible fool, and a weakling for not being able to fight them off.'

'That's terrible.'

Berard laughed, memories of his childhood coming into sharper view. 'It wasn't so bad. Eventually, they'd feel so guilty that they'd take me to the training ring and have the slaves feed me sweetmeats while I watched them fight.'

'How generous of them!' Hanna snorted.

'I do miss it.'

'What? Being locked in a chest?'

'No, Hest.' Berard looked around the dark and smoky King's Hall. 'I'm glad we're here, but I miss my home. I miss the castle and my chamber. The view of the harbour. The heat.' He leaned forward, wrapping his hands around his empty ale cup. 'I miss Meena.'

***

Meena showed Amma to her new chamber.

She felt happy for Amma, who was elated to have been removed from Jaeger's, and even more elated with the news that Jaeger wanted to stay far away from her until the baby's birth. Meena smiled, though she did not feel happy because Jaeger had told her that she would be moving back into his bed immediately.

Amma didn't notice as she explored the softly lit room. It was on the opposite side of the castle to Jaeger's chamber, and she felt herself start to relax for the first time since her arrival in Hest. Then she saw Meena's face. 'I'm sorry for you. I didn't expect this,' she said apologetically as Meena carried Amma's things to the bed.

'It's not your fault,' Meena mumbled. 'I'm used to Jaeger.' And she was. She was almost dulled to the feel of him. The smell of him. The way his hands grabbed at her, forcing her to do things that made her cringe. Uncomfortable things. Swallowing, she looked at Amma's worried face. 'You need to focus on your baby and staying away from Jaeger. Just because you're in separate chambers now, it doesn't mean you won't be together. You'll eat in the hall, be by his side, stand by his throne.'

'Why doesn't the Queen of Hest have a throne?' Amma wondered, not liking the idea of standing near Jaeger for hours on end.

Meena shrugged. 'Perhaps the Dragos kings didn't think much of their queens?' She eyed the door, feeling Draguta's need for her like a dark shadow creeping around the castle. 'I'll come and see you in the morning, but I must go before Draguta sends Brill looking for me. Jaeger doesn't want her finding out where you are. She would be... cross.'

Amma walked Meena to the door. 'I'll stay here until supper, out of everyone's way, don't worry.'

Meena turned to her, dropping her voice. 'Draguta sees everything. She hears everything. You may not be alone for long.'

Amma gulped, nodding. 'Then I'll make the most of it. Don't

worry, Meena. You've done enough to help me. I'll be fine.' She didn't feel fine.

And Meena didn't feel fine, but she slipped through the door and out into the corridor, her knees almost knocking together as she thought about the potion she had drunk and how she needed to find a way to test whether it had worked.

***

Draguta was stalking the corridors, growing more and more irritated by her unreliable assistant who had a habit of disappearing just when she needed her most. Swinging around a corner, she barrelled into Evaine who fell on her backside with a yelp. 'What are you doing standing there?' she bellowed, her temper spiking. 'Hiding from someone?'

Evaine looked up in surprise. 'I... I was walking.'

'Too slowly!' Draguta snapped, striding around Evaine's sprawled figure. 'Far too slowly! Now get up and come with me. I need to find your slovenly cousin! We have work to do, and I refuse to be delayed by her!'

Evaine's ears were ringing as she scrambled to her feet, smoothing down her dress, suddenly aware that Draguta was already halfway down the corridor, shouting Meena's name, not wanting it to be dawn before they began the spell.

And rolling her eyes and hitching up her dress, Evaine ran after her.

***

Bram was not prepared to let anyone else take first watch that night. In fact, if he'd had his way, he would have taken second and third watch too, but that was silly, he knew.

A sleep-drunk man had little chance of being alert or effective.

He sat by the hall doors, thinking about Fyn, trying not to think about Runa. It hurt his heart to remember the night of the barsk attack and the moment he'd found her body. He knew that the only thing he could do for her now was to keep her son safe. Their son. Bram smiled, thinking about that.

His son.

Everyone who was staying in the hall was settled into their beds now, he could see as he scanned the room. Two large fires burned low, and a third, smaller one was crackling in the middle of Edela's little circle. The smoke was pumping like the bellows tonight, he thought, reaching for the cup of ale he'd kept beside him.

Like a great fog.

The fort had been covered in it for weeks.

Stinking smoke. And death.

And his mind was right back at Runa, and he sighed.

Edela watched Bram with one eye open, pleased that he was there - that all his men were - though weapons and burly men did not make her feel safe. Magic was powerful. It was secret and hidden, and Edela had her doubts that magic would knock on the door and demand to be let in.

She shivered, pulling the fur up to her ear, missing her cottage.

Vella was sleeping next to her, tucked up against her stomach and she felt happy about that, her mind wandering to Jael and Axl. To Aleksander. To poor Amma, who would be the most scared of all, wondering when they would come and rescue her.

Closing her eyes, Edela held Amma's face in her mind, wanting to find her in a dream, though she knew that she couldn't. For tonight, she had to try and find Draguta.

***

'And when did you arrive?' Draguta roared, striding into her chamber, Evaine panting behind her, already wondering when she could head for her bed. 'I have been all over the castle looking for you, and you certainly weren't here before!'

Meena swallowed, quickly flustered. 'I... I didn't have enough dragons blood,' she mumbled, dropping her pestle into the bowl. 'I had to... go and get some more.'

'Hmmm.' Draguta's eyes were sharp, unimpressed, quickly alert to what else needed to be prepared. 'Well, do you have everything now? Everything I asked for?' And reaching for the Book of Darkness, she laid her hands on it, feeling an unexpected jolt. It popped open her eyes, shooting down her spine and Draguta blinked, trying to remember what she had been about to do. Meena was busy nodding at her, and she snapped. 'Get stirring! And while you do that, Brill, you will poke that fire. It will not survive long by the look of it, and I will soon have need of those flames.' She took a deep breath, trying to calm herself, still not sure what had happened.

Turning her attention back to the book, Draguta lifted the cover, opening it slowly, feeling nothing but the familiar cool leather, and the crisp texture of the vellum pages as they crackled between her fingers. But she frowned, her limbs tense, sensing that something was wrong. Reaching the page she was looking for, she inhaled a sharp breath, frowning at the unpleasant smell emanating from Meena's bowl. 'Do hurry!' she growled. 'I would like to begin!'

***

Aleksander yawned. 'Hope you get some sleep tonight,' he murmured, rolling towards Jael. The fire was crackling between them, but he could see that she was wide awake. 'You need some sleep.'

'I do. But I need dreams too. It would be helpful to know what

Draguta is planning. Why she didn't try anything today.'

Aleksander's eyes closed. 'Not sure I'd want those kinds of dreams,' he admitted, thinking about the Widow. About Dara Teros. She had been in his head once, but hers had been a comforting voice. A protector. He often wished she would come back, but then, he smiled to himself, that would likely mean they were about to be attacked. He grabbed his fur, trying to get comfortable. 'I wish you luck with your dreams. If you need any help, let me know.'

Jael didn't say anything. Aleksander could fall asleep mid-sentence, she knew. Something he had in common with Eadmund.

Her face changed.

She hadn't thought about Eadmund all day. Not since she'd left Eydis behind. Eadmund, who was out there somewhere. Waiting.

And when they found each other?

Jael's eyes moved to Thorgils, who was sitting with Karsten by the mouth of the cave. They had argued over who would take first watch and, in the end, they'd all agreed that it made more sense to take it in pairs, which by the droop of Thorgils' big head, had been the right thing to do.

Reaching down, Jael placed a hand on Toothpick's moonstone pommel.

Waiting.

Waiting for whatever surprises Draguta had in store.

***

The wind picked up.

It had been a relatively fine day – nothing threatening a storm – so Gant was surprised by the rattle of the window; the strong breeze shaking the door. He edged towards Gisila, who was moaning in her sleep. 'Ssshhh,' he soothed, his eyes still closed, a hand out, smoothing down her hair. 'Go back to sleep. It's just the wind.'

CHAPTER TWENTY FIVE

'There are many ways to hurt someone,' Draguta breathed, her eyes narrowing to slits. 'You can take their life with a knife, a whisper... ' She eyed Meena and Evaine who sat opposite her. 'You can destroy everything they love, one at a time. Until they go mad. Until they have nothing.' She smiled. 'Or... you can take everything all at once.'

Meena's eyes widened in horror, the smoke from Brill's fire making them water.

'But where is the fun in that?' And dipping a finger into the bowl of bloody potion, Draguta placed it on the table and started to draw.

***

Axl was lying in the cave near Fyn. There were three caves beside each other. Theirs was the largest, certainly the most accommodating, though the ceiling was dripping and the noise was so irritating that Axl couldn't sleep. The rain was still falling, less heavily now, though the wind was whipping the trees in the distance where the horses were tied up between them along lengths of rope.

Rork was sitting by the mouth of the cave, looking out into the darkness. Axl wondered if he should join him, though Rork wasn't one for conversation. Perhaps that made him the perfect company, Axl thought, watching the dark shapes of the trees in the distance as they waved from side to side.

Listening to the horses whinny.

***

Edela scrambled to her feet, staring at the hall doors, her hips clicking, the flames from her tiny fire disturbed by the breeze.

'Edela?' Bram started walking towards her.

She pointed at the door. 'Something is wrong, Bram. Eydis, Ontine, wake up!' The girls were sleeping by her feet, curled into her circle. The puppies too. 'We must stay here. Biddy!'

Biddy had been sleeping on one of the beds that lined the walls, near Derwa and Alaric. She stumbled towards Edela, trying to peel open her eyes, struggling out of a deep sleep.

Gant was there quickly, belt already wrapped around his waist. 'What's happened? Edela?'

'Something is wrong,' she whispered. 'I don't know what, but I cannot leave the circle. You must go.'

Biddy stepped into the circle, bending down to stop Vella who was eager to follow Gant. She gripped the whining dog to her chest, happy to see that Eydis was holding onto Ido. 'Do you have everything you need?'

Edela didn't know, but she quickly bent down to close the circle, trying to think.

She didn't know what was coming.

***

They were just like the wind.

Draguta smiled, watching as her tiny whisps flew through the fort. She could control them with the sweep of a hand, the delicate flick of a finger. They were almost invisible as they slipped around corners, sliding under doors, squeezing through keyholes.

Just innocent little whisps.

But in her hands, oh so devastating.

***

Gant and Bram strode across the square, armed with axes. They'd left Bram's men behind, not wanting to leave the hall vulnerable.

Gant thought of Gisila lying in her bed, half-asleep.

He should have moved her into the hall.

'Albyn!' he called up to the ramparts. 'I need some men! Send down a dozen! Let me know if you see anything out there!'

They strode onwards, wishing for some moonlight, but the moon was hiding, and their journey was even more uncertain because of it.

Bram's skin was prickling all over as the twelve men hurried down from the ramparts to join them.

'Spread out,' Gant ordered. 'Either side of us. Weapons drawn.' He heard a whinny from the stables, quickly followed by another, and then the pained roar of a horse, and his attention was quickly on the long shadow of a building in the distance. He sniffed the air. 'Come on! Let's check the stables!'

***

Eydis sensed that something was happening, just as Edela did, but neither of them knew what.

They stayed inside the circle, trying to focus, wanting to determine if they were in danger. Ontine sat opposite Edela, Eydis to her right, Biddy behind them, one eye on the doors. She held a spear, wishing Jael was there to protect them all.

Edela's eyes were closed. She felt as though she was standing on a beach, the chill of a breeze sweeping over her body, winding around her, making her shiver.

She was so cold.

But it was not cold.

A breeze? A cold breeze? In the hall?

Entorp came over to the circle, wondering if he could do anything.

'Go to the doors!' Edela ordered suddenly, her eyes springing open. 'Is there a storm? Is the wind blowing? Hurry, Entorp!'

Entorp could hear the terror in Edela's voice, and he raced to the doors as two of Bram's men hurried to open them. Running down the steps, Entorp paused for a moment, taking in the dark night.

The perfectly still dark night.

***

Meena watched Draguta move her finger across the seeing circle, her dark ring almost humming as it slid around. Draguta's eyes were closed as she swayed from side to side, murmuring under her breath.

Evaine yawned from her seat beside her, wondering how much longer she would take. She couldn't see or hear anything, but she could smell the horrific stink of the smoke pumping from the hearth. It had her eyes itching, and she found herself growing sleepier by the moment.

Meena glared at her cousin, trying to get her attention but

Evaine ignored her, yawning again.

Draguta was deep in her trance, though, oblivious to anything that was happening in the chamber as she watched the whisps dart through the air like tiny sparks exploding across a night sky. The glint of a blade, the blink of an eye, as they readied their attack.

***

'There is no wind, no wind at all!'

Edela was reaching for the Book of Aurea as Entorp ran back into the hall. She thought about Gisila, realising that she was still in her chamber. 'Get my daughter!' she yelled to the nearest man. 'You must carry her in here! Into the circle! Hurry! We are under attack!'

***

Her grandmother woke her.

Jael sat up, confused. She hadn't heard a voice, but she could suddenly feel Edela's terror. It was as though her grandmother's heart was beating in her ears, racing with panic. Peering around the cave, she could see Aleksander staring out into the dark night, muttering to himself, trying not to fall asleep. She was supposed to be keeping watch with him but knowing Aleksander, he hadn't wanted to wake her.

'What is it?' He turned, hurrying towards her. 'Did you have a dream?'

Jael blinked, trying to see his eyes. 'We need to check outside. See if everyone's alright.' She had a terrible headache, and as she stood, her ears started ringing.

Something was wrong.

'You check on the horses. I'll go and see Ayla.'

***

Pushing open the stable doors, Gant and Bram stepped inside, hands out, axes ready. The horses were upset, moving around in their stalls, banging into the sides, whinnying. There was a real sense of panic.

And a smell.

Gant was panicking too. He smelled death.

It was almost pitch black in the stables, but Gant quickly found his way to Gus' stall, relieved to see that he was alright, but the horse next to Gus suddenly collapsed to the ground, and then another and another. 'What's happening? Bram, hurry! Something's killing the horses! Spread out! Spread out!'

***

'Whisps.'

Entorp's eyes bulged. 'Whisps?' That made no sense.

Eydis had no idea what a whisp was.

Biddy did, her eyes quickly scanning the hall, trying to see one. They were spirits. Sprite-like spirits, so malleable and fine; invisible to the eye unless revealed by moonlight. Shy land spirits with a reputation for random acts of kindness.

That made no sense.

Then they heard a scream, and suddenly one of the men who had been guarding the doors collapsed to the ground, hands around his throat, blood pouring over his fingers.

'Edela!' Biddy shrieked. 'They're in here!'

Edela could hear that. She had not seen anything about whisps in the Book of Aurea, though. Not a single thing. Why would she? They were not creatures of the darkness. Panic tightened her dry throat, and she looked at Ontine whose eyes were blinking, and at Eydis, who was awake, alert, and not in a trance at all.

And then another scream.

'Mother, do something!' Gisila panicked, lying in the circle, gripping her stomach. 'Hurry!'

Edela tried to shut them all out, closing her eyes.

Needing to think.

***

Gant clung to Gus' neck. 'Help me!' he urged one of the men. Nyk. 'Hold his other side! Keep him covered!' Nyk was a good man. A horse-loving man like him. They needed to keep the horses safe. Protect them somehow.

Another thud as a horse fell.

'Can you see anything?' Bram was bellowing to their men. 'Anything?'

And then the clouds parted, and the moon revealed itself. Bright white moonlight shone through the thatch. It streamed under the doors, down the smoke holes, in through the holes in the walls.

And they could see them.

'Whisps?' Gant was momentarily confused, his eyes on the lethal-looking daggers in the sprites' hands and the dead look in their pale-green eyes. 'Kill them!'

***

It was as though dawn had arrived. The hall was suddenly flooded with light, and they could see the luminescent whisps flitting around their heads, glowing like fireflies, holding glinting blades in their tiny hands.

Poised to strike.

Marcus, who had been sleeping in the hall with Hanna, unsheathed his new sword and hurried to stand in front of her, tired eyes suddenly alert, head swivelling.

'Keep the doors open! We need more light!' Entorp yelled, then just as quickly. 'Behind you!'

And a whisp slid out from behind the door, aiming its blade at Marcus' neck. Hearing Hanna's scream, Marcus spun around, cutting it in half.

They could see them more clearly now.

The tiny creatures were everywhere. Swarming like flies.

Entorp drew his knife and charged, yelping as a whisp sliced its blade across the back of his hand.

'You need a sword! Get a sword!' Biddy panicked from the circle, watching him stagger backwards, scanning the room, trying to see everyone who was in danger, which was impossible as everyone appeared to be in danger.

'Where's Gant?' Gisila panicked. 'Where is he?'

'Father!' Hanna shouted, drawing her eating knife and slashing at a whisp aiming for Marcus' back. 'Behind you!'

***

Jael had reached the wagon, and she popped her head inside, not surprised to find Ayla awake, bent over a fire, Astrid and Bruno looking confused and half asleep on either side of her.

Ayla was relieved that Jael had come.

'Stay inside the wagon,' she breathed. 'I must go outside quickly and try to make us safe before Draguta brings them here!'

'Brings what here?' Jael couldn't catch her breath as she moved to one side to let Ayla pass.

But Ayla wasn't listening as she hurried out of the wagon, knife in hand.

***

Gant could feel Gus shuddering as the whisps stabbed and slashed his rump. 'Edela!' he yelled, hoping she could hear him somehow. 'Please!' He couldn't be everywhere. Couldn't keep Gus safe. Couldn't save the other horses. Couldn't save his men.

Bram was trying to be everywhere, cutting the whisps to pieces, but more and more swept into the stables, attacking the horses, trying to hurt him. 'Aarrghh!' he screamed, stumbling forward, just holding onto his sword, not wanting to imagine what was happening outside the stables.

***

They were still in the tiny, windowless cottage, and there was not enough room to swing a sword, but Ulf was trying.

So was Berard.

The creatures glowed, pale like moonbeams. Berard could almost see through them. Whisps. But not the whisps he'd heard tales about. Their tiny eyes were oddly dead; the eyes of killers.

The children were gathered on a bed, crying, terrified, and Bayla was trying to keep them all calm, but they could feel the cold breeze swirling around the cottage. They could see the little whisps darting around the room, blades out, trying to hurt them.

And then one of them did.

A whisp slid its blade along the back of Kai's chubby leg. He yelped, blood running, tears stopping as the shock set in.

'Kai! Bayla, take him!' And Nicolene was up off the bed, slipping her eating knife from its scabbard, standing in front of her two sons and their three cousins, and Bayla who was working hard to hold onto them all. Swinging around, Nicolene slashed her knife from side to side, trying to keep them safe.

'Open the door!' Ulf yelled, surrounded by six whisps who dove and swooped and tried to stab him. They were so fast, though, moving wherever he wasn't. 'We need to see! More light, Berard! Aarrghh!'

***

Meena's head was spinning, her ears ringing with Draguta's laughter as she peered into her circle, lost in the chaos, enjoying the entertainment.

Andala.

Meena felt that strongly.

Draguta was doing something to Andala.

***

Ayla dragged her knife through the dirt, making a circle around the wagon, hunched over, murmuring under her breath, the noises in Andala loud in her ears. She had studied the Book of Aurea until its vellum pages were seared into her memory. She knew how to make a circle of protection, though whether it would keep out Draguta's magic was yet to be determined.

Straightening up, she saw a flash of Edela, her pale face aglow in the flames, worry etched into the lines of consternation across her brow.

She was confused, uncertain, Ayla could tell.

She needed help.

***

'Gus!' Gant couldn't hold him up. His horse collapsed onto the straw with a groan and a thud. 'Gus!' Gant dropped down to the ground beside him. He could feel Gus' blood oozing through his hands as he tried to staunch its flow; as he tried to find his horse's wounds, knowing that there were too many. 'It's alright,' he soothed, running a hand down Gus' cheek. 'I'll go and find Entorp. He'll get those stinking salves of his, don't worry.' But he was worrying, not wanting to lose his loyal horse who had been by his side for nearly twenty years.

Straightening up, Gant knew that he had to leave.

He had to get back to the hall.

Bram was shouting, yelping, working with their men to try and kill the whisps, but they were everywhere, lethal blades hissing through the air.

And Gant couldn't see a way through.

***

Ayla rushed back into the wagon, squeezing in between Astrid and Jael. Bruno sat on their bed with the drum, waiting expectantly, eyes on his wife.

'I need to slip into a trance now! Throw those herbs onto the fire! Hold my hand, Jael. You will help me reach Edela.' And gripping Jael's hand, she turned her eyes to the flames. 'Bruno, start drumming.'

Jael's eyes closed, and she heard the beat of her grandmother's heart again, sensing her confusion, hoping that Ayla could get to her in time.

***

Entorp spun, listening to Derwa and Alaric yelping and shrieking from the beds along the walls where Alaric was trying his best to fight off the swirling whisps. Marcus was on his knees, blood dripping from his head, his arms. Hanna, pale-faced and panting, stood by him, knife in her bleeding hand, trying to keep the whisps far away from her father.

The noise in the hall was a clattering panic, and Edela was working hard to shut it all out. She dipped her finger into the bloody mixture she had prepared earlier, and bent over the floor, inhaling the smoke. There was no symbol in the Book of Aurea that dealt with whisps, of that she was certain now. But the gentle sprites had been possessed by Draguta, and she remembered a symbol from her time in Tuura – the one they had used during the raven attack – though she could not remember the chant.

Not yet, anyway.

Leaning forward, she started painting the bloody symbol, suddenly aware of Ayla's voice vibrating through her. And feeling encouraged, Edela drew with confidence now, repeating Ayla's chant in a loud voice. 'Say it with me, girls!' she called to Eydis and Ontine. 'Say it with me!' And sitting back on her haunches, she grabbed Eydis' hand with her right, Ontine's with her left, squeezing tightly as their voices lifted up her croaking one.

And the shimmering lights that were the whisps suddenly went out, their tiny bodies falling to the floor like a cloud of dust, their glowing eyes as dull as stones.

***

'One by one, you will be gone.'

Draguta stood with a smile, her eyes on the seeing circle glowing around the table. It had been amusing. Enjoyable. Destructive.

She was content to let the Andalans live in a permanent state of terror now.

Happy to let it be that way until it was done.

For soon it would be.

And leaving Meena and Evaine at the table, glassy-eyed and light-headed, she moved towards the fire, hands extended, inhaling the smoke.

So fragrant. So powerful.

Just as she was.

***

The moon was gone again, lost in the clouds, but so were the whisps.

Marcus collapsed to the ground, bleeding. He heard the intense ringing in his ears, the pain in his body quickly overwhelming him as everything went dark.

Entorp hurried to him, dropping to his knees. 'Marcus?'

Hanna rushed to his side. 'Father!' She leaned over Marcus' body, grabbing his hand. 'Father?'

Edela could hear the panic in the hall as she tried to catch her breath, dropping her head, inhaling a mouthful of smoke. Biddy brought her a cup of water, her hand shaking as she waited for Edela to take it.

Edela took a quick gulp. 'We need to make sure everyone's safe. Biddy, help me up! Those whisps may have been everywhere.

Likely they were. Gant hasn't come back.'

Gisila looked terrified, worried eyes blinking in the flames.

She wanted to stand.

'No!' Edela glared at her. 'I will go and find him on my way to Branwyn. I need to make sure that she's alright. Kayla and Aedan and the baby too. You stay there. I'll send Gant back when I find him.' Biddy grabbed Edela's arm, leading her to Marcus, who remained unconscious. Derwa had quickly shuffled over to check on him, though she was trembling so much that she couldn't decide where to begin.

'How is he?' Edela wondered, peering down at Marcus. Hanna was sobbing, cradling his body, which was not the best sign. Nor was the amount of blood leaking through his clothes. She squinted. It was suddenly so dark. 'We must get these fires higher! Alaric!' Edela saw him perched on a bed, his pale face bleeding, too afraid to move. 'Grab some wood! Get the fires going! Find more lamps! Hurry now!'

***

'Nicolene?' Ulf leaned over her body, confused.

Her dead body.

But how was she dead?

'What happened?' He reached out to Bayla, tapping her arm, trying to get her attention but Bayla was too shocked to move. Her mouth was ajar, her grandchildren screaming and sobbing around her. Kai and Eron had crawled out of her lap, down onto their mother's lifeless body.

They had kept the fire going, and there was enough light to see that Nicolene was most certainly dead. Her eyes, fixed open, were staring up at the rafters in surprise.

Berard tried to wake himself up, hurrying towards his tiny nephews. 'Eron, Kai,' he called. 'Here now, come here.' And dropping his sword, he grabbed Kai's arm.

Ulf picked Eron up, getting an ear-full of terrified wailing. 'Ssshhh,' he tried, looking down at Nicolene's body. There wasn't a cut on her. No blood. He couldn't see anything.

But she was very much dead.

CHAPTER TWENTY SIX

Jael sat back, leaning against the side of the wagon, staring at Ayla. 'I don't know what happened, but it was something, wasn't it?'

Astrid and Bruno looked on in confusion, wanting to know themselves.

'It was whisps,' Ayla breathed, seeing the flashing images in her mind. 'Sprites you can only see in moonlight. They can make themselves thinner than vellum, as small as ants. But they're friendly. Supposed to be friendly.'

Jael had heard of them. 'And did Edela stop them?'

'She did,' Ayla nodded, breathing out a sigh of relief. 'She used a symbol. Edela knew it, but not the chant. I helped her, but...' Her voice trailed away.

'What?' Bruno touched his wife's arm, sensing her distress. 'What happened?'

'They killed a lot of animals.'

'Animals?'

'Livestock,' Ayla said. 'I saw a lot of dead livestock. Horses too. They were in the stables. I felt the horses dying.'

Jael sat up straight. 'What can we do?'

'We've done all we can, Jael,' Ayla insisted. 'I've drawn a protective circle around the wagon, which I hope will keep us safe. The whisps in Andala are dead, and if Draguta sends them here, we know how to stop them.'

Jael wanted to leave and check on Tig. 'Did you see anything else?' she wondered, standing up, whacking her head on the roof.

Ayla's ears were ringing with a chorus of terrified cries, and she was struggling to concentrate. 'No, but I'll find you if I do.'

Jael left the wagon, walking as quickly as she could in the darkness, hurrying to find Tig who appeared distressed but unharmed. The horses were all disturbed, moving about, pulling against their ropes, making noises, not sounding sleepy at all.

Convinced that they weren't in any immediate danger, Jael headed back to the caves, carefully winding her way through the fires which were higher now, burning brighter, men alert, watching as she passed.

Aleksander came out to meet her, Karsten too.

Karsten gripped her arm. 'What happened?'

And for the first time, Jael saw a flash of the whisps, and her mouth dropped open. 'I...' She blinked.

'Jael?' Axl was there too, Thorgils and Rork behind him. 'What happened?'

'There was an attack in Andala,' she said, her eyes on Axl, eager to get away from Karsten. 'Draguta sent some creatures. I don't know what happened, but Edela stopped it. Ayla saw that.'

Nobody spoke. Minds whirring, full of worry.

Jael took a deep breath. 'I've checked on the horses and the men, and they're fine. There's nothing we can do for Andala from here. Best we all go back to sleep if we can. Those keeping watch should stay alert, though. I'm going to take one more walk around the fires, just to be sure. Axl, you take the other side.'

Her brother nodded, disturbed by the strain he could hear in his sister's voice, but certain that she wouldn't have been able to even speak if something had happened to Gisila or Edela.

'I'll come with you.' Thorgils quickly strode away from the caves, leaving Karsten behind to keep watch, wanting to know more. Wanting more assurance that Isaura was safe. Jael had sounded strangely evasive. 'What did you see?' he asked when they were out of earshot. 'You can tell me.'

Jael sighed, turning to him, grateful for someone to talk to. 'I saw Nicolene Dragos.'

'Oh.'

'She looked dead.'

Thorgils didn't say anything for a moment. He could hear men murmuring around the fires, restless, wondering why everyone was wandering around. 'Don't tell him, Jael.' He placed a hand on her arm. 'He doesn't need to know now, does he? I wouldn't want to.'

'You wouldn't?'

Thorgils shook his head. 'Here? Where we can't do anything except face our own destiny? Likely death? I wouldn't want to know. If you see anything about Isaura, keep it from me. Let me die believing that she'll live long after I've gone. Let me think I did something to save her.' And feeling sad for Karsten, and worried about Isaura, he strode off ahead of Jael towards the horses.

Jael watched his hulking shadow merge into the darkness, knowing that he was right. Hoping that she'd be able to hide it from Karsten.

She was a terrible liar.

***

When they rolled Nicolene over, they found her wounds. Two in her neck. One in her back. Two more in her waist. Tiny, tiny holes, but they must have been deep, sharp, quick cuts. She'd never even cried out.

That was wrong, Ulf realised, shaking his head. She had been crying out the whole time, but they'd both thought that it was in anger, warning the whisps away from the children as she fought off their attackers.

The floor was wet with Nicolene's blood now, the cottage stinking with the smell of death, and Berard could hear the children becoming more and more upset. Eron had worked himself into such a state that he sounded ready to vomit. 'We need to go,' he whispered, imagining Karsten's face. 'To the hall. We should go. Away from here. The children need to leave.'

Bayla didn't move, and Ulf realised that she was still in shock.

Eron was flailing his arms, snot running from his nose, his face drenched in tears. Kai slipped out of Berard's grasp and threw himself on Nicolene's body. Berard had to drag the boy off his mother, though he didn't want to. But they needed to leave the cottage, to see what had happened to everyone else.

They needed to get to safety.

***

Marcus had opened his eyes for a time but lost consciousness again as Derwa started stitching him up. He was bleeding from too many wounds to count, and Derwa had quickly employed Entorp who stood on the other side of Marcus' long body, working away with another needle and thread, lamps burning all around them as they struggled to see.

Hanna had stopped weeping, but she shook uncontrollably, praying to all the gods that her father would survive. She sat on a bench, watching, not wanting to get in the way.

Edela stood beside her, a hand on her shoulder. 'He is a big man,' she murmured, not wanting to distract Derwa and Entorp. 'Losing all that blood will not affect him as much. They just need to sew him up quickly, which they will, don't worry. Derwa is a fast worker.' She was worried, though, having seen no sign of Gant on her visit to check on Branwyn. And glancing at Gisila, who still lay in the circle, she could tell that she was feeling the same.

Ontine was on her knees, helping to hold down a young woman, a servant who'd been stabbed in the leg. Her wound was bleeding profusely, and she was panicking as Biddy tried to stitch her.

'Press her ankle down, Ontine,' Biddy grumbled, knowing that she didn't sound sympathetic, but she needed to stem the bleeding which was gushing like a waterfall. 'Please.' Eydis was beside her. 'Can you help? Eydis? Move around to Lysette's head, there you go. Now see if you can hold her shoulders down. Keep her steady now.'

Gisila looked around as the hall doors burst open and Gant came in, relieved to see her trying to sit up in Edela's circle, reaching out for him. He ran to her, dropping to his knees. 'You're alright?'

Gisila nodded, grimacing as he held her close. 'You?'

Gant sighed. 'I've a few cuts. Nowhere important by the feel of it. But Gus...' He shook his head. 'The whisps were in the stables, killing the horses. I need someone to look at those that are left. If there's anyone?'

Edela came to join them, her brow furrowed. 'The horses?'

Gant nodded. 'The horses, the goats. Chickens and pigs. Looks like Draguta went after the livestock more than us, though I've come across some dead too. But the animals...'

Edela frowned, a chilling realisation sinking in. 'It's a game. A slow death. One cut at a time. Kill our livestock, and what will we eat? A slow death.' Her voice was low, and only Gant and Gisila could hear her.

'But whisps are supposed to be friendly, aren't they?' Gisila whispered. 'How did they have blades? What else will she turn against us?'

Edela didn't know, but she realised how truly impossible it was to protect themselves now. If Draguta could turn a harmless creature like a whisp into a weapon, any dark thing was possible.

She stared down at the circle for a moment, looking up as Isaura entered the hall, all four children in tow, an idea popping into her head.

A way she might be able to keep them all safe.

***

Morning dawned bright and warm, and Jael and Ayla walked through the forest together, eager to talk away from everyone else. They were both tired, neither having gone back to sleep after the whisp attack, and they were struggling to think of what to do.

'I wish I knew more,' Ayla said. 'I wish I could see more about what happened.'

Jael wasn't sure she wanted to know. It was hard enough to keep themselves safe; impossible to keep their attention and everyone else's focused on what lay ahead without worrying about what was happening back at the fort. 'She could have crushed us, but she didn't.'

'It seems that she's waiting for something.'

'Or someone.'

Ayla frowned. 'What do you mean?'

'I mean me. Draguta wants me.'

'So perhaps we are in less danger here, then?' Ayla mused. 'Perhaps I should have stayed behind? Edela needs me.'

Jael turned to her, eyes up on the tree canopy. 'And you helped her from here, so you can again. We just have to stay alert. Focus on getting to Vallsborg. Hopefully, the Iskavallans are on their way, and nothing has happened to them.' She felt a sudden fear for Raymon, knowing that he was inexperienced, nervous, and without many allies. And then there was Getta, who was a nagging problem that would have to be addressed at some point too.

If they survived long enough to have that conversation.

***

Raymon wanted to go back to sleep. He missed his own bed, the comfort and privacy of his chamber. And his mother.

He missed her most of all.

He had dreamed of her again, and her terrified cries were still echoing in his head as he sat on his bed, trying to find the will to start the day. This time he'd seen Getta too, a knife at her throat, but he had run for Ravenna, wanting to save his mother.

Not his wife.

Raymon listened to the creak of his cot bed as he contemplated standing; the sounds of the men outside his tent, preparing for the day. He needed to be outside, organising them, but he could barely make himself move.

Death made him want to hide.

Remembering his mother's. Facing his own.

He dropped his head to his hands as grief bubbled up, tears wet on his palms.

'My lord?'

Raymon was quickly sitting up, rubbing his eyes, hurrying off the bed, shutting it all away. 'One moment.' He waited before the tent flap, trying to breathe. And pushing back his shoulders, he dragged open the flap and strode out into the morning.

***

Bayla wasn't sure how many more goodbyes she could endure. She had the very real sense that soon it would be her lying on a pyre being wept over.

If there was anyone left to mourn her by then.

The bodies of the dead had been brought into the square, awaiting the pyres that Bram and Ulf were organising with haste. The bodies of the dead livestock and horses were another question entirely.

Gant had joined Bram and Ulf to discuss a strategy.

Gus was alive, though his body was shredded, and he remained lying still in his stall while Biddy and Isaura tended to him. Amidst all the injuries, Gant was grateful they'd found time to care for his horse. Isaura had insisted. Her children and servants were safe, and she knew Gus had saved Thorgils and that Thorgils had formed a deep attachment to the horse as a result. She wanted to help.

'Edela says we can't eat them,' Gant announced.

Ulf frowned. 'All that meat going to waste? It needs to be cured. Salted. It will feed us through winter.'

'She's worried those blades were poisoned. Maybe cursed. We have no way of knowing. Draguta killed our livestock because she wants us to suffer. Otherwise, why bother? It would make sense if she'd poisoned the animals to make it even worse.'

Bayla and Berard walked over to join them. Nicolene's pyre was almost ready, and they were debating whether to find the children and give them a chance to say goodbye to their mother. Or perhaps that would only terrorise them further? Neither could think clearly enough to know what the right thing to do was.

'But if we burn all those animals, what will we eat?' Bayla panicked. 'Does she mean to starve us?'

'I would think so,' Ulf frowned. He was still in shock, not understanding how Nicolene had died. The heartbroken wails of her two little sons had stayed with him all morning. He couldn't shake the sound of their unbearable pain. 'The animals killed were mainly the ones we'd eat.'

'Or the useful ones, like the horses,' Bram added, the picture of all those dead and dying horses vivid in his mind.

'We can't eat them,' Berard agreed. 'It's too much of a risk. But maybe we need to harvest everything else now? Everything. Keep it safe somehow. If Draguta tries to spoil our fruit and vegetables, we'll be in an even worse position than we are now.'

Gant nodded. 'We can do that today. Though I'm not sure there's anything we can do to keep it out of Draguta's hands. If creatures like those whisps can crawl through cracks in the floor, how can we keep her out of the fort?'

***

Marcus had been moved into one of the bedchambers. Hanna wondered distractedly if it had been Aleksander's. She hadn't slept, and her thoughts kept wandering into a maze, going around in circles, getting lost.

She was trying not to worry about what was going to happen to her father. He looked so very weak. His face was ashen, his body completely still. She had to keep checking to make sure that he was breathing.

Derwa came in often.

Hanna peered at the healer in the faint light of the lamps as she stooped over her father, trying to read her expressions. Derwa grunted and groaned, belching sometimes, but she didn't speak until she was done, and then she curled a finger in Hanna's direction, motioning her towards the door.

'Your father is weakening,' Derwa began, quickly reaching out to calm Hanna's panic. 'But that is to be expected. He lost a lot of blood, but your fears won't help him get stronger. He must rest to heal. Peace helps. In here it is calm. And you can help him by being calm yourself.'

Hanna didn't look convinced that that was possible, but she nodded.

'I'll bring you something to drink. Some food,' Derwa decided with a yawn, heading for the door. Hanna looked bereft and so alone. She didn't know what else to do for her. 'You just sit there. I won't be long.'

Hanna turned back to her father, picking up his limp hand, Derwa's words sinking in. Calm, she thought to herself, fighting back tears.

Calm.

***

Edela was animated. Optimistic. It was not how she'd expected to feel after the whisps had sliced their way through the fort, but the more she thought about what had happened, the more she realised that they had a way to keep themselves safe.

She tracked down Isaura and Biddy in the stables, horrified by all the dead horses being dragged out; pleased to see that Gus was still hanging on.

Biddy stood up, wiping her bloody hands on her bloody apron. 'You look brighter than I would've expected after last night,' she sighed, staring down at Gus, dark lines of stitches zigzagging across his still, white body. 'We need to get some salves from Entorp. It will stop these wounds festering, and help with the pain.'

Isaura nodded. 'I'll go and find him.' She wiped her own hands and turned to leave the stall.

Edela stopped her. 'Wait, I came to see you both. About something I want to try. A dream walk. Tonight. I want you to help me.'

'A dream walk to who?' Biddy wondered.

'Jael or Ayla, I can't decide. Either way, we need to be ready to do it tonight. Isaura, I want you to drum for me. And Biddy, I think we need a few more herbs. Why don't you come and see what we're running low on.' She rubbed her cold hands together. 'We must act quickly now. Whatever Draguta is planning next, I don't believe she'll delay. Not with Jael and the army on their way to her.'

***

Draguta strode across the square, inhaling the smell of unwashed bodies and the overpowering reek of fear, her sharp eyes on the ragged huddle of Followers who shuffled closer together, away from the Hestian soldiers and their gleaming swords.

Her prisoners.

She ignored the pleading eyes and the outstretched arms of the most pathetic. Those weak few appeared to have abandoned Briggit Halvardar altogether, ready to do her enemy's bidding rather than face another day imprisoned under the burning Hestian sun.

Smiling, Draguta turned to Amma and Evaine who walked with her. They were heading down to the harbour, eager to greet their latest arrivals. 'What do you say, then, ladies? Should we leave them to fry like little eggs? Looking at that sky, I predict the hottest day of the summer so far.' She eyed one Follower who was dripping with sweat, though it was only mid-morning and the sun was some way from its zenith. 'I imagine you'd like to remove that heavy woollen robe, wouldn't you? You must be steaming beneath it.' And turning away with a satisfied smile, Draguta headed for the piers, listening to the pitiful groans rising behind her.

And then a murmur wound its way around the Followers, all eyes fixed on the harbour.

To where Briggit Halvardar had just been helped down onto a pier.

Evaine hadn't been sure how she would feel when she saw Eadmund, but her body shivered with excitement as he walked towards her. She glanced at Amma, feeling so plain beside the overdressed queen, yet Sigmund was in her arms, and hopefully, that would be more appealing to Eadmund than any new dress.

Eadmund's attention was on Draguta as he walked, but he could see that Evaine was there with their son.

That was oddly confusing.

Amma was there too, and he smiled briefly at her before Draguta took sole command of his attention as she approached.

'Eadmund, dear Eadmund,' she sighed, looking from the weary King of Oss to the tiny Queen of Helsabor. 'You have returned! Though it was hardly a test for you, was it?' She considered Briggit with interest, still talking to Eadmund. 'And I have a reward for you as you can see. Your son! Returned to you, at last!'

Eadmund was conscious of how wet he was, though feeling the oppressive heat from the sun, he realised that he wouldn't be for long. Trying to avoid looking at Evaine, he reached for his son, taking him in his arms. Evaine's eyes didn't leave his face, but

Eadmund continued to ignore her as he dropped Sigmund into the crook of his arm, pleased that he'd remembered how to hold him. Happy that he was safe.

'He's missed you,' Evaine murmured. 'We both have.'

Briggit burst out laughing, drawing a look of irritation from Evaine who suddenly noticed how close the queen was standing to Eadmund, and how attractive she was. For a prisoner.

A Follower.

Someone Draguta was hopefully about to kill.

Draguta herself said nothing. She was taking everything in.

Letting it ruminate.

'Hello, Amma,' Eadmund said gently, watching her trying to shrink away.

Amma looked up suddenly. Eadmund was spellbound, she knew, though what that meant she wasn't sure. But there he was, looking at her kindly and he reminded her of Jael and Axl and all that she missed about Andala. Trying not to cry, she smiled. 'Hello, Eadmund.'

Briggit eyed the girl queen impatiently, eager to be taken into the castle which she could see in the distance. The castle, where she would find a chair, a goblet of wine, something to eat, and hopefully, something dry to wear.

Draguta emerged from her daze, clapping her hands. 'We shall head into the castle, get you out of those wet clothes, Eadmund. Perhaps Evaine could go with you, while Amma and I take care of the former Queen of Helsabor.'

Eadmund scowled, not wanting Evaine's company.

Briggit thought about scowling, though she didn't really care who said what about whom. She had made it to Hest, not quite in the way she had foreseen, but now she was here, within reach of Draguta and the Book of Darkness.

And both of them were going to help her bring Raemus back.

CHAPTER TWENTY SEVEN

After the disturbed night, they had taken some time to get going that morning, but once they were on the road again, minds quickly turned to what would be coming next.

Jael had sent Aleksander to ride up front with Axl, hoping he could keep her brother's mind focused. She was trying to stay far away from Karsten by riding with Thorgils and Torstan, though the Dragos' were not far from her thoughts. She kept seeing Nicolene lying on the floor of her cottage, hearing the wailing children as they crawled over her lifeless body. She swallowed, glancing at Thorgils, hoping he could take her mind off Nicolene, but he was talking to Torstan, reminiscing about Oss, telling stories about Eadmund and Eirik. About their fathers. Their friends. Jael wasn't paying attention to anything they were saying, but, eventually, she started to think about Oss too.

About whether she would ever return.

They were riding down a narrow road that cut through a sparse wood. Not Hallow Wood. They wouldn't be near that terrifying maze of trees until they reached Vallsborg, thankfully, but it felt so far away from the bleak and sharp terrain of her island home that she felt wistful.

She smiled sadly, thinking about Eadmund.

Remembering her fight with Ivaar.

Wondering if her husband was practising ways to kill her.

***

Hest's grand hall looked different, Eadmund thought, though he couldn't put his finger on how. He was too tired to even try. Hungry too, he realised, handing Sigmund back to Evaine who smiled sweetly at him, hovering near his elbow, wondering where Tanja was. She patted Sigmund's back as Eadmund followed Draguta to the throne where Jaeger sat, waiting for them all, looking much improved from the last time he had seen him.

'My wife!' Jaeger exclaimed, his hand extended. 'My queen!' And he encouraged a nervous-looking Amma to come closer.

Amma frowned, her eyes instinctively darting to Eadmund who was watching Jaeger, a wary expression on his face, his body tense.

Draguta waited, interested to see how Jaeger would act. He almost looked like himself again, she noted with pleasure, though perhaps still a little glassy-eyed. But he dragged himself out of the throne, slipping Amma's hand through his arm as he approached Briggit.

'My lady,' Jaeger said with a mocking bow. 'You appear in great need of a towel.' And he winked at Draguta who smiled her approval. Snapping his fingers, he ordered a towel brought for Briggit, who did appear soaked to the bone, her shining dark hair plastered to her face, wet on her neck. She was still dressed in her hooded robe from the attack on Angard, and it stunk of sweat and seawater and things she didn't want to remember.

'A towel?' Briggit looked offended. 'After that horrific journey, all you have to offer me is a towel?'

'Be grateful you're still alive to need a towel!' Draguta snarled, shepherding Briggit to the table. 'Not like those charred dogs out there. I've already had to send for a cart. It seems that the lords and ladies of Hest do not enjoy staring at the crispy remains of your Followers as they go about their business.'

Briggit swallowed. 'And what will you do with them? Leave them out there all day? That is your plan? Sunstroke?' she laughed.

'I'm quaking in my boots! What evil will you conjure up next, oh dark mistress?'

Draguta's right eyebrow lifted to a sharp point. Though she prided herself on her sense of humour, she detested being mocked. Especially by a compromised Follower queen in chains. Lunging forward she wrapped a hand around Briggit's neck, lifting her off the ground.

Amma's eyes bulged as she stumbled against Jaeger.

Eadmund's mouth dropped open, wondering what Draguta would do next.

Briggit stayed perfectly calm, though, blinking, waiting for Draguta to release her.

Which, eventually, she did.

'Sunstroke?' Draguta spat, throwing her to the ground. 'No, Briggit Halvardar, that is not what I have in mind at all!' And spinning around, she headed for the table, searching for a goblet of wine.

***

Gant felt sorry for the Dragos'. It was hard not to. Sorry enough to hastily find them the house that Bayla had wanted so much.

It was one of Andala's finest, newly built in wattle and daub, with a thatched roof and two reasonably sized windows. There was a generous storage room at the back stocked with vats of ale and jars of honey; preserved meats and fruit, shelves of fish hooks and tools, and a few spare soapstone lamps too. There were enough beds for the five children. Enough for Berard, Bayla, and Ulf.

There would have even been enough room for Nicolene.

Bayla felt tears coming. She hadn't liked Nicolene. No one had, though Karsten had seemed fond of her at times; attached to her, at least. They had been a family, as Haegen and Irenna had been. And now they were gone, and here she was... mother to all five of her grandchildren.

It was too much. Too horrible to take in. But tears would not help, she knew.

Turning to Gant, Bayla rubbed her eyes. 'Thank you,' she sighed, and she meant it.

He nodded, indicating for Ulf to follow him outside, and, when they were standing away from the door, Gant stopped and turned to him. 'It's bigger, which will please the queen, but it will be harder to keep trouble out. You should block up the windows. Make barriers for the door. Make sure you've got buckets of water nearby at all times. Spears and torches to burn too.' He was suddenly overcome with exhaustion, struggling to think. 'I've a feeling Draguta will try again soon.'

'She seems to be having fun, so I imagine she will.' Ulf turned back to look at the house. It was a fine house, and he would be sharing it with a fine woman. Not something he'd ever imagined for himself... whatever it was. 'I'll get things ready in there, then I'll go and retrieve the children and the servants. Once they're settled, I'll come back to the hall. We need to get the stores sorted before nightfall.'

'We do. Though they're not going to be safe wherever we put them. And as for all the carcasses...' Gant frowned, worrying about Gus. He needed to go and check on him again.

'They're digging an enormous pit out in the valley,' Ulf said. 'Another one.'

'They are. And who knows what else we'll need to fill it with soon.' Gant didn't want to sound so morose, but he was struggling to see how there would be anyone left standing by the time Jael arrived home.

***

'Safe? You're sure?' Biddy's weary eyes sparkled with hope. 'Inside the circle?'

Ontine had not spoken all morning. Not more than a few mumbles to her hovering mother, at least. Eydis was much the same, but Biddy was full of questions, eager to act, not wanting to feel so vulnerable.

'We were not touched inside that circle. The whisps couldn't enter it,' Edela said, leaning towards the flames, her hands numb with cold, though it was another warm day.

The hall was once again ringing with the sounds of pain, shock, and grief, and Edela was struggling to keep a firm hold on her thoughts and not get drawn back into the bleak pit of terror.

She couldn't grieve or fret.

She could only focus on what was coming next.

'The symbol Marcus showed me worked. It worked! I'm sure of it.' Her elation was dampened by the knowledge that Marcus was barely clinging to life now.

'So we make the circle bigger?' Biddy wondered, seeing where Edela was going. 'Big enough to fit more people inside?'

Edela nodded. 'I made a circle of protection using that symbol. Cast by a dreamer. Held by a dreamer. It was not broken. Once Gisila was inside, I sealed it again. The circle was not breached. Every time I saw a whisp approach, it turned away. They couldn't even fly above it.'

'And do you need a dreamer inside the circle?' Ontine wondered, frowning at her mother who was trying to ply her with food she didn't want. 'Or could you have circles everywhere?'

'Circles are powerful,' Edela mused, watching Sybill who stopped fussing over her daughter, her enormous eyes bulging with interest. 'But their power comes from the dreamer who casts it. A dreamer holds a circle. Without the dreamer, there is no power, and the more dreamers, the more powerful the circle becomes.'

'So we could be in a circle with you, and we would be safe, but everyone outside it would be in danger?' Biddy asked, not feeling good about that idea.

'Yes, though we have three dreamers here,' Edela smiled. 'We could make three circles. Three big ones.'

'Or just one,' Eydis suggested shyly, sensing everyone turn to her. 'We could make one around the whole fort.'

Edela's eyes were suddenly wide with possibilities. 'Around the fort? Besiege ourselves, you mean? Lock ourselves in?'

Eydis nodded. 'We wouldn't be able to go out.'

'No, not unless I closed the circle again.'

Sybill finally got Ontine to take a bowl of nuts. She was eating from nerves, nibbling on anything she could find, yet it was almost impossible to get her daughter to eat. 'It sounds as though it would take some time. A circle that big?'

'Oh, I imagine so,' Edela said, quickly on her feet, energised by the idea. 'So we should get moving, then, shouldn't we?'

***

After Draguta had generously provided Briggit with a goblet of her best wine, and a plate of quail eggs and crispbreads, she took her upstairs to the bedchamber she had chosen for her prized prisoner: a large room looking directly over the square.

Jaeger came with them.

Eadmund had excused himself, wanting some dry clothes and a chance to escape Evaine. Amma had run away to the kitchen, out into the garden where she thought she might vomit again.

Briggit was silent, her neck aching from where she'd been hoisted into the air, too furious to speak, and wise enough to keep her mouth shut. Upon entering the bedchamber, all thoughts of Draguta and her vice-like grip left her as she took in the welcome sight of a bed, piled high with soft furs and thickly-woven blankets; plump pillows stuffed to bursting with feathers; new hides covering the flagstones surrounding it. It was not the level of luxury she was used to, and the bed was small, barely big enough to stretch out in, but it did look inviting, and after the deprivations of her time on the ship, she was eager to sink into that mattress.

'We will burn them.'

Briggit shook her head, wondering if Draguta had actually spoken. 'Burn who?'

Draguta had stepped out onto the balcony, Jaeger dragging Briggit behind her. 'I'm sorry?'

'You just said you would burn them. Burn who?'

Draguta laughed, turning her attention to the square. 'All of them, of course!' And she swept her arm across the balcony to where the Followers crouched and lay, some wandering around, trying to find any patch of shade in the cobblestoned square. There were enough guards to create a fence around them, and those guards looked just as miserable as the Followers. Draguta turned to Briggit, enjoying the horror contorting her face. 'Tonight! It shall be the entertainment. I have invited our guests. A feast is being prepared as I speak. The hall will be resplendent with food and wine, music and festivities. And, of course, you will be there. My very special guest of honour!'

Briggit could not shake the confusion she felt. This was not what she'd imagined would happen. This was not what she had seen in her dreams. 'But why would you do that? Kill them? Why bring them all the way to Hest to kill them? Why go to the trouble of attacking us at all?'

Draguta's face was suddenly serious. 'You and your mangy dogs wish to lead us all into a pit of darkness from which there is no return!' She shook with rage. 'No! This is where it ends! Where I end The Following once and for all. You have been like cockroaches all these years. Always creeping around, hiding, multiplying in the shadows. Shaking with delirium for a dead God of Nothing! Impossible to kill! Spreading like a plague! But this will be the end of you once and for all!'

Jaeger was listening with a grin, enjoying the twists and turns on Briggit's mesmerising face. 'But what about the queen?' he wondered. 'What will you do to her?'

Inhaling sharply, Draguta spun back around. 'Briggit?' And she stared into those conniving golden eyes. 'Well, after I make her sweep up all the ash, we shall have a little talk. About the future and whether she'll have any part to play in it.'

***

Though it was hard to feel cheered by anything after the whisp attack, the announcement that Edela may have found a way to keep them safe had roused a small show of enthusiasm and a lot of head-scratching as Gant, Bram, Ulf, Edela and Entorp tried to decide on the best approach to creating the giant dreamer circle.

'It will take some time,' Edela acknowledged. 'It needs to be cast carefully. Accurately. If it isn't, we won't be able to protect ourselves.'

'We'll need to guard the fort carefully too,' Bram decided. 'We can't let anyone out, though many might want to leave. Some aren't handling things well.'

It was true, Edela knew. She didn't blame anyone who wanted to run for their lives, though it would likely not end well for those who left the safety of the fort. Not if Jael couldn't kill Draguta. 'Yes, we will have to be prisoners inside here. For our own good. No one must leave.'

'So we bring in everything we might need,' Gant said. 'Abandon everything else.'

'Including the ships,' Ulf mumbled, not feeling good about that.

'True, but we won't need them if we're dead,' Entorp reminded him. 'This way, we have a chance of living. Edela's right, our only hope is to be locked inside the circle. We thought symbols would keep Draguta out, but they won't. All that work around the walls? Rebuilding the hole? None of it's made any difference. She can creep inside whenever she likes. Wherever she chooses.'

'And she very well may creep in tonight,' Edela warned, her voice low. They were in the hall, talking around the map table, and though there was enough noise to drown out even Mads Skalleson,

Edela was still conscious of not worrying anyone unnecessarily. 'So I must work in here first. Create a circle big enough to fit in as many people as we can. And food. We don't want her spoiling everything we need to sustain ourselves.'

'But if you draw that circle and then leave?' Gant wondered.

'Oh, I can close a circle after I break it. That is easy enough. The girls and I will work in here this morning, preparing for tonight. And then, this afternoon, we'll start outside.'

Gant frowned, thinking about how large the fort was.

How little Edela was.

It was going to take some time.

***

Fyr was back.

Jael was glad. The raven rode on her shoulder, black feathers shimmering a deep inky-blue in the afternoon sun. She was surprisingly light, her claws hooked around Jael's armoured shoulder, swaying in time to Jael who swayed in time to Tig.

In silence.

No one had much to say. Tired eyes kept a close watch on their path ahead. Scouts rode in all directions, checking for any signs of danger, returning regularly to report that there were none.

Which unsettled them further.

Armoured bodies were tense, hot, fidgety; tempers fraying as they rode and marched beneath the beating sun, worrying about what would come for them, but most of all, worrying about Andala.

Axl wanted to talk to his sister, but they had not spoken since Aleksander had slipped back to check on his men.

Jael turned to him. 'You're worrying about Amma, aren't you?'

'Always.' Axl wasn't surprised that Jael could tell. It was all he could think about. 'Have you... seen anything about Hest? Have you... seen Amma?'

'No. I wish I had, but you have to believe that she was captured as a prize. You don't go to all the trouble of organising that just to kill someone.'

'I suppose not.'

'They'll be caring for Amma. For their own reasons, of course. But she'll be safe. And Eadmund's there, isn't he?' Jael didn't know if that was either true or comforting, but she saw her brother's eyes brighten, his head rise, happy to give him something to hold onto.

***

Having changed into dry clothes, Eadmund felt almost refreshed as he headed down the corridor looking for his son. He had no idea where Evaine's chamber was, but he was certain he would hear her before long.

Evaine had a way of making her presence known.

Thinking about Evaine led Eadmund to Morana, and he was knee-deep in a daydream, remembering the bright glow of his mother before he'd thrown the knife. Remembering what Dragmall had said about the shield.

'Eadmund!'

He looked up just before he ran into Amma.

'I thought you saw me coming,' she smiled, hands in front of her dress.

Eadmund's eyes went straight to Amma's stomach. 'I'm sorry, I was dreaming.' He looked up at her face. 'I'm sorry for you too, being Jaeger's wife. I wouldn't wish that on anyone.'

It was nice to hear.

Amma glanced around, lowering her voice. 'Jael is coming for you. Axl will come for me. I... I just hope there is time.'

Eadmund sighed.

Amma stared into his eyes, looking for any sign that he still loved his wife, for if he did it would give her hope. Hope that

Eadmund would protect her in this terrifying place where Draguta could simply lift someone off the ground and strangle them to death.

'Draguta will not be stopped,' Eadmund said firmly. He didn't want to give her any hope.

'She hasn't met Jael yet.' Amma could see the defeat in his eyes, and it worried her. 'Jael will stop her.'

'Amma.' Eadmund grabbed her arm, pulling her out of the way of a train of servants who were struggling down the corridor with armloads of bedding. 'Draguta sees and hears everything. Talking like this won't help you here.'

Amma suddenly felt incensed, wanting him to be different. Needing him to be. 'Then what will? What will help me, because I want to go home, Eadmund. To Andala. To Axl. I can't stay here. I can't!' And sobbing, she dropped her head to her hands, wishing more than anything that she could feel a pair of arms around her. A pair of comforting arms.

And then she did.

'I can't be Jaeger's wife,' Amma sobbed quietly against Eadmund's chest. 'He'll kill me. Somehow, I know he'll kill me!'

And feeling her shudder against him, Eadmund knew that she might be right.

CHAPTER TWENTY EIGHT

Briggit was starting to panic, imprisoned in her chamber, listening to the wails and moans of her distressed Followers expiring in the afternoon sun. Hest was hotter than anywhere she'd experienced, and yet she had the luxury of a ceiling above her head. She hated to think how many would be left standing by the time Draguta had put on her little show. How alone she would become in this wreck of a place.

Her hands were still bound in the iron fetters, and she was becoming irritated by the cumbersome weight of them. She wanted to scratch her back, to itch her nose, to not feel as incapacitated and helpless as she was.

Turning towards the balcony, Briggit thought she heard someone call her name, wondering if it was Sabine or Lillith. It didn't matter now. Those who weren't baking to death would soon meet their end. And though an end in itself wasn't something Followers feared, the idea of dying at Draguta Teros' hands made her want to scream.

That vain, ridiculous ghoul.

She was not about to let herself be killed by Draguta Teros.

Briggit crawled onto the bed, wanting to shove a pillow over her ears, hoping to drown out the voices of those who sought her help. She couldn't help them now, but she had to quickly find a way to help herself.

***

Draguta was trying to stay calm, but she felt as though she was rocking from side to side, unable to keep her balance. Yet she was sitting on the throne, her shoes pressed firmly against the flagstones, her hands gripping the smooth skull armrests.

She didn't know what was happening.

Meena stood before her with an ever-deepening frown. Draguta had opened her mouth to speak, but no words had come out. She wondered for a moment if she was trying to communicate with her mind.

'What are you gaping at?' Draguta barked suddenly, pushing herself upright. 'You could stuff a lemon in that mouth!' And standing up, she stalked towards Meena who jerked backwards. 'I need you to prepare this potion for tonight. It is the same as the one that removed Yorik Elstad and his Followers, but with a time-saving twist. There are so many of them out there. Or there were, last time I looked. I'm sure you remember that potion?' And suddenly feeling like herself again, Draguta eyed Meena, enjoying the spark of terror in her eyes. 'Good. And get it done quickly, girl, for if not, I shall make you drink it too!'

Meena was nodding as she backed away, stumbling into Jaeger who had entered the hall.

He smiled, grabbing her around the waist. 'You should try walking forwards. Might make it easier to see where you're going!'

Draguta frowned, her eyes on his hands which had lingered on Meena's waist. 'And where is your wife?'

Jaeger shrugged. 'No idea.'

'Well, do make sure you spend some time with her, Jaeger. It is not my place to show her around the city, to introduce her to your people. And tonight many will be here, wanting to meet her. As curious as they will be about Briggit and her scum, from what I hear, your lords and ladies are more interested in meeting your wife.'

Jaeger looked bored, but he nodded, thinking about the Book

of Darkness. He felt strong again, but his desire to lay his hands on it had only increased. He was finding it hard to concentrate on anything else. 'I will, of course.'

'Good!' Draguta glared at Meena. 'What are you standing there for? Get into those gardens! And if you see Brill or Ballack, send them to me! No!' And seeing a servant walk away from the flowering centrepiece on the high table she had spent hours deliberating over, Draguta strode towards her. 'That looks like a pile of overgrown weeds! Come back! Immediately!'

Jaeger turned around, grabbing Meena as she tried to leave, his arm around her waist again, ushering her through the entranceway, towards the doors. 'I'll walk with you,' he whispered in her ear. 'Into the gardens. I'm sure we can find something to do that's more exciting than digging in the dirt.' And dropping his hand, he squeezed her buttock, laughing as Meena squeaked.

***

'My belly says food!' Thorgils declared. 'Food and a fire. A few cups of ale too.'

'Mmmm, that would be nice.' Jael hadn't felt her arse in hours, and it was becoming hard to stay as focused as they needed to. The landscape had remained unchanged for some time: mountains to the left, gentle and sloping, dark with shadows as the afternoon dragged on; pastureland to the right, flat and wide, a stream running through it, a thick line of dark-tipped trees in the distance signalling the start of Hallow Wood.

And before it, Vallsborg.

They would be there soon.

Jael had been watching those trees since midday. Fyr had flown off regularly, disappearing into them, returning to her shoulder often.

Nothing seemed amiss.

But now the sun was low in the sky, and they all knew how much trouble Draguta liked to stir up in the dark.

Jael stared at Aleksander as he turned around in his saddle. 'Nearly there?' She hadn't been to Vallsborg in years, and everything suddenly appeared less familiar.

'Nearly there!' Aleksander smiled before turning back around, talking to Axl.

Thorgils sighed, wishing they were already there. His tension was building as quickly as his hunger pains. They were finger-tip close to having made it to Vallsborg without any trouble. That should have made him feel relieved, but he just felt more unsettled. He couldn't stop thinking about Isaura either. About how they were going to stay safe in the fort. If Draguta kept sending creatures to kill them, how much longer could they all hang on?

***

Edela was exhausted, Biddy could tell. She had been rushing around all day, and her cheeks were bright red from the effort. 'Take a moment,' she insisted, almost forcing Edela down onto the nearest bench. 'Sip this tea and just take a moment, Edela. You need some energy for tonight, don't you?'

Edela sighed, impatient to get going. She had completed the dreamer circle inside the hall. It was large, stretching as close to the beds that framed the walls as possible. They had moved most of the tables and benches outside to the square which was almost empty now that the bulk of the catapults had gone. That would leave space inside the hall for more people to sleep on the floor, inside the circle.

She hoped it would keep them safe.

It had to keep them safe.

'I do need energy for tonight, yes,' Edela conceded with a weary groan. 'I do. I've decided to see Jael. I want to see her. I only hope she will be asleep.'

'And that Draguta won't attack them tonight.'

'Mmmm.' Edela sipped the tea, smiling as her body started to relax. 'Thank you, I needed this.' She caught sight of Sybill staring at her from across the hall where she stood talking to Ontine and Derwa. 'She's a strange one, that Sybill,' she whispered. 'I can't tell if she's shy or evasive. What do you think?'

Biddy resisted the urge to turn around. 'Strange? No, I think she's just nervous. Looks like nerves to me. And after last night, who can blame her?'

Edela cleared her mind as Ontine approached, having left her mother behind.

'I don't mean to interrupt,' Ontine said, staring down at Edela.

'Not at all, have a seat,' Edela smiled encouragingly as Biddy slipped away. 'I'm only sitting down for a moment, just to rest these old feet of mine. You look as though you've got something to say. I've been watching you today. Listening to your thoughts.'

Ontine looked surprised. 'You can read people's thoughts?'

Edela frowned. 'Sometimes, yes, but yours are a little hazy, though I get the feeling you have a lot of them. That you're quite confused.'

Ontine sat down with a sigh. 'I am. I see many things, but I'm not sure whether they're real, or just my imagination. I don't want to mislead anyone if all I'm seeing is just something I've made up.'

'It can be confusing at first, I know. But seeing the difference between a real dream and your imagination is easy enough once you learn how to calm down. To listen to your body. It talks to you. When you have a real dream, you tend to get a reaction. Some dreamers shake or shiver. Others feel as though they're falling. Some can't catch their breath, as though they've been running. Your body will talk to you, so you must relax enough to listen.'

'Oh, perhaps I did have a real dream, then, as it felt as though I couldn't breathe. I've felt that way before.'

Edela placed her cup on the table. 'Tell me, then, what did you see?'

***

'I can see you!' Draguta shrieked from the throne, watching Meena creep up the stairs, a basket in her arms. She was wild with irritation. No one and nothing was moving quickly enough for her liking. She had a castle of snails to command.

A castle of utterly useless snails.

Meena shuddered to a stop, almost throwing the basket up the stairs. She turned ever so slowly back to Draguta, her feet remaining on the step, hurrying to clear her mind. Then she blinked, realising that she was never going to know if the potion was working if she didn't test it.

'And you expect me to walk over to you?' Draguta growled, eyebrows sharp. 'Is that what you'd like?'

Meena hurried down the stairs with speed, almost running into the hall, her face as red as her hair, wondering what Draguta had seen.

Dreading the answer.

She tried to swallow.

Draguta's eyes were on the basket. 'Is that everything I require?' Her nose was up, sniffing. 'And Jaeger? Helped you, did he?'

Meena wondered if that was a question that required an answer.

It wasn't.

'My plans for tonight must not be held up by your inability to work with haste. I shall not delay my entertainment because of your slow pace. So hurry along, little mouse, or I shall have Ballack throw you out a window!'

Meena's mouth dropped open, Draguta's sharp tone like a knife at her throat.

She nodded, thoughts of the ring suddenly at the forefront of her mind.

'Well?' Draguta was staring at her. 'What are you waiting for?' And standing up, she pinched Meena's mouth closed and spun her around. 'Go! Now!'

***

Edela had led Ontine to an open door, but Ontine appeared reluctant to walk through it. 'If I can help you, I will,' Edela promised. 'But not unless you tell me what you saw.'

Ontine nodded. 'I saw your granddaughter. Jael.'

Edela felt terror grab her from behind. She froze, knowing that whatever Ontine said next was not going to be good. 'You did?' Her voice broke. 'What about her?'

Ontine could sense Edela's unease. 'I saw her fighting her husband.'

'And?'

'I saw no one else. Just the two of them. She was screaming at him. Trying not to kill him. But he was different.'

'How do you mean?'

'I saw Eadmund Skalleson when he was here, in the fort. My mother pointed him out to me, said who he was, but in my dream he seemed different. Stronger than Jael.'

'Oh.' Edela was surprised. 'That was the feeling you had?'

Ontine nodded. 'He was killing her. I think he did kill her. Someone was laughing. A woman. I couldn't see her. I heard people calling for Jael. I think he killed her.'

Edela's hands were on her legs, and she could feel her body shaking beneath them. 'I see. Well, thank you, Ontine. I am... grateful to know this. It will... help.' She wasn't sure how. 'You did the right thing.' Edela couldn't breathe. 'I must hurry along now and get back to that circle out there.' And she stood, needing air.

Needing to get away from the dreamer who had broken her heart.

***

Jael smiled, not surprised that Raymon wasn't waiting for them in Vallsborg.

'He's paying us back,' Thorgils grinned, his eyes on the big hall they had stopped in front of, sniffing the air to see what was cooking. 'Cheeky little shit.'

'No doubt Getta had some part to play,' Jael said, stretching her back, smiling as the Lady of Vallsborg approached. 'Beryth!'

'My lady,' Beryth smiled, pleased to see the Furycks, though not pleased by the circumstances. 'It's been some time. And now you are a queen, as you were always meant to be.'

'Hello, Beryth.' Aleksander shook his damp hair out of his eyes and smiled. 'Still hanging on?'

'Seems that I am.' Beryth Ulrik was a rotund middle-aged woman with more living children than most – eight by their last count. A woman who'd had the misfortune of losing three husbands, the last of whom had been the Lord of Vallsborg, murdered in his bed by a vengeful lover. Beryth had been attacked too, and the scars could still be seen stretched across her throat in thick pink lines. She had lived to see her husband's murderer put to the sword, and then assume his place on the high seat, from where she had ruled Vallsborg for nearly seven years now.

'Well, I'm glad to hear it,' Jael said, eyeing the hall herself. 'Everything looks bigger. Or perhaps I've shrunk?'

Beryth laughed, her smile bright, blue eyes twinkling. 'The hall's bigger for sure. I always thought it was a little pokey. So now we'll have room for some of you, at least.' Her attention moved to the long trail of horses and wagons and men she could see coming to a stop outside her gates. 'Niel, get out there and help move everyone to where they need to go,' she said to her eldest son who hovered behind her, shyly eyeing the Furycks. 'I've had the livestock moved, so you'll be able to camp out back. We've had a few dry days, but it might be a little boggy.'

'Sounds perfect,' Axl lied, thinking about how exposed they would be, sleeping out in the open fields. 'Hello, Beryth.'

'My lord,' Beryth smiled, bobbing her head. 'Congratulations on your new position. Vallsborg will always be here to provide you with support whenever you may need it.'

'I think you might regret saying that,' Jael said with a lop-sided grin. 'Let's get inside, and we can talk about what we need from you. Fyn, can you see to Tig for me?' And checking that Fyn had heard her, she inclined her head for Aleksander and Axl to follow her inside.

***

Almost happy with the state of her festive-looking hall, Draguta returned to Briggit's chamber, throwing a golden dress on the bed. 'I doubt it will fit, but Evaine is a similar size, though you have much wider hips. Still, I'm sure you'd prefer to greet our guests in something that didn't smell like you'd been sleeping in the latrines.'

Briggit stood by the balcony door, watching the sun sink towards the sea. The plaintive sounds of her Followers had lessened with the diminishing heat of the afternoon. The cart had been creaking back and forth all day, removing those who had not been able to withstand it.

She didn't turn around.

'Is it so hard to accept that you have been defeated?' Draguta wondered, gliding forward, her white silk dress, freshly delivered by the tailor, sliding around her legs. 'It is certainly obvious to me. Can you not hear it? Smell it?'

Briggit turned to her then, and Draguta was surprised by the defeat in her eyes. Those yellow eyes had no fire in them now.

'You will kill them all. For what? Applause? Horror? What is it that you gain by killing my people like that... by burning them alive?'

Draguta couldn't see inside Briggit's mind, which surprised her, though she didn't need to; the anguish Briggit felt was all over her face. 'And what would they have done to me?' she scoffed.

'Kindly let me live? Ha! You wanted my book. Wanted to destroy all of us to bring Raemus back. I saw that. You think I'm the enemy? The villain? You would have killed everyone, Briggit Halvardar! I am merely removing the threat you and your Followers pose to Osterland. To my Dragos'. To me.'

Briggit walked over to the bed, trying not to show how distasteful she found the plain dress Draguta had brought her. 'You want to rule Osterland? That's what you want? To be the queen of everyone? The most powerful woman in the land?'

Draguta laughed. 'Woman? I shall be the Queen of the Gods themselves. Soon they will bend to me, their ruler, more powerful than any creature, living or dead.' She didn't know why she was revealing anything to Briggit, but she felt a need to justify her ambition.

Briggit spun around, her eyes aflame again. 'How? How will you rule all these kingdoms you plan to conquer? By leaving Jaeger Dragos in charge? Ha!'

'I shall have rulers in every kingdom. Those I trust. And yes, Jaeger will be one of them. Of course. He is Dragos born. Our noble bloodline will command this land forever. I will make it so.'

'You will trust mortal men and women? You will watch them? Daily? Watch how they conspire to take more power? To defeat their rivals? To steal land? Isn't that always the way? Power breeding greed? It has been the downfall of kingdoms throughout history.'

Draguta ignored her. 'The Furycks will die. The Vandaals. Those Tuurans still scraping about in the ash of their precious temple. Those who betrayed my family. They will all die. And I will be left only with those loyal to me,' she insisted, hearing a loud howl of pain from outside. She smiled. 'Why is it any of your concern, Briggit dear? Are you worried for me?'

'I don't want you to burn my Followers.' There was no smile in Briggit's eyes as she walked forward, stopping just before Draguta, suddenly conscious of her own smell. 'They could be useful to you. They could help you rule. The dreamers, at least. They see through lies and deceit. They can ferret out disloyalty. They know spellwork. Curses. Pain. They can be your weapons. An army of dreamers at your beck and call.'

Draguta frowned, not expecting that. 'Why?' She felt as though she was rocking again, and glancing around, she moved to sit on a fur-covered bench. 'The Followers' love of Raemus will not be denied, just ask Morana Gallas, who is lying headless in a dark hole. Ask her how eager she was to abandon that God of Nothing!'

Briggit blinked. That was a surprise, though not an unwelcome one. The more she'd thought about it, the more convinced she was that Draguta had sent Morana to Angard to break her circle. She was the weak link, the only possible reason that powerful circle would have faltered. 'Morana was loyal to Raemus until the end,' Briggit continued, 'but my Followers are more malleable. More able to adapt –'

'You should get dressed, Briggit dear,' Draguta cooed, bored with talk of The Following. 'My guests will be here soon. I shall send Eadmund to collect you when it is time. Unless, of course, you'd prefer Jaeger to accompany you down to the hall?'

Briggit dropped her eyes as another loud wail emanated from out on the square, followed by a dull thud. 'Whomever you want,' she mumbled, turning towards the bed.

***

It was nice to sit down, Jael decided, which was an odd thing to say after two days of sitting on Tig, but Beryth's benches were draped with sheepskins, and her tables were lined with cups of the most refreshing mead she had ever drunk.

It was nice to sit down.

Thorgils lifted his cup, winking at her as he threw the frothy mead back in one big gulp, turning to Rork and Karsten who were already assessing what fun they could conjure up to distract themselves from the fact that they were edging closer to the precipice of certain death.

'Jael?'

Jael turned around, noticing Beryth's frown. 'Sorry, I drifted off. We've had a long couple of days.'

Having listened to Jael and Aleksander explain what was happening in Hest, and what had been happening in Andala, Beryth wasn't surprised. She glanced around the hall at her children who were as young as six, as old as twenty-two, anxious for their safety.

'We'll not stay long,' Jael promised, sensing her unease. 'We wouldn't have come if we'd had a choice, but we had to meet the Iskavallans somewhere, and your fort is one of the best defended in Brekka.'

'It is,' Beryth agreed. 'Even more fortified than the last time you were here. But against dragons or whisps, or anything in between?' She shook her head, struggling to comprehend how much danger they were in. 'I'm not sure how we can protect ourselves against such creatures. Seems to me they'll find a way through the thickest walls or the smallest holes.'

Jael didn't want to think about walls.

She forced a smile. 'Lucky for us we have some dreamers on our side. Here, and in Andala. We'll do what we can to keep us safe, don't worry.' She felt worried. More worried than she could remember feeling before.

Away from Andala, unable to help them.

Waiting for night to come.

PART FOUR

Allies

CHAPTER TWENTY NINE

As soon as supper was over, Biddy hurried out of the hall with Ontine and Isaura to prepare the cottage for Edela's dream walk, while Edela went for an actual walk. She had wanted a moment to think on her own, though at the last moment, she had brought Eydis along, deciding that she was old enough to know everything.

It might be the only way to save Jael.

They walked up to the moon-watching bench, where Edela revealed Ontine's dream.

Eydis was quickly dismissive. 'And you believe her?'

Edela sighed. That was not the response she'd been hoping for. Perhaps she'd been wrong to think that Eydis was mature enough to help. 'Why would she lie?'

Eydis felt incensed, ready to go on the attack, but then she slumped back against the bench realising that her dislike of Ontine was colouring everything with a darkness she wasn't sure was real. 'I don't know,' she mumbled. 'But Eadmund wouldn't kill Jael. He wouldn't.'

'He would, Eydis. If he had no choice, he would. Someone who is spellbound can't stop themselves from doing what their mistress requires. They can't. Not unless the spell is broken. Eadmund loved Jael but he couldn't stop himself being with Evaine, could he? Not until we cut that binding rope.'

'So we have to cut the other rope, don't we? Both of us. Together. Before it's too late. Before...'

Edela nodded, relieved that they were no longer talking about

Ontine. 'We do. Somehow, we must find a way to stop Eadmund from killing Jael. Draguta wants that to happen. I feel it very strongly. I cannot find that woman in my dreams, but I can almost feel her in the darkness. Watching.'

'But how can we cut the rope? You couldn't even touch it.'

'No, I couldn't,' Edela remembered. 'But I will dream on it tonight, and look in the book again too.' She squeezed Eydis' hand. 'For all that we fear the force of dark magic, there is great power to be found in love. We will not be defeated by this evil. We won't, Eydis. We won't.'

Eydis could hear the strength in Edela's voice. And the worry. A lot of worry. But they were here, in it now. All of them. There was no turning back.

They had to find answers.

They had to save Eadmund before it was too late.

***

Eadmund was hesitant as he approached Briggit's door. He hadn't enjoyed any of the celebrations he'd endured in Hest – not a single one of them – and this one, Draguta had promised, would be the greatest of all.

He knew what she was planning, and he felt sick at the thought of it, though Briggit and her Followers were no victims. They would hurt and kill them all if released. At least that was what Draguta had said. He sighed, reaching for the door handle, realising that it was nothing to do with him either way. He had done what she requested – conquered Angard, captured the Followers – and now there was only one thing left to do before he'd be allowed to leave for the islands.

Just one more thing, he tried to convince himself.

'You look handsome,' came the familiar voice behind him.

Eadmund spun around with a frown. Evaine confused him.

She was the mother of his son, and as much as he knew that she was a manipulative witch, he couldn't help but see Sigmund when he looked in her eyes. 'You're going downstairs?' Eadmund wondered, noticing how different she looked from the girl who had followed him around on Oss. Evaine had always been beautiful, but now she appeared elegant in a way that he wasn't sure suited her.

'Yes, Draguta insisted I come. Though, I would rather not have to endure it. I'd much rather be at home.'

'Home?' Eadmund was surprised. 'You mean Oss? You aren't really dressed for Oss.'

'This?' Evaine looked down at her new silvery-blue dress, feigning distaste. 'Draguta chose it for me. I imagine she thought I would embarrass her if I wore my own clothes, though it is too much for me. Not my taste at all.'

The torches along the walls burned low and Eadmund was struggling to see Evaine's eyes as she moved her head around, fussing with her hair. 'Well, I hope you enjoy your evening.' And he turned the handle.

Evaine blinked. 'You could walk me downstairs? We could go together?' she suggested, working to keep her voice light. 'It might make it easier for us both.'

Eadmund nodded. 'Yes, alright. I just need to collect the queen first.' And disappearing inside Briggit's chamber, he left a disappointed Evaine staring after him.

Disappointed but hopeful, for Eadmund was still talking to her.

She smiled, fingering her hair, waiting for him to return.

***

Draguta stood on the castle steps, flanked by guards and flaming torches, welcoming her guests as they made their way around the sizzled mess of sun-stricken Followers who lay and sat in the square, enjoying the darkness. She was amused by the horrified faces of the ladies, their noses in the air, frowns digging deep canyons into their sagging faces; the confusion in the eyes of the men whose arms they gripped; merchants she recognised; guildsmen; lords.

'Wait until you see the entertainment I have in store!' she said to one. 'You must try the mead, ' she told another. 'Have you met the queen?' she wondered, nudging Jaeger forward to introduce his wife.

Amma looked perfect. And Jaeger stood powerfully beside her, behaving like a king. Draguta was pleased to see it, her red-lipped smile genuine and wide, but then another cry of pain, followed by a kick from one of the soldiers, and her smile slipped, doubts starting to nag her.

She had made her plans.

Death to the Followers. Death to The Following.

They would all be ash come sunrise.

But Briggit's words were whirling around her mind in a completely unexpected way.

'Welcome!' she exclaimed as another bemused couple mounted the steps. 'Don't you look so... quaint.' And turning her attention away from the Followers, she ushered her guests inside, wanting to see how Meena was coming along with her preparations.

***

Meena was working faster than she had in her life. The stink of Draguta's potions and the stuffiness of her chamber had her gagging as she worked, her sweat-stained dress stuck to her back, her hair limp and plastered across her forehead. She had ground the long list of ingredients for Draguta's ritual into a thick paste, adding it to four enormous bowls of blood that were now waiting by the door. Draguta would come soon, she knew, so she was racing to make another dose of her own potion, just to be sure that it was working. She didn't even want to think about how to get the ring until she knew that it was working.

Gulping, Meena glanced at the door, worried that Draguta would throw it open at any moment, and discover what she was doing. She had to finish chopping the angelica quickly, then she could drink it.

And then a knock on the door had Meena yelping in fright.

***

'I would like to see them,' Briggit muttered as Eadmund led her down the stairs towards the entranceway.

'What? Who?' He had been thinking about Jael. He wasn't really listening.

'My Followers. To say goodbye. Before Draguta kills them.'

Eadmund stopped on the last step, looking down at the tiny queen, oblivious to Evaine who stumbled to a stop behind them. 'Well, that would be up to Draguta. It's nothing to do with me. Or you.'

Annoyance flashed in Briggit's eyes, intensifying as Jaeger approached, almost dragging his wife with him.

'Isn't that Evaine's dress?' Jaeger laughed, looking Briggit over, eyes on the straining bodice of the finely embroidered golden gown. 'I remember it well.'

Evaine glared at Jaeger who glared at Eadmund, daring him to try something.

Eadmund bit his tongue, watching Amma who was wishing she could disappear back to her chamber. Seeing how frightened she looked cooled his anger. He couldn't change what Jaeger had done. And while Draguta wanted Jaeger alive, there was nothing he could do to make him pay.

'I think you're referring to another dress,' Evaine snapped. 'I burned the one you ripped off me. I was never going to wear that again!'

Jaeger looked as though he'd been spat on.

Briggit smiled, though she did not feel happy about anything, except, perhaps, the look on Jaeger's face.

Amma blinked, horrified.

Ignoring them all, Eadmund motioned towards the hall. 'Shouldn't we be in there? With your guests?'

Jaeger clenched a fist, anger bubbling inside him like water, flooding his veins. But, thinking about the book, and how unlikely Draguta was to let him anywhere near it if he laid a hand on her precious Eadmund, he stood aside. 'We should. Come on, let's go and start the festivities!'

***

Meena hurried to stow the bowl of potion under her bed, standing up, trying to still her trembling hands before she opened the door.

To Ballack.

She almost fell over in relief. 'Yes?' she panted.

'Draguta sent me with a trolley,' he mumbled, looking down at the small wooden cart he had taken from the kitchen. 'For the bowls. She said it would not make such a mess.'

Meena frowned. 'But what about the stairs?'

Ballack looked puzzled, his mind not as quick. 'Stairs?'

'How will you get it down the stairs?'

'Don't you worry about that,' he grunted dismissively, wiping a hand across his flat nose. 'Now, hold open the door, so I can come inside.'

Meena nodded, grabbing the door, hoping she had shoved the bowl far enough under the bed for it not to be seen.

***

'We have some time before the dream walk,' Edela yawned. 'You are all welcome to have a little sleep. I can wake you.'

Biddy appeared ready to nod as she caught Edela's yawn, but she shook her head. 'No, no, you look wearier than all of us combined. We'll wait up together, won't we, girls? We don't want to miss out on you seeing Jael.'

Ontine had lost some of her shyness as the dream walk approached, and she was full of questions. 'But will you actually be with her? Jael? I don't understand how it works.'

Edela smiled, wiggling her toes which had gone to sleep. 'We are a version of ourselves in our dreams, aren't we? But we are not really there, not experiencing it in our physical body. So what Jael will see is me, as she imagines me to be. Will I be there? Only in spirit. I will go into a trance. And that trance will send me into the dream realm.'

Ontine looked impressed. 'And how will Jael know it's not just a dream?'

'Well, because it won't be the first time I've visited her. And she's a dreamer. She will know. You've nothing to worry about there. We just need her to be dreaming. That's the key. Nothing will work unless she is asleep.'

***

'You look ready for bed!' Aleksander grinned, knocking his shoulder into Jael's, one eye on Karsten and Thorgils who had their heads together with a couple of Beryth's warriors. He wasn't drunk, but he was enjoying the night; all of them pretending that something wasn't lurking outside the hall doors; pretending the people they loved weren't in danger in Andala.

It felt nice to pretend.

'I don't think so,' Jael said, trying not to yawn. 'I want to go outside. See how Ayla and Astrid are doing in their wagon. Check on the horses.' She frowned. 'It worries me that Draguta went after the animals in Andala. She's playing games. For her it's all a game, I suppose. I just wish she'd go after me. Leave everyone else alone.'

Aleksander's face was suddenly serious, all of his attention on Jael now. 'And if she killed you? She wouldn't be finished, would she? You can't win this fight on your own, Jael. Not against Draguta and the Book of Darkness.' He lowered his voice, leaning close to her ear. 'And that ring. You need us. You need all of us.'

Jael shrugged. 'Maybe I do. Though by the size of that man Karsten's about to fight, I may have one less of you come tomorrow.' She took a sip of mead, feeling strange, as though she was slipping away, removing herself. Taking herself to a place where she could make hard decisions.

Draguta had all of the power for now, and likely till the end.

She thought of her baby, Lyra. Her helpless little baby.

Draguta had all of the power for now.

But that wouldn't keep her safe forever.

***

'Done already?' Draguta was impressed as Meena unloaded the last bowl from Ballack's cart. 'That was a good idea of mine, wasn't it? We do need so much for tonight's fun, and I remember how sloppy you are, Meena Gallas. Like a drunken duck as you waddle behind me, dripping my precious potions all over the ground.' She eyed Ballack sharply before glaring at Meena again. 'I don't want any spilled, do you understand me? Not a drop! I want every last bit of that potion. We are going to cast a circle, you and I. A circle around those Followers. And while my guests are enjoying themselves with their king and queen, we shall be preparing the entertainment!'

Draguta blinked, that odd feeling returning again.

It was unsettling, unfamiliar, as though she was unwell. But quickly dismissing that notion, she straightened her spine and strengthened her voice. 'Hurry up, my girl. I want you right in front of me so I can give you a sharp kick if you walk too slowly!'

***

The Vallsborgian warriors were not playing the game.

Both Karsten and Ivaar had been returned to their bench, bloodied in defeat.

Frustrated.

Jael frowned at them both. 'Hope you can still see to save yourselves when Draguta sends her creatures tonight! I'll be too busy trying to save those not stupid enough to risk an injury!'

'We were hardly fighting,' Karsten grumped, feeling his face. 'A bit of grappling isn't going to get us hurt.'

'Yet you're bleeding all over your tunic, and Ivaar's eye is closing up.'

Neither of them said anything.

Jael stood. 'Well, I only hope most of you are standing in the morning. Or whenever Draguta decides to attack us!' And squeezing past her men, she made her way towards Beryth who was deep in conversation with Rork Arnesson. 'I'll head off now,' she said. 'I want to check on my men. Make sure they've got a good understanding of who's on watch when.'

Beryth nodded, cheeks flushed pink from the warmth of the packed hall, or perhaps, Jael realised with a smile, perhaps it was Rork's company? She looked around as Fyn approached, yawning, before turning back to Beryth. 'Make sure you guard the hall. Lock and guard it all night long. Stay alert. You need to keep your children safe in here.'

That woke Beryth up. She glanced at her eldest daughter, Fritha, a confident young woman who had been serving mead all night long, catching the eye of a few of the Brekkans. Fyn included. 'We will. Don't worry. We'll lock ourselves in tight.'

Jael grabbed Fyn's arm. 'Come on, walk with me. We'll run our eye over the horses. Check the ramparts.'

Fyn nodded eagerly, happy to get away from Karsten and Thorgils who were trying to lure him into a fight.

'See you in the morning!' Jael called out as she headed for the doors. 'Hopefully!'

There were a few jeers, but they quickly faded into low murmurs as their queen slipped away.

Hopefully.

CHAPTER THIRTY

Amma couldn't stop staring at Eadmund who had spent the evening trapped between Evaine and Briggit. Draguta had wanted her prisoner to take centre stage for some reason, so she had placed her at the high table, keeping a close eye on her, enjoying how Briggit had to eat with her hands bound in the iron fetters.

Briggit didn't appear bothered. She held her head up like a queen, ignoring those who peered at her, curious about this woman who had ruled the hidden Kingdom of Helsabor. They had barely heard of her, so quick had her rise been. So sudden her fall.

'Would you like to go and sit on Eadmund's lap?' Jaeger snarled, bending towards Amma, his cracked lips near her ear. 'You seem more interested in him than your own husband tonight.'

His voice was a sharp rebuke, louder than the other voices at the table and Amma sat back, embarrassed.

Eadmund heard him.

As did Draguta, who, after finishing her circle on the square, had taken her place at the high table, waiting while her guests ate their meals. She scowled at Jaeger before turning to her prisoner. 'You did not eat enough, Briggit dear. I do not require food myself, but a mere mortal like you must eat.'

'For what purpose?' Briggit wondered dully. 'So you can set fire to me? Are you hoping to fatten me first, like a suckling pig? Eat me once you're done?'

Draguta laughed. 'You think I want to burn you too?' She

shook her head. 'Oh, Briggit, but I have something much more enjoyable planned for you.' And leaving Briggit to wonder what that might be, she stood, goblet raised. 'Now that you have eaten the finest of meals prepared by the most accomplished of cooks, it is time to head outside for a little night air and some entertainment! Come along, come along! Feel free to bring your goblets with you. I shall have my slaves serving you out there. And we have seating too. It shall be a sight to behold, I promise!'

Briggit felt sick, and reaching her bound hands towards Draguta's dress, she grabbed hold of it. 'Please, don't do this. Please. You are making a mistake. Don't do this!'

Draguta turned to sneer at her, but something in Briggit's eyes made her stop.

And pause.

Her goblet in mid-air.

***

Jael sent Fyn on his way after she found Tig.

It was never good to form an attachment to an animal, she told herself. It was never going to end well, though she couldn't deny that she'd always preferred the company of her horse to that of most people.

Resting her head against Tig's cheek, she stroked his wiry mane. 'Stay safe, my friend,' she whispered. 'And fight. You have to fight. Whatever happens, I will try and save you.' Standing back, Jael held out her hand, watching while he gobbled up an apple she'd taken from the hall.

It was a still night.

Fires glowed around the field, voices murmuring in the distance, the groan of whetstones sharpening blades, the occasional shout. A subdued night.

They were all waiting.

Jael had thought about taking up Beryth's offer of a proper bed in the hall, of stabling Tig with her horses, but she had wanted to be outside the fort with her men. Not bringing trouble to Beryth's door.

'Sleep well, Jael.'

It was Ayla, walking with Bruno. They had not gone into the hall, wanting to take some time alone together as Ayla rummaged through Vallsborg's gardens, seeing what plants she could find that might come in handy. They had eaten in the wagon with Astrid before going for a walk through the field, just the two of them.

'Sleep well.' Jael turned away from Tig, grateful for the bright moonlight which would hopefully remind her exactly where Aleksander had pitched their tent. They would be sharing it. Taking turns keeping watch.

Jael yawned, her shoulders tense, finally ready for bed.

***

Draguta waited while her guests made their way out to the square to take their seats. Meena was hovering near the bottom of the castle steps by the cart, Brill beside her. Both of them waiting to be called upon by Draguta. Ballack too.

But Draguta was busy talking to Briggit Halvardar.

Too busy to notice that they were there.

'I have promised an event. A grand show,' Draguta insisted, hissing as she glared down at Briggit. 'For all the sense your argument may make, I have promised my guests a grand show!'

Briggit could feel a change, a hint of the wind turning, and she raced towards it. 'You should still have one, of course. But as a warning. A threat. You do not need hundreds to die to achieve that aim. And besides, that can be cumbersome, can't it? Having to contend with so many people? But what if you killed a handful. Say... ten?' Her eyes were glowing with fervour now. 'It would still be the spectacle you need, but you would also demonstrate how merciful you are. An admirable quality in a queen, wouldn't you say? Especially one who wished to be beloved by her people.'

Draguta's eyes were up, looking at Meena who dropped hers immediately. 'Mercy? You think those scurrilous Followers deserve mercy?'

Briggit looked indignant. 'Of course. They can be shown a new way. They can become useful tools. To you. Weapons to unleash upon your enemies. Your own army of dreamers, bound to do your bidding.'

Jaeger walked up the steps to see what was holding everything up. Though he was not eager to witness Draguta kill the Followers, he was impatient to get it over with so he could get Meena upstairs. It would stop him from thinking about Amma and what he wanted to do to her. 'Are you ready?' he demanded. 'Draguta?'

Draguta looked from Jaeger to Briggit – pleading, desperate Briggit – and she nodded. 'I am.'

***

'You won't come back.'

Jael spun around, feeling Toothpick in her hand, ready to kill whoever that was. Ronal? She didn't know. It didn't sound like Ronal.

The forest was moonlit, shadows of tall oak trees dwarfing her as she crept across the dewy pine needles, trying to find the owner of that voice. 'I will come for you,' she warned, edging closer.

'And then what?'

Jael could feel her heart banging in her chest as she followed moonbeams towards the sacred grove. Was he hiding in there? By Furia's Tree?

'Jael.'

Jael spun around, coming face to face with her grandmother,

who stood before her wrapped in a dark-red cloak. She froze, not sure what to do. 'Are you dream walking?'

Edela nodded, noticing the sword in her hand. 'And you?'

Jael glanced down at Toothpick. 'I'm busy.'

'Well, not too busy to listen to me, I hope. Sit down, please.'

Jael was about to protest that there was nowhere to sit when she saw that Edela's moon-watching bench was behind her and her grandmother was already waiting on it. 'What's happened?'

'We were attacked by whisps. Those poor creatures. Draguta possessed them somehow, armed them with blades, sent them to kill our livestock. And she succeeded. There is barely a cow, a pig or a chicken that lives. They killed people as well. Nicolene Dragos. Marcus was badly injured. I'm not sure what will happen there. And poor Gus. He is still hanging on, though Gant is beside himself with worry.'

'Oh.'

'But we were safe in my circle. I used a symbol Marcus found in one of the scrolls he rescued from the temple. An ancient symbol the Followers used to protect themselves. Perhaps a symbol Draguta doesn't know about. Here.' And she handed Jael one of her river stones with the dark symbol twirling around its smooth surface. 'It is intricate, I know, so you must work hard to remember it. See it in your mind now, and know that when you wake you will find it again. You must tell Ayla. She knows how to cast a circle using symbols. She can show you.' Edela took a deep breath, feeling her chest tighten. 'If you are able, if you are under attack, you can cast one, and everyone inside it will hopefully remain safe.'

Jael didn't look convinced. 'But you don't know it will work. Not for sure.'

'No, it's a hunch,' Edela admitted, trying to suck in some air, suddenly hot all over. 'More than a hunch, but it may not work or work for long if Draguta has her way. But it is worth trying now.'

Jael gripped her hand. 'What else? There's something else, isn't there?'

Edela nodded. 'Ontine had a dream. She saw Eadmund... kill you.'

Jael stilled in surprise.

'She is not an experienced dreamer. It may not have been a real dream,' Edela added. 'But more likely it was.'

'Kill me?'

'Eydis and I are going to try and help Eadmund. We will try and cut the rope binding him to Draguta.' Edela's ears were buzzing, everything starting to blur.

Jael wasn't listening. 'He really killed me? Eadmund?' She felt mad that she'd let anyone kill her, especially Eadmund. Sad that he was so lost that he'd want to.

'He is not the man you remember. Or even the man we saw in Andala,' Edela croaked. 'You must not let him near you, Jael. Do not fight him. We need time! We will try and help him!'

Jael held on tighter, feeling her grandmother's hand trembling but in another breath, Edela was gone, and she sat on the bench alone, hands empty, staring into the darkness. 'Kill me?' She shook her head, quickly turning it again as that voice called to her.

'You won't come back.'

***

Eadmund could feel Amma squirm as Jaeger returned, joining them as they waited near the guests; none of them wanting to sit down on the benches Draguta had ordered moved out onto the square.

'They're coming, apparently,' Jaeger grumbled under his breath. 'Though I wish Draguta would hurry up. Does anyone really want to watch this? Smell this?' He shuddered, remembering what she had done to Hest's Followers at the Crown of Stones. 'It won't be pleasant.'

'Perhaps we should go back inside?' Amma wondered, glancing back at the open castle doors. 'I don't think I feel very well.'

Evaine was just as eager to head inside. She had no need to see anyone killed for entertainment. Her father's death still haunted her. The shock of it. The smell of it. 'Yes, I should check on Sigmund,' she lied, smiling at Eadmund.

He ignored her, his attention on Draguta as she swept down the steps, Ballack dragging Briggit behind her.

No one was leaving now.

'Oh, what a lovely evening!' Draguta exclaimed, her voice quieting the noisy conversation of her guests who turned to her with expectant faces. 'Not even a breath of wind!' She glared defiantly at Briggit who looked defeated, her broad shoulders curling forward.

'The entertainment will begin shortly!' Draguta promised, indicating for Ballack to release Briggit, before turning to Meena. 'Bring that remaining bowl of potion down here! Hurry now!'

Briggit stumbled, losing her balance, falling against Draguta who grabbed her shoulders, righting her.

'You will show me the dreamers,' she whispered in Briggit's ear.

Briggit froze.

'The rest will die. I will save the dreamers, for I am merciful,' Draguta smiled. 'More merciful than any of those Followers deserve. Perhaps soon they will wish they had died? Now, come along, Briggit, my fallen queen, and show me which of your loyal dogs will die.'

***

After the dream walk, Edela felt like being tucked up in her bed, but she was shuffling back to the hall, down the dark road, away from her cottage, Biddy's arm firmly through hers, both of them following Isaura who held a flaming torch.

Eydis and Ontine were not far behind, the puppies running

beside them, sniffing out the cats who were crawling around in the dark looking for mice.

The whisps hadn't killed any of those.

'And what did she say?' Biddy wondered, her voice low. 'About Eadmund?'

Edela felt as though her head was stuffed with feathers. She couldn't think. 'I... she sounded mad.'

Biddy grabbed Edela as she swayed away from her. 'Mad? Well, I like the sound of that. Sounds like Jael. I'd be mad too if I thought someone had killed me.'

'Especially someone you love.'

'It's very sad,' Biddy sighed, listening to someone crying in the cottage they were passing. 'So sad to think that anyone could be so cruel, so evil that they'd take pleasure in watching others suffer. As if it's a game to be enjoyed. Not people's lives. It makes you wonder if Draguta ever loved anyone. If there's any part of her that's still human.'

'I doubt there is. To do what she has done? I doubt there is.' Thinking about Draguta made Edela pick up her boots. 'We should hurry,' she mumbled. 'To the hall, Biddy. We need to get into that circle!'

***

Draguta was enjoying the game, though she could see that it had dragged on, as some of her guests were now yawning in the distance. 'Hurry along, Briggit dear. Show me the last of your dreamers, and then we will begin!'

Briggit had separated the Followers into two groups, taking most of the dreamers to one side. They would be saved. And as for the rest...

She walked amongst them, hearing their cries, their desperate pleas as they begged her to spare their lives. Stopping before Sabine and Lillith, Briggit's face remained blank as she turned to Draguta. 'These are the last two.'

Draguta peered at the sisters, the flare of flames bright on their terrified faces, neither one knowing where to look. 'Hmmm... I don't think so.' And striding into the middle of the Followers, leaving Briggit behind with one of the castle guards, Draguta aimed straight for a large middle-aged woman and her equally rotund daughter whose sunburned faces suddenly shone with hope. 'You seem to have forgotten these little dumplings!' She curled a finger for Ballack to come forward. 'You will take them to my dreamers. And as for these two...'

Briggit's mouth was suddenly dry. She couldn't even blink. Her face revealed nothing, though her heart was a beating storm in her chest as Draguta walked back to her.

'I'm not sure why you think your symbols can keep me out,' Draguta growled, bending down to her, lips brushing against Briggit's freckled cheek. 'I am showing mercy, yes, but not to you.' And flicking a hand at Ballack, she strode up the steps to Meena. 'Take them to the others!'

'Briggit!' Sabine and Lillith cried in unison, panicked eyes brimming with tears. 'Please! No! Briggit! Please!'

Briggit felt sick as she stared straight ahead, listening to the scrape of Lillith's boots, smelling Sabine's fear, hearing their hysterical cries as they begged for their lives.

She closed her eyes, trying to reach them over the panic of the square as those doomed to die wailed and begged for mercy. 'Stay calm, my loves. Death is not your enemy. It will free you. Stay calm now, for we will be together soon.'

CHAPTER THIRTY ONE

Another night had passed, and everything was starting to feel even harder.

No attack. No attack on Andala that Ayla or Jael had felt. No odd dreams. Well, yes, odd dreams, Jael thought to herself, remembering what Edela had said as she dropped a cloudberry into her bowl, watching it slowly sink into the porridge. She had found Ayla as soon as she'd woken, scratching out her memory of Edela's symbol, hoping she had remembered it correctly. 'We should train this morning. Raymon will likely arrive today.'

Axl turned to his sister. He'd barely slept, and his eyes were almost closed as he considered her with a frown. 'And if he does?'

'Then we'll leave first thing tomorrow. We don't want to delay.'

Aleksander was happy with the sound of that. Pushing away his bowl, he reached his arms over his head, stretching out his legs. 'Training sounds good.'

Ivaar nodded as he made his way to the table, one hand out in front of him.

'For those of us who can see, at least,' Jael frowned, staring at his bruised face. His broken nose was still a swollen mess, and his right eye was completely closed up, yellow and purple and painful looking.

'Mmmm, perhaps I had too much of that mead last night,' he grimaced. 'Though it was good mead.'

Aleksander yawned, thinking much the same. It had felt good to relax, though. The pressure of what was coming was like a pair of hands around his throat. He could feel that they were there, knowing that soon they would start squeezing hard. He blinked, smiling at Beryth who walked in from the kitchen with two bowls in her hands.

'I have figs! Any takers?'

Thorgils, sitting next to Aleksander, leaned forward immediately. 'I'll have some of those. And how about some soft cheese? I do like a bit of soft cheese on my porridge.'

Axl screwed up his face. He had no appetite at all. His thoughts were swirling around his tired head, and his fears were griping in his belly. The longer it took to get to Hest, the more danger Amma would be in. She was smart, he knew, but how could she possibly defend herself against a monster like Jaeger Dragos?

***

Jaeger smiled from his seat at the centre of the high table, watching as Meena slipped down the stairs, no doubt heading for the gardens. Though Amma continued to tempt him with her body, he was content to spend his nights between Meena's accommodating thighs. Draguta had promised that he could touch the book again, and he was determined to stay far away from trouble, eager for that to happen.

He turned to his right where Briggit sat, wearing Evaine's dress, sullen and bound. Trouble. Trouble Draguta didn't need. Jaeger wondered what she was thinking, keeping her alive. Keeping so many of the Followers alive too. All of them dreamers. Yet, it had been bad enough watching her turn the rest of them to ash.

The smell still lingered.

He peered at Briggit who was staring blankly at her plate. Nothing had been touched. 'Feeling bad, are we?'

'About sitting next to you?' Briggit wondered tartly. 'I am. Yes.'

Eadmund laughed. 'Who could blame you?' He looked down at his own plate with some discomfort, staring at the thick slices of roast pork, charred around the edges, reminded of the mess Draguta had made in the square.

The leadup had been so terrifying: the hysterical cries of the condemned; the mix of curiosity and disgust from the watching Hestians; the glee with which Draguta had performed her grand show.

The piles of smouldering ash.

Eadmund could sense Evaine staring at him again. He wondered why Draguta had invited her into the castle. Why she was keeping Evaine around at all.

For him?

He certainly didn't want her company.

'Will you be training today?' Evaine asked sweetly. 'I expect you will, what with the Brekkan army coming our way.'

Eadmund didn't want to think about that. 'I imagine I will. It's something to do.'

'You'll have to improve if you hope to defeat your wife,' Jaeger grinned, biting into a crispbread. 'From what I've seen, you don't stand a chance against her.'

Eadmund took the bait. 'You've no idea what Draguta has planned, so shut your mouth or stuff a sausage in it, so no one has to suffer the sound of your voice!' And pushing back the bench, he smiled at Amma, ignored Evaine and strode out of the hall.

Straight into Draguta.

'Just the man I wanted!' she exclaimed with a triumphant smile, leading Eadmund back into the hall. 'After the success of last night, we must put you to work today. Our enemies are on the march, so it is time to choose our battlefield, and I have the perfect place in mind!' She could see Jaeger's interest pique as he left his breakfast behind to join them at the map table.

'Choose our battlefield?' he wondered, licking his lips. 'You don't want to make them come here?'

'I do not. Not at all. This is no place to stage a momentous battle, is it? There is no room. Too many mountains. Nowhere to view the carnage.' And she bent over the table, murmuring deeply, running a finger around the little lines and shapes that designated where each village and valley, every river and stream lay. 'But here,' she smiled, placing her finger on a clear patch between Saala and the Helsaboran border. 'Here is perfect.'

Jaeger looked over her shoulder. He shrugged. 'It's as good a place as any, though there'll be little advantage for either side. As long as you're confident in what you can do.'

Draguta turned towards him with a raised eyebrow. 'You were in Angard, weren't you, Jaeger? That wasn't some other bleary-eyed, dull-witted king I sent there?'

Jaeger stood back, irritated. 'Well, if you're able to do the same, then we shouldn't have a problem.'

Draguta moved her attention to Eadmund. 'I may not need to. After you kill their leader, I doubt anyone else will have the stomach to face me. Not once they see what I can do.'

Eadmund didn't have the stomach for the conversation. He turned his head away from the happy gleam in her eyes.

Draguta grabbed his arm. 'We will all be there, Eadmund. All of us. But it is you who will get it done. Kill your wife, and I will allow you to return to your son. I will allow you to go back to your little island rock, if that is your wish. But fail me...'

The look in Draguta's eyes was as threatening as a newly sharpened blade and Eadmund found himself nodding, realising that he had no choice.

No choice at all.

***

'That would be your brother, I think,' Ivaar panted, happy to distract Jael from launching another attack on him. He was struggling to breathe through his broken nose, and he couldn't see out of his right eye either.

Jael didn't turn around. 'Why would I care about that?' she wondered, readying her wooden staff, sweat trickling down her brow. Then her face cleared as she got Ivaar's meaning. 'Oh.' And banging the staff onto the ground, she wiped a hand across her brow, turning as Raymon Vandaal rode through Vallsborg's gates, ragged columns of weary-looking Iskavallans traipsing behind him. 'That brother.'

The idea that her father had had another child had still not sunk in.

A secret family.

She didn't feel angry about it now, just constantly surprised by the notion, and – she realised, looking at Raymon as he dismounted – worried. He was so young. In charge of the most turbulent kingdom in the whole of Osterland, with a disloyal wife who had been tangled up in the last botched attempt on his life. 'Hello!' Jael called, striding forward, leaving Ivaar to catch his breath. 'Decided to keep us waiting this time, did you?'

'I did!' Raymon grinned. He stood awkwardly before his sister, neither of them knowing what to do, and Jael not liking most forms of affection anyway.

Axl seemed to have no problem, though, as he joined them, clapping Raymon on the back. 'We were going to leave without you! This afternoon, even.'

Raymon looked mortified, glancing at Jael. 'I'm sorry. It's my fault. I just couldn't organise everyone in time. After what happened in Rissna... it put us all behind. I had to find new leaders. It took some time.'

'He's joking,' Jael said, whacking Axl. 'We weren't leaving without you.'

'Oh.'

Raymon was a serious boy, Jael realised, though he appeared to have aged five years since they had last seen each other. Even the hair on his face looked to have thickened into something resembling a beard.

A man came to join them. He reminded Jael of Gant, which gave her a good feeling.

Raymon introduced him. 'This is Soren. The new head of my army. A man I can trust.' He smiled confidently, though he wasn't entirely sure if that was true. Soren was a man with a solid reputation, but he had thought the same about Tolbert. Memories of Garren Maas' betrayal started to stir, of his mother's death too, and he swallowed, trying to bring himself back to Vallsborg. 'We don't have as many men as I'd imagined, I'm afraid. I've left a solid garrison back at Ollsvik.' He glanced at Soren. 'We thought it was important to protect the fort.'

Jael nodded. 'It is. We've done the same. We'll be picking up warriors as we march down to Hest, don't worry. Word has been sent. Everyone will be required to turn out their best to help us defeat Draguta.'

Raymon looked relieved. 'I wouldn't mind something to eat,' he said, his eyes on the smiling red-cheeked woman who emerged from the hall, a gaggle of children hanging off every limb. She didn't appear to notice them as she bustled forward, her bright eyes fixed on the new arrival.

Another king to accommodate, Beryth sighed. Another army.

Vallsborg would be bursting at the seams for sure.

'How about something to eat, my lords, my lady?' she smiled. 'The kitchen has been busy all morning, so if you're hungry, please do come and get something to eat!'

***

Meena was starving as she waited by the door for Draguta to finish talking to Brill. The breeze from the balcony was almost cool, and she looked longingly towards it, wishing she could stand in that open door. Her eyes drifted to Draguta who lifted her goblet, drinking deeply before setting it down beside her seeing circle.

'What are you staring at?' Draguta grumbled as Meena blinked herself upright. 'Come closer. Come into the light. Hiding in the shadows won't keep your lies from me!'

Meena edged forward, dragging her boots across the flagstones. 'I... I was just thinking that I was hungry. Thirsty. I didn't have anything to eat this morning.'

Draguta stared at her. 'Why? What have you been up to? Skulking around the castle? Slipping in and out of Jaeger's bed?'

Meena forced herself to look in Draguta's eyes. 'He... I don't have a choice.' She thought about Berard, about how much she wished that she was with Berard instead of his violent brother.

Draguta studied her face. 'Well, you will keep Jaeger amused when he requests it. But out of sight. Far out of sight. I have no wish for anyone to see the two of you together.' Try as she might, she couldn't see anything more. Nothing she needed concern herself with, at least, not while there was so much to do. 'This will be your task for today,' she said, handing Meena a folded piece of vellum. 'I shall need to bind the Followers to me. And Briggit too. I only hope the gardens can withstand such a pillage!'

Meena crumpled the vellum into her purse, heading quickly for the door.

'And when you're done with that, I shall be sending you down to the catacombs with Ballack. I'm sure you'll enjoy that little adventure!'

Meena could almost see Draguta's smile growing behind her as she reached a shaking hand towards the door handle.

***

Jael drew a map on the ground to the right of the hall steps. The scratches in the dirt were enough for them to get a sense of the Vale of the Gods and how they could set up their warriors and weapons.

'Will they wait for us, do you think?' Raymon wondered. 'Sit back and defend?'

Seeing how earnest he looked, Jael tried not to laugh. 'No.' Shaking her head, she smiled kindly. 'No, they'll come out and attack us. They've no reason to feel defensive at all. Not with the strengths they have.'

Karsten poked a stick around the marks that indicated the border between Brekka and Hest. 'They won't go through the pass. They'll come out here. The pass is faster but too narrow. If they're bringing siege engines or creatures of some kind...' He paused, frowning at the thought of that. 'They'll come this way. Through the back of the vale. There's a wood there, a stream, leading up to that big tree.' He moved his stick to the other side of the vale. 'This is where we'd come in. No point doing anything else. We can't surprise dreamers.'

Thorgils grinned. 'Who knew you'd come in so handy?' He didn't have a stick, but he did have a cup of exceptionally fine ale, and he raised it to Karsten, getting a half-hearted scowl in return.

'We're talking as though we're going to get there,' Ivaar interrupted, quickly dampening everyone's mood. 'We've got days of marching ahead of us just to make it that far. They could come at us anywhere. Any time.'

No one looked pleased to have received that piece of information.

'Ivaar's right,' Jael said. 'Sometimes you choose where you stand and fight, but often that choice is out of your hands. We'll aim for the vale, but we need to be ready for whatever happens. Whenever it happens. We can't imagine everything Draguta might do, but we can be sure she wants a fight, so we need to be ready to give her one.'

***

The thought of going to war beside Jaeger turned Eadmund's stomach. As an Islander, it didn't make sense to him. Yet, he stood beside the Hestian king as they inspected the vast trove of weapons they'd brought back from Angard. Eadmund had never seen so many arrows in his life. Spears. Axes. Swords and shields. Yet to use them on his wife? His friends?

He could barely bring himself to join in the conversation, but he had to. Jaeger's thoughts did not extend far past his own plans for glory. 'We've a lot of weapons, but what use are they without a solid plan?'

Jaeger snorted. 'After Angard? You really think Draguta is concerned with a plan? You saw what she did to that wall. Seems to me we just turn up and leave the rest to her.' Though that didn't sit right. He wanted to be a victorious king. A king with a reputation for crushing his enemies. Not a man who hid behind a dreamer, killing with magic. And he certainly wasn't going to be content letting some half-dead beast or possessed bird kill Karsten and Berard.

That was personal.

The last of his brothers? That was not a fight he was going to miss.

'They have dreamers,' Eadmund reminded him.

'We have dreamers,' Jaeger laughed. 'Now that Draguta has saved them. And we have the most powerful dreamer of all. Not to mention the Book of Darkness. I hardly think we need to worry about what they'll do. We just have to go along. Shut our mouths and go along, and hope to find our own victories along the way.' He studied Eadmund, sensing his unease. 'Unless, of course, you're planning to lose? Go against Draguta? Save your bitch wife?'

Eadmund was impatient to leave. He wanted to talk to Berger, someone who would be interested in making actual plans. 'I can't. And nor can you. Ever. So smile all you like, Jaeger, but for the rest of your life, you'll never be free. Know that.' And he strode out of the armourer's, heading down the road that led out of the city, towards the Crown of Stones, wondering how long he could walk before he found himself unable to go any further.

Knowing that, eventually, he would have no choice but to turn back.

***

Jael put the combined armies to work, practising how they would respond to an attack. An imaginary attack. Of anything they could think of.

Astrid would keep a fire burning in the wagon. It seemed both impossible and dangerous but in the panic of an attack, fumbling with tinder and trying to set a brazier alight outside in a storm seemed like an impossibility.

They would have water too. Swords, spears, axes. Catapults.

Sea-fire.

And they would have Ayla. She had taken notes from the Book of Aurea, and she was studying them intensely as she sat at a table opposite Bruno, who smiled at her, watching a deep frown of concentration furrow her brow. 'The elderberry cake is good,' he said, pushing a plate towards her. 'Never tried it before, but it tastes good.'

Ayla looked up, puzzled. 'Cake?' She shook her head, her eyes quickly back on the pieces of vellum again. 'I'm just trying to concentrate. I don't want cake.'

Bruno wanted to help. 'Can I do anything? Get you something?'

'I've everything I need,' Ayla muttered, though what she really needed was more time and more useful dreams. 'Though I'm sure I'll remember something I should have thought of when we're under attack.' She smiled, trying to hide her worries from him as she broke off a corner of the cake and popped it in her mouth.

'You'll be fine,' Bruno assured her. 'When the time comes, you'll know what to do.'

'I keep thinking about Briggit Halvardar,' Ayla mused, wanting to change the subject. 'If her mother bought that scroll from you, then Briggit knows things about the prophecy. But what? What does she know about what will happen? What does she know that we don't?'

Bruno smiled at Astrid, who brought over a jug of small ale and a bowl of apples. 'Well, whatever she knows is useless to her now if Draguta has defeated her, wouldn't you say? It didn't help her. She's either a prisoner or dead.' He took the jug and filled a cup, pushing it towards his wife. 'Briggit isn't the enemy we need to worry about now. You saw her defeated, didn't you?'

Ayla frowned, remembering the Briggit Halvardar she had seen in her dreams. That woman was not about to be defeated easily. Those eyes were calculating and clever.

The eyes of a queen who always had a plan.

***

'Tonight I will bind you,' Draguta purred, circling Briggit who stood in the middle of her chamber, shackled hands resting in front of her dress, still thinking about Sabine and Lillith. 'Then you will be mine. You will all be mine. My weapons. My dreamers.'

Briggit wanted to spit on her, but her eyes were suddenly on the knife Draguta had slipped from her belt. She froze, the hairs on the back of her neck rising.

'Did you think you could keep me out, Briggit? That you have some magical protection I cannot penetrate? Ha!' And grabbing the top of Briggit's dress near her right shoulder, she tore it off her arm, revealing a line of faded blue tattoos that ran all the way down to Briggit's elbow. 'That these little scribbles can stop me?'

Briggit jerked away from her, but Draguta moved faster, her hand around Briggit's neck, keeping her steady as she brought her blade up to the tattooed symbols, cutting across them, one after the other, blood beading quickly, trickling down Briggit's arm.

'One more to go!' Draguta smiled, twisting her around again. 'And then I'll go and attend to your friends!'

CHAPTER THIRTY TWO

Edela had worked on the circle around the fort all day. She was making it inside the walls because the outside was a mess of barricades and ditches; sharp stakes threatening any who came close. Though, she thought on reflection, it may have been easier than trying to go around the myriad of structures inside the fort itself. Over the past few years, thanks in part to Lothar's poor management, new buildings had been constructed in a ramshackle manner, cramped together, many of them then crushed by the dragon. It was a real challenge.

Sighing in frustration, and struggling with the nagging pain in her back, Edela straightened up, leaning on her staff. 'Oh, to be ten years younger. Or fifty!'

Biddy smiled, handing her a cup of water. 'Drink this. The sun is hot today.'

'It is. Even my toes are warm!' And taking a quick sip, Edela waved at Gant who was approaching. 'How is poor Gus?' she wondered, noticing how drawn his face was.

'Holding on,' Gant said. 'So far. The salves might be helping. And your quick stitching,' he said to Biddy.

'Anything to help.'

'And how about you, Edela? Are you holding on? Do you want me to bring over a bench?'

'Oh, yes, good idea. I was about to collapse onto the ground in a heap, though that won't get me very far, will it?' she smiled wearily. 'It is taking a lot longer than I'd anticipated. In all my years in this fort, I'd never really considered how big it is.'

Gant grinned. 'Too big is the obvious answer, especially now with the army gone.' He felt odd. Worried about Gisila and Gus, thinking about how to keep the fort safe, but mostly it was hard not being with Jael. With Aleksander and Axl. They needed him, and Gant was struggling to accept that he had made the right decision. He shook his head, trying to focus on what he had stayed behind to do. 'I'll grab you that bench, then I'd better go and find Bram. We've got to bring in as much wood as we can before you finish your circle. I want fires burning in the square day and night. We need to be prepared for whatever's coming. Whenever it comes.'

Edela stared into his weary grey eyes. 'Thank you for staying, Gant. We are all glad for it. Glad you're here. Though I don't doubt that Jael is missing you.'

Gant was surprised, embarrassed even. 'Missing me? Not sure that's true. Knowing Jael, she has everything under control.'

***

Jael frowned, watching the battle of the shield walls from the top rung of the railings she was sitting on. 'Don't break them!' she growled. 'We're not trying to wreck our shields! Just try to push each other back. Push!'

Thorgils grumbled from behind his shield, crouching near the ground. 'What does she think we're doing in here?'

Rork grunted beside him, shunting harder, knocking his Iskavallan opponent over.

'Breach!' Raymon called from beside Jael. 'Fill the breach!' And in a moment another Iskavallan had plugged the hole.

'We need to change it around,' Jael muttered, turning to Aleksander. 'It may come to a battle of shield walls, but likely we'll just need to defend whatever creatures come our way. Especially flying ones.'

'Houses?' Aleksander suggested.

Jael nodded, jumping down from the railings and striding into the boggy stretch of field just before it rose to a generally flat platform. Thankfully, it was dry enough to train on. 'Let's make houses! Iskavallans, you attack my men! Twenty shields along each side! Three rows inside! Shields on top! Karsten! Thorgils! Rork! Ivaar! Take your men! One house each!'

Axl came to join her, reminded of the Battle of Valder's Pass and what it had felt like to be trapped in one of those long shield houses. 'I'll go join in.'

'You should. You need the practice. Aleksander! You and Axl in the same house!' And happy to see that Aleksander was heading for Axl, Jael walked back to Raymon. 'Soren seems useful. Best you get him organised for shield houses when it's your turn. It helps everyone to know who they'll be with so it's not a complete panic. Though I imagine it'll be nothing but panic when we're in the vale.'

Raymon stared at Jael, noticing the smile on her lips, and the hardness in her eyes. 'Jael.' He glanced around nervously, but no one was near them. 'If...' He dropped his head. 'I've never been in a battle. I... if something happens to me...'

Jael felt sorry for him. No father. No experience. No mother either. And Getta for a wife. As impatient and tense as she was feeling, she tried to sound sympathetic. 'I survived my first battle,' she said, turning to her men who had scrambled their shields and spears into an impressive array of defensive houses which the Iskavallans were poised to attack. 'All those men out there survived their first battles too. Some of them are grey-beards. Old enough to have more arm rings than could fit on both arms. Nothing to say you won't survive just because you're inexperienced. We're all inexperienced to begin with.'

'I suppose so. But if I don't survive... I don't know what will happen to my kingdom. To my son. He'll be in danger, won't he?'

'Your son will be in danger whether you live or die, Raymon. It's the nature of that kingdom of yours. But if something happens to you, don't worry. Your son is a Furyck. We're bound to care for him. We'll do everything we can to get him onto the throne when the time comes, I promise.'

Raymon nodded, his attention drawn back to the field as his men started to attack the shield houses. 'Thank you, though I hope it doesn't come to that. I want to go home. Be a real king. Make my fathers proud.'

Jael stared at him, watching his skittish eyes dart around, hoping he was going to get the chance.

***

Briggit's arms ached, blood still leaking from the cuts Draguta had made across her tattoos. Her back was stinging too. She was bubbling with fury as she stood on the balcony, watching the guards grapple with the remaining Followers while Draguta took her knife to them; ripping their filthy robes, cutting through their symbols. Opening them all up to whatever spell she was going to curse them with.

Binding them. Making them hers.

But Draguta was not the only powerful dreamer, Briggit knew, grimacing as she lifted her bound hands up to her left shoulder, wanting to stem the flow of blood.

Draguta was not the only powerful dreamer.

***

Meena and Amma crossed the square, heading for the castle. Amma had been desperate to avoid Jaeger, so she had followed Meena into the winding gardens where she'd enjoyed a pleasant morning helping her gather Draguta's herbs. It had reminded her of Edela's garden and Andala, and she'd felt a lift just thinking about what it would feel like to be home again.

Draguta strode towards them, white dress whipping around her in the warm breeze, eyes aflame. 'I wasn't aware that I had employed you as an assistant, Queen of Hest!' she snapped, peering at them both.

Amma shuddered to a stop just before her. 'I asked to come along. Meena didn't really want me to. But everyone is so busy, I... just wanted to help.'

Draguta was distracted by a sudden panic as one of the Followers tried to escape. She turned around, pleased to see that two of the castle guards had rushed forward to tackle the white-haired old woman. Turning back, she frowned. 'You may help as you see fit, of course. But do realise that you are the queen, not a servant of the queen.' And impatient to finish what she had started, Draguta marched towards the wailing Follower who was still being restrained on the ground. 'Brill!' she barked at her servant who had emerged onto the steps, looking for her mistress. 'Go and get Evaine! She will help Meena with the preparations while Amma goes to find her husband! I am tired of the lot of them. I will bind them all now!'

The sunburned Followers looked like a huddle of beggars with their torn robes; blood drying in red stripes down their arms. Defeated. Tortured. And soon to be helpless.

Meena hurried Amma towards the castle, avoiding the terrified eyes that bulged out of blistered, battered faces, eager to do whatever she could before it was too late.

Before she became as helpless as them.

***

Entorp took some time off from tending to the wounded; from helping to lift the bodies of the dead animals onto carts to be transported out into the valley; from bringing in wood that had been chopped in the forest and carried back into the fort.

Some time to tattoo Ontine.

'Dreamers need to protect themselves,' Edela smiled as Ontine squirmed, lips clamped together in pain, hoping her tattoos would offer some protection. Entorp had been oddly unconfident, noting that the moon was in a particularly weak phase, though Edela had insisted that the moon was not their most pressing concern and that he should just get on with the tattooing.

'Not much longer,' Entorp promised, feeling Ontine shrink away from his needle. 'I'm nearly done.'

Eydis sat nearby, crushing rosemary into a bowl with a heavy pestle. The scent was overpowering, and both the aroma and the grinding sound reminded her of her mother. Which reminded her of her father, her brother, and Jael, and she felt lonely.

Edela peered over her shoulder. 'You're doing a good job there, Eydis. I'll get Biddy to keep an eye on you. I need to head back outside. Back to my circle.'

Biddy was busy nodding, but her attention was elsewhere, watching Bayla Dragos struggling with one of her grandsons who had just thrown a flatbread at her and was now attempting to grab another weapon. 'I will, of course. You go.' And leaving Entorp with Ontine and Eydis, and Edela to head for the doors, she made her way to Bayla who looked ready to cry or scream, or perhaps both at the same time.

'Here,' Biddy said, trying to get Bayla's attention, her hand out. 'Why don't I take the boys? Isaura's children are always looking for new friends. I think they're out the back. Outside the kitchen, in the garden, with Isaura and Branwyn. I'll take them.'

Bayla blinked at Biddy, not even able to form an answer, but she managed to nod her head, happy to have a break from the noise and the bad behaviour. She couldn't even remember how to be a mother, how to make children do what she wanted. If she ever had. Her shoulders slumped, her body and mind aching with weariness. Thoughts of Hest were lost in the past now. She felt defeated.

Her husband gone. Haegen and Irenna dead. Nicolene too.

Berard crippled.

And Jaeger.

Jaeger...

Finding a bench, Bayla sat down as the hum of the hall continued to flow around her, oblivious to everyone, tears flooding her eyes.

***

Meena was going to take some time with her binding potion, so Draguta ordered Jaeger and Eadmund back to the map table to finalise their plans for the vale. She felt a sudden urgency to be prepared, sensing that her enemies were getting closer. 'Jael Furyck will come here,' Draguta mused, her finger on the line that marked the entrance to the Vale of the Gods. 'I have seen it.'

'If she gets that far,' Jaeger grunted, certain that Draguta wasn't going to make it easy for her.

Draguta didn't look up; her eyes were all over the map table, trying to see what was happening, but she couldn't. Her seeing circle had stopped working. She would need to begin again, but she frowned, bothered that she was unable to sense where Jael Furyck was without it. 'I want her to come,' she insisted. 'We want her to come, don't we, Eadmund?'

'Well, no, I don't,' Eadmund admitted, earning himself a sharp-eyed stare from Draguta and a look of surprise from Jaeger. 'I don't want to kill her.' It was no secret. Why pretend otherwise?

'But for me?' Draguta cooed, running a fingernail over his beard, bringing his face towards hers. 'You would kill her for me, wouldn't you, Eadmund?'

Eadmund tried to fight the words that wanted to come out of his mouth. He could almost see his mother watching him, and he pressed his feet down into his boots, determined to fight. But he couldn't. 'Yes. For you, I will.'

'Wonderful!' Draguta turned back to the table. 'Then we will make sure you are waiting for her. That we all will be. They will have delays, I'm sure.' She laughed. 'More than sure. But we will need to leave soon.' And closing her eyes, Draguta tried to find that certainty again, but she couldn't. Opening them, she glared at Jaeger who was looking on eagerly. 'Within days!' And hurrying away from the table with a scowl, she headed for the entranceway, deciding to find out how long Meena was going to be. 'Jaeger, why don't you accompany me? I have a feeling it's time for you to see the book again.'

Jaeger spun around, a hungry gleam in his eyes, following after a quickly disappearing Draguta, leaving Eadmund by the map table.

Eadmund ran a finger over the map, conscious of Jaeger and Draguta talking in the distance as they climbed the stairs.

Jael was out there somewhere.

He saw Andala. Saala. Hallow Wood. He traced his finger down towards the Vale of the Gods, wishing that Jael would come into his dreams.

He wanted to warn her away.

She couldn't come. He swallowed.

She couldn't come.

***

'Useful day,' Karsten mumbled, slopping mead over his moustache. He drained the cup, then tried to squeeze the liquid from his long blonde beard. 'The Iskavallans know a thing or two about shield walls.'

Jael wasn't listening. They were leaving in the morning, and she was trying to think of anything else they needed to organise before she headed off to her tent.

Karsten nudged her. 'You don't agree?'

'I do. It was.'

He laughed. 'Got things on your mind?' It struck him then that he was sitting beside the woman who had taken his eye. The woman he'd wanted to kill ever since. And yet, he had a smile on his face.

Jael didn't. 'Not sure my mind is big enough for how many things I've got on it.'

'Guess that's being a queen. Thinking about everything. Everyone.'

'It is. Being a leader. Leading all of them.' She pointed to the Brekkans, the Islanders, the Alekkans, the Iskavallans, all mixed up together with Beryth's Vallsborgians, enjoying the endless flow of mead in the heaving hall and the promise of the entertainment to come. 'It's a lot to think about.'

Karsten held his cup up to Beryth's rosy-cheeked daughter who was carrying the mead bucket again, eager for a refill. 'Or not. You're a warrior, Jael. More experienced than most. Better than most. Well, better than some.' He winked at her. 'Why not think less, and just trust that you'll know what to do when the time comes? Besides, you're a dreamer. And you've got that raven. You'll get some warning. You'll be ready.' And taking a quick sip of mead, he raised his cup to Thorgils who was standing on the other side of the hall, wedged in between Rork and Torstan. 'Perhaps what you need is a good fight?'

Jael lifted an eyebrow. 'Against you, you mean?'

'Me? No, but Thorgils and I were talking. Rork too. We've an opportunity tonight to make ourselves a little coin.'

'You want me to fight? For you? Ha! Not likely. I'll give you Briggit Halvardar's gold, or you can take your own, but I'm not going to fight for you lot. Nope. Not a chance.' She could see Thorgils approaching, his eyes full of intent, bushy red eyebrows almost meeting in the middle of his face. 'Nothing you can say is going to convince me!' she called, looking for Aleksander and a quick escape.

***

Drips of sweat fell from the tip of Meena's nose as she leaned back and considered the bowls on the table. She was panting with effort, her arm aching from grinding all the caraway seeds into a fine powder. There were so many Followers to bind and such vast quantities needed for the ritual that Meena was worried she was either going to run out of ingredients or time.

Likely both.

She glanced back at the door, but Draguta had still not arrived.

'Why don't you open it?' Evaine wondered, coming in from the balcony where she had been sitting, enjoying the hint of a breeze wafting up from the noisy harbour. 'If you're so desperate to know if Draguta is coming, why not open the door?'

Her cousin was a problem Meena didn't have time for.

Ignoring Evaine, she turned back to the table, trying not to let her eyes linger on the ring box which sat inside one of Draguta's seeing circles. It was all she could think about. All that had been on her mind since she'd opened the chamber door.

It was as though Evaine was reading her thoughts as she flounced over to the table and flicked open the lid on the box.

Meena gasped, her eyes rounding. 'What are you doing?' she hissed.

Evaine ignored her, running a finger over the smooth black stone. 'How plain. Not the sort of ring I would ever choose.'

Meena was frozen to the spot, listening as the door creaked open.

Draguta strode inside in one, two, three quick movements, Brill shuffling behind her. 'And not the sort of ring that would ever choose you, Evaine Gallas!' she snarled, her eyes boring holes into Evaine's as she quickly dropped the lid and stepped back, away from the table. 'How mistaken I was, leaving my precious possessions out in the open for anyone to touch!' And she scooped the ring box into her hand, holding it close to her chest.

Evaine was quickly slouching backwards, her eyes on

Draguta's left hand which was flapping against her leg. 'I... I was curious. I... didn't realise.'

Draguta exhaled loudly, her desire to injure Evaine not as strong as her need to bind the Followers. 'Well, I do hope you teach your son how dangerous curiosity can be, Evaine Gallas. I would hate to have anything happen to him or his mother.' And popping open the lid, her body started to relax. The ring was still there.

Still perfect.

Evaine swallowed, the threat in Draguta's voice like a block of ice slipping down her back. She nodded, dropping her head.

'Good!' And seeing that she had suitably terrified Evaine, Draguta spun around to Meena who had been looking on with an open mouth. 'One day, I will look inside that mouth to find a bird has made a nest!'

Meena quickly pressed her lips together, watching as Draguta turned her attention to the bowls arrayed across the table.

'Well, at least you have made progress here. That is good news... for you.' She glared at Evaine again. 'You will help carry these bowls down to the square and then you may go and tend to your neglected son. Meena will finish here then help me bind the Followers. And I will go and find a new home for my ring. Somewhere far away from your curious fingers!'

Evaine was surprised to be dismissed so abruptly, and though she did not wish to stand out on the square with those smelly dreamers, she needed Draguta to find her useful. More useful than her dolt of a cousin.

Glaring at Meena, she stepped forward to pick up one of the bowls, avoiding Draguta's eyes as she headed for the door.

***

Jael scanned the hall. All eyes were on her. She glowered at Karsten and Thorgils; at Aleksander and Axl.

They were all cheering for her to fight.

And Jael wanted to tell them to go to bed. To put down their cups. To get some sleep. But for many, this would be one of their last nights. Some would never see their homes or families again. And despite knowing that, they had still come to fight. For their homes and families.

And for her.

'Alright,' she grumbled, unbuckling her swordbelt. 'Alright, I'll do it.'

And the cheer nearly took the roof off Beryth's hall.

Aleksander put an arm around her shoulder, but Jael quickly shook him off. 'You think I need you to tell me how to fight?'

'Well, she's not the most polite contender we've ever had,' Thorgils grinned, his eyes on Beryth who was busy organising which Vallsborgian would fight the Queen of Oss. 'Though all that fire might help get us a victory.'

Aleksander couldn't see their logic. 'No one's going to bet against Jael, are they?'

He had a point, Karsten realised, though he'd already decided to. For all that he was no longer looking to rip out Jael's eyes, it wouldn't hurt her to be put on her arse.

Jael frowned. 'You've just cursed me, big mouth.'

Aleksander laughed, his eyes widening as the contender was revealed.

The hall hushed as the tall young woman strode forward, dressed in a tunic and trousers; white-blonde hair tied back in two beaded braids, sleeves rolled up past her elbows. Bare feet. A cut lip.

And then everyone was yelling and cheering, rushing Karsten and Thorgils, waving their coins.

Jael turned to Aleksander. 'Can you tie back my hair?' she muttered, wiping her nose.

Aleksander had had enough cups of mead that his fingers felt like sausages as he quickly tried to pull Jael's dark hair into some sort of braid while Jael eyed her opponent. She was young. Taller than her. Broad shoulders that she pushed back as she walked into the space that had been cleared for the entertainment.

Jael recognised the look in the girl's pale-blue eyes. It mirrored her own.

'Marissa,' she said shortly. 'My name is Marissa, my lady.'

And frowning, Jael walked away from Aleksander, the sound of her boots scuffing the floorboards drowned out by Thorgils' whooping.

She was not prepared to be anyone's entertainment.

CHAPTER THIRTY THREE

Ivaar pushed his way into the front row, squeezing in between Thorgils and Karsten, both of whom looked at him with happy grins.

They'd not been expecting this.

'She's tall!' Ivaar yelled.

The cheering was so raucous that neither man heard him, their eyes quickly back on the action as Marissa and Jael circled one another.

Jael wondered if she should have taken off her boots. She didn't want to hurt the girl with the knife stuck down her sock. And then Marissa was on the floor, grabbing for Jael's ankles, writhing around like a worm, and Jael was hopping and dancing back, catching a wink from Aleksander who looked as though he was enjoying himself.

Marissa jumped back onto her feet, sensing that Jael was faster than she'd anticipated. She quickly launched herself at Jael's middle instead, arms flailing.

Jael was halfway through thinking how amateurish the girl was when she heard Marissa's thoughts, loud like a thundering waterfall. 'I'll gut you, bitch! I will gut you!' And ducking Marissa's long arms, Jael grabbed her around the thighs, knocking her to the ground. 'You want to gut me, do you?' she growled in Marissa's face, working to control her hands. 'Do you?'

'On the ground!' Thorgils clapped Ivaar on the back. 'Jael's on the ground!'

Marissa was slippery, and she wriggled out of Jael's hold, grabbing her wrist, twisting it until Jael was grimacing. Taking control, Marissa rose onto her knees, cracking her elbows against Jael's as she used the length of her long arms to dominate the queen.

Jael was on her knees now too, sliding out her right leg, smacking Marissa's waist. Marissa was taller, her legs longer and she couldn't react as quickly. Jael had spent years fighting men taller than her. Very rarely could they untangle themselves with speed.

But Jael could.

And collapsing backwards, Marissa's hands wrapped around her arms, she brought them both crashing back onto the floorboards again, roaring as she flipped the girl over like a fish.

Fyn and Axl knocked their cups together, cheering for Jael.

Karsten frowned.

Marissa slid out of Jael's hold again, rolling away, grabbing the bottom of her tunic. Twisting it around her hand, she yanked Jael towards her, slamming her knee into the side of Jael's leg. Jael stumbled onto the ground, Marissa flopping onto her back, pushing her down to the floorboards.

Jael growled, cross with herself, though Marissa was no Tarak, and she was quickly rocking from side to side, pushing her over, onto her back, straddling Marissa now, securing those writhing arms again, holding them tight.

Marissa kneed her in the back, and Jael grunted, tipping forward, loosening her grip, giving Marissa enough time to free her right hand, aiming a punch at Jael's jaw. But Jael dropped to the left, grabbing Marissa's hand, bending it backwards, still straddling her, knees digging into Marissa's sides.

Marissa yelped in pain, throwing her head forward.

'Not the headbutt!' Thorgils laughed, but Jael had rolled away to avoid the blow, both women on their feet now. 'Watch out!' he yelled as they came charging towards them, scattering the crowd of mead drinking men and women back to their tables and benches.

Jael ended up banging into Thorgils, who righted her,

whispering hoarsely in her ear. 'Disappointing, Jael. Thought you'd have knocked her senseless by now.'

'I'll knock you senseless if you want,' Jael panted before lunging forward again, listening to the merry din, conscious for one moment of how happy they all were.

***

Amma had left the hall early.

Draguta was still out on the square with Meena, binding the Followers, and Jaeger had taken the opportunity to drink too much wine. It had started to worry her, as had the way he was leering at her, touching her all the time. Eadmund had been distracted, not paying much attention, lost in his own thoughts, and Amma wasn't confident that he'd step in to help her anyway, so she decided to extract herself before it came to that.

She wanted to get to her chamber quickly, hoping to fall into bed and find Axl in a dream, though she had bumped into Evaine who seemed intent on keeping her company.

'It won't be long till the army marches,' Evaine said cheerfully, her eyes on the end of the corridor in the distance. 'And who knows if Jaeger will ever return?'

Amma frowned, wondering what Evaine wanted. 'You're not worried about Eadmund?' That felt strange to say.

'Well, Eadmund doesn't want anything to do with me, so it doesn't matter what I think. But we'll all be happy without Jaeger here, won't we? I'm not sure there's a person in this castle who would welcome his company. Or his return.'

'I don't imagine Draguta will let anything happen to him. He's a Dragos. She wants him to rule the kingdom.'

'Perhaps,' Evaine mused. 'Or perhaps now that you're carrying a Dragos, she may decide that he's more trouble than he's worth? He's hardly the sort of king anyone would miss. And without him, you could be a queen in your own right, couldn't you? Free, like Jael Furyck.'

Amma froze, and Evaine sensed that she'd made a mistake.

'You think Jael is free?' Amma hissed, rounding on her. 'You think she wants to come here? That she's choosing to? You took her husband, and then Draguta did, and then she killed people.' She thought of Runa, still hearing the sound of that blade puncturing her chest. 'A lot of people! Jael is coming because of that. She is coming to make us free!' Amma trembled, realising that she was talking so loudly that Draguta was likely to emerge from her chamber and do something to bind her too. So, ducking her head, she turned and hurried away, leaving an open-mouthed Evaine staring after her.

***

Marissa yanked Jael's hair until it came undone.

That made Jael mad. She hated anyone pulling her hair.

'Grrrr!' she roared, spinning around, slamming her elbow into Marissa's throat. She hadn't wanted to hurt the girl, but she was both an octopus and a leech; Jael couldn't get away from her writhing limbs and her grabbing hands.

'Oooohhhh!' came the cry weaving around the hall.

Jael saw Beryth's shock, Fyn's approval, Aleksander's wary eyes urging her on. Then she heard Gant. 'What are you doing?' he was grumbling in her ear. 'Being nice? We don't fight nice, Jael. Knock the bitch out.'

Jael smiled, watching Marissa stagger, hand at her throat, and she stepped forward, eyes never leaving that furious red face. One step, two, and on the third step, Jael kicked, smacking her boot into Marissa's chest, launching her back into Rork, who grabbed the girl by the arms, pushing her towards Jael, who promptly slid across the floor, kicking Marissa's right ankle out from under her, knocking her to the ground with a bang.

Marissa wasn't done yet, though, and she kicked out with a bare foot, flicking it, trying to unbalance Jael. But Jael jumped over her leg, throwing herself on top of Marissa before she could get up, arms around her throat, legs wrapped around her body.

Squeezing. Just enough.

Marissa slithered around the floorboards, arms and legs flapping, trying to gain some purchase, wanting to knock Jael off her, but Jael kept her arms around her throat, her legs controlling Marissa's body, keeping her pinned to the floorboards.

If Marissa didn't concede the fight soon, she was going to pass out.

Karsten looked on, worried.

'Too late to change your bet!' Thorgils warned him.

Struggling to breathe now, everything going black, Marissa tapped the floorboards with the tip of a reluctant finger.

And Aleksander was cheering, Axl, Fyn, and Raymon with him, as Jael sat down with a thump, brushing hair out of her eyes. She glared at Marissa, who had given her a tougher fight than she'd anticipated, and who now lay there, panting, embarrassed.

Jael stood up, happy to feel like her old self again. She held out a hand, and despite wanting to punch the jubilant queen, Marissa took it. 'Are you coming with us?' Jael wondered, watching the girl's eyes, which lost their anger, brightening quickly.

Marissa looked towards Beryth, who nodded, smiling. 'Yes, my lady, seems that I am.'

***

Amma was happy to leave Evaine behind. Evaine who had stabbed Edela and stolen Eadmund. She was more than happy to leave her behind, but in the very next breath, she wished she hadn't because as she rounded the corner, she could see Jaeger lurking outside her chamber door.

She thought about running in the opposite direction, but he would only catch her, so dropping her head, she started walking towards him.

'I wondered where you were,' Jaeger slurred, eyes on her breasts. 'Taking a tour of the castle, were we?' He tipped forward, reaching a hand to her cheek. 'Or perhaps you were lost?'

Amma glanced down the corridor. It was dark, and they were entirely alone. 'I... I was with Evaine.'

'Evaine?' Jaeger's mind drifted to thoughts of Evaine's naked body lying amongst the bushes. 'Why Evaine?'

Amma swallowed; Jaeger's hand was moving across her collarbone, as though he was examining her, though his eyes didn't leave her face. 'She... is...' Amma ran out of words. 'I don't know. She was speaking to me. Following me.' The words tumbled out quickly now as Jaeger's hand continued its journey, slipping inside the bodice of her dress. She gasped, trying to edge away from him. 'Draguta wouldn't like it!'

Jaeger laughed. 'This?' He leaned in, pressing his lips to hers, pushing himself against her, his tongue inside her mouth. Stepping back, he panted, his body pulsing. 'You think Draguta wouldn't like this? A king and a queen? We are her king and queen, Amma, my love. Of course she'll like it.'

He pushed his hand down far enough to grab a handful of breast, tearing her dress, and Amma grimaced. 'Please.' She was panicking. 'Stop. Please!'

Jaeger leaned back again, noticing the distaste on her face, the fear in her eyes, and he remembered their wedding night: Amma running away with Axl Furyck, leaving him lying on the square in a humiliated heap. And growling, he shoved his hand back down her dress, tearing it some more, squeezing harder, his other hand on the door handle now, yanking it open, pushing Amma inside.

Watching from the end of the corridor, Evaine shuddered, turning away.

***

'I wasn't sure you could tame that wild cat,' Thorgils yawned. 'She seemed to have you worked out easily enough. Still, at least I bet on you, unlike poor Karsten here.'

Jael eyed Karsten. 'You didn't bet on me? You who told me I couldn't lose?'

Aleksander laughed. He was squeezed in between Fyn and Axl. The hall was packed to the gunwales thanks to the Iskavallans, and there wasn't room to move. He wasn't sure when he'd last been able to lift an arm. 'You were being too kind. As usual.'

Now everyone turned to stare at Aleksander, bemused.

Except for Fyn. 'Well, Jael didn't want to hurt her or humiliate her, did you?'

Jael laughed. 'You mean by kicking her in the head?' She shook her own head. 'It was a bit of fun, and no, I didn't want to hurt her. We need her. We need everyone. A leader shouldn't try to injure her warriors before the biggest battle they've ever faced.'

That had heads nodding.

'Still, it was a good show, watching you fight a woman,' Thorgils winked.

'A girl,' Jael reminded him. 'She was just a girl.'

Aleksander had a grin on his face. 'I remember when you were just a girl. You weren't so nice then. Just ask Ronal Killi.' He'd drunk too much, he knew, and he shouldn't have said it. He watched the flash of darkness in Jael's eyes as she turned them to her cup.

'Who's Ronal?' Fyn asked.

'Ronal's ash, so let's not drink to him,' Jael said, looking up, shutting away all thoughts of the past. 'But let's drink to us, for tomorrow we edge closer to destiny!'

Ivaar leaned forward, clanking his cup against hers. 'To destiny!'

'Oh, you think something good's waiting for you now, do you?' Thorgils wondered, eyeing him blearily. 'Thought you were already planning your pyre?'

The mead had made Ivaar merry enough to see some hope, though he doubted that feeling would last. 'Might be. But hopefully, it's one that will send me to Vidar's Hall.' He sat back, thinking about his father, who would no doubt be waiting for him; whether with a fist or an embrace, he didn't know.

Their table was quiet for a moment, though the hall wasn't, and an arm-wrestling bout between Rork and Beryth's eldest son soon caught Thorgils' attention, and he wriggled away from the table, giving the men left on his side a chance to breathe.

'Thought he'd never leave!' Aleksander joked. 'Next time, you're sitting next to him.' He grinned at Jael who was watching Ivaar, thinking about Eadmund.

And Eydis.

Wondering which one of her brothers she would bring back to her.

If any.

***

Amma was scared. She wanted to scream and fight, but the voice in her head told her that Jaeger was a madman who would only be urged on, or so angered by her resistance that he'd get more violent.

But he was hurting her. Laying his weight on her belly.

'The baby!' she panicked, listening to him grunt in her ear. 'The baby!' She squirmed, trying to move him. Trying to move her stomach away from his bony hip, which was digging into her. And then a shooting pain. 'Aarrghh!'

Jaeger pushed himself up, panting, his trousers around his ankles, bile swirling in his mouth. He glared at Amma, trying to focus, to see just one of her. Dishevelled, red-faced, panicking Amma, her torn dress pushed up over her belly, staring at him as though he'd slapped her. 'What?'

Amma froze, not knowing what to do, then another stabbing pain. 'Aarrghh!' And she curled forward, suddenly not worrying about Jaeger at all.

Jaeger could hear the clanging of angry voices in his head taunting him. An explosion of noise. 'What did you do?' he yelled, grabbing Amma's arm, panicking. Images of Elissa lying on the floor, bleeding, flooded his mind.

His dead son too.

'What did you do?' he screamed, dragging Amma off the bed, throwing her onto the floor.

***

Meena had been trudging through the castle looking for Ballack. The remaining Followers were all bound - all one hundred of them - and she felt ready to fall down, wishing she could escape to the coves for a swim. The humidity out on the square, even in the dark had left her dripping. It was the last thing she'd wanted to endure after a day on her knees, scraping in the dirt, blending endless potions.

But now, Draguta was sending her down to the catacombs with Ballack to retrieve all her boxes. Meena didn't even want to imagine how terrifying that place was going to be.

Hearing a scream, her head was up, and she was quickly running down the corridor.

***

Evaine had wandered the castle thinking about Eadmund. As

much as it made sense to go back to her own chamber, she couldn't contain her desire to see him again. She stopped outside his door, wondering if he was inside.

He would not welcome her company, she knew, but perhaps she could invite him to see Sigmund? To come and say goodnight to him?

Eadmund was so fond of his son.

She knocked on the door.

***

Meena pulled open the door, mouth gaping at the sight of Jaeger, trousers around his ankles, towering over Amma who cowered on the floor, sobbing, her face bloody. 'Jaeger, no!' she cried, running forward, trying to grab his arm. 'Stop it! Stop! You must stop!'

Jaeger swung towards Meena, confused and surprised. 'What are you doing here?' His eyes were wild. Deranged.

Meena hadn't seen him that way before. He wasn't there at all.

'No!' She stared at him, trying to get his attention. 'The baby! You don't want to hurt your son, remember?'

But Jaeger lashed out, shaking Meena off with a roar, knocking her to the floor. 'Get out!' he yelled, pointing at the door. 'This is nothing to do with you, Meena!' And he turned back to Amma who had scrambled away, huddling by the wall, blood dripping down her chin, shaking all over.

***

'Evaine,' Eadmund sighed, staring down at her. 'I was about to go to bed.' That wasn't true, but he wanted her to leave.

'Already?'

'I need to get some rest. We'll be leaving on a long march soon.'

Evaine thought quickly. 'Well, that's why I'm here. I thought you might like to come and say goodnight to Sigmund. Spend some time with him before you leave.'

'He's awake?'

'Tanja is always feeding him. I'm sure he is.'

Eadmund wasn't going to play Evaine's games. He would see Sigmund in the morning. He turned suddenly, hearing a shout. 'What was that?'

***

Meena wasn't going to let Jaeger hurt Amma. 'Jaeger, please! What would Draguta say?' She felt her face, her bleeding, aching face, wishing she had a knife as she tried to grab his arm again.

'Draguta?' Jaeger yanked up his trousers, tightening his belt, feeling a pain in his fist. He heard Amma whimpering for the first time, and his anger cooled slightly. 'Draguta?' It was as though the mist had cleared and he could see. 'Where's Draguta?'

Meena swallowed, seeing his eyes change, sharper now. 'In her chamber. With the book.'

'Aarrghh,' Amma groaned.

'We need to get Draguta,' Meena tried. 'Amma needs help!'

'No!' Jaeger yelled, his eyes on fire again. 'No!'

The door swung open, banging against the wall, and Eadmund stood there, taking in the scene, but not for long. 'What the fuck are you doing, Jaeger?' And he ran to Amma, lifting her into his arms, noticing the pain twisting her bleeding face. 'Is it your baby?'

Amma nodded and Eadmund carried her straight out the door past a shellshocked Jaeger.

'Where are you going?' Jaeger ran into the corridor, Meena chasing after him, trying to pull him back.

'Stop!' Meena tried. 'Let him take her. She needs help.'

Jaeger turned back to Meena, ready to scream before slamming his fists into the sides of his head. 'No! No! Fucking no!' And he banged his back against the wall, sliding down to the flagstones. 'No!'

Meena stood there watching him, shaking, wanting to go after Amma, to see if she was alright, but knowing that she couldn't.

Her place was with Jaeger.

Always with Jaeger.

And sighing, she sat down on the floor beside him.

CHAPTER THIRTY FOUR

Jael went to bed with a headache, and no matter how many times she yawned, the pain in her head wouldn't allow her to fall asleep. It was as though someone was banging on the walls of her mind, and she couldn't relax at all.

Eventually, she sat up. 'We should swap. There's no sleep coming for me.'

Aleksander was pleased to hear it. He was struggling to force his eyes open as he sat by the entrance of the tent, keeping watch. 'You're sure?'

Jael nodded, creaking out of her cot bed, wrapping a fur around her shoulders. 'I'm sure.'

Aleksander stood with a yawn. 'I liked watching you fight tonight.'

'Ha! Not sure why I did that.'

'Because you're a good queen. You made everyone happy for a moment. It was nice. Brought us together.'

'Really?' Jael sounded doubtful.

'Maybe.' Aleksander crept over to his bed, stumbling into it with a grateful groan. 'Better than sleeping on the ground,' he mumbled into the pillow. 'We should have thought about travelling like this in Hallow Wood.'

'Not really the sort of place to pitch a tent,' Jael whispered, listening, waiting, and there it was: the first rumble of a snore. She shook her head, smiling, enjoying the pleasure of familiarity. The comfort of certainty. The last moments of peace.

Her shoulders tightened, and Jael put her hand to her head, trying to take her mind off the pain.

***

Draguta was surprised by the bellow outside her door and even more surprised when Brill opened it to see Eadmund hurrying inside, a sobbing Amma in his arms. She had not seen what was happening.

That was a worry.

'Put her there,' she ordered, pointing to the bed, her voice as cold as a wind at sea.

Amma looked terrified, keeping her eyes low, not wanting to see the anger she could hear in Draguta's voice. Then the pain in her belly exploded again, and she couldn't help the moan that escaped her bleeding lips.

Draguta stood by the end of the bed. 'You may go,' she said to Eadmund. 'Return to your chamber. There is nothing for you to do now.' She waited until Eadmund stepped outside, closing the door. 'Oh, Amma, Amma,' Draguta murmured, leaning over and pulling up Amma's dress, placing her ice-cold hands on her belly. 'What am I going to do with you?'

***

Eadmund stood in the corridor, hands shaking by his sides, curling into fists, banging against his legs, his anger rising.

And he thought of Axl, who loved Amma.

And his shoulders tightened into rocks, and still he stayed

there, staring at Draguta's door, listening to Amma crying out in pain. Eventually, he dropped his head to his hands, his shoulders sinking in resignation.

To hurt Jaeger would go against Draguta.

Every part of him wanted to fight against that inescapable fact, but he couldn't.

He couldn't fight it.

He couldn't go against Draguta.

And turning down the corridor, he slowly made his way back to his chamber.

***

Meena helped Jaeger into bed, still trembling, in shock.

Worried about Amma.

Jaeger hadn't spoken in some time. He didn't protest as Meena encouraged him to lie down, dragging a fur over him. It was a cool evening, and she could see that he was shivering as she stood next to the bed, not knowing what to do.

That was a lie.

Shaking her head, she sighed and slipped off her hole-ridden boots, hopping into the bed beside Jaeger, pulling the fur over her too.

***

It was such a still night.

Jael couldn't hear anything but Aleksander's rhythmic snoring, which made her smile. Her headache wasn't going away, so she bent over, rubbing her eyes, pushing her palms against them, willing the pain to stop. And when she looked up again, Fyr was walking towards her. More like hopping, she thought, seeing the way the bird's black feathers glistened as she jumped closer.

Jael frowned, hearing a voice.

She stood up, off her tree stump, moving out into the night, listening. Fyr flew up onto her shoulder, turning her white eye towards Jael's face.

And Jael recognised the voice.

Amma.

Feeling her headache intensify, she stayed perfectly still, closing her eyes.

Listening.

***

Amma couldn't stop sobbing. The terror and shock of Jaeger's attack had receded, and now she was becoming hysterical. 'My baby!' she cried. 'What about my baby? It hurts. It hurts!'

'Your baby,' Draguta growled, her eyes sharp, 'is Jaeger's baby. And you will do well to remember that, Amma Dragos. Jaeger's baby who you must care for. Who you must keep safe. He is the Dragos heir to the throne. A very special child indeed.'

'The baby is alive?'

'Yes, he is. I can feel him. Your son is still in there. Still strong. As I would expect from one with his bloodline.'

Amma felt a wave of relief soothe her taut body. She hadn't imagined that she would feel so attached to something she couldn't see – something she shared with Jaeger – but she did.

Brill came towards her with a wet cloth.

'Brill will tidy you up, and you will sleep here tonight. And in the morning...' Draguta took a deep breath, irritated that Jaeger continued to be such a problem. 'In the morning, we shall think of what to do.'

Amma looked terrified, eyes blinking, shrinking back onto the pillows.

'You will remain here when we leave to meet the Brekkans. It will be a chance to rest, undisturbed. I will find a way to keep Jaeger more... contained by the time we return. Do not worry.'

Amma shivered, nodding, agreeing that it was the best she could hope for. Grateful that Eadmund had come in when he had. Worried about what had happened to poor Meena.

Wishing that Axl was here.

***

Jael decided not to say anything to her brother, though she realised that she needed to become better at hiding things. Axl had to keep his head. So did Karsten. And though Amma still appeared to be very much alive, she could only imagine how her brother would react to hearing about what Jaeger had done to her.

She sat outside the tent for some time, trying to clear her mind, relieved when her headache finally eased. And then Aleksander emerged with a half-asleep grin.

'Go get some sleep, Jael,' he croaked. 'Find us a dream.'

***

It was smoke.

Or fog.

Clouds?

They were thick and heavy, and she couldn't breathe. They were inside her, suffocating her and Edela couldn't breathe.

Bending over, she crumpled to the ground, onto her knees,

desperate for some air.

And then that voice, cackling with laughter.

'You think you'll see me coming, Edela? Ha! But I am already here. I am everywhere!'

Edela jerked awake.

Silence. Snuffling puppies.

A loud snort from someone. Eydis breathing heavily beside her.

Gant was moving around the hall, checking the fires, which crackled loudly, hissing flames as rain dripped down the smoke hole.

Smoke.

Edela needed to cough, but she didn't want to wake anyone up.

The smoke was trapped in her chest. In her throat. Lingering from the dream walk, she knew. But what else?

What had that dream been about?

***

Jael eyed Beryth with a grin, shielding her eyes from the morning sun. 'Looks like Marissa's pride is still intact.'

Beryth nodded. 'She's young enough to be spurred on by defeat. Not like some who'd hide away, afraid to show their faces. Or perhaps that's just the men?' She winked at Rork, who was braiding his beard beside her as he prepared to mount his horse.

'She's a fighter,' Jael admitted. 'A good one.'

'She is, so bring her back to me, please. And my sons.' Beryth's eyes lost their sparkle. 'I may have eight children, but once I had thirteen. And losing any more is not something I could bear.' Her eyes were desperate as they stared into Jael's. 'I'd come if I was any use with a sword, just to keep an eye on the little beggars, but I'm better here, looking after the rest of them.'

'You are. And don't worry, I'll try to keep them safe.'

The weight of how many people she had to keep safe was like an anchor across her shoulders, and Jael felt her body tighten, watching the wives and mothers saying goodbye to their sons and husbands; confused and scared children crying as they clung to legs and hands. There was some excitement too, she could see. The chance to claim glory in victory, to build a reputation, to share in the prizes on offer.

But mostly, everyone appeared anxious.

Thorgils farted as he approached. 'Not sure about that cabbage,' he grumbled, sniffing the air. 'My belly's been griping all night.'

Beryth laughed. 'Well, from what I remember, you had four helpings, so I'm not surprised!' And she turned away to say goodbye to Rork.

'Get away from me!' Jael grimaced, walking far away from Thorgils and his cloud of cabbage-infused gas. 'You're not riding anywhere near me today!'

Thorgils stared after her, his face contorting in discomfort as he farted again.

'Ready?' Raymon asked as Jael approached, leading her horse. He had eaten a big breakfast, thinking it would help him for the ride but he was suddenly regretting it, wondering if he had time to head for the latrines.

'Almost. I've got Aleksander and Karsten checking the wagons. We've taken on more supplies with the Vallsborgians coming along, so I just need to know they're secure.'

Raymon nodded, not really listening. Now that they were heading south, he felt acutely aware of the danger they were in. 'And do you expect an attack? On the way to the vale?'

Jael smiled. He was tall, and his armour was slightly too big for him. It was new and beautifully made, but he still looked like a boy dressing up in his father's clothes. A boy who was not ready for the test he was about to face.

But Raymon Vandaal was a king. And he did not have a choice.

'I do. Always. And so should you. But an attack is an

opportunity. Don't worry, we're ready to fight whatever comes our way.'

Raymon still looked worried as he mounted his fine grey stallion, who skittered in the dirt, tail flicking, big eyes bulging, eager to be gone. Jael's attention moved from her youngest brother to her other brother who strode towards her, twitching in anticipation. This brother she knew. And she knew that Axl was bound as tightly as a trap.

'Where were you?' Jael asked, giving Tig a pat. He was just as tense and impatient, nudging her constantly.

'I couldn't find my boot.'

Jael laughed.

'A dog ran off with it. Found him with it in his mouth.' He shrugged. 'It's a bit wet now.'

'What did you have in your boot?'

'My sock. Can't find that.'

Jael smiled, sticking her own boot into a stirrup. 'Well, come on, now that you're all dressed. We need to get going before people start changing their minds!'

'They'd better not,' Karsten grumbled, striding past with his horse. 'We're going to need every one of these bastards to defeat Draguta.' And he lifted an eyebrow at Rork, who appeared far more interested in kissing Beryth than mounting his horse. 'What are you doing, Rork? Put your tongue back in your mouth and let's get going!'

Jael nudged Tig towards the gates where she would head up to the front of their long line of warriors, horses, and wagons, leaving Rork to peel himself away from Beryth, and Karsten to snarl at everyone he passed.

She took a deep breath, inhaling the crisp morning air, the ripe smell of manure, the sour tang of ale, and something else...

Anticipation.

It was time to head for the vale.

***

Biddy handed Edela a cup of small ale. 'Sure you wouldn't like to sit by the fire for a while? Have a rest? The circle making is going to take a lot out of you today.'

'How is Marcus?' Edela wondered, abruptly changing the subject.

Biddy frowned in surprise. 'Oh. Well, I've just been in to see him. Hanna won't leave his side. Poor girl. She's very upset.'

'I'm sorry to hear that.' Edela handed back the cup, stifling a yawn. She didn't feel like small ale at all. 'I will go and see him soon, but I must keep going with my circle for now. I had a lot of dreams last night. I saw Jael leaving Vallsborg with Raymon Vandaal and his army. They are on their way to meet Draguta.'

Biddy shivered. 'Well, then, you'd better finish that circle. We need to be able to help them, but not if we can't keep ourselves safe first.'

***

Evaine was the only person sitting at the high table when Eadmund came down for breakfast. That both worried and irritated him.

Evaine, though, looked delighted to have his company all to herself.

'I saw Sigmund,' he mumbled, taking a seat beside her, reaching for a slice of bread. 'He looked happy.'

'He's happy you've returned. He missed you.'

'I doubt that's true, Evaine. He's barely seen me before.' Eadmund had decided that he might have to endure her company, but he didn't have to endure her nonsense.

Evaine hid her annoyance by ducking her head, suddenly interested in pushing her dried apricots into a pile. 'Well, he seems happier when you're around, I know that. Whatever you may think, a child needs his father.'

'Unless that father is Jaeger Dragos,' Eadmund muttered, eyes turned to the entranceway, wondering how Amma was. 'No child needs that bastard around.'

Evaine shuddered, never wanting to talk about Jaeger.

'I know what he did to you,' Eadmund said awkwardly, adding some cheese to the bread. 'And I'm sorry for it.'

Evaine sat up straighter, surprised. 'You are? I thought you'd be disgusted with me.'

'Why?' Eadmund folded up the bread and shovelled it into his mouth, reminded of Thorgils and Torstan, who had once had a competition to see how many pieces of bread they could fit inside their mouths at once.

Unsurprisingly, Thorgils had won.

Evaine didn't have an answer. 'I thought... perhaps... it was my fault.' She didn't want to talk about it. 'Though it doesn't matter now.'

The bread was doughy, not quite baked through, and Eadmund was quickly reaching for a cup of buttermilk. 'Not sure that's true since he's now raping his wife. Beating her too.'

'Oh.' Evaine almost felt sorry for Amma as she leaned closer, enjoying the familiar smell of Eadmund, resisting the urge to touch him. 'But what can anyone do while Draguta wants him on the throne? She won't get rid of him, will she, so what can anyone do?'

Eadmund frowned, rubbing a hand across his beard, knowing that the answer was nothing.

Nothing at all.

***

Jaeger rolled over, expecting to touch Meena. He jerked upright, surprised to see Draguta sitting on his bed.

Glaring at him.

He grabbed his head, thundering pain crashing in on both sides.

'You may need this,' Draguta said coldly, handing him a goblet of water.

Jaeger took it silently, afraid to look in her eyes. 'Thank you.'

'Your child lives, and your wife is unharmed, apart from a cut lip, a bruise and, of course, the humiliation of being raped by her husband. And in front of everyone too.' She shook her head, her body rigid. 'A man like you? A king? Handsome. Young. Powerful. Why should you feel the need to force yourself on every woman you see?' And standing, Draguta strode to the window, inhaling the strong odour of wine. 'It is unacceptable, Jaeger!' she snapped, spinning around. 'I endure you as I see no alternative to you, but I shall not endure you much longer!' Her eyes narrowed to slits as she considered him. 'You may no longer touch the book or your wife. Do what you wish to Meena Gallas, for she is nothing, but you will not lay your hands on the Queen of Hest. Not while she carries your son. Do you understand me?'

Jaeger could only nod, relieved that he had not killed either Amma or his unborn son. He couldn't even remember what had happened, though Meena's and Amma's screams were suddenly ringing loud in his ears. 'I do.'

'Good, then dress quickly and head downstairs for breakfast. Eadmund will be there, I'm sure, and I shall retrieve Briggit on the way.'

Jaeger wanted to groan. The splitting pain in his head was so intense that he was working hard just to keep his eyes open. He spilled the water on the fur, not noticing. 'Briggit? Why Briggit?'

Draguta smiled for the first time all morning. 'Oh yes, you were far too busy ranting and raving and beating women last night to hear about what I was doing, weren't you?' she purred. 'Briggit Halvardar is all mine! Briggit and the Followers. They are my army now. My army of dreamers. Jael Furyck will not know what hit her. She is bringing a dreamer with her, you know. Two dreamers against one hundred. Ha! Never in my long life have I encountered a more arrogant creature. Thinking she can come for me? With men and boys? A few manly women? Two dreamers and some jars of fire liquid? Ha!' And gliding towards the door, Draguta turned back to Jaeger, her smile gone. 'What are you waiting for? Get dressed now!'

CHAPTER THIRTY FIVE

Jael could see Hallow Wood looming on their right, but though it would have saved time to cut through it, the tangle of trees would trap their wagons and catapults, and no doubt end up terrifying their armies. And after her recent experience of that wood, she wouldn't have blamed them. She shuddered, remembering the decomposing dragur crawling out of their leafy graves, stone-like fists trying to kill them.

'Rain's coming,' Aleksander mumbled, chewing on a hard biscuit.

'You'd think the gods would be on our side,' Jael frowned, not looking forward to a soggy journey. 'Clear skies and warm air, thank you!' she called out, eyes on the gathering clouds.

'Where's Fyr?'

'No idea. She comes and goes. Keeping an eye on everything, I hope.'

To their left, flat pasture and boggy lowland stretched to a low ridge. And beyond that ridge?

Aleksander's body was tense, Jael could feel it. She could almost hear his fears as they tumbled around his head. He was worried. About her mostly. 'What will you do when we get back?' she wondered, trying to relax him.

'Back?' Aleksander was surprised by the question. 'I hadn't thought about it.'

'You should,' Jael said. 'Think about it. We can't act as though this is it. That we won't return. We should make plans. Think about what will come next. With Draguta dead and the Book of Darkness destroyed, we'll be free. We should make plans.' She was telling herself as much as him. 'Destiny can be what we make it, can't it?'

Aleksander watched Fyr flying towards them, black wings glistening as she aimed for Jael. He smiled. 'With the gods on our side, why not? Let's make some plans!'

***

Briggit had no desire to get out of bed. She lay on her back, eyes on the ceiling, listening as the sounds of hammering started down on the piers.

She was unhappy. Angry. Wanting to scream.

Her arms ached where Draguta had cut her; tiny little cuts down both arms. They stung, and she grimaced for a moment, rubbing her feet together.

Her bare feet.

She smiled.

Her feet were small and delicate, much like her.

The perfect place to hide the rest of her tattoos.

Her Followers were lost now. They were Draguta's.

But as for her...

***

Meena was happy to see Amma.

'Are you alright?' she asked quietly, edging into Draguta's chamber. Draguta wasn't there, but Ballack had let her in. He was guarding the door, keeping Jaeger far away.

Meena thought he looked able to handle him.

Amma nodded, pleased to see Meena but not pleased to see the mess Jaeger had made of her friend's face. 'I'm so sorry!' she exclaimed, sitting up, wriggling forward.

'You should stay there, shouldn't you?' Meena panicked. 'The baby?'

Amma sighed, easing herself back onto the pillows. 'I should, but your face? It's all my fault!'

Meena sat down on the bed. 'That's what it isn't, I promise you. Jaeger was wild. The book does that to him. It stops him seeing clearly. He can't control himself. When something gets into his head... he, he can't stop.'

'But what can I do?'

'Stay away from him.' Meena lowered her voice, knowing that Ballack was just outside. 'Go back to your chamber when you can. Lock the door.'

Amma looked terrified. 'And will you go with Draguta when she leaves?'

Meena could hear the worry in her voice. 'Yes, but so will Jaeger. You'll be safe here with him gone.'

'And you?'

Meena had not taken her tea in some time. She wanted her dreams to come now. Finally, she felt strong enough to face them. And what her dreams had revealed was darkness. Not the darkness when you closed your eyes, but the darkness that lived in the depths of your soul. A hidden, depraved, crushing darkness that sought to consume all light and life. 'I will fight,' she said simply, dropping her eyes to her chapped hands which she clamped together in her lap. 'When the time comes, I will fight.'

***

Briggit was much changed, and Draguta was relieved to see it as she ran her eye over the tiny queen who stood silently beside her, next to the map table.

Draguta had been feeling oddly unsettled since Jaeger's attack on Amma. It had been some time since she'd had a dream. And not having had any warning about Jaeger's attack on his wife disturbed her. But, she supposed, she had been busy working her binding spell on the Followers at the time. Even a woman as powerful as she was could not possibly see everything that was occurring all at once. Still, she reached for the goblet Brill offered her with a desperation to calm her fractious mood. And turning to stare at Jaeger, the main reason for her irritation, she dared him to cause any more trouble.

But Jaeger was too busy watching Briggit, who appeared quite changed from the spitting, snarling queen he'd captured in Angard. She stood silently by Draguta, red marks on her wrists where the fetters had been. Jaeger frowned, not convinced that Draguta should have freed her at all. Eadmund appeared to be thinking the same thing, for when he wasn't glaring at Jaeger, he was eyeing Briggit with suspicion.

'We will get to work quickly,' Draguta announced, her bloody symbols glowing around the table, revealing exactly what she needed to see. 'They may be bringing an enormous army to us, but I'm sure we can trim it before it arrives!'

Eadmund's attention moved to Draguta, his discomfort growing. 'We need to decide when and how we're going to get to this vale. If they're already marching, I can't think we'll have long. Not if you want to stop them there. If you want to fight them on your own terms.'

'No, we won't have long,' Draguta agreed. 'But never fear, I'm sure Briggit and I can do something to delay them. What do you think?' And turning to her right, she watched those golden eyes spark into life for the first time all morning.

***

Bram and Ulf had been organising everyone in the fort to do their part: chopping wood; harvesting what was left of their summer crops; stripping the ships of everything they could use to protect the fort; foraging for berries, mushrooms, and plants. They had groups out hunting, hoping to find an elk, rabbits, deer, boar, wild pigs. Anything that would help sustain them throughout the summer and the coming winter.

And now they had come together with Gant to prepare a solid plan of defense.

'Anyone who stays up there is risking their life,' Gant began. They were walking outside the fort in the drizzle, staring up at the ramparts, watching the warriors on the wall hunching their shoulders, eyes on the valley in the distance. 'They'll be outside Edela's circle, so we'll need volunteers, those who don't have families. When the time comes, they'll need to ring the signal bells.' He frowned. 'The dreamers will be busy, perhaps too busy to open and close the circle. They may not make it inside.'

Ulf nodded. 'If even one person breaks it, we're all in danger.'

'Mmmm, I'll have to think about that. Talk to Edela. But until then, Bram, seek out volunteers. If you need help finding any, let me know.'

Bram ran a hand over his bushy beard, realising that he was no longer one of those men. He had no plans to volunteer. He needed to be waiting when Fyn returned. And he stopped his mind from wandering, not wanting to go any further. 'Everything we need must be inside the circle come dark.'

'Edela won't be done,' Ulf warned. 'Poor woman. It's a weight to carry on her own. And at her age too.'

Gant grinned. 'Well, I'm not sure there are many stronger than Edela Saeveld. She's survived a lot lately, and I've got faith that she's going to keep us safe in here,' he said, strengthening his voice. He believed in Edela, just as he believed in Jael. They were made of the same blood.

And that blood was iron-strong.

***

'I just can't do it!' Edela wanted to fall on her face. She was on her knees, and the desire to flop down onto the ground was suddenly strong.

Eydis and Ontine were by her side.

'You can, Edela,' Eydis promised, wishing Biddy was there to offer some support. 'Perhaps you need a rest? Some sleep might help?'

'And a change of clothes,' Ontine suggested. 'You're very wet.' She too glanced around, looking for Biddy.

Edela sighed, sitting back on her heels. 'Oh, girls, I am simply old. And weary. But this circle must be finished by me. If the rain doesn't wash it all away.' It was just a light drizzle, though, and Edela could see the sky was lightening rapidly. 'Perhaps a bite to eat would help? I did see Branwyn wandering around with a tray of something. You could find her for me, Ontine? And, Eydis, I wouldn't mind my other cloak. Perhaps you could see if Biddy would fetch it?'

The girls nodded, standing up, Ontine reaching out a hand. 'Here, you might need to stand for a while. Stretch your legs?'

Edela shook her head, staring up at her. 'Thank you, but no. That will not get this circle drawn. You hurry along now, and I'll get myself in order. Talk like this isn't going to get me anywhere today!'

Ontine watched Eydis who was turning around, trying to get her bearings. 'I think Biddy went to the hall,' she said kindly, wondering if she should touch Eydis and point her in the right direction. 'Perhaps we could walk together?'

Eydis tensed all over, immediately wanting to refuse the offer, but she could hear how friendly Ontine was trying to be, and remembering her talk with Edela, she nodded. 'Yes, alright.'

Edela looked around in surprise, smiling. 'Good girls, now off you go and leave me to it. Perhaps something hot to drink would be nice!' she called after them. The smoke was still tickling her throat, reminding her of her dream. And shaking her head, realising that her thoughts were drifting like a cloud across a wind-swept sky, she took her knife, and pushed it into the earth, continuing the circle.

***

The Followers were still being corralled on the square, though Draguta had insisted they be given water and shade. Some food too. She didn't want her army of dreamers to perish before she could deploy them. 'They do not look much,' she sneered, eyeing the tattered black-robed group of women. 'Not worthy of assisting me, at least.'

Briggit was walking beside her, in front of Eadmund and Jaeger who followed some distance behind them. 'What you did demoralised them. Not knowing if they would live or die? Watching everyone collapse around them? They need food. They need to bathe. Somewhere to sleep. Some comfort and certainty.'

'How very charitable you are!' Draguta laughed, turning to her. 'I had not picked you for that sort of queen at all. You look like the type who enjoys a little torture. A little depravity.' Briggit eyed Draguta with a look she couldn't read, saying nothing. 'Though you are not wrong. One cannot expect beaten dogs to do anything other than want to kill their torturer. So, yes, I shall see that they are taken care of, never fear. And besides, we do not wish to look like a gaggle of beggars standing before our enemy, do we?'

'Why let them stand before you at all? After what you did in Angard? A woman that powerful should not even need to send an army. Why use men when you have the Book of Darkness?'

Briggit's eyes were sharp with urgency, Draguta could see.

It was both encouraging and disconcerting. Briggit was powerful, but her place was not to lead. And she would need to realise that quickly. 'How sweet you are to try and help me,

Briggit dear. Though what I intend to do is not your concern.' And snapping her fingers at Brill who lurked further back, she watched as her morose servant hurried forward. 'And how is Amma this morning?'

Eadmund's eyes were immediately on Jaeger, who jutted out his chin, determined to deflect any blame before it arrived.

'She is well. Meena is with her. Sitha is on her way to tend to them both.'

'Both?' Draguta spat. 'That woman needn't concern herself with Meena Gallas, you can tell her that. A few bruises will hardly matter on that face. Get back upstairs, then send Meena down to me. I have work for her to do!'

***

There was a lot of sympathy in Sitha's eyes as she laid her hands on Amma's rounded belly. 'I am no dreamer,' she said, 'but I've felt my way around a lot of pregnant women, and you seem fine. I'll apply a salve to your lips and bruises, then I'll look at you, Meena.'

Meena's eyes were on Draguta's tables, disappointed to see that the ring box hadn't returned. She sighed. 'Me?' And spinning around, she was suddenly aware that her face was aching, her head was pounding, and her throat was tight with fear. She shook her head. 'No, Draguta would not like it. I must go. She will need me.' Meena stood up straighter, surprised to realise that she knew that for certain.

Amma looked disappointed. 'Will you come back? I don't want to be stuck in here all day alone. Not if Draguta returns.' She glanced at the door, not wanting it to open.

'I don't know. But if I can, I will. Or perhaps Brill will come and keep you company?'

'They were in the square,' Sitha mumbled, heading for her basket. 'Draguta and that Halvardar woman. Inspecting the

Followers. No doubt making plans.'

Meena shivered, her eyes wandering towards the tables again, wondering where Draguta had hidden the ring.

They were all making plans.

***

Ayla was struggling to settle her nerves. It had been a trying time, and she did not doubt that the stress of the past few weeks had taken a toll on both her mind and body, but she needed to think of how she could help. Of ways to protect them all. Of how to keep her and Astrid safe while she tried.

The noise of the wagon wasn't helping. The creak of the wheels as they clattered along was hammering a hole in her head, and eventually, she threw her hands in the air and gave up.

Astrid, sitting opposite her, laughed. 'It's awful, isn't it? That noise?'

'I thought the fish oil would help. I can't believe it sounds just as bad!'

Bruno was riding up front, talking to the driver. Four more men walked on either side of the wagon, another two at the back. They were surrounded by warriors, yet Ayla felt exposed. She could see Hallow Wood through the window, which unsettled her further. It felt as though they were being watched. By who, she didn't know, but she could almost feel eyes following them. And she needed to think about what she could do if someone was out there.

Or something.

'Perhaps you should try and sleep?' Astrid suggested, though she wasn't sure that was even possible. The road continued to be a lumpy, bumpy mess and they were jerking and rattling about inside the wagon, sliding up and down on wobbling stools.

'I think that sounds like the perfect idea,' Ayla declared with a grin. 'As long as you're keeping watch. I don't want to roll into the fire!'

Astrid nodded. 'I will, don't worry. I'm feeling wide awake and certain that my head's about to hit the roof at any moment!'

Ayla wasn't listening as she stood, heading for her bed in the left corner of the wagon, already letting the thump and creak of the wheels become a rhythmic chant that would hopefully lull her to sleep.

***

'Is it safe?' Jael wondered as Thorgils approached, nudging his horse alongside Tig. She didn't look pleased with the company.

'Might be the last time we see each other, Jael,' Thorgils said. 'Imagine if that were true and your last memory was of being so mean to an afflicted man?'

'Afflicted by what?' Jael snorted. 'Your own greedy eyes?' And peering at Thorgils, she could see him squirming, his left hand hovering near his griping belly. 'Don't even think about it,' she warned, 'or I'll send you out with the scouts. You and Torstan both.'

Torstan, who had come up with Thorgils, looked indignant. 'What did I do?'

Jael laughed. It was a warm day, though the sky was still grim and the heat clung to them in a way that made them wish they weren't wearing armour. 'You have the misfortune of being next to Thorgils. The smell of him lingers on everyone he's near, didn't you know?'

'Speaking of smells,' Thorgils grinned, ignoring Jael's insults, 'how good did that venison smell? Tasted even better. Beryth has a fine cook. Apart from the cabbage, of course. She did something wrong there.'

'Well, looks like Rork agreed with you,' Torstan said, turning around to Rork and Karsten who had their heads together behind them. 'Never heard him talk so much.'

Jael could see that it was true as she turned around. Rork's mouth was open, his face and hands animated as he chatted to Karsten. He almost looked happy.

How odd, she thought, that amidst all this terror, anyone could be happy. But as she glanced around, she saw Fyn and Axl sharing a joke; Ivaar was riding with Aleksander, and they both had smiles on their faces; even Raymon looked happy.

Shaking her head, Jael lifted her eyes to the clouds, watching Fyr circle above them all, wondering what she could see.

***

Gant and Gisila were alone.

'Just for a moment,' he insisted, fidgeting. 'I shouldn't be here.' He was lying on top of the bed, next to her, their faces almost touching.

'Why shouldn't you be here?' Gisila was feeling better. More comfortable. Able to move without yelping. She was ready to get out of bed, but her mother was keeping her prisoner awhile longer, and she was eager for the company. 'Surely, others can manage without you for a moment? Bram? Ulf? They're capable, aren't they? And if not, why keep them around?'

Gant burst out laughing. 'When did you become so bossy? Though now that I think about it, there's a definite resemblance to Edela I seem to have overlooked.'

'You think I'm turning into my mother?' Gisila was horrified, brushing strands of greying hair out of her blinking eyes. 'An old woman?'

'Or your daughter, who is not an old woman, but just as bossy as the two of you.'

Gisila's face dropped as she thought of her children. 'I wish

I knew if they were alive. Though it's not only death to fear, is it? Who knows what those people will do to them.' Tears were quickly leaking from her eyes. 'I feel so worried, Gant. They are my children! My children, and what can I do to help them? Ranuf isn't there to protect them either. And you're not with them.' She rubbed her eyes. 'Perhaps you should have gone? You could have brought them back. You could have kept them safe as you did Ranuf.'

Gant took her hand away from her face. 'I trust Jael.' He didn't say any more, but he stared into Gisila's eyes, urging her to believe in that one thing. 'We can't predict what will happen, but we can hold on to what we have right now. And we have this. A second chance.' He shook his head, amazed at how well she looked. How alive. 'I thought you were dead. Thought I'd wasted all those years. That I'd run out of luck. But look at us now.'

Gisila cried some more, freeing her hand to smooth down his eyebrows which were growing out of control, she thought, grinning through her tears. 'Mmmm, two old people about to die.'

Gant laughed. 'Yes, possibly. Or two people about to begin the rest of their lives together.'

'Is that so?'

'Well, if you'll have me?'

Gisila's teary eyes sharpened. 'Are you asking me to...'

'Be my wife?' Gant nodded. 'I am. Unless you have other plans? Other offers?'

'I do not,' Gisila whispered. 'And if I did, I would still choose you, Gant Olborn.'

Gant smiled, pleased to hear it. Leaning closer, he kissed her softly. 'It's not so bad being old, is it?'

'No, it's not. Not at all.' And closing her eyes, Gisila edged closer, not noticing the ache in her stomach for the first time in days.

CHAPTER THIRTY SIX

Once Draguta and Briggit had disappeared, Eadmund had hurried away from Jaeger, not trusting himself in his company. Draguta's eyes had warned him away again, and he felt the threat in them. He couldn't ignore it, as much as he wanted to. So, instead, he did the only thing he could do: he visited Amma.

Amma was pleased to see him, disappointed to hear that he hadn't killed Jaeger, but well aware that Eadmund was trapped. She could see it in his eyes. They were kind eyes, she thought, noticing them properly for the first time as he sat on the bed with her. Kind but troubled. 'I want to get up,' she said. 'I feel embarrassed about it all... what happened.' She tried not to grimace, but now that her belly had stopped aching, she could feel every other part of her body that Jaeger had hurt.

'You shouldn't feel that. What Jaeger did? He did it to Evaine. He tried to do it to Briggit. He's likely done it to Meena. I imagine he raped his first wife too. You shouldn't feel embarrassed, Amma.' Eadmund felt embarrassed, seeing her discomfort, wanting to change the subject so she could relax.

Amma could see, so she changed the subject herself. 'When will you leave?'

'Tomorrow. You only have to survive one more day, then Jaeger will be gone.'

'For good?' Amma almost joked.

Almost.

Eadmund frowned. 'I don't think Draguta will let anything happen to him,' he said slowly. 'Though... perhaps she won't always be watching.' His eyes drifted to the curtain floating across the door to the balcony. Even with the door open, the chamber was stifling. Sweat was soaking his tunic again, and he felt wistful for Oss' cold weather. 'I can't. But his brothers...'

'Axl too.'

Eadmund nodded. 'Jaeger will have a target on him for sure, so you never know what might happen.' He felt hope surge at the thought of what Karsten might do to Jaeger. He had less certainty about Axl. Axl was barely a man, though Eadmund remembered how he had taken off Lothar Furyck's head, and run back for Amma when it had looked impossible to save her.

And his mind was quickly back on the night they had escaped from Hest.

And Jael.

***

They stopped to take a break.

Jael dropped to the ground with a groan, unable to feel her arse. She grimaced as Axl approached, swigging from his water bag. 'I feel like some of Beryth's mead,' she admitted. 'I don't usually like mead, but that was delicious.'

Axl was distracted, his eyes on the clouds. 'Do you think a storm's coming?'

Jael looked up. Fyr had disappeared into the clouds again, which were thick but not threatening. 'I doubt it. If the gods still control the weather, then I doubt it. A storm wouldn't help us now.'

Axl handed her his water bag, and Jael took a long drink, reminded of Gant. 'I wonder how everything is going back at the fort.'

Fyn joined them, a look of pain contorting his sunburned face.

'Are you alright?'

'Cramp,' he grimaced. 'My leg.' And bending over, he tried to straighten his left leg.

'Oh, poor us!' Aleksander laughed, walking up to the moaners. 'Poor us who've been sitting on our arses all morning. It's hard work, all that sitting!' And he looked back at the red-faced warriors who were trudging to a stop behind them.

'Fair point,' Axl agreed, his attention drifting back to Andala. 'I hope they're alright back in the fort. It's a lot to ask of Edela, looking after everyone.'

'But there's Eydis,' Fyn insisted, more comfortable now that he'd stretched out his leg. 'And Ontine,' he added shyly.

'Ha!' Axl was roused out of his dour mood by the look on Fyn's face. 'Knew you liked her!'

Fyn's cheeks quickly reddened like two apples. He didn't say anything.

'Leave him alone,' Jael said, handing back her brother's water bag. 'Nothing wrong with that. Ontine's a nice enough girl.'

'Pretty too,' Aleksander added.

'Oh, noticed that, did you?' Jael frowned.

Thorgils arrived with Karsten. 'Anyone got anything to eat? My saddlebag's empty.'

'Already?' Aleksander never failed to be surprised by the size of Thorgils' appetite.

'We've been riding for hours. All day!' Thorgils insisted.

'It's not even midday,' Jael laughed as Torstan and Ivaar approached, Raymon and Rork behind them.

'Midday?' Thorgils was horrified, looking up, trying to see the sun through the clouds.

They all laughed then, except for Jael whose attention had wandered to Ayla and Astrid who had walked from the wagon to stretch their legs. 'Maybe Astrid can find you something to eat?' she suggested. 'It'll save us all the headache of having to listen to you moan for the rest of the afternoon!'

***

'Well, they are cleaner,' Draguta admitted, running her eye over the orderly rows of bathed and brushed Followers. Not Followers, she reminded herself. Dreamers. They were her army of dreamers now. She did not wish for them to follow her like dull-eyed fiends. She simply wanted them to obey her.

To have their unwavering, submissive obedience.

Briggit had taken the Followers down to one of the coves for a long-overdue bath, a refreshing dip in water cold enough to soothe sunburned faces and chill overheated bodies. It had washed away the filth and the grime of the attack on Angard, the terrifying journey to Hest, the torturous days in the baking sun.

But it could not remove the stench of fear.

Draguta could smell it. 'How long did the tailor say it would take to make them new robes?' she wondered. 'Longer than we have, I imagine. Unless we wrap them all in sheets!'

Briggit didn't smile. The Followers were clean, but they were still prisoners. Though, she realised, staring at some of the dark patches on the cobblestones, at least they were still standing.

Not like poor Lillith and Sabine.

'The tailor said many days, my lady,' Brill mumbled, coming forward.

'What's that? Speak up!' Draguta demanded, irritated by her servant's habit of talking into her clothing. 'I am up here, Brill! Up here!'

'Many days,' Brill repeated, her eyes up and blinking now. 'He does not have enough cloth to make so many robes.'

'No, I don't suppose he does,' Draguta realised, eyeing the tattered robes with distaste. 'So we shall have to make do. Though what they are wearing is hardly as important as what they will do, is it?' she smiled, turning to Briggit.

And for the first time all day, Briggit smiled back.

***

Eadmund had left the castle through the kitchen door, wanting to be alone. Yet there was Evaine, right where he had not expected her to be, talking to Tanja who was bent over, washing Sigmund's clothes in the stream. Sigmund was lying on a swaddling cloth in the grass, naked and wriggling, enjoying the attention of one of the cooks who was cooing over him, an apple in her hand.

The sun glared at him and Eadmund frowned back, turning to leave, but he heard his mother's voice, and he saw her blissfully happy face as she cradled him in her arms, Eirik standing by her side. And he turned back, heading towards his son.

'Eadmund!' Evaine almost squealed in delight, lifting her shoulders and pushing out her breasts, wishing she was wearing her most flattering dress, but Tanja was washing that too. 'I didn't expect to see you here.'

The cook made a hasty exit, and Eadmund bent down to smile at Sigmund, who seemed to recognise him. He wanted to think that he recognised him. And squatting down, he held out a finger for Sigmund to grip hold of, which his son eagerly did, trying to stick it in his mouth.

'I told you he'd missed you,' Evaine breathed, crouching beside him.

Eadmund sighed. 'Evaine.' He glanced at Tanja, who quickly looked away. He didn't mind speaking in front of Tanja, but he didn't know what to say.

'Yes?' Evaine's face was bright as she sat down next to her son, looking up at Eadmund expectantly.

'You don't care about Sigmund. You never have. I'm sure there's a part of you that feels something, but I imagine that part is so small you can barely see it. You only care that he can help you get what you want. Which is me.'

Evaine almost toppled backwards.

'But he can't. He can't help you because I never loved you, Evaine. Not once.' She looked as though she'd been stabbed but

Eadmund kept going. He reminded himself what Evaine had done to Edela. How she had trapped him, bound him, pushed him away from Jael. And he kept going. 'I was sad and lonely after Melaena died, and mostly drunk. I didn't say no when I should have. I didn't really want to be with you. I just didn't want to be alone. I never loved you, Evaine, and I never will.'

'But...' Evaine spluttered. 'But...'

Eadmund leaned in closer, trying to get her to see. 'Even if Jael was dead, I wouldn't choose to be with you. If she chose someone else, I wouldn't choose to be with you. I can't love you, Evaine because I can't find anything to love about you.'

Evaine couldn't speak. She couldn't find a way to twist and turn Eadmund's cruel words into something resembling hope. She couldn't find any part of what he'd said to cling to. Lifting her head, she stared into his eyes, seeing the truth laid bare, feeling her life's purpose unravel, pain flooding her heart. And standing up, she turned and strode across the grass, heading far away from Eadmund and everything she had believed in.

Everything Morana had promised her since she was a girl.

***

Ontine and Eydis were talking.

Biddy was amazed. 'That took some time!' she exclaimed, plonking herself down next to Edela who had taken a break and was enjoying the company of Selene and Leya Skalleson. They had brought her a kitten to play with, and she was happy to take some time to talk to them, eager to rest her aching arm which had been circle making all day long.

'When my Jael was little, she used to play with my cat,' Edela smiled at the girls. 'She was a very special cat. Not like this kitten. My cat was a magical cat. Have you ever seen a magical cat?'

The girls shook their heads, big eyes blinking.

Isaura watched, smiling, not worrying about Thorgils for a brief moment.

'Well, a magical cat can talk, you know,' Edela went on. 'But only a dreamer can hear it. Only a dreamer can understand what it says.'

'But what does it want to say?' Selene wondered, frowning. 'Why do they talk to you?'

'To help. They want to help. Sometimes they want something to eat, of course. A tickle. A bowl of milk. But sometimes they have a warning.'

'What about?'

'Well, a magical creature will warn you if you're in danger.'

'Oh.' Selene looked down at the black kitten who was starting to get heavy in her little arms. 'Are we in danger?' she asked the squirming creature. 'Can you see any danger?'

***

'Where'd the sun go?' Thorgils grumbled, shivering. 'How is it this cold?'

Torstan looked worried beside him. 'Those clouds look thick enough for snow.'

Thorgils had no appetite for the first time all day, which was another bad sign, he knew. Looking ahead to where Jael rode by herself, he wondered if he should go and have a word. He hadn't seen that raven for a while, though the clouds were low. Perhaps she was lost in them?

Jael could feel the chill of the afternoon air too. She could hear the silence of on-edge warriors trekking behind her. Even the horses were quiet.

And as for the birds...

They were crossing a meadow dotted with pretty flowers. White and yellow. Red and blue.

It was so quiet.

Jael was waiting for a storm. Listening for thunder.

The clouds were a deep, dark grey, thickening and swirling like billowing smoke. She pulled on the reins, waiting while Axl, Fyn, and Raymon joined her, wondering how far back Aleksander was.

'What is it?' Axl looked worried.

Jael didn't answer. The hairs on the back of her neck were up, and as she turned around, she could see that the clouds were moving towards them at pace.

Not clouds.

It was a fog. A thick fog, coming in on each side of them.

'Thorgils!' Jael spun around. 'Blow the horn. Let's stop! That fog's coming in fast! Fyn, ride down the line and warn everyone to bunch up. We need to stay together. Get to the wagon. Tell Ayla what's happening!'

She heard the wail of the horn as she turned around and then the loud warning cry of Fyr as she flew out of the fog, aiming straight for them.

***

Draguta made Meena join in.

'You will watch and learn,' she insisted, sensing Meena's discomfort grow as she peered at the Followers who had formed a circle around them. 'I shall be in the centre. You may stand on one side of me, Briggit on the other. Three dreamers at the centre of a circle of power.' Her eyes sparkled in anticipation for she had made the most intriguing discovery in the Book of Darkness, and she was eager to put it to the test.

Slipping the Ring of Taron from her purse, she slid it on her finger.

Meena watched, suddenly cold all over. Surprised that it felt cold.

That was never a good sign.

They had walked to the Crown of Stones, and though it was day and not night, Meena was shaking all over. The sky was grim, cloudy, threatening rain. Not even the bright light from the fire could dispel the terror she felt to be standing in the middle of those ancient stones again, surrounded by Followers.

And then Draguta's smile flashed through the gloom. 'Now, we dance!'

CHAPTER THIRTY SEVEN'

'Shield! Houses!' Jael screamed, though by the time she'd finished yelling, the fog had consumed them all.

She couldn't see Axl.

'Jael!'

Her brother sounded far away.

'Axl?'

'Jael!'

Jael drew her sword. She couldn't see anyone. She couldn't even see Tig beneath her, but she could feel him trembling.

Fyr was up above them somewhere, warning them.

She tried to listen, spinning around, faced with wall after wall of fog. Suffocating, panic-inducing fog. Was it fog? She could smell something odd, her head suddenly hazy. 'Aleksander?' Slowly turning Tig around, Jael nudged him forward, one cautious step at a time. 'Thorgils?'

No one was there.

Nothing was there.

Just fog.

And then a face. Ivaar.

And he was swinging his sword, trying to kill her.

***

Ayla and Astrid had been building up their fire as the temperature dropped. And just before the sound of Thorgils' horn, Ayla had thrown one of her bundles of herbs onto the flames. 'Into the circle!' she cried to Astrid, dragging her inside, closing it after her. 'Bruno!' she called out. 'Bruno!'

He didn't reply.

They heard the sudden clanging of swords as the fog seeped into the wagon.

'What is it?' Astrid whispered, shaking as she edged closer to the fire. 'Ayla, what's happening?'

***

Draguta chanted loudly, drawing a symbol in blood on her forehead, more symbols on her bare forearms. She spun around in the centre of the circle, flames crackling behind her, blood splattering her dress, eyes mad with ecstasy as the power of the spell surged through her. And dropping to her knees, bloody knife out, Draguta saw the symbol clearly in her mind, and eyes blinking now, she hurried to scratch it into the earth with the tip of her blade.

Meena tried to see what she was doing as she swayed near Briggit, but the herbs were pumping powerfully in the fire, and she could barely keep her eyes open. Draguta was just a white-and-red blur as she came back to join them, and they were quickly moving again.

Meena found herself tripping over her boots as she clumsily followed Draguta and Briggit in a dance that everyone seemed to know but her. Her feet felt too big, too slow, and she stumbled again and again, following after Draguta, listening to her deep voice thumping like a drum.

Like a beating heart.

It was inside her chest. Echoing in her head.

Draguta was inside her.

***

'Ivaar!' Jael shouted, bringing Toothpick up to block his strike. 'What are you doing?' And then the fog shifted, and Ivaar was gone.

Hearing screams, she spun around as a man she didn't recognise ran towards her with an axe, aiming for Tig. 'No!' And reaching down, she started to bring her blade towards his arm when she felt a bite on her own. 'Aarrghh!' And spinning around, Jael saw Fyr digging her beak in through the tiny links in her mail. 'Aarrghh!' Turning back around, the man with the axe was gone, but another was there, and he yanked Tig's bridle, trying to climb up to her.

And then Fyr pecked Jael's other arm, and her mind cleared as she kicked the man in the face, knocking him back into the fog, spurring Tig on. 'Wind!' Jael yelled as Fyr flew off, black wings quickly lost in the stinking fog. 'We need wind!'

***

Ayla gripped two symbol stones, trying to let her fears for Bruno dissipate, hoping she could release all thoughts of him from her mind. She needed to find Veiga, the Tuuran Goddess of Weather.

She needed help clearing the fog.

Astrid's head was swivelling, eyes moving from Ayla to the thick white mist which had settled just outside the circle, almost touching her. It smelled so strange that she tried not to inhale as she leaned in, listening to Ayla chant.

***

'Faster! Faster!'

Meena could hear Draguta's voice riding her like a horse, urging her on, her feet skipping now, as light as air, faster than she imagined possible. Her eyes were open, watching the Followers as they wove around her in circles; dark robes merged into a fog so thick she couldn't see.

She couldn't see out.

She had to keep going.

She had to keep dancing.

***

Thorgils was off his horse.

He couldn't see her anymore, but he could see Torstan who had his sword out, aiming for his throat. 'What?' He was furious. 'What are you doing?' And unsheathing his own sword, Thorgils reversed it, slamming the pommel into Torstan's chin. His friend stumbled backwards, just keeping to his feet, and Thorgils surged through the cloying fog after him.

'Thorgils!' Jael had heard him. She was trying to get to him. She had to stop him. She had to stop all of them. And then Aleksander was behind her, his hands around her throat.

Jael threw herself forward, rolling him over the top of her, onto the ground, pointing Toothpick at him, wanting him to stay down. 'It's the fog! It's doing something to us! Stay down! Stay down! Swords down!'

'Aarrghh!'

Jael heard the scream of agony, and distracted, she turned away just long enough for Aleksander to slide away from the tip of her sword. He was quickly up on his feet, slashing at her with his own sword, and then Fyr swooped in through the fog and bit him on the neck.

'Fuck!' Aleksander spun around, swinging for the raven who

flapped away from his blade, biting the other side of his neck before disappearing back into the fog. Aleksander grimaced, shaking his head, blinking at Jael. 'What happened?'

'It's the fog! It's making us kill each other!' Jael exclaimed. 'Come on! I can hear Thorgils!'

***

Bruno's roar drew Ayla out of the trance. She lurched forward, close to the flames. The wagon was not large and nor was the circle she sat inside with Astrid.

The tense look on Ayla's face told Astrid that it hadn't worked. Whatever Ayla had been trying hadn't worked.

'Bruno!' Ayla couldn't leave the circle, but she could hear more screaming.

And then the door to the wagon slammed open, and Bruno stood there, blood dripping down his arm, a knife in each hand.

Ready to kill them both.

***

Edela had been sitting before her fire in the hall, the Book of Aurea open on her knees when the visions of smoke started coming again, just like her dream. But now she could see that it wasn't smoke at all. It was fog.

Draguta's fog.

Edela was confused, wondering what that meant when she heard the sound of a furious battle ringing in her ears. She tried to stay with the vision, letting the flames twist before her, revealing everything she needed to see. And then she was off her stool, the

Book of Aurea dropping to the floor with a crash that had everyone turning to her.

'Gant! Clear the hall now!' She spun around. 'Biddy! I need more wood! Herbs smoking! Entorp!'

He hurried to the edge of the circle.

'Find Eydis and Ontine and bring your drum!'

And hurrying to pick up the book, Edela sat down, slightly dazed, hoping she could find an answer.

***

Thorgils swung a fist at Jael. He'd lost his sword. Someone had thrown themselves on top of him, and he'd had to fight them off. He didn't know who it was, but he might have killed them.

Jael ducked, slamming her fist into his balls, hard enough to suck the air through his teeth. Thorgils dropped to the ground with a plop, knees together, screeching in agony.

Raymon lunged out of the fog, teeth bared, blood in his mouth. 'You bastard!' he screamed at Aleksander. 'You killed my mother! You killed her!'

'Raymon!' Jael spun around, wanting to see Fyr but there was no sign of her. She could see the fog shifting, though, swirling around them like a whirlpool. 'Fyr! Fyr!' And then Raymon punched her in the stomach.

Aleksander whose head had cleared, hit Raymon in the jaw, knocking him back into the fog. Shaking his hand, he turned to Jael. 'Look out!' And there was Ivaar again.

'You bitch!' Ivaar yelled, blood running down his face from a cut above his eye. 'You took everything from me! I'll gut you!'

Jael ducked the blow, slamming her fist into his ribs.

More screaming.

All around them, they could hear screaming. Horses in a panic. Swords and shields banging and crashing all around them.

And the whistle of the wind.

Jael kept turning, watching, listening.

She could definitely hear the wind picking up.

***

Entorp's tapping on the drum was a steady, pulsing rhythm, so much slower than the frantic beat of Edela's heart. She took four deep breaths to steady herself, knowing that she needed to be calm. Calm enough to see what Draguta was doing.

Fog was made by Veiga, Tuuran Goddess of the Weather, yet Draguta appeared to be controlling it herself. Edela frowned, needing to know more, feeling her body sink further into the trance, deeper into the fog. And there she saw Veiga, helpless in the midst of it all. She was a powerful goddess, but she appeared to be bound, wound tightly into a spell that Edela couldn't see a way through.

She recognised that familiar dark cackle of Draguta's in her ears as she swept her poisonous fog around Jael and the army. And she saw the raven, Fyr, flapping her wings, trying to create a breeze.

And then a memory flickered.

Faint at first, then it surged to the front of her mind.

'On your feet, girls!' Edela urged, clicking and cracking off her stool. And dragging her knife from its scabbard, she cut her palm and dug her finger into the wound. Painting a symbol quickly on Ontine's forehead, she turned to Eydis and did the same, before drawing one on her hand. 'We must be the wind! We must help Fyr! We must save the army!' And she led the girls around in a circle, worried that she couldn't go fast enough. But Ontine and Eydis were younger, stronger. They had not been casting circles for days.

And they spurred Edela on.

***

'Bruno!' Ayla pleaded, her eyes on the sharply carved line of the circle she and Astrid were huddling inside. The fire crackled between them, pumping a heady mix of fragrant smoke as Bruno stepped into the wagon, eyes fixed on her. 'Bruno! Stop!'

Bruno edged closer, dead eyes peeled open, bloody knives glinting in the flames. 'You left me in that hole!' he growled, his gentle voice suddenly full of threat. 'Left me to die! I'll kill you for that! For what you did with Ivaar! For all of your disloyalty! I'll kill you!' And clenching his teeth, he lunged at his wife.

***

The fog was swimming around them now, and everyone was screaming at Jael. Thorgils was up on his feet, fists in balls, aiming for Aleksander. Raymon had Axl around the throat. Jael saw Rork felling Fyn with a vicious headbutt.

And then Fyr was back, struggling in the wind, snapping her beak, tearing some of Thorgils' flesh, then Axl's and Raymon's. And finally Rork, who bent over Fyn, blinking, feeling his head. 'Fyn?'

Jael's braids were snapping behind her, the hem of her tunic flapping beneath her mail shirt. And soon she was struggling to stand. 'Hold onto each other!' she cried, reaching for Raymon who was shaking his head, hair all over his bleeding face. 'Hold on!'

'Help! Help me!' came a voice and they turned to see Ivaar leaning over Torstan who was bleeding from his belly, blood gurgling from his mouth.

'Torstan!' Thorgils blinked in horror, running to his friend. 'No!'

***

'Hurry, girls! Faster!' Edela was struggling to breathe as she swept around the circle, holding Eydis' and Ontine's hands, worried that she was about to tumble over in exhaustion. But feeling a cool breeze against her back, and listening to the flap of the raven's wings, she took a quick breath and kept going.

***

Bruno fell backwards, straight through the wagon door, down the step, onto the ground, knives clattering from his hands.

Ayla scrambled to her feet, leaving the circle.

'Ayla! No!' Astrid panicked, but she could see that the fog was clearing. The strange smell was lessening too, and she dared to leave the circle herself, listening to the retreat of the wind and the sudden loud wail of injured men.

***

The fog was dispersing, leaving them in a meadow of bodies.

Riderless horses. Confusion.

Thorgils was fumbling, trying to tear his tunic, but his hands were slippery with blood. He tugged, but it wouldn't rip.

Jael tore hers, pressing the cloth against Torstan's bleeding belly. 'Someone get Astrid! Hurry! Torstan, stay with us. Please!'

Torstan's eyes were full of panic, blood running from his nose, his mouth.

He couldn't speak.

Thorgils was in shock, finally tearing a piece off his tunic. 'Here, take it. You need more!'

But Jael could see that she needed more than two strips of cloth.

Torstan's eyes bulged, his body jerking. He couldn't breathe. Couldn't swallow.

'I'm so sorry!' Thorgils sobbed, grabbing his friend's hand, trying to get him to focus. To hold on. 'Torstan! No!'

Torstan suddenly tensed, stiff for a moment.

And then he went completely limp.

'Torstan! Torstan!'

Jael laid a hand on Thorgils' back.

Nobody spoke.

***

Edela collapsed against Ontine, unable to speak.

Seeing that they had stopped, Biddy raced inside the circle, helping her down onto a stool. 'Stay there now. Try not to speak. Just rest.'

Gant held his breath, standing just outside the circle, hand hovering near his sword, helpless. He didn't know what had happened.

He didn't know who was safe.

***

'Edela Saeveld has become more than an inconvenience,' Draguta snarled, her breath a smoky rasp as she drew herself out of the trance. 'She has become a problem. And I dislike problems, Briggit, so we will need to work on removing that one, won't we?'

Briggit couldn't focus on Draguta, but she nodded nonetheless. 'It will not be easy. The gods will work hard to protect them all now. To keep them safe from you.'

Draguta laughed, her eyes sharper than any of them. 'But you saw our power. We claimed Veiga herself! A goddess! Now she is ours! Ours!' She felt elated. It was another step. Another step towards claiming ultimate power. 'Soon, those gods will be impotent,' Draguta purred, her eyes on Meena. 'As helpless as slaves. My prisoners, every last one of them!'

Meena looked towards the stones, struggling to halt the sway of her body as it rocked from side to side, still wanting to be moving in that whirlpool.

Draguta could control a god.

Meena couldn't breathe.

Draguta could control a god.

***

Ayla threw herself onto Bruno who was blinking, his head clearing, not sure what had happened. And then he was.

'I killed him,' he panted, staring into her eyes. 'I killed him.'

'Who?' Ayla panicked.

'The driver. Thorvar. I killed him. I... tried to kill you!' Bruno's eyes were bleary and bloodshot, but his mind was alert. 'That fog. It was that fog!'

Astrid hurried down the wagon steps, a basket in her hands. She could hear the cries of pain and distress all around the meadow.

And then Ivaar was there. 'You have to come!' he panted. 'We've got men dying. Everywhere! You have to hurry!'

***

It was too late for Torstan.

Thorgils sobbed over his friend's body.

Beorn was there. Some of the other Islanders too. Orvar and Erland, friends with Thorgils and Torstan since they were boys. All of them stood around Torstan in shock.

'I killed him.' Thorgils couldn't make it any less real, no matter how many times he said it. 'I killed him.'

Fyn was still unconscious.

Jael left Thorgils to check on him. She wanted to find Tig too.

Panic rose in her chest as the horror of what had happened came into full view. As the fog dispersed and the clouds parted, the late afternoon sun revealed the bloody path of destruction the cursed fog had wrought.

'Fyn?' Jael shook his shoulder, listening as he groaned, turning suddenly at a familiar whinny, and there was Tig, black mane flying in the strong breeze, stamping his foot impatiently.

Relieved to have found her.

CHAPTER THIRTY EIGHT

'What does it mean?' Gant wondered, peering at Edela's ghostly face. She was trembling, barely speaking since Biddy had forced her onto a stool. 'What did she do?'

Edela took a deep breath, focusing on Gant's reassuring face, taking strength from him. 'She trapped Veiga. Bound her. Through her, Draguta made that fog, cursing it, wrapping it around them all. The army was lost in it, seeing threats that weren't there.'

'And?'

'They killed each other.'

Gant's face blanched. 'They did?'

Edela nodded. 'Even Jael was lost in it for a time. The raven, Fyr, helped. Pecking them. Cutting them. Breaking them out of the spell. But for some, it was too late. I fear they have many dead and injured.'

'Who?'

'I don't know.' Edela's head was still lost in that swirling fog. She glanced at Eydis and Ontine who sat beside her, swaying on their stools. 'I don't know.'

Gant's shoulders tightened further. He ran a hand over his beard, seeing the worry on Edela's exhausted face. 'You did what you could,' he tried to assure her.

But Edela didn't even nod her head.

***

Astrid and Ayla hurried around the meadow, trying to respond to every cry of pain. The wailing was not just from the injured, though. The distress of those who had killed their friends and allies rang through the late afternoon, the horror too shocking to make any sense. The fog had cleared, but they remained thick-headed, confused, struggling to understand how they had been tricked into murder.

'We pile the bodies,' Jael said, trying to find the path forward. 'Away from the trees. In the centre. Over there.' She pointed Aleksander and Raymon towards the flattest part of the meadow. 'We need to burn the dead quickly, help the wounded, then leave.

'Burn them?'

'We'll use sea-fire,' Jael muttered, turning away, her head down, trying not to think about Torstan. About Thorgils who was a mess because he'd killed Torstan. 'We have to get out of here quickly. We're too exposed.'

Aleksander nodded in agreement, turning to Raymon. 'I'll get some of my men. You get yours.'

Jael left them to it as she headed for Fyn who was sitting up now, an enormous purple-hued bump rising out of the middle of his head.

'Are you alright?' she asked, squatting in front of him.

'Think so,' Fyn mumbled, his ears ringing so loudly that he could barely hear her. 'What happened?'

Jael held a hand over her bleeding arm, trying to staunch the determined flow of blood. 'The fog tricked us into seeing things that weren't there. Nightmares. Threats. I thought Ivaar was trying to kill me. Thorgils thought Torstan was doing the same to him.' She swallowed. 'He killed him.'

Fyn's frown cleared, his eyes bulging. 'No!'

'Thorgils isn't the only one who's going to have to live with what happened in that fog, I'm afraid.' Jael's eyes drifted to where Bruno was helping Ayla. He looked shellshocked as he handed his wife some strips of cloth, unable to focus, continually shaking his head.

Jael shook her own head, grateful that she wasn't going to be burdened with the same guilt; grateful to Fyr for releasing her from the spell so quickly. Looking around, Jael couldn't see the raven, but hopefully, she was up in the sky again, watching for what else might be coming. 'We have to move. Can you move?'

Fyn nodded, grabbing Jael's hand as she pulled him to his feet. 'I want to see Thorgils.'

'You should. He's over there. Come on, I'll take you,' she said, watching Fyn stagger, amazed that he could stand at all after being felled by Rork and his enormous head. 'Then we have to go. Once we round up the horses, that is.'

They passed Karsten who still hadn't closed his mouth, tugging on his beard, unable to comprehend the scene around him.

'Get your men to find the missing horses,' Jael ordered. 'We have to leave!'

Karsten nodded, forcing himself to move, overcome with relief that he was still standing.

That there was no blood on his hands.

***

Draguta was pleased with her dreamers' first effort, knowing that their presence had enhanced the power of her spell. And once they were dressed in something less dreary, she would almost be proud to claim them.

Briggit stood beside her on the castle steps, her eyes on the Followers who had been returned to the square, once again surrounded by armed guards. 'They need shelter, somewhere to sleep, away from that sun.' It was warmer than it had been all day, and she could feel sweat trickling down between her breasts.

'Well, I suppose they earned it,' Draguta decided. 'So yes, I shall have someone move them. They have freed themselves with their performance today.' She turned, motioning for Briggit to accompany her inside. 'As have you. Though I am always watching. Always. One sign that my binding spell is under any threat and I shall tighten the noose again, my dear. Tight enough to strangle you all!'

Briggit swallowed, her eyes on the steps as she mounted them. 'I have no wish to be in those fetters again.'

They walked into the hall where Jaeger was helping himself to wine.

'Well, those of you who behave yourselves have no need to be imprisoned at all. But no one should ever think themselves above punishment,' Draguta added, her eyes on Jaeger. 'I demand complete loyalty and nothing less.'

Briggit nodded, taking the goblet Jaeger handed her.

Draguta turned away from them, heading for the map table. 'We have wounded our enemies! Jael Furyck's army will now limp towards us, and the people of Andala will quake in their boots tonight and every night to come, wondering what we will take from them next...' She inhaled, feeling a surge of contentment flood her body. A peace like nothing she had ever known. 'And the gods!' Draguta laughed. 'And the gods!' And spinning around, she eyed Briggit. 'Soon, I will be their queen. They feel it. They know it is coming. They felt the unfamiliar loss of control, the shock of vulnerability. Ha! Those gods will soon be mine. Every last one of them!'

***

Edela missed Ayla. She was a dreamer with experience; someone she felt comfortable talking to. And looking at a clearly terrified Ontine and Eydis, she didn't feel that there was anything she could gain by sharing her fears with either of them.

But there was always Biddy.

Not a dreamer, but one of the wisest women she knew. So Edela took her into the kitchen garden, wanting a breath of air and a chance to escape the clamour of the hall.

She was glad when Entorp asked to join them.

'We are in deep trouble,' Edela said solemnly, her eyes running up and down the perfectly straight rows of radishes. 'Deep, deep trouble, and I do not know what we can do. We knew, of course, that the gods were powerless against the magic of that book, though I'm not sure we knew that Draguta would be able to control them with it.'

Entorp, though unsettled, was not as troubled as Edela. 'But with the girls' help, you were able to fight back. Draguta did not win, did she? You and the raven stopped that fog.'

'We did, yes, but we don't know what happened to Veiga. Likely she is bound for good. And what will Draguta do next? She appears to be growing stronger. Perhaps she will go after all the gods now?' Edela felt sick. 'I don't believe that Dara Teros foresaw her sister becoming this powerful.'

Biddy looked more worried and much less confident than Entorp. 'If she was brought back to life by the Book of Darkness, she must have been weak in the beginning. Perhaps now she is starting to realise her true power?'

They walked through the garden, hazy beams of sunshine guiding them towards a bench under an apple tree. No one spoke for a while. Edela appreciated the silence, her shoulders finally relaxing, though her legs were still trembling as she took a seat next to Biddy.

Entorp stayed standing, his eyes on the sinking sun. 'My wife told me stories about The Following. Their quest for that book drove many mad. Their desire to claim it was greater than anything. They believed it was the key to Raemus' return. That the book could bring him back, and he would, in turn, set them free.'

'But they didn't anticipate Draguta's reluctance to part with her power,' Edela said. 'Did they?'

'No, but perhaps the book controls her now?' Entorp wondered with a frown. 'Perhaps she has no choice?'

'And without it?' Biddy asked. 'Do you think she would just be a dreamer?'

'She was once, from what I saw in my dreams,' Edela murmured. 'She was a dreamer like her sisters. But when she was given the book, I don't imagine there was any way back. It appears to have consumed her.'

'Which makes her even more dangerous,' Entorp decided. 'She must be at the mercy of the book now. As though they are one. Bound by evil to destroy everyone they perceive as an enemy.'

'Which is every one of us,' Biddy said. 'Isn't it?'

Edela nodded. 'It is, I'm afraid. We can only hope that Jael kills her before it's too late. Before she destroys us all.'

***

Draguta had quickly returned her attention to preparing for their departure to the vale, and that gave Meena a chance to slip away to see Amma.

'What happened?' Amma was bored and curious, eager to escape the traumatic memories of what Jaeger had done to her. 'I saw you all leaving. Where did you go? What did you do?'

Meena felt embarrassed to say, but, in the end, lying to Amma didn't feel right. 'We went to the Crown of Stones. It is a magical place where the Followers make spells and rituals. Draguta too.'

'Oh.' Amma lay back on the pillows. She was tired of being imprisoned in Draguta's suffocating chamber. Though she felt safe, locked away from Jaeger, she was starting to panic, knowing that soon they were all leaving to try and kill Axl and Jael. She was worried that they would succeed and she would be stuck in Hest forever. 'What did you do there?'

'We... Draguta... I...' Meena felt like vomiting, the bitter taste of the smoke still strong in her mouth. 'She bound a goddess. Then she made a fog. She... cursed it.' It was all such a blur. Meena still wasn't quite sure what Draguta had done.

'What?'

'It made the Brekkans see things that weren't there. They killed each other.'

Amma threw her hands over her mouth. 'No!'

Meena's cheeks reddened, ashamed that she had been there, helping to swirl the deceptive fog around Jael Furyck and her men.

On the wrong side once again.

'I saw Axl,' Meena whispered, eyes on the door. 'He was alive.'

'You're sure?'

Meena nodded.

'We have to do something.' Amma's voice was lower than Meena's, her eyes on the door too. 'We have to do something to stop her before it's too late.'

Meena shuddered, knowing that Amma was right. But now they were leaving, and Draguta had hidden the ring thanks to Evaine.

She needed to find it and destroy it.

But how?

Those two words crashed around her head, not finding any answers.

But how?

***

Jael dropped her head, remembering her fights with Torstan. She had beaten him every time, though he'd kept turning up to face her with a wobbly grin, trying to look confident. She smiled sadly, patting Thorgils on the shoulder. 'There'll be time when we're done with all of this. Time to talk about him. About those we've lost, those we'll lose along the way. But now isn't it. We have to hurry. We need to get away from this place before nightfall.'

Thorgils stood beside her, Beorn next to him, his eyes on the pile of bodies they had made. And it was a pile. At least one hundred men, and Marissa, the girl Jael had fought in Vallsborg; her throat slit, an arm missing, her eyes closed.

Thorgils wanted to reach out and touch Torstan's bloody hand. His most annoying of friends had always been one of his best. The guilt of his death would be a heavy weight to carry for the rest of his life. He thought about what Eadmund had done to him, leaving him for dead in Hallow Wood as he had. He would never let him feel guilty for it. It wasn't his fault – Thorgils felt that more strongly than ever – it wasn't Eadmund's fault.

Though, he would never absolve himself.

He couldn't.

Rubbing his eyes, angry and sad, he turned to Jael. 'We should leave.'

She nodded, looking for Axl and Raymon who had been gathering their men into some semblance of order. 'It's not far to go to get away from these open fields. Somewhere we can regroup. Talk about what we can do.'

'What can we do?' Karsten wondered, arriving with a frowning Fyn who could barely open his eyes against the pain in his head. 'What?'

'Keep going, and hope that those left standing will be enough. Fight to live. Expect to die. Believe that together we'll not be stopped in the end. Know that somehow, those left will make it all worth it. That's all we can do.'

Karsten nodded. It was what he needed to hear. And turning to Fyn, he clapped him on the back, noticing the enormous lump in the middle of his head. 'And try not to ride anywhere near Rork. Not unless you want to be knocked out by that block of stone!'

***

As night fell, the tailor arrived with a chest full of white silk dresses for Draguta to take on their journey, and she felt an immediate rush of excitement. Preparations for their departure were complete. The Hestian army had not expended much effort in Angard, with little loss of men or weapons during the attack. In fact, they had gained more weapons and ships. Gold and dreamers too.

There was little to organise in theory.

Their men were drilled, equipped, prepared. Eadmund and Jaeger had discussed their plans. Briggit and the dreamers were ready. Bound. Hers.

Just like Eadmund and Jaeger were hers.

Ballack and Meena had retrieved everything from the catacombs.

And now she had her dresses.

But, Draguta realised, walking into the baths, her eyes on the steam floating above the hot water, there were some problems she still needed to attend to. 'I'm not surprised Eadmund doesn't want a wretch like you, Evaine Gallas.'

Evaine looked up in confusion, seeing three white figures moving before her. It was dark. Flames dancing in sconces highlighted only snatches of colour and Evaine was too drunk to tell what was going on.

'Were you planning to drown yourself? Or slash your wrists and then drown yourself?' Draguta wondered coldly, stalking around the edge of the pool, her eyes on the knife Evaine was trying to conceal behind her. She was naked, submerged in the water, her face red, eyes bloodshot and swollen. 'I despise weakness,' Draguta hissed, crouching down, ice-blue eyes sharp and unsympathetic. 'And this is perhaps the weakest display I have ever witnessed. Certainly the most pathetic!' She stood, irritated, as Evaine hunched over, eyes hidden beneath her wet hair. 'Were you hoping Eadmund would suddenly realise his love for you while you were burning on your pyre? That you would finally get what you wanted by being dead?' She laughed, walking to a bench, where she brushed off a small bug and sat down.

Evaine didn't know what to say, and she realised that she was too drunk to even form words.

'Did you know that your ancestors can be traced back to the very first Followers? A coven of desperate sycophants, the lot of you! But ultimately, powerful dreamers. So many dreamers of great skill and reputation. And you and your idiot cousin are the last of them now. She is the most pointless dreamer I have ever met and you... well, what use were you ever going to be, except as a decoy?'

Evaine was too curious to be embarrassed as she lifted her head. 'What do you mean?'

'You didn't know?' Draguta laughed. 'Oh, you, Evaine Gallas, were bred to be a pot of honey for Eadmund to dip his finger into. To be so distracted by your beauty that he would stay far away from Jael Furyck, the woman he was destined to be with.' Draguta watched as Evaine started blinking rapidly. 'Your demented mother cursed both you and Eadmund, and now, here you are, ready to end it all. Life without him holds no meaning to you because being with Eadmund was all you were born to do.'

Evaine wasn't sure she understood Draguta at all. 'But I want to love Eadmund. I do love him.'

Draguta shook her head, standing. 'Then why are you trying to kill yourself, you idiot girl?' She picked up Evaine's dress from the bench and threw it at her. 'I gave you a chance, and despite humiliating yourself before me, that chance is still there. Prove yourself worthy of my help, and I will show you how to bind Eadmund again.'

'Prove?' Evaine pulled herself out of the water, reaching for her dress. 'How?'

***

The silence was heavy and somber as the army arrived at their campsite that night. And though they knew they should try to shake themselves out of it and look ahead, they stumbled around, setting fires, pitching tents, tending to horses. Silent. Numb. Struggling to raise their heads.

Ayla left a morose Bruno in the wagon and came to find Jael, who, having sorted out her tent, was making sure that Tig was secure for the night. She wanted him close. They had brought the horses into their campsite, knowing there was a possibility that they would have to leave in a hurry; worried that Draguta would try to hurt them.

They had to keep them safe.

'We're not safe,' Ayla sighed.

'No, we aren't,' Jael agreed. 'We've not been safe since Draguta returned. And we won't be till she's gone.'

'But we can try to make ourselves safe tonight,' Ayla insisted. 'You and I. We're the only two here who have a chance of keeping everyone alive. Tonight, tomorrow, the day after that. You, me, and your raven.'

Jael nodded. 'We need to make those circles Edela mentioned. A dreamer circle with that symbol. If you can show me, I'll make one too.'

'Yes, that's why I've come. We'll make one each. I only wish we could make one around all of us, but that would take all night. It would be impossible to keep it intact with so many men. Drunk men too. I imagine there'll be some drinking after what happened today.'

'I imagine so.'

'We can make them here,' Ayla said, glancing around in the nearly-dark, pleased that the ground was reasonably flat and amenable to circle making. 'You can invite whomever you want inside. But you will need to close it and guard it. I'll show you how.'

Jael followed Ayla, her empty stomach rumbling, but with the smell of their burning men still in her nostrils, she didn't want to think about food.

Not tonight.

CHAPTER THIRTY NINE

Jael woke before anyone was stirring.

It was dark, and the walls of her tent were still. For a moment, she wasn't sure it was morning, though she felt anxious to get moving, wanting to ensure that everyone had made it through the night. Sitting up in her creaking bed, she saw that Aleksander had gone. He had taken second watch and was no doubt wandering around outside, trying to keep himself awake.

It felt cold, and Jael shivered as she dragged on her boots, trying to clear Torstan's face from her mind. Torstan's face, Thorgils' face. She couldn't even imagine how bad he felt.

But not as bad as Torstan, she imagined with a sad grin.

Spinning around suddenly, Jael saw Fyr watching her from the end of the bed. It was becoming less shocking to see the raven now. More comforting. 'Thanks to you,' she mumbled, turning away to pull her swordbelt out from under the bed. 'Thanks to you, I don't have to feel like Thorgils today.' And sitting up, she came face to face with a woman standing in the corner by her bed, draped in a shimmering black cloak, her long white hair almost touching the ground.

Daala, Mother of the Tuuran Gods.

She had come to Jael the night of the barsk attack, warned her then.

Daala stepped towards the bed. 'What happened yesterday...' Her distress gave her voice a heaviness, a weight she had not felt in centuries. If ever. 'It was a change, Jael. For all of us. We must protect ourselves now. If Draguta captures any more of the gods, she will use us against you. We are powerful, and in her hands, weapons that will cause great devastation. My gods, Vidar's... we must hide.'

Jael wondered if she was dreaming. She moved her right hand to Toothpick's pommel, wanting to feel some certainty in what she was seeing. 'I... you saved me. Us. You helped. You protected us against Draguta.'

'As Fyr?' Daala barely blinked. 'I did what I could in the moment, and so did Edela. Her and the Book of Aurea, which, thankfully, has had enough answers up until now.'

Jael frowned, worried for her grandmother. 'Won't Draguta try again? To take it?'

Daala clasped her hands in front of her cloak. 'Draguta no longer feels constrained. She has much that makes her powerful in her own right. Perhaps she has no need to fear the Book of Aurea any longer? Not now that she has found that evil ring and claimed an army of dreamers. Their power makes her even stronger. Strong enough to claim any man or god she chooses.'

'But how do we stop her, then? How do we fight her without the gods to help us? She's going to pick us off, one by one, isn't she? Until there's just me standing.'

'She wants you, yes. You are the symbol of all that she despises. You and Eadmund. Because you are ours. Our weapons. She will pit you against each other until one of you kills the other. Then she will claim victory. Victory over the gods, the Furycks, and Osterland. We will all be hers.'

Jael's mouth hung open in surprise. 'You see this happening?'

'That is what Draguta believes will happen.'

'I have no magic,' Jael tried. 'No way to stop her. My sword...'

Hearing a noise, Daala spun towards the tent flap, and when she turned back, Jael could see that her face had softened. 'There came a time when I realised that to save everyone, I had to kill my husband.'

Jael froze.

'It was something I avoided for longer than I should have,' Daala admitted. 'I had heard the rumours, seen some of the evidence myself, but I was not prepared to face it. I hid from my fate for a time, but eventually, I killed Raemus. I had no choice. His love for me had corrupted him. His obsession with the Darkness had destroyed him. Killing him was the only way to save everyone else.'

'But Eadmund isn't corrupt. He's bound to Draguta, a prisoner. We can help him. I don't have to kill him.'

Daala held out a hand, helping Jael to her feet. 'That may be so. For your sake, Jael, I hope it is. But I came to tell you how it feels to be faced with that very choice. Your husband or your people? Who will you save? When the time comes, who will you save?' She watched Jael's eyes working hard to avoid hers, worrying for a moment that Jael Furyck was not who they had always believed she would become. 'Eadmund is lost. Perhaps you will find him again? Perhaps his sister will? Or it may be that he is Draguta's forever. Time will tell, Jael. I will be with you until the end. I will not retreat from this fight, and nor can you. Not now.'

Jael shivered, seeing the times Eadmund had looked straight through her; the memories of him with Evaine; the nights in Eirik's hot pool; sitting outside Ketil's, listening to Thorgils' terrible jokes.

Closing her eyes, she tried to hold onto the image of his smiling face, and when she opened them, Aleksander was there, light streaming through the tent opening.

'Jael? Are you alright?'

She stared at him, her memories slipping away.

Just as Daala had.

She nodded quickly. 'I am.'

***

It was dark when Briggit woke.

Or was she still in a dream?

She could smell jasmine strongly, and reminded of where she was she sighed, rolling over. Then her dream rushed back to her, and she shivered, eyes blinking as the first hint of light crept in through the balcony door.

She smiled.

How much clearer everything suddenly appeared after the right dream.

***

Dawn had only just broken when Draguta yanked a sleep-drunk Meena out of bed, and threw her out of the castle, into the winding gardens to pick some herbs for the last spell she would cast before their departure. And when Meena returned, wide awake and hungry, Draguta led her back up to the horrible little chamber at the top of the castle, where they sat on stools, waiting for Brill to arrive. She did, eventually, bringing one of Eadmund's old tunics with her.

'Excellent!' Draguta exclaimed, rubbing her hands together. 'This is not something I want Briggit's help with. Nor any of my new dreamers. And especially not Evaine. Not for this. I do not wish anyone to see how I bind them.'

She was speaking so quietly as she tore Eadmund's tunic into little strips that Meena wasn't sure that Draguta intended them to hear her, but she looked at her just the same, waiting to respond.

Draguta sat up, eyes on Meena. 'Eadmund is straying far from where he needs to be, wouldn't you say? Fighting against his destiny? It is not good enough for him to simply be here. I require him to be on our side. Our warrior. Our hero against the gods and the pathetic woman they think can defeat us. Poor lovesick Eadmund is under her spell as much as mine, but it is time to put an end to that!' She smiled, her eyes on the licorice root Meena was grinding in the bowl. 'Another slice, I think, don't you? And then you may hand me the vine.'

***

Breakfast was porridge, and though there was little enthusiasm to be found, most forced it down, knowing that they had another long day ahead. There wasn't much conversation either, but there were a lot of tired eyes straining in the sunshine, peering around, searching for the next trouble heading their way.

'I'll keep you by me today, Ayla,' Jael said, pulling off her boot, trying to find the tiny pebble rolling around in it. 'You and the wagon. Just in case.'

'Do you think she'll try something today?' Ayla wondered, stirring her porridge. Bruno had tossed and turned all night, disturbed by nightmares he couldn't escape. He'd had no appetite for breakfast at all.

'I don't know. I hope not. I'd like to get through the day without having to burn someone I care about.' Jael frowned, remembering her talk with Daala about Eadmund.

Had that even happened?

The shivers running up her arms quickly told her the truth about that.

Ayla lifted her head as Astrid arrived with a basket of berries. 'I found these,' she said mutely. 'It might make that porridge taste better.' She had been off in the forest since dawn, wanting to give Bruno and Ayla some space to be alone. And herself. She was struggling to cope with the increasing terror gripping her body, knowing that she needed to find a way to be useful. To fight against the desire to simply hide in the corner of the wagon and sob.

'We're going to bring the wagon near Jael today,' Ayla told her. 'At the front.'

Bruno squirmed. 'Think I'll ride. Near the back. There are plenty of spare horses now. I don't want to be with you today. I want you to be safe. From me.'

Jael could see Ayla's distress as she nodded. 'It makes sense. If there's someone you care about, it makes sense not to be too close to them. Just in case.'

'But... but...'

'I'll keep you safe,' Jael assured Ayla, her eyes on Thorgils who was tipping his porridge onto the ground. 'Don't worry. I doubt Draguta will try the same spell again. She seems like the sort of woman who wants to keep us guessing right up until the end.'

'The end?' Aleksander wondered, reaching for his water bag. 'And what do you think that will be, then?' His eyes met Jael's, and he frowned, unable to read her look at all.

She shrugged. 'I'm not sure anyone knows. Not after all that's happened. Perhaps not even Dara Teros herself?'

***

'I must go to Andala.'

Dara felt it strongly.

Eloris wasn't convinced. 'You are not safe, Dara. Not once you leave here. This cave is the only place we can hide you now. These symbols are keeping you from Draguta.'

'For how long? You have kept me safe, I know, but this is the end. Can't you feel it, Eloris? This is the end, and I must be there. I must help. And you must help me get there.'

Eloris was the Tuuran Goddess of the Forests. She was timid, gentle, nurturing, but not especially brave. 'But Daala wanted you to stay here, with me. She wanted to keep you hidden from Draguta.'

'Unless I was needed. Which I am.'

Eloris frowned. 'You are sure you dreamed it?'

'I feel it,' Dara insisted. 'I feel a darkness shifting inside me. It is loud and terrifying, as though it is reasserting the balance of the entire world. And if that balance shifts, it will not be in our favour, will it? We will all die. Humans will die. Creatures too. And as the keeper of the forests, you are bound to care for and protect them, aren't you?'

Eloris looked towards the mouth of the cave, watching rain streaming down like a waterfall. She liked the rain. The sound of it was helping to hide them away, masking their voices, keeping them safe. 'I am, yes, but leaving here? Making that journey? We will need to protect ourselves. If you wish to leave for Andala, there is much we need to think through. Draguta is growing more powerful. She has trapped Veiga and bound her. She may find us and kill you.'

Dara smiled, knowing that despite her fears, Eloris was bound to help Jael Furyck too, just as she was. And now they had no choice.

They had to get to Andala.

***

Bayla was not enjoying her new house.

It had floorboards, two fires, and separate bedchambers which gave her more privacy. She had two servants helping her with the children. Ulf was in and out; Berard too. But mainly, she was all alone, waiting for the next terror to strike down her family.

She worried about Karsten, knowing that he was her only chance for a return to her old life, though when she thought about it, she realised that even if Karsten were to reclaim Hest from Jaeger and the rest of them were able to defeat Draguta, her life would never be the same again.

Bayla sat on a stool in front of the fire, watching Ulf walk through the door. His face broke into a weary grin at the sight of her, slumped forward, not a child in sight. No servant either. Berard, he knew, was up on the ramparts, and they were actually alone for the first time in memory. 'Enjoying the peace and quiet?' he wondered with a wink, plonking himself down on the stool opposite her.

'I am not. No.'

Ulf frowned. 'Not even enjoying the bigger house?'

Bayla studied him, her shoulders sinking further. 'I feel like a wild boar running through a forest, knowing the hounds are after me. The hounds and the horses and the men with their spears. All after me. And I keep running, listening to my own heart beat. Running with my family, until they're all killed, one by one, and then I'm alone in the darkness. Waiting. Hiding. Knowing that they will kill me too.'

Ulf blinked, watching the terror in her eyes. The resignation.

'And who will care for the children when I'm gone? Berard? You?'

Ulf nodded. 'We will.'

'Why?' Bayla spat. 'Why would you? They're not yours. Not your children. Not your grandchildren. Why would you care?'

'I... I just do. I care about you, Bayla. They are your family, so I care about them too.'

The look in Ulf's eyes was one of such gentleness and concern that Bayla burst into tears, burying her face in her hands. Ulf was quickly off his stool, wrapping an arm around her. He felt her flinch before she relaxed, and he squeezed her tightly, not wanting her to feel alone.

***

Eadmund found Sigmund in Amma's chamber, which was handy as he wanted to say goodbye to her too.

Tanja had left to take a break, and Amma was happy to have

Sigmund's company. He wriggled on her bed, pulling on his toes, making happy baby noises. For a moment it stopped her from thinking about what was coming. But then she looked up at Eadmund, who stood silently by the bed watching his son, and she shivered. 'He will miss you,' she said. When she stared at Eadmund closely, she could see that something was different about him.

It troubled her.

'He's too young to notice me either way,' Eadmund insisted, holding his finger out for Sigmund to grab.

Amma wasn't going to argue. 'Well, I hope...' She stopped, realising that she didn't know what to say. 'I hope you'll stay safe, Eadmund.'

The door swung open, and Evaine flounced in, bleary-eyed, nauseous but determined to ignore everything that had happened since she'd last spoken to Eadmund. 'There you are!' she exclaimed, smiling at her son. 'Tanja said she'd left him here.'

Eadmund turned to Evaine, eyes blank. He studied her face, seeing only anger and resentment. Perhaps a little desperation too. 'Missing him, were you?'

Evaine stiffened. 'Yes, I will miss him when we leave.'

'You're coming?' That was a surprise.

Evaine looked pleased to have claimed Eadmund's attention. 'I am. Draguta requires my help, so she has insisted that I accompany her.'

Amma looked just as shocked but immediately relieved to think that she wouldn't have to suffer Evaine's company for a while.

Eadmund sighed, bending down to kiss Sigmund's head, surprised by the sudden tears on his son's cheeks. 'Take care of yourself,' he said, staring at Amma. 'We will return soon, once it's all done.' He turned to Evaine. 'You should get the baby to Tanja, then. Draguta will be waiting for us.' And without waiting for her, he headed to the door.

Evaine didn't even look at Amma as she scooped a now crying Sigmund into her arms, hurrying after Eadmund. And though she felt ready to sleep or vomit, and though Eadmund kept glaring at her as though she was his enemy, she knew that, with Draguta's help, she still had a chance of claiming his heart.

***

'I don't think you should be riding next to me,' Thorgils mumbled as Jael nudged Tig alongside him. 'Best keep your distance.'

Jael smiled. 'You don't think I could beat you in a fight?' She saw a hint of humour in Thorgils' eyes.

Just a hint.

'Well, you've been looking a little rusty lately. That Marissa could've embarrassed you if you hadn't gotten lucky.' He frowned suddenly, remembering that she was dead too.

Jael was quiet for a moment before shoving his arm. 'Really?'

'I didn't want to say anything earlier, you being so moody, but somebody had to.'

Jael laughed out loud, wanting to forget all about Marissa and Torstan and the image of their burning bodies. 'Got any salt fish stuffed down your trousers today?' She was trying to cheer him up, which would then cheer her up. Nobody made her smile as much as Thorgils.

'No. Just a very big sausage.'

Jael shook her head. 'Well, serves me right for asking.'

Thorgils burst out laughing, slapping his thigh. He felt terrible, but at the same time, it was a relief to feel an emotion that wasn't guilt.

They rode on, skirting Hallow Wood, heading south towards the vale, the sky a dull grey above them. There were trees on both sides now. Rows and rows of young silver birches bordering a wide, well-ridden path that made for fast travel, though Ayla's wagon was clattering loudly behind them, not coping well with the pace.

'I've been thinking about Eadmund,' Thorgils said, no humour in his eyes now. 'About how we're going to get him back.'

'Me too.' Jael was watching Axl and Aleksander who rode ahead of them, heads together. It was odd to see them without Gant. She kept expecting to turn around and find him there, lifting a stern eyebrow, watching over all of them.

'We can't leave him behind, Jael, whatever happens. Whatever state he's in, we can't abandon him.'

Jael remembered her talk with Daala and her shoulders tensed. 'I'll do everything I can to save him, you know that.'

That didn't sound reassuring, and Thorgils peered at her, trying to smile again. 'So will I. You're not alone in that, even though I'm sure it feels as though you are. You're not. Your Islanders are all with you. We want you to bring Eadmund home too.'

Jael pulled gently on the reins, guiding Tig around a deep hole. 'Then we'd better hope I'm not as rusty as you say, or else I'm going to be in big trouble when Eadmund gets hold of me!'

***

Draguta's army of dreamers would be walking to the Vale of the Gods.

Though she knew that they were now bound to her, the taint of their fanatical loyalty to Raemus remained, and she couldn't hide the joy she felt in thinking of how much they would suffer on their trek over the mountains, into the south of Brekka.

Briggit would be riding beside her, behind Jaeger and Eadmund.

Though not overly fond of horses, Briggit was grateful that Draguta viewed her as important enough to keep by her side; relieved that she would not have to endure the discomfort of swollen, blistered feet.

It was another unforgiving day of burning sun, absent any breeze, and Draguta was thrilled, not bothered by the heat, or the look of annoyance on Jaeger's face as he peered down at the rows of dreamers who would be marching near the front of their columns. 'Why aren't they further back?' he grumbled. 'I wanted them further back.'

Draguta eyed him with irritation. 'Sometimes, it would benefit you to think more than you talk. For if you did, you would realise that keeping our prizes close by makes sense. Say we were to be attacked. Should I then wait for all the dreamers to hurry up the line to find me? And how would that even be possible when we are crawling around some of those perilous paths as we head into the mountains? Do think, Jaeger! Just for once!'

That almost put a smile on Eadmund's face as he came down the steps with Evaine.

'Been crying, have we?' Draguta mused, staring at Evaine's cheerful face. 'Sad to be leaving your son behind?'

Evaine looked confused as she followed Eadmund to her horse, which, she was unhappy to see, appeared larger than any she had ridden before. 'I am, yes. But I know he will be well taken care of.'

'I'm sure he will,' Draguta laughed, turning to Meena who was wobbling nervously on her pony which was so fat that she could barely see its legs. 'You will ride in front of me, little mouse,' she smiled. 'It will give us some entertainment on the ride, I'm sure!'

Briggit's black stallion reared up, throwing back its head, forcing her to grab the reins as she slid out of the saddle, taking everyone's attention away from Meena. She turned around to peer at Brill, sitting atop a small grey pony who was becoming increasingly terrified by her loud sneezes.

'Are you alright?' Meena wondered. 'Brill?'

Draguta spun around, watching her. 'What are you doing back there?' she grumbled, eyes narrowed. 'What are you talking about?'

'I'm just seeing how Brill is,' Meena spluttered, moving her eyes back to Draguta as she spurred her pony forward.

'Is there anyone else you would like to help, then? Anything else we can do for you, Meena Gallas? Please, do take your time!'

And happy to see that Jaeger had sorted Briggit out, Draguta turned around to Eadmund who had mounted his horse, impatient to make a start.

He took a deep breath, feeling the certainty of his destiny enclose him like a cloak, leaving all thoughts of his mother and the shield, and Jael, far behind.

PART FIVE

Enemies

CHAPTER FORTY

Edela had finished casting her circle around the interior of the fort, and now they were trapped inside it, which was inconvenient, though slightly comforting. Nothing had come for them since the whisp attack, and though the shock of it still reverberated and the implications of the slaughter of their livestock were sinking in, some Andalans were starting to relax.

Which wasn't making Gant feel at ease.

He left the stables with Bram, an intense frown digging a canyon between his eyebrows. 'What do they think? That she'll just stop? Leave us alone?' He hadn't been sleeping, and his temper was fraying, though he doubted he was alone in that.

'I think there's a need to feel something other than fear. To not be on edge every moment of the day and night. They want to forget what has happened. To feel safe,' Bram said, nodding at Berard who was walking with Hanna, trying to entertain his nieces and nephews, and take her mind off her father. 'Perhaps Draguta will be busy now? Worrying about the army?'

Gant didn't like that thought either. He sighed, coming to a stop. 'I can't read the woman's mind, but it seems to me that she's determined to conquer us one way or the other. She won't let us be. We can't sit back and think we're safe. That a few nights without an attack means we're free from Draguta.'

'No, we can't.' Bram hadn't stopped thinking about Thorgils and Fyn. They were his family now. Isaura and the children too.

They needed to return. He wanted the chance to bring them all together. To go back to Oss. To start a new life.

Berard watched Bram and Gant walk past, muttering to each other. They looked worried, and though they were enclosed inside Edela's circle now, he did not feel safe at all. Not in the slightest. He had lost so many members of his family since that night in the castle when Jaeger had taken his arm, that it was hard not to feel as though it would continue. And looking down at the children, he was terrified that before long it would be one of them.

'They are being very brave,' Hanna said, her eyes on Halla who was toddling along beside her, holding her hand, not interested in running after her brother and sister or her cousins. 'You all are.'

'I'm not sure we have any choice,' Berard admitted. 'Doesn't feel like we do. Just one foot after the other. Hope for some luck.'

'It feels like that, doesn't it?' Hanna thought about her father, who was not improving. She glanced at the hall, wanting to get back to his chamber. 'But I think we're all due some luck, don't you? Something must go our way soon. It can't all be like this. It can't be the end of everything.'

The gloom descended upon them both, which only made the children more miserable. Realising it, Hanna lifted her head. 'There are strawberries on that table over there!' she exclaimed with a weary grin. 'Why don't we go and help ourselves? Looks like someone's put them out just for us.' No one looked interested in strawberries, but Hanna didn't notice as her attention was suddenly drawn to Entorp who was aiming straight for her. 'What is it?' She hurried towards him, her heart throbbing in her chest. 'Has something happened?'

'It's your father,' Entorp panted. 'You need to come!'

***

After being forced to ride at the front for much of the morning,

Meena had finally been sent behind Draguta who had grown bored with the plodding pace of her rotund pony. Now her pony was struggling along beside Ballack on his giant white horse. Meena didn't want Ballack for company, but at least he was better than Evaine, who had, thankfully, slipped back to ride near Eadmund. Nor did she want to be close to Briggit Halvardar, who kept turning around to stare at her.

She swallowed as Briggit spun around again, keen eyes roaming her face before dropping to her breasts. Briggit winked, turning back around, confusing Meena entirely.

Ballack chuckled, noticing how flustered she was becoming. 'You're never safe with that one,' he grinned, revealing only a handful of brown teeth. 'I'd watch where you're sleeping tonight. Make sure you're far away from her. She can't keep her hands to herself from what I've heard!'

Ignoring Ballack and his toothless mockery, Meena glanced over her shoulder at the two wagons clattering behind a morose looking Evaine who had been rebuffed by Eadmund and was now riding alone. One was filled with most of the contents of Draguta's bedchamber, the other contained the boxes they had retrieved from the catacombs. The decaying reek emanating from that wagon was strong, overpowering even the smell of Ballack who didn't appear to be a man familiar with the concept of washing.

But which boxes, Meena wondered, letting her mind wander. The Book of Darkness was in there, she knew, locked in an iron chest.

But the ring?

She had not seen what Draguta had done with that.

And when she found it...

Meena swallowed, sweat pooling along her upper lip. She wiped it away, thinking about how quickly night would come. Once they stopped and set up camp, she would have an opportunity to find out where it was.

***

Edela had been visiting Kayla and Aedan, taking some time away from the hall and the worries of trying to outmanoeuvre dangerous dreamers and the dark magic of their ancient books. Biddy's urgent face at the door had her on her toes, though, racing back through the square.

And when she arrived in Marcus' chamber, Hanna was sobbing, holding her father's hand. Entorp and Derwa stood at the foot of the bed, silent. Edela took one look at their faces, and her shoulders dropped.

Hanna's tears flowed with even greater force as she looked at the old dreamer. 'Someone has to do something. Please! Edela? Someone has to do something!' Letting go of Marcus' hand, she rubbed the tears out of her eyes, reaching for Edela. 'Please!'

Edela grasped her hands. 'Let me see. Let me see.' And she allowed Hanna to lead her to the bed where Marcus lay. She caught Derwa's eyes and saw the resignation in them. And when she reached out a hand to Marcus' head, she felt that he was slipping away. 'Hanna,' Edela soothed, squeezing her hand, trying to get her attention. 'Come here now, and say goodbye. Tell him everything. Do it now.'

Hanna looked horrified, shocked. 'But... I...'

Edela pushed her forward and slipped out of the way, leaving Hanna to take Marcus' hand again.

'I love you,' Hanna sobbed. 'I wish... I wish we had... I wish...' She couldn't go on, not believing that any of it could be real. 'I don't blame you. I love you.' And she threw herself onto her father's chest, wrapping her arms around him, wanting to hold onto him, to keep him with her. 'Please don't go. Please! No!'

Biddy came into the room with Berard who watched as Hanna suddenly stopped crying, standing up, realising that her father had stopped breathing.

She was in shock. She didn't know what to do.

'Hanna.' Berard's voice was soft, and she turned towards it, seeing him, bursting into tears again as he hurried towards her.

'Berard!'

'Oh, Hanna, I'm so sorry for you,' Berard murmured, his arm around her back as she leaned towards him, seeking comfort. 'So very sorry.'

***

They followed a babbling stream throughout the afternoon, Jael keeping her eyes on Fyr in the distance, looking back occasionally to check on Ayla and Astrid's wagon whose wheels were squeaking and creaking behind her.

Raymon had left his men to ride beside Jael, and she was debating what to say to him. Getta and Garren Maas had been lovers. Or perhaps that was only in Garren's head? She didn't know, but Garren had insisted that Getta supported his rebellion against her husband. It was something Raymon needed to know.

But not now.

She heard her father's voice booming in her ears, warning her away.

Their father's voice.

'Getta's not a Furyck.' Jael couldn't help herself. She wanted to say something.

Something truthful.

Raymon was surprised. 'She's not?'

'Lothar wasn't a Furyck. The elderman told me. A dreamer told him. My grandmother had a lover. Lothar's father.'

'Oh, that explains a lot. Getta was quiet after we came back from Rissna... about you.' Raymon looked awkward. 'Before we left, she was different, angry. I... thought it was just about what had happened in the forest. But perhaps it was more?'

Jael was suddenly focused on Tig who threw up his head, snorting. She glanced around, scanning the trees, listening for anything out of the ordinary. 'I don't imagine what happened in the forest helped, but what I told her about Lothar wouldn't have helped either. I just thought you should know.'

Raymon nodded, though he didn't say anything.

Jael's attention wandered.

'Though likely she was upset about you killing Garren too.'

Jael froze, her eyes fixed straight ahead.

'They were... close,' Raymon almost whispered, 'before we were married. I know that. I suspect it never stopped. Perhaps she was even involved in what he did?' He looked at Jael, wanting to see some confirmation of his fears.

Not wanting to see a confirmation of his fears.

Jael tried to mask her feelings. 'She's your wife. Mother of your son. If you love her, that's a good thing. You need to think about getting back to her. There'll be plenty of time to talk about everything then.'

Raymon was almost relieved, wanting to put all thoughts of his wife behind him for now. He needed to concentrate on what was coming. If he didn't, he wouldn't stand any chance of making it back to his son.

Hearing a thunder of hooves, Jael turned around as Thorgils pulled his horse in beside her, an attempt at a smile on his face. 'What?'

'Oh, nothing, just wanted to stretch out our legs,' he grinned, patting his chestnut mare. 'Thought you might like that salt fish now?' And handing Jael a hard sliver of fish, he gave her a wink before spinning his horse around and thundering back down the line, splattering mud all over her.

'It's hard to keep up with him,' Jael smiled, wiping her face, relieved to have seen a sign of life in Thorgils' eyes.

***

Marcus' death cast a shadow over the fort. There had been so much grief to cope with, but the loss of the Elderman of Tuura affected them all.

Hanna didn't notice as she stood by Berard who was handing out slices of apple to Halla, Valder, and Lucina Dragos who were orphans, just as she was an orphan now.

It hurt too much to cry. Her throat was sore, her eyes ached, and she wanted to fall down and sleep until the pain went away, but she stood there, beside Berard, listening to the chatter of the children as they munched on their apple slices.

'Here,' Biddy said, handing her a cup of ale. 'Something to drink.'

Hanna took the cup, though she felt sick. She wondered how many cups it would take before she stopped feeling anything at all. 'Thank you.'

'All gone!' Berard exclaimed, holding up his hand. 'Why don't you go outside, see if you can find your cousins?'

None of the children looked excited by that idea. Halla shoved the last piece of apple in her mouth with one hand and grabbed Hanna's hand with the other, squeezing hard.

Hanna blinked, looking down at the little girl, remembering Karsten's offer. And suddenly, the desire to run away from Brekka and Tuura and the memories of her father was overwhelming. 'I'll come with you,' she said, turning to Berard. 'When you go home. If you go home. Karsten asked me to come and help with the children. I will. I'll come with you.'

Berard looked surprised, glancing down at his tiny niece who was now leaning against Hanna, hoping to be picked up. 'You will?'

Hanna thought about Aleksander, but he was not hers and never would be. She knew that now. Tears stung her eyes, and she wanted to run back into the chamber where Derwa and Entorp were preparing her father's body for his pyre, but Halla had her hand and Berard reached out and took the other.

She nodded. 'Yes, I will.'

***

Meena wished she'd been left behind with Amma. She thought of how it would feel to be alone in the castle. Alone but for the quiet and amenable servants who would bring her food and then leave her in peace. Who would make her bed and wash her clothes. Perhaps even brush her hair which was a wild bush of matted knots, slightly limp in the heat, sticking to her neck, making her feel even hotter.

She frowned, wondering about Else and Dragmall, hoping they were safe. Though, she realised, glancing around, no one was safe now. Draguta was leading them all to their deaths. Perhaps Jaeger and Eadmund too? They continued to ride up ahead in silence, side by side to please Draguta, ignoring each other, Briggit and Draguta behind them, chatting occasionally. And Meena was left to ride further back with Evaine, who had gotten her horse under some control now, though she refused to even look at her cousin. She kept her eyes ahead, sometimes looking up at the jagged red cliffs, muttering to herself.

'Wine!' Draguta declared, turning around. 'Don't you think it's time for wine, Briggit?'

Briggit nodded, her bronzed face shining with sweat. The heat was growing more unbearable, though Draguta didn't appear affected. Her skin remained pale and luminescent, not a hint of sun touching it.

Brill was quickly turning her pony around, heading for the first wagon as Draguta called for Eadmund and Jaeger to stop. They all needed a drink and somewhere to shelter from the intense beating of the sun, but there wasn't even a cloud and on this long, straight and narrow path, no tree either.

Handing her reins to Ballack, Brill dropped down from her pony and hurried into the long covered wagon, returning quickly with two silver goblets of wine.

Draguta stretched out her elegant neck, reaching for one of the goblets. 'Take some to my kings,' she ordered 'I'm sure they are just as parched.' She made no mention of the equally perspiring Meena and Evaine as she turned back to Briggit. 'We must think of something to entertain ourselves with on this tedious journey. I want to keep our friends on their toes. We cannot let them think that we've forgotten about them, can we? No, that will simply not do!'

Briggit lifted an eyebrow, excited by the thought of it.

Meena didn't like wine, but she would have drunk from a puddle at that moment, watching Brill hurry past her with two more goblets; red liquid slopping over silver rims. Her mouth dropped open, and she could taste the dust in her throat.

Draguta turned around to glare at her. 'Close that gaping mouth. I do not wish to look inside it!'

Meena wanted to scream. She blinked, surprised by the rush of anger that pulsed inside her melting body, surging towards her temples. Holding her breath, she waited for Draguta to spin around and glare at her some more.

But she didn't.

***

Dragmall and Else's journey had been beset by problems. Everything appeared to be conspiring against them making any progress. Their most recent mishap had been an issue with a wheel that had stranded them in a tiny village dug into the side of a mountain for nearly two days.

Dragmall was beside himself at the delay, frantic to get going again, because he'd had a dream. He had been up at dawn, urging the wheelwright to finish his repairs, and now, as the sun was heading for its peak, they were well on their way again, leaving the village of Gamla far behind.

'If only I'd known you were a dreamer,' Else grinned, bouncing along on the seat next to Dragmall, trying not to bite her tongue as she nibbled on a flatbread. 'I'd have come to you for some advice years ago, and not ended up in Draguta's clutches!' She frowned suddenly. 'Why did you stay in Hest? Did you not see what was coming?'

Dragmall looked uncomfortable, his attention on the path ahead. Their wagon was wide, and the path appeared to be narrowing to a rather challenging degree. He had travelled this way before but not for years, and rockslides had changed the landscape over time. Many of the paths were new, dug around those which had fallen away or been blocked by boulders, but none were as wide as the older ones, he was sure.

He was starting to worry that they would have to abandon the wagon, and if that happened, they would most assuredly not arrive in time.

'I did not see everything, Else. I would have intervened if I had. But I always knew that the shield would be required one day. I knew that I must keep myself safe, able to help when the time came. And returning to Helsabor would have been too dangerous. There are no volkas left there anymore.'

'No. And no Followers now that Draguta has captured them.'

'Well, I doubt anyone will cry about that.'

'And what was this dream you had last night, then?' Else wondered suddenly. 'Something good, I hope? Something about Meena?'

'It was.' Dragmall gave Else his first smile of the day, and he was pleased to see how happy it made her.

'Really? Is she alright?' Else almost stood up. 'Is she safe?'

Dragmall shrugged, sweltering in his cloak, though better to be sweltering, he'd decided, than burned to a crisp as Else was. Even his hood was up, trying to hide his face from the scorching sun. 'I don't think Meena will be safe while Draguta lives. But she is alive, riding with her, I saw that.'

Else slumped backwards, relieved. 'Oh, I'm so pleased, Dragmall. So pleased!'

'Yes, but now we must get to her.'

'Must we?'

'Mmmm, Meena is on her way to the Vale of the Gods. And that, my dear Else, is where we must head, and quickly!'

Else shivered, biting her lip as a wheel hit a rock. 'The Vale of the Gods?' She'd heard stories about that sacred place. A place where the gods had waged their battles.

Few humans ever went there.

Until now.

CHAPTER FORTY ONE

Nagging thoughts were not just nagging thoughts for dreamers.

Edela knew that.

They were lost memories that needed to be reclaimed. And not reclaiming them was starting to become a bad habit. It was age. And weakness. Both of those things were true. The exhaustion of terror and panic. Worry too.

But there was no time for any of it. She had to find a way through. Back to the place where her dreams were waiting for her.

If only she could get more sleep.

Ontine and Eydis had been dreaming, and some of what they had seen was helpful, but Edela was struggling to make herself fall asleep. She wondered if Draguta was doing something to her?

Keeping her away from her dreams?

Biddy crawled back under her fur, lying opposite Edela. 'What are you doing awake?' she whispered, conscious of how late it was. Bodies were strewn around the circle in the hall, sleeping foot to head, elbow to back: Branwyn and Hanna; Gant and Gisila; Kayla and Aedan and their daughter; Derwa, Alaric, and, of course, Ido and Vella who remained alert, heads popping up occasionally, hearing an odd noise.

'Trying to go to sleep,' Edela whispered back irritably. 'Or it could be that stew. I don't think onions agree with me anymore.'

Biddy smiled, closing her eyes which felt heavy, just like the rest of her aching body. 'Sounds about right. Freya's getting too heavy-handed with the onions. I'll talk to her tomorrow.'

Edela closed her own eyes, imagining how that would go. Freya had always ruled the kitchen with a whip of a tongue. Even Jael was afraid of her.

Sighing deeply and trying to stop thinking about food, Edela pulled her hands to her chest, curling into a ball, wanting to feel the sense of security that had eluded her for so long; the confidence that the answers were waiting to be discovered in her dreams. And then sighing, she opened her eyes.

Wide awake.

***

'It's not cold!' Karsten snorted, heading for his tent, watching Jael shiver by her own. 'How are you cold?'

Thorgils had drunk more ale than his legs could handle, and he wobbled, slapping Karsten on the back. 'You've never met a colder woman than Jael Furyck. Some say she's made of fire, but I think ice runs in those veins!' And he stumbled into his tent, Karsten's smile flashing in the moonlight as he followed him inside.

'You can have my fur,' Fyn offered. 'I'm not cold.'

Jael was starting to feel as though she was imagining the drop in temperature. Or perhaps she was ill? 'You're sure it's not cold?'

Aleksander laughed. 'Take Fyn's fur and go to bed. I'll take first watch tonight. You try and stay warm.'

Jael glowered at them both, not wanting to feel like an old woman, but she grabbed the fur Fyn had retrieved from the tent he was sharing with Axl, and draped it over her shoulders. Turning around, she watched Tig's head drooping by her tent, Sky just as still beside him. They were inside her circle. She had made one that encompassed their four tents; Raymon's tent as well.

'Goodnight, Jael!'

Jael lifted a hand to Ayla and Astrid who were heading for their wagon. Ayla had made her own circle for all the wagons, including hers and Astrid's. After what Draguta had done to Andala, they didn't want to lose their food stores.

There was still too much of the journey ahead of them to risk that.

***

They had camped for the night in another crumbling village. Hest was full of them, it seemed; each one clinging more precariously to the familiar red cliffs than the one before. Eadmund was looking forward to seeing something resembling a tree. A bush. Some grass.

He yawned, trying to get comfortable in his cot bed, happy to be alone.

Draguta had relented and let him leave Berrick behind, but she had brought Evaine, who had been far more irritating than his fussing steward ever was; riding beside him, trying to draw his attention to her appearance, constantly needing to be helped with her horse. Well, the last part was true, he realised. Evaine couldn't ride, and her poor horse looked ready to bolt.

He wondered if he should just let it.

Eadmund rolled over again, trying to smile, but he couldn't. He felt empty of everything but the need to keep going.

There were chanting voices rising outside his tent. Part of him felt curious, but most of him was tired, and all of him was so bound to Draguta that he knew he had no right to know what was going on.

Whatever she was doing out there, he would not stop her.

He couldn't.

From now on, Eadmund knew that he could only help Draguta.

It was all he wanted to do.

Eskild stood watching her son, helpless. He would not have dreams. Not now that Draguta had tightened the binding rope. He would not see anything now, but that evil woman.

And closing her eyes, she realised that she had to leave Eadmund.

For the first time since her death, she had to leave her son.

It was time to find him some help.

***

Eydis could feel Vella stir beside her. She thought she'd heard a noise, though most of her was trapped in a dream, and she wasn't even sure where she was.

But Vella was worried, and her head was up, eyes on the doors, ears alert.

'What is it?' Biddy had sensed that something was wrong too. Ido had tucked himself into her chest, and his low growling had woken her up. She blinked, trying to see in the dim orange light of the fires.

She saw Vella, dark eyes fixed on the doors, and crawling towards Edela, she shook her shoulder.

Edela was sure that she hadn't even fallen asleep. 'What?'

Biddy was just a shadow looming over her, but she saw her lift a finger to her lips, then move that finger towards the puppies, who had both crawled to the edge of the circle.

Growling.

Edela struggled to her feet, rubbing her eyes, trying to swallow.

No warnings, no dreams. She didn't know what was going on.

***

Aleksander had started counting his yawns. He was beginning to wonder if he'd ever been so tired. There were twenty-nine so far.

Twenty-nine yawns in a row.

He shook his head, laughing silently to himself as he walked around the circle, eyes moving from the trees in the distance, up to the moonlit sky.

Frowning, he noticed that it wasn't moonlit any longer.

He couldn't see any stars either.

And he was either getting sick, or Jael had been right.

It was suddenly so cold.

***

Ontine grabbed Ido, listening to him yelp. Biddy held onto Vella. Both of them watching Edela as she stood, her eyes on the hall doors.

Every part of her was vibrating with the certainty that something was out there. She swallowed, closing her eyes, trying to see.

Trying to hear something.

But nothing would reveal itself.

***

'What? What?' Jael shook as Aleksander grabbed her shoulder, his breath-smoke hiding his face. 'What's happened?'

Aleksander took her hand, glad that Jael hadn't removed her boots, and led her out of the tent.

To where it was snowing.

Jael's mouth hung open. Spinning around, she took in the sight of the trees that bordered their camp; the trees that were turning white in the rapidly falling snow. Her eyes were quickly on Tig and Sky who stood beside their tent, nickering softly, disturbed, but not touched by the snow at all.

No snow was falling inside the circles.

Ayla opened her wagon door, stumbling down the steps, half asleep. 'I had a dream,' she said, inhaling sharply. 'Oh.'

'You saw this?' Aleksander asked as Astrid followed Ayla outside, stopping in surprise.

Ayla nodded, blinking herself awake, wondering if she was still in a dream.

The snow was falling heavily, blowing now, swirling around. Settling.

Outside the circles.

Most of the army was sleeping outside the circles; men who didn't have the luxury of tents. They were nowhere near any caves. There was no shelter of any kind for their warriors or those warriors' horses.

Any fires were quickly buried.

It was freezing.

'What can we do?' Jael wondered, her toes numb in her boots. Fyr had disappeared again, and Jael hoped she was going to try and help. They needed to stop the snow.

The snow would slow them down. Freeze them.

Make everything even more impossible.

Ayla looked blankly at Jael, part of her relieved to see that the dreamer circles had held. 'You need to guard your circle,' she said suddenly, eyes alert. 'You shouldn't let anyone inside. There's too many of them. They will try to come. They will try to get out of the snow.'

Jael could quickly see how that would unfold. 'Aleksander, get everyone up! Bruno, you take charge of your circle. I need weapons out. Surround the perimeters. No one can break them. We need to stay safe! Secure the wagons! We don't know what's coming next!'

***

Draguta had so many dreamers now, an abundance of riches, so she had divided them into two groups and set Briggit to work with one, while she commanded the other, determined to slow Jael Furyck and her rag-tag army down. She did not want them arriving at the vale before she did.

That would not do at all.

She had spent much of the evening at her seeing circles, searching for the other gods, but they appeared to have vanished entirely; all of them masking themselves from her.

Cowards.

Though she still had one goddess bound to her, and that goddess was proving to be very useful indeed.

Turning away from the dreamers who were bunched up along the cliffside clearing they had camped in, Draguta motioned for Meena to follow her into her tent. 'I sent Brill to watch over Briggit,' she murmured, her eyes unable to focus. 'So I shall need someone to find me more wine and turn down my bed. I almost feel ready for some sleep.'

It was strange not to know if that were true.

Though, Draguta realised, it was not sleep she was after as much as dreams. Dreams about her sister. About the gods. She wanted to find every last one of them, so she needed to dream of a way through their pathetic symbols. 'You will sleep in my tent tonight in case I require anything.'

Meena nodded mutely, still lost in the smoke from the fire she had danced around, watching with an open mouth and wide eyes as Draguta had made it snow; listening to the painful cries of Veiga, who was helpless to stop Draguta using her gifts as weapons. The ring had glowed like a dark hole on Draguta's finger as she'd chanted, her eyes alive with power.

And Meena shuddered, knowing that soon she would use it to crush Jael Furyck and her army. Andala too.

***

It was the middle of the night, and Edela's body was urging her to find a pillow and a fur, though her mind was busy insisting that something was happening. Something she needed to remain alert and ready for.

'Edela.' Ontine touched her sleeve. 'I saw something.'

Edela spun around, peering up at the girl. 'What?'

Ontine looked nervous.

'This is no time for dithering. You are a dreamer now, Ontine. You must trust in what you saw. Do not be afraid. Was it a real vision? Could you feel it?'

Ontine nodded.

'Well, then, come here, sit down.' And Edela led her to a stool by the fire. 'Tell me. Tell us.' No one in the hall was asleep now, Edela could see. They were all awake and listening, though her certainty that something was happening had no sound. Not one that anyone appeared to hear, except for Ido and Vella who had to be restrained from leaving the circle.

Edela turned her attention to Ontine, whose mother stood beside her, long eyelashes fluttering with worry. 'I saw snow. The army. They were covered in snow. It was falling heavily. Jael is trapped.'

***

They were trapped in a valley. Deep forest on one side, Hallow Wood a dark wall in the distance on the other.

And the snow was rising fast.

'Can anyone stop it?' Thorgils shouted. The wind was whipping around the circle creating a screaming blizzard, and nobody could hear a thing. Though they all caught glimpses of those stuck outside the snow-less circles, wanting to get in.

'We'll try and stop it!' Jael yelled, looking past Thorgils to the white warriors who were gathering in rows before them. 'I'll close the circle after me. You have to protect it!' And leaving Aleksander to take charge, she ran out of her circle and into Ayla's. And when both circles were closed, they headed inside the wagon.

Astrid had one eye on the spluttering flames struggling under a pile of herbs, and another on the drum Ayla wanted her to use. Snow was falling down the tiny smoke hole in a constant stream of thick white flakes now, and she didn't think the fire would last long.

Ayla didn't notice. The herbs were already working on her. 'Drum, Astrid,' she breathed, reaching for Jael's hand. 'We must see if we can find a way to free Veiga from Draguta's hold.'

***

Edela's indecision was wasting time, she knew. Help Jael or help themselves? 'Eydis, where is Dara Teros? Can you hear her?'

Eydis hadn't heard anything from Dara in some time.

She shook her head.

The sense that something was happening in Andala was palpable. Undeniable. But perhaps it was only a distraction, trying to prevent her from helping Jael and the army?

'Bring me the book, Ontine!' Edela hurried to the fire, sitting on a stool, taking the book which Ontine had quickly retrieved. 'There must be something in here that can help us free Veiga.' Though she could almost hear Draguta laughing as she quickly flicked through the pages.

How to free a goddess?

She didn't imagine that was something Dara Teros had foreseen.

***

Fyr was outside the wagon, cawing with urgency.

It didn't distract Ayla, who had slipped away into a trance. It stopped Jael from joining her, though; the sounds outside the wagon did as well. She could hear angry voices over the roar of the blizzard now.

Squeezing Ayla's hand, Jael hoped that she knew what she was doing.

***

They had been moving from cave to cave.

Edging their way towards Andala, hoping not to be seen.

Dara was panicking. 'I need to help them. I...'

Eloris laid a delicate hand on her arm. Her skin was a light, golden colour, sprinkled with tiny freckles. 'Your sister will find you if you do. She is looking. She searches for you in her dreams and her seeing circles. I can feel it.'

So could Dara.

'If you need to get to Andala, let nothing stand in your way,' Eloris warned. 'Stop Draguta now, and she will come here. Kill you. Both of us. You won't be able to help Jael then. Neither of us will. Daala has sent all the gods into hiding now. If we reveal ourselves, there will be no one left to help when the time comes.'

Dara frowned, turning back into the cave, shaking her head. 'But what if Jael is dead before she ever gets to the vale?' Her eyes were pleading, but Eloris had turned away, seeking out the flames of their meagre fire.

***

Veiga was blind. A blind goddess who saw in her dreams.

She drifted with the clouds, cried rain to quench the earth, shot lightning bolts of anger, roared thunder from her belly.

Veiga could control the weather, until Draguta had bound her in a spell, wrapping a mask around her face until she saw nothing but darkness. The blizzard swirled around her, but she was unable to stop it.

And Ayla could see that she was powerless to help her.

She could feel Jael beside her.

'The chant is not working.'

Veiga was bellowing helplessly, though there was no thunder, only the slightest of murmurs.

Astrid was still tapping on the drum.

Fyr was cawing outside the wagon.

But Draguta's magic could not be undone.

CHAPTER FORTY TWO

They saw what had happened in the first pink-tipped streaks of morning light.

From the ramparts, it was apparent that something was wrong. Those men up there had felt it in the night, but the darkness had cloaked the valley, and not even a fire arrow had penetrated that cloak. But now, it was vividly clear to those who had left the circle with Edela and walked through the main gates.

Her shoulders heaved at the sight of the destruction, her mind quickly skipping through the implications of what Draguta had done.

There wasn't a living blade of grass. Not a plant, a bush, a flower. Not a tree.

Everything surrounding the fort appeared to have died.

Biddy gripped Edela's arm. 'What are we going to do?' she wondered, her body humming with terror, her eyes on the dead grass.

Brown. All of it, as far as she could see.

Edela was trying not to freeze. She could feel everyone's panic rising around her, and she didn't need to add her own to it. 'We have enough in the fort,' she said firmly, knowing that that was true for now, but not for long. 'We can grow more, can't we?' And turning to Biddy, she smiled, catching the worry in Ontine's eyes as she walked behind them with Hanna. 'I'm just so relieved that the circle worked. That the fort was spared.' And smiling some more, she shut away every other thought for now. 'The circle worked! We are still standing. We have food and plants in here, which means we can start again out there. We are safe.'

But no one looked consoled by that.

Everything outside the fort was dead. And now they knew that the only thing that stood between them and certain death was a circle scribbled in the dirt.

No one was comforted by that.

***

Dawn ushered in a clear sky, which revealed how trapped they were. Everything and everyone outside the circles was buried in high drifts of white powder.

Freezing white powder.

'Draguta means to destroy us! To break us!' Jael bellowed from a wobbling stool.

Fyn bent down to grab it, sensing that she was in danger of toppling over.

'We may be cold!' There were grumbles and dirty looks at that statement, seeing as how Jael and the rest of the leaders of the army, the healer and the dreamer, and all of their horses had not been snowed upon, safe in their circles as they had been all night. 'And you may be covered in snow!' Jael could read their mood, and it was dark. 'But we've only got one enemy and one chance of making her pay!'

Thorgils stood to one side of Jael, wrapping his hands across his chest, clapping his arms. Aleksander stood beside him, eyeing the angry crowd which surrounded them. They had broken the circles, though Aleksander was now wondering if that had been a good idea, noting the looks on some of the red-nosed, frost-bearded faces before them.

'You need leaders!' Jael growled, her voice breaking, irritated and freezing. 'Kill us and then what? Good luck getting home!

Good luck fighting Draguta and the Hestians! Good luck against the dreamers!' She glared at the men in the first few rows who quickly looked away from her tired eyes. 'You don't think we're suffering? Fyn whose mother was murdered by Draguta's men? Or Axl whose woman was taken? Or Thorgils who was tricked into killing his friend? Or me...' And she stopped, shaking. But not from the cold. 'Draguta took my husband! She killed my baby!'

That stunned everyone.

Everyone outside the circle. Everyone inside it too.

Except for Thorgils, Aleksander, and Fyn who all looked surprised that Jael had mentioned it. But they could see that she'd had little choice.

Ayla dropped her eyes, feeling Jael's fury burn across the frozen ground.

'So, yes, you are cold! Freezing! I know! But what choice do we have now? We need to fight! And if you want a chance to win this fight, you need me! Alive! You need them!' And she swung her arm around, pointing at Rork and Karsten, Ivaar and Axl, Aleksander and Thorgils. Ayla too. 'You need all of us! We will give you a fighting chance! A chance to win! A chance to return home!'

Murmurs grew into nods and nods grew into a smattering of agreeable grumbles, and though they sounded weak coming from the mouths of such terrified, cold men, they were welcome, and Jael breathed out a smoky sigh of relief. 'Come and warm yourselves by the fires! We will make food, find what we can, but then we must start digging! We must get to the next caves by nightfall! We have to find shelter!' And jumping down from the creaking stool, Jael looked around for something to drink. Her mind wandered to Andala and Biddy's smiling face as she stooped over her cauldron, stirring a drop of honey into hot milk with a wink.

No one would meet her eyes. But Jael wasn't in any mood for explanations or sympathy. They were going to have to spend the morning shovelling snow, making tracks for the catapults and the wagons. They needed to get some warmth into their bodies quickly.

***

It was early, but already warm enough for Meena to worry that she might be about to faint again as she swayed precariously on her pony. She glanced at Brill who was frowning at her, sweat dripping from her furrowed brow.

'You need water,' Brill mumbled, her voice low, not wanting Draguta to hear. But Draguta was too busy talking to Briggit to notice what they were doing behind her, so Brill shoved her reins into her left hand, opening her saddlebag with her right. 'Here.' And she pulled out a water bag. It was a small skin, not big enough to hold much liquid but Meena looked at it as though it were a lake.

Grabbing the skin, she lifted it to her cracked lips, drinking in a panic, convinced that Draguta would turn around and make her give it back.

But she didn't.

Eventually, Meena handed the water bag to Brill, who took a sip before stowing it away again. Ballack was riding behind them, keeping an eye on Draguta's wagons and they were both grateful for that, not wanting to share what little water was left with a giant like him.

It was comforting that Draguta had still not spun around.

It gave Meena hope that she would have the chance to think of a plan to take the ring. Once they got to the vale, she would think of a plan.

Meena held her breath, but Draguta remained facing forward, turning occasionally to Briggit who was regaling her with some tale.

Draguta squinted. 'You thought that you would rule all of Osterland? From behind that wall? How?'

Briggit shaded her eyes from the sun, revealing little. 'It was my grandfather's intention to remain locked behind the wall. He believed and made us believe that we lived in our own world. The sea, the wall, and the land between, that was our kingdom. He did not believe in anything but the sea and the wall. By the end, he didn't even believe in the gods.'

Draguta laughed. 'He was cleverer than I realised! Though that is not saying much. Those gods have been manipulating us since the beginning of time, and now, I have a chance of ending them. Every last one of them.'

'And will you?' Briggit was curious, her eyes alive again. 'Will you kill them all?'

Draguta had not decided. 'I may. They deserve to be punished. But perhaps, like my new dreamers, I can use them to my advantage. They can help me claim Osterland. My family's land. Tuura's land.'

Briggit was intrigued but confused. 'You destroyed Tuura.'

'You have misheard that tale, Briggit dear. Jael Furyck and the Followers were to blame for that, though I do not mourn the place. Those black-robed idiots did not care for Tuura. They cared about their quest for Raemus. It was always the same since I was a child. Since before then. Those in power always sought Raemus.' She almost spat with disgust. 'Blind fools! They did not see who he truly was beneath all his lies. They gave him their souls, so desperate to serve him, but he only wanted to serve himself!'

Briggit shivered with anger, though she looked at Draguta with a need to please her, and to be pleasing in return, a dull-eyed smile fixed upon her shining face.

***

Edela escaped the panic in the hall with Gant who was on his way to the stables to check on Gus.

'Is there any way to get rid of the snow?' he wondered, tired eyes scanning the path ahead, men and women walking past them, shell-shocked, faces drawn, sleepless and worried. 'It will take some time to dig themselves out.'

'No way that I can see,' Edela sighed, struggling to piece

together her thoughts, though she had barely slept all night and it was making her feel muddled.

'Well, if Draguta can control the weather now, then anything's possible.' Gant didn't want to let his mind wander too far, but just the thought of all that snow made him feel sick.

Edela nodded. 'I'm afraid it is. Our only hope now is that Draguta wants to keep playing her games. That she wants Jael to come to her. Though as for us...' Fear had a firm grip on her and she froze, not knowing what to do. 'I... I don't feel as though I've even been having the right dreams. It's been hard to sleep with all that's going on. Hard to find a way to the answers.'

Gant was concerned. Edela was almost slurring her words. He stared at her as she mumbled away beside him, worried that it was simply too much for her: the pressure to keep them safe; working on those circles. She looked more tired than he felt. 'Perhaps that's the answer, then?' he suggested. 'Sleep. If you're going to be kept up at night with Draguta's games, why not go back to your cottage? Try to get some sleep today?'

Edela could feel the heavy clarity of Gant's logic as she slipped on the soggy straw, and she nodded.

'Needs to be mucked out,' Gant muttered, snatching her arm. 'Though I suppose we've all been a little too busy panicking today.' He grinned at her as they came to Gus' stall.

Gus, who was standing, staring at them.

Gant's body sunk in relief. 'Hello, boy,' he smiled, holding out a carrot. 'Nice to have you back.'

***

Despite the misery of the cold and the setback of being snowbound, Jael almost smiled as she dug in the snow next to Beorn. It reminded her of Oss, and Eadmund, and then she was frowning again.

'I was about to ask why you looked so happy,' Beorn grumbled, shaking snow from his bright-red hands. 'But you don't look so happy now.'

'Thinking about Oss,' Jael admitted, blowing on her hands, wishing for some gloves. 'Good and bad memories.'

'No doubt.' Beorn's eyes were evasive. 'Sorry to hear about your baby. That was a surprise.'

Jael stiffened, bending over to dig in the snow again. 'It's done now. Over. I just need to make Draguta pay. We all do. So we keep going.'

Nodding, Beorn ducked his head, feeling just as awkward as Jael.

Astrid and Ayla had hot water. They'd been melting snow, boiling it over the two fires they had built up in their circle. It was helping to warm everyone up. Astrid handed Jael a cup, but despite constantly thinking about being warm, Jael shook her head. 'Give it to one of the men instead,' she said, eyes on the trough she was digging, eager to see some earth beneath all the white powder.

Ayla nodded, walking away, her dress buried in the snow, Astrid struggling behind her, a bed fur tucked around her shoulders.

Jael straightened up, sensing a shadow on the ground and when she saw that it was Fyr, she sighed, wondering what the raven could do to help them.

Ayla was watching the raven too, and after handing out her cups of hot water, she motioned Jael away from the catapult.

'What is it?' Jael asked, breath smoking around her numb face.

'I think I have an idea,' Ayla said hesitantly. 'It may not work, but perhaps it's worth trying? Something my mother used to tell me about one of the gods. Something that might work in our favour... if you can help me?'

Jael nodded, eager to do anything to help free them from their frozen prison.

***

Ontine's mother, Sybill, sipped her small ale, unable to stop shaking. Her protruding eyes were on Alaric, who blinked back at her, on Branwyn who was walking around with a small bowl of nuts, conscious of rationing, and on Gisila, who had not wanted to return to her bedchamber.

'I fear that we cannot survive much longer,' Sybill said nervously, nibbling on a walnut. 'With what that woman is doing? How long will it be before she grows tired of the circle and just sends more dragons?'

Gisila's eyes were up, away from her cup of dandelion tea. 'I think we have to believe in the circle. My mother spent a long time making it, and look at how it protected us last night.' She lifted her voice, attempting to quell the nervous muttering around her. She couldn't see Edela, but she doubted that her mother would appreciate Sybill spreading her fears around the camp like headlice. 'We have food to eat because of it. Think of what would have happened without that protection.'

Sybill looked ashen-faced. 'I'm sorry, yes. I... I am grateful for the circle. Of course. Very grateful. But what will come next? That is my fear. That which we cannot see.'

Gisila frowned. For all her fear-mongering, Sybill was not wrong. Edela had revealed no dreams about what was coming. Nor had Eydis or Ontine that she knew of. She had thought the dreamers would have had more insights, more visions about what Draguta might do next, though she didn't want to share her worries with Sybill. 'We are lucky to have dreamers,' Gisila declared, staring at the throne, deciding that it was time she was sitting on it. Everyone needed to see strength, whether she felt any or not.

She was a Furyck – by marriage, she knew – but she was the only one left in the fort now, and she needed to do something to hold them all together.

It would only get worse.

'We are lucky to have dreamers like your daughter, Sybill. We must do what we can to support them while they work hard to keep us safe.' And Gisila eyed her with a look that reminded

Branwyn of Jael.

'Here,' Branwyn said, holding out a hand, sensing that her sister was about to stand. 'I'll help you.'

Alaric was on his feet too.

'Thank you. I think it's time I started doing some work. I can't lie around all day when we're elbow-deep in trouble now can I?' Gisila scanned the hall. 'Biddy, can you bring me some wine? I'm sure we could spare a small cup. Just a little something to set me right.'

Biddy spun around, smiling at the sight of Gisila Furyck back on the throne, before scurrying away, searching for a wine jug.

***

'Your dreamers did well last night,' Draguta purred from her chair which Ballack had positioned just outside her tent. It was not a comfortable chair, but at least she wasn't having to perch on rocks, or squat in the dirt like everyone else.

Briggit looked up from where she was organising the tiny jars of herbs Brill had unpacked. 'They did. Though they could not penetrate the circles.'

Eadmund listened with a blank face, drinking from his goblet.

Wine again. Always wine.

He looked around, seeing if there was anything else on offer.

There wasn't.

He was hungry, inhaling the smell of food cooking down past the wagons, and his attention wandered, his eyes meeting Evaine's as she strode towards him in an elegant blue dress, looking as though she was heading to a feast rather than another long day in the saddle.

'I hardly think their symbols will keep us out for long,' Draguta smiled confidently. 'But we don't want to crush them yet, do we? They would simply wave a white banner. Beg for mercy. And how dull would that be?'

Jaeger crunched into an apple, tired and hot. His mood was ebbing and flowing, his eyes darting around, unable to focus. The book was closer than it had been in days. On Draguta's lap. He was trying not to look at it, or her, but he could feel it pulling him closer. Eventually, he stepped forward. 'But why delay Jael Furyck?' he wondered, trying to stop himself from resting his hand on that black leather cover. 'If you're not going to kill her, why keep her away? Don't we want her there, waiting for us?'

Draguta stared at Eadmund, but there was no reaction in his eyes now, she was pleased to see. 'Waiting for us? No.' She shook her head. 'We must be ready for her. A little delay is just what we need. A little delay and I'm sure she'll be on her way again. Never fear, Jaeger. You will get your chance with that woman if Eadmund fails. If,' she mused, narrowing her eyes, 'if you can fight your way through the army of people who wish to kill you!'

***

Karsten helped Bruno work on building another fire. Ayla had asked for the biggest fire they could make, positioned in the middle of her circle which she had now closed, keeping everyone else out. Curious onlookers stopped and stared, but they were quickly put back to work with a bellow from Rork.

Ayla needed bright, dancing flames that would smoke her herbs high into the clear morning sky. The trance she would enter had to be deep. She glanced at Jael, who had her head down, fussing with her swordbelt. 'I'm not sure it will work,' Ayla admitted. 'I'm not someone a god would choose to reveal themselves to. And perhaps he'll be in hiding now with the rest...'

Fyr was on Jael's shoulder, and Jael sensed that she was listening.

'The gods have spoken to you before, though, haven't they?

Helped you?'

Ayla nodded slowly. 'Yes, they have. But not the Oster gods. I am Tuuran. I'm not one of theirs.' She had a lot of knowledge of the gods, passed down from her mother; enough knowledge to know that she was not the right person to enter the trance. 'I think he's more likely to listen to you, Jael,' she said. 'You must do it. You must go into the trance and find Darroc. If he wants to help us, he'll be there, waiting for you.'

Jael leaned forward, enjoying the warmth of the flames. 'Who?'

'Darroc,' Ayla smiled. 'A lesser-known god, though don't tell him that. He's a reclusive creature. The God of the Seasons. If what I've heard about him is true, I can help you find him.'

'Do you think he'll want to help us? He doesn't appear to be watching what's happening here if that's the case.'

'There's only one way to find out. Now, come here, and I will show you what to do,' Ayla said quickly, realising that they needed to hurry if they were going to have a chance of moving the army before nightfall.

***

Ontine looked worried. Edela hadn't spoken since she'd returned from her cottage. Biddy had rushed in and out of the circle, checking on her, but Edela had her head buried in the Book of Aurea, and she didn't even look up.

Eydis was worried too. 'Edela, is there anything we can do?'

'Do?'

'To help you,' Ontine added, grateful for an end to the silence. Everyone was rushing in and out of the hall in constant motion, and she wanted to do something to help, though she didn't want to be gone when Edela needed her.

Edela shook her head. 'Not unless you've had some useful dreams I don't know about. Mine have not been very helpful at all.'

Eydis sat up straighter. 'I've seen Eadmund.'

'You have?' Edela leaned forward, hearing the worry in Eydis' voice. 'And?'

'He is worse,' Eydis said sadly. 'So much worse. There is no light in his eyes now. He's not there at all.'

'Draguta has strengthened her hold, then,' Edela declared, sitting back. 'I'm not surprised. Eadmund would have been fighting it ever since we freed him from Evaine.' Edela was getting a headache. She squinted, though the light in the hall was dull. 'And you, Ontine? Have you seen anything?'

Ontine nodded. 'I saw the Followers. They were divided into two groups. One of them had a tall woman in charge. She wore a white dress. I think it was Draguta. She seemed very powerful. The other group was commanded by a dreamer with golden eyes. Dark hair.'

Eydis gasped.

'What is it?' Edela asked.

'That sounds like Briggit Halvardar,' Eydis breathed. 'Was she small?'

Ontine nodded.

Eydis waited.

'She was,' Ontine added, realising that Eydis couldn't see her nod. 'And powerful. I sensed that. She had great power.'

Edela wondered if anyone would mind if she screamed. Then she noticed her daughter sitting upon the throne, a frown on her pale face as she ordered everyone about, and she felt a lift. 'Well, then we are going to be quite busy, I imagine. If Jael can get her army out of that snow, they will arrive at the Vale of the Gods within days. That does not give us long.'

'Long for what?' Eydis wondered, her hands around the warm cup of marshmallow tea Biddy had just put into them.

'Careful,' Biddy whispered. 'It's hot.'

'It doesn't give us long to save Eadmund, so we must work quickly now, for if we can't save him, I don't think Jael stands a chance of stopping Draguta!'

CHAPTER FORTY THREE

They sat in front of the fire.

Ayla insisted that Jael should sit.

Aleksander was busy shooing everyone back to work, urging them away from the circle where Jael needed to concentrate.

But Jael couldn't concentrate at all. 'How will I know what to say?'

Ayla smiled, wanting to instil her with confidence. 'You'll know once you find him, don't worry.'

'But how? How will I find him?' It seemed implausible. Impossible. But Ayla was looking at Jael with such determination that she almost started to believe that she could do it, just with the sheer strength of her will.

'You'll hear me. I will be with you. I'll guide you.' The smoking herbs were in Ayla's throat as she watched Jael yawning. That was a good sign. 'Deep breaths, Jael. Listen to the drum. Hold my hand now, and we will see where the smoke takes us. Don't worry, I'll be there.'

Jael closed her eyes, yawning again, Ayla's voice drifting away from her into the darkness. She thought of her grandmother, as she always did when she closed her eyes now. Hoping she was safe in Andala. Wishing she was back in the fort, protecting her.

'Breathe deeply.'

Ayla's calm voice wound itself around Jael's thoughts, untangling them as she tumbled into the darkness, flames occasionally flickering around her now. The sound of dripping. The pop of a fire.

And then that voice.

'You won't come back!' A booming warning, chilling her blood. 'You won't come back, Jael Furyck. I won't let you!'

***

Eydis missed Amma. She missed Jael. She missed Fyn. But most of all, she missed her brother, and she was determined not to let him slip away from her. She thought of their father and how much he had wanted Eadmund to sit on the throne of Oss after he was gone. And though she couldn't save Eirik anymore, and though everyone was scattered around Osterland, on opposite sides, facing danger and death, Eydis was certain that she could do something to help.

So, leaving the hall, she shut herself in Jael's bedchamber, determined to find a dream. They had been taking turns napping, knowing that they needed information. They needed to find the right path to take.

The one which led out of the darkness.

Eydis could feel Jael as she lay on the bed, curling onto her side. She could smell her too. It made her smile, feeling closer to her sister-in-law for a moment. And thinking about Jael led her back to Oss and the sound of Eadmund's voice as he sat next to his wife, laughing with her at a table in the square, happier than he'd ever been.

Eydis remembered that sound, and closing her eyes tightly, gripping Eadmund's wedding band, she let herself drift away.

***

'Sun's heading for its peak,' Thorgils panted, frozen hands on his thighs, wishing he could feel the sun on his feet which were buried in the snow as he dug out one of the catapults.

Beorn sighed, turning to Rork who grunted, wishing he had a cup of ale. But the ale was frozen, no use to any of them now.

'We have to get moving. We don't need some magical help. Just feet and hooves. We need to get moving,' Beorn grumbled.

Ivaar nodded, unable to stop his head from shaking. 'It would w-w-warm us up.'

'It would,' Thorgils agreed, tired eyes surveying his red-nosed Islanders who were all used to the cold weather; almost at home. 'But what if Draguta tries it again? Jael has to see what help she can get. Surely you'd like a bit of help?'

'Magical help?' Beorn's scowl wouldn't budge. 'Magical help will just tie us up in more knots, won't it? What we need is fire. Set the whole place on fire. Throw a few jars in the air!' he grinned.

Thorgils didn't. 'Think the snow's frozen your brain. You do remember the dragon, don't you? How that went?' He snorted. 'From what I remember, snow beats sea-fire.' And he glared down at Beorn, wishing him back to work on his digging.

'But what beats snow?' Ivaar wondered, staring back at Ayla's circle, his eyes jerking quickly away from Bruno Adea who was walking around the perimeter, staring him down.

'Hopefully, a god,' Thorgils said, bending back to his hole, turning to look at Jael who was somewhere in the circle, doing something that would help them. 'Hopefully, a god.'

***

The chant in Jael's ears sounded like a lullaby. A song. A rhythm that spurred her on as Ayla's voice rolled and dipped, dancing up and down, keeping her moving, tumbling, and she gradually lost all sense of where she was until she landed.

It wasn't hard. There was no noise that she could hear, but Jael had stopped.

And so had Ayla's chanting.

She scrambled to her feet, looking around, but there was no Ayla. And as the darkness revealed its secrets, she saw that she was in a forest.

Jael's eyes were immediately drawn to a sprawling tree. It looked oddly familiar, or perhaps it was the little holes dug into the trunk from which tiny owls peered back at her. Grey, white, white-and-brown. Big eyes blinking. Wide awake.

Hundreds of them.

Jael's attention was so transfixed by the tree that she didn't hear the figure behind her until it was too late, and he was towering over her like a range of hairy mountains.

Darroc.

'This is no place to come uninvited,' the god growled, bulging eyes all white and angry, bursting out of a hooded face as he glared down at her. Thick neck, meaty shoulders, his voice a deep, tree-shaking boom. 'Especially not one of your kind.'

Jael was taken aback, not expecting that any god would be so rude. 'Well, there was no time to send a note,' she grumbled.

Darroc's glare intensified, then relaxed suddenly as he burst out laughing. 'I've heard all about you, Jael Furyck! Seen you too. You are quite like Furia, aren't you? That goddess is all fire. A belly full of anger, too, just like you.'

'And you?' Jael asked. 'You seem quite angry yourself.'

'I don't think so.' Darroc stepped back, indignant. 'I just don't like uninvited guests. Humans. I have no idea how you found your way here...' He looked around, sensing another presence. 'Likely Eseld gave away my location. Fair enough goddess, but a very big mouth.'

'Well, if she did, I'm grateful. I need your help.'

'Ha!' Darroc bellowed, his enormous girth jiggling, shaking the earth beneath their feet. 'You want my help? As though I'm a servant? Like me to come and tuck you in, would you? Bring you some mead?' He shook his head, his hood slipping down, revealing a thick thatch of grey hair braided with tiny bones, framing his ruddy cheeks. 'I am no servant, Jael Furyck. And I do not live deep within this wood to be sought out by the likes of you. It is a long time since I cared what any god thought. And even longer, any human.'

Jael was impatient. Her ears were a buzzing frenzy, and she found herself struggling to concentrate on being polite. Whatever you do, Ayla had warned her, make sure that you're polite. 'If you don't come and help me, we'll all die,' Jael tried.

Darroc belched so loudly that Jael had to hold her hands over her ears as the noise reverberated around the trees. 'I don't care if you all die!' he laughed, gripping his round belly. 'In here? In my forest, with my owls, how would I even know? Why should it bother me?'

Jael's frown was severe, her toes curling in her boots, the noise in her ears painful now. 'Don't care? Who made someone like you a god if you don't care about anyone? What sort of god are you?'

Darroc was finding it hard not to like Jael Furyck. He'd almost missed the pleasure of a disagreement with Furia, and before he'd left the gods behind and become a recluse, he'd had many. But still, it would not do to have a human break into his hidden grove and insult him.

It would not do at all.

'I can send you back!' Darroc snarled, bulging eyes transforming into predatory slits; no white to be seen now. He lifted a thick hand, shoving it at Jael. 'A click of my fingers and you're gone, Queen of Oss.'

'Do it!' Jael dared. 'You can't help me, so do it. We're all out there fighting. Dying and fighting. We'll sacrifice our lives to save Osterland, and we're not even gods. We have no power to hide in a forest or keep our families safe. So do it! Send me back. I want to go, far away from you! A god so cowardly he won't fight for anyone. Not even for his owls.'

Darroc froze, Jael's words cutting him deep. None more so than those last five. 'What do you mean, my owls?'

***

Rain fell.

It was a soft, steady rain, gentle and soothing and Eydis felt a welcome peace as she walked along the beach, her eyes on the stone spires guarding the harbour. She'd always liked the rain. It put her to sleep. Made her feel happy.

'You were Eirik's pride and joy.'

Spinning around, Eydis saw a woman who looked familiar, yet she didn't know her. But she did know who she looked like. 'You're Eadmund's mother. Eskild.'

Eskild smiled sadly. 'I am. And I have come for your help, Eydis. For Eadmund. I cannot find my way into his dreams anymore. For a time I could, and I almost thought I was getting through to him, but now?' Eskild tried not to panic. 'Draguta has bound him tighter. Even his dreams belong to her now.'

'Edela and I tried to help him,' Eydis said. 'We cut his binding rope to Evaine, but Edela couldn't even touch the other one.'

'But what about you?' Eskild asked gently. 'You are his sister, Eydis, so perhaps you could try? You are connected to Eadmund by blood. By love. A bond that powerful is strong enough to overcome many things.'

Eydis wasn't so sure, though it sounded similar to something Edela had said. 'Draguta's power is growing. She can control the gods now.'

Eskild nodded. 'Yes, she is like a storm about to explode above you all. And you need Eadmund for this fight. He must be there. Eadmund and his shield.'

Eydis wasn't convinced that there was anything she could do about that, but Eskild held out her arms, and she crept into them, longing to feel her embrace.

She had such kind eyes.

Just like Eadmund.

***

'Enjoyed yourself, did you? Sitting by the fire?' Thorgils frowned as Jael stumbled towards him through a cloud of smoke.

She could barely stand, and eventually, she bent over, hands on knees, trying to breathe in some fresh, cold air. It helped, and standing up, she sighed. 'No, I didn't, but it appears that I did waste a lot of time.' And surveying the deep snowdrifts they were all still wading through, she felt a stab of regret.

Perhaps if she hadn't been so rude...

'Well, we've cleared out half the catapults, and all of the wagons,' Aleksander panted, rubbing his frozen hands together, blowing on them. 'Hopefully, we can make a start later this afternoon.'

Jael turned to where Ayla and Astrid were struggling away from the fire, eager to escape the smoke themselves. 'I'm sorry,' she muttered. 'He... he wasn't interested in helping us. Or me. He didn't seem to like me.'

'Can't understand why,' Thorgils winked. 'You being such a charmer.'

Jael couldn't even raise a smile as she headed out of the circle into the glare of sunshine reflecting off the white snow. Sunshine that became warmer as she walked, her shivering body suddenly not as cold. And turning around, wondering if she was imagining it, she caught the look on Ayla's face.

On Thorgils' and Aleksander's too.

That sun felt like summer.

***

Draguta smiled, enjoying the heat of the sun, imagining the Brekkans traipsing in the snow. With the Ring of Taron and the

Book of Darkness, there was nothing she couldn't conquer. No one she couldn't command, man or god.

It was an uplifting feeling, yet there were problems.

Her dreams had gone. She could make plans, but those plans were generated by ideas instead of visions. She was even struggling to read minds. Her seeing circles worked, and she stopped often to check her tables that banged around in the wagon behind Meena and Evaine.

But that was all.

She was blind, which was inconvenient and troubling, but, Draguta realised, as much as she didn't feel the need for sleep or food, perhaps the human part of her still required such things to function? And, of course, how could she have dreams if she was never asleep?

'Meena!' And spinning around, Draguta eyed the bright-red face of her assistant burning in the sun under a limp mop of hair. 'You will come here!'

Meena kneed her pony forward, manoeuvring her way in between Draguta and Briggit, who did not look pleased for the company.

'You will tie your pony to the wagon. Get inside it and start preparing a tea. Something to help me sleep.' She eyed Meena who appeared to be shrinking backwards. 'You know all about teas, don't you, girl?'

Meena wasn't sure if she should nod. She stared down at her hands, waiting.

'Agrimony and bergamot. Jasmine too. Add in some marshmallow root...' Draguta's mind went blank. Frowning, she tried to bring some thoughts into that dark void. 'Thyme!' she snapped. 'You have brought all of those, I assume?'

Meena nodded this time, starting to panic, not wanting Draguta's dreams to return.

'Good! Then hurry along, for I shall be looking forward to a long and deep sleep this evening. Evaine can go with you. She can watch you. That should keep your hand steady.'

Draguta's eyes were so cold and insistent that Meena found

herself unable to stop shivering as she spun her pony around, banging into Briggit who scowled at her some more before turning her attention to Draguta.

'Do you trust her?' Briggit wondered, looking over her shoulder, watching Meena awkwardly making her way back up the road. They had crested the top of the mountain range and were now heading downhill, which was even more of a challenge for the wagons and the horses, as wheels and hooves skidded in the dusty gravel, slipping dangerously.

'I trust no one,' Draguta smiled, her eyes fixed straight ahead. 'Not even you. And you are no more to me than Meena Gallas, so do not presume to have an opinion about anything, Briggit. Your opinions are not wanted until they are requested by me. Though, that in itself is highly unlikely, I assure you.' And clicking her tongue, and leaning further back in her saddle, Draguta moved her white horse ahead of Briggit's, deciding that she would rather spend her afternoon in Eadmund and Jaeger's company.

***

The smiles on everyone's faces as they left their camp behind made Jael happier than she had been in some time.

'Now, if only you could sweet talk Draguta like that,' Ivaar mused, relieved to be walking his horse through harmless dregs of slush rather than wading through knee-high snow. 'Maybe we could all go home.'

'Home?' Thorgils was on Jael's other side. 'And where's that going to be, then? When it's all over? Where will you go?'

Ivaar shrugged. He had been on a sharply defined path for revenge since he could remember. Nothing had shaken him from it. He had lived and breathed the quest to reclaim Oss' throne, the defeat of his brother, revenge against his father. But now? 'I don't know. Seems like a long way to go yet to think about that.'

Thorgils nodded. 'You're right there. Don't imagine Draguta will be happy that your friend Darroc melted her snow.'

Jael smiled. 'I'm not sure she'd care. She didn't send dragons to burn us alive, so I don't think she's trying to kill us. Maybe just slow us down.'

'What about the fog?' Ivaar asked, frowning.

Thorgils' head drooped.

'The fog was a terrible game,' Jael said, happy to have Fyr on her shoulder again. 'She could kill quickly if she wanted to. I saw what she did to Angard.' It made sense to warn them, Jael realised. To give them time to reflect before they arrived at the vale. To say what they needed to before it was too late.

'Angard?' Ivaar heard the bleakness in Jael's voice. 'What did she do?'

So Jael told them about the dragons and the broken wall.

About the ring.

Neither Ivaar nor Thorgils spoke after that.

'So, when Draguta brings us snow or fog, it's just to play with our minds. To get us fighting each other. To weaken us. She knows she could end us now, but she hasn't.' Jael could almost feel cold hands creeping up her back, clawing into her shoulder blades, and she shivered. 'The game will end when Draguta says it will, or when we defeat her. But not until then. For now, we just have to keep playing along.'

***

The afternoon was turning to dusk as Biddy stared at the sky, noticing how low the sun was as it dipped behind the newly repaired wall. She dropped her eyes back to the square, watching Bram throw a couple of treats for Ido and Vella who ran towards them. Or, at least, Vella did. Ido spun around trying to find where they had gone, eventually tumbling over, yelping as he twisted his broken leg, giving his sister enough time to gobble up all the treats herself.

Shaking her head, Biddy hurried over to him. 'You big baby,' she grumbled. 'Come here, then.' And picking him up, she smiled. 'I may as well put him in a child's cart. Wheel him along.'

Bram laughed. 'Mads has one of those. I can fetch it for you if you like?'

Biddy shook her head. 'Think I'll leave him hobbling around for now, poor thing.' And she placed Ido back on the ground as Bram bent down, offering him his last bit of bread.

'Strange feeling, isn't it?' Bram said from down on his haunches, watching the shadows lengthen across the square. 'Fearing the darkness. That sense of dread when the sun goes down.' He straightened up, missing the sea. Missing the freedom of surging across the waves, not a cliff nor a harbour in sight. Just his men, his ship. The unknown adventure to come.

'Terrifying, you mean,' Biddy grimaced.

'They must be at the vale soon,' Bram thought, running a hand through his beard. 'Gant said another few days. Won't be long now.' He felt sick at the thought of it.

'If they make it there. If they make it that far.'

Bram saw the fear in Biddy's eyes, and it diluted his own. 'There's one thing I know,' he said. 'One thing I've learned too late, and that's that life is worth the fight. This life. Our families. It's worth fighting for. So I can't imagine anything's going to stop them from getting there and facing whichever enemy is trying to take all of this away.' He wrapped an arm around her shoulder. 'And you know Jael, better than most. I don't think she's going to be stopped easily, is she?'

Biddy found a smile. 'No, I know Jael. She won't be stopped. Ever.'

CHAPTER FORTY FOUR

The Hestians stopped for the night in the middle of nowhere. Nowhere suitable for hosting an exhausted army and their sunburned servants. Draguta didn't notice as everyone ran around, making sure that she was comfortable, pitching her tent, ensuring that her furniture was ready and waiting. She sat on a chair, her eyes on the slow journey of the setting sun. That big orange orb was sinking towards the Adrano Sea, taking all its warmth and light with it. Though Draguta no longer dreaded the coming darkness.

She no longer feared anything at all.

Smiling, she watched as Meena stumbled towards her with a cup, working hard not to spill a drop of the tea she had been slaving over.

Meena bit her tongue as she slipped on the gravelly path, her eyes up quickly, listening to Briggit's snort of derision, conscious of Evaine watching her.

Evaine, revolted by her cousin's sweaty face, turned and smiled at Eadmund who edged away from her. She tried not to frown, but she felt herself growing more impatient with every moment spent on this tedious journey.

Not even the thought of him killing Jael improved her mood.

She needed to find a way to prove her loyalty to Draguta quickly.

She had to get Eadmund back.

Draguta finished the tea, one eye on Meena. Though she could smell some of the herbs, she couldn't taste it, and that bothered her.

'I hope for your sake it works, Meena Gallas,' she snarled, handing her the empty cup. 'It would be such a shame if you proved entirely useless. A shame for you and that flapping tongue of yours.'

Meena gulped, trying to still her shaking hand, forcing her eyes to remain on Draguta as she waited to be dismissed.

If Draguta's dreams returned, what would she find waiting in them?

But if they didn't...

'Now, go!' Overwhelmed with irritation, Draguta waved an impatient hand at Meena, wanting her gone. She turned her attention to Jaeger whose eyes were on Briggit, admiring the way her sweat-soaked robe clung to the curve of her hips. 'We must discuss what we will do once we arrive at the vale. How we will prepare for our guests.' And leaving her chair behind to stand in between Briggit and Jaeger, Draguta smiled. 'We have so many weapons at our disposal, but they will be rendered impotent if we are not fully prepared with a plan for how to utilise them.'

'What weapons?' Jaeger wanted to know.

'My weapons. None of which concern you. You have a sword. A shield. An army of men required to follow your orders. That is all you need concern yourself with, Jaeger.' She turned her head, watching her dreamers sitting along a low ridge, resting their blistered feet, no doubt wishing for a pool of cold water or a horse.

Draguta smiled. She had weapons. Many weapons.

If she were Jael Furyck, she would turn around now.

***

Jael yawned, scratching her nose. Something had bitten it. They had gone from shivering in the snow to sweltering in a cloud of hungry midges.

'Grrrr!' Aleksander slapped his neck. 'I think they're living in this cave!'

'Must be a stream somewhere back there,' Axl said, finishing up his plate of cheese and bread, a few slices of smoked pork too.

Jael wasn't listening. Her mind was on tomorrow and the next day and the day after that. She was thinking about how long it would be before they ran into their enemy. How long before she'd be standing in front of them, trying to kill them all. 'We need to imagine what Draguta will do,' she muttered, scrambling to her feet. 'We're plodding along, expecting her to be waiting at the vale. Maybe she is. Maybe my dream was right. Who knows? But what then? We can't treat this as if we're simply going to fight the Hestian army. It won't be the same.'

Karsten held his tongue.

'She's sent a dragon and a serpent, the barsk and the dragur, the whisps too. So what will Draguta do when she finally has us where she wants us?'

Axl stood, a cup of ale in his hand. 'Everything.'

Jael nodded. 'I think so too. Why hold anything back? It's the end, in her mind, at least, so she'll want to finish us. She'll give us everything she has.'

They stood around the fire in the cave: Ivaar and Karsten; Aleksander and Thorgils; Axl, Fyn, and Raymon; Rork, and Raymon's man, Soren too.

'She'll want an end, that's for sure,' Karsten growled. 'She knows we won't stop until we finish her.'

'So she'll come at us with everything she has,' Aleksander said, missing Gant's voice, realising that everyone had turned to him. 'But we can't give her all of us. Not at first.'

'No,' Jael agreed, watching his dark eyes, reading his thoughts. 'We can't. We need to separate our forces. We've brought a number of horns, flags too,' she said, watching Thorgils' eyes brighten, thinking about their successful attack on Skorro. 'So we should use them. We don't know what we'll be facing, but it almost doesn't matter. We assume the worst. That there'll be fire. Something will be flying. There'll be teeth. Danger to us all. So we separate, coordinate, and fight as though we're one. Each one of us a different limb of the same creature.'

Karsten looked enthusiastic. 'Assume the worst,' he agreed. 'Prepare to be attacked by a fire-breathing dragur serpent.'

Thorgils laughed. 'The size of a whisp!' His face fell, looking at Karsten.

'What?' Karsten was quickly frowning.

Thorgils glanced at Jael, his face reddening. 'Just thinking about Andala. It's not really funny,' he mumbled into his beard.

Jael jumped in before Thorgils could shove any more of his foot into his big mouth. 'No, it's not. None of it is. But we shouldn't sit around and feel sorry for ourselves or them. They'll be fighting just as hard as we are. Best thing we can do is focus on us, and what's ahead, not on what we've left behind. We're powerless to change any of that now.' She grabbed a stick, drawing a circle on a patch of dirt by the fire, trying not to look at Karsten, though she could feel his eye on her.

Watching.

***

Edela had thought she'd only nodded off for a brief time, so it surprised her to discover that it was dark and that Biddy had her supper waiting for her, though the soup was lukewarm.

'I can heat it up,' Biddy said, hands on the bowl.

Edela's hands were also on the bowl. 'It's warm enough for me,' she insisted, pulling it towards her.

Biddy wasn't so sure, but she saw Ontine laughing at them, and she let go of the bowl. 'Well, whatever you want,' she grumbled, heading back to the kitchen to find some crispbreads.

Edela smiled at Ontine, who sat next to Eydis, which made a nice change. They almost appeared to be enjoying each other's company.

'You look well-rested, Edela,' Ontine said, patting Vella who had her paws up on her knee. 'Did you have any dreams?'

Edela's smile faded. 'No dreams, but I'm almost grateful for that. Dreams are hard work, as you girls know. I think my sleep was more useful because there were none. It should keep me going tonight.'

Eydis could hear the uncertainty in Edela's voice. It was as though she was saying the opposite of what was true. Being blind helped her to see those things people tried to keep hidden. Being blind and being a dreamer.

Edela was worried she couldn't find the answers in her dreams.

But Eydis still had her dreams. 'I saw Eskild,' she remembered. 'She told me that I should try to save Eadmund. That I should cut Draguta's binding rope myself.'

'Did she?' Edela gagged, her spoon in mid-air. The soup really was cold. 'Why did she say that? Why did she come to you?'

Eydis' face fell. 'She said that Draguta had tightened her hold on Eadmund, just as you said. She can't get inside his dreams anymore. She wants me to help him instead.'

'Oh.' And looking up, Edela grabbed one of the crispbreads from the plate Biddy had brought out of the kitchen. 'We must try then, Eydis. If you feel you want to? When I touched that rope, it felt like an explosion. I'm not sure how safe it is.'

Ontine looked on in confusion.

'I don't care,' Eydis declared. 'We don't have time for safe, do we?'

'No, I suppose we don't,' Edela admitted, looking up at Biddy. 'I wouldn't mind if you heated up the soup. It really is cold.'

***

Draguta had retired to her tent, wanting to have a private talk with Jaeger. They were getting closer to the vale. Closer to the battle that meant so much to her.

To Hest too.

'You must play your part, Jaeger,' Draguta purred, her body growing heavier as her desire to sleep grew more pronounced. 'Your reputation must be enhanced by this battle. Surely, you can hear the whispers? No one respects you, and no one who knows you admires anything about you. And as for your reputation with women.... well, that will only deteriorate further when the rumours spread.' She eyed him disapprovingly. 'No, you must fight with your sword beside my beasts. You must prove yourself worthy of sitting on the throne. Of being a Dragos king. So far we have all been disappointed in you. Gravely so. But this is your chance to change our minds.'

Jaeger sat forward, his amber eyes aflame, not appreciating the insults that Draguta had delivered so casually. 'And I will take it. I want it. I want the Furycks. Both of them.'

'Jael is Eadmund's problem to solve, as you well know. I won't have you anywhere near her, do you understand me? Not until we have seen what Eadmund can do.'

Jaeger scowled, remembering how the bitch had cut his ankles, held him prisoner, humiliated him. But then he thought of his brothers. 'I want Karsten.'

Draguta looked bemused. 'You will have Karsten, don't worry about that. You will have anyone you want. If you can get to them in time. If you can fight your way through my carnage. And you must, Jaeger. I will be watching. I will be there.'

Jaeger narrowed his eyes. 'And Eadmund?'

'Eadmund?' Draguta smiled. 'Once he has killed Jael Furyck, you may end him, though having witnessed the two of you fighting, that may be beyond you.'

Jaeger ignored her, puffing out his chest as he stood, heading for the wine jug, imagining slitting Eadmund's throat. 'I won't let you down.' He stared at Brill who was bringing another jug of wine into the tent, a plate of cheese and figs too. 'I won't let you down,' he murmured, smiling.

***

Karsten ran the whetstone down his axe blade. One of his axe blades. He had two. Two blades with which to carve his brother into tiny pieces. Chunks of something once resembling a person. He could almost taste the victory in that image.

Thinking about his father. Berard.

Haegen and Irenna.

They were all victims of Jaeger and that book he had been so desperate to find since he was a boy.

'You can tell me,' he murmured, his eyes on Jael. Everyone else was asleep. She'd been checking on the horses. Now she was fussing around the fire, looking as though she had no intention of sleeping at all.

Jael turned around, studying his face in the flicker of flames. All in shadow. Just the glint of an eye studying her.

The eye of an enemy? The eye of an ally?

Sometimes, it was hard to tell.

Sighing, she left the fire and took a seat beside him on the ground. 'I don't think I should.'

Karsten's smile was sad. 'Thorgils is a terrible liar.'

'He is.'

'Who was it?'

Jael paused before taking a deep breath. 'Your wife.'

The shock flooded Karsten like a waterfall bursting over the side of a mountain. He couldn't breathe. Couldn't speak. Tears came, his hands not moving. Whetstone on blade. Shaking. 'Nicolene?' It was a whisper. 'Nicolene?'

He thought of his sons. His motherless sons.

'She didn't love me,' he mumbled. 'Did she?' Looking up, he sought that confirmation in Jael's eyes.

She blinked, then shrugged. 'I don't know.'

'But you're a dreamer!' Karsten's voice rose, but he barely heard the irritated grumbles of those lying around the cave, trying to sleep. 'You can see inside people's heads. Why not their hearts?' More tears, streaming from only one eye.

'She loved you,' Jael lied, hoping she was better at it than she believed. Staring into Karsten's eye, she tried to strengthen her voice. 'She did.'

Karsten thought of how much he wanted to be back in Andala with his sons. He dropped his head to his hands.

Jael reached out awkwardly, a hand on his back.

He jerked around in anger. 'You did this! You! It's all because of you! You took my eye! She didn't want me after that!'

No one was asleep now.

Jael put her hand back on her leg. If someone had just told her that Eadmund was dead, she would have wanted to put a sword through them. The pain would have broken her into tiny pieces. Though Jael could see through Karsten's grief, and she could feel that his love for Nicolene had withered long ago.

He grieved for her, but his heart had not broken.

'I'm sorry,' Jael said. And she was. 'I'm sorry about your eye too, Karsten. I am.'

He hadn't been expecting that, and all the energy was sucked out of his anger. His body slumped forward in a heap. 'There's going to be no one left, is there? No one left for me to go back for. No one.'

'I don't know,' Jael admitted. 'But Berard will be doing what he can to keep your children safe. And Bayla. Ulf too. They'll do whatever they can to be waiting for you.'

Karsten didn't hear her, he didn't see the pairs of sleepy eyes staring at him in the darkness. Scrambling to his feet, he sniffed loudly, rubbing his eye on his sleeve, adjusting his eyepatch.

Leaving the cave.

***

Edela wanted to find something in the book, some way to help Eydis break Draguta's hold on Eadmund. Eydis was so determined but young, she thought with a smile, watching her sleeping on the opposite side of the fire.

She didn't want to put her in danger.

'Can I help?' Ontine wondered, wrapping a fur around her shoulders as she took the stool beside Edela.

'I thought you were sleeping.'

'I should be, but it's hard. I keep waiting for something to happen. And the waiting keeps me alert. Too alert for sleep to come.'

'You have been helpful,' Edela smiled. 'Your dreams have kept our eyes open, which is lucky as mine are in an inconvenient muddle.'

Ontine looked worried. 'Has that ever happened before?'

'Oh yes,' Edela sighed. 'It has. There are just too many things to think about, so it's become a real tangle in here.' She tapped the side of her head before returning to the book, edging it closer to the flames. 'What I really need more than a dream is to find a way to help Eadmund.' She ran her hand over the roughly drawn symbols on the page, her attention drifting. 'Though sometimes it feels as though this book is a forest of trees and I keep going around in circles, certain I've seen that one tree ten times before.'

Ontine laughed softly. 'Shall I look? Perhaps a new pair of eyes might help? Though I'm not sure what I'd be looking for.'

Edela shook her head. 'No, as you say, you wouldn't know what to find. And, in all honesty, I don't think there's anything in here that can help Eadmund. Dara Teros imagined a lot of what would come, but it was always going to be impossible for her to see everything, wasn't it?'

***

Eloris felt sad, Dara could tell.

They had both seen what had happened to Veiga. And though Draguta's growing power had come as no surprise, the shock of it had left them struggling to choose a path forward.

'She will find us,' Eloris fretted, twirling her long brown curls around a finger. 'Her seeing circles reveal more and more to her. It is only a matter of time before she finds us. Binds me. Kills you.'

Dara didn't know how to comfort a goddess, a being more powerful than she was, but not, it seemed, more powerful than her sister in command of that book. 'We cannot give up, Eloris. The dreamer circles have held. They have held, and so have our symbols, so we must keep going.'

'But the Ring of Taron? You never saw that in your dreams, Dara. Raemus hid that from all of us. All of us except Taegus, it seems.'

Dara nodded. 'Yes, Raemus' son has a lot to answer for. If only he hadn't fallen in love with Draguta all those years ago.' She shook her head, trying not to dwell on the past, her past, which stretched back centuries. 'But now Draguta has revealed it, we can think of how to stop her. It gives us a chance.' After all this time, she was numb to fear, but she could feel a desperate loss of hope in Eloris, and she was trying her best not to sink with her.

Eloris turned to Dara, light-green eyes moist, golden skin bathed in moonglow. 'It does. And yes, we can try,' she sighed, though her hopelessness was like a bleak cloud over them both and neither of them could even raise a smile.

***

Eydis lifted her head, listening. Edela was awake, she could tell, and feeling around the floor, she pushed herself up, onto her knees, crawling towards her.

Edela turned, watching her. 'What are you doing?' she whispered. 'It is too early to be up yet. Go back to sleep.'

But Eydis couldn't go back to sleep, for she'd had a dream. 'I found it, Edela,' she whispered. 'I found a symbol to save Eadmund!'

CHAPTER FORTY FIVE

The Vale of the Gods.

A sharp break in the rugged landscape surrounding southern Brekka and northern Hest. A dry, barren arena of dirt and gravel nestled in between two vast mountain ranges. A place of war and death where the gods would come to battle each other, and though the arena was soaked with the blood of ages, nothing ever grew there.

Draguta inhaled slowly, turning to Meena who looked happy to be standing beneath the Tree of Agrayal; its deep green leaves keeping the sun at bay. 'You and Brill will set my tent up here, beneath the tree. Bring all the wagons close. Have Ballack help you. I want everything unpacked quickly. My boxes too. All of them ready for me.'

Meena nodded, backing away, eager to make a start.

'Get Evaine to help you too!' Draguta barked. 'I don't want to be waiting around all day!' She frowned, irritable, for though she had certainly seen flashes of images in her sleep, no dreams had stuck, and upon waking, she couldn't remember any of them. Squinting into the sun, she saw Eadmund approach. 'I want men everywhere. Eyes on every corner of this place. Up on those cliffs. Along the ridges. Stationed at both entrances. Scouts too. Send them north, east, and west. We must know when our enemies are coming, though I doubt they have any choice but to find their way here. If they want me, they must come.'

Eadmund nodded, turning to leave.

Draguta stopped him with a hand on his arm. 'And when you're done, you will meet with Jaeger, then I want you training. You must be sharp, Eadmund. Well-rested. Prepared.'

Eadmund's eyes registered some awareness now; the crease between his eyebrows deepening. He thought about Jael. About how he had to kill her. 'I will,' he muttered. 'Of course.' He felt nothing. Nothing at all.

'Good! And send Briggit to me when you find her. Make sure she brings my dreamers. They can sleep out there, on the grass. All those eyes must be watching, keeping us alert.' She smiled, trying to imagine when Jael Furyck would arrive, but she couldn't.

Her shoulders tensed as she realised that she couldn't see a thing.

***

There was no opportunity to breathe a sigh of relief at having survived another night. Concerns about food were becoming Gant's biggest headache. One which he reluctantly shared with Gisila.

She smiled, enjoying his frown. She had always liked that frown which had only improved with age. 'We have food in the fort. Plants and trees. Enough to start again. And we can. Once this is over, we can start again. I doubt Draguta did this to Iskavall or Tuura. Or even to the rest of Brekka. We'll be able to find livestock and food elsewhere. Not to mention those who'll come to trade. Once we can escape the circle, of course.'

Gant agreed. That had been his thinking too. 'My worry,' he said, happy to see Gisila's smile; it distracted him for a moment. 'My worry is that we won't make it till then.'

'Oh?' Gisila leaned forward.

'I've been checking our stores. They were depleted during

the attacks. Depleted in more ways than I think we realised. We were so busy looking after the injured and helping Jael prepare the army. They took a lot with them. A lot. And now...' He shook his head. 'There's not enough left, Gisila.'

'Oh.' She wasn't smiling now. 'Can you show me?'

'It's a long way to walk.'

'Then you may have to carry me,' she said tartly, already on her feet, feeling weak but determined. 'Come on, then, I've a lot of people to talk to today.' And striding off through the hall, she left Gant gaping after her.

***

Meena and Brill were enjoying the shade as they worked to erect Draguta's tent beneath the ponderous branches of the ancient tree. The pleasure of not being on their ponies and the silence of each other's company was a welcome change from the noise and constant demands of their journey.

It was nice to be away from Draguta too, though they were both aware that if they didn't finish her tent quickly, they would not be enjoying the peace and quiet for long.

Ballack had left to bring the wagons closer to where they had pitched the tent, just behind the tree, and Meena and Brill were preparing the interior, on their hands and knees, checking for any stones or pebbles that might get under Draguta's feet.

Evaine was watching from the comfort of a chair, one eye on the tent flap, wondering when she could leave, though that would hardly endear her to Draguta. She leaned forward. 'You're taking too long!' she barked imperiously. 'Put those furs on the grass and stop fussing. Draguta will want wine and somewhere to sit. Her tables too!'

Meena rocked back on her heels, brushing hair out of her eyes, scowling at her lazy cousin, though if Draguta were to arrive now, she would be furious that there was nowhere to sit. Nowhere she could draw a seeing circle either.

And then Jaeger came into the tent, scanning the vast space, glancing at Evaine before resting his eyes on Meena. 'Just the woman I wanted!'

Meena tried not to sigh, but she could feel her cheeks redden as Evaine looked on. 'I have to get the tent ready,' she mumbled.

'Isn't that what Brill's for? And Evaine?' Jaeger turned to wink at Evaine before bending down to grab Meena's hand, yanking her to her feet. 'I'm sure you'll be back before Draguta comes looking for you.'

Meena was quickly stumbling after Jaeger as he headed towards the tent flap, looking helplessly back over her shoulder at Brill, trying to avoid a smirking Evaine.

***

Biddy had taken Ontine and Eydis to Edela's cottage. They were going to discuss the ritual to break Eadmund's binding rope. Edela was supposed to be inside too, but she had stopped in the garden, picking herbs for a tea to calm her busy mind.

She heard footsteps approaching. A nervous cough.

'Hello!'

And turning around, she saw Sybill Ethburg.

Edela was struggling to find any reason to like the woman, which was not very charitable, she knew, but it was hard to know what to say to her. Her big blinking eyes made her look like a hungry rodent, always trying to please with her conversation, revealing little about herself in the process, not making it easy to form any sort of friendship. Edela frowned, standing up, making no move to head down to open the gate. 'Are you looking for Ontine?'

'I am!' Sybill called. 'She did not eat her breakfast again. I am fussing, of course, but I do worry about her. She has become so thin since Victor died. Once she had such round cheeks, but now she is fading away. I brought her some flatbreads and cheese. They're still warm!'

Edela's stomach rumbled at the thought of warm flatbreads. 'I will take them if you like. We are meeting inside my cottage, and I need Ontine to concentrate.' Her voice was firm as she headed down to the gate, taking the covered tray. 'I will try to get her to eat something.'

'Thank you.' Sybill looked disappointed not to be invited in. 'You have a lovely garden, Edela. I'm sure everyone will be turning up, hoping to share in it soon. I imagine it will be hard to keep them away.'

Edela wondered what she meant. There was just something about those eyes that made her doubt whatever came out of Sybill's mouth. 'Well, they're more than welcome to,' Edela said, turning away. 'Anything I can do to help!' And scurrying up the path, she decided to forget about her herbs and head inside, wanting to focus on Eadmund and what Eydis had seen.

***

Ayla was sitting beside Bruno, who was driving the wagon. It was nice to have a moment, just the two of them. Astrid was good company, but living in such close quarters had them all hankering for some time alone.

'Did you have any dreams?' he wondered, enjoying the way his wife's head was resting on his arm. 'You were making a lot of noises last night.'

'Was I?' That surprised Ayla. She smiled. 'Could have been that stew!'

Bruno had been determined to make her a stew, having foraged for the mushrooms and nettles himself. 'Well, it's been a few years since I cooked anything, though I thought it tasted alright.'

Ayla's attention strayed to Thorgils and Karsten, who were riding ahead of them with Ivaar. It felt odd that everyone seemed to have forgiven Ivaar. What he'd done to them was obviously not as scarring as what he'd done to her and Bruno. It couldn't have been.

She squeezed her husband's arm, hoping to distract him. 'I couldn't have done any better.'

'I doubt that's true,' Bruno said, not distracted at all. He could see Ivaar. He could see how expertly Ivaar had made himself palatable now; so much so that even Thorgils could stand his company.

It made him feel isolated. And motivated.

If he could just get through this battle at the vale, keep Ayla safe, have a chance to begin again, then he could...

Sighing, Bruno leaned his head down until it touched Ayla's, reminding himself that focusing on Ivaar was a waste of time. And Ivaar had already stolen enough of his and Ayla's time. 'Though I might have another try tonight. If we come across a river, I'll get out a spear, see what I can find.' And he felt his heart swell as she looked up at him with a smile.

Ivaar watched them, quickly turning back around before they could see. It irritated him how happy they looked. How in love. Bruno Adea was a half-dead cripple of an old man. He couldn't imagine what Ayla saw in him.

Jael turned around and glared at him, motioning with her head to Thorgils and Karsten who looked as morose as each other. Ivaar nodded irritably until she turned back around. He had been trying to keep the conversation afloat, but he'd run out of things to say, and their dark moods were threatening to sink him too.

He thought of Mads. Thumb-sucking, red-faced Mads. His only son.

Wondering if he would ever see him again.

***

Bram and Ulf had been lumbered with the children.

All nine of them.

Isaura and Bayla had gone somewhere to do something, though likely they just wanted a break. And having endured only a few moments in charge of the gaggle of children, Bram didn't blame them. He couldn't hear Ulf over the shouting, whining, arguing noises. 'We need to put them in a pen!' he grinned, bending down to take the stones out of Mads' hands. 'We don't throw stones at our sisters!'

Mads was shocked by the sudden growl in Bram's usually cheerful voice, and he burst into tears. But before Bram could try and comfort him, Kai bit Halla who screamed and hit him.

'Do you need some help?' Hanna wondered. She had gone for a walk to find Berard, wanting some company, and though she hadn't found him, she had found his nieces and nephews. And more.

Ulf and Bram looked at Hanna as though she was the sun after a storm.

'Yes!' Bram exclaimed. 'Help would be good. We really should be...'

'We have to...' Ulf added.

'It's alright,' Hanna smiled sadly. 'You don't need an excuse. Kai!' And she grabbed his hand, yanking him away from Halla who he appeared ready to kick. 'I don't mind the noise.'

'Well, you'd be the only one,' Ulf laughed, though one look at her face and he was frowning. 'I'm sorry about your father. He was a good man.'

'Thank you,' Hanna mumbled, trying not to cry again. Her eyes were sore, and she was desperate for a break from all the tears. Nothing felt real yet. She didn't want to hide in the hall, but she didn't want people to talk to her about her father either.

Bram lifted an eyebrow at Ulf, trying to get him to leave but before either of them could escape, the cat Annet was attempting to kiss scratched her face, and she screamed, bursting into tears.

Both men looked at Hanna, who smiled. 'Go! I'll be fine. I promise.'

And nodding quickly, feeling guilty but relieved, they headed to the ramparts to check on their men.

***

Entorp didn't have a lot to say as he worked at a small table in his cottage beside Edela, making another batch of salves, which was just as well as Edela's mind was whirring away, working through the ritual, trying to think of what else they might need.

And then there was the constant worry about Jael, who would soon be arriving at the Vale of the Gods.

'Edela? You seem distracted,' Entorp said suddenly, turning to her, realising that she hadn't spoken in some time.

'Oh, I'm nothing but distracted at the moment. There is so much to think about. I have never had such a heavy load of dreams, and it takes a lot of sifting through them to find a clear path.' She smiled, hoping to convey some sense of control. She didn't want everyone to worry that she was losing her mind. 'I have a tea which I will try tonight. That might help get things in order.'

'Sounds like just what you need. There is so much to worry about. Especially for you.' Entorp picked up the pestle and pushed it against the basil leaves, inhaling their sweet scent.

'For me, yes, I suppose there is. Being a dreamer has always been a great responsibility.'

'But you have Ontine and Eydis to share the load now, and you must let them.'

'Yes, Eydis is always trying to help, and Ontine is becoming more confident, which is good to see.' Edela frowned suddenly, her thoughts darting from Ontine to her mother. 'What do you know about Sybill?'

'Sybill Ethburg?' Entorp looked up. 'Nothing at all. I don't remember her from Tuura.'

'No?' Edela was surprised. She'd received the same answer

from most of the people she'd asked, and though Branwyn did remember her faintly, she had no information to impart, which in itself was unusual.

'I left Tuura some time ago, so perhaps I saw her when I was younger, but my memory is not what it was.'

'Oh.'

'Though she seems pleasant enough. She comes in regularly to check on me, offering her help. I've enjoyed our conversations enormously.'

Edela looked perturbed, realising that there was no point in digging any further. 'Well, Ontine is proving useful, so I shall stop worrying about her mother and focus on helping her.'

'Sounds sensible. The more we can do to help Jael, the better,' Entorp yawned.

Edela's eyes twinkled at the sound of her granddaughter's name. 'I miss her,' she said suddenly. 'I fear that I'll never see her again.'

Entorp looked surprised. 'You have more faith in her than that, don't you?' He was determined that Edela not see how worried he was himself. 'Jael's exactly where she's supposed to be. Where Dara Teros saw her being, isn't she?'

Edela nodded.

'Then remind yourself of who she is. The woman who has fought since she was a girl. Who was taught how to survive. To win. Try and remember her, Edela, because if there is one thing you need to believe in now, it's your granddaughter.'

***

Jael's attention kept wandering as the landscape became more challenging. They had left behind the meadows and fields as they headed deep into the south of Brekka. The terrain was becoming jagged, rising in places now, stone ridges bordering them on their left, Hallow Wood still on the right.

She was looking forward to seeing Rexon. He would meet them in Verra, just before the vale. They had already been joined by warriors from Tornas and Folstad. More were coming from Rosby and Skorn. If they made it to the vale, they would be an army some four thousand strong.

But it wouldn't be enough.

Not if Meena Gallas didn't take that ring.

And not if she couldn't stop Eadmund, though Jael could feel that he was further away from them than ever. She scratched her head. After the chill of the snow, they were all steaming in their armour, and she had taken off her helmet for the first time all morning, trying to shake her damp hair away from the back of her neck.

'What are you thinking about?' Aleksander asked with a smile.

She turned to him, surprised to see him beside her. 'Thought you were up there. With Axl.'

'Ha! Are you riding asleep? I've been here for some time.'

Jael blinked, wondering if she had drifted off. 'There's a lot to think about.'

'There is. For you.'

'Not just for me. We've all got a part to play, haven't we? In Draguta's show.'

'We do. But Draguta's not bothered about any of us, is she? She just wants you to come.'

'Well, she'll regret that I'm sure.'

Jael winked at him, but Aleksander knew her well enough to see the doubt in her eyes. He had been watching that doubt grow over their journey, and it worried him. They needed her to be the best she could be. At her fiercest. Full of anger and burning fire. That was the Jael who could defeat Draguta.

If she could get through her husband first.

And that's when he realised what was wrong. 'You don't think you can defeat Eadmund, do you?'

Jael froze. 'Defeat him?' She shrugged. 'I imagine I can. But kill him?' Her voice was a whisper. 'I don't know if I can do that.

Could you kill me?' She peered into his eyes, no humour in her own. 'If you had no choice, could you kill me?'

Aleksander didn't know. He stared into her deep green eyes, feeling his stomach flip. 'I would die to save you, but would I kill you?' He shook his head. 'I don't ever want to find out.'

Jael dropped her shoulders, reaching out to pat Tig. 'I could kill you, but Eadmund?' And looking around, she grinned at him, not wanting to dwell on the darkness that was coming to claim them. It would come regardless.

Let them enjoy whatever time they had left.

Aleksander shoved her arm, trying not to smile. 'Not sure why I ever loved you, Jael Furyck.'

'Yes, you are. Still do, from what I can see.'

'Oh, really?' He tried to remove any emotion from his eyes.

'Being a dreamer is more useful than I ever realised. Can't believe I spent all those years fighting it. Now I can read minds!'

Aleksander frowned, reluctant to keep playing, but with Jael, it was always hard to resist. 'And what does my mind say, then?'

Jael studied him, swaying with Tig who was keeping a slow, plodding pace behind Axl and Raymon. She thought about creeping around the edges of the truth, but it was Aleksander. She owed him more than that. 'That you're confused. Afraid. Sad. Lonely.'

'That sums it up perfectly,' he laughed, though he didn't look happy.

'You're thinking about Hanna a lot. I feel that.'

He grew awkward.

'But you're finding it hard to let go of me.'

Even more awkward.

'If I were you, I'm not sure I could let go. Even if I knew I had to,' Jael admitted. 'I'm not sure I can now.'

Aleksander's eyes were full of surprise. 'You can't?'

'I'm used to you being there. Here. Next to me. When I was on Oss, I missed you.' He looked confused, and Jael realised that she was tired, making a mess of things.

'But you love your husband.' Aleksander knew her. He wasn't that confused.

'I do, though I may kill him, so don't forget about me just yet,' Jael laughed.

It was strange, how things were between them now, though being together had always felt right. It was what they knew. It was comfortable and easy.

It made sense.

'You need Eadmund,' Aleksander said after they'd ridden in silence for a time. 'They all say that. But I want you to know that I'll be there too. My name may not be in that prophecy, but I'll be there too.'

'I hope so. You might have to yell at me. Remind me of what I'm supposed to be doing. There's no Gant to scream orders this time.'

'I will, don't worry. You'll be fine. You'll do what you have to do. What you were born to do. Don't worry.'

And looking into those familiar dark eyes, Jael felt herself relax for the first time all day.

***

Despite having gone over the ritual many times now, Edela still felt unhappy about what Eydis was going to try.

Not unhappy. Unconfident. Nervous. Anxious.

She had the overwhelming feeling that it wasn't going to go well.

Ontine had not been at the first ritual when she'd cut Eadmund's binding rope, but she looked just as worried. Her dark-blue eyes were jumping back and forth between Edela and Eydis.

'I don't care if I die! I don't care if it kills me!' Eydis insisted. 'I would do it, Edela. For Eadmund, I would do it!'

Biddy, standing behind all three of them as they sat on stools around the fire in the hall, looked horrified. 'And why would you say such a thing? Eydis! Eadmund would never want that. And your father? Jael? They would never want that for you!'

Eydis sat taller on her stool, wishing she could stare into Biddy's eyes. Anybody's eyes. She wanted them all to know how determined she was. For them to see her as she saw herself. She would not back down or walk away. They had to free Eadmund before it was too late. It didn't matter if it was dangerous.

It didn't!

Edela was quiet. Eydis was fourteen-years-old. Not a girl. Not a woman. Something awkward in between. But that something was a dreamer, filled with purpose and Edela would not deny her. 'We will go ahead tomorrow, then. We will try it. There is a lot to prepare, though, so you must help me, Biddy.'

'Tomorrow?' Eydis sat forward, anxious, hoping they were not running out of time.

'Tomorrow,' Edela insisted firmly. 'And in the meantime, I will decide how safe it's going to be for you. I will decide, Eydis. I will think on it, and, hopefully, dream on it. But we will be ready nonetheless.'

Edela spoke with the certainty of a boulder dropping from the sky and Eydis could only nod her head.

Tomorrow.

CHAPTER FORTY SIX

The ring was on her mind.

Draguta was talking to Brill who stood next to Meena, and the ring was on her mind.

And Draguta didn't look her way once.

Meena didn't want her confidence to trip her up, though. It wouldn't help if she made a mess of everything now. The potion appeared to be working well, keeping Draguta away from her thoughts, and the tea she had given Draguta appeared to have made no difference.

She glanced around at the Followers sitting in a circle on the grass verge beside them. A large group of dishevelled looking women. No men. No man had survived Draguta's purge. None of them were looking at her suspiciously either. And Briggit appeared far too interested in pleasing Draguta to bother terrorising her anymore. But Evaine?

Evaine's eyes never left her alone as she waited to be called upon.

'I want this to be a grand feast!' Draguta was insisting in a sharp tone. 'We have more than one table, don't we?'

Brill looked ill. They had brought as much as they could from the castle, though she had not expected her mistress to want more than one dining table. 'We could only fit one big table in the wagon,' she mumbled, eyeing the Followers.

'One? Well, we don't really need more, I suppose. Just enough for us. Those of us who matter, at least.' And her eyes snapped to Evaine who was becoming so attentive now, though still as useless as ever as she stood there while everyone else worked.

'Draguta.'

Eadmund was there and she spun around with a smile. 'You have found Jaeger, then?' He nodded, and Draguta felt her confidence renew. He was compliant, so very compliant, and it made her happy. 'Good, well, then come along with me. Let these little helpers organise our supper. We will discuss how I expect it to unfold, and what I require from each of you.'

Eadmund turned away and Meena felt the change in him, realising that he was no ally anymore, if he ever had been.

'Are you dreaming?'

Meena bit her tongue, shivering as Briggit crept up behind her. 'I...'

'You appear to be in such a dream,' Briggit smiled, walking around to face her. 'But then, you are a dreamer, aren't you? Not a very good one, though, it seems.' And she lifted a finger to Meena's face, running it around her jaw, down to her chin, over her lips. 'Or are you? With a grandmother like Varna Gallas? An aunt like Morana? Perhaps it's all an act? This little mouse everyone thinks you are?' She took her finger away, enjoying the sudden red hue that coloured Meena's face; the stink of her sweat as she panicked.

'Little mouse, little mouse...' Briggit mused. 'Oh, but what a shame it would be if the little mouse got herself trapped. Jaeger would be so sad to lose a friend like you.' And swinging around with a smug smile, Briggit strode away after Draguta and Eadmund.

Meena stood watching her, wondering what she could see.

Wondering what she knew.

***

Supper was delicious.

'If I hadn't asked Isaura to marry me, I'd ask you,' Thorgils grinned, beard dripping with the mushroom stew Aleksander had been slaving over since they'd made camp for the night. 'Not sure anything's ever tasted so good!'

Karsten was nodding beside him, quiet but enjoying the hot meal after a day spent gnawing on salt fish and stale flatbreads. He hadn't said much since his talk with Jael. Nothing felt real, and he was choosing to pretend that it hadn't even happened. As though the only thing that existed was this army of warriors on a journey to the greatest battle Osterland would ever witness. One they would embroider in gold thread on long tapestries that would hang on the walls of his castle; tales of great feats and heroic battles that Warunda would bellow from every stage, and from every hall in the land.

Karsten hoped he would live to hear it.

Ivaar frowned, surprised that Thorgils was going to marry Isaura. He felt nothing except the relief of no longer being married to her himself. His eyes wandered to Ayla, who remained the most beautiful woman he had seen since Melaena, though he had ruined that. Treated her badly.

He tried not to look at Bruno.

That wouldn't help.

Aleksander was pleased with the compliment and the happy faces of the stuffed bodies that slumped around the fire, occasionally glancing at the cauldron, wondering if there was any more.

There wasn't. Thorgils had already seen to that.

'Do you think she'll come again tonight?' Fyn asked. They were sitting inside Jael's circle. Ayla had made her own. It felt reassuring to have the protection, but the circles were not helping to ease the tension amongst her warriors.

The eyes that drifted towards Jael and her men were hooded.

Resentful.

She noticed, hoping they would arrive at the vale before that resentment dug in too deep. 'Draguta? I don't know. Perhaps. We're not far away now, so maybe, or maybe not. Just make sure you go to sleep dressed in everything you want to keep with you.

Have your horse saddled. And stuff some food in your trousers!' She smiled at Thorgils, who looked as though he was taking the idea seriously.

No one spoke, and Jael was conscious of the slow wail of the wind flapping tents behind them. She wondered whether that was the sound of Veiga, still bound by Draguta.

'Well, I hope she gives us a chance to fight her,' Axl muttered, placing his empty trencher on the dirt. 'After what she's put us through? I hope she lets us come. I don't want to be stopped now.'

Low grunts of agreement, nodding shadows, a loud fart.

Thorgils' grin was bright in the darkness, his eyes suddenly sad as he thought of Torstan who he had killed, and Eadmund who he'd let go.

If it hadn't been for him, Eadmund would be here, preparing to fight with Jael as he was meant to.

Fyn tapped him on the shoulder. 'Thorgils?'

And Thorgils blinked, realising that Fyn was trying to hand him the ale jug. Shaking his head, he took it, filling his cup. 'Who's ready for a few tales, then?' he called, trying to shut away the memories and the voices of his friends.

They were gone now. Both of them.

But he still had a chance to help bring Eadmund back.

***

'Draguta's keeping you busy,' Jaeger smiled, slipping his arm around Meena's waist, pulling her close. They were walking into the trees that formed a small wood behind the Tree of Agrayal. Meena didn't know why.

She sighed, her shoulders tense. She knew why.

Jaeger's appetite for her was only increasing, and Meena was petrified that it would get her in trouble with Draguta. She knew that it would get her in trouble with Draguta. 'There's a lot to do,' she insisted, wanting an escape, but her face still ached from the last time she'd displeased him, and she knew that it was better to do whatever he wanted. All of it. No matter how much she loathed it.

'There is, but in a few days we'll be heading back to Hest, and everything will be different.'

He sounded so confident.

'Unless it goes wrong,' Meena mumbled. 'What if Jael Furyck defeats Eadmund? She could, couldn't she?' Jaeger had stopped, his attention on the ground, clearing away pine cones and rocks with his boot, and she was trying to distract him.

He frowned. 'She could. Though Eadmund is not the useless piece of shit he once was. But don't worry, I'll finish her if she ruins Draguta's plans. Eadmund too.'

'You?' Meena blinked. Jaeger sounded as bold and strong as if he'd been holding the Book of Darkness in his hands.

Jaeger grabbed her arm, pulling her down to the ground. 'Do we really need to be talking about Eadmund and Jael now? When we're here, together? Why worry about them? Neither one of them will survive what's coming. Draguta and I have spoken about it. Whatever happens, I'm to ensure that neither of them lives. You've nothing to worry about, Meena. Nothing to worry about at all.' And stroking her face with one hand, he pushed her backwards with the other.

***

'Jaeger took her,' Brill tried to explain as she stood in front of Draguta's turned down bed in her very comfortable looking tent.

Draguta's raised eyebrow was unimpressed.

'But she made the tea before she left,' Brill hurried to add, her shoulders hunching up to her ears. 'I have been keeping it warm for you.'

'How kind you are, dear Brill,' Draguta cooed, though her eyes were hard. 'And so... loyal. I am grateful to have you by my side, tending to my needs.' She stepped closer to the tall servant, studying her in the glow of the tent. Brill had been keeping all the candles and lamps alight too, despite the sudden determination of the wind. 'Loyalty, as you know, is very important to me. Above all things, I must trust those around me, like you and Meena.'

Brill's throat was so dry that she couldn't swallow, and she was attempting not to. Instead, she spluttered, coughing all over Draguta. 'I... I am sorry! It is... I am hot!'

Draguta laughed, knowing how terrified she made the girl. It was amusing, she supposed. 'Grab yourself something to drink, then. Hurry along. And bring in that tea. I may even try two cups of it tonight.' There was a hint of desperation in her voice, and she scowled to hear it as she spun around, her eyes on the small tables. On the new seeing circles she had just drawn.

Taking a seat before one, she ran a finger around the symbols, setting them aglow. 'Oh, how I wish we were on the same side, Sister,' Draguta murmured, searching through the forest, certain that Dara was hiding in it somewhere. 'How much more fun everything would be with you by my side.'

The forest was warded with symbols. Draguta could see them shimmering as she ran her eyes over the trees; dark, tall shadows, swaying in the wind. She thought about Darroc. That smelly old buffoon. She would have to find him before that pointless god decided to play any more games. He thought that he could hide from her like the rest of them. From her?

She would find him. And Dara. And every other god cowering in the shadows.

There was no place for any of them in what she had planned.

No place at all.

***

Dara was crying out in her sleep, and Eloris didn't know what to do.

Eloris did not sleep. She was immortal, like Dara, though Dara needed dreams, which came to her more powerfully when she was asleep. And though she appeared distressed, Eloris didn't want to wake her before she found the answer to whatever had been eluding her for days.

'Aarrghh!' Dara sat up, head swivelling, confused.

They were in another cave. She didn't even remember where.

They journeyed in the dark, hiding in dense thickets, woods, forests, far away from where anyone would find them.

She hoped.

'Dara?' Eloris kneeled down beside her. 'What is it?'

Dara shook her head before closing her eyes. Her dream had gone, the threads dangling far from her reach. Sighing, she hung her head. 'I don't remember. I don't remember. It was there, on the tip of my tongue, and then... gone.'

'But it was troubling? Something was wrong?'

Dara nodded slowly, lifting her head. 'Yes.' It was like an ice-cold hand on her shoulder. As though someone was there, whispering to her in panicked tones.

A warning.

'Stop her!'

***

Edela felt refreshed when she woke. Her back was stiff, and she couldn't turn her head to the right, but her mind was brimming with renewed energy.

'Any dreams?' Biddy wondered, handing her a bowl of steaming porridge.

'No dreams,' Edela admitted. 'Though I shall take that as a good sign. We are all still here to fight another day, and neither of the girls had any either, so perhaps there was nothing to dream about?' She was determined to sound positive. It was not in anyone's interests for them to feel defeated yet, though it was hard not to let the constant terror and grief gnaw at their spirits.

Biddy smiled, sitting down with her own porridge, sprinkling some chopped hazelnuts into the bowl, her eyes on Entorp who was very quiet as he sat opposite them. 'What about you, then? You don't look as though you slept at all.'

'Oh, no, I slept,' Entorp sighed. 'I had terrible dreams all night long.'

'You did?' Edela's attention shifted to the doors where Ontine was helping Eydis inside, the two of them having taken the puppies for a walk. She smiled, pleased to see how well they were getting along now; frowning as she caught a glimpse of Sybill who was approaching her daughter with those ferrety eyes of hers. Realising that she was staring, Edela turned back to Entorp. 'What did you dream about, then?'

'My wife. My children.'

Biddy stopped eating. Entorp rarely talked about his family, and she could see how disturbed he was.

'I saw what The Following did to them.'

'What do you mean?' Edela wondered. 'As though you were there?'

Entorp rubbed his heavy eyes. 'Yes, I was there in the dream, the nightmare, watching the Followers kill them.' He shuddered. 'It was very distressing.'

'Oh, Entorp.' Biddy reached out a hand, patting his, a sympathetic look in her eyes. 'That must have been awful.'

'I agree, but you're no dreamer, Entorp,' Edela said. 'It was not real, so likely not anything that actually happened. Best you try to pretend you never saw it. Imagine them as they were. You cannot help them now.'

'No, I can't. But it made me think about The Following. About how secretive they were. Even Isobel didn't know every Follower in Tuura.'

'She didn't?' Edela was surprised.

'No. They worked to shield themselves from discovery. To

remain hidden from each other, separated, so that if one Follower was discovered and forced to reveal what they knew, they couldn't expose everyone else.'

'But they're dreamers,' Biddy said. 'Couldn't they tell? Couldn't they see the truth?'

Entorp shook his head. 'No, they could mask themselves. I'm not sure how, but Isobel told me they could. Our neighbours may have been Followers, and we would never have known.'

Biddy's eyes were full of worry as she scanned the hall. 'But that means we could have Followers among us,' she hissed. 'Couldn't we?'

Entorp nodded. 'It is possible, yes, I think so.'

Biddy turned to Edela wondering just what they were going to do about that, but Edela's eyes were on Sybill who was watching her, a smile on that insipid, rodent-like face of hers.

***

There was no tent for Evaine, and she watched Eadmund emerging from his with a weary scowl from her bed of grass. Her dress was damp, and her neck was twinging, and she thought longingly of her chamber in the castle. Even Yorik Elstad's revolting cottage would have been preferable to sleeping outside.

Frowning, she reached for her father's satchel. She had brought it with her, though she didn't really know why. She had packed a spare dress inside, a comb, another pair of shoes, though Eadmund would not have looked at her if she had been made of gold. She knew that now.

Searching through the satchel, looking for her comb, Evaine blinked, her fingers on a book. And dragging it out, she smiled, remembering Morana. It was her book.

Help, she'd said.

Help for when she needed it.

***

Karsten had joined the scouts, wanting to get away from everyone who felt the need to offer some sympathy for the loss of his wife. He didn't want sympathy, though. He wanted some ale. A bed with a thick mattress. A throne.

He thought about Hanna as he rode back to the head of the line, to where Jael was riding with Aleksander; Aleksander who'd made his feelings for Hanna known now. Or perhaps it was the other way around? Karsten wasn't sure.

'Any sign of a murderous, monster-wielding witch?' Thorgils called. 'Any dragons or possessed goats?'

Raymon laughed. He'd come to join Jael at the front, leaving Soren to command the Iskavallans. 'I don't think a possessed goat would be scary, would it?'

They all looked at him as though he was their annoying little brother who had tagged along somewhere he wasn't invited.

'Well, possibly not,' Jael said, watching Raymon's cheeks flush pink. 'Though, they've got those little horns. I wouldn't like to be jabbed by one of those.'

Karsten slipped in beside Jael. 'Nothing to see out there. Feels a bit odd.'

'Does it?' Jael's body tingled all over. 'Why?'

'Didn't see any sign of animals. Couldn't hear any either. Not even a bird.'

It was true, Jael realised. They had been so busy talking, trying to keep their minds off what lay ahead that they'd barely taken a breath since they'd left their campsite that morning.

It was disconcerting.

'But surely we're days away?' Raymon wondered. 'Aren't we?'

'We're aiming for something I saw in a dream,' Jael reminded him. 'It doesn't mean Draguta had the same dream or any intention of making it come true. But if we carry on at this pace, we should reach the vale by tomorrow night. Or, at least, we'll be close. We still have to get those catapults over a few hills. Might take some time.'

'Perhaps the gods warned them?' Raymon suggested, already regretting that he'd opened his mouth again.

Jael turned to her youngest brother with a frown. 'You might be right.' She looked up, not having seen Fyr since she'd flown away that morning.

Hoping she would see her again soon.

***

Edela was finding it hard to concentrate. 'Yes, yes,' she muttered. 'Two of those.' Her eyes were briefly on Ontine before she turned back around, watching the hall doors opening and closing. It was warm enough to keep them open, she thought irritably, feeling a sudden rush of heat.

'I thought you were feeling better today?' Biddy smiled as she passed. 'You look as though you need some fresh air. It's getting a bit hot in here.'

'Is it?' Edela was relieved. 'I thought it was just me.'

Biddy laughed. 'Why don't you come with me and we'll step outside for a while?' She could see Edela recoil from her hand. 'Just for a while. Take in some sun. Inhale something that doesn't smell like sheep fat and whatever is in that cauldron.' And screwing up her nose, she leaned forward, grabbing Edela's hand.

'I've never known anyone as bossy as you,' Edela grumbled, though she quite happily followed a bustling Biddy out through the doors and onto the hall steps, where a cooling breeze and a dull grey sky greeted them.

'Not exactly sunshine!' Biddy grinned. 'But it will do you good to stop squinting over that book for a while.'

Edela panicked, not wanting to leave the book behind.

'The girls are there,' Biddy assured her. 'It's just for a moment.' And she lifted a hand as Sybill approached, helping a limping Derwa to mount the steps.

'What happened?' Edela was too concerned to be bothered by Sybill's presence. 'Derwa?'

'Oh, nothing much. I twisted my ankle. A hole that wasn't a hole. I misjudged it and down I went. Silly old fool.'

Derwa looked flustered, and Edela quickly took her hand. 'Let's get you inside and have a look at it. I think you've cut your arm too.' She could see blood seeping through the sleeve of Derwa's grey dress.

'Oh, I did make a mess of myself then, didn't I?' Derwa sighed, letting Edela and Biddy help her up the steps.

Sybill hurried ahead of them, opening the door, her eyes meeting Edela's as she passed, surprised by the harsh look on the old dreamer's face. And blinking, she dropped her head, following after them.

***

Draguta scowled at Jaeger as he headed towards her with Meena who looked embarrassed and in need of a comb. 'We must find you other forms of entertainment, Jaeger. Or, at least, someone else to entertain you, for I did not bring Meena Gallas here to service you day and night!' She saved her fiercest scowl for Meena as she approached, jabbing a finger at her chest. 'And you will hurry to find Brill who has been left to assist me all morning with only Evaine for help! And I'm sure you can imagine how that has gone?'

Meena nodded, bobbing and weaving past Draguta and Eadmund, trying to make her way to Brill.

'Straighten up!' Draguta barked after her slumped assistant. 'You are not a weeping willow!' And turning back to Jaeger, she inhaled sharply. 'There is a stream. Do not forget to use it, before we are all forced to smell what you've been up to.'

Jaeger didn't bother to feel offended. He felt invigorated, knowing that Karsten was coming. That Jael Furyck and her army were coming too.

But when?

'You will ensure that everything is in place by the end of the day,' Draguta snapped, her mood more fractious than ever. 'And then, perhaps we will hurry the Furycks along. We don't want to wait here forever, do we? No harm in giving them an incentive to march faster!'

CHAPTER FORTY SEVEN

They wrapped Derwa's swollen ankle in cabbage leaves and left her resting on a bed near the grey curtain. Biddy brought her a cup of rose hip tea, and Alaric, who was getting in everyone's way and would be better use as company for Derwa. Edela returned to the circle where Ontine and Eydis were chatting as they worked; Ontine stirring the cauldron, Eydis sniffing the herbs before picking the leaves and handing them to her.

'Well, this is impressive teamwork!' Edela grinned. 'I'm not sure you needed me to come back.'

Ontine looked horrified. 'Oh no, we can't do it without you, Edela. I'm just reading the words, but I doubt they'll have much weight to them with my lack of experience.'

Edela bent over the cauldron, inhaling the potent blend of herbs and spices, relieved that they had managed to save the gardens inside the fort. Relieved too that they had foraged in the woods before Draguta had killed everything.

She frowned, thinking about the sacred grove; wondering if she had destroyed Furia's Tree too; worrying about the gods, and whether any could withstand Draguta now. 'I'm sorry?' Edela smiled at Ontine. 'I drifted off, I think. Must be time for my nap.'

'That sounds like a good idea,' Eydis said, standing up. 'You should go.'

'Not yet, but once we're done here, I will. And so will you, Eydis. Tonight will drain us both. To sustain that sort of trance whilst attempting to cut that powerful rope?' She took a deep breath, doubting whether it was even possible, then, looking at Eydis' hopeful face, she exhaled, smiling. 'But we had some success last time, didn't we? I'm sure we can go one step further tonight.' She wasn't sure at all. And she wanted Entorp to help keep them safe. He would be coming to add more tattoos of protection to them soon.

Edela wasn't looking forward to that.

'We'll finish up here, then a nap, and then we'll be ready for Entorp,' she decided, reaching for the Book of Aurea, comforted just to touch it again.

Hoping it would have all the answers she needed to the battle that lay ahead.

***

Draguta sat at the table, her hands placed on either side of her seeing circle, watching Jael Furyck and her sprawling army trudge towards the vale, where they would...

Meet their deaths.

Draguta smiled.

Where they would meet their deaths, and she would kill her sister, who would be forced to reveal herself to save them.

Draguta drained her goblet, feeling the wine heat her chest. In fact, she felt warm all over, a heat that charged her. Turning to the book, she laid her hands on it, feeling it pulse beneath her fingers.

Ready to begin.

'It has been a long journey, my friend,' she sighed. 'You and I have come to this place together, but this is only the beginning. Once we show them what we are capable of, there will be nothing to stop us. No man, woman, or god will stand in our way!'

***

They had stopped in Verra just in time for lunch, much to Thorgils' delight, and while Jael and Aleksander sat with Rexon, explaining everything that had happened since they'd last seen him, Thorgils filled plate after plate with the bounteous food on offer in the smoke-stained hall.

The Lady of Verra had stood anxiously by the door to the kitchen, hoping the giant red-headed warrior wasn't going to barge past her looking for more. She had put on a feast in honour of the Lord of Saala and his men, but she had not been expecting to entertain the vast swathe of the Brekkan army, including some very hungry Islanders too.

Eventually, Jael had sent Thorgils outside to get everyone ready, leaving a relieved kitchen staff behind. And now they were back on the road with the Saalans, making plans with Rexon whose eyes were bright and alert, looking out for any of the terrifying creatures Jael had described.

Fyr returned that afternoon, and Jael could feel the raven's tension as she perched on her shoulder, twitching, eyes blinking, turning to Jael, back to Thorgils, looking ahead and behind.

Never still.

It made Jael twitchy too.

She sucked in a long breath, eyes up on the clouds in the distance.

Aleksander's eyes were there too. 'Just clouds,' he decided.

'Or smoke?' Rexon wondered from beside him, not convinced; more on edge than he had been in some time. He was used to looking for enemies with swords and shields. Not fangs and wings. 'Maybe fog?'

Jael shrugged. 'Could be either. I like clouds, though. Let's stick with clouds.'

Aleksander smiled, glancing around at a worried Axl who rode behind him with Karsten, eyes on the clouds too, feeling his tension mount. They were getting closer to the vale, and he could only hope that Jael was right. That Draguta was leading them to her.

Her and Jaeger.

Karsten spat on the ground. He'd had no appetite since eating that stew, convinced that Aleksander had poisoned them all. 'You're going to have to fight me.'

Axl was surprised, turning to Karsten with a frown. 'What? Why?'

'You're thinking about your woman. About what you'll do to Jaeger, aren't you?'

Axl nodded. 'Not hard to see why.'

'No, but you won't be able to kill him. I've seen you fight. He'll blow you over. Tear you to pieces on his way to me.'

Hearing where the conversation was headed, Thorgils nudged his horse in between them. 'You've got a better impression of your arse brother than I have. We all saw him on Skorro. Jael knocked him down before he'd even opened his mouth to cry for his mother.'

Karsten laughed. 'You don't think he's improved since then? Since he was stuck in that smoking bowl with a crew of half-drowned men?' He spat over the side of his horse again, bile swirling around his mouth. 'I've fought him, you haven't. I know you want to take him, Axl. Have him. Kill him. But you can't,' Karsten insisted, his eye on Thorgils, eyebrow raised, wanting his help convincing Axl not to even try.

'Karsten's got a point,' Thorgils said, watching Axl's frustration mount. 'I know what it's like to want to kill a man. To think that you can. Believe in your reputation so much you kid yourself into becoming the hero you're not. I almost got myself killed with thinking like that.' Thorgils' mind wandered to Tarak. 'Lucky for me, Jael finished what I couldn't even start.'

Axl wasn't about to retreat, though. 'In battle…' He stopped, shying away from Karsten's fierce glare and Thorgils' sympathetic eyes.

'In battle, you're never as good as you think you'll be. It's slippery and loud. It stinks. Your friends die. You can't see. Can't think. Guts everywhere. A bloody nightmare.' Karsten's voice softened. 'You're a king. I'm not, but I will be when I defeat my brother. You need to ride into battle like a king who cares about his kingdom. Not one man. Jaeger's not worth it. You want to avenge your woman? Then live. Leave Jaeger to me.'

Axl saw the sense in that - surprised that it was coming from Karsten Dragos - and he realised that Amma meant more to him than killing Jaeger ever would. That and going home to Andala, to his mother and Gant.

His grandmother and Biddy.

And he stared at Karsten, who was adjusting his eye patch, looking as though he was about to spit again, but he didn't say a word.

***

Jael's bed was big enough for two. She had slept in it with Aleksander for many years, and Edela felt sad that time had moved on so quickly. From Jael and Aleksander being together, to Jael being on Oss, to this. Edela could smell the faint aroma of lemon balm, a hint of sheep fat, and she smiled as she helped Eydis lie down, grabbing a fur for her, moving Vella out of the way as they made themselves comfortable.

Jael would come back.

Edela held onto that thought as she closed her eyes. 'Good luck, Eydis,' she murmured, patting her shoulder. 'I wish you some useful dreams.'

Eydis opened her eyes, though there was only darkness. She could hear the worry in Edela's voice that she wouldn't find a dream at all. 'I wish you the same. And don't worry, Ontine will come and find us if there's any trouble. You need to relax.'

Edela chuckled softly. 'Can you hear my worries now? You are getting to be a very good dreamer, Eydis Skalleson, if that's the case. Though it's not really Ontine who worries me as much as her mother.'

'Oh, why is that?' Eydis rolled towards Edela, too curious to feel tired.

Edela felt silly. 'I'm not sure. You didn't like Ontine, did you? At first?'

Now Eydis felt silly. 'I think it was because of... Fyn,' she admitted. 'Ontine is a pretty girl. A woman. I've seen her in my dreams. I can see why Fyn would get tongue-tied around her.'

'But you don't mind her now?'

'She's been helpful and kind. And the puppies like her. The children, too, so no, I don't mind her now. I haven't spoken to her mother, though. I haven't seen her in my dreams.'

'No?'

'No. Why are you suspicious of her?' Eydis wondered, yawning. It was a comfortable bed, and she was starting to feel sleepy. 'Did she say something to you?'

Edela could see that Eydis was ready for sleep, and she didn't want to distract her; she needed as much rest as possible before the ritual. 'No, nothing at all. Don't you worry, now. I've a feeling it's just me letting my imagination run away with itself.' She caught Eydis' yawn and closed her eyes. 'Get some sleep. See if you can find that brother of yours.' And yawning some more, Edela waded into the darkness, hoping to find a useful dream of her own.

***

Though the sun was out and the wagon was a constant wobbling noise, Ayla was trying to fall asleep. She desperately needed more dreams, though lately, they had been confusing. She always saw fire.

It had been that way since long before she had taken ill with the sickness. Always fire. It was unsettling. Smoke lingered in her nostrils, in her hair, on her clothes, reminding her of her dreams.

Astrid was the perfect company. She was a quiet, industrious worker with an agreeable disposition. Ayla had enjoyed getting to know her, but she was always most grateful when Astrid left her alone with her thoughts.

Even Bruno had been quiet. He was still struggling to understand how he had killed that man in the fog; struggling with Ivaar's constant presence too. It was hard to ask him to hold himself back when Ayla could feel how desperately he sought a reckoning. And one day, perhaps, he would get it. She hoped so.

Rolling onto her side, she inhaled the lavender she had stuffed inside her pillow. It was the perfect remedy for a troubled mind.

And closing her eyes, Ayla let the creaking wagon rock her to sleep.

***

'Our enemies are hiding in plain sight,' Dara warned the young woman. 'Yours and mine. They tried to steal the prophecy, but I destroyed it.'

'You did?'

'I was a child when I wrote it. So naive. I believed in people I shouldn't have. The Following was like a magical creature that could regrow a severed limb. They shifted and hid and twisted themselves into new shapes so that we never knew who they were. They cloaked themselves from even the most talented dreamers.'

'Like you?'

Dara smiled, handing Samara a cup of lavender and rose tea. 'Well, yes, even me. I wrote the prophecy as a warning. I imagined a warning as dire as that would be heeded, that the elderman would act. We trusted her, my aunt and I. But Sersha was a Follower. She killed her own kind to protect her identity. That's what they do. Anything they can. They are desperate for Raemus. His return is the only thing that matters. The one true goal, they call it. Their lives are devoted to the search for the Book of Darkness and to the destruction of those who stand in their way.'

Samara was seventeen-years-old. This was her first visit to Dara Teros on her own. She had come with her mother over the years, but she was only just beginning to learn what a responsibility being a protector of the Book of Aurea was. How she must work to keep it out of the wrong hands.

'And they are all the wrong hands,' Dara said, interrupting her thoughts. 'You must trust no one but your own family. Our family. You will have a daughter, Samara, and she will have a daughter, and one day that daughter will become the most powerful dreamer in all of Osterland.'

Samara blinked. 'She will?'

'Her name will be Eydis. I have seen that. And though the gods will deprive her of her sight, they will give her the greatest vision of all, for she will be able to see in the Darkness.'

***

Meena's eyes were grainy. Jaeger had kept her awake for much of the night. He was acting as though he needed no sleep at all. His energy was surging, and she suspected that it was something to do with the Book of Darkness.

Draguta was letting him touch it again, encouraging him to, sensing that he would need its power before the battle.

It worried Meena.

She could see the change in him after he'd held it. His eyes were peeled open wide, blinking rapidly, his movements fast and jerking. It was as though he was turning into someone else. Something else.

'Is it ready?' Brill asked, nudging her.

Meena blinked, peering at the dark liquid. Everything appeared to have blended together as best that she could see. She nodded. 'You can take it to her.'

Brill grabbed the copper bowl, eager to be gone. She almost ran into Evaine who stood in the entrance of the tent, watching with hooded eyes. 'Everyone is rushing about today,' she purred, her eyes on Meena.

Meena swallowed, wishing Brill hadn't just run away.

'Draguta told me to come and see what you were doing.'

Meena frowned. 'I have a list,' she mumbled, pointing to the curling piece of vellum. 'I'm making potions for tonight.'

Evaine's eyes did not follow Meena's arm. 'And what else are you making?' she wondered. 'What are you doing that Draguta doesn't know about?'

Meena shook her head. 'Nothing.' Though she had no fear of her cousin, she could feel her legs shaking beneath her dress. 'N-nothing.' Looking up at Evaine, she cleared her thoughts. 'I'm preparing everything as quickly as I can.'

Evaine was enjoying the game. 'And Jaeger? What will you prepare for him?'

Now Meena was confused. 'Prepare? For Jaeger?'

'You want him to live?' Evaine spun around, dropping the tent flap, revealing the real reason she had come. 'In this battle where there is a chance he could die...'

Meena froze.

'You hate him as much as I do,' Evaine murmured, her voice a deep hum. 'And you could finish him without anyone ever knowing. He could die on that battlefield. No one would ever know it was because of you. Draguta will be too busy with the Brekkans. She won't notice how he dies.'

Meena remained frozen, hiding her thoughts behind a stone wall, her face impassive. 'I have to make the next potion. You should go before Draguta gets angry. She wants Jaeger to live. You should go.'

'I will,' Evaine smiled, pulling a torn piece of vellum from her purse. 'I found this spell in a book. A book Morana gave me. She said it would be useful one day. And with your help, maybe it will.' Evaine left the vellum on one of Draguta's tables before turning with a smile, slipping through the tent flap, leaving Meena caught in a world of deception and danger and magic so dark that she was beginning to wonder how she would ever find her way out.

***

Eadmund was fighting Berger in the middle of the arena, both men stripped of their soaking tunics, struggling in the oppressive heat of the afternoon. Wooden staffs in their hands, they paced back and forth in front of each other, sweating and panting, long past ready for a break, but Draguta was watching from a chair on the grassy ridge, so they kept going.

Jaeger was sitting next to Draguta, refreshed after a quick dip in the stream that cut through the back of the secluded forest, holding the book on his knee.

Draguta kept glancing at it, not wanting a clumsy oaf like Jaeger touching it, but she hoped that the power of the Book of Darkness would help him to overcome his error-ridden ways.

'You think he's good enough?' Jaeger wondered, reaching for a plum from the tray Brill was holding. 'Eadmund? He seems slow today.'

Draguta was not interested in what Jaeger thought about anything. 'He appears to be struggling in the heat. I enjoy it myself, but I do worry that it is too hot for you mere mortals to endure. And when you're dressed in all that armour? I can't imagine it is pleasant.'

'No, I'd gladly see the back of the sun. Something cooler would help us.'

'Would it?' Draguta hummed, her eyes on the bowl of potion that sat on the table beside her. 'I shall see what I can do about that. Once I attend to this.' And standing, she handed the bowl to Brill. 'Take it back there.' She pointed to the Tree of Agrayal, almost feeling it twitch its disapproval at the thought of what she had planned. 'Such a perfectly powerful place, though I don't imagine the gods thought it would help the likes of me.' She turned back to Jaeger. 'I shall take that.' And impatiently tapping her toe, she waited while he stood, handing the book to her. 'Do not worry, you will touch it again before we begin. I want you ready, Jaeger. It will do none of us any good if you continue to play the fool. It is time for the Dragos inside you to come alive. You are descended from a powerful god, and it is time that everyone saw it!'

Jaeger felt a charge crackle through his body, as though every part of him was suddenly stronger. He nodded. 'They will. I can feel it. They will.'

Draguta peered into his eyes. 'Good. Then go and practice. Not with Eadmund, though. That is not a fight I wish to see. Yet. Find someone else to pull apart. Kill them if you must. But win the fight. Test yourself. Grow your power, Jaeger. You will need to use it when the Brekkans come. The Iskavallans and the Islanders. The Alekkans too. They will all be here soon, and we must be ready to face them.'

CHAPTER FORTY EIGHT

Edela tried to clear her mind for what lay ahead.

They had prepared everything they would need for the ritual. Entorp had tattooed her and Eydis, and the pain of those new symbols was still in their eyes, though they both felt energised and ready to begin.

'Eadmund needs to be asleep,' Edela insisted. 'We must wait. It is only supper time. We must wait, girls.'

Eydis was impatient. 'What if he doesn't fall asleep? Maybe he's keeping watch, or walking around?'

'We could try and tackle him to the ground,' Edela grinned. They had walked away from the hall, taking the puppies around the square. It was all starting to feel so claustrophobic, for though the fort was large, and the army had left, it felt like a prison with the gates shut all day long; warriors guarding Edela's dreamer circle, warning those who dared come close to step back.

'Could we do that?' Eydis wondered seriously.

'Tackle your brother?' Edela laughed. 'I don't think you remember the size of him. Now, Berard Dragos over there? Yes, I think together we could tackle him. Perhaps with Ontine's help.'

'I think we could,' Ontine agreed with a smile, watching Berard help Hanna with the army of children who appeared to be playing a game of hide and seek. 'But you want to focus on cutting the rope, don't you, not on trying to restrain him?'

Edela nodded. 'That is a daunting enough task for us to

manage, I can assure you.'

'And what if he sees you?' Ontine asked. 'What will he do?'

'If he does, he will likely try to stop us. He will want to protect Draguta. If that happens, I will pull you back, Eydis, and we'll drop out of the trance, don't worry.'

'But he won't hurt me,' Eydis insisted. 'Not Eadmund.'

'I'm sure Jael believes that too,' Edela said sadly. 'But it's no longer true, I'm afraid. Eadmund has no control over himself anymore. No free will at all. If he catches you cutting Draguta's rope, he will come after you. We will both have to be alert. And careful. Whatever we do, we mustn't wake him.'

***

'I thought for certain today was going to be the day!' Thorgils announced, leaning his head back against a tree, watching the sun set in the distance. They had stopped for the night just off the road, bordered on one side by a dark forest that had kept them on their toes all afternoon. It was not Hallow Wood, and there was some comfort in that, but still, none of them felt good about camping near such a hidden place. 'Guess she plans to keep us hanging like an apple on a tree.'

'Mmmm, but eventually, that apple's going to fall,' Karsten sighed, eye closed, seeing Nicolene's face. And opening his eye, he threw back the last of his ale. 'And who knows what it's going to land on. Or who.'

Jael had gone for a walk with Fyn and Axl, checking their men, wanting to speak to Raymon about the next day.

Karsten could just see their shadows in the distance. 'You think she can do it? Jael?'

'What?'

'Kill Eadmund. Kill Draguta. Get us out of this cauldron of shit we've been swimming in. Save us.'

Thorgils pulled out his comb and attacked his beard, picking out a piece of salt fish and popping it in his mouth. 'Jael?' He turned to Karsten, watching the doubt in his gleaming blue eye. 'What do you think?'

Karsten licked his lips, wanting more ale. 'I hope she can, but you'd have to be made of iron to kill someone you love. Nothing but iron.' He saw the pain in Thorgils' eyes and he tried a hasty retreat. 'On purpose, I mean.'

Thorgils nodded sadly, thinking about Torstan. He'd always just been there, ever since he could remember. Like a faithful, slightly forgetful, clumsy dog. A beloved dog.

His friend.

'Jael won't kill Eadmund,' Thorgils insisted. 'Not unless there's no choice. But if anyone can do something that hard, Jael can. I saw what losing that baby meant to her. Saw what she went through. She nearly died.' He shook his head, remembering. 'But she dragged herself out of bed to fight off the dragur, to get us out of Harstad. If anyone can prepare herself for this fight, it's Jael. And she might be trying to save all of us, but I've a feeling she wouldn't mind a bit of revenge for herself.' His eyes wandered to where Jael and Axl were standing almost head to head, arguing beneath a tree, Fyn looking on awkwardly.

Jael grabbed her brother's arm. 'It's not about revenge!'

Axl scowled at her, but he knew she was right.

'It's about going home.'

Fyn felt awkward, wanting to leave them to it. They had been away from Oss for so long now, and he was worried that when they returned, nothing would be the same. He wondered if Bram would come with them.

He hoped he'd live to find out.

'It's about fighting together for what matters most. Our homes. Our families. The ones we love,' Jael insisted. 'This might be revenge for Draguta, but it can't be revenge for us. If we focus on who we're angry at, we'll lose sight of what we're trying to achieve. If one of us breaks, it will damage all of us.' Jael was telling herself as much as her brother. Axl, she knew, was too young to have a firm grip on his emotions, and even she was working hard to stop her mind wandering to what she wanted to do to Draguta.

'Like Skorro,' Fyn said, remembering that brief victory.

'Yes, like Skorro,' Jael agreed. 'That island hadn't been claimed by anyone until we took it from Haaron Dragos. But working together, we captured it. If it hadn't been for Lothar and Osbert, things might have been very different today.'

Axl didn't want to remember what had happened in Valder's Pass while his sister was attacking Skorro, though he realised that he could learn from it, and not make the same stupid decisions Lothar had. And they were his decisions now. Jael would command them, but he would still be there, in the panic of battle, making those life and death decisions for his Brekkans. 'Tomorrow,' he almost whispered. 'We'll be there tomorrow.'

Jael nodded. 'Though, I doubt Draguta is done with us yet.' When those men had raped her mother in Tuura, she'd felt powerless. Trapped. Wanting to rush to her rescue. To pull them off her.

But she hadn't.

She had hidden under the bed with Axl, trying to block out Gisila's terrified screams. And turning to her brother, she shut it all away and smiled. 'We're Furycks, you and me. The Furycks of Brekka. So tomorrow, we'll go and save our people. Tomorrow. And the day after that and every day for the rest of our lives, Axl. Because that's what we were born to do.' She had a sudden fear for him, imagining how their father must have felt the first few times he'd ridden into battle with her, wondering if she would be good enough.

She hadn't heard his voice in days, but she needed to.

Now more than ever.

They both did.

***

'Can't sleep?'

Gant had followed Gisila into the kitchen, worried about her.

She spun around in shock. 'You gave me a fright!'

He smiled. 'Sorry. I wondered where you'd gone. I woke up, and you weren't there.'

'Well, you fell asleep as soon as you lay down,' she sighed. 'I've been lying there for hours. I thought I'd find something to eat. There wasn't much to supper, was there?'

Gant frowned. 'No, there wasn't. It's how it has to be, I'm afraid. We don't know how long this will last. How long till we're free.'

Gisila's tiredness had her feeling morose. 'If we'll ever be free.'

Gant's head was up, hearing a noise outside. 'Wait there.' And moving Gisila behind him, he crept across the kitchen, around the enormous spit in the centre of the long room. He wasn't wearing his swordbelt, so he grabbed the axe hanging behind the door in his left hand, turning the key with his right. And swinging the door open, he brought the axe into both hands, staring out into the dark night, watching two cats bounding away, a tail dangling from one of their mouths. Puffing out a long breath, Gant turned around to a pale-faced Gisila with a smile. 'Just cats.' He shook his head, feeling his heart pound. 'Just cats. Doing Freya's work for her.'

Gisila's face didn't release any tension at all.

'Come on, I'll find you something to eat, then we'll go back to bed. Sleep will help you see things more clearly, I promise.'

***

It was a cold night, and after the extreme heat of the day, Eadmund was relieved not to be sweating. The back of his neck was throbbing with sunburn, though, and he had an odd headache that wouldn't go away.

Lying on his back, he tried to fall asleep, but everything was conspiring against him. He rolled onto his side, which was more comfortable for his neck, but the chanting from the Followers outside his tent was becoming louder, and he closed his eyes, wishing it away.

That and the smoke he could feel tickling his throat.

***

Jael was too tense to sleep. Her body was rigid, her mind like a glowing bar of iron she kept hammering at, trying to see how to keep them all alive. It wasn't possible, she knew, but who would die and who would live was partly in her hands. She had to make the best decisions possible.

Closing her eyes, she thought of Fyr.

Who was Daala.

Neither of them were in her tent.

***

'I think we should begin,' Edela decided, watching Ontine and Eydis struggling to keep their eyes open. 'If you girls are ready?' She suppressed a yawn, not wanting to give Eydis the impression that she felt ready for bed.

Biddy and Entorp were there too. They had insisted, both of them wanting Ontine to be free to help Edela if needed. Entorp had the drum, and he started tapping on it, Biddy anxiously scanning the hall as Ontine threw a bundle of herbs onto the healthy flames of the fire. Though the privacy of Edela's cottage would have been preferable, it was safer for everyone if they remained close by, able to help if needed.

Gripping Eydis' hand, Edela took a deep breath, inhaling the smoke. It was a strong mix – more potent than last time, which had given her a sore throat for days. 'Slowly now,' she spluttered, slowing down her own breathing. 'Take it very slowly, Eydis. And listen to the drum, the gentle beat of the drum. Like a horse running, pounding its hooves onto the earth. The warm, soft earth. Keep breathing, there you go, slowly now. And think of how soft that earth is. How easily you can push your fingers through it. Feel it in your fingers, Eydis, pushing through. All the way through now, finding Eadmund. We are going to find Eadmund...'

***

Fyn was on watch.

He had been walking around Jael's circle, trying to hear anything that might be a problem, his mind wandering back to Andala, hoping that Bram was safe.

Thinking about Eydis. And Ontine.

He smiled, feeling stupid. Surely a girl that pretty wouldn't even look his way? Not like that.

He spun around suddenly, sure he'd seen a flash of something, his eyes on Jael's tent as Fyr flew inside.

Straight through the wall.

***

The smoke was so intense that Biddy's eyes watered as she held onto Ido and Vella who had started to wriggle. She'd quickly realised that she should have shut them in Jael's chamber, but she couldn't move now. She didn't want to pull Eydis and Edela out of their trance, so she squeezed them tightly, trying to stop them moving, frowning as Vella started growling, her furry belly vibrating beneath her hand.

***

Jael hopped out of the tent. One of her boots had come off while she was sleeping, and she was struggling to shove it back on. Fyr flew out of the tent, over her head, wings flapping, disappearing quickly into the night sky.

Fyn ran to her. 'What's happened?'

Jael spun around, eyes up. No moon. Thick clouds. She inhaled, spinning some more. Thick clouds... or fog.

Or smoke.

'Fire.' It almost sounded like a question. There were fires everywhere, most burning low, but then Jael saw Ayla running towards her.

'Fire! Hurry! Get up! Fire!'

***

Vella wriggled, growling. Ido would have wriggled if he could have moved quickly enough.

He started whimpering.

Entorp glared at Biddy who shrugged at him, losing her grip on Vella, who ran out of the circle, towards the hall doors, barking.

Edela dropped forward, out of her trance. Vella's barking was far away, like a heartbeat, merging with the drum. She felt lost. 'What?' she rasped. 'What happened?' And then the barking became louder, and Edela yelped, dragging herself up off the floor.

Gant ran for the doors.

Biddy struggled to her feet, Ido limping after her, both of them following Entorp.

'Wait!' Bram was there first, sword drawn. 'Get behind me. I'll take a peek, see what she's upset about.' His head was spinning from the smoke, and he stumbled, his hand missing the door he was about to push open. The two men on either side of it had already lifted the beam, and placing it on the floor, they drew their own swords. 'Behind me!' Bram croaked as Vella slipped past him, charging out into the night.

'Vella!' Biddy panicked. 'Come back!' She quickly turned and picked up Ido, not wanting to lose him too. 'Vella!'

***

'What is it?' Aleksander's eyes were heavy with sleep.

'Fire's coming!' Ayla kept turning, looking for clues.

Rork was there, sniffing the air. 'We've all got fires burning. You sure?'

Ayla nodded, eyes bright with terror.

'Ayla's right. Fyr warned me too,' Jael said, trying to think. 'We have to leave.'

'Leave? Now?' Ivaar looked incredulous. 'In the dark?'

'We've no choice. Go to your men. Get them ready! We can't sit around and wait for it to come!' Raymon was hurrying towards her, tying up his swordbelt, Rexon and Soren behind him. 'We have to leave!' she yelled at them. 'There's a fire!'

And that fire was Draguta.

She was not done with them yet.

***

Bram's head cleared in the cool night air as he hurried up to the ramparts. 'What's happening?' he called to the men on watch. 'What can you see?'

Vella was racing around barking, and Bram leaned down over the rampart wall, his eyes on Ulf who was hurrying towards them with Berard. 'Ulf! Grab Vella! Stick her in the hall now!' Bram couldn't see anything moving out in the valley. He couldn't hear anything either as he hurried around the ramparts one way, Gant going the other, and when he reached the eastern side, he stumbled to a stop. 'Fire! Fire!' And turning, he ran in the opposite direction, aiming for the signal bell. 'Fire!'

***

'We need water!' Jael yelled, doubting how much they could collect from the stream before they left.

'We need rain!' Ivaar called back. 'Snow! A storm!'

Her heart racing, Jael started to think.

Darroc.

'Ayla! Get back to the wagon! Find Darroc! He may be able to help us!' She spun around, looking for Fyr who had not returned. 'Leave the tents!' she yelled. 'There's no time!'

Karsten wasn't sure how he felt about that. There were no flames that he could see, and he didn't want to be sleeping on the dirt.

'Karsten!' Jael grumbled, sensing his reluctance as she ran for Tig. 'Leave the tents! Get the catapults and the wagons attached! I'm going to ride back and see how close it is!' They'd always prepared to leave in a hurry, and though their tents would be missed, there was not much else that they'd have to leave behind.

She spurred Tig on, down the road before quickly pulling up on the reins, her eyes on the thirsty flames reaching up into the night sky.

The forest was burning.

***

Edela was up on the ramparts, her eyes on the forest, the trees aflame.

Ulf and Bram were down in the fort organising buckets of water. Gant was beside Edela, wanting to know what he should do. It looked like a fast-moving fire. The trees were crackling in the distance, louder than the panic in the fort, the smoke already creeping towards them.

'Can you stop it?' Gant wondered. 'Can the gods?'

Edela's head was still hazy from the herbs smoking her fire. 'I will go and see. But you must come with me. I need to secure the circle again.' They had been in and out through one hole, and Edela wanted to seal them back inside and keep them safe; all of them except those men who would stay on the ramparts to keep watch.

Gant was worried. Locking them inside the fort didn't sound like the best plan with a fire bearing down on them. 'It's not magic, though, is it?'

'It's Draguta,' Edela breathed, certain in that knowledge. 'That fire did not start on its own, but fire in itself is not magical, so I'm not sure what we can do to keep ourselves safe from it.' Edela needed to think quickly. 'Come, let's get back to the hall. We need a plan!' She swallowed, hoping she would be able to come up with one quickly.

***

Astrid was trying not to panic. She kept reminding herself that Jael was out there, working to keep them safe. And Ayla was crouching in front of the fire, seeing what she could do too.

Bruno had been given the drum. He tapped slowly, though his body was shaking and he kept wanting to go faster, but he knew that what Ayla needed more than anything was a steady rhythm, something to keep her in a trance. He held his breath, trying not to cough, though the smoke was intense, from their fire and now, from the one outside too.

Ayla could hear his thoughts, and Astrid's, and it wasn't helping her as she stepped into the darkness, wanting to find her way to Darroc, who was no friend of any Tuuran. She kept turning, looking for some sign as to where she was, but she was confused, not sure where she had ended up. She could hear the loud crackle of a fire tearing through the trees, branches snapping, leaves sizzling.

But she couldn't see anything.

Smoke was swirling around her, and Ayla was almost swimming through it as she pushed on, finally coming out the other side. Out of the forest.

And there she saw a fort.

Andala.

CHAPTER FORTY NINE

'We must stay,' Edela decided as she walked back into the hall. She cleared her throat, wanting to strengthen her voice. 'We will stay inside the fort! Inside our circle! The circle will stop the fire!'

She saw the terror in Gisila's eyes as she gripped Branwyn's hand.

The fire in the middle of Edela's circle was still burning, Eydis and Ontine standing behind it. 'Girls! We will get to work. There is much we can do to disrupt Draguta, I'm sure.' She felt fear, but anger was also coursing through her veins now. And motioning for Entorp and Biddy to hurry back into the circle, she closed it after them. 'Drum, Entorp! Drum!' she demanded, easing herself down onto the ground. 'Close your eyes, girls! Quickly now. More herbs, Biddy! Throw that second pile onto the flames! Hurry!'

***

Ayla stumbled down from the wagon towards Jael who was off Tig, organising everyone to leave.

'What happened?' Jael grabbed her arm, disturbed by the look on her face. Then she saw it herself. 'Andala.'

Ayla nodded. 'I couldn't find Darroc, but I saw Andala. The forest is on fire.' She shuddered, listening to the crashing of burning trees in the distance. 'We can run but they can't!'

Bile rushed into Jael's mouth. 'Darroc!' she yelled. 'Darroc!' Her eyes were up on the smoky clouds. 'Darroc! Your owls will die! Your home will burn! Darroc!' But even if he heard her and helped her, what could they do for Andala?

Then she heard his voice, booming in her ears. 'You have to choose, Jael Furyck! Who will live, who will die. I cannot help you all.'

Jael felt the earth moving beneath her, and turning, she saw Darroc standing by her tent, watching her. 'My owls for your family? You think I would choose that?' He didn't blink, his hooded eyes studying her in the darkness.

'Your owls can fly,' Jael reminded him. 'Save my family, please! Save Andala. You're an Oster god. Save your people. We will run!' And watching him nod slowly, she turned away, doing just that. 'We have to leave! Now!'

Aleksander didn't know who Jael had been yelling at, but he was immediately by her side as Ayla hurried back to the wagon. 'The catapults won't move quickly.'

'No.' Jael grabbed Tig's reins, throwing herself up into the saddle. 'So we'd better get them moving, hadn't we?'

***

The cackling voice told Edela that she was in the wrong place.

She was nowhere.

Smoke was pumping in her lungs, and she was nowhere.

'You will live, Edela. Your granddaughter chose you. You over herself. You will live, but Jael?'

And Edela was falling, tumbling through the air, wind rushing past her ears. They ached, and she felt as though she would vomit. Flashes of light. Bursts of heat and she fell onto her elbows, crashing to the ground.

Her beating heart, her struggling lungs.

Edela spun around. Alone.

Alone in a vast pit, like a long riverbed, stretching towards an ancient tree.

But there were voices. Like a hum.

Chanting.

Edela crept towards the tree, slipping on loose gravel, feeling the sharp rocks jabbing into the soles of her boots. Moonlight glowed brightly, and she could see shadows, hooded figures who circled the tree like standing stones. Dark, mysterious shapes. And one dressed all in white.

And then that voice.

'Your granddaughter is coming for me, Edela Saeveld! And when I have finished with her, I am coming for you!'

***

The flames were moving faster than the catapults. Three had been abandoned already.

'We're going to have to leave them!' Axl cried, panic in his watering eyes. He had raced to the back of their quickly escaping train to see what they needed to do. They could ride, and the men could run, slowly, in their armour. And the wagons could even move at pace if pushed, but the catapults? Axl looked sick. 'We'll have no chance without them!'

'I suspect that's the point!' Jael shouted over the noise of the hungry fire and the yelling men who were trying to pull the catapults away from it. 'She wants us hobbling towards her! She wants us broken!' But Jael was not about to lose those catapults. 'You go! Get up front! Send Karsten and Ivaar to keep an eye on the sea-fire! Get it far away from the flames! Send Thorgils back to me! I need his help! We're bringing these fucking catapults with us!'

The fire was hot.

Jael could feel its heat threatening them in waves that had her dripping in sweat. But after all they'd endured to bring them along, she was not riding away without those catapults.

***

Gant was in the square, inside the circle, calling up to the men on the ramparts, listening to the hungry flames devouring the dead trees. And then he felt the snow; tiny flakes, wet on his face. One, two, and then a furious blizzard descended upon the fort with an angry roar.

Rubbing snow out of his eyes, Gant ran for the hall.

***

'We're going to help them!' Jael was screaming.

And Thorgils was nodding, trying not to focus on the fire raging towards them. 'Hurry!' he yelled at Rork, who released the oxen, slapping their rumps, sending them running. He had power in his arms, and so did the men he'd brought with him. They were going to drag the catapults. Six men on each side.

Ropes were tied to the frames from the times they'd had to pull the catapults over challenging humps or out of deep holes. Those men were used to the weight of it. But now they were going to have to move it running.

'Faster!' Jael cried as more men arrived. 'Pick up the ropes and run! Fast as you can!' She stared at Thorgils who grabbed his own rope, thick-necked Islanders on either side of him.

'Go!' he told her, grunting as the weight of the catapult bit.

'I'm not going anywhere!' Jael yelled back, watching the

flames, her eyes bright. 'Now, pull!'

***

Draguta was getting tired of Darroc.

How was it possible that that ridiculous god could mask himself from her? A bumbling fool like that? A god no one had even heard of before now!

Still, she thought, trying to cool her rage, her goal had been to hurry the Brekkans along, and, as it stood, they would be hurrying all through the night. The fire was still burning, chasing Jael Furyck and eating her catapults, and there was some pleasure to take in that.

There would be no rest for those scorched men.

Not tonight.

***

Thorgils tripped. The flames behind him were bright but in front of him lay nothing but shadows and he was on his knees, the man behind him tumbling straight over him. Theirs was the catapult at the back. Perhaps the heaviest. One of only three untouched by the fire now.

They needed more men.

Jael was on Tig. 'Throw me a rope!' And grabbing it, she looped it around Tig's neck, sliding off him. 'Come on! Come on, boy!' she called, tugging him forward. 'Pull!'

Aleksander was there, worried. 'We're going to have to leave it!' he cried, seeing how close the flames were. One look at Jael's face, though, and he dropped off Sky, grabbing a rope to tie around her reins, tugging her along. 'Come on!'

He was right. Jael was worried that he was right. Any breath of wind and the flames would swallow them whole. But they couldn't lose any more catapults.

They couldn't.

***

Edela opened her eyes, surprised by how bright the flames from her fire were as they danced and popped before her. She stared at them for a moment, trying to force herself out of the trance.

'What happened?' Ontine was the first to ask. 'I didn't see anything.'

Edela's head was spinning. 'I... I was at the vale. Draguta was there with Followers... so many Followers. Chanting. I heard her... Draguta... she said that Jael had saved us.'

'Jael?' Biddy was confused. 'How?'

Edela coughed, bending over. 'Water,' she croaked, eyes watering.

And Biddy was off, searching for the water jug.

Gant came back into the hall, ushering in a cloud of smoke. 'It's snowing. A real blizzard,' he reported with relief, shaking his hair. 'The fire's going out.'

Edela exhaled, sipping the water Biddy had hurried to her, Draguta's warning still booming in her ears. 'Well, it seems that Draguta was right. Jael did something to save us.'

Gant looked troubled. 'But what about Jael and the army? Are they safe?'

'I don't know,' Edela admitted. 'I saw nothing.' She turned to Eydis, who was swaying beside her. 'Did you, Eydis? Did you see Jael?'

Eydis' head was hazy. She had been searching for a way through to Jael or Dara Teros, but she'd been unable to break through the clouds. 'No. Nothing.'

It was troubling, and nobody spoke for a time; the sound of the snow sizzling the flames suddenly the loudest noise in the hall.

'Well, we can't attempt the ritual again, not until tomorrow, so there is only one thing for it,' Edela decided, glancing at the worried faces peering expectantly at her. 'We must try and get some sleep.'

They all blinked at her in surprise.

'Sleep?' Gisila shook her head. 'After that? I think I need some wine!'

***

Having finally rescued their last three catapults from the immediate threat of the flames, Jael gave Tig to Aleksander and hopped into the wagon with Ayla and Astrid. The burning forest could still be heard crackling in the distance, and they knew that they couldn't stop if they wanted to outrun it, but Jael needed to know what had happened in Andala.

'Darroc stopped the fire before it got to the fort. He made it snow,' Ayla said.

Jael looked surprised but relieved, grateful for the water Astrid handed her; her mouth was so dry that it hurt to swallow. 'And they're alright?'

Ayla nodded. 'I think Darroc likes you.'

'Well, if he saved the fort, I like him too.' The wagon hit a rock, and Jael jerked forward, splashing water into Astrid's face. 'Sorry!'

Astrid wiped her eyes. 'Don't be sorry. I'm just relieved that the fire is behind us.' Her heart was still racing with panic, her hands shaking.

'For now,' Jael said, suddenly exhausted, ready to collapse into one of the comfortable-looking beds in the corners of the wagon. 'Though we can't stop. Not now. We have to get to the vale before Draguta conjures up something else. We have to keep going through the night.'

It felt odd to say. Part of Jael didn't want to get to the vale at all.

The idea of seeing Eadmund kept her body tingling with both nerves and excitement and the trepidation of what was to come.

The end, she knew.

The end was coming.

***

After the irritation of Darroc's interference, Draguta couldn't sleep, therefore no one else would sleep either. 'Our enemy is running towards us, so we must prepare! We must be ready and waiting!' Her voice rose, cutting through the heavy darkness like a blade. 'Your weapons! Your armour! Make them shine! We are Hestians! The pride of our kingdom stands here, ready to be victorious! To crush our enemies! To write our names in the great sagas!' She motioned for Jaeger and Eadmund to join her. 'Now is no time for sleep. Not when our enemy is breathing down our necks!' And turning for her tent, she curled a finger in Briggit's direction.

Meena and Brill were already inside, working away under Evaine's watchful eye; Ballack standing guard to ensure that no one disturbed them.

Meena could hear them coming, Draguta's raised voice peeling through the air like a screeching bird. Brill blinked, panicking as she handed Meena a bowl of blood, trying not to retch.

'You will need to work faster than that!' Draguta barked as she swept into the tent. 'Ballack!' And frowning as the big man ducked his shaven head and stepped inside, she rounded on him. 'Find more light! How are my assistants expected to see in this dark pit? Hurry!' She felt a sudden rush of energy, as though the night had been illuminated by thousands of stars. Everything she had worked for and dreamed of... everything was coming together for that one perfect moment when she would defeat her enemies. When she would claim victory over those who had murdered her family. Those who had been disloyal. Those who sought to defeat her.

It was time to crush them all.

***

Dara burst out of a dream, launching herself onto her bare feet. She felt neither hot nor cold, but her body was vibrating. Spinning around in the darkness, she almost lunged at Eloris. 'I must do something now! Now!' Looking down at her hands, she tried to think. 'We have to get through to Edela!'

Eloris was confused. She held out a hand, trying to calm Dara down. 'What is it? What has happened?'

But Dara shook her off, hurrying towards the fire. 'There is no time! Help me, please! I must try to reach Edela!'

***

Ontine had gone with Biddy to make some hot milk and honey in the hope that it would calm them all down enough to fall back to sleep, though Biddy had her doubts. She couldn't stop shaking, and though the blizzard had stopped the fire, it hadn't stopped the great clouds of smoke choking the fort.

She couldn't stop coughing either.

Edela took the opportunity to lead Eydis to a corner of their circle where they were able to talk privately. Her eyes followed Sybill who was talking to Derwa, checking her sprained ankle.

'We will keep things to ourselves from now on, Eydis,' Edela whispered. 'I feel as though we are being watched. Perhaps from within the fort itself. I don't have a good feeling.'

Eydis nodded. Her distrust of Sybill was growing too. Whether that was because of Edela's fears or because she could feel herself getting more worried with every passing moment, she didn't know. But she did know that she'd do anything to keep Eadmund and Jael safe. 'What about Ontine? Do you trust her?'

Edela turned around, her eyes meeting Sybill's. She smiled quickly, looking back to Eydis. 'Ontine has given us no reason not to trust her. She has been helpful. Kind. But I cannot shake the odd feeling I have about her mother, so we will keep things between us. Any discoveries we make, we must hold them close to our chests. Until we know more about Sybill, we will keep them both at a distance.'

'Yes,' Eydis agreed. 'Perhaps you should try to dream about Sybill? Take something of hers?'

'Oh, yes, I will. Thank you!' Edela exclaimed loudly as Ontine approached with a cup of milk. 'That is just what my poor throat needs.'

'Eydis, perhaps you should sit down?' Ontine suggested. 'The cup is quite hot.'

Eydis blushed, embarrassed that they'd just been gossiping about her. 'Thank you,' she muttered, chin on her chest.

'It's been such a terrifying night,' Ontine sighed, helping her to a stool. 'I'm just so glad the fire is out. I can't imagine what it would be like now if Jael hadn't stopped it.'

Edela nodded, thinking about Jael, worry gnawing deep inside her. She could hear Draguta's cackles and threats echoing in her ears, but most of all, she could feel her power. She had felt how immensely powerful Draguta was as she stood there, commanding the vale from her grassy ridge, surrounded by those Followers; each one a dangerous dreamer in their own right.

Edela shivered, worrying that they hadn't been able to reach Eadmund.

Wondering how they were going to help him now.

***

'They're going to be tired,' Aleksander yawned, feeling tired himself, despite the welcome appearance of the sun, his eyes on their straggling columns of warriors who were almost stumbling behind them.

'They are,' Jael agreed as she rode alongside him, thinking about her bed and the tents they'd left behind. 'But it's quite motivating when a horde of bloodthirsty Hestians are running at you. I'm sure they'll wake up in time.'

He grinned. 'I think they will. Especially if there's a dragon or two swooping down over their heads.'

Raymon frowned from Jael's other side. 'Do you think she has more?'

'Dragons?' Jael shrugged. 'Seems like a shame to have just the one. Marcus said that Aros made Thrula for Raemus, but he didn't say if he'd made any others.' She didn't feel good about lying, but she wasn't sure Raymon's nerves could take the jolt of knowing that there were certainly more dragons about.

'I wouldn't mind a dragon,' Raymon said. 'On our side.'

'They wouldn't need us, then, would they?' Aleksander mused. 'We could take a seat. Watch from the sidelines. Karsten and Thorgils could organise the betting. A battle of the dragons!'

Jael's mind was wandering all over the place, and she wasn't really listening. She could sense the beat of her heart quicken, knowing that she was getting closer to Eadmund. And she knew that Draguta wouldn't be thinking about dragons. She'd be preparing Eadmund to kill her.

And Jael didn't know if she was ready to face him.

***

Eadmund was patiently receiving his instructions.

After having set everybody to work, Draguta had stared into her seeing circle for what felt like hours, looking for the gods. Looking for her sister. And now dawn was breaking, and she had drawn herself away from her tent, taking him for a walk, far away from the Followers and their open ears.

Eadmund wondered why Draguta needed them.

With all her power, and the magic of the Book of Darkness, why did Draguta need Briggit and the Followers?

'Eadmund!' Turning to him, Draguta grabbed his sleeve. 'Now is not the time to be falling asleep. After all that I have done for you? All that training? Saving you from Evaine's desperate clutches? Giving you that potion for Morac? Sending Morana to Angard?'

Eadmund looked surprised. 'You sent her there? For me?'

'Well, not for you exactly,' Draguta admitted. 'But if I hadn't...' She laughed. 'That revolting witch is only dead because of me!'

'I...' Eadmund didn't know what to say, but he knew that he didn't want to think about Morana. 'I feel fine.'

Draguta lifted an eyebrow, studying him in the faint light of the morning. The sky was awash with an eye-catching display of warm colours, and soon the sun would come to brighten the vale, though Eadmund appeared to be shivering. 'Are you cold?'

He nodded.

'Is it cold?'

He nodded again.

Draguta felt as though she was on fire. 'Well, the sun is rising and no doubt soon you'll all be complaining about how hot it is, but in the meantime, being cold is irrelevant. You must hear what I need you to do, understand what I require from you, and know that if you fail me, Eadmund, your son will be raised by another man. Another man. Could you imagine such a thing?'

Eadmund couldn't.

'Fail, and there is no coming back, I promise you that. No coming back at all.'

Eadmund watched as Draguta abruptly turned away from

him, stalking towards the broad, lichen-covered trunk of the old tree. The need to please her pulsed in his veins, and lifting his head, he tried to focus on what she had said.

'Eadmund?' Evaine looked frantic as she approached. She felt exhausted but too terrified to think about sleep now. 'They say the Brekkans will be here soon. Your wife too.'

Eadmund frowned at Evaine, wondering what she wanted. She placed a hand on his new leather arm guard, and he flinched. 'I have to prepare for the battle.' He moved his arm, wanting to leave.

'You do, I know, but I... you must stay safe... for Sigmund.'

Eadmund stared at her. 'Sigmund?'

Evaine wanted to throw herself at him, not wanting him anywhere near his wife or all those men who would try to kill him. But she thought of Oss. Oss where she would be Eadmund's queen, with Draguta's help. And she blinked away the tears that were threatening to come like a flood. 'Your son needs you to return to him.' She bit her teeth together, stopping herself from saying any more.

Eadmund nodded, his eyes on the vale entrance, wondering how long it would be before Jael was there. 'I will. You have nothing to worry about, Evaine. I won't be defeated today.'

CHAPTER FIFTY

Ontine had been the only one to fall back to sleep. Edela had sent her to Jael's chamber as she kept nodding off, almost falling off her stool. And when she returned, she told them about her dream.

She had seen Jael and the army approaching the Vale of the Gods.

They had not stopped. They had marched through the night, hurrying to stay ahead of the flames that Draguta had sent to terrorise them too.

Eydis panicked. 'But how can we dream walk to Eadmund now? If they're getting that close, perhaps there'll be no more time? Perhaps they will fight today?'

After a sleepless night, Edela was struggling to think clearly. Eadmund needed to be asleep for them to cut the binding rope. And Eadmund needed that rope cut to help Jael.

To help all of them.

'Can't you try while he's awake?' Biddy wondered, immediately feeling foolish. 'Will he see you?'

'Eydis has to put her hand into his soul,' Edela muttered, trying to come up with another solution. 'So, yes, I think it is preferable if he's asleep.'

'They may not fight today,' Eydis said hopefully. 'Don't armies take their time to prepare for battle?' She turned to Entorp, who was sitting next to her.

'Well, I'm no expert on what armies do,' Entorp smiled wearily, 'but yes, there's usually more to consider than just arriving and heading straight into a battle. Though Gant would know more about that than me.'

'We must stay alert,' Edela insisted. 'Or asleep. One of the two. I can't decide!'

Gisila, who stood outside the circle listening, looked worried. 'Can't you dream of something, Mother? Some way to do it? To see what's possible?' She was so used to Edela having all the answers, but her mother suddenly looked frail and confused. 'Why don't you go and get some sleep? You haven't slept all night.'

'That's a good idea,' Sybill said as she stopped beside Gisila, her eyes moving from Edela to her daughter. 'It helped Ontine, didn't it?'

Edela's lips were tight. 'Yes, I think you may be right. It was a long night.' She didn't blink, watching Sybill's eyes, which, for the first time, did not appear nervous at all.

Gisila was surprised that her mother seemed so compliant. 'Here, come with me, then. I'll tuck you in.' And she put her arm around Edela's shoulder, leading her away to the grey curtain.

***

After riding through the night with barely a break, Jael was hungry. Really hungry.

'You need to keep your strength up,' Thorgils fussed, handing her a rock-hard flatbread that he'd sawed in two and filled with smoked cheese that smelled a bit off. He couldn't stand still. His nerves were working away at his body and his mind, and not in a way that made sense. He was worrying about dragons and bloodthirsty creatures, and powerful dreamers who could attack them with who knew what. His mind was overwhelmed with terrifying images that had nothing to do with warriors and shield walls.

Jael took the flatbread, and with some effort, bit into it. 'I think you're right,' she mumbled, mouth full of food. 'Being tired makes me want to eat.'

'Surprised you have any appetite,' Axl said, feeling nauseous. 'Aren't you nervous?'

Jael laughed. 'About dying?' She shook her head, eyes scanning the mountains in the distance, noticing the clouds thickening now, hiding the sun.

They had finally taken a break alongside a stream. Weary legs. Drooping heads. Sore feet. Thirsty horses. After the long march through the night, they all needed a moment to rest and gather their thoughts. 'Dying doesn't bother me. As long as I've ended Draguta and destroyed her book, I'll gladly die. But I'm not going anywhere till that bitch is ash.'

'And when she is?' Karsten wondered, swigging from the water bag he'd just filled up. 'When you've killed her and burned her book? Will that be that? What about all those Followers you saw with her? All the creatures she can conjure up to attack us?'

Jael thought back to her time in Tuura. To Gerod Gott and his circle of chanting dreamers, reminded of how they had controlled the temple guards, not letting them die. 'The Followers will be trouble, but I'll have my own dreamer working on that. You need to focus on the Hestians. On Jaeger. He'll be commanding them, and an army usually loses its way when its leader falls. Although, I can't imagine anyone will care if Jaeger dies.'

Karsten couldn't disagree with that.

'You shouldn't be at the front, Jael,' Aleksander insisted, not liking her plan. 'I don't want you out there.'

Everyone turned to Jael who looked irritated. 'Well, tough luck for you. I need to be out in front. I'll have a shield. Toothpick. Don't worry.' She suddenly did worry, remembering the shield that Eadmund didn't have; the one supposed to protect them from Draguta. Her own shield was new, made of linden wood, iron-rimmed, with a gleaming domed boss. It would hold off an attack from a sword, an axe, a spear, but it would not withstand magic.

But Eadmund's shield...

Where was Eadmund's shield?

Everyone else looked worried too, Jael could see, especially Fyn. She patted his shoulder, trying to focus him. 'You'll be with Thorgils,' she smiled. 'He'll keep you safe.'

'But who will keep you safe?' Thorgils wondered, eyebrows knitting together, stomach in knots. 'Draguta will have everyone on you. Like you say, an army is vulnerable when its leader falls, and you're ours.'

'I'm one of ours, and I'm not planning on falling. But look,' and she swept her arm around the anxious, sooty faces before her. At Ivaar and Rexon. Rork and Karsten. Axl and Thorgils. 'We've enough leaders here to get us through what we need to do. More than enough. We need to trust each other now.' She stared into each pair of eyes. 'Trust.'

And, eventually, a few heads nodded, and she coughed. 'Now, is there anything to drink? I think that flatbread's choking me!'

***

Dara and Eloris had travelled at night. Only at night. For days they had crept towards Andala in snatches of moonlight, slipping through the trees, sheltering in protected caves, hiding in warded forests, but now they had run out of time.

Dara had tried to get through to Edela. And then Eydis.

Jael and Aleksander too.

When she had failed, Eloris had tried, though she could not reach anyone either.

Something was wrong, they could feel it.

Dara wondered if they were all using symbols to keep Draguta away. Hiding, trying to stay safe. She didn't know. She hoped it was that, not something more sinister.

This time they had not taken shelter before dawn started filtering through the forest canopy. They had kept going, hoping the symbols they were using would keep them hidden long enough to get to Andala.

It was still raining, and Dara was wet through, though she couldn't feel it. Her boots had holes in them, letting in tiny bits of dirt, but she didn't care. She kept going, knowing that after waiting for centuries for this moment, she was in danger of running out of time.

And if she did?

Dara jumped as Eloris gripped her arm. 'We have to leave the forest now. We must cross the meadow.'

'I know.'

They could both see how wide and exposed that meadow was as they peered through the last trees of the forest.

'Draguta may see us,' Eloris panicked. 'If our symbols aren't working, she might come for us.'

'And if she does, you must leave. Please, Eloris, promise me. This is too important. If she comes for me, you must keep going to the fort. Tell them what I've seen.'

Eloris nodded. 'I will, I promise. But please, let us hurry!'

***

The boxes that had been retrieved from the catacombs were arrayed across the grassy ridge. Draguta had kept Ballack working all morning, lifting everything into place. He had built a great fire, and the heat from its sparking flames had him sweating as he rushed around it, bringing Draguta everything she needed.

Her certainty had returned with the sunshine, and she looked Briggit over with a smile, noting that, despite wearing her hideous black robe, her face was glowing, her dark hair smooth and gleaming. 'How lovely you look this morning,' she purred approvingly. 'Almost like a queen. Not like that ragged doll over there.' And she inclined her head to where a red-faced Meena was lugging a heavy basket towards her.

Briggit laughed. 'I've always found that the most useful people are the ugliest. Still, Jaeger doesn't appear to notice. He has quite... peculiar tastes.'

Draguta wasn't pleased to have that pointed out. 'The book is more powerful than any mortal can handle. He is not a dreamer. A dreamer can absorb its power and maintain control. Jaeger... struggles. It is hardly his fault. Raemus designed the book that way.'

Briggit flinched, incensed to hear Draguta use Raemus' name so casually. The sound of it on her tongue made her toes curl. Swallowing, she quickly tried to calm herself.

Draguta glanced at her, surprised by her silence, though none of Briggit's thoughts revealed themselves. Her body was tense as she turned away, watching Eadmund approach. 'Well, how handsome you look! I imagine you are pleased?' She ran her eye over his gleaming new suit of armour.

It was not what the King of Oss would have worn, and Eadmund twitched uncomfortably as he stopped before her. He was used to his heavy mail shirt, his well-worn leather arm guards, his comfortable old tunic. But the shining plated armour Draguta had given him made him feel like someone else.

It made him feel like a killer.

Draguta ran her eyes over Eadmund, noting how snugly the plates of metal hugged his impressive frame. He was a powerful-looking man now. A king finally worthy of his title. 'This is a good start!' she declared. 'And where is Jaeger? I want him down in the arena with his men. We shall not be delayed by his tardiness!'

'I'm here,' Jaeger grumbled, approaching from behind. He'd been pissing in the trees, wanting a moment to think, to gather his thoughts. He couldn't understand the rush. His scouts had been back and forth all morning.

There was no sign of anyone approaching.

Draguta's face cleared. Jaeger looked just as impressive as Eadmund, and his surly scowl only made him appear more threatening, as did his new helmet which covered most of his face.

'Well, this is good to see. My two kings. So terrifying! I would not want to face either one of you. I'm sure Briggit agrees?'

Briggit looked on blankly.

'Now, Eadmund, you can go. Find your men. Jaeger, come to my tent. I think we need a final word, don't you?' Her eyes followed the disappearing figure of Eadmund Skalleson before she turned away, heading for her tent.

Briggit watched Eadmund go. He was so lost in Draguta's spell that he could no longer compel an independent thought, and Jaeger was so consumed by the Book of Darkness that he would do anything for Draguta just to touch it again.

Prisoners, both of them.

She smiled, smoothing down her dark robe, feeling her stomach flutter.

***

Edela had no intention of sleeping when she lay down on Jael's bed. She had just wanted a moment to think, free of the noise in the hall.

Being a dreamer often felt as though everyone was living inside her head. There was no choice but to listen to the demanding fears and worries, hopes and wishes of those around her; all of them tumbling around her mind, waiting for her to pick and choose what was important. What stood out as something she needed to explore further.

The clouds.

Edela smiled, yawning. She had to fight her way through those clouds, through everything that was stopping her finding answers; ignoring what she had read, imagined, and dreamed about.

All the faces. The secrets and lies.

Were they lies?

She didn't know. She thought of Marcus, Entorp, Alaric,

Branwyn. All of them Tuuran. Yet none of them had known Sybill or Ontine in Tuura. They had seen them, recognised them, yet they didn't know them. Not even Branwyn – who was the sort of woman to stick her nose in everywhere – could tell her much about Sybill.

Edela rolled onto her side, coming face to face with Vella who tried to lick her nose. 'What do you think, then?' she wondered. 'You know more than anyone, perhaps? Much more than me...' And she patted that soft fluffy head, wishing she could read her thoughts.

Vella had growled at Evaine, she remembered. Both dogs had.

But she had never seen them have a problem with either Sybill or Ontine.

Edela sighed, frustrated now, doubting her sanity again.

And what were they going to do about Eadmund?

It was all too confusing, she realised.

She would have to try and find a dream...

***

Meena hurried after Eadmund, her back dripping with sweat. The clouds had come in, swirling moodily above their heads, making the air more humid as she ran from one end of the ridge to the other, stirring cauldrons over hot fires, grinding and chopping and mixing until her hands were blistered. She felt ready for a dip in Fool's Cove.

That was the last thing she needed to think about, she realised, reaching out to touch Eadmund. He flinched, spinning around in surprise and Meena was horrified to see how dead his eyes looked.

'What is it?' He stared at her bruised face. 'Is something wrong?'

Meena shook her head, fighting the urge to leave. 'Draguta asked me to give you this.' She reluctantly handed him the goblet.

'She said it will help you.'

Eadmund sniffed the liquid.

It wasn't wine.

'Help me?'

Meena shrugged. 'Draguta wants you to drink it.'

Eadmund shuddered, throwing the dark-red liquid down his throat, quickly gagging, blinking, wishing he had something to take away the horrific taste of whatever it was.

He handed back the goblet.

Meena took it, but she didn't leave. 'Thank you,' she said quietly. 'For saving me from Jaeger. Amma too. I'm grateful.'

Eadmund frowned, seeing how swollen her right eye still was. 'I didn't save you from anything. I wish I had. Jaeger...' He knew what Draguta thought of Jaeger. He couldn't say any more.

'He will kill you!' Meena blurted out. 'Draguta told him to. Whatever happens, she wants him to kill you.' And blinking three times, she spun around, almost tripping over her flapping boots as she scampered away.

Eadmund stared after her, the iron tang of the potion coating his tongue, Meena's words echoing in his head.

It made no sense. No sense at all.

Draguta needed him. She wanted him to kill Jael.

She needed him.

Didn't she?

***

They were edging ever closer to the vale, and Jael felt a growing sense of urgency to know what Draguta's plans were. Or Daala's. Anyone's. She had her own, but as for everyone else...

She wondered what Edela was doing. Whether her grandmother had freed Eadmund yet?

Her mind kept wandering to Toothpick too, her hand resting

on his cool moonstone pommel. Toothpick felt like part of her now – the most powerful part – yet she feared that he wasn't. She felt Tig beneath her, and she knew that she would have to say goodbye to him before they entered the vale.

If they made it that far.

And then Fyr returned.

Fyr was Daala's animal form, and when Fyr was on her shoulder, Jael felt a sense of certainty that kept her moving forward, believing that for the next moment, they weren't in danger. Though, Jael realised, shaking her head, that would not be true for much longer.

She glanced back at the wagon, bouncing along too quickly for its own good just behind her. She hoped that Ayla was feeling focused.

They were all going to need her.

***

Astrid hit her head on the roof of the wagon, yelping.

Ayla didn't notice. She was too busy trying to calm her mind.

They were walking into the dangerous arms of a woman so powerful that she could bind the gods themselves. And Ayla knew that, as a dreamer, her mind was her weapon. Her sight. Her senses. The warriors walked and rode in their armour, weapons banging against backs and thighs, hanging from belts. Weapons they could draw at the first sign of trouble.

And Ayla needed to be just as prepared.

She had been in and out of a trance for hours, ignoring Astrid, inhaling the herbs the healer regularly threw onto the flames. She came and went, looking for clues, for signs as to what Draguta would do. When she would come.

How?

But she also kept thinking about Andala. Whenever she drifted into a trance, Ayla found herself inside the fort, looking for Eydis, the pounding urgency pulsing through her body.

The need to find Eydis.

***

'Edela doesn't seem like herself today,' Ontine said, pouring water into two cups. 'Though, perhaps I don't know her well enough to say such a thing?' She pushed a cup towards Eydis' hand.

'No, but I do, and she doesn't,' Eydis said. 'I'm not sure any of us are. What is about to happen is...'

Ontine smiled, squeezing her hand. 'I only hope I can do something to help. I feel useless. You and Edela have to do everything. I'm not much help at all.'

Eydis lifted the cup to her lips. 'I used to think that. To feel as though I wasn't a real dreamer because I had no training.'

'What changed?' Ontine wondered. 'You don't appear to think that anymore.'

They were sitting on stools on opposite sides of a small table in the middle of the circle.

Eydis shrugged. 'There was no time. When we were in danger, under attack from The Following in Tuura, there was no time for worrying about how I felt anymore. I just stopped thinking.'

'That sounds like good advice.' Looking up, Ontine noticed her mother standing by the hall doors, motioning her over. 'Will you be alright by yourself for a while? My mother wants to see me. I'm sure Edela will be back soon, and Biddy is coming and going from the kitchen. Gisila too.'

Eydis nodded, taking another drink.

'Good. I won't be long.' Ontine hurried up from her stool, heading for the doors.

Biddy watched her go, eyes fixed on both women as they disappeared outside.

***

The craggy vale arena was carved through long, rugged, red-rock mountains; shelves stepped into each side forming platforms from where the battle could be witnessed.

Or joined.

Draguta smiled, watching Eadmund talking to Berger. She could feel his aggression bubbling like a cauldron of hot water, and it pleased her. There was no hesitation in him now. No doubt. Inhaling sharply, she turned to Briggit. 'You are troubled?'

Briggit swallowed. 'I am... not.'

'No?' Draguta eyed her closely. 'You cannot stand still. Cannot sit. And I am certain you have bitten every one of your fingernails by now.'

Briggit turned to Draguta with a smile. 'I am impatient. Eager to begin. They are getting closer.'

'They are.' Draguta looked down into her seeing circle, watching the long worm of warriors creeping towards them. 'And when they arrive?' She smiled, sweeping her hands across the arena. 'They'll wish that they had never come!'

PART SIX

Sacrifice

CHAPTER FIFTY ONE

Their journey had been uncomfortable, terrifying, arduous, and yet, for Dragmall, it was just the beginning.

Else gripped his hands. 'I don't want you to go.'

The shield was on his back, warded against any dreamer who would seek it. And Draguta. He hoped the symbols would keep it hidden from her long enough to get it to safety.

'I must, Else. And you must stay here. Stay safe. I will return when it's done.' He wasn't sure that that was true, though he tried to smile and Else seemed encouraged by that.

Dragmall was leaving her in a cave. He had taken his knife and scraped symbols around its stone mouth, around its dirt entrance. Symbols he hoped would keep her safe.

She nodded, looking up at him, eyes watering, and suddenly Dragmall felt like a fraud. 'I... I may not make it back,' he admitted, feeling the weight of the shield as it tried to pull him backwards. He saw the panic in her eyes now, bright white against the darkness of the cave. 'It will be dangerous. Very dangerous. I want you to stay safe here. If I do not return in a few days, you must move north. Escape from this place. Start again.'

Tears rolled down Else's cheeks. 'But...'

Dragmall pulled her to him. 'You are strong, Else Edelborg. Always have been. Strong and brave. You will find a way, I know.'

'Do you see something?' Else mumbled into his chest, smelling the smoke from their fire in his long beard. 'Have you seen what will happen?'

Dragmall stepped back. 'No,' he admitted, looking down at her, wishing it wasn't the truth. 'No, I haven't. But I will try my best to get this shield to Eadmund. I will do everything I can to help. And then... well, that is in the hands of the gods. Or perhaps, Jael Furyck.'

***

The morning dragged on, and everyone was so quiet that they all had a chance to contemplate what was about to happen.

Which was a bad thing.

No one needed more time to think of what could go wrong, though Jael was trying very hard to anticipate what she needed to do to keep Draguta guessing.

Was that even possible anymore?

'Getting closer.' She turned to Aleksander, who looked as though he wasn't breathing. His shoulders were raised, his mouth hidden beneath his dark beard. 'We need to get ready. Draguta won't necessarily wait for us to arrive.'

Aleksander nodded. 'I'll head down the line.' And with one quick look at Jael, he turned Sky away, dust and dirt flicking everywhere.

Jael barely noticed as she turned back around, trying to listen to Fyr who rode on her shoulder, balancing herself with splayed claws, hoping to get some warning. She had her sword, Ayla, the sea-fire and three catapults. Weapons too. And in Andala, an old lady and two girls with a book who would hopefully be more useful than anything.

Though she would still like to hear from the raven, who was the Mother of the Tuuran Gods, about what she thought was coming...

***

Edela woke from her nap in a fluster.

Arms flailing, she rushed around the hall ordering everyone about in a rasping voice. Her sense of urgency had heightened so much that she was vibrating all over. Eventually, Gant took her towards a stool inside her circle, while Biddy made her a cup of chamomile tea and Entorp arrived to try and calm her down with a soothing lavender salve.

'I think that sounds impossible,' he said, glancing at Biddy who had taken a stool beside him. 'To perform the ritual while Eadmund is awake? I don't see how it can be done, Edela.'

'But it has to be!' Edela lurched up from her stool, spilling her tea, eyes on Derwa who stood outside the circle, listening. Derwa had gifts, and though she was not a trained dreamer, she knew how to enter the spirit realm. How to traverse those hidden places.

Edela stared imploringly at her.

'It could be done,' Derwa decided calmly, fingering her long braid. 'I don't believe that Eadmund must be in a dream state, though it would be helpful if he wasn't walking around, or in the midst of a battle!' She lifted a snowy eyebrow at Edela who sat down again, wobbling impatiently on her stool.

'He would have to be held down, restrained in some way,' Entorp said, his frown deep. 'It seems unlikely that you'd be able to keep him still for what Eydis needs to do. That will take some time.'

'Unless Jael injures him,' Edela wondered out loud. 'If he can't move, can't walk, then we could try.'

'But then what use would he be?' Biddy asked, watching the three faces fall. 'If he's injured he won't be able to help Jael, will he?'

'Not to mention the shield,' Entorp sighed. 'There is no shield.'

It was as though a storm was raging overhead, bringing nothing but dark clouds and doom crashing down upon them.

No one could see a way through.

'I will try,' Edela insisted, at last, the fire before her bright and comforting. She thought of her cottage and her granddaughter and the night she'd told Jael what she had seen about her and Eadmund.

Nothing had changed in her heart, or in her dreams.

Whenever she saw them, it was as though they were bathed in golden light. Together. Meant to be. And that light would defeat the darkness.

That is what the gods had intended.

So she would simply have to go and talk to Jael.

***

The clarity of sleeping without nightmares had made Meena feel stronger, and that strength had encouraged her to abandon her sleeping tea and return to her dreams. They had welcomed her back, coming with great frequency whether she was awake or asleep. She kept seeing visions of Berard in Andala; of Jael Furyck on her horse, dressed for battle; of Amma back in Hest.

It was distracting, and she blinked, trying to concentrate on the vast quantities of potion she was finishing for the Followers.

Brill walked towards her, lugging another bowl of blood. 'This is all. I...' she panted. 'This is all. I can't kill another horse. Please.' She looked ready to cry.

Meena shuddered, nodding in agreement. There had been enough sacrificing since they'd arrived at the vale. The cool morning air was thick with smoke and tainted with the stink of blood. 'It will be enough.' And motioning for Brill to leave the bowl on the ground, she turned back to her basket, thoughts of Else on her mind. And then a flash, and she was staring into a dark cave where Else stood, sobbing as Dragmall disappeared in the distance.

Meena screamed suddenly as Brill touched her arm. 'What? What is it?'

Brill shivered in surprise, peering down at her. 'Nothing. I... you weren't answering me. Are you alright?'

'Oh. Yes. Yes.' Meena couldn't breathe. She glanced around, back into the forest, out towards the edge of the ridge where Draguta was talking to Briggit and Jaeger; around to the right where the mountains bordered the vale, jagged and sloping. Her skin prickled, and she knew for certain that Else and Dragmall were nearby.

But where?

'Girl!' And then Meena was spinning and stumbling, and hurrying towards Draguta.

***

Thorgils and Fyn were riding beside Jael, talking to each other, both trying to take their minds off the fact that they were fast running out of road. They could see the mountains in the distance growing more imposing by the moment.

Axl had left to ride with Aleksander.

Jael was daydreaming. Or, at least, she was trying to, but her mind wouldn't wander anywhere.

She wanted to find Eadmund. To see if she could get through to him somehow.

'Jael.'

Jael spun around. Fyr was flying ahead of her. Ayla was in the wagon.

'Grandmother?' she whispered, though Fyn and Thorgils were too busy talking to each other to hear her. 'Grandmother?'

'I need your help,' Edela breathed. 'Eydis and I will try to cut Eadmund's binding rope again so we can break Draguta's hold on him. You must get him to the ground, Jael. As soon as you can. Hold him there for us. We will be waiting.'

Jael found herself nodding, though she didn't know if Edela

could see her. 'I will, I will. We're nearly there.'

'Jael, I love you.' Edela's voice was faint, disappearing.

Jael shivered. 'I love you too.'

'You do?' Thorgils was staring at her. 'Well, this is unexpected, Jael, though I'd long suspected your feelings for me ran deeper than you let on.'

Jael rubbed her eyes. 'Fuck off.'

Fyn laughed, frowning suddenly as Fyr came diving back towards them.

Jael was distracted, expecting the raven to land on her shoulder, but Fyr veered away, aiming for a dense wood to Thorgils' right.

'What's she seen, do you think?' Thorgils wondered.

Jael's shoulders tightened, her senses alert. 'Hopefully, she'll come back and tell us.'

'Maybe she's gone to find the gods?' Fyn suggested. 'To help.'

'A nice thought, Cousin,' Thorgils sighed. 'But the gods have no love for each other, nor of playing nicely. Not at all.'

Jael glanced at Thorgils. 'If the gods are smart, they'll all stay away. It won't help us if Draguta imprisons any more of them. She can already make it snow and as for that fog...' Jael shook her head. 'We don't want her near any of the gods.'

Thorgils frowned at the reminder of the cursed fog. 'No, you're right there.' His eyes were on his horse's brown ears which had not stopped swivelling in hours. She could sense things, he knew; hear things they couldn't. His attention wandered to the swirling grey clouds sinking in the midday sky, wondering whether they would get enough warning about what was coming.

Hoping a dreamer would see something before it was too late.

***

Meena had been rushing from one end of the ridge to the other in such a blur that she didn't even notice Jaeger until his arm slipped around her waist. She jumped, biting her tongue.

'Stop.' His voice was low as he pulled her into his tent.

Meena stumbled after him, trying to wriggle away from his arm, trying not to spill the cup of potion in her hands.

'The Brekkans will be here soon,' Jaeger said, turning her to him. He had taken off his helmet, wanting to see her. Wanting her to see him.

But Meena's eyes were on the tent flap which had just dropped closed after them.

She didn't respond.

Jaeger lifted her chin. 'Don't worry, I'll keep you safe. And so will Draguta. They won't get anywhere near you.'

Meena squirmed, staring into his eyes, a mix of emotions bubbling in her chest. Mainly she thought about Jael Furyck and whether she could still find a way to take the ring. She needed to do something to help her and Berard.

'I will be victorious, Meena. Draguta will be victorious. And then we'll go home, all of us, back to Hest. Together.'

Meena nodded, feelings of guilt and anger and fear tumbling around her mind as he pushed his hands through her nest of red hair, finding the sides of her face and kissing her roughly.

Pulling back, Jaeger peered at her, trying to see what she was thinking. 'You want that, don't you?'

Meena tried to smile. 'Yes. Yes, I do.' She looked down at the cup. 'You should drink this. Draguta wanted you to have it.' The lie tingled her tongue, and she couldn't help twisting her lips in discomfort. 'She said it will help you.'

Jaeger took the cup, gulping down the liquid. He grimaced, wiping his short blonde beard as he handed it back to her. 'I should go. I need to be waiting down in the arena.'

Meena was eager for him to leave, hoping he wouldn't pass Draguta on his way. Her heart started galloping, her legs trembling. 'Good luck.'

Kissing her one more time, Jaeger smiled confidently, his insides churning with anticipation as he headed out of the tent, ready to begin.

Meena watched him go, holding her breath for a moment before hurrying to the nearest bed, throwing the empty cup underneath it. She scrubbed her mouth, wanting to remove the taste of Jaeger and any remnants of potion from her lips. Taking a deep breath, and straightening her shoulders, Meena dug into her purse and pulled out the tiny scrap of vellum Evaine had given her, going over the chant again, seeing the symbol she had to draw.

Checking that she had her knife.

***

Edela took a deep breath, making sure she had everything for the ritual, trying to still her shaking limbs, hoping she would be able to keep Eydis safe.

She glanced at Ontine, who smiled back.

Edela frowned.

She could see nothing lurking behind those pretty eyes, which appeared nervous, though that was to be expected. The sense of anticipation in the hall had them all mumbling and stumbling around. 'Are you sure you feel ready, Eydis?' she wondered. 'When it begins, there will be no time. No time for nerves. We will need to act with urgency.' Edela didn't feel ready herself. Slipping into a trance to find Jael had exhausted her, which wasn't an auspicious beginning to what would be the most challenging ritual she had ever attempted.

Eydis looked excited as she nodded, though, and Edela smiled. 'Well, I'm glad to hear it. Now, Ontine, you will be left behind when Eydis and I enter the trance. You must keep alert to anything that threatens us here, do you understand?'

'Yes, I will.'

Edela had kept Derwa in the circle. Biddy would keep the fire going, Entorp would be drumming, and Derwa would be the extra pair of eyes she needed.

Just in case.

'Mother!' Gisila called, trying to get her attention. 'Will you have something to eat?'

'Now?' Edela was puzzled. 'Why now?'

'We're organising food for those who are hungry,' Branwyn said.

Edela turned away before they could bother her further.

Gisila rolled her eyes. 'You need sustenance,' she tried. There was no reply, so she turned to her sister. 'Well, no surprise there. Dreamers!'

Branwyn smiled, following Gisila to where Hanna, Bayla, and Isaura were organising the children into pairs in an attempt to control the noisy chaos. 'Alright, line up, line up, and we'll go outside and see what we can find to eat! We need to leave the dreamers in peace now.' She glanced at the circle, trying not to feel anxious about what was coming. Her mother was working hard to keep them all safe, she knew. And she hoped more than anything that she could.

She didn't want to lose anyone else.

***

There was an opening in the forest to Jael's right, and she could see Fyr sitting on the drooping branch of an ash tree, waiting for her.

She was definitely waiting for her.

'Keep going!' Jael called to Aleksander, heading for the trees. 'I just need a piss!'

Aleksander blinked after her. 'We should wait!'

'Eyes open!' she shouted, disappearing into the forest after Fyr.

Aleksander watched her go, hesitating.

'Where's she going?' Karsten wondered from behind him. 'Who's in there?'

'Well, she's a lady, so she's not going to just piss over the side of her horse like you,' Thorgils said from his right.

'When have I ever done that?' Karsten snorted. 'You think I'd piss off the side of my horse? Is that what they do on Oss?'

Aleksander left them to it, his eyes on the trees, wishing he'd gone with Jael.

***

It was not the dragon throne, but the chair upon which Draguta perched, running her eyes over the flurry of activity in the arena, was grand. High backed, carved in an ebony so dark that it matched her hair; angry dragons roaring above her broad shoulders, all tongues and teeth; polished until it glistened, even in the increasingly dull light of the afternoon; lined with white furs, which she rubbed her back against, feeling a sense of peace calm her expectant mind.

Briggit, who stood beside her, continuing to fidget, appeared anything but. 'Are you going to stay seated?' she wondered impatiently, jiggling from one foot to the other. 'We should form the circle now. Have the dreamers ready.'

Draguta reached out a hand, patting Briggit's twitching arm. 'Do not fret, Briggit dear. The hard work is already done. I have cast my circle, so we only need to walk into position. I'm sure those dreamers of mine can manage that.'

But Briggit was fretting.

Draguta smiled, enjoying her distress. 'They have an impressive army, despite the challenges of their journey, but so do we. You can see how intimidating our Hestians look. How ready for war.' And standing, she strode to the edge of the grass, her attention on the rows of finely turned out warriors who were being moved into position by Eadmund on one side of the grassy ridge, and Jaeger on the other, polished helmets glinting, spear-tips sharp and threatening.

Waiting.

'Perhaps you'd like some mead?' And Draguta walked back to her chair with a smile, picking up a silver goblet from the small table that sat beside it. 'You look as though you need it.' And she stalked away to where Meena and Brill were frantically finishing their preparations. 'Are we ready, ladies?' Draguta dipped her finger into one of the bowls, lifting it to her nose. 'Smells revolting. Ballack!' And turning around, she pointed her bloody finger in her trusty slave's direction. 'It is time to move everything into place. Into the circle. You will help the girls with the bowls. Then the boxes. And where is Evaine?' She spun around, frowning. 'Always missing when there is work to be done!'

Briggit drank the mead, enjoying the sweet honey coating her tongue. It made her relax, and glancing around, she realised that everything was falling into place. She smiled, her golden eyes peeking over the rim of the silver goblet, gazing to where the Followers sat, curled into a large circle around the Tree of Agrayal.

Ready to begin.

CHAPTER FIFTY TWO

'Where are we?' Jael wondered. Fyr croaked at her, but she could not read the raven's thoughts. She drew her sword suddenly, spinning around as a man emerged from the trees to her left.

A tall old man with a long white beard.

'I know you!' Jael called out, though she didn't know how. 'Who are you?'

Dragmall's bright-red face broke into a weary grin as he approached, his aching back ready to break in two. And creaking forward, he eased himself down to the ground, onto his knees, revealing the shining round shield on his back.

Jael's mouth fell open. She gripped Toothpick tightly, though she didn't feel fear as much as a surge of relief.

'I married your cousin to Jaeger Dragos,' Dragmall panted, unstrapping the shield from his back with a groan. 'You were there, I remember, for that miserable occasion. Poor girl,' he mumbled, thinking of Amma Furyck. 'I am Dragmall Birger. A volka and a dreamer. Protector of Esk's shield, like my father before me and his before him.' And gathering himself together, he stood, presenting the shield to Jael, who quickly sheathed her sword. 'It was not meant for you, of course, though it appears that there is little choice about that now.'

Jael took the gleaming shield in both hands, amazed by how light it felt. Well, not that light, she supposed, glancing at the pain contorting Dragmall's red face, but a shield that large, made with that much iron should have felt heavier in her hands. 'No, but I still hope to get it to Eadmund.'

Dragmall smiled, encouraged by the fire in her eyes. 'Good. He should have it. The prophecy said as much, didn't it?'

'From what I hear, it did.' Jael glanced back over her shoulder. 'I can't stay.'

'No, you can't.' Dragmall stepped towards her. 'Here, let me help you with it. It is warded against dreamers. Hopefully, against Draguta too, though she is like no dreamer I've ever met. Not anymore.'

Jael could hear the creaking wagons heading past the trees, and she knew that she needed to hurry back. 'Go and hide,' she warned. 'Stay safe.'

'Safe?' Dragmall chuckled. 'An old man like me? I have done safe. Now I think it's time to do something more. I will come with you, Jael Furyck. I will help.' And pointing Jael towards the trees she had slipped through to find him, he smiled. 'Perhaps you can even find me a horse!'

***

A man was standing on one of the stone viewing platforms that bordered the vale arena.

Not a man.

A god.

'Interesting,' Draguta mused, surveying the unexpected arrival from the edge of the ridge. 'Wouldn't you agree, Meena Gallas?'

Meena's mouth had flapped open. She couldn't speak. She had never seen a god in her life, though she knew without question that the giant standing watching them was Esk, Tuuran God of War. Varna had told her stories of the gods she had despised almost as much as Draguta did. The gods who had been Raemus' enemies. Those who had worked with Daala to end him.

Meena squinted, her eyes on the glinting bronze spear Esk

held in his right hand. Glowing symbols wrapped around its thick haft; the barbed iron tip itself as long as his arm.

'An audience, do you think? Or perhaps our first victim?' Draguta wondered, turning back to Briggit.

Briggit's eyes were sharp, her thoughts focused. 'He cannot stop you,' she hissed, holding Draguta's gaze. 'Your magic comes from Raemus' book. And his magic was more powerful than any god! More powerful than that pathetic God of War!'

There was an odd look in Briggit's eyes, but it was gone in a flutter of dark eyelashes leaving Draguta to wonder if she had imagined it. 'No, but he may try. Rouse my dreamers and let us see what we can do about our guest. We don't want him ruining our entertainment, do we?' She spun towards Meena and Evaine, who had finally dragged herself away from peering at Eadmund. 'You will assist me. Both of you. Stand behind me, right there, ready to help.' And Draguta pointed to just past the small table where the Book of Darkness sat, open and waiting, before spinning back around to her trusty servant. 'Brill, you will go with Briggit, to the other side of the circle.' She leaned down, her nose almost touching Brill's hair. 'Watch her closely. Do as she requires, unless...' And straightening up, Draguta felt her body tense, as though someone had their fingers inside her, pulling her backwards, forcing her around.

She glanced towards the arena as Esk entered it, carrying his giant spear. 'I will have the first potion. The first box too.'

Swallowing the bile flooding her mouth, Meena headed for the row of boxes that Ballack had laid out inside the circle. The first box was small and long, made of dark wood, and oddly heavy, Meena thought as she headed back to Draguta who had quickly drained her goblet.

'Wonderful!' she exclaimed with a smile, eyeing Ballack over Meena's shoulder. 'You will go down into the arena! Have Eadmund ready and alert! Jaeger too!' And Draguta took her position at the head of the circle, near the edge of the grass.

Esk might think that he could disrupt her fun.

But as he would quickly discover, all the fun was going to be hers.

***

After hiking through the forest with the shield to find Jael Furyck, Dragmall felt relieved to be sitting in a wagon with such pleasant company, though after a brief introduction, Ayla had returned her attention to the fire and her stones.

Astrid bustled about, shaking with nerves, knowing that they were edging closer to the vale. She tried not to make any noise as she moved around the wagon, offering Dragmall some water. He was breathing heavily as he made himself comfortable next to Ayla, coughing as the smoke from the fire filled his throat.

'You know Draguta!' Ayla announced suddenly, blinking herself away from the mesmeric flames, her large brown eyes demanding answers. 'What can you tell me? What can we do to stop her?'

Dragmall coughed some more, sipping the water. 'She is powerful with that book. It commands her as much as she commands it.'

Ayla frowned, taking the cup Astrid offered her, eyes on Dragmall. 'And does she need to use it? To read from it? Is there any way we can get it away from her?'

'I would think it near impossible, but Draguta doesn't have twenty pairs of eyes, does she? If she's busy fighting Jael and her army, we may be able to do something without her seeing us. I have this.' And he pulled a comb from his pocket. 'It belonged to someone who may be able to help us.'

***

Edela and Eydis entered the trance.

They needed to be ready. There would be the smallest of opportunities for them to act. It was better to be prepared.

Arriving in the vale arena, Edela could see soldiers dressed in highly polished armour, eyes hidden beneath helmets, shuffling their feet in the gravel as they waited. She spun around, looking for Jael, trying to find anyone she recognised.

And then a gasp from Eydis, who had stilled beside her.

Eadmund.

Edela grabbed Eydis' arm, pulling her away. 'We cannot let him see us,' she hissed, dragging Eydis past the soldiers, hiding behind them.

'But won't the soldiers see us?' Eydis panicked, glancing back over her shoulder, aware of the shimmering bodies towering around them. The smell of sweat and fear mingled with smoke that drifted towards them from fires on the ridge.

Edela shook her head. 'We are here for Eadmund. This is our trance with him. I...' She sucked in a deep breath, trying to clear her foggy head. 'I believe it is only Eadmund who will be able to see us. It is that way in a dream walk... I think.'

Eydis could hear the hesitation in Edela's voice. She sounded confused, which worried her further. 'How long can we stay here, Edela? Jael's not here yet. Maybe we should go?'

'Ssshhh.' Edela held up a finger, watching as Eadmund strode past them, his eyes directly north, looking to where the mountains parted, opening an invitation, a route towards the battle arena.

He looked so different.

He felt so different.

'Something's wrong with him,' Eydis whispered. 'Look at his eyes.'

Edela couldn't see Eadmund's eyes, but she was struck by how he was almost jerking as he walked. She could feel anger seething through his body like a hot lake of fire. 'Stay here, Eydis. Just stay here. We must try and hold on for Jael.'

***

Aleksander kept eyeing the giant shield on Jael's back as she rode beside him. 'I'll use it,' he insisted. 'You need someone to use it.'

'I need Eadmund to use it,' Jael muttered, her chest aching, familiar pains darting in from everywhere, tension building. The mountains were rising directly in front of them now, and the afternoon sky was darkening further, increasing her tension. 'You've enough to think about without worrying about the shield.' Aleksander didn't say anything, and Jael turned to him, grabbing his arm, staring into his eyes. 'If I can't save Eadmund, you'll use it.'

He nodded. 'You need to stay safe.'

'I do.'

'And you trust the old man?' He inclined his head towards the wagon following just behind them.

'Yes. He brought the shield all the way from Helsabor. I don't imagine he'd have gone to that much trouble just to trick me.'

Aleksander watched Fyr flying down towards Jael. 'I...' He glanced around, but Axl and Karsten had their heads together, not looking his way. 'I need to say something, in case...'

Jael tried not to laugh. 'You say this before every battle!'

'I know. And you've never said anything back. Not once!'

'Why would I? I know I'll see you again.'

'You do?'

Jael blinked, suddenly not as certain. Her mind was a storm of things to remember, and she couldn't see through the darkness. 'I do,' she smiled, hoping it was true. 'There's no need to say anything.'

Aleksander patted Sky, running his hand over her mane, wanting to steady his nerves. As much as he enjoyed riding into battle beside Jael, the fear of losing her had always been impossible to shake. 'Well, I won't say anything, then. Hard to say something to a woman like you anyway. You're like one of those stones guarding Oss' harbour.'

'What? Fearsome and dangerous?'

'Sharp and unforgiving.'

'And nothing else?'

Aleksander scratched his head. 'Thinking...'

Jael laughed. 'Well, don't think for too long, or we might –'

Heads were up, eyes scanning the mountains as the sky darkened dramatically, thunder crashing down on top of them, panicked horses skittering in the dust.

Fyr launched herself off Jael's shoulder, flying towards the vale.

Jael could see the entrance in the distance now. They were almost there.

And she could feel Eadmund waiting for her.

***

Briggit wanted to be at the head of the circle beside Draguta, helping her defeat Esk. She wanted to watch that pathetic god beg for mercy as he was cowed by the power of The Following. Conquered by the magic of the Book of Darkness. But she was stuck on the far side, amongst the Followers who were weaving around the ridge in a slow dance. Weaving around Draguta, who had drawn a bloody symbol on her forehead and was now howling to the sky.

Esk had been unable to stay away. He had heard Daala's warning – they all had – but he was never going to be convinced that Raemus' spells and symbols could defeat the brutal, raw strength of a war god with a mighty spear. And striding towards the shrieking woman in white, he dug his right boot into the gravel and drew back his arm, releasing the spear. Standing up, arms at his side, he watched the blur of golden light as it shot towards Draguta who suddenly turned her eyes towards it and swung out her arms, stretching them out on either side of her before snapping them back together with a loud clap of her hands.

And Esk's famous spear clattered to the ground, broken in two.

He blinked slowly, not understanding what had happened,

feeling oddly vulnerable as Draguta's eyes locked on his.

'I won't kill you!' she promised with a growing smile. 'No! What I will do will be much worse than that, Esk, Daala's son! Feel free to run! Run and hide like your mother told you to! You will not get very far. Not now!'

Esk drew his eyes away from the broken spear, shutting out the sound of Draguta's taunting voice and the chorus of dreamers who kept moving, their chanting reaching a crescendo now. 'Hide?' he laughed, stomping forward. 'No, woman, that is what you and your kind do. Your Followers? Raemus'? They've always been nothing but cowards! Hiding beneath their hoods! Hiding in the shadows! And here you are, hiding in that circle! Come out and face me, Follower Queen!'

Draguta's eyes popped open, rage flowing up into her throat, hot and urgent, and gritting her teeth, she spun around, heading back into the circle as the Followers enclosed her like a black cloak.

Esk frowned in surprise, certain she had been about to attack him, but in the very next breath, he realised that she was. He tried to lift an arm, but both were pressed firmly against his thighs. He tried to move a boot, but they were pushing against the gravel, keeping him where he stood. And he turned his head, searching for a way out, stopping suddenly, unable to turn it back.

And then a smell, a burning smell, and though he couldn't move, Esk sensed that something was on fire around him. He could almost see the glow of symbols out of the corner of his frozen eyes.

Draguta cackled with pleasure as the power of the Followers charged through her hands. She pressed a bloody finger to the table, making symbols in a circle, watching as they burst into life, sizzling.

Burning.

Esk bellowed in pain, and Draguta threw back her head, joining the Followers in their chant, her body pulsing with ecstasy.

'Edela!' Eydis panicked, listening to the noise coming from the ridge as Esk roared, trapped in the circle burning around his feet. She gripped Edela's hand tightly, afraid that she would slip away from her. That she would be left alone in the vale.

Edela was worried too. Her ears were buzzing, and her body was tingling, but she pushed her boots down hard on the earth, trying to hold on. 'Stay still now,' she murmured. 'Just stay here. Look.' And she pointed to Eadmund who appeared oblivious to Esk and the Followers and Draguta as he strode towards the centre of the arena, his sword drawn.

Eydis pointed to the vale entrance. 'Fyr!'

'You can see her?' And it was only then that Edela noticed Eydis' eyes, which were no longer milky, but a clear cornflower-blue, big and blinking with terror.

They watched the shimmering feathers of the black raven as she swept into the arena, flying towards the rocky shelf where Esk had been standing only moments before. Flapping her wings, Fyr shot up into the dark clouds, disappearing before Draguta could turn her magic on her.

Edela exhaled, her heart stammering. 'Jael is close.'

***

'Can you feel that?' Thorgils was riding beside Jael now, worried eyes flitting around, seeking out any threat. 'The ground's shaking. Look at the horses.'

Jael gripped Tig tightly with her leather-covered thighs. He shook his head, throwing his black mane over her knees. 'Ssshhh, boy,' she murmured, feeling his tension mount. 'Ssshhh.'

Aleksander dropped the reins, shoving his helmet onto his head, tightening the strap under his chin as the ground rippled beneath them. 'What is it?'

'A god,' Jael said quietly. 'Esk is in the vale.'

Thorgils swallowed.

Jael turned to him. 'Blow your horn. Blow it loud. Three times!' And checking that her own helmet was on tight, she slid out of the saddle, eyes up on the opening in the mountains ahead. An opening that wasn't as wide as she'd remembered. Wide enough for catapults, yes, but then what? It looked like the perfect place for an ambush. Though, she supposed with a tense grin, with Draguta, it was always going to be an ambush.

Aleksander dismounted, leading Sky towards Thorgils; Axl and Fyn behind them. They would leave the horses now. The vale was a place for shields and swords, fire and arrows. The horses would only get in the way.

Aleksander watched Jael slide off Tig, standing close to him, her hand on his cheek. He could sense that she needed to be alone. To prepare herself for what would come next.

So could Jael.

Lightning shivered across the sky, bright golden shards exploding above her head and Jael suddenly wondered where Fyr had gone.

'You were born to fight, Jael.'

Her father.

She could almost feel him standing beside her, and she remembered how it had felt going into battle together; Ranuf on one side, Aleksander and Gant on the other. She had taken it for granted for all those years. And now her father wasn't there anymore, and nor was Gant. 'To fight my husband?' she muttered. 'I wasn't born for that fight. This is Draguta's game, and we're all her pawns.'

'You?' Ranuf's laugh was deep. 'A pawn? You don't think you chose this? All of it? Eadmund? You could have run, Jael. You could have killed Lothar, turned the army to your favour when I died, but you didn't. This was your choice. It's always been your choice.'

Jael frowned, wondering if that was her father's voice at all.

She twisted Tig's reins in her left hand, fingering Toothpick with her right, wondering whether she could keep him safe from Draguta.

'Good luck, Jael.'

She shivered, sensing her father's presence fade, and turning around, she walked to where Fyn was helping Thorgils organise the horses. 'Find me a full quiver of arrows.' Fyn blinked, his face suddenly pale. 'Throw in some fire arrows too.' Turning back to Tig's saddle, she unhooked her bow.

Thorgils looked concerned. 'How will you fight with that on your back?'

'I won't take it now.' She handed him the bow. 'You keep it. Give it to me when I'm ready. Take the shield too. If anything happens to Eadmund, Aleksander will use it.'

Thorgils swallowed, grabbing the bow as Jael slid the shield off her back. 'Jael... I...' He rested the bow on the ground. 'If you have to kill Eadmund...'

Jael stared at him. 'I won't. Don't worry, I won't.' Her lie was spoken slowly, with great care, and she hoped it would convince them both.

Thorgils nodded, not convinced at all. There was so much more he wanted to say, but she needed to go. 'Just remember Tarak. You defeated that bastard when no one else could. But you did it. Because it mattered.' Fyn was back with the quiver, and he turned to his cousin. 'It mattered to all of us.'

Jael scuffed her boots in the dust. She needed to make sure that everyone knew what they were doing. That Axl did. She handed the shield to Thorgils, her eyes on both him and Fyn. 'Bring this to me when I'm ready... and, Fyn, stay safe. Listen to Thorgils. And if not Thorgils, then Aleksander.' Fyn blinked, turning to Axl who arrived having checked on his men.

Jael drew her brother away, out of earshot. She could feel his tension threatening to explode into panic, and she tried to focus him. 'We don't know what they're going to do,' she said, inclining her head towards the entrance. 'But we know what we're going to do. And we're going to stop Jaeger and Draguta and destroy that book and get Amma and Eadmund back.'

Axl took a quick breath, nodding.

'You're a Furyck. A king. Born to lead. Ranuf chose you, remember that. He chose you to lead Brekka when he couldn't. So you must, Axl. I have to focus on Eadmund and Draguta now, but you have to kill the Hestians.'

'I will.' His voice was a croak, and he coughed, clearing his throat, wishing he had some ale. 'I will, Jael.' Leaning forward, he pulled his sister into his arms. 'For Brekka. For Ranuf.'

Jael nodded, pulling away. 'Don't stop thinking. Looking. Anticipating. Eyes everywhere. There'll be no time for panic. Only action.' She rested her hand on Toothpick's pommel, calmed by the familiarity of that cool stone.

There was nothing more to say as she turned back to Thorgils and Fyn, feeling herself disappearing now. She was going to that place where there was no fear.

No love. No safety. No certainty.

She was going to a place of death.

And grabbing hold of Tig's bridle one last time, she leaned her face against his warm, soft cheek and whispered goodbye.

CHAPTER FIFTY THREE

Esk was hers.

Draguta laughed, watching as he stood, trapped, back on the viewing platform. There was no ridiculous spear in his hand now. No fire in his spellbound eyes.

He was broken, just as Veiga was broken. Broken and bound.

And this was just the beginning.

Draguta doubted that any other gods would venture into the arena now, trying to disrupt her plans, though she did not allow that thought to distract her. There would be time after she had ended Jael Furyck and Dara.

Time to claim every last one of them.

Her eyes drifted from Esk to Eadmund who waited in the arena, sword in hand. He wore no helmet, and that bothered her. He would have looked far more regal with a shining helmet upon his head, though Draguta doubted he needed it against his wife. She had seen him practice. He was ready.

Her attention was suddenly drawn to the dark figure striding into the arena.

The Followers hushed expectantly, all eyes following hers.

Jael Furyck.

Dressed in black leather, a fitted mail shirt hugging her body, polished helmet upon her head, dark hair flowing beneath it. 'How very sleek,' Draguta purred, turning to Meena. 'My ring,' she smiled. 'I will be needing my ring.'

Meena froze, hands in fists, chest aching with panic. 'I...'

Draguta cocked her head to one side. 'Yes?'

Swallowing, Meena turned to the table, picking up the tiny ring box which sat beside the Book of Darkness. Hands shaking, she turned back to Draguta, holding it out.

Draguta was too busy watching Jael Furyck to even glance at Meena. Too busy watching Eadmund's reaction as he walked towards his wife, vibrating with power. She slipped the ring on her finger and handed the empty box back to Meena. 'You will be ready. When it is done, you will be ready for what comes next.'

Meena nodded, her eyes on the Book of Darkness, Dragmall's familiar voice suddenly loud in her ears.

***

Edela and Eydis had been in the trance for what seemed like hours, though Biddy knew that it hadn't been long at all. Still, she wasn't sure how much longer she could keep her eyes open. As terrified as she felt, the smoke and the steady rhythm of Entorp's drumming echoing around the hall was starting to put her to sleep.

Ontine smiled at her. 'Perhaps water would help?' she whispered, reaching for the water jug, feeling thirsty herself. And hot. Her eyes met her mother's, and she blinked. The light in the hall was dull, but Ontine saw a glint of panic in Sybill's eyes as she inclined her head towards the grey curtain that led to the bedchambers and the kitchen. Taking a deep breath, she turned back to Biddy and Derwa with the cups. Entorp was still tapping on the drum, eyes closed, as much in the trance as Edela.

Coughing, Ontine reached back for the jug, pouring herself a cup of the cool water, her eyes on the curtain her mother had just disappeared behind.

***

Dara turned to Eloris as they reached the end of the scorched forest. 'I have to get to Edela!' she panicked. 'You must hide! Hurry! Get to the caves!'

Eloris looked past Dara to the large stone fort in the distance. 'You cannot pass. There is a dreamer circle inside the wall. It is warded with a powerful symbol, Dara. I cannot pass either. It must be why we couldn't get through to Edela.'

'But I have to!' Dara ran away from her, out of the forest, panicked breaths pumping in her chest. 'I have to! Just go! Leave me!'

'Dara!' Eloris watched her disappear, knowing that she couldn't help her now. She could feel the threat of Draguta looming over them, and she had to get to safety quickly. 'Be careful!' she cried, spinning around, running back through the blackened trees.

***

Jael's eyes were on Eadmund, who was striding towards her, though she was taking everything else in as she walked. The clouds were sinking over the arena, hiding the clifftops on either side of the vale which made it easier to see. And what she could see was Draguta standing on the grassy ridge at the head of a circle of Followers. She could see the Hestian army arrayed on either flank, deep rows of warriors tightly packed together behind shields, shining metal stretching far back to the woods in the distance, spear tips pointing towards the clouds. Jaeger Dragos was no doubt lurking somewhere near the front, though those men wore so much armour that she couldn't see their faces.

Fingering Toothpick's pommel, Jael lifted her eyes to the

stone shelf where Esk stood, trapped and bound, his famous spear snapped in two. She tried not to think about what Draguta might be planning to do with him.

Turning her attention back to Eadmund, Jael saw a glimpse of the ancient tree spreading its branches over the hoods of the Followers; dark-robed, all of them, except for Draguta who was dressed entirely in white. It was as she had seen in her dream, and there was some relief in that.

Fyr was close by, Jael knew, though she almost wanted her to stay away, hoping that Draguta wouldn't imprison her too.

Axl was leading the Brekkan army into the arena, filling the space behind her, shields slapping over shields as they took their positions in long rows; spears, swords, and axes at the front, archers in the back. Ivaar was bringing the Islanders, and Rork had command of his Alekkans, leaving Beorn outside the vale to command the catapults. Jael could hear boots shuffling across gravel as the army fanned out in silence.

She didn't need to look. They had planned this out.

Jael didn't need to look at Draguta either now. She could feel her. She could feel the power of the ring pulsing in the distance, and she knew then that Meena Gallas hadn't taken it.

She hadn't taken the ring.

Jael lifted her head, shutting that thought away, taking a deep breath.

Hopefully, Draguta would want to watch her fight before she used it.

She turned all of her attention to Eadmund as he stopped before her, sword in hand.

He scuffed the dirt, eyes on Jael.

His wife. His queen.

He felt nothing.

Nothing, except the desire to bring Draguta her head.

***

'Let me in!' Dara cried up to the ramparts. 'I must see Edela! Or Eydis! Please! Hurry!'

'I can't!' a man called down to her, tugging on his braided blonde beard. 'No one can come in or out!'

Dara wanted to scream, though that would hardly encourage his help. 'I must see Edela Saeveld! If you can't let me in, please find her! Bring her to me!' She was panicking, trying to think of what she could do. Of what magic she could use to break the circle before her sister found her. But, she realised with a shudder, Eloris was right, the symbol being used was too powerful.

She couldn't see a way through it.

The guard turned to his friend with a perturbed frown. 'I'll go to the hall. See what Gant thinks.'

'Far as I know, they've locked down the hall. It's happening. Now.'

'We can't let her in on our own, though,' the first guard grumbled. 'I'll be back.' And feeling increasingly unsettled by the woman's panic, he hurried down the rampart walk, towards the stairs, where he disappeared, coming quickly into the gatehouse, emerging out onto the square.

Just before the dreamer circle.

He lifted a hand to one of the circle guards who approached quickly. 'Need to get word to Gant. Someone's outside the gates, wanting to come in. A woman. She needs to speak to Edela. Says it's urgent.'

'What is happening?'

Both men turned to see Sybill Ethburg bustling towards them, grey curls bouncing around an alert face. 'Did you say that someone needed to see Edela? But why have you left them outside? It may be important!'

The rampart guard felt even more disturbed. 'I can't break the circle.'

'I will take her inside,' Sybill said, big eyes blinking. 'I'll break the circle and send Edela out to close it. We must see what this woman wants. Bring her to me. Quickly!' And she stared at the frowning guard until he spun away, running for the main gates.

***

Bruno had driven the wagon into the vale, stopping it just past the entrance, to the right of the long rows of silent warriors and archers who were still moving into position. Ayla hurried out of it, casting a small circle near the mountainside. Astrid and Dragmall followed her, arms loaded with everything they needed to start a fire.

'Jael doesn't need our help yet,' Dragmall assured Ayla who had pushed herself up on her tiptoes, trying to see what was happening in the arena, catching a glimpse of a man who did not look like the Eadmund she remembered. 'But we must be ready for what will come next.'

Ayla nodded, her eyes on Bruno who stood outside the circle, guarding it, sword in hand. He turned to her and smiled, and she smiled back, her eyes already watering from the smoke.

'Magic is as magic does,' Dragmall winked. 'And being exceptionally old, I know more magic than I would wish to. See up on that grassy ridge there. Beneath the Tree of Agrayal.' And he pointed at the hooded figures circling the tree. 'Briggit Halvardar is in there somewhere. She is our enemy. We will leave Eadmund to Jael, and you and I will work on Briggit and her Followers. That circle will protect Draguta. It will enhance her power and stop Jael from getting anywhere near her, so we must try to break it.'

Ayla could feel the hammer of her heart, but Dragmall's calm words focused her, and she nodded, closing her eyes, inhaling the smoke, hoping that Jael would stay safe.

Jael wanted to run. To throw her arms around her husband.

But this wasn't Eadmund. This man she might have to kill.

He wasn't wearing a helmet, so Jael could clearly see those familiar hazel eyes which looked oddly cold and emotionless. She could see his sharp cheekbones, the line of his jaw beneath his beard. He looked nothing like the man she had married, though Jael tried to convince herself that that Eadmund was still in there somewhere.

He had to be.

'Eadmund.' She shuffled her boots in the dust, feeling an unwelcome tremor in her hand as she unsheathed Toothpick. 'Been training, I see.'

'To beat you? I'd have to, wouldn't I?'

That voice. It didn't sound like her husband at all.

Eadmund's eyes roamed her body, sizing her up as though they'd never met.

Or perhaps as though he was preparing to kill her.

'We don't have to fight,' Jael tried, searching his eyes for any sign that he felt something for her. That he recognised her. 'I've brought one or two warriors with me. Some you might know. Join us, we can free you.'

'Free me?' Eadmund laughed. 'And what do you think I need freeing from, Jael?' He was edging closer now, his eyes on her face, noticing the bruises, perhaps a new scar or two. Her new armour.

She looked tired.

Jael smiled. 'Not that tired.'

Eadmund frowned. 'I don't need to be saved by you. I've no wish to be yours or Evaine's.'

'But you want to be Draguta's?' Jael firmed up her grip, sensing that he was about to move. She could suddenly feel Edela nearby, and she lunged, Toothpick swinging.

Eadmund blocked her strike, swapping his sword into his left hand, sweeping it towards her right shoulder, knowing that Draguta was watching, remembering what Meena had said.

He had to kill her.

'I need you!' Jael shouted, dipping away from his blade. She jumped back, throwing her weight onto her left leg, kicking her right into the side of his knee.

Eadmund's leg buckled, and he stumbled, growling, still on his feet. Jael didn't let him go. She charged him, sensing her grandmother's impatience growing.

She needed to get him down to the ground quickly.

Eadmund dodged her next strike, sword still in his left hand, coming back, punching her shoulder with his right. Now it was

Jael's turn to stumble, grunting at the pain of his knuckles hitting bone. She kicked out at him, her boot cracking his hip, spinning away before he could touch her. Stopping, turning back around, Jael parried his blade, kicking him in the knee, needing to weaken his legs quickly.

Draguta, watching from the head of the circle, could feel Eadmund's anger growing. The sun peeking out from beneath the low clouds was in her eyes, and she lifted a hand to her forehead, sensing Evaine straining to see, creeping up beside her.

Aleksander, Thorgils, Fyn, and Karsten started edging towards where Jael and Eadmund were fighting, leaving Axl and the army behind. Aleksander rested Esk's shield on the ground, and they crouched behind it, pausing before continuing.

Edela and Eydis followed behind them. They didn't know if the dreamers could see them. If Draguta could. They were not real, merely dream versions of themselves, though this was no dream and Edela found herself trying to see what was happening, terrified that Ontine had been right about Eadmund killing Jael.

Eadmund was trembling with rage now.

Jaw clenched, he burst forward, almost spitting at his wife.

Jael could see that his eyes were as dead as the temple guards in Tuura. Dead like Baccus who she'd killed more times than she could remember. Ducking Eadmund's blow, she kept her eyes on his, punching him in the throat. Eadmund fell back, just keeping to his feet, stirring up clouds of red dust as she came at him again, sheathing Toothpick.

Thorgils inhaled sharply. 'Not sure that's the right thing to do,' he muttered nervously to Fyn, barely able to breathe as they crouched down behind the shield again. 'Eadmund looks ready to kill her. Capable of it too.'

Fyn was too tense to speak as he gripped his spear. He didn't take his eyes off Jael who slipped around a gagging Eadmund, elbowing him in the lower back, following up as he turned with an elbow to the cheek. Bellowing, Eadmund lashed out with his sword, watching sparks of gold flash in Jael's green eyes as she ducked his blade, dropping low, punching him hard in the balls.

Edela gripped Eydis' hand as Eadmund fell to the ground, loosening his grip on his sword. Jael kicked the sword away, throwing herself on top of him, slamming her fist into his nose, slicing the side of her hand into his throat again, hoping to keep him gasping for air as she fought to control his arms.

She needed to secure them quickly.

Shoving a hand down her trousers, she reached for a rope, but Eadmund, eyes watering, balls throbbing, throat aching, flicked his boot into Jael's ankle, knocking her sideways. Scrambling to his feet, he threw himself at her, shunting her to the ground, pushing all his weight down onto Jael's chest, wrapping his hands around her throat.

'I'm not sure this is going to plan,' Thorgils panicked, turning to Aleksander who was vibrating beside him, ready to run.

'Jael can stop him,' Aleksander insisted, trying to shake some confidence into himself. 'Just wait.' Though his voice wavered and his hand shook. He firmed up his grip, preparing to move.

'Can't breathe,' Jael rasped, hands working, trying to push Eadmund off her chest. He looked at her blankly, squeezing her throat with greater force. There was nothing in his eyes but hatred. Hatred and the need to end her.

Jael could feel her heart almost bursting beneath Eadmund's weight. And then that voice in her head. 'You won't come back.' Laughter. Dark and malevolent. And she was back in the forest with Ronal Killi lying on top of her, sweaty, fumbling hands trying to get down her trousers, up her tunic. And wriggling, dragging her knife from its scabbard, Jael stabbed it into Eadmund's left arm, in the gap between the top of his arm guard and his armour plate. He jerked back, screaming, his hand releasing her throat, and Jael swung her left leg into the side of his head with the crack of the knife down her boot.

'Ooooh!' Karsten grimaced as Eadmund toppled forward, his face slamming into the ground with a thump.

Eadmund shook his head, dazed, trying to roll over. Everything had gone dark, though, and he couldn't see. Jael jumped onto his back, rope out now, needing to tie his hands before he moved, but Eadmund pushed himself off the ground, and she was in the air, hands around his throat as he spun, throwing her back to the ground.

Jael rolled onto her stomach, crawling for his ankles, but Eadmund aimed a boot at her head, missing as she swerved, slamming it into her shoulder. She grunted, gritting her teeth, rolling quickly, jumping back onto her feet. Doubling the rope in her hand, she snapped it at his face. Eadmund swayed back, dropping his shoulder, swinging his fist at Jael's ribs. He could see that he'd hurt her, and he wanted to do it again. He wanted to hear her bones snap.

Jael darted to the side, slipping on gravel, Eadmund's fist smacking into her ribs. 'Aarrghh!' Bright shards of light burst in front of her eyes, anger surging, ears ringing as he swung at her again. She ducked, snapping the rope at his heavily protected chest, trying to think of how to get him down to the ground again.

Eadmund roared, fists clenched, throwing himself forward.

Ready to kill her.

***

Dara barely looked at the woman as she followed her, the knots in her stomach tightening with each step. 'You will take me to Edela?'

Sybill nodded, leading Dara through the busy square, where the afternoon was turning to dusk, and the braziers were smoking; happy children chasing after each other, ignoring their parents' calls to watch where they were going. She turned before the hall, heading around the back. 'The doors are locked. We must enter through the kitchen.'

Dara was so panicked that she paid little attention to what she was seeing until she was inside the kitchen garden. 'Wait.' She stopped, her eyes on the ominous clouds sinking towards the fort. 'Who are you?' She felt odd, as though there was a fog around the woman, concealing her.

'Me?' Sybill had one hand on the kitchen door handle. She didn't turn around. 'I'm no one. Not important at all. Just someone helping.'

Dara stepped closer. 'Helping who?'

And spinning around in a flash, Sybill stabbed her knife into Dara's chest, then, drawing it out, she slit her throat, watching horror bloom in Dara's eyes as she collapsed to the ground, blood falling from her throat like a bright-red curtain.

Bending down to clean her blade on a patch of grass, Sybill stood, sheathing her knife. And, smoothing down her blue dress, she smiled, heading into the kitchen.

***

Gant's voice was loud in her ears.

'Nothing fancy.'

Jael saw his eyes, grey and hard. And she remembered him battering her over and over again in the training ring, forcing her to keep going. To think. To see a solution for every problem.

'Nothing fancy, Jael.'

Her lip was cut, bleeding. She was struggling to drag in enough air to breathe. Her ribs were broken. She was choking on dust.

Then she saw her baby daughter, dead in her arms.

And she knew that the woman who had killed her was there.

The woman who had done this to Eadmund was there.

And she just had to end her.

But she had to stop Eadmund first.

'Fuck!' Jael screamed, anger shaking her arms. 'You are not going to fucking kill me, Eadmund Skalleson! Not today!' And spinning away from him and his bleeding fists, she ran towards the ridge where Draguta and her Followers stood, watching.

Aleksander's eyes popped open. He could hear Thorgils'

sharp intake of breath as he leaned forward, wondering what Jael was doing.

Eadmund ran after his wife, charging across the arena.

Jael heard him coming. Boots crunching gravel.

She could hear how close he was.

Getting closer. Closer.

And suddenly she stopped, spinning towards him.

Eadmund couldn't stop in time. He skidded helplessly, flying over Jael as she crouched down, throwing out his arms, sword lost again.

He smashed into the gravel, face first, mouth full of dust.

Jael grabbed his ankles, wrapping one length of rope around them, tying it into a tight knot before he could kick out at her. She threw herself onto his back, punching him in the neck before dragging out the second length of rope she'd tucked down her trousers.

Eadmund roared, trying to roll her off him, but Jael dug her knees into his waist, slamming her helmet into the back of his head, knocking him forward. Fingers working quickly, she tied the rope around his wrists, pulling it tight, securing it in a knot.

'Let's go!' Aleksander urged, running to her. 'Hurry!' And Karsten, Fyn, and Thorgils ran behind him, shields up, heading for Jael and Eadmund; Edela and Eydis, unseen, struggling to keep up with them.

Draguta clamped her teeth together in displeasure, running a finger over her ring. 'Hand me the second potion!' she growled at Meena, who appeared to be trying to leave. She frowned suddenly, her attention drifting away from the arena. 'Where are you going?'

Meena's mouth opened and closed. 'To get the potion?'

'Yes, you are!' Draguta shouted, not wanting to be distracted for a moment. 'And it is not in that direction!' She quickly turned back to the soldiers who waited on the left flank, watching as Jaeger strode forward, unsheathing his sword.

CHAPTER FIFTY FOUR

'Karsten!' Thorgils could see Jaeger striding towards them, the Hestian army on the march behind their king. 'Karsten! You have to go!' Thorgils grabbed his shoulder, staring into his eye. 'Go! Kill your brother! Don't let him through! We need time to save Eadmund!'

Karsten turned back to Jael who wasn't looking his way as she tried to keep Eadmund on the ground. He could see Aleksander on her other side, one hand on the shield that would become Eadmund's if his sister could save him. And she could only save him if he stopped Jaeger from getting anywhere near them. Nodding, he rose to his feet, pulling an axe from one of the scabbards crossing his back. 'Good luck.' And adjusting his eye patch with his left hand, Karsten stepped away from them.

Thorgils nodded. 'Kill that bastard!' And he turned back to Eadmund who was now on his back – uncomfortable, tightly bound, hissing and spitting at them - and he punched him in the face.

'Harder!' Jael yelled. 'I have to make a circle!' And Thorgils happily obliged, slamming his fist into Eadmund's jaw, knocking his bellowing friend's head back to the ground with a bang. 'Well, not that hard!' Jael had her knife out, hiding behind Aleksander and Esk's shield as they crept around Eadmund, Thorgils, and Fyn, casting a circle in the gravel.

Thorgils looked indignant, jerking as the first wave of arrows whistled through the air. He frowned in surprise. 'Arrows? I'll take arrows!'

'Not just any arrows,' Draguta murmured, watching the arrows slam into the gravel around Jael Furyck and her men in a perfect circle, white goose feathers fluttering in the breeze. 'Not just any arrows.' And running her finger across the ring, she closed her eyes.

Opening them immediately, Draguta strode to the edge of the ridge, squinting. 'What is that?'

Meena shuffled forward, squinting with her, trying not to let her eyes wander to the book whose pages were suddenly flapping in the breeze. She didn't understand what Draguta had seen. Evaine, on her other side, was too worried about Eadmund to care.

He hadn't gotten up.

What were they doing to him? Why hadn't he gotten up?

'That shield! How did it get there?' Draguta shrieked, her pale-blue eyes as round as full moons.

Jaeger shut out Draguta's furious screeching as he strode across the arena towards his brother, his heavily-armoured body fizzing with anger, the bloody-potion still thick on his tongue. He'd left Berger in charge of his men, warning him to stay alert but not to attack until he was done. He wanted Eadmund and Jael all to himself. And he wanted Draguta to witness it all.

But first, he would end his pathetic one-eyed brother.

Karsten was charging towards him now, no helmet, no shield, though Jael had convinced him to wear a mail shirt which slapped against his thighs as he ran. He held his axe in two hands, bringing it up to his shoulder, poised to strike, and Jaeger watched him with a smile, knowing that he was running towards his own death.

'You bastard!' Karsten spat, almost frothing at the mouth. And then he was there, axe flying, not even taking a breath, enraged by the smirk on his brother's lips, the mocking look in his crazed amber eyes. 'You bastard!'

Jaeger laughed, swaying away from the winking axe blade. 'You think you can win, Karsten? Against me?' He lunged, all humour gone now. 'I'll rip out your other eye before I kill you! You can die blind!'

Axl looked from Karsten to Jael, panic thrumming in his

chest, urging him to act. He shuffled impatiently in the gravel, eyes jumping up to the clifftops, then back down to the arena as Jaeger threw Karsten to the ground. He could feel his men getting impatient behind him, their eyes on the Hestian army who edged forward on either side of the ridge, swords banging on shields in a rhythmic fury. They wanted to engage, just as much as he wanted to. But Jael needed to get Eadmund off the ground first.

Karsten rolled, scrambling back to his feet, axe in both hands, teeth bared. He thought of Nicolene. Nicolene in Jaeger's bed. Dead Nicolene, who wouldn't have been in Andala at all if it weren't for Jaeger, and he roared. 'My wife is dead, you fucking prick!'

Jaeger didn't care.

He was up on his feet, swinging for Karsten's exposed middle. Karsten's teeth hammered together as he lurched back, away from the scything blade, his eye on his brother, watching him coming, sensing the power surging through those massive arms which looked to have doubled in size since he'd last seen him.

Anger swallowed him whole now, and he saw his father's face.

Berard's. Haegen's. Nicolene's. His mother's.

And thinking about Jael, Karsten skidded across the ground, slamming his boots into Jaeger's weak ankles, knocking him over with a cracking thump.

Jaeger barely felt it as he jumped back to his feet. 'Oh you think you're Jael Furyck, do you, Brother? Ha! But my ankles don't bother me now!'

Karsten could see that as Jaeger threw himself forward, blade slicing through the air, taking Karsten on the shoulder, slipping past his ear. He staggered back, firming up his grip, ducking low, aiming for Jaeger's legs. But Jaeger had anticipated it, and he jumped away, spinning around, coming back at Karsten, sweeping his sword in a wide arc. Karsten threw his axe up to meet the blade, the clanging impact sending shocks down his arm. And then Jaeger was shunting and shunting, steaming towards him, sword whipping through the air, knocking him over.

Raymon crept towards the edge of the clifftop, neck straining, trying to see what was happening, his eyes on the banner flapping from Fyn's spear.

Blue. Still blue.

He chewed on a fingernail, his guts griping, creeping back to where his archers waited, bows down, eyes on their king. They had been waiting there for some time, having left the bulk of the army earlier in the afternoon, making their way up the mountains, alert to the danger they would be in once discovered. Though with all those hooded dreamers on the grassy ridge, Raymon knew it was likely that their presence was no secret.

Dragmall could hear Draguta's voice crackling through the air as she tried to break through Jael's circle. 'She will attack now,' he warned Ayla, gripping her hand as they sat before their belching fire, his voice just a hum. 'We must break that circle!' He was growing frustrated. Nothing they had tried so far had worked. No symbol or chant had found a way through.

Ayla nodded, her eyes on the twisting flames, feeling herself separate; as though her body and her mind were drifting apart. She could feel Briggit Halvardar's power growing. She could hear her whipping the dreamers into a chanting frenzy in support of Draguta, the sound of their combined voices reverberating around the vale, Draguta's screams of displeasure rising above them.

'Jaeger! Finish him!' Draguta shouted, watching as Jaeger punched Karsten in the eye, knocking him to the ground again, throwing himself on top of him. His rock-like fists crashed into Karsten's face, blood and skin flying through the air. 'Hurry, Jaeger! Finish him!'

Meena eyed Evaine as she stepped back, away from Draguta, but Evaine was far too busy trying to see what was happening with Eadmund to care. And Draguta was far too busy screeching at Jaeger to notice.

Quietly sliding her knife from its scabbard, Meena tried to steady her nerves as she cut her hand, aware of all the Followers around her. Many of them had their eyes closed and those who didn't appeared to be lost in a daze. Dropping the knife, Meena dipped a finger into the blood beading across her palm, making a shaky symbol on her arm, chanting the words from Morana's spell under her breath.

She remembered the nights in Jaeger's bed, crushed by him, abused by him, hurt and humiliated by him. And she pressed her finger against her skin, tears in her eyes, her body shuddering.

Karsten could barely see out of the one eye he had left, but the mammoth shape of his brother loomed over him like a bloody mountain. He couldn't lift his arm. Couldn't move at all. He thought of Berard, who he would never see again. His children. And Hanna. He tensed, waiting for the final blow, wishing he had a weapon, something to hold onto.

Meena blinked, her eyes on Jaeger, watching as nothing happened.

She pressed her hand against the symbol again, repeating the chant but nothing happened. And her eyes snapped to where Evaine was smiling at her as she edged closer to Draguta.

Meena panicked, her body convulsing, stumbling backwards, trying to see an escape through the circle.

'Hold Eadmund!' Jael shouted at Fyn, feeling Karsten's life hanging in the balance. And pulling the bow over her head, she drew an arrow from her quiver, eyes on Jaeger who was leaning over his brother, hammering his bloody fist into Karsten's face.

And Jael thought of Berard as she released the arrow, knowing that with all the armour protecting Jaeger, she had the smallest target to aim for. 'Jaeger!'

Jaeger turned his face towards her, his mouth open in surprise as the arrow shot straight through it, lodging in the back of his head. The shock was greater than any pain, and he tried to lift an arm, wondering where his sword was before his legs gave way and he collapsed beside Karsten, unable to move, his father's laughter ringing in his ears.

Karsten could hear him gurgling wetly beside him. He could smell the stink of his brother as death came, and he closed his eye, knowing that soon death would come for him too.

Seeing no obvious escape, Meena tried to wipe her bleeding hand on the back of her dress, hiding her arms, shuffling forward to where Draguta was spinning around.

'Jaeger is dead!' Draguta screeched, ignoring Evaine who was trying to get her attention, her eyes on Briggit who stood on the opposite side of the circle. Despite being lost in the smoke, Briggit was working hard not to enjoy the moment. 'Dead!' Draguta's anger rolled like waves as she spun back around, striding forward, her voice rising as she ordered the army to advance; the Hestian army, no longer under the control of a Dragos at all.

She hoped those men knew what they were doing.

Rexon watched from up on the eastern clifftop, eyes on the arena, trying not to draw the Followers' attention. They seemed focused on Draguta, though, who was focused on Jael and Eadmund and the Hestian army which was now starting to advance. His eyes moved to the tiny circle where Jael was working to save Eadmund, watching the blue banner flying from Fyn's spear.

Waiting.

Eadmund could hear Draguta's fury as he writhed on the ground, head pounding, legs and arms bound, Thorgils leaning over him, all bushy red hair and darting eyes.

Eydis panicked, realising that she had to act before Eadmund escaped.

'Eydis.' Edela's voice was faint. 'You must shut out all the noise. All of it. Eadmund is your brother. Your love for him is deep. Your connection to him is strong.' She paused as Thorgils rose to his feet, alert to the Hestian army's advance. 'You know what to do, Eydis,' Edela panted. 'You know what to do.' She almost screamed out in pain, the strain of holding the trance suddenly overwhelming her.

'Edela? Edela?' But there was no answer. So, taking a deep breath, Eydis leaned over her raging brother and placed her hand against the plate of armour protecting his stomach, feeling how smooth it was. How tough. It worried her, but pushing gently as he squirmed beneath her, she eased her hand down, through the metal, inside her brother.

Into his soul.

'Is anything happening?' Aleksander cried, glancing back, one eye on Draguta in the distance; on Karsten who hadn't moved since Jaeger had fallen. 'Jael? Is Edela doing anything?'

'I don't know!' Jael shrugged, her eyes on the Hestian army edging closer under Berger's steady command. She could hear boots shuffling behind her as Axl led their army forward; shields protecting chests, swords and axes poised to strike. 'Fyn!' she shouted over the wailing chants of the Followers. 'Black flag!'

Fyn turned away from her, lifting his spear, a black banner flying now, raising it above his head for everyone to see.

Everyone inside the vale.

Everyone above it.

And suddenly, the air was filled with the high-pitched whistle of arrows, bowstrings snapping as the Iskavallans standing atop one clifftop fired. Rexon's Saalans on the other quickly joining in.

Draguta's eyes were up, followed by her hands. She pushed out her palms, sweeping them quickly around as the arrows shot towards her chanting dreamers, stopping just before the circle, dropping harmlessly onto the grass.

Eydis, hand inside Eadmund's soul, was trying to shut out the terrifying noises; panicking as she heard men shouting about sea-fire and catapults; hoping she would hear Edela again or even Dara Teros.

She could feel the rope in Eadmund's soul, and she gripped it, carefully at first, feeling its texture, frozen and hard. Her body started shaking, her ears ringing, black patches in front of her eyes. Eadmund twisted, throwing her to the side, but Eydis held onto the rope, pulling and tugging it until she had a firm grip with her left hand.

'Hold him down!' Jael shouted to Thorgils, sensing that Eydis was close. 'Keep him still!'

And then Edela was back, reaching for Eadmund, her finger covered in blood. Eydis watched as Edela bent over him, trying to draw the symbol on his constantly moving forehead. She could hear Edela chanting as she turned to her. And holding her breath, Eydis lifted her knife with her right hand, cutting through the rope.

Draguta's attention was on the archers lining the clifftops. This was not their fight, and they would pay dearly for their interference. She shivered, feeling a sudden loss jolt her body, her attention shifting to Jael Furyck's stubborn circle.

Eadmund.

And moving her eyes to the centre of the arena, she watched Eadmund rise.

'You'll be needing this,' Aleksander said, handing the shield to Eadmund.

Eadmund was too confused to speak.

His stomach was stinging as though he'd been stabbed. His head was throbbing, his face aching, but suddenly he was wide awake. Arrows whistled above his head, screams reverberating around the stone bowl as Axl led his bellowing Brekkans forward; Ivaar on his right flank with the Islanders; Rork on his left commanding the Alekkans.

Eadmund took the shield without even looking at it, his eyes on Jael.

Jael who he'd just tried to kill.

He could see the angry red marks around her throat. Her bloody lips. The pain in her eyes.

He wanted to reach out and touch her.

But there was no time.

'We're going for Draguta,' Jael said, her hand on his arm, unable to experience any joy or relief that he was there again. 'I'm going for her. You're going to keep her away from me with that.' And she pointed to the shield.

Eadmund nodded, firming up his grip, surprised by how light it felt. How familiar.

'Here,' Thorgils smiled, handing him the sword Eadmund had lost earlier. 'You may need this too.'

'Thank you,' Eadmund mumbled, feelings of guilt and gratitude mingling uncomfortably.

More confusion too.

'Fyn!' Jael yelled. 'Red flag! Red flag!'

Sea-fire.

But just as she yelled it, Draguta stuck out a hand, pointing to the Brekkan army. Then another hand. And she lifted them both into the air before slamming them down towards the grass.

Jael spun, horrified eyes on Aleksander who turned back to Axl. 'Run!' And she charged out of the circle towards her brother. 'Run! To me! To me! All of you! Run!' And shocked into action, the confused Brekkans, Islanders, and Alekkans abandoned their shield walls and started moving towards Jael. 'To me!' she screamed at Ivaar. 'Hurry! Ayla! Dragmall! Run!'

Rexon heard her, and he spun to his right where his archers were positioned above the entrance to the vale. Sheathing his sword, he flapped his arms, shouting, trying to get their attention.

On the opposite clifftop, Raymon could see him. He could hear Jael shouting as she ran, and he could feel the clifftop shudder.

The two dazed dreamers were already scrambling to their feet, leaving their fire and wagon behind, running forward, Bruno and Astrid with them, listening to the ominous rumble as the mountains started collapsing on either side of them; rocks and boulders crashing down on the warriors who were boxed in with nowhere to run. Stuck in lines, trapped, unable to move quickly; catapults behind them, men in front.

Men who could only scream, hands above their heads as they were buried alive.

***

Ontine was giving Edela some water, helping her up onto a stool when Eydis burst out of her trance, head spinning, not knowing where she was for a moment.

'Eydis?' Ontine looked worried as she left Edela and hurried to help her to her feet. 'Are you alright? Did you do it? Did you free Eadmund?'

Eydis staggered backwards, unable to hear anything but the screams of the army as it was crushed by the crumbling mountains. Her head ached as she felt her way to a stool, sensing Entorp nearby. Edela and Derwa too. She bent over, coughing uncontrollably.

'Here,' Ontine smiled, handing her a cup. 'Drink.'

And Eydis did, draining the entire cup. 'Eadmund is back.'

Entorp's smile of relief was wide. 'Well done, Eydis! And you too, Edela.' But even in his slightly befuddled state, he could see that something was wrong. 'What happened?'

'Draguta.' Eydis couldn't sit still. She put her cup on the ground and stood, trying to think. 'Draguta has trapped them. Separated them. Crushed them. Half of the men and all of the catapults are trapped outside the vale.'

'Oh!' Entorp was quickly waking up.

'What?' Gant was at the edge of the circle, frustrated by how helpless he felt. He ran his hands down the sides of his face, scratching his beard, eyebrows knitting together. 'Can you do anything from here?'

Edela could barely see, but she could think. 'Yes. Always. Bring me the book, Ontine. Let us get to work. And Gant, stay alert,' she urged, her eyes struggling to focus on the men who had joined him. Berard was there. Ulf and Bram too. She coughed, hearing Jael screaming, bellowing at her men. 'All of you in here! We cannot help you while we are helping them, so stay alert. If you sense anything is happening in the fort, you must let us know.'

Gant nodded. 'I'll go outside. Check with the men on the ramparts. Make sure they're watching closely.' He glanced at Gisila who had come back into the hall and was now whispering to Sybill. 'I won't be long.'

Sybill stiffened, eyes on Gant. 'If you'll excuse me,' she smiled at Gisila. 'I must just check on something in the kitchen.'

Eydis and Edela were trying to focus, Ontine hovering behind them.

Derwa was hobbling around the circle, attempting to breathe deeply, feeling herself panic. She was not a real dreamer, though her senses were greater than most, but she had not been admitted into the temple as a girl. The elders had decided that her skills were better used for healing. The dreamers, they'd said, had seen that. And Derwa had believed them, though she was often surprised by the vivid clarity of her dreams; further surprised when those dreams then came true.

Perhaps there was something in her?

A way that she could help.

***

'Help!'

Jael could hear the screams of her injured and dying men as she turned to Thorgils and Aleksander. 'Go! Help Axl!' She could see her brother beside Ivaar and Rork, trying to drag the remainder of the army into formation again, dust clouds swirling around their shocked faces.

Her mind was tumbling.

The catapults were lost or trapped outside the vale now. She scanned the collapsed clifftops, not seeing much movement. She couldn't get a sense of Raymon or Rexon at all. Turning around, she grabbed a shell-shocked Fyn, and, pulling him close, she whispered in his ear, pushing him away, urging him to hurry.

The Hestians were approaching, the dreamers were chanting, and Draguta had extended her arms, readying another attack.

'We have to kill her!' Jael shouted. Clouds of dust were pumping towards them, and she was struggling to breathe. 'It's the only way to stop it!'

Eadmund nodded; there was nothing he wanted to do more.

Jael urged him forward, towards where Karsten and Jaeger lay, neither of them moving.

Draguta inhaled slowly, her hands up to the sky, parting the clouds and the dust, bringing back the sunshine. She smiled in the bright glow of it. Carnage everywhere, and not all of it desirable, admittedly, but Jael Furyck's army was in ruins, her catapults gone, her archers dead, and as for any help she might get from those gods...

There was nothing they could do now.

The sword and the shield?

Jael and Eadmund?

Draguta laughed. All those centuries of planning... for what?

She called out to Berger, demanding his attention, urging him to finish the Brekkans. He could keep them busy while she focused on killing Jael and Eadmund.

Brill swallowed, listening to Draguta.

She had been positioned behind Briggit, waiting to be of use, knowing that Draguta wanted her watched carefully. And now she had seen something.

She had to get to Draguta now!

Picking up her feet, Brill started moving around the Followers, trying not to be seen.

Ayla and Dragmall had hurriedly made a new circle, though another fire was proving more difficult. Bruno had found some wood burning amongst the rubble, though its flames were barely flickering and there were no herbs to help them into a trance. But the armies were moving again now, and they knew that they were running out of time to try and break the Followers' circle.

Bruno had quickly rallied a dozen dust-covered Islanders to help him and the wagon guards keep Ayla, Astrid, and Dragmall safe. Shields up they stood around their circle watching as Axl led his men forward again.

The noise in the arena was deafening now as Brill started to move faster towards Draguta. It was so loud that she didn't hear the footsteps behind her or the swish of the knife as it swept through the air, straight through the back of her neck.

She fell to the ground, the pain like an explosion of lightning.

And then nothing but darkness.

Despite the choking dust and his own panic as the noise of the warriors intensified all around him, Dragmall's mind cleared. 'She broke the mountains with a ring!' He could almost see the black stone on Draguta's finger pulsing in the distance. 'Ayla, we must get that ring!'

Meena had crept up to stand near Draguta, avoiding Evaine, whose desire to get her cousin in trouble had suddenly become far less important than her need to see if Eadmund was safe. She could see him with Jael, working together now, freed from Draguta's spell. Evaine panicked, knowing that if Eadmund had turned against Draguta, she would surely kill him.

Meena froze suddenly, hearing Dragmall's voice in her head again. And not even stopping to think, she threw herself forward, knocking Draguta sideways, onto the ground, the ring flying off her finger. And then, from out of the Tree of Agrayal flew Fyr, glistening in the sunshine as she swooped down in a furious flash of black feathers, grabbing the ring in her claws before flapping away.

Draguta scrambled back to her feet, screeching in horror, searching for the raven. And then the arrow struck, straight through Draguta's right shoulder. She jerked backwards, her attention snapping to Jael Furyck who stood inside a tiny circle in the arena, bow in hand, readying another arrow.

Draguta screamed, and the arrow popped out of her shoulder, falling harmlessly to the grass. 'You think that you can kill me?' she laughed, though she was confused, wondering how the arrow had penetrated her circle.

How had it struck her? And who had knocked her over?

But she couldn't look around to see what was happening now. All of her attention was on Jael Furyck.

'No,' Jael said softly, knowing that despite the crashing noise in the arena, Draguta could still hear her. 'But I can distract you.' And she smiled, watching as Draguta's eyes bulged, realising that the raven had gone.

Taken her ring and flown away.

'Draguta!' Evaine called, her hand around Meena's wrist, yanking her cousin forward, hoping to distract her from killing Eadmund.

'You!' Draguta yelled, spinning around to glare at a trembling Meena who was trying to slip out of Evaine's pincer-like hold. 'You did this?' Her eyes drifted to Meena's bleeding hand, noticing the outline of a symbol on her arm. 'You disloyal little bitch! Kill her!' she snarled at Evaine, realising that as much as she wanted to end Meena Gallas herself, she was losing control of the fight in the arena. 'You want me to save Eadmund? Take your knife and kill her!' She spun back around, her attention returning to Jael Furyck. 'You think I need that ring? To hurt you? Ha!' And leaning forward, Draguta lifted the lid on the smallest of her boxes, picking up something too tiny for Jael to see. Adding it to a bowl, she started stirring with a finger, chanting, indicating for her dreamers to join in.

Evaine grabbed Meena by the hair. She was taller than her cousin, and despite being slighter, she was stronger, and she dragged Meena towards her, teeth clenched, eyes wild. Meena fought back, panic thundering in her ears, wanting to run. She needed to escape before Draguta finished what she was doing, but Evaine wouldn't let her go.

Wrapping her hand around Meena's hair, Evaine held her in place, drawing her knife from its scabbard, sweeping its sharp blade towards Meena's throat.

Meena despised her cousin. She hated everything about her.

And there was no way she was going to let that preening, self-obsessed girl kill her. Gritting her teeth, she jerked away from the blade, swinging her head into Evaine's face, smashing her in the nose. Evaine cried out as her nose broke, still gripping the knife. She blinked away the pain, trying to see, jabbing the blade forward again, but Meena didn't care about the knife. She felt it cut her arms as she pushed her cousin backwards, onto the ground, pinning her there, hands around Evaine's long neck.

Evaine tried to scream, her eyes bulging but Meena squeezed even harder, sitting on top of her now, squeezing until Evaine's face turned pink and purple and her eyes almost popped out of her head, and she released the knife, her hand going limp by her side.

Meena fell off her, panting, eyes up on Draguta who was watching the arena.

She had to hurry.

She had to try and escape before she spun around.

CHAPTER FIFTY FIVE

Sybill slipped through the kitchen door, racing around the back of the hall, intercepting Gant. 'Over here!' she cried. 'Quick!'

Gant turned away from the guard he'd been about to speak to and hurried towards her.

***

Axl slammed his shield forward as the armies came together. The noise intensified, warriors smashing against each other, bellowing and cursing as they tried to gain purchase in the slippery gravel, spears jabbing over the top of shields, knives and swords slipping through gaps between them, stabbing unprotected legs.

Axl tried to keep his head clear, conscious of the need to know what was happening. He couldn't get lost in the battle. He had to lead. 'Push!' he yelled. 'Push them back! Push!'

Draguta didn't notice the noise. She didn't notice that Evaine was dead or that Meena had disappeared. All of her attention was on the centre of the arena, watching as the ground suddenly burst open, dirt and rocks flying into the air.

The clash of armies was quickly disrupted as warriors on both sides froze, bloody weapons in mid-air, the ground undulating behind them, around them, all around the vale.

Thorgils had joined Aleksander and Axl at the front of the Brekkan shield wall, and he was confused, his heart galloping like a runaway horse. 'What is that? What's happening?' And looking down in surprise, he saw creatures wriggling around his boots. 'Worms?'

Jael jumped towards Eadmund as their circle cracked, the ground beneath them breaking open. 'Get back!' she turned and screamed, her eyes meeting Aleksander's. 'Back to the mountains!'

***

'More herbs, Derwa,' Edela yawned, trying to push herself back into another trance. It was proving difficult, though she had no idea why. She felt ready to sleep for a year.

But Derwa wasn't listening. She had backed away from Ontine, Edela, and Eydis. Entorp too.

Something was bothering her.

Or someone.

She had seen Sybill. Watched her eyes. Saw her disappearing into the kitchen again. And something about those enormous eyes continued to disturb her. Colour, she realised. She had seen a colour, and though Sybill's eyes were pale blue, Derwa had seen black.

She stepped out of the circle.

***

The tiny black worms wriggled across the gravel, searching for each other, and when they found another worm, they joined together.

One by one, fewer and fewer worms.

Making bigger and bigger worms.

And then there was only one giant worm, throwing itself around the vale at Draguta's command. It crashed down onto the earth, jaws prising apart, sharp fangs dripping with thick saliva, its dark body shivering with spiky fins as it surged forward.

Aiming for Jael and Eadmund.

Dragmall scrambled to his feet. Head up, he scanned the arena, his eyes bulging. 'It's a where-worm!' he yelled, ducking down again, scarcely believing that Draguta had conjured up such a creature. And grabbing Ayla's hand, he pulled her towards him. 'Quick! We have to do something!'

***

'Derwa!' Biddy hissed, watching the old healer shuffle towards the grey curtain. 'The circle! What are you doing?'

Bram's eyes were on Derwa too, wondering much the same. 'I'll find out what's going on.' He turned back to Ulf who was sitting by Bayla. She had left the children in the square with Isaura and Branwyn, following Hanna back inside the hall, both of them eager to see what was happening. 'Ulf, with me.' His eyes went to Berard and Hanna. 'Keep an eye on that circle.'

Bayla grabbed Ulf's hand, feeling her heartbeat skip. She squeezed tightly. 'Don't leave.'

'I'll be right back,' he smiled distractedly. 'Don't worry.'

Bayla watched him go, her eyes drifting back to the circle as Biddy tried to wake Edela out of the trance she'd finally slipped into.

***

'How do we kill it?' Eadmund yelled at Jael as they ran away from the where-worm.

The worm crashed around the vale, chasing them, its high-pitched screech piercing their ears. And though Jael's chest was pumping and her heart was racing, she suddenly felt calm. She saw her father and the path before her cleared. All the noise and distractions were gone as she turned and ran for the worm whose head was up, its long fangs dripping, its slithering body slamming onto the arena, ready to crush anyone it landed on. 'Come on!' she cried, waiting for Eadmund, who, realising that Jael had changed direction, spun around after her.

Eadmund's sword was drawn, Esk's shield banging against his chest, wondering how he could keep Jael safe, or anyone else for that matter. He watched in horror as the worm swung its giant head into the army's left flank, sending the shield-bearing Alekkans flying through the air, smashing against rubble and each other, landing on the ground with sickening thuds, bones breaking, necks snapping. And wrenching open its jaw, the worm kept going, crunching its way into the Alekkans, trying to devour those broken, terrified warriors whole.

'Over here!' Jael screamed, and the worm swung around, long tail flicking angrily, red eyes glowing. Toothpick was sheathed now, and she had her bow in her hand, drawing arrow after arrow from her quiver, aiming for the worm's spiky head. It screeched in anger as the arrows struck, lurching forward. 'Run!' And Jael turned, throwing away her bow, lungs burning, ribs aching as she charged towards the Followers and Draguta.

Leading the where-worm far away from her men.

***

'What is it?' Gant was worried and confused. Sybill appeared to be shaking as she led him into the garden.

'I found a woman! Dead! Over here!' Sybill looked horrified, but as Gant ran towards the blood-soaked body of Dara Teros, her expression changed. 'Someone's murdered her!' she cried from behind him, watching as he bent over, hands on Dara's head, pushing hair away from her face, trying to see if he recognised her.

And then Sybill was behind him, knife out.

'No!'

Derwa's cry from the kitchen door had Gant spinning around, but not in time as Sybill lunged for him, blade jerking, stabbing him in the thigh. Gant yelled out, grabbing her wrist, her knife falling to the ground with a dull thud. 'You?' He grimaced, the sting of the wound sharp. 'Who are you?'

'Gant!' Derwa screamed as figures appeared from around the back of the kitchen. Hooded men. Six of them. 'Behind you!'

Gant spun, dragging out his sword, blood coursing down his leg.

Limping.

'Who the fuck are you?'

'Followers!' Derwa could see everything clearly now. 'They're Followers!'

***

Meena couldn't escape through the Followers. Their circle was tightly bound, black robe to black robe. She didn't want to attract Draguta's attention by trying to force her way through. She didn't want to attract Draguta's attention at all, so she hid around the back of the Tree of Agrayal, hoping its leafy branches would shield her as she tried to think of what to do, her eyes drifting to the Book of Darkness.

Draguta's eyes were following Jael and Eadmund as they ran towards her, jumping over gaping cracks, and deep worm holes, losing their balance as the screeching creature smashed the earth behind them, surging closer.

Jael could feel the rhythm of the Followers' chanting now and Draguta's voice like water, rippling around the vale, urging the worm on. And if she could just keep them all busy, perhaps Edela or Ayla could kill it.

***

Edela was panicking. Nothing was coming to mind. 'Eydis, can you hear Dara Teros? Can she help?'

Eydis was mumbling, though, and her voice sounded muffled, too far away for Edela to understand anything she was saying. And then Biddy broke into her trance, and Edela was quickly back in the hall, inside her circle.

Her broken circle.

'What happened?' Edela coughed, glancing around, blinking. 'Derwa? Where's Derwa?'

***

Jael had to try and slow the worm down quickly. It would crush every Brekkan, every Islander, every Alekkan too. She turned and ran at it, Toothpick extended to her left, dragging his blade through a thick fold of black skin, dropping to the ground, rolling quickly away. The worm squealed, its sharp cry drilling into her ears. Eadmund was behind her, stabbing his sword into the where-worm's snapping tail as it turned.

In and out. Dropping and rolling away.

Aleksander could see them and reminded of how they had killed the serpent in Andala's harbour, he turned to his men. 'We need to help Jael! Her sword can bring it down! Her sword can bring it down!' And leaving Axl to pull his men back into formation, and Thorgils and Ivaar in charge of the Islanders, he grabbed ten Brekkans and ran after Jael.

***

Ulf and Bram rushed past Derwa, down the kitchen steps, running to join Gant who was fighting off six sword-wielding Followers. His arm was bleeding, his leg wound gushing blood into his boot now. He kept turning, eyes darting around the garden, knowing that Gisila was in the hall.

He wasn't letting any Followers inside.

Bram's sword was drawn, his eyes on the black-robed figures. 'Need a little help?'

Gant didn't show how relieved he was. 'They're Followers! Thought I'd killed that one,' he growled, pointing to the stocky man on his right. 'Slit his throat, but he got up, no wounds on him. Not sure what's going on!'

Derwa had seen it herself, and she turned back to the door, realising that they needed more help. But suddenly, Sybill was there.

And she had her knife.

***

The where-worm flicked its bleeding tail at Eadmund, sending him flying, shield spiralling away and Jael roared, lunging forward, stabbing Toothpick into its side, smelling the stink of the creature as she rolled away, jumping back to her feet, running to grab the shield.

Thinking about Fyn.
Now, Fyn. Now!

***

'Aarrghh!' Derwa stumbled back down the step, pulled over by Sybill who had hold of her long white braid.

'Derwa!' Bram spun around, but he was trapped between two Followers, and he couldn't get through to help her. 'Derwa!' He elbowed one in the eye, lashing out with his sword, but another sliced his blade towards him and Bram was jumping back, falling against Ulf who tumbled over.

'You?' Berard was at the kitchen door, eyes popping open in surprise. Quickly taking in the bloody scene, he slammed his boot into Sybill's face, sending her flying, knife gone again. But she scrambled back to her feet, drawing another, her bleeding mouth hanging open, big eyes blinking with frenzy.

'Kill her!' Gant panted, ducking a scything blade. 'Berard! Kill that bitch!'

And Berard gripped his sword tighter in his left hand, ignoring the throbbing in his stump and his discomfort about killing this woman, who, up until now, had been so friendly. He saw the evil look in her strange eyes, though, and he saw Derwa on the ground, blood pouring from her head, her eyes fixed open, Gant, Bram, and Ulf fighting out of the corner of his eye.

And jumping over Derwa's dead body, Berard lunged for Sybill, pushing his sword through the folds of her sagging neck, forcing it straight out the other side as he fell on top of her.

***

Raymon had an arrow through his shoulder. Another in his thigh. The pain was blinding, and he thought he might pass out, but he was trying to see how he could help Jael. She needed help killing the giant worm, but though they still had some arrows and archers to fire them, he wasn't going to risk hitting her and her men. They were running too close to the worm, slashing it, trying to kill it, but he didn't see how they could. It was longer than his hall, almost as wide.

And as for those fangs...

Fyn's eyes were up, scanning the clifftops as he climbed the rubble, spear down, close to his body, slipping occasionally, hoping no one was watching him. He thought of Eydis and his mother. And he kept climbing. He needed to get high enough to raise a flag. And then Jael's voice was suddenly ringing in his ears, and he stopped where he was, balancing himself against the uneven rocks as he shoved the spear in the air, red flag fluttering from its tip, hoping someone would see. He wasn't high enough yet for those on the other side of the rubble, he knew, but if someone on the clifftops was watching...

***

Edela felt torn. She didn't understand what was happening in the hall.

Where had Derwa gone? And why had she broken the circle?

But she could feel Ayla's panic back at the vale. They needed help urgently.

Jael and Eadmund too.

So closing the circle, she hurried to join Eydis and Ontine.

***

Both armies were back behind their shield walls now, flattened against the mountains, more concerned with keeping out of the where-worm's chaotic path than trying to kill each other.

Thorgils held his shield to his chest, eyes on the terrifying black creature throwing itself around the arena, making holes near Karsten who was flopping up and down beside his brother. He didn't know if either of them lived, but the way that worm was bounding around, soon it wouldn't make any difference. He ran to Ivaar who'd been knocked flying by the worm, yanking him to his feet, handing him a shield. 'We need to see if Karsten's alive. Come on!'

Karsten's body moved helplessly, launched into the air as the worm slammed its dark belly down onto the arena and then its tail. He couldn't see what it was, but he could smell it, and he could hear it, and he knew that soon it would land on top of him. He tried to close his eye, though it made little difference. He couldn't see a thing.

And then a voice.

'Thought you'd be more use than this, but I guess you're a Dragos, so we shouldn't have expected much.' And Thorgils quickly had hold of one side of him, Ivaar the other, and together, they dragged a limp Karsten away from the where-worm, past Jael and Eadmund who were tearing holes across the worm's leaking middle with their blades.

Jael stopped, sensing something, and hearing shouts from the clifftops, she spun towards Eadmund. 'Run!' And they charged away from the worm, which slithered after them, banging onto the ground, the impact knocking them over.

They were quickly back on their feet, running again.

Aleksander ran with them, one eye on Thorgils and Ivaar who were struggling to get Karsten behind Axl's shield wall.

Three jars of sea-fire flew over the rubble, two smashing onto the earth, one breaking open on the worm's spiky head.

'Fire!' Jael bellowed, hoping someone could hear her over the chanting Followers and the shrieking worm. 'Fire!

Draguta spun around in fury, surprised to see Evaine sprawled on the ground behind her, stinking of death, Meena Gallas nowhere to be seen. Her anger spiked as she scanned her chanting dreamers. 'Briggit! Come up here! Beside me! I have grown bored! We will end this now! Together!'

Briggit nodded, hurrying forward, her body humming.

Draguta's head snapped to where Axl had stepped out of the shield wall, bowstring to his ear, flaming arrow nocked and ready. She smiled, one hand twisting, as though his heart was in it, trying not to be distracted by her missing ring. Turning her hands again, she aimed the bleeding wreck of a worm at the King of Brekka. 'Goodbye, Axl Furyck!'

***

Edela heard her.

That taunting, evil voice had been in her head for as long as she could remember. She knew that now. That voice had always sounded so victorious, so confident that she would never be stopped.

But they could stop her.

Jael could.

And so could she.

And lurching out of her trance, Edela dragged her knife from its scabbard, slicing across her palm. Bending down, a clear vision of the Book of Aurea in her mind now, she drew a circle, seeing the words on the vellum page as she chanted them softly, listening as they rumbled in her chest like thunder rolling in the distance; seeing herself drawing a dreamer circle of protection around Axl.

***

'Edela Saeveld,' Draguta growled, cocking her head to one side. 'What's that you say? Old, but not dead yet?'

And Axl's arrow struck the where-worm in the jowls of its black neck, igniting it in an explosion of flames; more fire arrows shooting down from the clifftops.

Jael, Eadmund, and Aleksander threw themselves to the ground; Thorgils, Ivaar, and Karsten behind them. Flames everywhere.

More explosions.

Waves of heat surging over their heads.

The worm lurched forward, flames bursting from its nearly severed tail, its mouth open, bellowing in pain, fangs dripping with blood. Balls of fire shot up into the darkening sky - gold and red, hot and loud - and it toppled over, smashing down onto the arena, rocks and gravel flying, coming to a shuddering stop just before an open-mouthed Axl.

Draguta didn't even blink. 'Birds! Where are my birds?' she screeched at Briggit, who nodded calmly, pointing to the wall of rubble in the distance.

Jael's eyes were on the woman with Draguta, and she was on her feet and running. 'Thorgils! Take Karsten back to Axl! Get behind the shields! Eadmund! Come on!' She turned to Aleksander. 'Go with them!'

He looked hesitant, his eyes darting around, watching the Hestians on the move again, arrows flying. 'No! I'm coming with you! You need me!'

Jael frowned, but there was no time to argue.

She ran after Eadmund, heading for the grassy ridge, Aleksander right behind her.

Dragmall watched them running, his eyes drifting to the circle of Followers, confused, muttering to himself before squatting back down beside Ayla again. 'Their circle is open, I can feel it. The Followers' circle is open!' He didn't understand it at all. 'Don't they realise it?'

Ayla wasn't listening. 'Something is coming, Dragmall!' Her eyes were up, trying to see past the clouds. She couldn't see anything yet, but she could feel it. Despite the cloying heat of the late afternoon, she couldn't stop shivering.

'Keep guard!' Bruno growled at the Islanders around him. 'Close up!' He peered at Ivaar, who had joined him, leaving Thorgils to get Karsten somewhere he could lie down. More Islanders hurried forward with more shields, making a tighter house around the circle. Bruno didn't even feel irritated by Ivaar's presence. He needed all the help he could get to keep Ayla safe. He spun around, eyes on his wife, watching as hers popped open, pointing to the sky. Pointing to the giant red birds flying towards them in squawking waves, diving over the rubble wall, wings flaming as they descended into the vale.

Gripping his shield tightly, locked into place with Bruno, Ivaar felt all the air leave his lungs as the birds swooped towards them, cawing angrily. 'Higher!' he shouted. 'Lift your shields higher!'

The shrill cry of the birds rang in Eadmund's ears as he ran. 'Behind me!' he yelled as Draguta lifted her arms, slamming her hands forward, shards of light crackling through the air towards them. He threw up his shield, an explosion of light sparking off the rim. Keeping his head low, Eadmund charged forward, Jael running just behind him.

Draguta screamed in frustration, dropping her hands low, throwing them to the right, and Eadmund with them. He was back on his feet quickly, though, shield at his chest again, in front of Jael, moving forward with speed now, Aleksander keeping watch from behind.

CHAPTER FIFTY SIX

Ulf was on the ground, two Followers on top of him and then one fell forward, a blade through the back of his neck.

And he didn't get up.

Bram panted, drawing out his bloody sword, spinning at the sound of footsteps behind him, hoping that Ulf could help them finish off the final three men who appeared quite able to die now.

'Gant!' Ulf rasped as the bigger of the three crept around behind him, drawing a knife. 'Watch out!'

The Follower spun, flicking his knife at Ulf who was too surprised to move. Even more surprised when it lodged in his shoulder.

Mad too.

'Fuck!' Ulf roared, leaving the knife where it landed, charging forward with his sword. 'Kill them!' And he ran, screaming, his body vibrating with an anger he'd never experienced before. He thought of Bayla inside the hall, the children outside in the square, one-armed Berard who was struggling to see how he could help, and poor Derwa, dead on the steps.

He wasn't going to let them past.

Gant swung his sword with both hands, chopping off the still-hooded head of one man, while Bram who'd been knocked to the ground, stabbed his knife through the eye of another. And Ulf lunged, chopping his sword into the waist of the last Follower, throwing himself on top of his collapsed body, knife out, dragging it across his throat.

The four men staggered together, glancing around, scanning the garden, making sure that no one else was coming.

***

The worm was dead, but the vale was now under assault from flaming birds.

Berger was holding the Hestian army behind their shields, until a screech from Draguta urged him to engage. He lifted his sword, trying to make himself heard over the noise of the birds as he led his men forward.

Axl could hear him, but he didn't want to engage at all. He had to keep his remaining men alive, though they wouldn't be alive for long if they stood there, waiting to be attacked. 'Forward!' he yelled, trying to swallow. 'Move forward!'

Dragmall felt the warriors moving all around him as he crouched on the ground inside the tiny circle. He had tried two symbols already, but neither had worked, and he glanced at Ayla, hoping she had some ideas.

The birds swooped around the circle, wings flaming, long beaks jabbing the warriors who couldn't get their shields up in time. And through all the chaos and panic, a memory of a symbol flickered in Ayla's mind, immediately slipping out of reach as Astrid shrieked next to her, watching as two flaming birds barrelled towards their circle, shearing away at the last moment, unable to penetrate it.

Bruno screamed, and Ayla spun as he fell, gorged through the leg by a bird which drew back its beak, aiming for Bruno's chest. Ivaar was quickly there, butting his shield boss into the bird's head. It exploded in a ball of flames, knocking him over, singing his face. He shook his head, struggling back to his feet, aiming for the next bird who was coming for Bruno, stabbing it through the neck. He could feel the heat of flames surging towards him, and his attention drifted to Ayla who was shouting at her husband. He didn't hear the bird behind him until it was too late and the beak had punctured his back, severing his spine. He didn't even cry out as he collapsed to the ground, trying desperately to keep hold of his sword as the darkness came.

The Islander on Bruno's left caught fire as a hammer bird knocked him into Bruno, both of them falling to the ground. Bruno lifted his sword, trying to protect himself, but not in time as more birds dove towards him, one piercing its beak through his chest, another tearing a hole in his throat before they both flapped away.

'No!' Ayla cried, her heart stopping. 'Bruno! No!'

Dragmall's eyes were full of sympathy, but he had to get her attention before everyone was dead. 'We have to stop the birds! Ayla, we need a symbol now!'

Ayla heard the waves of chanting from the ridge, louder now, like the crashing boom of a waterfall, like the surge of grief and pain threatening to drown her. But Dragmall's presence grounded her, and the pressure of his squeezing hand woke up some small part of her, and the symbol flashed in front of her eyes, clearly now.

Slipping her hand out of Dragmall's, she unsheathed her knife, cutting across her palm.

***

Gant and Bram stood over the dead woman.

'Who is she?' Bram wondered, staring down at Dara Teros in her blood-soaked robe. 'Do you recognise her?'

Gant shook his head, flicking blood onto the ground. 'No. Perhaps a distraction? A way to get me out here so the Followers could attack me? I don't know. We need to get back to the hall, though. Leave Sybill. She can rot where she lies, but let's carry the woman inside. See if anyone recognises her.' He froze, remembering Sybill's daughter, Ontine, and hurrying towards the kitchen, he tapped Ulf on the shoulder. 'Help Bram with the woman. Berard, head inside and get someone to carry poor Derwa.'

Ulf nodded, stumbling towards Bram, who was reaching for Dara's legs.

Which twitched.

***

Axl couldn't see through the flames of his burning men. He couldn't hear anything but the screams of those who were dying, injured, on fire, collapsing around him.

And the smoke. It was choking them all.

The Hestians were struggling just as much, he could see. There was little incentive to move forward for either army now.

Thorgils was beside him. 'The birds are dying!' he shouted. 'Look!'

And Axl lifted his eyes to the sky as the birds exploded across the arena in bright balls of fire.

Draguta barely noticed. Her attention was on Eadmund who was running towards her, hiding behind that ridiculous shield like the true coward he was.

Another crushing disappointment.

And what use had Jaeger been? What use had any of them been?

That shield was keeping her from Jael Furyck, and Draguta knew that she had to get past it, so crouching down, she dug into another box, pulling out a dark piece of rope. Dipping it into her last bowl of potion, she swirled it in the liquid until it was thickly coated, wrapping it around her wrist. Standing with a smile, she reached out towards the viewing platform, blood splattering her white dress as she pointed at Esk. And curling her wrist around, Draguta released the hulking god from his prison, drawing him into the fight.

Fyr cawed loudly, and Jael turned to see Esk stomping across the arena, batting Hestian warriors out of the way as he strode towards Eadmund. 'Eadmund! Run! Move!'

But in a few strides, Esk was there, his long powerful arms shunting Eadmund to the ground. Jael ran towards them, slashing Toothpick at Esk, who ignored her, stone-faced, dead-eyed and determined to kill her husband.

Eadmund roared, rushing back to his feet, gritting his teeth as he brought the shield in front of his chest, sword tip poking over the rim, charging for the god who swung out an arm and knocked him away with such force that Eadmund lost his grip on his sword and the shield. He flew through the air, crashing to the ground with a thump.

Draguta smiled.

No Eadmund. No shield.

She turned to Jael Furyck, licking her red lips.

***

Gant stood on the edge of Edela's circle, not knowing what to do. Edela and Eydis were in a trance. Helping Jael. Helping Aleksander and Axl.

He didn't know what to do.

'Gant!' Gisila gasped, her eyes on his blood-soaked trousers, his cut face. 'What happened?'

Edela fell out of the trance, drawn back into the hall, peering at Gant. 'What happened?' she croaked, bending over, coughing, Ontine and Eydis blinking beside her.

'We need to help Jael and Eadmund!' Eydis panicked, reaching out in the darkness. 'Edela! We have to go back.' Then she froze.

She could smell blood.

***

Esk had Eadmund in his arms, and he raised him above his head, throwing him away as though he were a cloak.

'Eadmund!' Jael cried, watching him crash to the ground again. She waited a heartbeat, eyes flicking to Draguta and back to her husband who wasn't moving this time. 'Eadmund!'

He wasn't moving at all.

Draguta raised her arms, pointing them at Jael who hesitated, then ran, Toothpick in front of her, slashing from side to side, charging straight for the woman in white.

Aleksander ran past her, ahead of her, his shield up as Draguta slammed her hands forward, lightning shooting from her palms, sending bolts of fire straight through Aleksander's shield, into his chest.

'No!' Jael screamed, stumbling to a stop, watching as he fell before her. 'No!'

She turned to her right where Eadmund lay, his shield lost, and now Esk was turning, coming for her.

And Aleksander wasn't moving.

'No! No!' Pain burned holes in Jael's heart, and she couldn't think.

Fyr dove down from the swirling clouds, aiming for Esk.

Her son.

Esk was her son. And she flew low. Low and fast, piercing her beak straight through the back of his thick neck, flying away as he staggered to a stop, mouth yanked open in surprise, before dropping to the ground.

'Jael!'

It was her father's voice, waking her up, and she ran to Aleksander, throwing herself on top of him. 'No! Please! No!'

His eyes were open. They were open, but he was dead.

'No!' Jael's head dropped forward, tears flowing. 'Oh, please! Grandmother! Help me! Ayla! Help me! No!'

'Jael! Jael!'

It wasn't her father. It was Eadmund.

Eadmund was limping towards her, shield back in his hand, Esk lying dead on the ground behind him now.

But Jael didn't see him. All of her attention was on Aleksander, wanting to believe that there was some way to bring him back. She couldn't fight through the pain that was drowning her. She couldn't feel anything but the agony of loss as she lay there, holding him, willing him to wake up.

Draguta laughed, watching her.

Her enemy. Weak and broken now.

Pathetic, useless Jael Furyck.

Jael could hear her, and she dragged herself off Aleksander's body, tears blurring her eyes, her body shuddering with grief, Toothpick still in her hand.

'Jael! No!' Eadmund screamed, sensing that she was about to move, trying to run. He needed to reach her.

She needed the shield.

Draguta was enjoying herself now. 'You thought the gods knew how to kill me? You and your little sword? Your useless husband? Your pointless lover? Ha! Nothing can protect you from me and my book!' And she twisted her hands, lightning exploding, shooting forward.

'You fucking bitch!' Jael roared, watching the sparks surge towards her. Everything slowed down, blurring around her as she dragged Toothpick up in front of her chest.

And then bright shards of light exploded all around her, sending her flying through the air, head cracking onto the ground.

'Jael!' And Eadmund was bending over her, the shield protecting them both, teeth bared, trying to fight back the waves of pain. His sword was sheathed, his hand was out, reaching for her. 'We can't stop! It's too late now! We have to kill her! Come on!' His voice was strained with urgency, but looking down, his face fell. Jael's sword was broken.

Tears in her eyes, Jael stared up at him.

Aleksander was dead.

And Toothpick was gone.

***

'The Following?' Ontine looked horrified. 'What do you mean, The Following?' She kept turning, eyes blinking, looking from Edela to Eydis, then back to Gant. 'You killed her?' She shook her head, tears falling quickly. 'You killed my mother?'

Edela could hear Jael screaming; her grief like rain, falling over her. She could feel her own heart breaking, tears in her eyes. 'Gant, take Ontine. Hold her, I...' And she turned back to the fire, stumbling, trying to focus. 'Hurry, Eydis. Entorp, more herbs. Hurry.' She was sobbing as she creaked down to the floor. 'We must... hurry before it's too late. Jael needs us! She must finish this!'

***

Dara Teros woke to the puzzled looks of two old men who leaned over her, bearded mouths hanging open, swords in their hands. She jerked away from them, dazed, then everything came rushing back in an explosion of noise. 'I must see Edela! Hurry! Take me to Edela Saeveld!'

Bram eyed her suspiciously. 'You were dead.'

'Hurry!' Dara insisted, scrambling to her feet. 'I must stop her. Hurry!'

'Stop her?' Ulf looked confused, reaching out to grab Dara's arm. 'Why?'

***

'I can't!' Jael sobbed, on her knees, broken sword in her right hand. 'I can't!'

Panic and fear throbbed in Eadmund's chest. He saw the tears in Jael's eyes. He felt her broken heart. 'We'll do it together. We can kill her together. We have to, Jael. We have to!'

Jael stared at Eadmund, knowing that this was the end. She gripped Toothpick, trying not to think about Aleksander, feeling that cool moonstone against her palm as Eadmund bent forward to kiss her.

'We were meant for this,' he murmured, his lips against hers. 'We have to stop Draguta. I can get you to her. Come on!'

Looking up, Jael watched as Draguta pushed out her hands, twisting them around, readying a final attack. And dragging herself back to her feet, she could feel anger exploding inside her now; nothing but anger as she gripped her broken sword, blinking suddenly.

Toothpick's moonstone wasn't cool.

***

'No!' Dara burst into the hall, eyes on Edela who was kneeling before the fire. 'Stop! Edela! Jael can't kill Draguta! You must stop her!'

Ontine slid out of Gant's hold, running for the circle, throwing her arm around Edela's throat. 'No! You won't stop her! You can't stop her now! It's too late! Can't you feel it, Dara? You were too late!'

***

Eadmund rose, shield in front of Jael, who took one last look at

Aleksander's body, sucked in a ragged breath and ran for Draguta.

***

Eydis remained perfectly still, as though she stood in two places at once; hearing the thudding beat of Jael's heart as she charged towards Draguta; feeling the surging panic of Edela who had a knife at her throat. Eydis could see that. She was dreaming, she knew. Not really there. She could see Dara Teros whose eyes did not move but whose thoughts were suddenly loud.

And silently drawing her eating knife from its scabbard, Eydis turned, watching Entorp; seeing Gisila outside the circle, terror in her eyes; Gant, whose face was full of guilt and fear; and Dara who was showing her everything.

Lunging forward, Eydis stabbed her knife into Ontine's back.

Ontine spun, screaming, reaching for Eydis who stumbled backwards as Gant threw himself forward, sword through the back of her neck.

Dara ran for her, dropping to the ground. 'We have to stop Jael!' she yelled, pointing Eydis back to the fire. 'We have to stop her now!'

***

The Followers didn't even turn their heads as Eadmund and Jael ran for the ridge. In fact, they started to move, bit by bit, slowly creeping backwards.

Eadmund ran just ahead of Jael, on her left, holding the shield high. Draguta's lightning barbs sparked off its shining dome, and she screamed, needing something else. She needed something else.

She felt weak. Unable to think clearly. Drained.

The book. She needed her book.

And turning around to her table, she reached for the Book of Darkness, but it had gone.

Jael felt Draguta's confusion and panic as she spun, searching for her book, and she urged Eadmund on, hoping he could read her thoughts. He blinked and stopped, dropping the shield, holding it out. And Jael ran for it, leaping high into the air. Jumping onto the shield, she threw herself at Draguta who couldn't get her hands up in time. And as she flew through the air, Jael could hear someone yelling at her to stop.

But it was too late.

She had jammed the jagged end of Toothpick's broken blade straight through Draguta's chest, his moonstone pommel bursting into flames, exploding in a rush of heat and noise.

Eadmund flew backwards, slamming against the gravel. He couldn't see.

Everything had gone dark.

He couldn't see.

***

'Quick!'

There was no time. Her life's work. Her sole mission. All a cruel trick.

But there was no time.

'There will be something we can do.' It sounded like a wish.

It was a wish.

Edela was confused. 'I don't understand. Dara? What has happened? Why didn't you want Jael to kill Draguta?' She looked around as everything became dark.

It was barely dusk, let alone night.

Gant looked up at the smoke hole. At the pitch-black sky.

There was no moon. No light up there at all.

***

'What's happening?' Fyn had stumbled down the mountain of rubble and found his way back to the Brekkans, to where Axl crouched behind a huddle of battered shields. The armies had drawn away from each other, waiting, unsure what was happening. The sudden darkness was disconcerting. Odd. The only light was coming from Ayla's tiny fire and the flaming piles of sea-fire burning around the dead where-worm.

Ayla shivered, desperate to go to Bruno, but Dragmall had hold of her arm, and he was pointing at the grassy ridge.

'Jael!'

Jael could hear Eadmund as she leaned over Draguta's body, dragging out her broken sword. Toothpick's flaming pommel was extinguished now; a grey void.

And Draguta?

'I warned you.'

Jael froze.

'If you made this journey, Jael, I said you wouldn't come back.'

Jael fell backwards as the black cloud consumed Draguta's white sheathed body. Twisting like smoke seeking an escape through the thatch, it rose into the darkness, turning into something.

Into someone.

'No!' And scrambling back to her feet, Jael blinked. 'No!'

Eadmund hurried to her. 'What. Is. That?' He still gripped the shield, though he could feel his arm shaking, suddenly cold all over.

'Raemus,' came the voice behind them.

And turning around, Jael saw Daala standing there in her human form.

'That is Raemus.'

CHAPTER FIFTY SEVEN

'How?' Edela couldn't understand it.

Dara's face was ashen. 'Raemus was in the Dolma, where Daala sent him when she killed him. There is no real death in the realm of the gods. Only the Dolma. The soul prison. But when Draguta was raised...' Dara shook her head, unable to believe that she had never seen it coming. Not until it was too late. And now it was too late. 'When Draguta was raised, Raemus came along. I had a dream. I saw it all.'

'He was inside Draguta?' Biddy's eyes were wide.

Dara nodded.

Edela shook her head. 'But she's dead now. Dead.'

'Oh, yes. Jael's sword, it was all a trick. The Following made it so. That moonstone hid a flame. A flame from the Fire of Light. And that flame brought Raemus back. Raemus and the Darkness. It is coming. Can you feel it?'

Eydis nodded. 'I can.'

Dara peered at her. 'Eydis, can you see?'

Eydis nodded again.

Dara grabbed her, pulling her forward, barely breathing. 'Hold my hand now. Edela, come and join us. I will cast a new circle. One to protect us all.' She glanced at Entorp, who still held his drum. 'We need a bigger fire! And Biddy.' She felt as though she knew them all. 'More herbs. And blood! I need a lot of blood! Hurry now! We must hurry!'

***

'Go.' Daala's voice was like stone. 'You cannot stop him, Jael.'

'And nor can you.'

They all turned to the right as Briggit Halvardar emerged from the darkness. 'None of you can.'

Jael stepped back as the man walked forward.

Not a man, she reminded herself. A god.

The God of Darkness. Father of Magic. He who was the first.

The sky felt as though it was suffocating them with its bleak heaviness, and she was struggling to breathe. It felt as though the air was slowly being drawn away from them, and turning to Eadmund, Jael could see his chest heaving. She looked past him to the dark shape that was Aleksander, and her heart broke again.

Raemus laughed, feeling her pain.

He was taller than Eadmund; bigger than Jaeger. Short black hair, a chiselled jaw, eyes like the night, teeth as bright as moonbeams, and Jael could sense the cold determination in Daala's body as she strode past them to meet him.

'And who is this creature to you?' Daala spat, glaring at Briggit. 'Another of your loyal pets?'

'This?' And putting his hand out for Briggit, Raemus brought the tiny queen towards him, bending down to kiss her smiling mouth. 'This creature is my most loyal Follower of all. The one I chose to help me. She opened the circle, and now I am free, so I shall reward her by making her my wife.'

Daala felt surprised. Surprised that she cared.

'You thought you were the only one?' Raemus laughed. 'You think I pined for you? After you killed me, Daala? Imprisoned me in the Dolma?'

Jael watched him, needing a plan. Her eyes were up, sensing something moving, and there, from out of the shadows came Meena Gallas, clutching the Book of Darkness to her chest, a hooded Follower dragging her towards Raemus, knife at her throat.

'Ahhh, my book! My book!' And reaching out, Raemus

snatched it out of Meena's trembling hands, eyeing her with distaste. 'I should kill you now, but you took it from Draguta at the perfect moment. Weakened her for me. Perhaps I should reward you for such a fine act of service? Make you a Follower?'

Meena closed her eyes, waiting for the punishment that was surely coming. But it didn't, and she opened one eye, peering at Jael and Eadmund and the goddess who stood before her.

Daala's eyes moved from the book to Briggit. 'You have chosen a new wife. You have your book.' She swept her arm around the vale. 'Your Darkness is coming! And then what?'

'You are right, my love, I do have everything. And no need for any of you!'

His voice was like the blood-curdling growl of a monster from her nightmares, and Jael closed her eyes, gripping her sun necklace – the one that Fyn had carved for her – trying to find her grandmother.

She stepped away from Daala, reaching for Eadmund's hand.

Eydis watched them.

Amidst the crushing fear and terrifying darkness in the vale, she could see Eadmund as he stood beside Jael, holding her hand. And she felt the warmth of happiness flood her body. She had saved him. Freed him.

After all these years, he was finally free.

And though Dara and Edela were with her, sitting in the dreamer circle, holding her hands, she knew that this was her path now, and she had to walk it alone.

For the Darkness was here.

And she could see.

And what Eydis could see most clearly of all was the Book of Darkness as Raemus placed it on the table before turning back to Jael.

Raemus watched Jael's eyes blinking in the glow of the flames that were slowly burning down as the air was sucked out of the vale. He peered at her until she felt as though she wanted to crawl into a ball and roll away from him. 'You will die, Jael Furyck. Soon all of you will die. That is the way of the Darkness. Can you feel it? Your burning lungs? The loss of all hope?' He laughed, feeling his power growing as the Darkness intensified around them. 'We gods do not breathe as you do. We do not eat or drink. We do not even sleep. But we do love. And we do need. And we do seek revenge.' His voice changed, and it was deeper, colder, as he reached out for Daala, who twisted around, turning back into Fyr, disappearing into the dark sky.

Raemus laughed. 'My wife was once so interested in saving her humans. Far too busy saving them to spend any time with me. Apparently that no longer holds true.' And he ran a hand down Briggit's ecstatic face. 'How well you have done, my love. How patiently you and your kind have awaited my return. How much you have sacrificed and lost for this moment. For me.'

Thunder crashed overhead, but Raemus barely blinked knowing that there was nothing the gods could do to stop him. He spun around, eyes on his loyal circle of Followers, and he stepped towards them, arms out, a smile stretching across his handsome face. They had helped bring him back to his rightful place.

And now?

Now he had everything he wanted.

Jael had the strongest image of Tig collapsing to the ground; of horses staggering in the shadows, falling with him. They couldn't breathe. In this heavy, airless darkness, none of them could breathe. She heard the rustling boots of warriors from both sides of the arena, shields banging as they stumbled against each other, weapons clattering to the ground. Jael tried to think, but she was dizzy, struggling to stand, and she swayed against Eadmund, who was barely standing himself.

Fyr flew above their heads, swooping low, making a circle, flapping her broad wings, creating a breeze, a cool, swirling breeze. And for a moment, Jael's head cleared.

Raemus didn't care what Daala was doing.

Delaying the inevitable?

He felt the relief of finally being freed from Draguta's body. Of no longer having to suffer that ridiculous woman's whims and her insufferable vanity. The joy of being reunited with his Followers was freeing. And holding out his hands, he started chanting, his voice a bone-rattling growl, watching the eyes of the dreamers as one by one they dropped to the grass.

Dead.

***

'What is happening?' Bayla gripped Ulf's hand, panic in her eyes. 'I can't breathe!'

'Gant?' Gisila wanted to sob, but her chest wouldn't move, her eyes wouldn't fill with tears. 'Gant...'

He was struggling to keep his own eyes open as the air thinned, as the effort to draw a breath became too much. He held Gisila close, knowing that whatever happened, they would never be apart again.

Gisila lay her head on his chest, watching Entorp who was still attempting to keep a steady rhythm on the drum, his eyes closed. She saw Edela and Eydis and Dara Teros who sat before the shrinking flames holding hands. 'Mother...' Gisila stretched out her hand, leaving it there as she passed out.

***

Eadmund leaned on the shield, feeling the strain of taking a breath, trying to focus on the cool air the raven was stirring, needing to stay alert. He felt Jael's body shuddering against his, and, for a moment, he was calm. Death, when it came, would mean being with her. He gripped her hand, squeezing it, feeling her body fighting to stay upright.

Raemus turned to Briggit. 'And you? Are you ready to die for me?'

Briggit could feel her body weakening as the air became thinner, but it was pulsing with need. For Raemus. For the eternal darkness he had promised her all those nights he had come into her dreams. 'Yes,' she breathed, head back, waiting for his kiss. And he bent down to her, pressing his smooth lips to hers, holding them over her mouth as she squirmed and wriggled, fighting for air, finally going limp in his arms.

And gently lying her tiny body down on the grass, Raemus straightened up. 'I was patient, Daala!' he cried, admiring the beauty of the Darkness. 'I waited for you. I wanted you! None of this.' And he swept his arms around the vale. 'None of this had to happen. If you had stayed with me as you always promised you would, none of this had to happen!'

Fyr swooped down towards him, ready to attack, but Raemus spun, snapping his fingers and the raven's neck broke, the bird dropping to the ground with a thud.

Eydis watched.

Hidden by Dara's symbols, she walked forward, Dara's voice a soft hum in her ears, urging her on.

The prophecy was a lie, Eydis. A trick.

What The Following wanted it to be.

Though, perhaps not all of it.

The son. The daughter.

They killed Draguta with the sword and shield as I saw they would.

But the third weapon...

I once had a dream, Eydis. The most powerful dream I ever experienced.

And in that dream, I saw you.

The son, the daughter, and the light.

You are the light, Eydis.

You are the light.

CHAPTER FIFTY EIGHT

No Follower was stirring. Not even Briggit Halvardar.

Eydis wondered if they ever would again.

Another promise? Another trick?

She didn't know.

Raemus dropped to his knees, scooping the dead raven into his hands, and as he did so, Fyr turned back into Daala, and he was carrying his wife's body away from the edge of the ridge, laying her on the patch of grass Draguta had been standing on only moments before.

'I only wanted you,' Raemus breathed, running his hand over Daala's shimmering white hair. 'You and this beautiful, perfect Darkness. Ours. Together.' He spun around suddenly, sensing movement, but no one was there, just the spark of a dying fire, the last breaths of a pointless human. 'I will make you again. Return you to me. I can. I can. And you will love me. Want only me. You will see.' And placing his lips on Daala's, Raemus breathed into her mouth.

Eydis could feel her heart beating so violently that she feared Raemus would turn around again and see her. She glanced back at him, but he was still bent over Daala, and as she turned, she stumbled, tripping on a rock, twisting her ankle.

Raemus straightened up now, frowning, searching the darkness, eyes seeking an answer. Something was out there. Someone. He stuck out a hand, wanting to feel whatever it was, to draw it to him, but he couldn't.

He couldn't find anyone.

Eydis could hear Dara.

You are the light, Eydis. You are the light.

And reaching out, she stepped towards the table, placing her hands on the Book of Darkness, screaming as light exploded from the pages, surging through her body, lifting her off the ground.

'No!' Raemus roared, lunging for the book, but the force and heat of the light pushed him backwards, and he couldn't get to Eydis or the book as they ignited before him. And then Daala was there, behind him. 'Thank you, Eydis,' she breathed, slamming her hands onto Raemus' back, knocking him into the column of light as the book caught fire, vellum crackling in the darkness, flames shooting up into the black sky.

And suddenly they could breathe, and Jael's head was up, watching the burning tower of light and Eydis in the middle of it all.

'Eydis!' Eadmund was on his feet, running for her. 'Eydis! Eydis! No!'

He could hear her.

And she was saying goodbye.

'Eydis!' Jael was beside him, and she could see Eydis disappearing now. 'Eydis!' She held out her hand, but there was nothing she could do.

'Little Thing! No!' Eadmund screamed, running for her, but the light shot up into the sky, taking Eydis with it.

***

Edela opened her eyes, turning to look down at her hand.

The hand that was holding Eydis'.

But Eydis wasn't there.

'No!' she sobbed, horrified eyes on Dara Teros who had

blinked hers open. 'No! Not Eydis! No!'

Biddy ran to her, frantic. 'Where is she? Edela? Where did she go? Eydis? Eydis!'

***

The light was golden.

The sun had returned, bathing them in a bright, warm, comforting light.

Or perhaps that was Eydis?

Jael turned away from Eadmund as he reached for Thorgils who had hurried forward; both of them in shock, neither understanding what had happened. She walked slowly towards Aleksander, still lying where he'd fallen, trying to save her life.

He had saved it.

She was still here.

Draguta was dead. And Raemus.

And she was still here.

'Oh,' Jael sobbed, falling to her knees, dropping forward, her arms around his still body, laying her chest on his. 'Oh, please. Please come back! Come back to me!' Her tears fell like rain, a lifetime of memories washing over her: that night in Tuura; their cottage: training; his face.

That face.

'Aleksander! Please. No!' She stopped suddenly, looking up, tears running down her cheeks, and she saw him.

With her father. With his father.

All of them, with Vidar.

And he was smiling.

Eadmund was there, and Jael blinked, struggling back to her feet. 'Eydis,' she sobbed. 'I should have saved Eydis. And Aleksander. And...'

'Ssshhh.' Eadmund held her gently, feeling her flinch. 'Ssshhh.

Eydis needed to save us, didn't she?' he tried to convince them both. 'And Aleksander... he would have wanted to die for you, I know that.' Eadmund pulled back, staring at her. 'I know that because I would have. I would have died for you, Jael.' He shook his head, pulling her close again, tears flowing. 'I'm so sorry for all of this. For everything. I'm so sorry.'

'No!'

Jael pushed herself out of Eadmund's arms, turning to Axl who was staring down at Aleksander in horror; to Fyn who ran for Thorgils, wanting to know what had happened to Eydis.

'Where is she? Where is she?'

'But why can't she bring them back?' Axl cried. 'Daala? Why? Why can't she bring them back?'

Jael shook her head, wrapping her arms around her brother, her face wet against his shoulder.

She didn't have an answer.

***

Gant held Gisila as she cried. Edela was there on his other side, too stunned to speak.

She couldn't understand what had happened.

'It should have been me,' Edela said, at last, thinking about Eydis, trying not to think about Aleksander. 'Why wasn't it me?' she asked Dara who sat on the bench beside her.

Dara held her shaking hand, squeezing gently. 'We are all born with a purpose, Edela. You know that. I had mine, you had yours, and Eydis... it was always in her. Her gift. Her vision. This was her purpose. She was always meant to be a light in the darkness.'

Biddy bent down before them. She had released the puppies from Jael's bedchamber, and they were licking the tears from her face. Entorp was there, bending down to her, tears in his eyes, wrapping an arm around her shoulder.

Edela looked up to see Hanna approaching with Berard.

And her heart burst with pain, seeing the question in her eyes.

Gisila noticed. 'Mother?' She pushed herself away from Gant. 'What is it?' she panicked, gripping her throat. 'What is it?'

Edela stood, lips wobbling, trying to gather herself together as she walked towards Hanna who suddenly froze, her face falling. 'I am so sorry, my dear.'

'No!' Gisila cried out, eyes full of horror, grabbing Gant. 'No!'

Gant was too stunned to move. 'Aleksander? Edela? No, no, not Aleksander. Please!'

Hanna turned and fell towards Berard, sobbing.

Edela was shaking too much to walk, and she couldn't see where to go if she'd wanted to. Gant stood quickly, grabbing her before she fell. 'He saved Jael,' Edela cried into his chest. 'Aleksander died saving Jael.'

Gant nodded, trying not to feel anything as Gisila joined them, arms around him. 'Not Aleksander,' he sobbed. 'No!'

***

Fyn was beside himself, and needing to comfort him stopped Jael from completely falling apart. And that made her realise that she had more than herself to think about. Turning around, she rubbed her eyes, trying to stop her tears, scanning the carnage in the vale: gaping craters, giant boulders, pieces of where-worm, dead bodies everywhere.

Trying not to look at Aleksander, and ignoring the rolling waves of grief for Eydis, Jael walked towards Daala who she could sense was waiting to talk to her.

'I am sorry for your losses,' Daala murmured, sadness in her grey eyes as she reached for Jael's hands.

'And yours,' Jael said, eyes on the body of Esk, lying where Fyr had stabbed him through the neck.

Daala nodded. 'This beautiful world is a gift we must all be prepared to sacrifice for. Though, I hope, not for a long time yet.' And spinning away, she turned back into Fyr, white eye blinking at Jael before taking to the air, soaring into the golden sky towards the wall of rubble, flying straight through it.

And, as Jael watched, the fallen boulders and rocks exploded, turning into bright light, and then disappearing entirely.

A cheer went up as Beorn and the Islanders on the other side of the wall rushed forward before staggering to a stop, confronted with the horrific mess Draguta and her creatures had wrought.

They moved forward quickly, seeing what they could do to help as the cries of the injured rose around them.

'That's it, then?' Karsten rasped, limping forward, leaning on Thorgils, his face a bloody pulp, his legs wobbling. 'No more Draguta?' He'd wiped the blood out of his mashed eye, though he was struggling to see.

Jael nodded. 'I think it is, yes. No more Book of Darkness either.' And she burst into tears again, remembering Eydis.

Eydis who had saved them all.

Karsten looked away to where a very awkward figure stood, shaking all over. 'Meena!' Thorgils helped him hobble towards her. 'Meena!' And happy to see that she was still alive, he wrapped a bloody arm around her.

Meena didn't know what to think, but Jaeger was dead, and there was no more Draguta. Morana was gone, the Book of Darkness, Evaine and Briggit Halvardar too. She shivered all over as Karsten stepped back, looking at her with a lop-sided grin.

'What do you think, then? Would you like to go home?'

***

Edela felt numb.

Voices in the hall echoed around her, getting louder as night fell; as the shock abated and the realisation that they were free from the terror sunk in. Fires burned, the smell of food wafting from the kitchen, the hall slowly getting put back together.

Edela looked down at the cup of ale Biddy had brought her.

'It might help.'

They both doubted that was true.

'My heart is in pieces, Biddy,' Edela admitted. 'I'm not sure it will ever be whole again.' She closed her eyes, not wanting to cry any more, but in her mind she saw her trip to Tuura with Aleksander; him cooking for her, crying with her, smiling at her; his arms around her when he was eleven; growing taller and taller until he was towering over her.

Saying goodbye.

'No,' Biddy sniffed. 'It won't be. It can't be. I feel as though I've lost a child.' Reaching out, she held Edela's hand. 'And poor Eydis... she was just a girl. A sweet, sweet girl. Why? Why her?'

'Eydis loved her brother. She loved Jael. She wouldn't be sad to think that she'd saved them,' Edela realised, turning to Biddy with a sad smile. 'Would she?'

Biddy shook her head. 'No, she wouldn't. She was strong. Brave.'

'She was. They both were.'

'And so were you. All that you did, Edela?' Biddy grabbed her own cup, desperate to feel some moisture in her throat. 'You kept us safe.'

'I'm not sure that's true. What about Sybill? Ontine?' Edela frowned. 'I didn't act. I knew something was wrong, but I was too slow to act.'

'We all were,' Gant agreed, filling his cup before sitting down opposite them, his eyes on Isaura who sat with Gisila, head in her hands, struggling, like they all were. 'Entorp said the Followers masked themselves from us. Perhaps there are more here that we don't know about?' He lowered his voice, glancing around. 'But how will we ever tell?'

Edela shrugged. 'I'm not sure. Though their book is gone, and so is their master. I would think it doesn't matter anymore. There's no way back for them now. No way back to the Darkness.'

Gant lifted his cup and stood, watching the men and women gather around the tables which had been dragged back into the hall. Most had cups in their hands, and they turned expectantly to him. 'To Aleksander!' he began, his voice breaking. Stopping, he caught Gisila's eyes, filled with tears, just like his own. 'And Eydis!' He tried to keep going, but he couldn't. His head dropped, and he shook it, unable to speak.

Bram was there, his eyes on Hanna who sat silently in a corner with Berard, still in shock. He held his cup aloft as he stood, grimacing at the pain in his chest. 'Those who have died today, died for all of us. A death we'd all happily sacrifice in turn. So we will keep their memories alive in this hall, and in every hall around Osterland and beyond!' He stumbled, thinking about Eydis. About Eirik who had loved that little girl so much. Tears came, and he bit his teeth together, trying to keep going. 'We'll never forget them. Never forget what they did for us.'

Silence. Heads nodding. Tears falling.

The fire crackled and popped, the puppies crawling under the table, licking Biddy's boots, hoping for crumbs.

***

There was no body to cry over, to touch and hold one last time. To lie on a pyre and honour with gifts for her final journey.

Eadmund hung his head, standing in the place he'd last seen his little sister, Thorgils by his side. 'I want to say goodbye,' he cried. 'For all this time, I was so far away from her. Bound to Evaine. To Draguta. So far away. And now I'm here, free, and I can't show her. I can't see her. She can't see me!'

Thorgils rubbed his grainy eyes. 'Eydis loved you so much. She would've felt proud to have saved you. To have saved all of us. The bravest Skalleson of all.'

Eadmund closed his eyes, the loss of Eydis digging a hole deep inside him. He opened them, turning to Thorgils. 'I'm sorry,' he said, nervous now. 'I left you for dead.'

Thorgils' face fell. 'You did. But I'm not dead. Not like that weakling Torstan Berg.' Tears filled his eyes, and he sighed.

Eadmund frowned, spinning around, realising that he hadn't seen him; he hadn't seen many of his friends. 'What happened?'

'I killed him,' Thorgils sniffed. 'There was this fog. It made us think things, see things that weren't there. We fought each other. I...' He banged his hands against his head. 'I killed him! I killed him!'

Eadmund was too shocked to speak. He reached out a hand, placing it on Thorgils' shoulder. 'Do you forgive me?'

Thorgils looked confused.

'Do you blame me? For what I did to you in Hallow Wood?'

'Well...'

Eadmund frowned.

'No, I don't,' Thorgils said, trying to smile. 'Of course I don't.'

'Then what do you think Torstan is doing now? Up in Vidar's Hall? Telling the tale of it to Aleksander no doubt, deciding who had the most fame-worthy death.'

'Or Ivaar.'

Eadmund froze, spinning around to Ayla.

'Ivaar's dead?'

She nodded sadly. 'I wanted you to know, Eadmund. He tried to save Bruno. I saw him. He tried, but he couldn't.' She burst into tears, thinking about her husband. About Eydis. It was too hard to imagine what had happened, though she could feel Eydis all around her and it was a warm, comforting feeling, even as night settled in.

Eadmund pulled Ayla into his arms, feeling her body shudder against his; not sure how he felt about the loss of his brother at all. His eyes drifted to where Jael stood with Axl, Karsten, and Meena, wanting to go to her but feeling oddly shy. She felt so far away, and after all this time, he didn't know if she wanted him anywhere near her.

'I'll send a ship for my family,' Karsten said, blinking his eye open, trying to see Jael. He needed to lie down. Everything was throbbing, and he thought he might be sick. 'I think I'll have a ship to send. You did burn my fleet.'

Jael didn't answer. She wanted to go back to Aleksander.

To be with him before...

'You have an enormous fleet,' Meena told him. 'Draguta brought the Helsaboran fleet to Hest.'

Now Karsten's eye did pop open. He turned, blinking at the scattered mess of Hestian warriors, none of them knowing what to do; bleeding, singed, dusty, but mostly confused, eyeing the Brekkans who were busy attending to their wounded, seeing to their dead. He nodded at Rork, who smiled back, half his face flapping open, but working too hard carrying his wounded men towards Astrid and Dragmall to notice.

Axl needed to go and help him, but not until he knew that Amma was alright. 'You're sure?' he asked Meena. 'Sure she's safe in Hest?'

Meena nodded. 'She was. Jaeger raped her,' she almost whispered. 'I am sorry. But Eadmund stopped him. He saved her. And me.' She smiled at Eadmund as he approached, his eyes on Jael.

'Who knew?' Karsten stared at the bushy-haired woman who seemed less timid than when he'd last seen her. Taller even. And no longer tapping her head. 'We've all come a long way since that night leaving Hest, haven't we?' And he looked at Jael. 'Thanks to you.'

Jael shook off the compliment, watching Fyn walk towards her with Soren, both of them carrying Raymon in their arms. She hurried to her brother as they laid him on the ground, relieved to see that his injuries didn't appear too serious, though with all those arrows sticking out of him, it was no wonder he looked pale, his eyes struggling to focus on her at all. He had lost a lot of men, just as they had lost a lot of men. And her heart twisted again, thinking about Aleksander. She swallowed. 'Ayla, will you look at Raymon? We need to get those arrows out.' Her eyes were darting around as Rexon approached.

Ayla nodded. She wanted to fall to the ground and sob, but she bit her teeth together, and rolled back her sleeves, lifting her eyes to try and find Astrid and Dragmall.

'Jael,' Rexon croaked, trying to get her attention. 'We're piling the bodies for a pyre. Beorn suggested we use sea-fire. There's plenty left. What do you think?' He thought of Aleksander, his eyes on Jael who suddenly looked as though she was ready to run.

She shook her head. 'I...' And then she turned and walked away.

Far away from all of them.

***

They were in Jael's chamber.

Edela had been surprised when Dara knocked on the door, curious as to what she wanted, but before Dara could speak, Edela knew, and the thought of it quickly pushed her down onto the bed. 'Dara, I...'

Dara smiled. 'I am old, Edela. You know how that feels. Imagine being over three hundred years old? Imagine watching your children, your grandchildren, everyone you've ever loved and cared about die? I am ready. Past ready.'

'Are you sure there's nothing more that you're meant to do? You have so much knowledge, Dara. What will happen when you're gone? When you're not there to help anyone?'

Dara sat on the bed beside her. 'They will have you, won't they? You and Jael, and one day, her daughter.'

Edela's head was up. 'Jael will have another daughter?'

'Oh yes, she will. And she will be a dreamer too. I have seen that. I have seen so many things, Edela, and my time is done. Draguta is gone. Raemus too. There is nothing for me to do. No need for me to keep living.'

'But how? How can I kill you? Sybill thought she had.'

Dara scowled, instantly angry. 'Yes, she did, didn't she, that horrible rodent, but don't you worry, I have a symbol, a spell.'

'Of course you do,' Edela smiled sadly, watching as Dara pulled a tiny scroll from her purse.

'This symbol will break the curse Draguta put on me all those years ago. If you think you can do it?'

Edela took the scroll with a heavy heart.

'I can.'

***

'I can't.' Jael didn't turn around. 'I can't.'

Eadmund reached out, his hands on her shoulders.

She flinched, moving further away. 'I can't say goodbye. I can't leave him here. I can't burn him.' Eadmund didn't say anything and she turned around, confused. He was here, back at last, and all she could think about was Aleksander. 'I...'

'You love him.'

Jael nodded. 'I do. Always. Always. He... I... I can't say goodbye.' Her eyes filled with tears, and they fell down her face.

Eadmund lifted a hand to wipe them away. 'I'm sorry. For you. For what I did to you. For Aleksander and Eydis. I'm so sorry, Jael.'

And she pushed herself forward, into his arms, remembering the feel of him, the smell, the warmth. Resting her head against his cheek, she saw images of Oss: the Pit; Ketil's; Tig and Leada; Eirik on his throne, Eydis sitting beside him; the puppies disappearing into the snow.

The cold.

Her cloak.

'I want to go home,' she breathed, closing her eyes, feeling his arms enclosing her, trying to ignore the ache of her broken ribs. 'I want to go home with you.'

CHAPTER FIFTY NINE

There was no one to tell Amma what was happening.

There had been no one to talk to at all, apart from Sitha and Tanja. Sitha had cared for her and Tanja had kept her company, and though Amma appreciated it, it did not make time go any faster while she waited to see who would return.

And when.

Her routine had been the same every day. After forcing down her breakfast, she wandered down to the harbour, watching the builders scrambling about, constructing the piers. Then she would walk past the ship sheds and the stables, out to the coves. Sometimes, she would take a quick swim. And then, refreshed, she would return to the castle, tired now, with a heavy heart.

Alone.

Until that one day when she wasn't.

Standing on the castle steps, already starting to feel too warm, Amma turned back to the harbour. She had never paid much attention to the ships as they came and went, but there was something about the ship that was being tied to the pier that captured her attention.

The children.

She could hear children.

And turning all the way around, she started walking across the square, hurrying now, her breath caught in her chest, worrying and panicking.

And hoping.

'Amma!' Berard's hand was in the air as she ran towards him. 'Amma!'

She stumbled to a stop, her eyes darting to a bedraggled looking Bayla Dragos who stood beside her son, and to Ulf and Hanna and the children who clustered around them all, tired eyes on the big castle in the distance.

Amma didn't know what to say.

'Edela told us everything,' Berard smiled, though he could feel tears coming as he stared up at the castle, thinking about his father and Haegen. About Irenna and Nicolene. 'So we came home.'

Bayla strode past them, ignoring her own tears, wanting to get inside. The smell of vomit and seawater clung to her, and she was desperate for a goblet of wine.

Wine in a goblet!

She almost fell down at the thought of it.

Ulf stood by Hanna who felt like turning around and hopping back on the ship. She didn't want to be in Hest, though she was working hard not to feel anything at all. She would just put one foot after the other. Concentrate on caring for the children. Not think. Not feel. Just be useful.

Bayla spun around, nose in the air, eyes sweeping her dishevelled-looking family. 'Well? Aren't you coming?' The children ran past her and Berard ushered Amma and Hanna forward, but Ulf didn't move.

He stared at her before looking down at his wet boots and the ragged trousers he'd worn for more years than he could remember.

Then he turned back to the ship.

Bayla pushed back her shoulders and strode after him. 'You aren't coming?' Her eyes were sharp, searching his face as it turned towards hers. A face that with a good scrub and some time spent with a comb would not be a bad face to look at.

Ulf squirmed. 'In there?' He pointed to the castle. 'With you?'

Bayla swung back to stare at the castle, almost seeing Haaron bellowing from the steps at their four sons, barking at slaves and glowering at her. She had loved him once, but they had not been happy.

And life, Bayla had discovered, was short.

Too short to waste any time.

'Yes. With me.' She bit her lip, which quivered. 'Why not? The children like you well enough. Berard too. And I'm sure Karsten could use a man like you when he returns.'

Ulf frowned, his boots stuck to the cobblestones. 'And you?' he mumbled. 'What about you?'

'Me?' Bayla froze, tears in her eyes. 'I'm sure I could find some use for you.' And she reached out, touching his hand.

Ulf grabbed it and didn't let go, even as he could feel Bayla start to pull away. He squeezed it tightly and stepped forward, slipping it through his arm as he headed for the castle beside her, shaking his head.

***

Despite the unexpected pleasure of having the Dragos' in the castle, Amma missed Andala, and she was desperate to see Axl again.

She needed to go home.

Berard could tell, and leaving Bayla to bark at the servants and the children to show Hanna and Ulf around, he took her for a walk.

'I still don't understand,' Amma cried as they headed past the stables, listening as he told her the story of what had happened in the vale. 'How could Eydis have disappeared like that? How?'

'I don't know. But Edela said that it was meant to be. That it was her purpose. And Eydis was very determined. Very stubborn. I can't think she'd feel sad.'

'No, she loved Eadmund more than anything.' Amma thought of Aleksander who had loved Jael more than anything too. Andala would not be the same without him. Nor would Axl. Aleksander had always been a big brother to him.

She felt sad and lost as she walked beside Berard, not noticing that his head was up, listening.

The sound was like a storm approaching, and Berard frowned, his eyes drifting to the clouds, which were dull and grey but did not appear to portend a storm. And then he realised that it did not sound like a storm at all, but the thundering of horses coming down the road.

Amma froze, holding her hands to her mouth.

The first horse carried Karsten Dragos. Amma recognised his eye patch, and though her hopes lifted, she did not dare give in to them until she saw that Axl was riding just behind him.

Axl.

Axl was there.

Axl was here!

And running towards him as he slid from his horse, limping and hobbling towards her, she launched herself into his arms.

'Amma!' Axl was trying not to squeeze her, though he very much wanted to. 'Amma!'

She pulled away, looking him over. 'Are you hurt? Are you injured?'

He shook his head, his eyes moving from her face to her bump. He could see it. And then he could see her fear as she backed away. 'He's dead,' Axl said quickly. 'Jael killed him. He's dead. Jaeger's dead.'

Amma shuddered, unable to look at him, remembering the feel of Jaeger's rough hands, his tongue in her mouth, the pain of what he had done to her. More tears ran down her cheeks. 'I'm sorry!' she cried. 'I'm so sorry!'

'For what?' Axl was incredulous. 'For being raped?' He tilted her chin, wanting to make her focus on him. 'Never apologise for what he did to you. Never.'

Amma lifted her eyes, staring into his. 'But the baby?'

'Is mine.' Axl said it without even thinking, but he meant it. 'He's mine. A Furyck. Isn't that right, Karsten?'

Karsten had been unable to stop staring at the castle in the distance, knowing that there was no father to snarl at him anymore. No Haegen or Irenna, no Jaeger or Nicolene. But there was a dragon throne, and he would sit upon it and rule the kingdom with Berard. Berard who was standing before him with tears in his eyes. 'Brother!' Karsten struggled forward, throwing his arms around him.

'Are you alright?' Berard mumbled into his shoulder. 'You don't look alright.'

Karsten stepped away, staring at him through his mashed eye. 'Oh, you think I look bad, you should see Jaeger!' He grinned, and it hurt. Everything hurt. It felt as though his brother had smashed every bone in his face.

But Berard didn't hear him because all of his attention was suddenly on Meena, who was struggling down from her little round pony.

She stumbled nervously, righting herself as she peered at him through her wild bush of hair, blinking, tears coming.

And Berard stepped towards her, forgetting all about the arm he didn't have as he pulled her close. 'You did it,' he whispered, feeling her body shudder as she wept on his shoulder. 'You did it, Meena. And now you're home. With me.'

Meena was surprised by how pleasant it felt to be held by him.

To be comforted.

To be loved.

'We all did,' she sniffed, stepping back now, wiping her eyes, worried about how terrible she smelled after all those days on her pony, trekking back from the vale. 'We all did.' And she blinked at Karsten, Axl, and Amma before leaning forward again, wanting to feel Berard's embrace.

And when his arm was around her back, she closed her eyes, sinking into him.

Home.

She was home.

And for the first time in her life, Meena Gallas felt safe.

***

The scorched valley was an unwelcome surprise. Every blade of grass was brown, every tree like a stick of charcoal marking where the forest had been.

'It's going to take some time to put this place back together,' Eadmund said, his eyes on the gates in the distance.

Jael rode beside him, her chest tightening as they edged closer to the fort.

'Are you alright?' Eadmund wondered, peering at her.

It had been a long ride home, though Jael had appreciated the time to think. To grieve. She could see Aleksander's pyre in her mind, remembering the feeling of letting him go, though she doubted she ever truly would.

Part of her heart would always belong to him. And she knew him.

He would never leave her.

Jael nodded. 'I'm not looking forward to seeing everyone.'

'You're not?' Eadmund was surprised, though he felt much the same. It was hard to return with such enormous losses.

The Brekkans had suffered badly, losing nearly a third of their army. The Islanders and Alekkans had fared better, as had the Iskavallans. They had lost many of their archers, but not their king, who despite being riddled with holes had survived his first battle. Raymon had been too weak to even sit up when they'd departed the vale, though, and he was returning to his wife in a wagon.

Jael sighed, remembering the enormous pyres they had built.

The smell of all those burning bodies.

She blinked as Ido and Vella raced down the path, flustering Tig, who skittered around irritably, Biddy chasing after them.

'Come back, you horrible creatures!' she yelled, her eyes on Jael and Eadmund, riding together, side by side. And she burst into tears as Jael slid off Tig and took her in her arms.

'Hello, Biddy,' Jael smiled over her shaking head.

'Oh, Jael,' Biddy sobbed, squeezing her tightly. 'My girl!' She could barely see Eadmund through her tears as he struggled down from his own saddle.

'Hello, Biddy,' he said quietly, not sure if anyone would want to see him again.

'Eadmund!' And releasing Jael, Biddy pulled him into her arms, her face breaking into a smile. 'You're back!' She thought of Eydis then and how much she had wanted to save her brother, and her tears fell even harder. 'Eydis would be so happy about that.'

More people emerged through the gates, and Jael froze, seeing Gant.

He froze too, watching her, trying to pull himself together. He'd had days to pull himself together, but Aleksander's death had hit him hard, and he was struggling to see the light.

Jael walked forward, and Gant stopped, waiting for her, and as she leaned towards him, he wrapped his arms around her.

'I'm sorry,' she cried into his shoulder. 'I couldn't bring him back.'

Gant hung onto her. 'He wasn't made to be without you, Jael, I know that. He saved you as he always wanted to. And now he's free.' It was true, Gant realised, remembering that ten-year-old boy who had watched his mother kill herself. Who had been given a bleeding, terrified Jael to look after that very night. And he had. For the rest of his life, he had. 'Now he's free.'

Jael hoped he was right. 'You're not staying behind again,' she mumbled. 'Understood? You're not staying behind again.'

'Understood,' Gant promised. 'I won't.'

Isaura ran past them. 'Thorgils! Thorgils!'

And groaning as he hopped down to the ground, Thorgils grabbed her, almost throwing her in the air with joy.

'You came back!' she cried. 'Edela said you were coming, but I wasn't sure. I wasn't going to stop myself thinking the worst till I felt you myself!'

Thorgils could smell her, and she smelled like sausages. 'I'm starving,' he grinned, sniffing her hair, kissing her forehead, her cheeks, her lips. 'I hope there's something to eat!' He saw Mads running towards them with his sisters, and his smile vanished, thinking about Ivaar.

They started walking into the fort, eager to get inside before too many people came out; wanting to rub down the horses, to get some food into their empty bellies. It had been eight long days of riding and marching back from the vale, and the idea of a bench and a cup of ale had spurred them on through the last few days.

That and the chance to see their families again.

Bram was waiting on the hall steps with Gisila, eyes scanning the returning warriors. Seeing him, Fyn dropped his horse's reins, hurrying forward.

'Fyn!' Bram's smile was hidden beneath his bushy beard, but it was wider than it had been in years. And bringing his son into his arms, he clapped him on the back. 'You're in one piece, then? Still standing?'

Fyn nodded, lips wobbling, trying not to cry. Trying not to but failing miserably. 'Eydis,' was all he could say.

'I'm sorry,' Bram said, stepping back. 'But she was so brave.'

'I... she... yes.' Fyn couldn't say any more, and seeing that, Bram took him in his arms again.

'Come on, why don't we sort out your horse, then you can tell me all about it over a cup of ale.' He saw Thorgils, and he winked at him. 'Before Thorgils gets there and drains the lot!'

'Where's Axl?' Gisila's eyes were frantic as she looked at Jael. 'Where's Axl?'

'Gone to Hest,' Jael said, feeling odd. 'To get Amma.'

Gisila's relief changed her face and relaxed her shoulders, and she smiled at her daughter, tears in her eyes. 'I was so worried,' she cried. 'So sad. Poor Aleksander. Oh...' And shaking her head, she held out her hands to Jael. 'I was his mother, you know. I was. For longer than Fianna. Eighteen years he was mine to care for. I can't believe he's gone.'

Grief was like the sun, Jael realised. You could never escape it.

It kept rising, no matter how many times you thought it had gone away.

Pulling herself out of her mother's embrace, she spun around and threw her arms around her grandmother.

Edela smiled through her tears. 'My, how big you've grown, Jael Furyck!'

'And my, how you've shrunk, old woman!'

'I may be old,' Edela winked, looking her over, 'but I'm not dead yet.'

Slipping an arm around her shoulder, Jael walked her towards the hall. 'I need something to drink,' she said. 'It's been hot. Dry. Sad. And I'm glad we're back.'

'Not just back,' Edela reminded her, 'but victorious.' She stopped and turned to her granddaughter, her eyes on Eadmund who was approaching with Biddy. 'You saved us. You and Eadmund. Aleksander and Eydis. Daala. Dara. All of you. Never forget that. The sun is out, and we are all still here, a little scorched and hungry, but still here, because of you, Jael Furyck.'

Jael turned back to Eadmund, watching Gisila embrace him, remembering that day in the hall when Lothar had sneered at her from his throne, gleefully announcing her impending marriage, that smug smile on his bloated face.

That day she had wanted to run.

Or had she?

It wasn't only Edela who had seen Eadmund in her dreams.

Jael frowned as her husband walked towards her.

It wasn't only Edela who had known that he would come.

That he would be hers. That one day they would be bathed in golden light.

She blinked, remembering Eydis.

'I'll go and rub Tig down if you like,' Eadmund offered. 'Fyn's a bit busy.'

Jael grabbed his hand. 'I love you,' she said quickly.

'What?' He almost hadn't heard her with all the noise as more people rushed out of the hall, across the square, welcoming home the visitors, grieving for those who hadn't returned.

'You're going to make me say it again?'

'Oh, I think so.'

Jael held her hands up to his face, her eyes seeking his. 'I love you. And I'm glad you came back, Eadmund Skalleson. I wanted you to.'

'You did?' Eadmund's smile brightened his battered face,

and he leaned forward, kissing her. 'I'm yours, Jael Furyck,' he whispered, his lips on hers. 'Always.'

THE END

THREE YEARS LATER

'She seems a bit rusty to me, don't you think, Fyn?' Thorgils called, nudging his cousin who stood between him and Bram, all three of them chewing on piping hot meat sticks from Ketil's as they leaned over the railings of the Pit.

Snow was up to their ankles, and though it wasn't particularly cold for Oss, everyone could feel that the Freeze was on its way.

'Shouldn't you be making more children with your wife?' Jael grumbled, numb hands wrapped around her wooden sword.

Thorgils laughed, raising an eyebrow at Isaura who was walking towards him with their three-month-old daughter, Elina, tucked inside a fur wrap; Ayla beside her, holding Mads' mittened hand.

'More children?' Isaura snorted. 'I think we'd have to move into a bigger house if we had any more children!'

Ayla laughed, letting go of Mads, who ran to Thorgils, eager for a boost up onto his shoulders. Thorgils handed his meat stick to Fyn and grabbed the little boy, throwing him up around his neck.

'Careful!' Isaura warned. 'He's not a cloak!'

Eadmund shut them all out, focusing on his wife, trying to ignore the blood in his mouth from where she'd struck him in the face. If anyone was rusty, it was him, which wasn't good with the problems in Alekka. He needed to be sharp, show the leadership his father had hoped was in him.

'Have you finished?' Jael wondered, hand on her hip.

'Anything else you want to fret about over there, King Eadmund?'

'Being married to a dreamer has its downsides,' Eadmund muttered under his breath.

Jael laughed. 'It does, especially one who knows every move you're going to make before you make it!'

'Ohhhh!' Bram laughed, nudging Fyn. 'Think we might need a drop of ale. What do you think, Thorgils?'

Thorgils was nodding, peeking inside Isaura's furry bundle, smiling at his tiny daughter with her shock of bright-red hair. 'I'd say so. Why not hop off and grab us some cups, Cousin?'

Fyn ignored both of them, leaning over the railings. 'Come on, Jael! Bring him down!'

Jael smiled, glancing at him.

And that was her mistake.

Turning back around, she was too late to see the boot coming for her head.

The boot on Eadmund's foot, attached to Eadmund's leg which had just knocked her flying.

No one said a word.

Fyn, Bram, Thorgils and Eadmund's mouths fell open, all four of them staring at the prone figure lying in the snow.

'Mama!' came the plaintive cries, as two children broke free of Biddy's hold and raced into the ring, Ido and Vella charging after them, quickly sinking into the white powder.

'Come back! Come back!' Biddy grumbled, sneezing. 'Get out of that ring!'

Eadmund shook his head, smiling at the sight of two dogs and two children smothering his moody looking wife.

'Are you alright, Mama?' Sigmund asked, worry etched into his little face. 'What happened?'

Bo was crying, red cheeks and nose, red mittens and hat. Two years old. As fiercesome as her mother. 'Mama, Mama!' she sobbed, throwing herself onto Jael.

'It's alright, I'm alright,' Jael muttered, her ears ringing. 'Your father just got lucky.' And she scowled at the hand Eadmund was holding out to her.

Eadmund pulled her out of the snow, onto her feet. 'I did,' he whispered, arms around her back, holding her close, feeling her try to squirm away from him. 'Very lucky indeed.'

READ NEXT

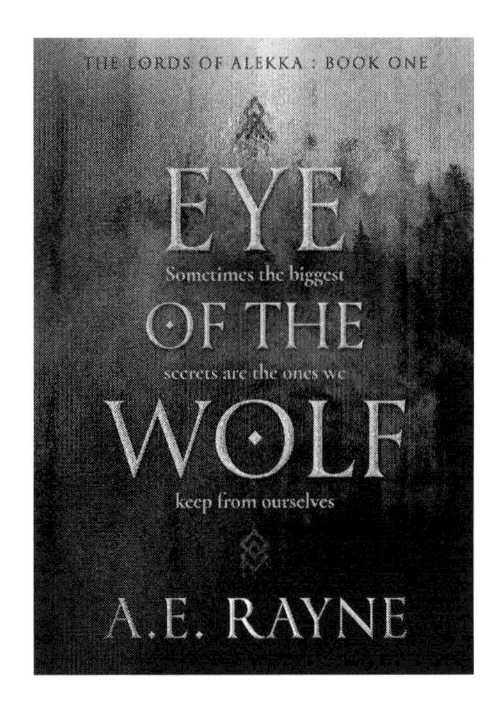

EYE OF THE WOLF

MARK OF THE HUNTER

BLOOD OF THE RAVEN

Sign up to my newsletter, so you don't miss out on new release information!

http://www.aerayne.com/sign-up

ABOUT A.E. RAYNE

I live in Auckland, New Zealand, with my husband, three kids and three dogs. When I'm not writing, you can find me editing, designing my book covers, and trying to fit in some sleep (though mostly I'm dreaming of what's coming next!).

I have a deep love of history and all things Viking. Growing up with a Swedish grandmother, her heritage had a great influence on me, so my fantasy tales lean heavily on Viking lore and culture. And also winter. I love the cold!

I like to immerse myself in my stories, experiencing everything through my characters. I don't write with a plan; I take cues from my characters, and follow where they naturally decide to go. I like different points of view because I see the story visually, with many dimensions, like a tv show or a movie. My job is to stand at the loom and weave the many coloured threads together into an exciting story.

I promise you characters that will quickly feel like friends, and villains that will make you wild, with plots that twist and turn to leave you wondering what's coming around the corner. And, like me, hopefully, you'll always end up a little surprised by how I weave everything together in the end!

To find out more about A.E. Rayne and her writing visit her website: www.aerayne.com

Printed in Great Britain
by Amazon

61640884R00452